The Royal Knights

Darius Heyward

Heyward_darius@yahoo.com

About 190,000 words

First paperback edition February 2020

Cover design by Rusbin Lopez
Characters designed by Milton Das and Kart Studios
Environments designed by Jun Steed, John Hsu, and Rick Bastos
Map by Rusbin Lopez

www.DariusBlazeh.com

A Special Thanks...

This book has been a long journey for me and those who helped me get to this point. First off, none of this would have been possible without my longtime friend, Zackary Pierce. Back in middle school while talking outside of David's house, we set up and created this entire world and story from nothing. I appreciate the constant consults on ideas, and discussions we have. This journey started there, and in no way is close to done, thanks 'Volt' for the help.

My family gave me a lot of immediate support when I wrote the very first version of this book in 6th grade, but no one took as much time out to help me as my grandmother. Grandma Joyce, I'll never forget you sitting me down and helping to type out different versions of the book I had written out in old composition note books. In everything I decided to do with my life, you were always there to support me, and I love you dearly for it, thank you.

The next person I'm thanking here annoys the hell out of me, but I do appreciate him a lot. Daniel Nunley. He is one of the only people to sit down and read through the book and talk about different ideas with me when I really need it. He gave support when I needed it, and he is a great friend for this and other reasons as well. Thanks Nun.

Matt Wright. Bet you'll be surprised you made it here, but your help has just meant that much to me. From talking me out of stupid ideas to making things in the book flow better, overall I'm very glad we reconnected after those years. You helped edit and question things I hadn't even thought about. A second opinion is always a good idea, and yours I respect very much. Thanks bro.

To the rest of my friends and family who held it down throughout the years and helped read through my story while I worked on it I love and appreciate each and every one of you! Thanks for helping making this possible. Enjoy!

1

Sylindra

Holy Ocean

The Aqua Graveyard

Mystic Ocean

Repshera

Peaks of Vladdim

Ship Graveyard

Sea of the Wicked

Kegato

Deepest Depths

Mystic Ocean

Basonali

Royal Grounds

Udalton Ocean

Udalton Ocean

Laix

Exile Sea

Eden

Kayard

Exile Sea

The Silent Islands

The Royal Knights

Table of Contents

5

8

The World of TRK

The following contains information about the realities and worlds that exist within *The Royal Knights* universe. *The Infinite Canvas* is the ever perpetually expanding space that holds the many worlds that get created by the five governing Deities. They will be categorized in several ways as they fall under certain subtypes. Most of the areas are marked as an "Open World" (possessing mystical pathways allowing travel between them freely). Some special locations are marked as "Closed Worlds" (Locked away and are sealed off by all but the governing deities and special individuals).

Luvenesyar

Type: Closed World
Deities: The Five Governing Deities (Lucinthis, Verafelt, Nefula, Sylindra, and Ardin)
Special Note: The birthplace of original Royal Knights (Volt, Blaze, Ocean, Void, and Sky)
Notable Races: Human, Angel, Demon

Luvenesyar, often referred to as "The Origin World" was the first to see life dictated by the hands of the Governing Deities. With the Governing Deities directly attached to Luvenesyar, it is a heavily mana saturated atmosphere, giving birth to a wide variety of animal life and having lush, bountiful lands. Mana is the underlying power that is in everything and gives life to all living things, both a life source and a power source. The five gods, who were still young in fleshing out their powers in the beginning, would manifest onto the land under a bizarre guise of colored orbs. The colors are believed to be associated with the ideologics of each individual and are reflected in the sentient beings birthed onto the world.

At the time of Origin, the gods were unable to communicate with each other directly. Despite that they seemed to have drawn lines internally against their compatriots and each opted to be more precise in what their direct influence would birth. Whilst their mana together created humankind, Lucinthis is the sole progenitor of the divine angel race, which has become present amongst many of the worlds in the infinite canvas but primarily reside in Ardin. (A world later created as a home for the angels).Verafelt used his influence to birth the demon race. Veravelt's influence as the "Evil God" dictated Demon Kind to follow suit; so as one would expect, Lucinthis being the opposite of Verafelt, had the Angels to do good. Humans were given the opportunity to decide which way to turn in this polarizing world and decided to side with the angels. This dissension began to affect the landscaping of the world, and molded it into what it eventually became.

As time passed and generations rose and fell through battle time and time again, the land began to wither away but the Gods chose not to interfere initially. The first to descend unto Luvenesyar was Lucinthis, the goddess of light. Her arrival brought about a great light, and in turn a great darkness as well. Stemming off of her power a great evil was formed in the shadows. This evil began to rise and destroy all, using the demons as its pawn. This evil came to be known as Chaos. After many bleak battles with Chaos and his new army, the deities realized how their mana too heavily influenced the beings of the world. Luvenesyar was losing its vibrancy, and the overload of mana began to evolve the beings in different ways. Those who could absorb and tap into the mana thrived. Such is the case with the original Royal Knights, who were born and formed in this world. Each of the five Governing Deities championed a Knight who could wield their mana with the most skill and purpose.

They had hoped to use them to erase their own mistakes and seal away the evil without having to get directly involved and pouring more of their mana into the world. While successful in sealing away Chaos, Luvenesyar had eventually begun to collapse upon itself. Seeing no other choice after eons of time had passed, the deities created other worlds and scattered them around the infinite canvas. The angels, humans, and demons had worlds created for them in order to keep them separated so there would be no disputes. These worlds in question were Ardin, Sylindra, and Armageddon. Only those able to withstand the strong mana influence stayed on Luvenesyar, the rest were sent off onto these other worlds with the pathway sealed behind. The remaining worlds had pathways open between them in the infinite canvas making it possible to travel from world to world. The years after this expansion are referred to as AE (After Expansion).

The Governing Deities matured throughout the time they spent taking care of Luvenesyar. They learned a way to properly communicate amongst one another, having taken a form akin to the Humans. The memories and power coming from Luvenesyar was so massive it leaked into the endless mana that created The Infinite Canvas and affected the worlds that were birthed from that mana. The influence of the deities was felt from all worlds because of this. They would grow in their own way, however, and the ideologies and memories of Luvenesyar and the god's experiences would be perceived differently in each world. This meant that there were endless possibilities for how each world would turn out but the fact that everyone came from

Luvenesyar was known throughout. It is the "Origin World" after all.

Sylindra

Type: Open World
Satellites: (Sun) (Moon)
Deities: Lucinthis, Nefula, Sylindra, Ardin
Continents: Kayard (E) Basonali (N) Kegato (W) Laix (Center) Eodon (S), Repshera (NE)
Notable Races: Human

Sylindra, the home of mankind, is often seen as the most productive and smartest of the worlds. Learning from their ancestors how to harness the mana, they trained themselves stronger, and built large city states in the center of the continents to gloat their power. The humans have also managed to create multiple pathways in and out of Sylindra connecting to other worlds using their incredible knowledge and understanding of mana. Sylindra is a world with earth like attributes that is also Governed by the five Deities. Each God represents its own fraction of human emotion, unique from those of the other deities. Each of the continents favored the traits/purpose/blessings of one of the Gods over the others, and dictated their lives and communities to worshiping that deity. This led to churches being erected to worship particular deities' dependent on where that area was. (Sylindra is worshipped near oceans or wetlands in order to help with fishing and such.)

The five Gods watch over the world as a council of sorts, and they can each disguise themselves as humans to blend into the different societies around Sylindra. Though they choose to stay back, relatively natural actions can still cause catastrophic consequences. The legend of the creation of the Royal Knights is passed down through generations as a motivator for kids to work their hardest to be the greatest because only the most worthy and fitting warriors will be chosen for the honor of being one of the knights. The legend taken from the memories of Luvenesyar goes: *when Lucinthis, the goddess of light first descended on the world, in turn the first shadow was also cast unto the world. When she departed back into the heavens, this shadow remained, and manifested itself into Chaos. Chaos is an entity that sought the ultimate annihilation of all life, and the complete darkness of everything. Over the many years, pieces of chaos broke away and became the shadow beings that now plague the world. These beings grow and evolve over time to become more dangerous. Their very presence absorbs the light around them, weakening all those around. The more light they absorb, the more darkness gets created. Even though Chaos had long been sealed away by the Gods, the shadows still roam around all worlds, and the shackles sealing Chaos will not hold him forever as his power is bolstered by the more darkness there is. For hundreds of years, Chaos has been locked away, and during this time the deities pondered ways to prepare for the ever-growing threat that awaits. They agreed to continue to use humans as vessels for the Gods' power. It was decreed that each deity would choose a young warrior in each region, and infuse them with parts of their own power and abilities. These 'Chosen Ones' would form a group, and lead the battles against the shadow beings. When one warrior would fall, or lose favor with the Gods, their blessings, as well as their 'name' or moniker would be passed down to the next generation. Each of the chosen warriors from different regions would then make expeditions across countries to combine forces, hone their skills and fight the darkness in*

the world. These chosen warriors are referred to as the
Royal Knights; Blaze, Volt, Void, Ocean, and Sky.

Armageddon

Type: Open World
Satellites: (Chaos Moon)
Deities: Nefula
Important Characters: Deces', Ruin, Scarlet, Scourge
Notable Races: Demons

       Though it is technically an 'Open World,' there is only one entrance to get in and out of Armageddon. Armageddon is the world formed of all of the darkness and evil after the split of the races on Luvenesyar. Savageness thrives in these wastelands as food is scarce for the demons here, who are forced to feast on each other and small creatures. Only the strong survive. Along with demons, the giant race also inhabits the harsh lands here as well. Giants and humans inhabited Sylindra together initially, but after a great war and many bloody battles later, the Armageddon has many large uninhabited areas, and some small demon villages but the one area of note is the area surrounding Exodus castle. While Armageddon is home to all of the most powerful demons, Exodus Castle is home to the most powerful of them all, Deces, or Demise as he is commonly referred to on Sylindra. The legend of Deces' and his dominance has expanded around worlds making travel to these lands very unintelligent. From his throne, Deces' is able to send demons and shadow beings across all worlds to kill and drain away all of their light. Armageddon has a moon called the 'Chaos Moon' orbiting it. This moon

13

enhances the powers of all beings of the dark, and drains the light from all other beings. There is a plethora of other dangers that await in the deep dark depths of Armageddon...

Ardin

Type: Closed World
Deities: Ardin
Notable Races: Angels

Ardin was created as a home for the angels after the split. Great peace was felt here for many years as the angels created tall cities and buildings as all the inhabitants could fly freely. Being the closest world to Luvenesyar, the large amounts of mana helped the plant and wildlife thrive on this world. The angels' peace was cut short by Deces' and his greed. On his path to absorb all of the light, he found a pathway to Ardin around the year 203 AE and brought chaos and massacre to the angels' simple lives. Deces' attacked Ardin with the full force of his dark armies in an effort to snuff them all out of existence. The angels did well to defend themselves, but after a while the onslaughts were too much and many of the angel's cities fell to Deces'. After watching these events unfold, and watching Deces' annihilate a league of angels, Einhale Ardin (The Deity watching over the world), stepped in and closed off all of the pathways into the world around 220 AE. This move forced Deces' back to Armageddon, but also closed off Ardin from the rest of infinite canvas. Since then, Ardin has been on its own similar to how Luvenesyar has been for centuries.

Chapter 0:
The Gods

Fourteen years before the events of the story, a group of children said to be the next generation of the world's leaders were led to the Aerial Citadel. The advisor to the Hiyama army in Laix acted as their teacher; the goal here is to educate these young warriors on the world around them, and the guardian deities that brought them to be. The Citadel floated high above the Eodic Sea, only accessible by unique gateways protected by the leaders of each continent. Inside of the first room of the Citadel, gigantic statues of the five deities in mighty poses reside, depicted as they were the last time they were in this world. Five children between the ages of ten and fifteen stand there staring wide-eyed at the massive structures before them while the guide approached.

Of the five kids, two stood out more than the others. A taller kid with small, angelic wings extruding out of his back, and tied back long white hair stood next to another slender, quiet kid with short, light blue hair. The two had known each other for a while, as they only talked to each other. The winged child chuckled and cracked jokes between them, causing the quiet one to snicker silently to himself. Guards from the Royal families all stood at the doorway throughout the lesson. King Hiyama steadied himself with poise focusing his attention on his son, Prince Sky Hiyama, the boy with the wings. He flanked Father John, a legendary warrior and religious figure in Sylindra. He would eventually be the guide to the Royal Knights, but for now, he looked after his adopted son, Volt, who joked with the

16

young Sky. After the long introduction, the instructor was finally ready for the lesson.

"Alright now! Listen up, young masters." The instructor swung his left hand up towards the first statue before them. The figure depicts a beautiful woman with a pirate captain's hat sat neatly on her head, who posed with her sword shooting forward in front of her. "My name is Arthur, and I will be your guide this afternoon. I'm here today to teach you about the deities that are responsible for everything we have here on Sylindra. Your work will be to lead others by the teachings and values set forth by these five. Speaking of, our first deity is Einhale Sylindra." He paused for a moment placing one finger into the air to make sure the kids were all paying attention. Every kid had given their guide full focus. The weight on their shoulders was understood all too well.

"Sylindra is the deity of the earth and oceans and keeps watch as the namesake of the world we reside in currently. Each God possesses their own uniquely colored wings, all except for Sylindra. As a dual-purpose deity, she has pure white wings and heterochromia; left eye is dirt brown, the other sea blue. Her knowledge and ambition are her strongest traits, leading and bestowing mankind with the insight to seek greater heights." Arthur stops for a breath; the sparkle in the kids' eyes was evident now, his calm but high energized voice was always said to inspire, maybe why he had received this role.

"This ambition also leads humanity to develop greed," Arthur says, continuing. "Sylindra possesses a moody attitude and can be difficult to please. We all know the Gods can disguise themselves as humans, yes? In this way, the Gods observe us sometimes." He stopped to wait for a response.

Sky raised his hand and immediately spoke. "I'm guessing she likes to be a pirate when she comes down to join us humans?" he said with a smirk.

"Actually yes, yes she does. Worshippers of Sylindra are usually druids or live in communities based around ports or islands. To finish up, she loves using a bow as her weapon, and her favorite animal is the turtle. An animal that thrives on both land and sea seems perfect for her, in my opinion. Any questions?" Arthur exclaims with a smile.

"It seems her qualities are most like that of a human as it is." Volt said lowly to himself mostly.

After a moment of silence, Arthur walked forward towards the next guardian deity statue. "Alrighty then, moving on." He holds his hand up, pointing. Next to Sylindra was a tall stoic student. He wore glasses, and held a book in his hand, close to his heart. Long robes decorated his body as well. "Einhale Ardin. The older brother of Sylindra rules the skies with his bright sky-blue wings." Arthur waves his hands up and down mimicking a bird. The other three kids in the group snicker a bit at this. Sky looked up at the statue with wide eyes, finally seeing something interesting to him. "Ardin values companionship and strength, presenting humans with their ultimate strength: leadership and bonds. Mankind has been able to draw limitless power from these traits, making them dangerous to other races. As a whole, Ardin is a lot more reserved and observant than his sister. When he visits the human world, he sticks to himself and studies unless those around him need help and guidance. Followers are often also scholars or even hunters who live off the wild. He prefers a sword in battle, and of course, his animal is the bird. Because of course!" Arthur finishes with a large breath. "Whew, that was a lot of talking," he says, stopping to look at Sky, who is still staring at the statue.

"I want to be able to get that strength one day. I want to be someone my partners can rely on!" Sky says earnestly. Arthur walks over and ruffles his hair a bit.

"Something tells me you will, Sky, worry not." The instructor backs away and walks towards the next statue in the middle, but is met by Father John.

"I've got this one; she is my favorite, after all," Father John says with both of his arms up into the air. Volt looked up at him curiously before noticing who it was himself.

"Ah, it's her," Volt says

"Euriphasia Lucinthis, the goddess of light!" John says enthusiastically. "This golden-winged embodies loyalty and love. Because of this, she is preyed upon for weddings at times. This angel is positive, friendly, and loves caregiving. For this reason, Lucinthis enjoys being a beautiful, elderly lady who takes care of people in need," he says with a huge smile.

"Wow she sounds awesome," one of the kids says..

"Yup. Her followers are very devoted religious leaders like me. Knights also find themselves supporting her as well, identifying with her strong sense of loyalty. Even as an elderly woman, she still loves riding horses with her legendary spear. One day you may find yourself wielding it, Volt," Father John finished to a silent nod from Volt.

"Ahem, may I continue now, sir?" Arthur said clearing his throat and walking over towards the next deity. The young warriors all refocused on Arthur and the tall, elf looking statue in front of him. "Euriphasia Nefula, the deity of darkness. Lucinthis's sister possesses purple wings and exemplifies revenge and jealousy," he begins.

"Wait, isn't this supposed to be a God? Those sound like negatives. Aren't our guardian deities perfect?" the last of the children spoke up.

"Well, neither are humans, right? Humans gained a piece of themselves each from one of the deities. So just how humans are imperfect, neither are they. But they are our Gods, and I personally feel it makes it easier to have something to strive for this way. Right?" Arthur nodded.

"I guess so." The kid responds.

"As I was saying, Nefula is unpredictable and cunning. She takes the form of a tall, purple-haired alchemist when she travels down to Sylindra. Always with her is a heart-shaped rose engraved eye patch though, as a part of her style. Shamans, alchemists, or paladins find themselves worshipping her for her strategic abilities. Nefula uses a staff mostly as her sorcerer side comes out, and she always keeps pet spiders with her for some reason. Bleh." Arthur says with a shiver. "I do hope you all keep these notes in mind. You most likely will need this information in your future." He nods again.

"Noted. We have one more right?" Sky asked, looking over at the statue furthest away from the front door.

"Our last deity is a bit of an odd one amongst the others. Elstanil Verafelt doesn't hold a key trait per se, though he does rule over creation, destruction, war, and rebirth. He is the Chaos that shows at the beginning and end of everything new. Most consider him the checks and balances of the guardian deities. They don't understand the flurry of emotions that he pushes onto humans very well. His influence can be the cause of anxiety, or inspiration, always changing with the seasons." Arthur holds his head, thinking about this one.

"I like the dynamic on him, but he seems to be the cause of a lot of inner struggles," Volt said to himself.

"Yes, sir, that is correct. He, himself, has a hot-blooded, arrogant personality that works in extremes. When Verafelt visits our world he will come as a tough barbarian or outdoor worker when he wants to relax, farmers for example. His followers are simple folk as well. His weapons vary from axes to claymores, but he always has a boar

20

alongside him," Arthur finished. "Do any of us have questions about our Gods?" he asks while looking around at his students and then to their guardians standing near the doorway.

"No, but I know more now that I want to meet these deities one day; however, that happens," Volt responds with determination in his eyes.
Sky put his arm around Volt's shoulders. "I'm with you on that bud," he says, nodding his head.
Arthur crossed his arms. "Yeah, well, let's hope it's while you're still breathing. Anyway, the lesson for today is over. Next week, we'll go over who Chaos is, and his effect on the world. Good day young men," he says, waving them off and heading back into the central part of the Citadel.

A bright portal opened just beyond the doorway behind Father John and King Hiyama at this moment. "Let's be off guys, a busy day ahead of us. And we need to make time for training as well. Thank you, Arthur." The king and the other world leaders leave out through the doorway, flanked by Volt and Sky, who fist bump as they walk through the portal.

As the guardian deities attempted to stop the calamity that would eventually occur, each generation of 'Royal Knights' were chosen wisely. They only selected those young warriors whose personalities and potentials best matched with that of the corresponding God. Around the age of eighteen, Volt, Sky, Ocean, Blaze, and Void all began developing their abilities granted from the blessing of the Gods. With the threat of Chaos looming more and more every year, the development of the knights had to occur

21

faster. The five Gods got together and agreed to have the knights begin their journey together by collecting special elemental orbs from all around Sylindra. These orbs are said to accelerate the progression and strength of those who possess them, allowing the knights to be more prepared when the time comes to step up. Each orb is found in a Shrine on a different continent. Each corresponds to a separate element. And we now join our Royal Knights on that long, perilous journey to defeat the ultimate evil...

Chapter 1:
The Deogrith

"What did I get myself into?" The rain was intense, almost drowning out the loud monstrous bellows that echoed into the open sierra…almost. Scorch marks plagued the ground, creating a beautiful yet devastating view with the sun setting in the background. Fire was everywhere, slicing into everything from the grassy patches to shrubs that were unlucky enough to be in the path. Beaten and bruised, a man with fiery red hair, now matted with blood, lied on his back in the middle of this terrifying sight. Red stripes decorated both his arms and the collar of his form-fitting black top. A gnarly scar went down the right side of his face and up his forehead, just past his hairline. Plenty more faint scars and burn marks decorated his chest beneath his ripped shirt. A red sword laid beside him, broken. He lied there, looking up and gasping for air, catching nothing but soot and ash in his lungs. Directly above him, a colossal mass eclipsed his view, increasing in size by the second as it drew near. The battered man's eyes began to glow a dim red as he lifted his right hand and pointed to his right, turning his body slightly in the process. "Not just yet, I'm not letting it end…not like this," he mumbled as a glow emanated through his gloves.

Suddenly, a short blast of fire shot out of his hand, propelling him to his left. Seconds later, a giant, scaly foot came crashing to the ground shaking the earth, narrowly missing the man who had been struggling to get to his feet. It slowly rose out of the crater it had just created and turned in his direction. The man, now back to his feet and gasping for air, slowly surveyed the beast that stood before him. The

24

pitch-black monster stood twelve feet tall, with dark red colored scales encompassing his back and wrapping around everywhere, except his midsection. Sharp spikes poked out of his knees, elbows, and the end of his head. Short, but muscular arms extended off to either side. Its head was long, almost resembling that of a tyrannosaurus rex's with green, slanted eyes on either side of its head. Steam erupted from its mouth as it revealed its sharp, curved teeth with a frightening growl. The man found himself stuck, staring into the eyes of his colossal adversary. Unfortunately, this left him open to a quick kick in the abdomen that sent him flying backwards, leaving behind a trail of saliva and blood mixed with dirt.

The man lay face down, coughing up blood. "Oh, this isn't good," he said, twisting his head to see the monster standing over him. The beast opened its mouth wide, smoke gushing out in the process. Small orange particles begin to appear and gather near the open mouth of the monster, forming a glowing orb. The man tried with all his might to push himself up, to no avail. The sphere was rapidly growing, becoming more prominent than even the mouth of the monster. The monster let loose an enormous, air shaking roar, as it turned its head towards the man.

The wind started to rush violently, causing even the monster to lose balance slightly. The monster's head forcibly cocked to the side as a powerful gust slammed into the side of his head. In effect, the orb dissipated. The beast wore an angry scowl as it looked in the direction of the attack.

"Blaze! What happened to all that cockiness you had before?" Hovering in the air was a slender man with long, silvery-white hair that flowed in the wind like leaves, a single bang covering one of his eyes. His pretty boy face matched the illustrious white, but slightly waterlogged wings that held him up, while green and black jagged scythe decorate his back. This man wore a matching outfit to the man on the ground, except with green instead of red.

"Hey, get ou—" Blaze started.

"No need to thank me, by the way!" The man in the sky cut him off, as he began to bombard the monster with more sharp, quick gusts of wind in rapid succession.

"Maybe you should look out for yourself, Sky!" Blaze said, finally able to make it back to his feet, holding his stomach and wiping rainwater out of his eyes.

Sky was looking down at Blaze, but the monster was glaring at Sky intently. In a single motion, the beast raised its arm and swatted at Sky. Sky crashed to the ground, right next to Blaze. The monster took in a quick, yet heavy breath, puffing out its cheeks. Slight puffs of smoke slipped out of the cracks on the corners of its mouth. Sky sat up wide-eyed as the monster let out a massive fireball right towards them.

"Oh, dammit!" Blaze yelled as he turned around, standing between Sky and the monster. "It'll be fine, I owe ya one anyway," he said to his companion, his body starting to glow a bright red. The blast hit Blaze's back and exploded. He barely flinched, however. When the smoke cleared, the back of Blaze's top was burned and torn apart.

Sky gasped as Blaze dropped to a knee, breathing heavily. "See? I told you," Blaze said, wincing in pain. The monster began to stomp over to them now, increasing its pace by the second. Blaze glared back at the monster, frustrated.

"This damn Deogrith... You're getting on my nerves!" Again, Blaze's body glowed red, but this time the flames started all around him, surrounding and spiraling around his body. As the Deogrith came into range, it lifted its foot to stomp down on Blaze's body. Blaze turned around and caught the foot, one hand on the sole, the other one in between the toes.

"Woah!" Sky rolled back and got to his feet. Blaze began to slide back a bit as the Deogrith started to gain traction.

His body violently engulfed in flames, Blaze screamed back, snapping Sky out of shock.

"I got you!" Sky then proceeded to pull the wind in his direction, increasing in speed incrementally. "Almost there," he said as the wind sped up and lifted the Deogrith slightly off the ground. With a shout of anguish, Blaze twisted the foot, raised, and flipped the beast back to the ground. It viciously slammed its head into the dirt and laid there. The flames surrounding Blaze simmered down. The rain slowed and eventually stopped.

"Hmm, did we do it?" Sky asked as he walked over to Blaze, put his arm on his shoulder, and looked down at the monster.

"I think so—," Blaze was cut off by the grumbles and rumbles of the Deogrith beginning to stir.

"Hey, uh, Blaze." Sky hesitated.

Blaze looked over at Sky. "What?"

"This is our first challenge as a team; I would appreciate not dying here." Dirt and rubble tumbled onto the ground as the massive monstrosity was nearly back to its feet.

"Well then…where is this team then, oh Captain?" Blaze paused, waiting for a response. Receiving no answer, he continued, "Maybe they ar—."

"They are coming, okay! I just…" Sky stopped mid-sentence as the Deogrith in a blind rage began swinging its arms and tail at the two, forcing them to dip and dodge out of the way. "I just had to fly ahead to help because…" Sky stopped to avoid, then continued. "I didn't want a member of my team to end up dead before we got started…or at all! You shouldn't have run ahead on your own, too."

Blaze jumped and pushed Sky out of the way of the monster's swinging tail. "Well, Sky, help me think of something before we're both dead by the time they show up!" Blaze dodged then continued, "Wait! I have an idea!" Blaze hunched over and surrounded himself in flames once again. "I got something for ya!" Blaze yelled as he leaped up and punched the Deogrith in the stomach. The monster didn't even flinch. It grabbed Blaze by the arm, lifted him, spun him, and chucked him at Sky.

Sky caught Blaze, yet they both still tumbled to the ground.

"Blaze," Sky started.

"Yeah?" Blaze was sprawled over the top of Sky.

"Get off of me!" Sky pushed Blaze off to the side and looked at him. "Any smart plans this time?"

Blaze had to stop and think. The Deogrith started swinging and breathing fire everywhere, forcing the two knights to get back up and dodge for their lives while they scrambled for a better plan.

"Actually! I have a plan. Blaze, go grab your sword." Sky motioned over to where Blaze's broken sword was lying on the ground.

Blaze turned and started to jog back, but a sudden epiphany stopped him. He called back, "Actually better yet, and I have enough mana to summon another one." Blaze lifted his arm into the air.

Sky looked over, confused while dodging an attack from the Deogrith. "Uh, what?" Sky switched focus back and forth between the two.

A small flame ignited a couple of feet above Blaze's raised hand. Slowly, it drifted downward like a flower petal in the breeze, and landed on his hand. In a flash of flames, a glaring silhouette of a sword formed out of mana above his hand. After a few moments, the fire cooled, revealing a heavy-looking sword with red plates on either side of the blade, a black handle, and an almost mechanical split on one side of the blade. The sword smoked out of the openings in the plates, and calmly landed in his firm grip. He looked over, sword in hand, "So you gonna stop messing around and tell me the plan, Sky?"

Sky tossed Blaze the scythe on his back. "Here, just follow my lead," he said. The white-haired knight flew over and picked up his companion before flying up and away from the monster. The Deogrith stopped swinging as Sky left its range, and instead lowered its head and stood there calmly. It appeared as if it were catching its breath.

"What's the meaning of this?" Blaze asked, struggling.

"Don't do that, or I will drop you." Sky smirked a little. "Let us see how this thing likes a flaming missile firing at it!" Sky started to fly towards the Deogrith, picking up speed.

"Wait, what?" Blaze yelled as he was pulled through the air.

Sky launched Blaze, who held both weapons at the ready. The knight of wind used his power to increase his partner's speed further. Blaze kept his body straight and released his flames, resembling a flaming dart. His body made a small whistling sound as it soared forward with incredible force.

This sound caused the Deogrith to pop its head up quickly. Blaze's skull hit the monster's jaw with such force, it caused the Deogrith's head to snap back, throwing the beast off balance. Blaze, still in midair, maintained his composure and slashed the monster's chest open in an 'X' shape. With its blood gushing out, the Deogrith slowly toppled backward onto the ground. Blaze began to drop as well, but Sky caught him and soared higher.

"Let's finish this, shall we?" Sky asked, nodding.

Blaze nodded back, and let Sky release him. He shifted his body to the side and aimed himself at the beast. Blaze's eyes lit up as the words of Verafelt begin cycling through his thoughts like a slideshow. Mana gathered into his right arm. "My right hand glows with God's power!" Blaze said, his eyes returning to normal, but his hand glowing intensely. The chant was now in his memories as if it'd been there from birth; second nature even. "Take this! My rage, my anger, and all of my fury!" Blaze spoke as if Verefelt's own tormented spirit stood beside him. Light pulsated as mana poured into the center of his palm. Flames spiraled up his arm, and a sphere of pure mana the size of his head gathered in his hand. Blaze was now gaining speed as he approached the ground, and the Deogrith, "Searing finger!" Blaze screamed as his attack made contact with the wound the beast had previously earned, the orb sliding quickly into its chest. Blaze stood on top of the behemoth as a giant pillar of searing light and flames arose. Blaze returned to the ground before collapsing to his knees. A sudden feeling of emptiness approached him. Sky flew down and stood next to him.

The monster's body fizzles away into the shadows. All that remained was an orange crystal orb with golden engravings on it. The ball rolled around a bit after the Deogrith disappeared and finally settled to one spot.

"Welp…one down it seems," Sky said, scanning their prize. "And four more to go, I think."

Blaze looked over and tried to get up, but Sky pushed him back onto his knee.

"Don't worry, I'll get it for you, man," Sky said as he walked over towards the orb. He stopped after only a few steps as the air in front of him seemed to shake and sputter before a doorway composed of pure darkness opened in front of him seemingly out of nowhere, standing to about Sky's height. Sky's heart skipped a beat it from shock. A mixture of sweat and water trickled down his head as he looked over to Blaze. *Damn, both Blaze and I are both spent, this is bad. Very bad.*

"Now now, we will be having none of that," a muffled voice was heard from inside the portal.

Sky summoned his scythe and backed up a couple of steps, his knees starting to buckle. Blaze stared at the dark opening, waiting to see what came out. He leaned forward, using his sword as a temporary crutch.

"I think I recognize that voice," Blaze said.

From the darkness emerged a tall, muscular, and armored, a malevolent entity. This fiend wore a white demon lord mask on his face, on which a permanent smile in red was painted. The mysterious figure carried a large, dark, irregular sword on his back. The weapon had an eye placed directly above the hilt, and from the blade itself dripped a black substance. "Hey Blaze, remember me?" The demon sarcastically asked as if talking to an old rival; after which, he let out a small chuckle, unable to hold it back any longer.

Blaze's eyes went wide. "Scourge!" "Dammit, I'll kill you!" Blaze got up and started towards Scourge.

Sky put his hand out to block Blaze's path, "Blaze wai—" Before he could finish, Scourge had teleported in front of him and buried his fist in his abdomen, knocking him out immediately.

Scourge caught Sky before he hit the ground, pulled him up by his hair, and leaned in close to his ear. "That's rude, you know, let the man try…and die…" Scourge laughed maniacally as he slammed Sky's head into the ground and kicked his body, sending the man flying back a few feet.

"Sky!" Blaze yelled as he looked back at Sky's limp body.

"Pay attention!" Scourge grabbed Blaze's head and shook it in place for a second before he slammed it into the

31

ground. He was then drug by his head across the field and tossed off to the side. Scourge grabbed the orange orb and walked back to him, squatting down.　　　　"Now listen here, Blazey, this right here is mine now." Scourge began twirling the orb around in his hand close to Blaze's face. "I have been instructed by my boss to stop you guys from getting these little trinkets for whatever reason."

Blaze grabbed Scourge's wrist and squeezed tightly.

"That's cute." Scourge smacked his hand away and put his knee on Blaze's chest. "I could crush you right now, boy!" Scourge yelled. Composing himself, he continued. "Ahem, but for an assignment like this, it could get very boring just to kill you all right now, so here is what I am going to do." He raised the orb in the air. "You guys need to get a hell of a lot stronger and faster because if you do not, the next time we meet will be the last. Make it fun, for me, give me a challenge, you weak bastards." Scourge slapped Blaze across the face.

Blaze's brow furred as his head shook with rage. "You know we are going to kill you, right? We are going to kill you!" Blaze's anger turned to hysteria as he began chuckling himself. "After…after what you did to my village, and who knows how many others… After all you have done thus far just know… We *will* end you!" The fiery headed knight let his rage seep out of the cracks of his smile. His body language remained calm.

Scourge cocked his head to the side as if in thought. "You know, maybe I will… start with you." Scourge put his face close to the orb. "I should just bash your head in with this orb here." Scourge began to chuckle to himself, before turning back to Blaze.

Suddenly, the loud boom of thunder caught Scourge's attention. A spear engulfed in electricity sailed through the sky as if it were lightning, passing Scourge, forcing him to dodge and drop the orb on the ground next to

Blaze. The giant demon turned his head, albeit unable to see anything. "Is that who I think it is?" he yelled into the distance.

"Hey, Scourge!" Blaze caught his attention while reaching for the orb. "This is mine!" Blaze slammed his hand into the sphere before Scourge could reach it. The glass shattered, and in place of the orb, a blinding light shone from inside of Blaze's hand, escaping through his fingers.

Scourge stepped back, bewildered." What did you do?" he yelled

The light moved into Blaze's body. His eyes began to shine for a split second as if confirming the mana had accepted him as its new host.

Scourge stood between Blaze and the sound of footsteps getting louder behind him.

"You guys are late!" Blaze yelled past Scourge.

"Shut up, you're lucky we came at all. Your impatience almost cost you and Sky your lives." An as of yet, an indiscernible figure responded as it walked closer with two others behind him.

Scourge looked over and smiled. "Oh it is you, Volt. How have you been? I think I owe you a beating for our last meeting." Scourge looked closer and saw the three grew closer. The white haired figured sombered up, with a massive great sword resting on his sturdy shoulders. Standing well over six feet tall, his attire matched that of Blaze and Sky, except black and purple. With a face warped with inner pain, and a muscular, tank like frame, this character was quite intimidating. The other was quite a bit shorter, with light pink, damp hair, wore a cocky smirk the entire time. He timed his quick strides to match pace with the slow and steady steps of his partner. Both figures had long cloaks reaching down to their shins. Stripes of color ran across the biceps of these cloaks, this character had black and blue for his color scheme. An odd weapon with blades on both sides and a sharp cylinder in the middle decorated the hip of this man. With his hands free he began rubbing his hands together faster at they approached.

Beside them stood a tough man with dark blue hair tied in a ponytail on his shoulder. He walked with a strong sense of justice; his feet slamming into the ground with each step. He was clean shaven, with a slender, quick moving body. A yellow sash ran across his waist, a green spear with two blades was held tightly within his firm grasp.

The blue-haired warrior began talking again as he neared Scourge. "You're surrounded now. You might want to rethink that."

Sky began to stir, and Blaze was already back on his feet behind Scourge.

Scourge chuckled again, "*Again*, it is so funny that you think numbers matter when you're weak." He looked down at the broken crystal on the ground next to Blaze. "But seeing as Blaze here was able to grab that orb successfully, my job is done here for today."

"Scared?" Blaze asked, punching his palm forcefully.

Scourge motioned to summon another portal. "No, I'd rather not pick my fruit before it ripens," the demon said, taking a step through the doorway. "Don't forget what I said Blaze… and you too Sky. You better get stronger, or else you're all dead." Then the dark corridor vanished just as quickly as it had appeared, taking the demon with it.

Chapter 2:
Reunion

The three in the distance came running over to Blaze as he lied back and closed his eyes. "Blaze, hello? Are you okay?" The warrior with the wet hair and blue accents looked him over, concerned.

Blaze smirked, "Don't worry, Ocean, I'm just taking a nap. Let's camp here tonight." He then almost immediately began snoring.

The tall warrior turned around and walked in the opposite direction. "I'll find some firewood, okay?"

Sky sat up and looked at him as he walked away. "Alright, Void, make it quick. It's getting dark."

****

The sky was black. Stars spiraled around the heavens like a dark snow globe. The moon stood front and center, only Ardin looking close in size. The wind blew cold air through the savannah, giving its residents a break from the smoldering heat of the daytime sun. This breeze blew a few blades of grass into the face of a dark knight about to doze off. It caused him to sneeze and he jolted awake. Void wiped his nose while he looked at Volt and Ocean lying across hastily chopped logs, groggy, using each other's company to keep awake. Sky and a now-awake Blaze were lying down next to a fire near an old, beaten down tree, across from the other knights. Blaze awoke to the sound of metal clanking, the crackling of the campfire and lightning. He glanced around, confused, seeing nothing but black sludgy remains in spots around the field. Gazing at the faces of all the knights, "What exactly happened guys?" Void peered down at Blaze, then stared into the fire. "Was a present from Scourge, it's all done, though."

"Thanks Void. Let's all have a seat, though," Volt says as everyone rests on the ground around the fire.

Sky sits up and leans over to Blaze. "Hey man, have you noticed how quickly you recover? It's been a couple of hours, and your injuries are already almost healed. I wish I was that lucky." A spark from the flame leapt over and landed on Blaze's leg as he stared into the fire.

"Well, you can dodge everything. You can fly, you have all of these nimble abilities." Blaze looked at his hands as they began to glow slightly, "I can only cause destruction." He heard footsteps approaching from behind as he finished his sentence. Everyone turned in anticipation.

Volt's eyebrows rose as he realized who it was. "Father John!"

"What?" Ocean looked over at the figure as well.

Approaching was a tall man sporting gleaming, slender white armor, and a sword on his hip, equally as brilliant. His thick grey hair slicked back, blowing in the breeze, added to his distinct persona. He came strutting up with both hands behind his back, and his head slightly rose with an air of importance. "Hello Knights, it has been some time since we last met." He began to fiddle with the hairs of his goatee. "Maybe months actually, since you began your journey to impress the Gods." Everyone stared at him in silence as he walked up and knelt next to Blaze at the campfire.

"So Blaze, I see you've gotten the first orb inside of you, somehow. Do you feel any different?" Father John peered over at Blaze, awaiting a response.

Blaze glanced down at himself, and all around his body. "I don't think so, Grandmaster, at least not yet." He clenched his fists and continued to gaze deeply into his hands.

"Do not worry, those orbs all unlock something deep within your soul. It may take time to manifest itself." Father John shifted his weight to his other knee to address the group. "Alright, guys, I came here for more than checking on your progress. There are matters that I have to attend to, so I will not be around for quite some time to relay this information later."

Sky scooted up, curious.
"After you get all of the orbs, you're going to have to go to Armageddon and face what lies there yourself," John continued.

"Wait, wait, are you sure we'll be ready for that? That'll be rough," Ocean says, sitting up now.

Father John's face grew unusually stern. "*Ocean,* you will have to be. Chaos will be reborn by the end of this year if we do not get those orbs, and that has to be stopped. The world's sacred beasts have begun losing control, attacking the very areas they should be protecting. We believe this is the plan of Deces', or Demise as he is known, in preparation for Chaos's rebirth." Calming himself, Father John continued. "You guys were chosen by the Gods for this purpose, and as your guardian through this, I have to make sure this is successful." John grabbed a branch off of the tree and cleared an area in the dirt. Void looked over at him sideways.

Volt noticed this and turned over to him. "You okay, man?" he asked.

Void shook his head, "I don't know."

"Come on, tell me, Void." Volt nudged him.

"Eh." Void shrugged and tried to look away.

"Void…" Volt shook his friend's arm. Causing the dark knight to shrug him off.

"It's just a lot, okay? This is a lot of responsibility; I don't deserve this." Void said, staring directly away from Volt now.

"Yeah...but this is something for all of us to share. We are here to help protect this world now." Volt started at Void seriously.

Void crossed his arms and turned towards the fire. "I don't believe I signed up for this Volt. I was forced into this coalition. *If* you even want to call it that," he said.

Volt leaned over near Void's ear. "Where are you gonna go, man? I brought you with us because you wanted a new purpose. You'll find that with us, I swear. Come on, just trust me."

Void remained silent but shifted his eyes to Volt for a second before looking away again. "Fine," he finally spoke up with a massive sigh.

"Okay, guys, your attention again, please." John drew a circle in the dirt using the branch. The knights gathered around him. "This is Sylindra." He drew lines around the ring and marked an 'X' on one area. "We are here in the middle of Kegato." He made a line from there to an area to the left of the circle. "You guys are going to go to Sky's home continent in Laix, and then to Kayard, then to Ocean's in Eodon." John pointed to the X he drew on the upper right area of the circle. "Oh that reminds me!" Father John dug under his armor on his chest plate and pulled out a folded piece of paper. He unfolded it and reoriented it to be upright, "This is a letter from a nice lady on the port of Kegos who said she would be nice enough to let you use her boat to get to Laix. It's a woman I used to know in a past life."

"Past life?" Volt asked.

Father John looked away slightly. "Yeah, she owes me a lot; I got her out of some bad situations before." John shook his head. "Anyway, just head in that direction in the morning."

Sky smirked at this statement as if taking the mantle for himself.

"After your journey around to all of those areas, you have to go here, Repshara."

Sky glanced at the 'X' in bewilderment. "What is there exactly? To my knowledge, there isn't much there but mountains and some elemental anomalies."

"That is where you will find the one gateway to get to Armageddon. Right in the middle of those anomalies is Polkera." Grandmaster was tapping on the 'X' now.

Blaze sparked at this statement. "Polkera? Isn't that place cursed or something?"

"I heard people who go there disappear or something," Ocean said, waving his finger.

John put his stick down and peered around at everyone. "You guys aren't scared, I hope?" After a plethora of head shaking and 'no's, he continued. "Good, you guys get some rest and good luck." An aura of light began to erupt around Father John. "Don't forget, I will always be watching." In a flash of light, he was gone.

"Whelp!" Sky said, clapping his hands. "We should sleep, for now, we have a long journey ahead of us tomorrow." Eventually, most everyone laid down and drifted off to sleep.

Blaze lay there with his eyes open, staring into the fire. Sky whispered over in his direction. "Hey Blaze, you up?"

Blaze shifted over slightly towards Sky. "What is it?"

"Well…we head over to Laix next, that means I'm next to get my orb." Sky murmured.

"Yeah, and?" Blaze rubbed his eyes.

"I just wonder what kind of power it'll be," Sky rolled onto his back and looked into the air. "You sure you don't feel any different yet, Blaze?

Blaze sighed. "No, I feel like it's the kind of thing that will show up during a big fight or something."

Sky groaned, "I guess we'll see. Anyway, night, Blaze."

Blaze closed his eyes, holding the area on his chest where his injuries were previously. "Yeah…"

****

The sun was shining bright the next morning, the sky was clear, and the route through the savanna back through the desert towards the Kegos port was as inviting as it was going to get. Sky opened his eyes and sat up, noticing everyone still asleep.

"Okay everyone up!" Sky clapped his hands until the knights began sitting up. "We've got a long day of travel ahead of us, so let's go!" Sky fixed his gear and attached his scythe to his back.

Blaze walked over to Sky. "What are we going to do about food?"

"We'll have to find something on the way, I guess. You won't die if you go a day without eating," he said with a smirk.

The knights packed up and set off towards the desert. For miles, the scenery was relatively the same: open fields, shrubs, and small creatures in many forms running amuck. On the ground around them, little ferret sized rats scurrying from brush to brush. Their faded green fur blended in well with the grasses they hid in. On the open fields, massive, thick-skinned felines ruled the yard. They sported long curved fangs on the top and bottom of their jaws, and a thick hide to protect against the predators from the skies. The mana was surprisingly rich in this area, allowing the animals to all grow to be large, and quickly evolve to deal with predators. This somehow led to several different forms of birds. The main ones being the dangerous ostrich looking Kravers on the ground and the omnivorous Favours that ruled the skies and hunted any animal they could get their beaks on. The latter resembled crows with all their black feathers but were the size of pterodactyls. Even the quick grazers of the area had protection for themselves. They were all tan and slim with three curved horns on the top of their heads, resembling gazelle but reared up on strong hind legs when it came time to run. Every animal was unique, but what they all had in common was their hesitance to approaching those whose auras were higher in mana than their own. As a result, the animals rarely went near the knights as they walked throughout the savannah.

"Man! Feels like we've been at this forever already," Ocean said as he glanced up at the sky. The sun was directly above them now, the heat blaring down.

"Hey look, the desert's just up ahead." Sky pointed to the sand dunes that were nearby.

Ocean looked around frantically, "And still no shade or food!"

Blaze sighed as he walked a bit behind the others. "My home town is around here, we'll be there shortly."

Ocean looked back at him with a smile, about to speak, but then saw the distraught look on Blaze's face and turned back around. "You think they have any food there?" he asked.

Volt peeks over at Ocean, shaking his head. Ocean's eyebrows rose as he mouthed 'oh.'

"No, my town was destroyed by Scourge," Blaze said, stopping. Ocean and Volt both prevented as well, looking at him, Sky and Void were not too far behind.

"Really, man? Damn." Ocean puts his hand on Blaze's shoulder. Blaze shrugged it off and looked past them.

"I got there to save Blaze just as he was confronting Scourge," Volt began. Everyone in his town had already been killed at that point; he did it looking for Blaze. Or maybe to trigger him in some way by—."

"And it worked; he killed everyone just to get to me, and it worked, goddammit." Blaze tried to hold back his anger. He proceeded to rush.. The knights followed behind at a steady pace, fearing becoming lost in this vast desert.

After another two and a half hours of walking, the sand began to thin, and the knights approached an arenaceous hill with a giant rock on the top of it. It overlooked a dilapidated town, torn apart and wholly overrun with sand. The building in the center had a massive hole caving it in. A large town square type opening sat in front. From the base of the building in the center to the market street, a significant black burn mark extended across it. It was slightly covered with sand, but it was still quite noticeable. To the right of the town, the giant rock stood tall like a bodyguard, watching over the town's inhabitants. The knights found the cave curious and decide to go check it out.

After arriving at the mysteriously large rock, the knights discovered the stone was the entrance to a small cave. The bottom half of the boulder opened up into a dark hole that dropped down slightly into what appeared to be a small room. "I think this is where he used to live," Sky said, strolling into the cave, the light from outside barely lighting the room enough to look around. There he found a small cot on the ground and a table pressed against the inner walls. Decorating the floor was a straw mat for sleeping tucked into the corner. Next to it was a decent-sized sack, weaved with a weak cloth judging from the various small holes along the bottom. In the center of the room was a small fire pit with a black pot haphazardly tossed off to the side. The pit had burnt wood inside, ash sat around the rim and came down the side of its circular base. Dust and sand from

43

outside blew inside from strong winds, creating a light layer of discoloration on the majority of the floor.

"Hmm, he had to live like this…" Volt spoke to himself softly as he peered around.

"Not everyone can live like royalty, Volt," Void scolded, coming in seemingly out of nowhere behind them. "He said he lived in a cave when we talked before, what the hell did you expect?"

Volt frowned slightly. "I don't know, I just...I guess I haven't left home enough."

Void walked out of the cave into the approaching sandstorm.

Sky strolled towards the exit behind him. "Maybe we should go look for Blaze now. This is the first time he has been back here since we took him away."

Ocean goes to the opening and looks around, noticing the quickly approaching storm, "It might have to wait, the sand might keep us in here," he said.

Sky immediately walked outside and used his abilities to blow strong winds through the sandstorm, breaking it up and revealing the town to everyone once more. "Do try not to forget who you have here with you," he gleamed, proceeding out and down the hill towards town. The others filed out and followed him, sliding down.

Emotions drop as the knights walked through the town, noticing most of the broken doors; dried blood was everywhere. Dried bones and personal belongings littered the streets while most homes and buildings were destroyed. Everything shifted every few moments with strong winds blowing down the streets. The market area was a mess; tables and tarps were thrown about. Spoiled foods and dead animals were almost etched into the ground, sand rings surrounding them.

Past the market area was a large opening surrounded by houses and one building with a crater near the side of it.

To the right, a wall was used to block off the area, the left led to a pathway towards the town entrance. Upon closer examination of the crater in the building, the knights noticed Blaze sitting inside of it, his head between his knees, a single tear in his eye.

The ground beneath the town square began to shake, causing the damaged buildings to fall. Rubble and glass crashed to the ground from all directions.

"What the hell is that?" Ocean looked all around, staying in the shade of one of the less damaged buildings. Less of a chance for it to come down on him.

Sky pulled out his scythe and pointed it towards the source of the tremors, the center of the square. "We are about to find out it," he said. The rest of the knights drew their weapons.

Blaze continued to sit there as a giant hole began to open up from the ground and split the town square apart.

"What the hell is that?" Volt shouted, pointing to a giant monster rising out of the hole. The beast resembled a scorpion but was all black, entirely covered in shadow. The monster burrows out of the sand, making a loud shrieking sound and frantically swinging its tail.

Blaze slowly hopped out of the opening he was sitting in and began walking forward calmly. Each step was careful and meticulous. Making it to level ground, the giant shadow scorpion began turning to stare at everyone and shrieking in the knight's direction.

"Oh boy, I guess we better get to work," Volt commented, readying his spear before starting forward. Behind him, the other knights begin to do the same.

Meanwhile, Blaze walked up to the scorpion, his sword still sheathed. He breathed calmly and held his hand out towards the monster. The scorpion snarled menacingly in his direction.

45

"Wait up, guys," Sky called out, running in front of the others to halt their approach, having noticed his fiery friend's actions.

Blaze's eyes glow a bright red as his entire body instantly ignited in flames. The flames pulsated up and down his body like a scanner. On cue they gathered up around his outstretched hand, bunching up there with pressure ready to be released. The mana grew massive here, and in a quick flash, it burst forward in a substantial stream of flames. The flow quickly collided and permeated the scorpion's chest, soaring past it, towards the marketplace. The insane blast's blinding light shone still as it began to stream out continuously even after the monster was dead. "Pitiful," Blaze spat, stopping the stream and watching the monster fall to the ground and fade away. The knights stood there, stunned and dazed.

"Whoa," Ocean said, walking up to Blaze. He put his hand on his friend's shoulder, before quickly removing it; the knight of fire was still hot to the touch. "Hey, you okay, man?" Ocean asked, shaking and blowing on his hand, steam now rising from it.

"Yeah, I remember that monster used to terrorize this town since my childhood. Sadly, there isn't even anything left here for it to kill or destroy," Blaze lowered his head in calm silence.

"Well, hey man, from now on, we are your family, alright?" Ocean put his hand back on Blaze's shoulder, ignoring the pain. He then turned him around, gestured to all the knights who smiledd and pose behind them, except Void, who stood stoic as usual.

"Thanks, Ocean. Anyway, the port is only about another day's walk that way, less if we hurry," Blaze said, pointing towards the exit of the town.

46

Sky walked out front and pointed his scythe in the direction of the entrance. "Well, let's hurry then! Maybe we'll make Kegos by nightfall."

They grouped up and started to head out of town, passing a beaten up 'Ryon town, the last stop you'll need' sign on the way out. They all stopped and peered around when they heard a low-toned grumbling sound, however. Everyone looked at Ocean, the source of the noise.

"Hey, I'm hungry. Sorry, we haven't eaten yet today." Ocean raised his shoulders, a guilty look on his face.

Sky glanced over at Blaze, "Well, while we are here, it wouldn't hurt if you knew anywhere we could find some food. There aren't exactly any animals or edible plant life around here."

"Oh, right! That reminds me, we do have…something I think. If it's still here, that is. Follow me." Blaze guided them back into town, and they went around the side of the building with the crater in it. It appeared to be a bank of sorts, currency littered the floor. He led them around the back and down a battered staircase. Down there they found two vaults on opposite sides of the walls. "My town has always had to ration food, being surrounded by the desert does that." Blaze began to fiddle with the lock to the vault on the back wall. "We specialized in dried foods, allowing us to preserve it for longer periods of time without going rotten." Blaze melted the lock and opened the door to the vault. Inside was an enormous stockpile of dried meats and herbs along with canisters that filled the shelves all around the walk-in safe.

"Whoa this is a lot man. How could you forget about this!" Ocean's mouth waters as he steps forward.

"Help yourself guys; what we don't eat here, we can try to take with us. I can't relock this vault anyway. Not like anyone would come down here anyway." Blaze's voice lowered as he spoke. The knights each grabbed some of the meat and a canister, and had a seat inside of the vault.

"What's in these, Blaze?" Sky asked, shaking one of the canisters and peeking inside to reveal a dark liquid. Blaze grabbed one and took a long, drawn-out swig. "That is some great stuff," Blaze said, his words slurring a bit. For the first time since they arrived in the town, a small smile crept up onto his face. Tears of joy joined afterward, rolling down his blushed face.

Sky took a sip then shot his eyes forward with surprise. "It's a brandy of some sort, but it's different. It's so refreshing, even though it isn't cold."

One by one, the knights began to try the mysterious drink while eating their meat.

"This special drink," Blaze started taking another sip, before continuing, "helps for desert travel by helping to hold in water...kind of like a cactus. Either way, it helps one's endurance out here." Blaze took another drink. "And it tastes great!"

They all raised their canisters and toasted.

Void looked at the vault on the other side of the room, staring at it after a while. "Hey Blaze, is there any money in the vault over there? We may need it at some point."

Blaze shook his head. "Nah, there most likely isn't anything in there. This town may have had these rations but we were very poor. Shouldn't we get going, though? If we want to make it to Kegos by nightfall." Blaze got up and packed some of the remaining meats and canisters in a sack that was nearby. "We're the Royal Knights after all, right? We shouldn't have to pay for shit...right?" He chuckled to himself.

"Ha-ha, you're right, let's go." Sky snickered before getting up, and waving the others to join him.

The knights headed out of town and back into the desert.

"Hey Blaze, I've meant to ask, why did you live in that cave instead of in the city?" Volt asked while looking back towards the town.

Blaze grumbled a bit to himself before answering "When I first got my abilities, it wasn't the easiest for me. I could not control them well, and I would cause damage to property…and people. We were already poor, so I didn't want to make it worse…so I decided to seclude myself until I could control my flames."

"Are you able to now?" Volt questioned.

"For the most part, except when I get angry. If I ever lose it, I'd appreciate it if you would stop me." Blaze looked at Volt, before ultimately turning around to Ocean.

"Of course, I'll do what I can," Ocean said, glancing away. The knights trekked through the sandy desert, taking swigs of the brandy along the way and enjoying the few traces of wildlife they saw.

Chapter 3:
Kegos Port

Night had befallen the desert over an hour ago. The crisp heat had been replaced by a bitter chill that breezed through the desert, even cooling the hot sand. The sightings of monsters increased with the darkness, but the knights pressed on.

They came upon a giant gate that extended across the horizon; two guards sat atop it. Behind it, the port city of Kegos sat mostly calm in the dark. In the night, all that could be seen past the gates were lights from the nearby buildings and the inns. These took up the front half of the city, while an expansive port and many seaside restaurants and pubs shared the docks on the further side; boats of all shapes and sizes parked accordingly. The knights looked up towards the guard box curiously. Two dark figures stared back.

One of the guards in the tower stared down at the approached knights. "Who goes there!"

Sky yelled back up. "Pay attention! It's the Royal Knights! We've come to see a Wendy Happilsfort."

The gates opened immediately, allowing the knight's passage inside. Upon walking through, towering buildings stared down at them in scads. They could feel the eyes of the town beaming down at them, although not a soul was shown. Long, perilous alleyways on either side seemed to invite them to hell. Passing the first few homes, one would have thought demons lived here. The knights peered along the deserted direct avenue that directed towards the docks. As they looked further forward, the eerie shadowed streets lightened as the town became livelier around the center in the city. One just needed to get past the outskirts.

The gate closed behind them, and the guards came down from the tower to the knights. "Hello, sirs, sorry about that. I am at your service," he bowed.

Sky tried feigning a fierce face, yet could not help but laugh. "Don't worry about it, man, we just need to know where to find Miss Wendy tonight."

The guard thought for a second. "Our Major, Miss Wendy, is out of town at the moment, unfortunately. She went on a hunt, but she was expecting you here." The guard pointed to a large inn sign on top of a building near the dock. "She has rooms prepared over there, and she will meet with you folk tomorrow morning after she prepares your departure."

"Well wasn't that nice of her," Ocean chuckled to himself in the back.

"Thank you, sir, you're free to go back to your post now." Sky waved for the knights to follow him as he began walking. "Come on, guys."

The knights cautiously walked through along the path past the eerie half of the town.

"This place is very…off at night, I don't know why," Void said looking around. It wasn't long before they got towards the center of the town, where the lights were on the brightest. Pubs and social gatherings livened up the area providing some well needed noise. It was very quiet going through those houses. It didn't take long to find the inn. All they had to do was look up.

The inn in question was huge. It was one of the tallest buildings in view, with servants outside and inside at the desk, standing ready. The knights walked in and greeted the concierge upfront.

"Hello there, there's a room ready for the Royal Knights, surely?" Sky said, leaning on the counter.

The lady flipped through her papers before looking up at Sky. "Why yes there is: it is the king's suite on the top floor." She handed Sky the keys.

"Thank you, miss," he said, flipping his hair and turning around to the knights. "So I propose we find a pub of some sort tonight, enjoy ourselves a bit. Hope y'all don't mind big crowds because it's late." The knights looked around.

"Yeah, that's fine. Sounds good to me." Ocean and Blaze both said looking at each other before grouping up with Sky. Void walked past them and out the door without saying a word.

"Here, give me a set of keys, I don't like drinking too much. I think I'll just get some rest tonight," Volt said, holding out his hand.

Sky tossed him the keys. "Suit yourself, man, let's go then." He, Blaze, and Ocean walked out of the inn. Volt made his way upstairs to their suite.

"So, where to?" Blaze asked looking at the town ahead.

"Mmmm, I don't mind, don't know this town at all." Ocean responded.

Sky spread his wings and flew forward ahead of the other two. "Onward to the most fun looking place!" he said, leaving them.

The knights found themselves at a pub down the street called 'The Weiss'. It was a tall, multi-floored pub with bars on each level, leading up to a rooftop bar with a great view of the port. It seemed like everyone in town was at this bar it was so busy.

"Well now, this looks fun doesn't it." Sky said landing gracefully at the front doors, Blaze and Ocean right behind him. The three walked inside, and immediately noticed how packed this first floor was. People were everywhere. From at the first bar to the left, to any of the many wooden lounge chairs and tables scattered around, it was difficult to move around. As soon as they walked in, a woman noticed and stood on a table and yelled at the top of her lungs.

"Hey! It's the Royal Knights! Everyone make way for them please!" The woman granted a slew of 'ooos' and 'yaays' from pirates and citizens of The Port alike.

"My my, what a welcome that was." Ocean said looking around. The party had continued, a clear path made for the them.

"Oyyyy, come grab a drink guys, on me!" The bartender waved them over and handed each of them a tall beer before sending them on their way.

"Thanks!" Sky gave a short bow before turning around towards the steps.

"Guess this knight stuff has its perks, huh?" Blaze said seconds before gulping down half of his beer.

"Ooo your wings are *so* soft. Hey Rachel, come feel this!" An inebriated harlot said as she stroked Sky's wing. Her equally cute friend came over and felt his other side.

"You're right! Hey chill with us tonight, we'll show you around Cap-tain." The friend whispered in his ear as they pulled him along.

"Uh guys?" Sky pleaded to his fellow knights nervously.

"What happened to all that confidence Sky? Go enjoy yourself captain, we'll be around." Ocean teased while taking a sip of his beer.

"Come on, Ocean, let's check out the roof." Blaze urged him on. They headed up the stairs and went all the way up to the top, taking a few shots with the locals on the way. Once on the top, they are immediately met with the cool ocean breeze, refreshing them. There were a couple people up here, but not nearly as many as downstairs. Even the bartender got a chance to relax. A couple of lounge

53

chairs and couches sat up there, but people mostly came for the view.

"Ah, fresh air. It's so stuffy in there, much less people out here." Blaze hung over the railing on the roof, looking out at the city at night.

"You're right, there's room to move up here thank goodness. Hope Sky's okay," Ocean lamented.

"He'll be okay, and can you please finish that drink! You've been sippin' all night, Ocean," Blaze said pointing his beer at him, swishing it around in place.

"Don't worry about my drink. I've got to get us back to the hotel in one piece, after all." Ocean flung himself next to Blaze. "Just, try to enjoy this time we have to chill. It's gonna be a hard road ahead."

Blaze shook his head. "I'm trying, man. All of this is just so new to me. I'm no prince, or church boy, or Ronin. I come from a small town in the middle of the damn desert. I could barely even interact with those people because they were afraid of my sudden powers. I still loved them though." He took a second to take another swig of his beer. "This life has been moving way too fast for someone like me, that's why I'm taking it day by day. Starting with getting to know each one of you guys," he finished with a slight smile.

Ocean chuckled a bit. "Meh, we aren't all that special really. We all have our own pasts. We all have our reasons for fighting. Fact remains we have people counting on us now. People are going to start getting terrorized by these sacred beasts as they awaken. That 'Deogrith' or whatever it was, that kinda thing could be loose in the middle of a city instead of in the open savannah."

"Yeah I know, the longer we take, the more lives could be lost. I think even so, we need nights like this. Keep ourselves humble, keep ourselves sane." Blaze said trying to back up a bit, and stumbling.

"Toast to that!" Ocean and Blaze clinked glasses and stared up at the moon. It was high above them in the center of the sky. Even in the chaos that was happening around them, it provided a calm they both needed to prepare them for what was to come.

"Hey, let's uhhh find Sky. Gotta make sure those harlots aren't taking advantage of him just yet," Blaze said with a snicker, his words starting to slur a bit.

"Yep, sounds good. Let's go." Ocean helped Blaze towards the stairs.

"Hey! Ya'll want another round?" the bartender on the roof shouted out to them.

"Yes!" Blaze yelled immediately.

"No, no thanks. We're okay, thanks though!" Ocean said dragging Blaze down the steps. The two knights never found Sky again that night in all the commotion at the bar, but they did catch him again in the hotel lobby much later that night; a plethora of lipstick kisses all over his cheeks.

****
*

Earlier in the night, upstairs, Volt picked his room, set his weapon aside, and lied down. The 'King's Suite' was beautiful. Royal decor littered the walls, expensive hand-carved symbols on the chairs, silk curtains and sheets, huge beds. It was worth every penny. The entire suite took up half the top floor, seven rooms in total. Each room was a little different; Volt choosing the one with a bookshelf housing reading material on the five guardian deities.

His room had a window overlooking the alleyway on the side of the inn. Volt sat on the bed after grabbing one of the books on Verafelt, flipping through it nonchalantly. He eventually dozed off, staring at the ceiling, the text face down on the floor next to him.

****

Volt lied there deep in his dreams. Extraordinary stories of Luvenesyar and the wars on the first world clenched his eyelids shut. Suddenly, a loud crash woke Volt from his trance. He jerked himself up in the bed and peered around, confused. A mysterious shadow dived out of the window before Volt could get a good look at them.

"What was that?" Volt jolted up, grabbed his weapon and rushed over. He looked out of the opening, spotting something jumping down. He sighed then grasped the open window seal. Spear on his back, Volt climbed out to find a drainpipe just large enough to shimmy down. When he got to the bottom, he heard movement on the roof. Volt glanced up towards the ceiling, frustrated. A deep breath helped him calm down a bit. Leaping from pipe to pipe, Volt quickly made his way up the side of the wall with ease. After each jump, the next was carefully played out in his mind before he leapt. It seemed to move in slow motion for him when he was most focused; as long as he was calm. In the back of his mind, he knew if he lost focus for a second, missed a jump, or made the wrong move, he would be in free-fall. The inn was seventeen stories tall, losing focus could mean death.

On the roof, a masked character dressed in an all-black cloak ran past him and jumped from the hotel's roof to the next rooftop, clearing the eighteen-foot jump with ease.

"Oh, come on…" Volt saw this, took a breath, braced himself, and tossed his spear at the next rooftop. As the spear was in midair, Volt turned his body into lightning, linking it to the spear. The spear arched with the trail of lightning and dug into the side of the roof. He turned back to normal as the spear hit, flipping them both safely on top.

Upon standing back straight, he snickered at his success. "That actually worked, lovely."

The figure kept jumping from roof to roof, followed by an irate Volt. The shadow leapt over an extra cloudy alleyway but stopped as soon as the two landed. Underneath, drunken pirates were smoking cigars and cursing. Volt got distracted by the smoke for a moment before he tossed his spear to the next roof as usual. Waiting until Volt turned himself into lightning; the mystery figure lowered their foot just a bit and swiftly kicked the tip of the spear downwards. The spear jolted down and stuck into the side of the wall, sending sparks flying. The back end of the spear slightly arched downwards right before the rest of Volt's lightning links to the handle. The masked person turned and continued running.

"Damnit!" Volt yelled as he reappeared, holding his spear gripped with one hand. His feet dangled over the alleyway, gravity threatening to land him on top of the drunks below. Volt peered around, noticing Sky and Ocean through a window in the pub behind them, enjoying themselves. Blaze walked over to the other two holding three large mugs of beer. Volt refocused on the roof and flipped himself up, using the spear as a balancing beam and jumping. The character noticed his pursuer still tailing and continued to flee from roof to roof.

They soon reached the end of the road as a large park came into view just past the last building before them. Five stories up, the two had been slowly descending as they passed the previous couple buildings. Volt was directly on their flank now. He wasn't going to let them get away after all this effort to catch up. Expecting them to stop as they reached the end of the building, Volt held his spear ready to stab. The figure didn't slow a bit however, and instead leaped off the roof without hesitation. Volt's mouth gaped open as he too approached the edge of the roof. He raised his spear above his shoulder and leaped straight up into the air. A small thud sounded in the distance, but the park below was dark, extremely dark. He had lost sight of the figure as soon as they jumped. Volt could just barely make out a park bench surrounded by low grass and decided if he was going to aim blindly; it would be the best place to.

He heaved the spear towards the ground to avoid landing directly. Volt turned into lighting shortly after to follow the spear. When his spear struck the ground, however, Volt received an elbow to the face as he reappeared, sending him to the ground. His weapon was kicked away, yet glowed from the excess lightning surging through it, creating a meager light source.

The figure walked over to the reeling knight of lightning and stepped on his arm. "Did you think that was going to work again, Volt?"

Volt's eyes lit up. "A woman? Wait, how do you know my name?" He looked at the figure up and down, confused. "Who are you?" Volt struggled to get his arm free but was unsuccessful. "Whoa, you're strong," he said, still straining to break free.

"Volt, I know exactly who you are. I've been following you for a long time," the female assailant responded.

Volt glanced around, wondering if they were alone. "Who are you?" he yelled.

"Hmm, Volt ey, not your birth name, of course, cause you changed it to match the hero of legend. You never knew your parents. You were raised by Father John. Religion was very important to you growing up. You got a goddamn castle. You also got Sigrun, that powerful ass spear as a coming of age gift, you privileged boy. And finally you got your powers bestowed to you by the oh so great and soft Lucinthis. Did I leave anything out?" The person rambled on, putting her hands on her hips.

Volt began to stumble over his words "But ho-, who-, wha, uh, how do you know so much about me?" He grunted as she put more pressure on his arm. She then got lower and put her face up to his. "You got your powers bestowed to you from the gods, but so did I." She then straightened up, and raised her arms. Volt could feel the ground shake. Suddenly from below the ground, stone and earth begin to rise and form around Volt's arms and legs, pinning him to the ground.

The woman took a step back, and removed the black clothing, revealing herself. She was beautiful, with long brown hair, large hazel eyes, and soft, tanned, light caramel skin. She was young, maybe freshly out of her teens. She had a certain glow about her. Her face said naive and innocent, but her body spoke stories of her numerous battles and fights she'd been in. She had many small scars along the sides of her arms and legs, open and on display in her yellow and black traditional outfit fitted tightly to her body. It was in one piece, sleeveless, with long and loose flaps being the only thing covering her crotch on either side; allowing her legs to move around freely. Her tight clothing revealed how muscular and toned she was. There was a beaded leg band around her right thigh, and she wore flats. Raising her hands again, "My name…is Gaia, and like your friend, Ocean, I also got my powers from Sylindra, as she governs earth and water. In…a different way, though."

Volt stared for a moment before shaking his head, getting back to struggling against his rock hard restraints, "Why are you doing this then if that makes you one of us?"

Gaia began to laugh. "I don't want to hurt you Volt, in fact, you may be kind of cute," She started to look closely at his face, blushing a bit. Gaia cleared her throat before continuing. "I just had to see exactly the type of people you were before I decided to approach you," she said, shaking her head. "I know you're supposed to be heroes, you can never be so sure. That's why I had to be so mysterious in stealing a meeting with one of you."

Volt channeled his lightning through the restraints to break free. His mana ended up being absorbed into the ground. "I can see why you chose to single me out now, I guess," Volt said, looking at his restraints.

Gaia walks over to him and kneeled near his face. "Of course, Hun. You'll find as we get to know each other that I may say whatever's on my mind, and maybe my emotions drive me sometimes. But I'm very loyal to those I love." She takes a deep breath before continuing. "I came to you because I need your assistance. There is another illegitimate chosen like myself out there; my brother. He may have gotten himself into trouble on Eodon, and I cannot stop him with my power alone." She looked away for a moment. "We aren't technically one of you, so I can't hope for help from you. It just couldn't hurt to try."

Volt sighed to himself. "Well, if your power truly has the same origins, in a way, it would make you Royal Knights. I don't know the specifics, but it would be my pleasure to help you two. Maybe you could join our ranks as well, make us stronger together," he finished with a smile.

Gaia let out a small, but hearty smile. "I hope one day we get to work together, but for now, I'll be seeing ya." She gave Volt a kiss on the cheek before summoning a platform of earth from underneath her feet. The ground under her levitated and pulled her away. As soon as she was gone from sight, the earth restraining Volt was released.

Volt, his face red, sat up and looked around, "Well, that was certainly odd. Maybe I'm just tired, maybe I just imagined it all y' know… I desperately need rest after all." He composed himself and headed back to the hotel afterward, questioning everything.

****

Morning came all too quickly when the door to the King's Suite busted open; in walked three figures commanding attention. "Wakey wakey, young knights, it is I, Wendy Hapilsfort and I have come to whisk you away into the sunset." A four-foot-tall elderly woman stood in the middle of the living room of the King Suite, with a large, burly guard on either side dressed in pirate garb. She had bright brown eyes, and long grey hair tied up under her frilled captains' hat. A long wooden walking stick accompanied her as well, nearly twice as long as she was tall. The staff was engraved with writing in a language that predated Sylindra. The shiny finish on the team sparkled from the slight sunlight sneaking out of the window in the suite. Groaning and shuffling was heard from behind the many doors surrounding the living room. Wendy tugged the arms of one of the men and pulled him down so she could whisper in his ear. He nodded his head and started to bang on the doors.

"Coming!" Sky yelled from behind one of them. he could hear tripping and crashing. Another couple minutes went by before the knights finally came out of the rooms at about the same time. Blaze didn't have his shirt on, showing the scars riddling his chest. He looked over and winked at Sky when he saw him come out. Ocean groggily stumbled over everything until he wobbled out of his room, placing a hand on Sky's shoulder to balance himself. Void simply opened his door, his head down, eyes closed.

Wendy walked around the room, surveying the knights one by one, "Man y'all look like shit! Ol' John told me you were the best and the brightest." She chuckled.

"Hey!" Blaze stepped forward, calling out to her.

She waved him down, "I'm only joking. Anyway, get yourselves together and meet me in the lobby. I'll take you to meet my crew." She and her pirate guards walked out of the room, slamming the door behind them.

Ocean fell back on his butt, "Whew, just who is this woman anyway, ha-ha."

"The most respected woman in this town, apparently. She has been here, running this dock for a hundred years or something to that extent," Void began talking, surprising everyone else in the room. "I did some surveying last night to find out who this woman was. Apparently she appeared here a hundred years ago and usurped power from the pirate guild that ran the place. She has the great fighting ability, with very...interesting powers." Void spoke as if he was presenting to everyone, using hand gestures, and speaking up for once. "She had a husband once too, and she had two kids from him, no one knows where the kids are now, but they both inherited special powers as well."

This triggered something in Volt as he started thinking about that girl he met last night. "Special powers, huh..." he said mostly to himself.

Sky walked towards his room. "Well ok, let's get ready to go down, guys." Void walks out of the room, grunting.

All the knights met Wendy in the front lobby, and with no words, she waved them to follow her outside and down the street, towards the docks. While they were walking, Wendy looked back to address the knights. "I've run my crew here for nearly a hundred years, for generations and generations. Yes, I'm old, deal with it. You'll have to trust my mates too, as they will be crewing the ship that will take you to Laix. I've got some of my best men set to accompany you, though they can be a little...rough around the edges..." Wendy trailed off as they approached a building next to the docks resembling a pub, but with boating equipment all around it. Off next to the pub was a large docking area with massive ships. Pirates were cursing and tending to them. Out in front of the pub was a large town square in the center with buildings spread out. People

62

were walking about casually in the beautiful sunlight. The port really was a different place in the daytime that calm creepiness vanished and was replaced with a sparkling happy aura. The dark alleyways turned into hideouts for stray cats and dogs. The air was filled with the scent of the ocean and fresh fish.

Loud yells and broken dishes could be heard from outside. Wendy and the knights stood there and watched as someone got tossed through one of the windows and crashed into a crate outside. " That's what you get for messing with my sister, you arsehole!" yelled a voice from inside. A crowd of guys rushed out, and before long, a brawl started between all the pirates there; beer mugs, people, even boots, were all flying everywhere.

"And she has the nerve to talk about us," Ocean whispered in Sky's ear.

Wendy looked back at him and shrugged it off before walking forward to confront the mob. "That is enough!" Wendy stomped her foot into the ground, creating a shockwave of mana and a large boom that rattled and startled everyone. The pirates all stopped what they were doing and paid attention to Wendy, who began again. "And here I was trying to show the Royal Knights here how homey and trustworthy you all were, and we come back to you guys fighting." She frowned and shook her head.

"Sorry, Wendy," the crowd all replied in unison with their heads bowed low.

"Yeahhh, sorry, Wendy, hahaha," The Knights all turned around quickly as a familiar voice appeared behind her, his hand on her shoulder.

"Scourge!" Blaze started towards them but was cut off and pushed back by dark waves of mana Scourge sent to throw everyone back, away from Wendy and himself.

"Not so fast, Mr. Blaze." From the ground, dark monsters came up through the shadows in enormous

63

numbers. They were completely dark, with figures similar to that of humans, with spikes on the appendages and armed with an array of bladed weapons and shields. The dark aura that emanated from them pulsed the more that appeared.

The pirates all picked up their weapons and formed up adjacent to the knights, desperate to reach their captain. The tallest pirate, armed with a great sword, and sporting an eye patch and long silver hair walked over next to the knights, who were preparing their weapons. "Hey, my name is Jax, and it's nice to meet you and all, but we've got some work to do. You know this guy, don't you?"

Volt looked up at him. "Yeah, he's an elite demon mercenary. We're his current targets, but we've had run-ins with him before. Don't underestimate that demon."

Jax gripped his sword tighter. "Yeah, well, you want to get to Scourge, and we need to save our boss. Both roads lead through this army of *very* unlucky shadows!" Both sides prepared for battle, all the while, Wendy stood silently next to Scourge. Her eyes were closed, and her head was down as if she was in a trance.

What came next was a full-scale battle between the knights and pirates and the shadow soldiers. With their overwhelming physical strength, the pirates pushed through quickly, but the demon side had numbers. New shadow soldiers were continually being formed and summoned to the battle; gaining ground became near impossible. While the pirates helped to keep the darkness at bay, the knights made constant attempts at Scourge before getting cut off every time.

"This doesn't seem to be working so far, there are far too many of them!" Jax yelled while fighting off multiple shadow soldiers, and tossing them into each other. "Hey, you guys got all this power, right? Don't you have anything big you can shoot at it?"

64

The knights peered at each other before Sky's eyes lit up, and he looked at Blaze. "Hey Blaze, do you remember that huge energy ball the Deogrith fired at us?"

"Hmm, I'll try it, give me a boost?"

Sky flapped his wings before hovering over to pick up Blaze. They then flew up in the air, high above the battlefield. This caught Scourge's attention.

"Oh, well, this should be interesting," Scourge glanced up, grabbing Wendy tighter.

"Well, here goes nothing!" Blaze held his hands out in front of him, gathering mana in front of himself. A molten orb began to form and enlarge. The ball expanded until it got as big as Blaze himself.

"Ok, hold on, I'm gonna go all out." Blaze engulfed himself in flames, expediting the amplification of the orb. Before long, the mana collected grew to the size of a house!

"Hurry! It's getting hard to hold you!" The flames began to burn Sky's hands.

"Ok!" Blaze's eyes light up as the words of the gods appear before him. With a shockwave, Sky was pushed away from Blaze, who grew large flaming wings made of pure mana. These kept him in the air as he raised fiery mana above his head. "Oh great lords grant me the power to create the ultimate destruction, kneel before the power of Lord Vcrafelt, Molten Nova!" Blaze yelled and heaved the gigantic orb towards the shadow soldiers. The pirates immediately retreated as they watched the attack travel towards the ground. Scourge grabs Wendy and teleports them back and out of the way.

The molten nova slammed into the ground; the impact blew pirates and shadows back. All shadows within range were incinerated, along with a large part of the dock as well. After it fizzled out, the large crater in the street could be seen for miles.

New shadow soldiers began to appear unto the battlefield, disheartening the pirates. Blaze lost his wings and went limp, forced to free fall out of the sky. Sky rushed over to catch him. Scourge appeared out of nowhere, swatting Sky out of the air and onto the ground. Blaze then hit the ground hard, behind them.

Seeing this, Jax instructs some of his men to hurry and get one of the boats prepared. A small crew of pirates rushed off towards one of the ships.

Scourge started beating on Sky mercilessly in the middle of the pirates' side of the battlefield. Volt threw his spear at Scourge, who caught it, and surprised Volt when he brought himself to his weapon. He then tried to force the spear into Scourge, but Scourge held the spearhead in place with little effort.

"No, no, no! You guys still aren't strong enough!" Scourge began to force his aura onto Volt through the metals in his weapon.

"Crap." Volt charged his spear with electricity, trying unsuccessfully to pull it away.

"Don't you touch him!" A female voice echoed. The earth beneath Scourge began to rumble and shake. Stone then began spiking out like stalagmites, traveling towards Scourge shortly after. This forced him to dodge and back up.

Gaia pushed pirates out of the way to stand next to Volt. "Hey Volt, I'll hold him off, take the knights to the boat and get away." Gaia looked at Volt, her face as red as a tomato, but very stern.

"I can't leave you here with him, he's too dangerous," Volt responded.

"Just go! If you don't go, we will all die right here. I'll meet again, and we can help my brother, but for now, get out of here." Gaia shoved Volt away.

Scourge pulled his sword out, furious. "You little wench, I will kill you, and feed you to my monsters!"

66

Volt looked at Gaia one more time, then picked up Sky and started towards the boardwalk. Void got the message. He grabbed Blaze and lead Ocean and Jax in the same direction. Wendy got up from the shockwave, turning her head to view the battlefield. Scourge trapped her in a prison of his dark mana before coming for Gaia.

"Come and get me Scourge," Gaia taunted while blocking and dodging his blows. The knights rushed onto the boat as the pirates finished getting ready to set off.

"Who was that?" Void asked glancing back towards the battlefield.

"I'll tell you later," Volt responded while he put Sky down.

The sails opened, and the boat started drifting forward. A sizeable shining light began to emanate from the battlefield. After the light's shine had faded, a gigantic boulder held shakily in the sky started crashing downwards towards the docks. It held so much mass; the booming sound reached the knights on the boat. They all looked up as mana, wood, debris, and bodies were flung into the air like sunflowers blowing in the breeze.

Suddenly, dark mana encroached from underneath the boat, clinging to the sides like moss. The ship and all its inhabitants were jerked forward at an incredible speed away from the port. Everyone had hit the floor hard as they rocketed out of range. "What the hell is going on?" The pirates start to freak out as they get forced out into the open waters.

Ocean walked over to the stern and leaned over the railing. "I don't know who or what that was, but I sensed Wendy's mana there...except...it was different; it reminded me of my own mana actually. Odd..." He trailed off as the boat drifted away.

Chapter 4:
Raging Waters

-Year 276 Udalton Ocean between Laix and Kegato,

Sylindra-

     The air was clear, as was the sky. The dot that resembled the port had disappeared half a day ago, lifting the tension from the crewmates. It seemed to reveal everyone's more lighthearted selves. Blaze brought out his 'special drinks' to share, and the pirates brought out rum to match. All who attended shared this moment of brotherhood, knowing it was something they could never forget. They enjoyed this respite in spite of the terrible events they just left behind.

     Jax slipped below deck and reemerged with an old, beaten down chest, slamming it down at Sky's feet.

     Sky eyed him, sitting his drink off to the side. "What is this?"

     Jax chuckled. "I have a proposition for you...*captain*!" He kicked open the lid of the chest; on top of the mound of gold, lay an all-black guitar. It was clearly well taken care of, barely any scratches, all of the strings were in good shape, and there was a soft glisten along the surface. "What say we show our crews what we can do." Jax reached in the chest below the guitar and pulled out a long wind instrument.

     Sky reached in and gingerly lifted the guitar, beginning to tune it shortly afterward. "You don't know what you're asking for, I've been training on this since I was a kid."

Jax played a single note from his instrument. "Aye, follow my lead, Sky!"

The shipmates all gathered around the two, waiting in anticipation.

"Come all ye young fellas that follow the sea," Jax started.

Sky began to play the guitar to match his pace. The pirates began to sing behind him in unison, "*to me, way, hey, blow the man down!*"

Ocean's eyes lit up for a moment. "Ooh, I think I've heard this one." He stood up, "Now, please pay attention and listen to me."

Jax and Sky looked over and smiled simultaneously, continuing to play and sing. "*O, give me some time to blow the man down, I'm a deep water sailor just come from Eodon.*"

One of the pirates took off his shirt, danced in the middle of the group while picking up the song. "*You give me some whiskey, I'll sing you a song. When a trim Black Ball liner's preparing for sea, On a trim Black Ball liner, I wasted my prime.*"

Volt pushed Void to the middle of the group, egging him on. "Go ahead, man!"

In a low, monotone voice, Void started recited the lines he knew from the song, "*When a trim Black Ball liner preparing for sea, you'll split your sides laughing such sights you would see.*"

Everyone stopped and stared at Void. He looked around and sighed before hearing a voice behind him. "*There are tinkers, and tailors, shoemakers and all...*" Void turned around to see Volt behind him picking up the song.

The instruments started back up, and everyone was merry again. "*They're all shipped for sailors aboard the Black Ball.*" Mostly arm and arm, drunk as hell, both crews finished strong altogether.

"When a big Black Ball liner's a-leaving her dock
The boys and the girls on the pier-head do flock

Now, when the big liner, she's clear of land
Our bosun he roars out the word of command

Come quickly, lay aft to the break of the poop
Or I'll help you along with the toe of my boot

Pay attention to orders, now, you one and all
For see high above there flies the Black Ball

'Tis larboard and starboard, on deck you will sprawl
For kicking, Jax Rogers commands the Black Ball."

"Haha, you were right. That was awesome, Jax! Thanks, I think we needed that," Sky said, holding out his free hand.

"Aye, I figured it'd help. Us Porter Pirates live to assist you knights," Jax reached out and shook Sky's hand, looking into his eyes.

Both crews enjoyed themselves as they carried on into the night, which approached quickly. The knights were in different areas of the ship, mostly resting, getting medical treatment, and enjoying the time with the pirate crew. Volt was leaning over the railing of the boat, staring out into the distance behind them. Sky was on the deck sitting with the captain of the ship, and some of the other shipmates, drinking and discussing things.

****

"Haha, so you're saying Wendy slept with your father, man?" Sky said, laughing wildly, clearly inebriated.

"Yeah, at least that's what I imagine happened. I was young, and my memory isn't the best," Jax said, slapping his leg. The captain leaned back in his chair and stretched. The back leg of the chair broke, and Jax crashed into the ground, spilling his drink in the process. "Damnit." Both the shipmates and the knights began laughing and cheering

"You alright, bud?" Sky said, helping him up. One of the young pirates went underdeck and retrieved a replacement chair for the captain, who nodded a thank you and refocused on Sky.

Jax leaned forward in his chair, the smile erased from his face, "So Sky, tell me what you know about this Scourge character we met at those docks, he seems very dangerous."

Sky thought for a moment, then leaned in as well. "Yeah, from what I've seen, he seems to be a demon-for-hire sent to kill us by Deces' himself."

Jax shook his head. "Why didn't he just outright kill you guys, then? I feel like he's had plenty of opportunities."

"He likes to play with his food, or his kill, I guess. He wants it to be fun, so he gives us chances to get stronger and prove ourselves to him. He's sick," Volt answered as he walked over from the railing.

"Oh my dear Volt, that's not very nice." From the bird's nest, Scourge could be seen sitting with his right leg crossed over the left, a dead pirate hanging over the railing next to him. Everyone on the ship stared up there in shock, speechless. The knights grabbed their weapons and gripped them tightly.

"H-how?" someone screamed from the back. Dark clouds began blackening the skies around the ship, unsettling the sea. The now aggressive waters tossed the pirates back and forth like a cradle.

"Fix this, Ocean!" A few of the crewmates yelled in unison over to him while attempting to hold themselves up.

Ocean glanced around frantically, holding his hands up to brace himself. "This isn't me, I can't fix this!"

Scourge was still up top, laughing hysterically, nearly falling off. "You guys forget whose ocean this is, all this time you've been sailing. I know you've read the legends. This isn't something you can control, Ocean. I hope you guys appreciate me pulling out all the stops for you!" Scourge gets up and stretches his arms out wide opening up his diaphragm. He appreared massive and threatening in his pose. "This is the Udalton ocean, you fools! Your disrespect of his territory shall not go unpunished! Now, get swallowed by the beast of legend!"

Void leaned over to Sky and whispered in his ear, "What is he talking about? Who is this Udalton? I haven't heard of him before."

"We may find out soon, Void. Be ready."

One of the shipmates hobbled over to the two, his wooden leg slipping and sliding on the soaked deck. "Udalton is a terrifying monster of legend created by Deces' in his earlier years by accident. Cursed, the monster was sent to the ocean, evolving and growing from there. Now more devastating than ever, the Kraken said to rise from his slumber in the depths of the sea once every decade now approached. When he awaked, Udalton not only swallowed ships in his territory, he had even demolished entire towns unlucky enough to be near him in his path of destruction. A couple hundred years later and no one had been able to also challenge him. In their rush away from the battle, they unknowingly began sailing right in the path of his sleeping body. He should had still been slumbering, though, so it is just their luck he has awakened while they sailed there." The mate finished.

Sky turned around wide-eyed, and smacked the hobbled pirate on his shoulder. "How did we make a blunder this large?"

Void placed his hand on Sky's shoulder, squeezing it tight to calm him. "The navigators were most likely just trying to get us out of there as quickly as possible."

After sighing and leaning back onto the rocking railing of the ship, Sky began to talk more calmly. "Well, Scourge still found us, so let's take care of that first." He flew up to Scourge in the bird's nest. "Scourge! How did you find us, and what did you do with Wendy?"

A broad, menacing smile grew on the Scourge's face. "I don't believe you should be worried about that right now. Worry about yourself." He pointed ahead of the ship where a whirlpool three times the size of the boat had opened up, and led downwards into darkness. The sea shifted to allow a monstrous being to rise up from the center of the whirlpool. Razor-sharp horns and spikes appeared first. Then the rest of its head exploded out of the water and shot up into the sky. The rest of the creature's serpent-like body followed, seeming to never stop. This horror of the deep was huge.

"What...in...the hell? We're dead. That's it, we're dead." Blaze's jaw dropped as he fell to his knees. The monster had finally extended its body fully out of the water, eclipsing the clouds with its massive head. It had a long, slender face, with two long and curved spikes ran adjacent to the sides of its lips. Large, slanted, red eyes beamed down at the ship as the water came seeping out of the opening mouth of Udalton. Then came a terrifying, ear-splitting roar so forceful it pushed the waves, and shook the entire ship. The cry resonated throughout everyone on board the vessel, finding its way through to their souls. The horrifying sound took any fighting spirit the crew had and dropped it as quickly as it took for their weapons to hit the ground. The defeat was in the air, not a single pirate had their head held high. The shriek had even forced Sky back down to the deck where he was before.

Scourge looked down at everyone and laughed. "Now, isn't this a site to see...lovely." He jumped off the railing of the bird's nest and drifted to the ground, right next to Sky and Volt. "I'm going to need you two to come with me." Scourge placed a hand on either of their shoulders and pulled them both into a dark portal.

-Year 276 Unknown Location-

Volt and Sky appeared in an area surrounded by darkness, on their hands and knees gasping and dry heaving. Nothingness surrounded them from all sides, so dark even seeing their own bodies was complicated. The thick air in here made breathing a chore, moving even more so. Their weapons appeared on the ground next to them. "What is this, Scourge?" Volt stopped coughing up to look up and around. Scourge was nowhere in sight.

Sky sat back and breathed heavily. "We need to get back to the others! Hmm, what is this place anyway? It's a whole lot of nothingness..." Sky finally got to his feet, and grabbed his scythe. "Woah. I can't...my head." He collapsed back down to his knees.

Volt held him in place. "You ok, man? Hey... I think I feel it too."

"This place is called Umbra, a shadow realm between your world and Armageddon." Scourge said, looking down at them before bending his knees to get closer.

Sky glared up at Scourge, annoyed. "I'm still waiting for you to tell us why you brought us here."

Scourge stood straight and turned away from them. "Well, I am planning to leave you two here while I go make sure Udalton finishes off your friends. I would hate for you two to help them out and with your oh so helpful abilities." Scourge shimmered away, leaving Sky and Volt in the middle of nothingness.

74

Volt sat up and crossed his legs while Sky was still attempting to get to his feet. "Well damn, I don't want to be stuck here forever; we have to find a way out. It'll be hard because if we just start walking, we'll certainly get lost." "Sky, it might be best if we stayed, just in case anyone can find a way into this realm." Volt sat calmly.

"I swear this…realm. I've never felt anything like this before. It's like it's sucking the mana away from me constantly," Sky said.

"Seeing as Scourge was perfectly fine, it must mean it only weakened us because we are warriors of light. We have to be careful," Volt responded as he then waited in silence, conserving his strength. Sky and Volt sat there for what felt like an eternity, for Sky anyway. Nothing changed in this realm, the darkness remained still.

Suddenly a loud, high pitched, ripping sound echoed throughout the realm. "Aghhh. Hey, Volt. What's that sound?" Sky said covering his ears. Just then, the shriek rang through twice more, slightly shaking the area around the two. "I am so tired of these high pitched sounds today!" he yelled in anger.

"I'm not sure what it is, but it sounds like tearing. What is going on here?" Sky and Volt searched frantically for something to place the sound too. Then it happened again, the ripping was close now. Before them, the tip of a lance appeared out of nowhere and ripped a jagged hole into the darkness. From the other side, the clear, blue sky and grassy plains could be seen. A man stepped through the opening, leaving the two even more confused than ever; they sat flabbergasted and speechless. The hole closed behind him.

The man had long, blond hair and sported shiny silver armor from head to toe. His lance had glowing insignias sliding down from the hilt to the point. "Hey, guys,

Volt and uh, Sky?" He pointed at each of them with his lance.

Volt and Sky stared at him. "Yes, who's asking?" they replied in unison.

The man put his hand on his chest and did a short bow. "Nice to meet you, captain, my name is Pierce. I was sent here by the Grandmaster to find you; he somehow felt your presence disappear."

Sky pointed at the lance, "What is that weapon you have, and how did you get here with it? Thought we were going to be here forever!"

Pierce lifted his weapon to his chest, "This is called a dimensional lance, it allows me to cut holes into space and time, and travel to different places. It also ignores many types of defensive abilities any enemy of mine might have. It's very dangerous, though, so only certain knights are trusted with these; well just me for now. Ha."

"Can we use that to get back to our other knights then?" Volt said.

"Of course, I just need a mental link to get us there." Sky looked at him sideways. "A what? Is that anything like a mana link?"

Pierce sighed then laughed. "Kind of…I guess. Just try to think about someone there who is still alive with all of your heart." Pierce went behind them and put his hand on Sky's shoulder. "Let's try it." Sky closed his eyes and calmed his breathing. After moments of this, Pierce's lance began to glow brightly, "There we go, links open, now to create a path." Piece grabbed the lance and began to swing it in the air, with strong diagonal strokes. The sound returned as he slashed at the sky.

"Oh, not this sound again," Sky winced at the loud ripping sound in front of them. After a few swings, a rift began to appear, showing a shallow beach.

"Hmm, a beach? Did they get across the sea already?" Volt spoke to himself.

"You two ready?" Pierce helped Volt and Sky up and guided them through the rift, staying behind himself.

-Year 276 Raptor Beach, Laix Sylindra-

Sky and Volt dropped down on a beach overlooking the ocean. Large wood chips and boards flooded the sand like a broken boardwalk. The water adjacent to the beach held shipmates scattered about underwater, floating on the water, and near the beach. Blaze was coughing up water lying on his back next to a makeshift raft, footsteps in the sand next to him, leading back into the water. Void and a couple of the others were checking on and trying to revive crew members as they washed ashore. In the not too far distance, the remains of the ship could be seen sinking into the sea. A loud roar was let out ferociously from behind as the last of the ship creaked away into the depths of the Udalton ocean.

"What the hell happened here?" Sky's voice trailed off as he looked around at the horror, deciding on what to do first.

Volt ran to Blaze, checking his vitals and setting him up. "I see you guys weren't able to defeat the monster."

Blaze coughed up more water. "Oh how much I hate the water, but no, it was a disaster. We tried our best, but with you two gone, we were at a terrible disadvantage against that thing." He took a second to breath, and continued. "We fought for survival, though it eventually got to the ship, we were approaching land at that point, so we tried to swim the rest of the way. It didn't go well. Ocean did his best when it attempted to follow us, giving us a chance in the water escape, but he couldn't protect

77

everyone." Blaze lowered his head and punched the sand under him.

Sky eventually got over there while surveying the rest of the scene.

"We lost a lot of Wendy's crew on the way," Void said as he led some of the others over and sat them next to the knights. "Welcome back! Now can you guys help us get these others out of the water." Void ran back towards the shore and shipmates who were drowning. Ocean was out there as well, swimming to those who were further out and bringing them in. The assistance of Sky and Volt helped get as many pirates to shore within the hour as they possibly could.

The sun shined bright directly above them, guiding the need for shade and directing the attention towards the jungle behind them. Sky guided everyone who was still alive and able into a group. They buried the dead on the edge of the forest, using Void's dark mana to move the sand away. A moment of silence commenced with the placing of the fallen pirate swords or mementos as gravestones.

Only about twelve of the pirates were left standing. A wave of sadness breezed through the beach as they all peered around to count their losses. The knights stood there in silence as Sky took up the mantle to speak. His hands behind his back, standing as straight as possible, "Alright boys…I know…whew…I know you just went through some rough hell, I know you lost some of your brothers, your family, and maybe even your home too. I know that you seek revenge." A tear rolled down Sky's eye as he yelled, looking around at the faces of all the men before him. "Well I do, too! I felt so powerless being taken away from you guys. Not able to help those I swore to protect. They are with us still though. They will always be in our hearts, helping us to persevere!"

Sky looked down and shook his head. After a moment, he raised his head back up and continued. "Even though it hurts, we still have a job to do. All of their sacrifices will be for nothing if we stop here crying." He paused to wipe off his eyes. "The Gods are relying on us to get orbs and defeat Chaos and dammit that's what we are going to do. Wendy tasked you guys with getting us here safely, and we got here. That means your job is done, you can stay here and wait for another boat to show up on that shore, or you can join us on our journey. Safety is not guaranteed, this is a dangerous land, but you guys are brave, right? What say, you pirates?" Sky held his hand out to Jax, who had his wet captain's jacket now over his shoulders, and a curved blade at his waist. He stood there staring at Sky's hand, then looked back at the rest of his crew, and again at his palm. "Well Jax?" Sky waved his hand back and forth.

Jax sighed and put his hand to Sky's, "We have lost a lot of men getting involved with this fight…with you and your 'holy' path. But dear, old Wendy gave us orders to protect you and to guide you, and we can't forsake that now. We will continue our duty, especially if those are her last orders to us." He shook Sky's hand firmly. "You have our support here. Don't worry; Wendy's pirates aren't going anywhere. And after we finish here, we will head back to Kegato and prepare a siege of our own on Scourge."

Sky smiled and turned towards the jungle. "Sounds good. Get ready boys, on me. This is my homeland; stay close, or you'll get lost or dead." Sky walked off, everyone filing in behind him as they embarked into the hell that awaited them.

Chapter 5:
Wind Phoenix

-Year 276   FenWentai Temple   Laix, Sylindra-

     Around the center of the continent was an area of great historical significance, Ville Ciel. With a modestly sized temple set at the top, this uniquely shaped city spiraled downward into a large hollowed out area in the earth. With an old stairwell going around the entire outer edge of the hole, it stretched down to the bottom. Platforms built up against the inner walls are used to hold up homes and small shops. Different levels of homes were seen as you progressed down the stairwell. The top had the more beautiful homes, closer to the temple of worship, while the less fortunate were forced to live near the dirt. Most of what were homes at the bottom before were there no longer. Ville Ciel hadn't been lived in properly since the times of old when humans had first come to Sylindra. Now only the aged priests live here in order to upkeep the temple where FenWentai sleeps, locked away. Over the past week, however, an uneasy feeling had fallen on the priests as Fen's vase had gradually become less stable.

     Violent earthquakes ran through the city, causing some older buildings to crumble and slide off into the center of the opening. The earth shook even more fiercely around the temple; the servants and priests to scatter in fear, most ignorant of the cause. Inside of the small, oriental temple, a person-sized metallic green vase with a phoenix and other golden insignia inscribed on it shined. It vibrated with the same rhythm as the ground, nearly falling off of its pedestal. "What's going on sir?" One of the scribes knelt in front of the head priest, his bright white and gold oriental robes flowing in the wind.

Wiping the sweat off his head, "The day we feared has come. FenWentai, the Wind phoenix, is being unleashed, and we cannot contain him any longer." The vase began to glow a bright green light that beamed forward, burning the temple walls in its path. "We must flee, or our lives, too, will join the casualties that await today." The two ran off along with the rest of the priests outside of the temple. A neon explosion went off behind them, followed by loud, high pitched shrieks.

-Year 276 Kritie Jungle southeast Laix, Sylindra-

"Oh man, it's so humid, is it always like this on Laix?" One of the pirates could be seen wiping sweat off his head only to have it replaced with more sweat. The coalition was now in the thick of the jungle, forced to use their swords to slice through the thick, harsh brushes that tried to impede them. Loud roars could be heard in the surrounding areas, causing them to pause and peer around before continuing. About every mile either a sign warning of dangerous beasts or one showing the distance to the nearest village could be seen.

"It's always gonna be humid over here, man, haha, but I do have to ask something." Sky turned around, looking directly at Blaze. "Can you refrain from using your fire mana here? This forest is significant to me, I'd rather not have it burned down," he finished with a fake smile.

Blaze's face turned red, almost tripping over a tree root sticking out suspiciously far. "Don't worry, Sky, even if you're being mauled by a wild beast, I promise not to use my flames," Blaze retorted with an equally playful smile.

"Who knows, if I have to fight back, I might just use my mana an—" Sky smacked him in the back of the head.

"Don't even think about it." Sky's face turned serious.

Jax came up and put his hand on both of their shoulders, pushing them along. "Come on, guys, let's not tear each other apart already."

Blaze and Sky glanced at each other, and then Sky directed his attention towards Jax. "No worries, we're just messing around right, Blazey?"

Sky matched Jax's smile as he patted Blaze on the shoulder. Blaze nodded and looked away, being mindful of his steps.

Their walk continued, deeper and deeper into the humid, heat trap. Sky used his control over the wind to keep a breeze blowing through the trees in their direction, easing their nervousness for moments at a time. He excitedly jogged in front of the group as they walked and turned around. "Come on, guys, imagine how my ancestors lived here years ago, and without the mana to help them as much." One of the pirates was taking off his top as he came into view from behind Jax, "Yeah, they probably had a lot less clothing too. Sheesh."

Sky laughed before turning back around. "I can't wait until you see my castle, and meet some of the interesting characters that make up my family! I know you remember, Volt, right?"

Volt faced away. "Yeah…they are sure something."

Blaze turned to Volt. "Oh, that's right, you're the only one of us who has been here before, other than Sky, of course."

Volt glanced around at the trees, shrubs, and down to another sign they passed. The wind breezed calmly through the trees at this moment. Volt looked at Blaze sideways before peeking around at the trees. Blaze's face changed a couple times as he inched towards Volt, waiting for a response. "Uh yeah. Father sent me here to train with Sky to be knights. They surely started us on this path early," Volt said.

The knights and pirates slid down a heavily bumpy hill, causing small nicks and bruises to those not careful. Upon reaching the bottom, running water could be heard off in the distance. Void got to the bottom first, brushing himself off while waiting for the others to come tumbling down.

"This is a thick forest; how do you even know the way?"

"Watch out!" Gaia yelled as she powered up and caught a beast leaping out of the bushes directly in the ribs as it lunged for Volt's face. The large, bear-like beast went crashing into a tree and whimpered off.

"Uh, thanks Gaia." Volt said, wide eyed staring at her.

"I got you babes." She said winking at him while also flexing her muscle.

"Hey, whose that?" Ocean asked, pointing at a random spectator hiding in the bushes wearing an all-black cloak. As soon as he is found out, the man proceeded to run back through the forest. Jax snapped his fingers and the pirates immediately chased after him. Moments later they drug the man before Sky and dropped him.

"Ugh what are you doing? Leave me alone!" The man yelled as he looked up to Sky.

"Sorry man, just had to make sure you weren't an enemy spying on us out here. I know my family has a lot of enemies," Sky said lifting the guy up to his feet.

"Are you a Hiyama? Heh. I can see why you're so cautious, but who are these people?" The man brushed himself off and pointed at Jax and the pirates.

Jax reached out and grabbed his finger. "First off, who are you?

"My name isn't important." The man snatched his finger back. "You guys have to be careful in these woods though, there have been reports of disappearances here lately. And your little family has done nothing to look into it." The man smirked at Sky in a demeaning manner.

"Hey! You see all of these guys we have here? I think we're good, man!" One of the pirates yelled from behind Jax.

"Either way, that's what I'm here looking into. So if you don't mind, I'll be on my way." The cloaked figure turned and dashed back through the jungle.

"What an interesting figure he was," Gaia commented as he walked off.

"Maybe we should heed his warning though." Void muttered under his breath.

"Worry not! We got this, let's continue though, time and daylight's wasting standing around here." Sky uttered as he skipped ahead down another hill.

"Hmm, you sure this is the right way?" Void motioned at Sky.

Sky snapped his fingers confidently. "Of course! I've been visiting this temple since I was a child. My family made frequent trips to pay respects to FenWentai. You know, when they weren't in the middle of fighting a war and had time to actually bond." A quick silence struck the group as they began to make way again down the path. Sky suddenly began checking around the group as they walked slower to match his pace.

"What's going on, Sky?" Ocean said, a bit worried. The group crept forward while loud footsteps tumbled through the bushes around them. Something bellowed off to their right, catching them off guard

The pirate behind Jax hopped up, nearly out of his boots and got to the other side of Jax, effectively hiding in his shadow. "What is that sound, Cap'n?" The pirate asked, looking at the tense Jax, who already had his hand on the hilt of his blade.

"Shall we?" Ocean continued past Sky to keep walking but jerked behind a tree after the next sound.

"Haha!" Blaze let out.

Another roar shook the jungle, closer this time. Footsteps echoed in their direction, approaching quickly. "Wait! Shhh… I hear something," Sky held his arms out and stopped everyone. Then, a large boar came burrowing through the bushes, crossing in front of them. This was no ordinary boar, however. This boar was massive, towering over the knights with its dark brown hide. Even so, the hog was running away from something, and the brushes got no mercy.

A few paces past where the boar crossed the knights, it stopped cold in its tracks. Ahead of the boar were thick, green, snake-like tentacles that shot down from above the trees, cutting the boar off. Only six showed themselves initially, then ten, and finally sixteen, the serpent-like tails had spiraled around and surrounded its prey. The tips of them split open slowly to reveal ten rows of teeth lined from long, slimy flaps resembling the mouth of a Venus fly trap. One of the mouths bit and attached to the boar's back right leg, stunning it and causing it to drop down on that side. The rest took advantage and what happened next was a savage feast. The tentacles munched the boar from all sides, tearing through its rough hide and burrowing through its body like earthworms in the dirt.

During this massacre, an enormous white-striped tiger had skidded to a stop right before the group, its attention focused on the boar or its remains. The group was so busy gawking, they barely noticed the feline. "That's some scary stuff. Sky what did you lead us into?" Ocean elbowed Sky.

"Oh," Sky looked over slowly to their left to see the big cat just as it noticed them. The two studied each other, the knights readying their weapons.

"Hey…guys…" Void spoke, but no one responded. He kept looking over at the empty carcass of the boar with no tentacles insight. "Guys!" Void yelled this time, but it was too late. Tentacles shot out from the trees above them and snatched up two pirates unlucky enough to be on their own in the back, pulling them up indefinitely.

"Waaa… help!" Everyone turned around to see them surrounded.

"Rye! Jae!" The pirate captain yelled up into the air, pulling out his weapon. "Damnit." Shredded clothing and bones came falling down through the trees around the knights; everyone stared, horrified. This switched to anger quickly afterward. The tiger had been surrounded as well during this time, trying to keep the tentacles away from him.

"Sky, what do we do here," Volt said, swinging wildly at the green demons.

"Try to cut the heads of the tentacles off!" Sky flew into the air and began slicing the tentacle in half, causing green and red blood to spray everywhere.

Void, using his massive sword leaped into the air, intercepting some of the heads coming in trying to bite and slammed them to the ground, splattering their heads.

"Yeah, that's the way, Void, off with the tips!" Ocean looked over in praise but froze in horror as more and more tentacles began popping up behind Void. "Guys! These things are multiplying at an alarming rate. We may have to make a tactical retreat!" Ocean set off and began running through the forest.

"Eh, we can't fight them here it seems, let's regroup!" Sky lead the group off towards Ocean, but some

86

godt bit and swipe along the way. Everyone ran off through the jungle with the serpents hot on their trails.

"They aren't slowing down at all, Whoa!" Blaze tripped over another root looking back at the skyline full of those creatures. Instinctively he begins to charge the mana in his hands ready to fire but paused and stopped. "Damn, that's right." Blaze leapt over to the side, dodging incoming strikes and caught up with the others.

Sky flew up. "I'll try to get a lo—" Sky got swatted to the ground and tumbled before being assisted up by Volt. He got Sky to his feet while blocking bites for him.

"Good try, but we have to keep moving," Volt parried a tentacle swipe and pushed Sky forward.

"Look! An opening!" One of the pirates out front pointed to a clearing in the trees. They tried desperately to skid to a quick halt when they saw the large cliff before them. "Oh, nooo!" The pirate in the front got nudged off the ledge, having only a loose root to hold on. The group looked behind to see the creatures gaining on them quickly.

Void walked up to the edge and looked down to a rough flowing river below rushing downstream to the left. "We might have to jump, guys."

Blaze looked down off the same cliff. "There's no wa—," Blaze got pushed off the cliff by Sky.

"There's no time, let's go!" Sky said.

Blaze's flailing body was followed by others as the rest of the crew jumped down one by one after him. "You piece of shiiiit!" Blaze yelled as he plummeted down towards the river.

Sky, in the air next to the cliff, noticed the last pirate got tripped up and caught by the tentacles before he could make it over. He got over to try and save the man, nearly getting captured himself. After a short struggle, they kept Sky back as the pirate got pulled away back into the forest. After a loud sigh, Sky was forced to fly down to the group before he go abducted as well, a solemn expression on his face. "Dammit!" He yelled as he flew towards the stream.

The knights and pirates were being shifted back and forth through the rough waters, attempting to avoid boulders and drowning at the same time. Sky and Ocean did their best to help keep everyone from drowning, pulling them out of the water when they went under. This worked for a while, but Sky couldn't get too far in, or it would soak his wings, nullifying his ability to fly. Ocean swam around, pushing people up to the surface from below, but it was impossible to get to everyone as the knights got priority. The pirates were naturally better swimmers, though. Their rough journey continued down the Rye River.

-Year 276 Base of the Rye River Laix, Sylindra

The water laid calm now, the river strolled downstream instead of rushing. The cliff and waterfall they came down had long disappeared from view and were replaced with hills and more forest to all sides. Boulders decorated the hands of the river base, giving something to grab onto to free yourself. Splashes of blood and bodies were sprinkled about in the water, some facedown, others floating head up, sucking wind. Along the shore, a dark-coated deer-like mammal surveyed the scene. It sniffed around while slowly walking past bodies crawling out of the water, and those still unconscious in the grass. Trotting up to one of the figures on his back, the jungle dweller began to lick their faces. Suddenly his eyes opened wide as he coughed out water and began to gasp for air. He sat up as liquid droplets started to fall onto his head from above. Leaning forward and holding his chest, he looked to his sides to see his wings waterlogged and sagging to the ground. Sky put his hand on the gentle beast's face as the rain picked up in intensity. seemed to cause everyone to stir a bit more.

"Hello there, Chansey, how did you manage to find me out here," he said while stroking its face.

Ocean, who had been facedown next to Sky, struggled to push himself up. He eventually succeeded and flipped onto his back, soaking in the rain. "Goodness that was rough. Hey Sky, I'm drained, how many were we able to save?"

Sky peered around noticing three pirates still breathing on the shore, and the pirate captain dragging two pirates out of the water and tossing them to safety.

"There are six of us left…" Jax said as he spit a mouthful of water off to the side. "Damn…demons nearly wrecked my entire crew." He scoffed angrily.

Volt came walking in from the woods behind them and stood next to Ocean, squinting, "Hey wait is that—," Volt cut himself off to jump into the water. "Blaze!" Volt swam over to Blaze, under the water, in the middle of the lake. "You guys are ridiculous," Volt said, throwing Blaze to the ground, who doesn't budge.

"Damn, is he dead?" Ocean smirked and rolled over to put his hand on Blaze's back.

Blaze shifted and picked himself up, spitting out an obnoxious amount of water, "Gah! I'm not dead asshole, I won't die that easily." Blaze stayed there in that position for a while, getting himself together.

Void walked over and put his hand on Blaze's shoulder, "Be better," he said in a low tone next to his ear.

Blaze shrugged him off and sat up. "You know how it is with me and water,…" Blaze, wiped rainwater off of his face.

"Don't be embarrassed Blaze, we all have our thing. Hmm speaking of…" Void walked over and kneeled next to Sky, "How far are we from the destination?

89

Sky got up and began shaking his wings to air them out, "One moment," He forcibly flapped his wings, throwing water in all directions. This was met with a bunch of groans and grunts as the water woke up pirates who were still lying there unconscious. Sky spread out his wings wide and began to flap them in place. He began to float. Up into the air he went, past the trees and out of sight. A strike of lightning, and hallowing crashes in the distance brought him back down swiftly. "Whew! I almost got hit!" Sky was caught breathing heavily; singe marks on the tip of his wing. "Yeah, the fiasco with those tentacles, and going down the river took a bit off the path, but a couple miles that way and we'll reach the town in question. Sky pointed up a hill to the northwest. The group assembled and started through the jungle again toward Ville Ciel, the Sky City. Chansey followed eagerly behind.

"Sorry about your crew, Jax." Gaia said slowly walking over, frowning

"Worry not las, we will press on. The time to mourn is later, for now you have a job to do," Jax said, holding back his quivering lip and wiping his eyes.

"I see..." Gaia trailed off.

"So, Sky, what's this place like anyway? I've heard a lot of legends about it." Jax walked up next to Sky, putting his hand on his shoulder.

"Well," Sky took a second to think before continuing. "When I was a kid, I was told Ville Ciel was the first place our ancestors settled in when they came to Sylindra. It is one of the oldest settled civilizations there is in this world. With buildings crafted using the trees as the base, Ville Ciel finds itself in one of the only true clearings in this jungle. Aside from the castle grounds and a few others, I think those are the only areas where the jungle lets up, albeit because of us. Either way, the Sky City is a beautiful sight to behold." Sky took a deep breath before

90

continuing," The rooftops are all rounded, and the structures streamlined to help against the constant rains. Most of the homes in the center are made of timber to keep them as light as possible…It has a unique setup, to be honest."

The group passed by countless animals as they trekked through the jungle, all of which shied away at the sight of them. Chansey trotted ahead for periods before rushing back. Sky slowed his pace a bit to continue. "It's mostly uninhabited now though, except for priests and others who have helped to keep it maintained over the years. That...and guard the shrine of the wind phoenix, who has been the guardian deity here for centuries. She became a symbol of Ardin's might since she came to be."

Jax was shaking the entire time in amazement, "Wait, so you guys are expected to take down this guardian deity? That's crazy!"

"Well, at the moment, I don't know if you noticed the earthquakes in the background, but the phoenix has been released from a long slumber, and in her rage, she is destroying the very land she once protected. So now we have more than one reason to stop her, we still must prove ourselves to the Gods," Sky looked up into the air and sighed. The rain eventually cleared up while they journeyed through the jungle, the ground shaking, and high pitched whistling sounds creating an uneasy feeling amongst the group.

The ground shook violently, causing most of the crew to lose their balance. Sky glanced around frantically as he heard a screeching wind sound coming in their direction. "Everybody down!" Sky tackled most everyone to the ground, but the pirate out front was slow to react. Almost instantly, a sharp gust of wind shot through the jungle in their direction, slicing trees, large rocks, everything high off the ground in two, passing by the knights and behind them off into the distance.

"*Shit,,* what the hell was that!" One of the pirates said as he turned around, horrified as he saw his buddy standing behind him stiff as a rock. Then his top half slid off his bottom half and splattered onto the ground.

"Damn…" Jax said, noticing who it was behind him. Everyone peered around, shocked, and disappointed.

"That was a warm welcome from our target." Sky got up and pulled out his scythe. "She knows we're here, ready up, guys!" Sky turns around to see the pirates mulling over their dead friend and began to say something, but Blaze stopped him short and went over to the pirates instead.

"I know you just lost your friend, but if you don't pay attention, one of this thing's next wild attacks will have you ending up just like him, sliced up into pieces, far away from home by something you can't even comprehend. We need your help here, so don't give up on us yet, ok!" The pirate he focused his attention on shook his head, tears in his eyes. "What's your name, man?"

Wiping his face, "Terry," he responded.

"Well, let's go, Terry, be a man, on to glory!" Blaze ran up next to the rest of the nights. The slice attack from the phoenix made an early clearing ahead of them, so they could see the city clearly. It was structured into a circular shape. Buildings around the outside spiraled down into a large opening in the center, with trees on the outside. Towards the back of the city was a vast temple with ancient writing on pillars and along the walls. Its roof was disheveled and broken in pieces scattered along the sides. A bright green light shone through the cracks in the building and a long stairway leading down to a path that went to other parts of the city.

Various buildings and homes along the stairwell path were blown over or were sliced into large pieces that slide off into the earth. There was a small horde of rubble packed together on the bottom level of the city. In the center of the destruction, a colossal bird made entirely of green mana in the form of spiraling wind. The mana was translucent, making certain angles harder to see it than others. A glowing green skeletal structure could be continuously seen, however.

The bones flickered and sparkle as it soared through the air, flaring blood-red eyes leading the way and streaking as they moved. While staring at the bird, the crew noticed priests and other residents still trying to evacuate by climbing the precarious stairwells, barely holding up under the damage and weight laboring on it now. Above them, was the safe haven of the jungles; below were the dark abyss and a long drop. Sky saw the phoenix noticed the survivors at the same time, and sprouted his wings in anticipation. FenWentai swung its massive towards the stairwell, letting out a furious burst of wind. "Shit, I knew it!" Sky gusted off towards the city, but he didn't make it in time, and that part of the stairs got destroyed, sending three of the civilians into free-fall. "Ack!" Sky hit them hard in midair, not able to catch them all. This shoved them across the opening and onto the stairwell a couple of levels below on the opposite side.

"Sky! You returned, sir!" One of the guys said, holding both of his hands and bowing.

Sky turned towards the group who started to run in his direction, "Guys i need you to help the civilians get to safety!" Sky yelled across the gap, then looked over at the phoenix who had focused his attention on Sky and the others behind him. "Void, assistance please!" Sky pulled out his scythe, as a dark portal appeared behind him.

"Why can't we just come with you to safety through that portal?" One of those behind him asked.

Sky peered back over his shoulder, "At the moment, only certain people can safely travel through his portals, those without a link to him he can't control where you'll end up. Don't worry, we'll get you guys to safety." At this Sky stepped back into the portal, disappearing. Another portal appeared behind FenWentai that Sky looked out of spinning around, scythe perched.

"Take this!" Sky turned around in the air multiple times before slashing at the phoenix and to his dismay it went phased right through Fen. "No way…" Sky flew back a few feet as he and the monstrous bird stared each other down. The pirates along with Blaze and Ocean went to protect the remaining priests and residents of the city as they attempted to escape. "Alright guys, expect a lot more destruction to come; we gotta make sure these guys get out of here alive and live to talk about the glorious Royal Knights who saved their lives!" Ocean did his best at trying to pep everyone else up as they ran, then he looked over at Jax. "Oh, and uh Wendy's pirates, too." Jax smiled slightly.

Sky flew over to Void and Volt, who still stood at the entrance to the city. They noted all of the destruction as he passed. "I might need y'all to support me any way you can."

"It would be my pleasure, Cap." Void stood there, weapon ready.

"Let me see if he can be hit by lightning, be careful up there." Volt waved Sky up.

Sky flew back up towards the winged monster and begins a midair fight, taking them all over the skies above the city. Sky's strikes with his scythe had trouble connecting; Fen did not have this issue. Her bursts of sharp wind combined just fine, blowing Sky back. "Ugh this is getting me nowhere." On the defensive now, Sky fended off wing slashes and charged attempts from the bird. The sky became increasingly darker as the fight progresses. On one last effort, Sky charged and swung full force at the bird, to no avail, as it smacked his now exposed body through the air and sent him crashing into the temple. The roof caved in a few seconds after impact, falling down on top of Sky. Volt and Void stood there eyeing each other as Volt gathered mana into his spear. It glowed dimly.

"You ready, man?" Volt said, spinning his spear in circles now.

Voids hands were glowing a dark purple as he punched his palm, "Yeah, man, let's do it!"

Volt nodded as a strike of lightning came cutting through the clouds, striking Fen and stunning her. The electricity surging caused her to shake and twitch in place while it coursed around her body.

"Now!" Void used his ability and created a plethora of portals surrounding her from all sides. Volt surrounded himself in lightning and with spear in hand jumped into a corresponding portal in front of him. This caused him to shoot out of an entrance near the monster. He struck her with a direct strike and a flash of lightning before soaring into another portal and repeating. Fen wailed and flailed its wings as it took damage from all sides repeatedly. Void smirked. "I think it's working," he said to himself with his hands up, maintaining the portals.

After minutes of getting pummeled, the bird let out a loud shriek, expelling a strong shock wave that disrupted Volt's path and sent him flying away. The portal's also dissipated at that moment, the angry expression on the phoenix turned into a furious rage. The green aura that surrounded the bone structure of Fen now expanded to his entire body, making visible the spiraling winds that encompassed the wind phoenix even more extensive than before. Volt crashed into the ground next to Void, knocking them both back. Sky flew up towards the bird only to get caught by her beak again. Fen found Sky and dove him back into the temple ruins, causing even more destruction to the area. Debris and blood from Sky flew everywhere, as Sky laid there still afterwards. Fen continued to fly high into the air above the clouds. A terrifying shriek filled the city as the bird soared through the air towards Sky's limp body. Sky opened one of his eyes, slightly regaining consciousness, "Oh shit!" At the last second, Sky was able to will himself over and push himself out of the way, flying somewhat to clear the temple but then tumbling out of the air and catching himself on the edge of the cliff, legs hanging off into nothingness. Behind him, however, the temple was utterly destroyed; a crater was left in the wake of the phoenix's landing.

The shockwave knocked one of the pirates —who were helping evacuate people— off the cliff towards Sky. Sky caught the pirate's leg at the last second and hung there for a moment as he got his wits about him again. He flew up and tossed the pirate back on the surface. He was thanked and turned around to see the phoenix coming in for another nosedive directly at him, "Wait when did he—" In a quick motion, Sky flew straight up, dodging the initial attack. Still, the shockwave hit his back, sending him flying towards the opening in the middle of the city. "Shit." Sky was unable to catch his balance as he flailed through the air. Suddenly a portal appeared in his path and teleported him back to Void and Volt.

"You ok, Cap?" Void said as the phoenix was flying back towards them now. He switched his attention from Sky to the incoming threat.

"Eh I guess, still can't touch this guy," Sky said.

"Volt and I have a plan, get ready to go all out, we'll create an opening for you," Void created a giant portal this time that caught the incoming phoenix, sending her back into the sky. Confused, she turned around for another dive-bomb. Sky and Volt got up and readied themselves, mana charging on both sides.

"Cut down the holy to protect the precious, cleave and devastate, God slayer scythe!" Sky's scythe illuminated

96

as it transformed and enlarged, now with a blade four meters long. The mana surrounding his scythe changed into a glittering gold that glowed intensely.

Volt put his left arm off to the side and began gathering his lightning mana all to that arm. "Lucin, grant me the power to strike down all who oppose you! Ringa Uira!" Volt's entire arm became engulfed in lightning as he got into a low stance towards the incoming attack.

"Hope you're ready because here it comes." Sky shifted his giant scythe back and waited.

"Eat this!" Volt swung up his supercharged palm and clashed with the phoenix, stopping her in her tracks. The force and power from the encounter caused shockwaves to flare out in all directions. Sky waited there, scythe cocked back for the perfect opportunity. Volt and Fen continued to struggle for supremacy, neither willing to give an inch. Finally, Void sent a dark blast hitting the phoenix in the side, distracting it just enough for Volt to take advantage. Volt grasped the beak of the bird with his free hand and forced it to the ground, coursing lightning throughout its body and stunning it in place. "Sky, NOW!"

At this, Sky charged towards the enemy full force swinging his gigantic scythe. "See if you can take this." With a fury of slashes, with increasing speed and ferocity, Sky laid an onslaught of blows causing the phoenix to curdle over in pain. Lightning still surrounded Fen, meaning it couldn't phase through any of the attacks. Sky walked up to Fen as she tried to back off. "Sorry, I've got to make up for you making me look like a complete fool!" Now raising his voice Sky took the sharp end of the scythe and in an upwards motion he stabbed the bird in her abdomen and pulled up slightly, catching the bottom of her ribcage. "Let's go for a ride, birdie!" Sky forced the phoenix up into the air, well above the opening, held up through the wound. He then pulled out his scythe and began to lay even more slashes on

97

Fen in midair. Green slush splattered left and right throughout this onslaught.

"This was for ruining this beautiful city you were supposed to protect! He slashed it more. Fen turned to fly away, but Sky caught her with the scythe blade around the bird's neck, jerking it back. He wrapped his free arm around her torso and pulled her back to his body. He narrowed his wings and angled them both backwards. "Say hi to Ardin for me on the other side!" While still holding on, Sky jerked them back and downwards in a spiral motion towards the opening in the center of the city. They soared down into the darkness, causing a massive, messy crash when they finally collided with the ground at the very bottom. Dust and debris flew everywhere, blinding everyone. After the collision, pieces of the stairwell crumbled away and dropped towards the ground, taking floors of the city with them. There was a long silence for what seemed like an eon while everyone awaited the conclusion to a stressful battle.

Chapter 6:
Hiyama Castle

An ear-splitting shriek echoed from within the hole in the center of the city. A sense of relief eased across everyone. The pirates high fived each other, the knights breathed a sigh of relief as they continued to evacuate people. However, suddenly, all of the celebrating stopped. A very familiar sound was heard coming from the opening to the city. Raging, slicing winds came burrowing through the hole and into the open air like a wind geyser. Everyone, surprised, stopped what they were doing and looked down to hear wings flapping and approaching slowly. The knights smiled, expecting their captain to be the one rising...until it wasn't.

"Volt! Your lightning ran out it didn't get him," a weak but loud voice yelled from inside the hole.

Volt's face lit up in dismay. Blaze enveloped his body in mana in preparation for the order that would come next. "Volt, Blaze...plan B! Hit him with the combo it should work down here without ruining the forest!" Sky yelled up through the opening. The others could hear him coughing up blood, while he repeatedly collapsed from trying to stand.

"Gotcha! Ready, Blaze?" Volt yelled to the other side of the gap.

"All good!" Blaze responded.

"TAO UIRA!" Volt yelled as his spear radiated with an electric aura reaching out further than the spear itself. Soon after, the mana began to circulate around the head like a drill. Perched back, he threw his spear at the opening of the

100

gap and caught the phoenix in the neck just as she resurfaced her head, stunning it in place. The bird was noticeably bleeding down her neck under cover of the green wind surrounding its body. It flapped there in place, unable to move with electricity caressing her body.

Blaze ran up to the edge of the gap, both of his hands glowing bright red. "Oh great lords grant me the power to create ultimate destruction, kneel before the power of lord Verafelt, Molten Nova!" A massive ball of molten lava and fire grew out of Blaze's hands as he hovered slightly above the opening with flaming wings made of pure mana. This ball was then thrown into Fen, who was forced back into the hole from the massive attack. Everything in its path was annihilated as the phoenix plummeted again down into the darkness. An explosion of fire shot up like a tower through the hole for all to see. "Man, why does that take so much out of me, I've gotta perfect it." Blaze said, as he collapsed from exhaustion.

Volt called his spear back to him and knelt next to Void. "Hey, uh, wasn't Sky down there, too?"

Void smirked as a portal opened up next to them, placing Sky gently down with a bright green orb in his hand.

Volt looked over. "Oh, I see."

Sky, breathing heavily, pulled the orb closer, and roughly shoved it into his chest. In a flash, the two had become one. The knights and the pirates began their route back to Sky, Volt, and Void, along with some of the priests, followed them over. Sky's body began to become translucent and resembled the same properties as the phoenix.

Void reached over to help lift Sky up, but his hand passed right through his buddy's body. It was a weird sensation when he gave it over where Sky should have been tangible; a sense of nothingness surrounded his hand. It felt like sticking your hand in a vacuum of space; the wind, rain, and every other element did not affect it. "Whoa, would you look at that, Sky."

Sky opened his eyes and looked at himself. "I love this, ha, I'm invincible." Sky's body reverted to normal, allowing Void and Volt to lift him up on their shoulders.

"Yeah maybe it'll help you not get hit so much, ha-ha." Don't forget the phoenix's weakness will be yours now; don't let your head get too big," Volt said.

Void spoke low to Sky as he watched the remaining priests stumble up to them with Blaze and Ocean close behind.

The priest with the most elaborate garb went to the front and sat on one knee in front of Sky. "Oh, Master Sky, we are forever in your debt! May Ardin bless you for passing your trial and saving us from our once peaceful protector."

Sky put his hand on the head priest's shoulder. "It's my pleasure, but I did have help as well." Sky looked back at his fellow knights.

The head priest gasped and went to shake the hands of the remaining knights as well. "Thank you, thank you, thank you."

"Think it's time we head out? Jax said, starting towards the exit of the city.

"Yeah, I guess so," Sky led the rest of the group out behind Jax. The priest headed back towards the center of the city, and the Knights and pirates walked out again into the jungle, taking another path off to the left, following Sky's lead. The sun began to sag off to the east, hiding behind the trees and limiting visibility.

One of the short and stocky pirates walked up next to Sky and ran into his wing, stumbling backward a bit. "Hey it's getting a bit dark out here, did you guys have any place in mind to stay for the night, so we aren't out in the open for the monsters in this forest." Sky chuckled and put his arm around the pirate's shoulders, "Worry not man, we are about an hour's walk from my castle."

"*Castle*?" All of the pirates say in unison.

"I didn't know you were royalty Sky, you don't really seem…like the type…" Jax trails off.

"I know, I know, but I've been groomed for this position since I was a young one. I also met Volt as a kid too; his church visited us and we kinda saw each other and our similar positions. We became friends instantly." Sky peeled back at Volt for a second while still walking forward.

"Hmm, really? I thought you guys just met each other," Jax questioned.

Volt walked up behind Jax, "Well, this is our first mission together as a group, but Sky and I have been through stuff before." Volt laughed a bit and then stopped short. "Wait, what's that sound?" Everyone stopped and looked around, confused. They had traveled about a mile from Ville Ciel after this point, making relatively good time through the rough forests.

A faint ripcord-like sound could be heard getting louder and louder. "How can this world be protected by such weak knights," A being shrouded in such dark shadows that none of his features could be distinguished other than his silhouette, appeared in the center of the crew. He was a giant, towering demon, at least half a foot taller than the tallest knight. He had what the group could barely make out to be a sizeable double-sided ax behind the billowing darkness. Everyone stared at the figure in silence as he snarled around at everyone. "This should be Scourge's job, but I decided to see you guys for myself…and I am not impressed," The demon said.

Sky's eyes widened upon realizing who stood before them now. "D-Demise…"

Blaze looked over to Sky, who was mumbling to himself. "What did you just say?' Blaze raised his voice, not believing his ears. The demon rushed forward, palming Blaze's head and shoving him back into the pirates who were standing behind him.

A dark, intense aura began to gather around the demon's body, forcing all around him to be pushed back instantly. "That's right, I am Deces' the King of Armageddon! Demise, the evil overlord! The reason for your existence! The end of your journey." Demise's giant armored fist hit the earth with such force, the resulting impact sent out a shock wave traveling along the ground and through the air, effectively destroying the surrounding area and sending the knights and crew flying. The ground directly around Demise was gone, leaving nothing but a gaping hole surrounding him.

Blaze landed in the thick of the forest around the same area as the pirates; Volt, Ocean, Jax, and Void in a small clearing in the jungle. A few abandoned log cabins in a clearing in the jungle unknowingly hosted Volt, Ocean, Jax and Void. A dilapidated low wooden fence surrounded the perimeter of this make-shift town. Sky landed on his own, closest to Demise.

Sky stared around at the devastation, then he searched for his knights, not seeing anyone. "Damn, I've got to get out of here," Sky peered back to see Demise rising up, focusing in his direction. Sky opened his wings and began flying up into the air but is suddenly stopped. A dark aura appeared around his body and slammed him to the ground.

"Oh no, no, no, Sky, you are with me today." Demise waves his hand back, and his mana dragged Sky back.

"What is this!" Sky struggled to break free, but is forced to his knees.

Demise wrapped his large hand around the back of Sky's head and forced it into the ground. Sky spits up dirt and made a feeble attempt to stand. "Let go of me!"

Demise laughed as he held down Sky's head, "Watch your tone, Sky." Demise started squeezing. Sky let out a shriek of pain and his arms went limp. Demise smacked Sky's head a few times. "Now now, don't die on me yet, I still need to get some fun out of this visit before I kill you guys." Demise loosened his grip slightly and Sky started bleeding from his ears, coughing again.

Chancey overlooked all of this from behind bushes, legs shaking in place, frozen.

Over in the middle of the jungle, Blaze got up and noticed the few pirates that remained all looking up to him. "Don't worry guys, we'll be fine." Jax could be heard yelling from a distance.

"Blaze you better keep my pirates safe or else!" The pirate captain shouted.

Blaze, his face scrunched in anger." I got it, don't worry J!" Blaze yelled back. As he finished, he looked over and noticed a tentacle stalking one of the pirates. "Hey, watch ou—!" It was too late; Blaze watched the tentacle as it wrapped around the pirate's torso, lifted him off his feet and pulled him back further into the forest. "Shit! Let's go, guys!" Blaze motioned for the rest of the crew to follow him.

Jax and the rest of the knights found themselves surrounded by beings shrouded in darkness in various spots in the trees and on the ground. The shadows in the trees had what appeared to be bows and dark arrows. The majority of them on the ground, stood straight with a blade in each hand. A few were larger shadows that wielded shields and swords. Volt pulled the knights closer into formation, while Jax stayed close.

"Keep it tight guys, we don't know how dangerous our enemy is this time." Volt addressed the group as he watched the archers ready arrows and direct them at the knights.

"Probably won't be any better than on the docks," Jax said, looking around. It was a moment of tension as both sides were still.

The wind blew through the trees, tossing leaves about, but one leaf caught Void's attention. It fluttered in front of his face, with an odd shape, "Is that…" The plant lowered itself gingerly and softly landed on the ground seeming to initiate the conflict.

As soon as it landed, a spray of arrows rained into the air towards the knights as the other shadow beings came at them as well. Almost in sync, the arrows were cut away as the group mostly remained in formation. Void's eyes were shaded with his dark aura as he rushed in, his dense dark shadow mana surrounding him and protecting him from incoming arrows.

"Void, wait!" Volt yelled after him.

Void had already approached one of the larger shadows with the sword and shield in hand. It swung it's sword down at Void, missing before defending itself. Void pointed his giant black claymore directly at the shadow and charged full force through the protection. His sword found its way on the other side of the thing's chest, who faded away after getting its body torn apart and violated by Voids weapon.

The faces of the knights were a mix of confusion and surprise. Void, now surrounded by shadows, stood all the way up, and rested his sword to his side, slightly dipping into the ground. He began to yell loudly. "Agh I am so tired of the darkness!" Void's emotional voice carried for miles, even Blaze and Sky heard him scream.

Volt looked over at him, "Void…" His spear raised high into the air, Volt called his knights, "Show them we weren't chosen without cause, Royal Knights charge!" The knights fought well against the shadow soldiers, cleaving them down with great force. This, however, seemed to be for

106

naught as new warriors appeared from the darkness to replace the fallen. The knights were bogged down by rains of arrows, making it hard to advance. Void's aggressive blows did help create some openings, however. With enough help, the bow shadow soldiers were thrown from the trees and cleaned up by Ocean's quick strikes. Fighting a seemingly never-ending battle, the knights slowly dwindled the numbers of the shadow soldiers.

Back in the center of the forest, Sky struggled to free his neck from beneath Demise's foot. "I'll kill you, dammit," he managed to choke out.

Demise pressed down harder. "I wonder who will die first, you or your subordinates." Demise laughed obnoxiously for a few seconds before continuing, "I have my gold on you, personally."

Sky struggled with all his might against the boot caught on his throat, channeling his mana. A green aura glowed all around Sky's body as his eyes closed, about to lose consciousness again. Suddenly, his entire body became intangible, and Demise's foot went straight through, slamming into the ground below. Sky's eyes shot open as he rolled off to the side and looked around at his body in shock.

Demise looked at Sky sideways. "What is this form?"

Sky grabbed his scythe, stood up and wiped the blood from his mouth, "I only have an idea, but I'm sure this fight just turned around."

At this, Demise, began his dark laughter again. "I highly doubt this will change anythi—" Sky's scythe cut him off with a swift strike to his face, only managing to break through the mana enough to cause a small nick to his cheek. Both stood still as Demise, with a face mixing anger and confusion, felt his face to check the damage. "You will not make it out of here alive, Sky, you realize that correct?"

Demise's massive mana began to expand and engross the area around him, killing plant life in its wake.

Sky flickered his eyes, and the sharp winds began to surround his body. "We'll see about that 'Deces,' I wasn't named captain of this team for nothing." Sky jolted into the air and flew around Demise, surrounding him with heavy winds. Growing closer, they began to nick away at the sides of Demise like ticks, causing minimal damage. He flicked the winds away like they were bugs.

The anger grew greater and greater on his face. Demise, silently lifted his hand and with a snap of his fingers, all of Sky's winds had disappeared, Sky soon began free-falling out of the air towards Demise. "Who do you think I am, Sky!? You think these tricks will work on me? Demise took his powered up fist, and he forced it through Sky's center as he was plummeting to the ground, penetrating his chest. Blood engulfed Demise's fist, as his arm now felt the inner lining of Sky's midsection, holding him off the ground.

"W-what…" Sky spat up blood as his body fell limp. The God slayer scythe tumbled to the ground.

Demise smirked as he threw Sky's body to the ground, splattering blood everywhere. "Face reality: I am a god!" Demise disappeared in a shroud of darkness soon, his complaints about being stained by mortal blood carried on the wind. Chancey trotted over and began licking Sky's face, to no reaction.

Blaze finally caught up to the tentacle monster. As soon as he arrived, a cloud of dark mana coming from beyond the trees caught his attention. A giant lizard-like creature, as tall as the trees, awaited them as the origin of the tentacles. It had a hunched back, with rough and scarred scales covering its body. Its back was littered with nubs where tentacles used to be, slowly moving in place like maggots. The tentacles still attached extruded infinitely into

108

the distance. Once it was surrounded by enemies, they retracted back to surround the pirates and Blaze.

"Up close, this thing is extremely gross," one of the pirates remarked, looking at the dead nubs. A previously captured pirate was on the ground next to the monster, fighting off being eaten alive by the carnivorous tentacles.

"Let's go!" Blaze and the pirates charged at the tentacles surrounding their comrade, helping him fight them off with their machetes. The spear-like tentacles soared at them from all directions. Dodging attacks this close became difficult. During the fight, Blaze continually turned back towards the clearing, concerned. "We have to make this quick… I'm so sorry, Sky…" Blaze's left arm began to glow brightly.

Void dropped to one knee, breathing heavily as he surveyed the wrecked battlefield before him. Trees were broken in half; the earth was scorched, and littered with gashes and blood. "These guys don't stop coming, do they?" Volt snickered over at Void with a long face as he too was resting himself for a moment.

Void shook his head before mean-mugging the ringleader, a shadow soldier with a pair of odd staffs in either hand while summoning another wave of shadow soldiers.

"That's the key, you know." Ocean walked over towards Volt and Void and knelt next to them. "We need to get through these…things. And kill that one, and fast. We are all nearing our limit. I think we have about one more wave in us," Ocean said.

Volt grasped his spear tightly, "I have an idea, Void can you throw this spear into one of your portals and get me close to him? I'll distract him and create an opening for one of you guys to take advantage."

Jax strolled over. "I'm ready for whatever guys."

Void grabbed Volt's Spear and stood up with force, "Alright, guys, get ready!" Void tossed the spear with great force directly at the ringleader. The knights mobilized behind his initiation and went to attack the freshly spawned shadows. The spear went into a dark portal, skipping all of the mobs and came out directly in front of the lead monster. The shadow covered up to defend. Right as it was to hit him, Volt teleported to his spear. A loud spark rang as Volt landed face to face with the shaman shadow soldier.

Volt lowered himself into a fighting his stance, but the shaman shook violently for a couple seconds before suddenly four muscular arms splashed out of his back, two on each side, armed with black machetes.

"Oh, you've got to be kidding me…" Volt sighed.

The shadow shaman began his deliberate evil laugh in Volt's face. The slow, but powerful swings of the six-armed Mahakala like shaman shadow soldier faced off against Volt's quick combos with his spear. "You're pretty tough, y'know. And since when can you guys show emotion. I guess you're an upgraded one, huh?" Volt caught four of the shaman's sword in his spears while he spoke. "Gotcha!" Volt spun his spear around, knocking the enemies weapons away in all directions leaving it wide open. It made a loud roar as Volt shoved his spear in the dirt, using it like a vault pole to get him into the air, he then flipped forward, his foot covered in lightning. "Spiral tap!" Volt gave the shaman an ax kick to the back of the neck, electrocuting it's entire body, causing him to drop down to his hands and knees.

"You're dead!" Out of the air, Jax came propelling himself off of a shadow soldier's back towards the shaman's. Sword out, he pierced the shaman's back, causing him to get shocked as well.

"Gahhhh damn, stay down." Jax forced the sword further into the shaman's back. After a quick shiver, it dissipated.

110

"There we go," Jax said, winded, as the electricity died down.

Volt stood up, brushing himself off, "Good job, and…uh, sorry about that."

Jax looked away. "It's alright, Volty." All at once, the remainder of the shadow soldiers disappeared into the darkness.

Void walked past the two towards the clearing, "We have to get back, let's go."
Both groups arrived back to the clearing to the same horrific sight. There was a darkened area in the middle where dead plants and blood mixed violently. In the center of the mass was Sky's body, lying on his side, facing away from them.

"Shit, Sky! Sky!" Blaze yelled as everyone rushed over to Sky's side. Blaze got down on a knee beside him and rolled him over onto his back. Blaze cursed as he surveyed Sky's body, noting all of the cuts and bruises along with the bloody fist-sized hole in his chest. Tears running down his face, Blaze looked up, hopelessly at the rest of the knight's damp faces.

Ocean got down and put his fingers on the side of Sky's neck. Ocean shook his head and waited there longer. "No…way…"

Blaze looked over quickly. "What?"

Ocean pulled back, shocked, "Somehow, he is still alive." Confusion rang through all of the knights.

Blaze put his hand over Sky's heart. "Maybe if I can channel my mana into him, it'll help his body recover in some way." He glanced at everyone hopefully. Blaze's hand began to glow, brighter and brighter the longer he held it there.

"Be careful, that's too much of the mana you need to survive, you'll die," Void snapped.

Blaze, his other hand now grabbing his own wrist, started to pour his mana into Sky's chest. Eventually, his

111

mana's color changed from red to white, beginning to sparkle like stars. "Whoa, what's this…" Blaze's eyes widened. The hole in Sky's chest began to close and replace itself with flesh.

"What, it's working…but that's not any normal mana, what is that power. I've never seen that before," Volt said, observing.

Blaze stood still, shocked as healing energy emits from his hands and commits a miracle in front of their eyes. The flesh grew back and reattached. After a minute or so, all of the damage on Sky's chest was recovered. Blaze's hand stops glowing, and he sat back. "Wow, for once, my hands were used for something other than destruction." Blaze's words began to slur and fade off as he spoke. He noticed unrecognizable figures in the distance on horses approaching as he drifted off to the side. "Who's that?" Blaze collapsed to the ground as Sky coughed a few times, still unconscious. The knights stared towards the approaching figures, weapons at the ready.

-Year 276 Unknown Location Laix, Sylindra-

"Mmm, it's pretty warm here...wait, where am I?" Blaze opened his eyes and looked around, dazed. He found himself in an enormous, extravagant bedroom. The sheets were made of expensive silk, hugged by a gold plated bed frame. Across the structure, golden engravings of oriental characters and symbols decorated the finished woodwork. In the corner of the room, smooth embers sparked off of the edges of the lit fireplace. It's warmth hugged the entire room, creating a calm, homely feeling. There was a lit fireplace in the corner that warmed the entire room.

He wore slight smile on his face as he looked around.

"This kind of reminds me of back at the castle," he mused to himself as he noticed his sword and clothes lying on top of a dresser that was off to the side. "Wait, what am I wearing then?"

Blaze looked down at himself under the covers to reveal all-black, soft nightwear. It was a two-piece silk set rimmed with golden sleeves and green symbols, one of which included a large bird.

"What the hell is going on?" Blaze started raising his head, but a sharp pain struck throughout his body. He felt weak and lightheaded the longer he attempted to sit up. "Oh, that's...unfortunate." He plopped his head back on the pillow. Loud clunks approached from down the hallway. Blaze looked at the open door, attempting to set himself up again in the process. A whistle rang through the hall shortly after, changing pitch multiple times throughout. It sounded like a sort of bird call, loud and unique.

"I wouldn't advise moving from there just yet, Blaze," Blaze heard coming from outside the door. In came a tall, lanky man with neatly groomed green hair and a seemingly permanent, and creepy, smile. His face twitched from time to time, but otherwise stayed the same. He wore a neatly fitted suit with the similar golden trim and pale metallic green base, littered with ancient texts. He moved his arms behind his back now. Blaze sat there, annoyed face and all, as the man stared at him for a few moments before speaking. "My name is William Ace Hiyama. Now I'm sure you have your fair share of questions. What happened to your friends? How you got here? Where even is here? Whatever," he said letting out a fake chuckle before regaining composure.

Blaze mumbled 'Hiyama' to himself, attempting to figure out where he heard that from before.

"I must say thank you, though," the mysterious face said, the smile becoming more earnest and sincere.

Blaze thought to himself for a moment. "Why?"

"For saving my cousin, Sky, of course. We watched your battles from above at our castle. We saw how Deces' nearly killed him, but you saved him with some ability that bewildered you," the smile on William grew and at the same time seemed more ominous. He raised his arm up and began scratching at his head.

"How could you even see us from there? And wait, so you are Sky's family? This is his house?" Blaze asked.

"Well castle, but yes. We helped groom Sky into the knight he is today, admittedly not the easiest task, though."

Blaze chuckled to himself. "Of course."

"This is our family's land, so to look over it, we have scouts who survey the land constantly. Our king can see through the scouts' eyes, truly having eyes everywhere." William spread his arms wide for emphasis.

"That is incredible. Will our cap get that sometime?" Blaze said, waking up more, marveling at William's words.

"It's in his blood, but it probably will not be realized as he will likely not be king and captain of the Royal Knights simultaneously. Too much pressure for any one man." Will went to put out a single finger but changed his mind, returning his hand to his head.

"Sky is a strong-willed man, I'm sure he could pull it off. Speaking of, how is he doing?" Blaze sat back in the bed, peeking over at William.

William bent his knees to get face to face with Blaze before responding. He watched Blaze's face to make sure he was calm. "He is alive, but he has not woken up yet. Even you were out for a week before yo—"

"A *week*?" Blaze cut him off.

"Yes, a week. It seems whatever ability it was you used took you out of commission for quite a while. Do be careful with it, ok?" William placed his hand on Blaze's arm staring into his eyes. "Until you have properly tested it." At this, Blaze broke eye contact and began eyeing over his

114

hands and his arms, deep in thought. After a moment, he looked back up and nodded. "And the rest of the knights?"

William stood back up and headed towards the door. "They are well taken care of and have been waiting here, planning in the meantime. You'll see them shortly for dinner, so get yourself dressed. Now that you're up, that weakness should go away slowly but surely. You bounce back quickly, don't you?" He took a couple steps back then stopped, "Oh, and yell out if you need any help, someone will come I'm sure." Will walked out waving behind him.

Blaze winced and sat himself up. "I think I'll be fi—" When he reopened his eyes, William was gone. After relaxing himself, Blaze stared at the ceiling and began talking to himself. "I guess no one said this would be easy. What would we have done without Sky's family coming to get us?" Blaze sighed to himself and closed his eyes for a bit.

****

Back in one of the dining rooms, Volt, Void, Ocean, Jax, the pirates, and William waited patiently at an oversized dinner table for the arrival of Blaze and Sky. The table was fully arranged with empty plates and cutlery, waiting staff rummaging in and out in preparation for the incoming meal.

Volt sat next to William at the table while Blaze's chair was over closest to the door. Sky had an open seat at the head of the table. "You sure he was ok enough to make it down here, Will?" Volt asked, whispering next to William.

William nodded and pointed towards the long stairwell. "Have faith, Volt, he will come. He has the perseverance to do so, it will be good to help him understand the extent of each of his new powers. Our father has told us of the evolution of such powers gained from those orbs. It starts with an ability that resembles that of the beast they

115

vanquished to get the orb, and evolves from there to other abilities based off of necessity, and life." He said staring at his own hand, a slight feeling of jealousy had shaken him for a moment. Will shook his head and refocused on the doorway.

Slow, but steady feeble steps echoed through the stairwell growing closer and closer. The entirety of the table looked at the base of the stairs in anticipation. After a minute of the slow-paced plops on the rough stairwell, he finally showed up. Blaze came around the corner into the center of the room, utilizing his sword as a cane. A few claps rang throughout the table, but everyone mostly sat there and watched him push his way onto the seat. After a couple of heavy breaths, "Thanks…for letting me do that on my own, my strength is coming back gradually." Blaze looked directly at William.

William stood up and gathered everyone's attention, but before he could speak, a servant hurried over and whispered something in his ear before rushing off again. William nodded and cleared his throat. "I regret to inform you guys that the king and the family will be unable to join us for dinner tonight; some things came up with a neighboring area and their presence was needed. It will just be just us…minus Sky. It appears he has still not awoken yet from his coma. We may have to wait another day for him to join us." A wave of disappointment struck through the group. Suddenly, from the back came servants rolling out several large carts with metal domes on top; steam seeped from beneath the lids. William stood next to the head chef. "My my it appears it is time to feast guys…so if you may." William gestured towards the head chef, and the servants began setting the trays onto the table, revealing the items shortly afterward. All at once, the aromas of fresh ham, chicken, rolls, potatoes, rice, and a plethora of other

116

delicious delicacies mixed and entice the senses of the guests.

"W-Whoa, this is crazy!" Blaze said, mouth-watering.

"Can't remember the last time I've feasted like this," Void said, grabbing a large piece of ham and putting it on his plate.

"Well here at the Hiyama household, we tend to do it big, and we eat well," William said while cautiously making his own plate, careful not to take too much or spill any. His nervousness went unnoticed.

"Hmm, William, tell me about this king of yours, I've only heard the stories," Hail said nearly done chewing his food.

"Hey now, while you're in this castle, on this continent, he's your king too." William said with a smile. Hail paused his eating for a second to listen. "King Hiyama is a strong, stern man. Now while he has truthfully spent more time fighting battles than raising his family, he does love his son."

"He doesn't show it certainly," Hail retorted, pointing a bone at him.

"You just…wouldn't understand! The king fights those battles *for* Sky. He wants the place left safe for when Sky takes over. He wears himself to the bone for his sake, don't question the intentions of that man! Ahem, thank you." Will cleared his throat and continued eating.

"He should tell him that, you know. I don't think Sky feels any of that love you shout." Volt spoke up. Will simply nodded and continued on. Everyone else ate in silence as well.

The knights and the pirates still enjoyed their hearty meals, stuffing themselves before being shown back to their respective rooms. Blaze seemed especially revitalized after having a great meal. The pirates were the first to make their

117

way back to their rooms, preparing to wake up at dawn to get a ship ready to head out the next day with the knights. Void was next to go, complaining about a big lack of sleep. Everyone else staggered out in time, leaving Blaze as the last one there, still getting a few last bites in.

Servants came by to clear out the area after Blaze left, leaving only William. He soon received a message from one of the family members who came in. "Hey Will, if Sky is up by tomorrow, they are planning on leaving for Eodon. I overheard one of the pirates talking; I think they plan on transporting them before they head home."

Will sat there shaking his head softly. "Well, the Farriage family can wait; we need Sky and his friends to help us now. We can't let them leave yet. Do what you must, Aura," he said with a nervous smile.

"Gotcha, Will." Aura nodded his head, and then paused. "You know Sky will object, right? This mission they have is vital to him."

William sighed. "Of course, but he will see our family's war is of more immediate importance. We are more than happy to support him afterwards." *I'm doing the right thing right? Wish I got a sign.*

The majority slept like babies as soon as they slipped into bed, but Void laid there staring into the ceiling, unable to drift away. "Damn, what does it take to fall asleep around here?" Void sat up in his dark room, and looked around. The lack of illumination was limiting visibility, even under the moon's light. After noticing the slight slit of hallway candlelight coming from his cracked open door, he gets up and starts towards it. "Hmmm, maybe I'll go for a bit of a walk," Void said, looking out into the dimly lit hallway.

Over in Sky's room, his body began twitching and shaking erratically. Afterwards, green mana gathered around his body, densely. The mana started to build erratically, as if preparing to explode. Sky's eyes shot open, and the mana surrounding him immediately dissipated.

Sky laid there unconscious and still. His breathing was steady, but deliberate. A chilly breeze blew through his open window and across his face. A pearl white dove fluttered its wings on the window, a tan parchment tucked under its beak. Suddenly, his eyes shot open. Panic and sweat was immediately painted on his face. He remained still and attempted to calm his breath until he got his head together. His eyes darting back and forth, absorbing information. "Shit...ok,ok,ok...I'm alive? But...how?" A tear unconsciously ran down his face beside the sweat. Sky jerked his body back and forth only to realize he was unable to move more than an inch.

"Ok so, can't move, cool, awesome," he said getting nervous again. "What's the last thing I remember?" Sky stared at the ceiling, attempting to access his memories. His face remained still for a moment before his mouth shot open. Images of the Demise snapshotted through his thoughts rapidly. Sky's face wrenched up in fear, his body shaking in place as he almost lost his head just thinking about it. He pushed himself past his thoughts and shook his head aggressively. "Demise...right..." he said getting his breathing back together. "I should be dead. It's a blessing I'm not." Sky focused his mind on finding any mana that remained in his body. "I must be home, we need to get out of here. I need Void, I need him now!" Sky's eyes rolled back into his head as he hummed to himself. More sweat began trickling down his head. "Void...Void...I need you...Void!" Sky's mana began to shine as he tried to tap into the mana that linked the knights all together. "Almost forgot about this ability our family has, I really hope he hears me. Void..."

As Void cautiously crept around the castle under the cover and shade of night, a dark aura stalked him. Void's mind jumbled, he walked on until he ended up in the maze-like basement dungeons of the castle, oblivious that he was being followed. After walking in the darkness for the entirety of his stroll so far, he finally approached a floor with lit torches whose light illuminated the end of the spiral staircase that laid before him.

"Wait, where the hell am I?" Void asked, the sudden flash of light snapping him out of his trance. He looked around, noticing the light slowly getting snuffed out from the few torches from the hallway ahead. One by one, the flames grew dimmer and dimmer, the light being sucked out of the room like a vacuum. "Good thing I'm so used to the dark…" Slowly but surely the darkness drifted towards him, again. Void stopped and stared at the shadows as they slithered to him and wrapped around his legs. "I-I'm drifting…again…no…" The room was completely dark now, but like a rock, Void didn't move for several moments. "No!" Void finally jolted back to his senses again and shook off the darkness. Then he began sprinting down the hallway, turning the corner and darting into the first room on the right.

Void slammed the door shut and sat down against the wall, looking up. The room was completely black. As Void sat there, he noticed echoing footsteps coming towards him.

"Hahahaha. What's someone like you doing pretending to be a good guy?" a mysterious voice directed at him.

Void looked up after hearing the familiar voice. "What?" he said.

"Do they know what you've done, Void? Do they?" Void's eyes widened when he saw that smiling demon mask come face to face with his.

"Scourge…how?" Void got to his feet quickly. Scourge took a step back.

"Oh, just embrace your roots, Void, let the darkness back into your heart." Scourge held out his hand.

Void summoned his claymore to him, pointing it at Scourge's face. "Leave. Me. Alone!"
Scourge began chuckling to himself, "I'm not here to fight you, Void, put that thing away." He shoved the sword downwards, lodging it in the cement.

Void still grasped his sword, beaming at Scourge's face. "I'm not afraid of the darkn—."

Scourge wrapped his hand around Void's neck and raised him into the air. "I don't want you to be afraid, I just want you to stop denying your nature." Scourge brought Voids face close to his own. Scourge could smell the fear and hesitation from Void's breaths at this distance. "You might as well join me now before you hurt your friends. You know the day's coming," Scourge whispered.

Void began losing consciousness, his fingertips still grasping the hilt of his sword, barely. Void's aura spiked just as he was to pass out, absorbing the darkness that surrounded them like a vacuum. This sudden burst of energy loosed Scourge's grip on his neck. Scourge let go and backed away a few steps, shaking his hand. He cursed under his breath.

Mana overflowing with darkness, Void lifted his claymore out of the cement with ease and pointed it back at Scourge. "I said, leave me alone!" Void's mana began to seep into his sword and overflow. With his sword in both hands, he arched it back and slashed at Scourge. "Be gone!" Void yelled as the sword phased through Scourge, who faded away like mist. The resulting energy from the swing

121

flew forward, gashing a hole in the wall in front of him. A mana residue resonated inside of the damaged part of the wall.

"There you go, embrace the dark," Scourge's voice echoed throughout the room even after his body had disappeared.

Void looked around, confused and angry. "Was he…really here?" He stood up, and relaxed himself. The dark aura that had surrounded the castle had begun to fade away, slowly. Void began to hear a voice from within himself that wasn't his own.

Void! Void! Answer me, dammit! Void heard from seemingly inside of his head.

"Uh Sky?" Void said, seemingly talking to the ceiling.

Finally! I thought this mana link wasn't working. I need you to come here to me now.

"Gotcha." Void created a portal in front of him and walked inside, leaving the darkness behind.

Chapter 7: Hail

-Year 276   Hiyama Castle   Sky's room   Laix, Sylindra-

Sky did not need to wait long for his companion to show. Void's portal opened in the center of Sky's room. He walked over and kneeled at Sky's bed.

"How are you feeling, Captain?" he asked, attempting to hide the fact he was shaken up himself.

Sky, finally regaining control of his hands, placed one on Void's shoulder. "I can't move much yet, but I'm alive, I guess. Thank you. Seeing a familiar face helped to calm me."

Void lowered his head and nodded. "I'm sorry I wasn't there to help protect you."

Sky shook his head. "I'm angrier you took so long to answer my calls, I feel so helpless like this." Void looked away. "Where were you anyway?" Sky asked.

Void took a deep breath. "I was…dealing with some stuff… sorry. Anyway, I'm here now, how can I assist you?"

Sky motioned for Void to help sit him up. "Thanks, now Void. I need your help. We all have to leave here tonight!"

"What? What about your family who will be back soon, what about the pirates?" Void said, raising his voice slightly.

Sky held out his hand to calm him. "I got an urgent message via dove from Gaia, do you remember her from the docks?"

Void nodded. "Well, she told me of serious incidents going down on Eodon that need our immediate attention. Meaning that will be our next destination, instead of Kayard," Sky looked outside the window, in the direction of the docks.

"Why can't we just have that as our next destination and leave together? I feel like that'd make more sense, "Void suggested.

Sky shook his head softly. "If only it were that easy. I know my family; they'll do whatever it takes to keep me around to help fight their battles. Don't have time for that, plus the pirates need to get back to their home. Prepare to teleport everyone to the docks, Gaia is waiting there with her own ship for us."

Void lowered himself all the way to the ground, and began locating the mana signatures of all the knights.

Sky's eyes rolled back into his head as he called the knights with his mana link. *Knights! This is Sky, wake the hell up!*

Confused, and dazed the knights all jolted awake, searching for the origin of the sound. It took the knights a moment to recognize the voice. Before long, they all understood and waited patiently for their captain's orders. Sky relayed to his knights the urgency of the situation, and the plan surrounding it. He needn't even plead for them to follow along or trust him; they had complete confidence in him. They had ten minutes to get ready before Void summoned a portal underneath everyone.

"Ok, Void hand me some paper and a pen." With a pen in hand, struggling, Sky jotted something down before folding the paper up and tossing it on the nightstand. After the agreed upon time had expired, Sky gave Void the nod to begin. After gathering a bit more mana, Void opened portals underneath all the knights, lowering them inside. They all disappeared at the same time.

A large portal opened up off to the side of a small beach. One by one the knight's tumbled out of the portal on top of each other. Groans and complaining rared up rather soon.

"Ow damnit, Void!" Blaze yelled out from the bottom of the pile.

Void lifted sky up over his shoulder, holding him steady. "Sorry, my first time doing such a large scale job. Least we all made it." Void said.

Sky lifted his head to look around at everyone. "Thanks for being ready guys, now let's find Gaia."

Volt's eyes lit up, "Gaia? She's here?" He took a second to adjust his level of excitement. A bush near them began shaking randomly garnering all of their attention.

"Volt!" Gaia came jumping out of the bush before running over and nearly tackling him with a massive hug. She squeezed until he could barely breathe.

"O-ouch," Volt let out.

"Thought I wouldn't see ya again!" Gaia said, making Volt blush a bit. Gaia walked back over to the bushes, "Here follow me guys, I docked my ship this way."

Volt smiled to himself. The knights followed Gaia into the bushes. It opened up into a long path that traveled through a cave and around a waterfall. Not far from the other side of the waterfall, a small beach sat peacefully in the moonlight. A small pirate ship brandishing Wendy's Jolly Roger appeared on the beach. Gaia dashed up and swung herself up onto the boat, pirate hat in hand. She put the cap on her head and gestured them over to her. "Come on, guys, we have to go."

Sky looked up at her hat as they walked over to join her, "Hey, isn't that…"

126

Gaia put her head down and nodded. "It isn't too long a sail, but it's enough to talk."

Void helped Sky find a seat on the deck, then went to help them set up. In no time, they were ready and had set sail. The sun could be seen struggling to rise in the horizon, lighting up the skies a bit but not enough. It would take hours for anyone to notice their disappearance as they sailed off in peace.

-Year 276 Hiyama Castle Sky's room Laix, Sylindra-

At the crack of dawn, William came bursting into Sky's room, Jax not far behind him. "Oh, Sky, where the hell are you! I know you can't walk," Will said, shaking his head, looking around at the empty room.

"Hey, what's that?" Jax pointed to the folded up piece of paper on the nightstand.

William walked over, curious, and picked it up. "Oh, a goodbye letter, that's not like you, Sky." Will opened the paper up and read it for a moment. After a minute, he grumbled, crumpled up the paper, tossed it into a waste container, and stormed towards the door.

Jax turned around. "Well, what did it say?"

William turned his head around, clearly flustered. "He said thank you, and for you guys to go home." He continued out the door.

Jax, curious, walked over and picked up the letter, opening it up and reading it:

Dear Jax, Will, or whoever finds this first,

I just wanted to thank you guys for your hospitality for my knights. William, I know you and my family, so yes, we had to make our way out before you could hold us up any further. Give my regards to father, who didn't even come to see me when I could have been dead, that ass. Also, make sure the pirates get out of here safely, they've been a great help to us. Don't even think about trying anything with them either.

Jax, I'm sorry for leaving so abruptly, I wanted to make sure you know we appreciate your service and your sacrifice for our cause. It will not go in vain, I assure you. Also, I did not want to burden you guys with our fight any further, Gaia gave me an update on the battle at the docks, they need you guys over there more than we do at the moment. So go! But be safe sailing that sea again, please...Anyway, I promise that we will get Wendy back from Scourge, it's where Gaia is leading us next!

Be safe,
Sky Hiyama

"Fuck…you better save Wendy, Sky…"Jax looked up with a slight smile. "You better keep Gaia safe too…" He left to relay the news to his subordinates.

-Year 276 Center of the Eodic sea near Thea, Sylindra-

The knights found 'seats' scattered around the deck of Gaia's boat. From crates to makeshift rope hammocks, everyone made sure to find a spot, even Sky, who was set up against the wall next to the below deck door. Gaia stood up top steering, her voice carrying across to everyone. "Ok, first of all, I hope you guys were able to get done what you needed because we lost a lot of my friends in that fight on the docks." A couple tears ran down her cheek before they got wiped away.

Sky looked up at her. "We made use of the opportunity you provided us, and we thank you and your pirates for your help... And your sacrifice. I'm sorry." Sky squeezed his hand, feeling almost all the way back now.

Volt walked up next to Gaia. "Can you tell us what caused the urgency to get here? We set sail pretty quickly, and the plan was for Kayard next."

Gaia turned her attention to Volt. "You remember when I said I might need your help?"

Volt nodded. "Yeah?"

"Well, during that fight, Scourge ended up kidnapping Wendy. Word is he dropped her off in Eodon somewhere; surges of power from that area lead me to believe she is there somewhere."

Ocean, who was in a chair next to the mast, looked up at Gaia as well. "Wait, Wendy's...in Eodon?"

"I think so, somewhere. But it's not my domain, so it would be harder to walk into foreign territory and start asking questions," she said.

Ocean put his head down. "I may not have the same pull there that I used to have."

Sky's head turned sideways. "Why's that?" he said, lifting his arms to swat away a bug on impulse. He stared curiously at his hand.

Ocean turned his body around in his chair, facing them. "In my home, it is a high-class felony for the prince to leave the Silcos islands. That's something I did ages ago when I began training before I was a knight. I left to look for a cure for my sisters... And well, my whole bloodline has this illness."

"Don't remember you talking about them before, what do they have?" Blaze said, lying back on a makeshift hammock hanging between two skinny barrels. He made it using cloth and rough animal skin he found on the ship.

"It's called the widow's curse; it attacks the bones of the females in my family, making walking nearly impossible, and giving birth even more dangerous." Ocean took a second to clear his voice before continuing. " It's one of the reasons it was so risky for me to leave our homeland. I am the only male born in our family in a very long time, and as such, I'm the heir… even though I've never met my mother."

Everyone looked at Ocean suspiciously.

"How have you never met your mom? Isn't she the queen there?" Sky said, continuing. "Even I've seen my parents, though quite rare."

Ocean sighed. "A lot happened when I was born, I had to be moved to be protected from the witch that cursed us, and my mother was in critical health for years. I honestly thought she died. I left for training, and when I came back, I met my sisters, but she wasn't around, then I left to look for a cure…to protect the innocent smiles on their faces."

Void walked over and stood behind Ocean, putting his hand on Ocean's shoulder. "Let's…change the subject a bit, Ocean. Gaia let us know where we are headed now."

Gaia held her hat on, protecting it against the massive burst of wind that blew through the ship. It began to snow shortly thereafter, increasing frequency by the minute. "Guess we're getting close, ha-ha, but our first destination is the southernmost island, Bora. We're going to pick up my brother, Hail." Gaia said, trying to steer through the heavy snow. With limited visibility, landmasses were just barely noticed in the distance. Docks with guards watched as they rode down the strait, past the snowy forests, and the castle high above in the background on the left landmass. "That's the main island to the left, and Thea of the Silco islands to the right. If we're going to Bora, we are headed to the coldest and most brutal of the islands. Ice everywhere, instead of the simple snow on the others. A lot of scary, icy creatures reside there. I guess the name Hail would fit if he lives there."

Blaze's typical annoyed look was back again. "Oh great…water *and* freezing cold. Oh joy."

Sky laughed by himself. "Ha, thought you were fearless."

Blaze glared at Sky. "I…just don't like it, okay? Just how you don't like stormy skies and how Volt can lose a fight with a rock."

Volt's head snapped over toward Blaze so fast his neck nearly snapped, "Hey!!"

"Sky…" Void said in a low tone.

"What's up Void?" He responded curiously.

"Why…do you act that way?" Void responded.

Sky's eyes lit up. "I don't know what you mean. Do you guys?" he said. The knights all silently looked away, not confronting it.

"You can be hurtful sometimes. The way you say things. Sometimes it just sounds so…lifeless. Like you don't care." Void said boldly. Blaze and Volt's mouths were both wide open in shock. Gaia avoided eye contact but eventually nodded a bit.

"I'm…sorry. If I do that, it's not on purpose. If anything it's just the things that got drilled into me growing up, my focus trumps all sometimes. Other than basic jokes, if I do act that way, check me. I'll listen. *I'm not my father after all.*" Sky said lowering his head. "Thanks for letting me know, Void. Let's go," he said as they continued moving forward.

"Heads up guys, it looks like we're arriving," Ocean shouted out as they cleared the landmasses on either side, with one approaching in front of them. It was a long strip, the end wasn't in sight. At that moment the snow turned into hail. Heavy hail. Ice hit the ship as hard as bricks, causing a minor panic amongst the knights.

"What the hell is this? Blaze yelled while putting up a screen of fire above the ship to melt the hail before it hit the boat. "Sheesh, did the temperature just drop again?"

"Yeah…we're close. Hail has held himself up on Bora ever since he left me on Kegato. He wanted freedom, I guess." Gaia said, staring straight ahead.

Ocean went over to Sky, tugging on his arm a bit, "You able to walk yet? We may need you a bit here."

Sky tested each of his legs, realizing he could stand, albeit barely. "I assume the ground will be super icy when we get there, I'd rather not slip, so I request a bit of assistance."

Void went over and stood next to him. "I'll be here the whole way until you regain your strength."

Sky looked over, and smiled. "Thanks, Void, you're very reliable." The ship had passed by Thea and approached the port at the island of Bora; the knights readied themselves for docking.

The docks at Bora were in rough condition, mostly for lack of upkeep. What wasn't falling apart was, at this point, frozen over.

No one was there to welcome them. It seemed more like a ghost town when they docked, anchored, and slipped their way to the mainland. A couple of voices and movements could be heard ahead, but not nearly enough for a major island. The stone cabins and shops before them held a homey feeling.. They weren't overly intricate or detailed, but they functioned well enough for these cold temperatures. The roads weren't paved, so only stone hard ground with a layer of snow and ice awaited the path ahead. After an initial survey, the knights started forward.

Blaze's flames coated his feet as he walked, making him the only one not slipping. "This is so annoying," he complained.

Gaia slid over. "Hey guys, let's ask around a bit to see where Hail is."

Sky nodded while being helped over by Void, showing signs of walking on his own now. The knights stormed the small town that awaited them, asking the people they actually saw if they've seen anyone named Hail.

Ocean and Volt did most of the work there, going from cold face to cold face, inquiring about this man. The temperature seemed to suck away the townspeople's desire to talk. Most simply kept walking along instead of indulging the knights in questions. The further they traveled into the frozen town, the less people they saw. Soon the streets were barren, with barely anyone around to even question.

"Hmph, this is harder than I thought It'd be," Ocean said looking back at Sky slipping in place. A thought struck his head. Ocean sent out a stream of water underneath Blaze, putting out the flames that kept him sturdy. He immediately plopped to the floor with a thud.

"Asshole." Blaze scoffed as he pounded the ground under him on his way back to his feet.

Sky stood behind him, visibly attempting to hold back his laughter, to no avail. "Bahahahaha," he burst out, causing him too to lose balance and tumble over as well. This made Gaia lose her cool as well, joining in the jitters.

"Ha, that's what you get, now come on." Void snickered while lifting Sky to his feet again.

"Worth it, I'd say," Ocean said turning back around towards the town.

"If you're done, I thought we had a time constraint here?" Volt broke up the fun with facts. He then stopped to think. It took him a moment to realize they had no idea what he even looked like.

"What's up?" Gaia commented, looking at Volt's pondering face.

Volt stopped and tapped Gaia's shoulder, "Wait. What does Hail even look like? Don't think we ever asked."

Gaia thought to herself for a moment. "Well, when I last saw him, he had long, spiky hair, super slim, a scar on his right eye. Hmmm, he also had black pants on and a light blue, fluffy, fur-collared jacket, if I remember correctly." The knights stopped and gawked as a man matching the description walked past them a street ahead.

Blaze summoned his sword and ran ahead, "I got this guys!"

Gaia swung her hand out to stop him. "Wait! He doesn't...like people..." Her hand dropped as her voice died down; he wasn't even listening.

Blaze followed him down the next street. "Hey! Who are you?"

The man stopped in his tracks and turned in Blaze's direction, sizing him up. Suddenly, as Blaze reached the man, several huge spikes of ice materialized around Blaze's head from all sides.

"Who's asking?" the man asked, straight-faced.

Blaze stopped in his tracks. His scorching mana surrounding him flared out, slowly melting the ice spikes.

"Some welcome to your ally," Blaze replied sarcastically, as he engulfed his blade in flames.

The man materialed a blade of his own, however it was smaller than Blaze's. It was as long as a rapier but broader and made of hardened ice. He then gathered more mana and brought forth an array of similar swords around him.

"I can see you will be a problem," the man said." I don't have time to deal with you, so I'll make this quick."

Blaze bent his knees, lowering his stance with his sword over his head, and both his sword and his fist flaming. "Sound's good to me, bud."

Both men rushed toward one another, clashing their weapons in the center. Shards of ice and steam erupted from the collision. The man's swords all began flying at Blaze one after another now. Blaze backed away and pelted them back as quickly as they approached.

"Wait! Blaze, Hail stop!" Gaia rushed over and punched both in the face to break them up. They tumbled to the ground and looked up at her in shock.

"Oh, hey, sis," Hail said in a low, monotonous voice as his swords dissipated.

Blaze stood back up and watched. Gaia slapped Hail's shoulder then hugged him. "Must you always pick fights with every one of my friends you meet."

Hail eyeballed Blaze as he rubbed his shoulder. "You know this guy?"

Blaze turned to face the others as they appeared behind Gaia. They walked around gingerly, trying not to slide. "Yeah, he's one of the knights. He's here to help, okay?" Gaia released Hail and grabbed his wrist, pulling his hand out in front of Blaze. "Let's get along, got it?" She squeezed his wrist. Hail winced, then nodded.

Blaze turned and shook the outstretched hand, "Yeah, lets."

Sky, finally able to walk on his own, came forward. "Nice to meetcha Hail, welcome to the group." Sky held out his hand.

"I'm sorry but who are you?" Hail said shaking his hand.

"Sky Hiyama, Captain of the Royal Knights. Your sister here requested we help you," The winged knight said with a beaming smile on his face.

Hail snared at Gaia, then refocused on Sky. "Sorry for the trouble, but I'm alright. Thank you, though," He said proudly, his chest poked out.

"But I heard you were over there getting your ass kic—" Blaze is cut off by Gaia covering his mouth and nose tightly. He struggled and wiggled free from her grasp, seconds before he was to suffocate. "GEEZUS. Aggressive woman, I nearly died." Blaze shouted panting. He tapped her with the side of his fist.

"What he meant to say was that we think even a bit of our help would aid in the protection of your town. I think you'll find joining us will help the longevity of your home if you'd let us assist," Volt said cordially, looking around.

Hail took a second and thought to himself. "Eh, I guess I can let you help me. Wait, does that make me one of these knights?" he said, fingering quotation marks.

Sky laughed. "Well, not officially. But it seems both you and Gaia's origins resemble ours, maybe a bit more direct. Think you guys should join us in our travels, it might reveal things for both of you."

"Hmmm, well I'll let you take a look at what I'm facing at least. Doesn't mean I'm joining you, though!" Hail said turning around.

Gaia looked at Sky. "I think we can live with being Royal Knight Extras for now," Gaia said as she grabbed Volt's arm and hugged it.

Sky peered at them questionably, before shrugging it off. "Well, anyway, Gaia has told me you've been fighting to protect this town from something. Let's see what this is."

As he finished, the ground began to shake violently. They held onto each other to keep each other upright. After regaining their footing, the knights began frantically looking around for a cause, all except Hail. He remained still, shaking his head. "That thing has a knack for timing."

Ocean looked at Hail sideways. "Hmm? I don't remember any monsters *that* wild on this island. What is that?"

"The locals call it 'Led Zmaja' the ice dragon. It appeared from beneath the frozen lake a couple years ago, and ever since, people have been somewhat afraid to leave their homes. I mean, people are used to the cold in this country, but…" Hail stopped as a massive blast of frozen mana rocketed down the street behind them, coming from the direction of the lake. The blast literally froze everything in its path; from the walkway to the sides of homes, to the unlucky victims who happened to be walking down, everything was now solid ice.

"Oh my god…" Sky walked over to the street to see the horrors around the lake.

"You've been fighting this thing?" Blaze asked, leading the walk down the slippery street. When they approached a man who got frozen in the path of ice, Blaze used his flames to free him. He looked dejected as it was unsuccessful in freeing the man.

"Yeah, I've been fighting this thing for a while now. Its ice doesn't melt by the way. The only way to free the people is by defeating it. Sorry, bud, but I don't think you'll be instrumental here."

Gaia smacked Hail upside the head to shut him up and turned to Sky and Ocean. "This is why I asked you guys to help, so he wouldn't die. His ice isn't strong enough to combat Zmaja's."

Hail turned around, frustrated. "Dammit shut up, Ga——."

"Ahh, Mom! Dad!" Hail was cut off by a loud shrieking scream from the direction of the lakeside.

"Shit, let's go, guys." With the flick of his arm, Hail shot his ice mana ice down the street, towards the lake. A slick, frozen slide sat before them now. He hopped on and slid his way down.

"Uh, ok?" Blaze said as he attempted to climb on the stream of ice, slipping on his bottom.

"Uh, know what, think I'll walk." Blaze took the long way and walked down the slippery road he couldn't melt.

Void cracked a smile then hopped on, sliding down the path with ease, followed by everyone else. Surrounding the lake, a cheaply made wooden barricade sat upon a step-up platform. Benches decorated the area, though they were all frozen solid and unusable. Paths to different parts of town could be found on either side of this area. A wooden sign picketed in the ice, slanted sideways, stood at the entrance of the lake reading: Caution: Lake not frozen solid.

At the lake was a little girl, around fifteen or so years old with an old, oversized, and torn jacket on. She stood at the edge of the barricades, crying. Two figures were next to her, frozen solid, in hugging positions with their backs facing the center of the ice lake. Hail walked over onto the ice next to the little girl and kneeled. "Hey, are you okay?" The girl shook her head and continued crying. Hail saw an enormous shadowy figure swimming underneath the ice beneath them. Despite the cold, he could feel a nervous sweat coming on. Stammering, "Uh, we might want to move from here."

The girl shook her head again. "Hmm."

Hail looked back and forth, frantically, "What's your name, at least?"

The girl stopped crying for a moment, sniffing, "Diana."

Hail nodded. "Ok, ok, let's move over there on the ground, please?" Hail tried to soften his voice now.

Diana shook her head again, "What's the point anyway..." She said in a low voice.

Hail looked up and sighed, low grumbles came from below them. "Well...you want to live, don't you?"

She shook her head, "I've lost everything." Tears began to run down Diana's cheek slowly. "All my friends

138

and their parents have been frozen or eaten by this thing already. Even my parents are gone now. I think I'll let it get me…so I can join them and play like we always used to." Diana looked up at Hail with a smile on her face, but tears still poured down her cheeks.

Hail looked at this girl, her sadness rubbing off on him. The ground began to rumble again, louder and louder. Hail looked down to notice the shadow directly below them approaching fast. "We'll all die one day. But you? Not today." Hail jumped into action, grabbing Diana and tossing her off of the ice, "Catch!" Hail yelled as the approaching Void opened his arms. He caught the girl flying at him. "Keep her safe, okay?" Hail jumped backwards while looking at Void as he nodded.

Just then, a large, sharp, dark object came crashing out of the ice around where Hail was standing before. Fins accompanied the thing on both sides, looking more like a tail as the water splashed off of it.

Hail turned around, facing the opening of the more giant hole at the center of the lake. The shadow began lifting itself out of this hole, revealing its monstrous form. "I'll take this thing down for you today, Diana. You will not die today, on my word…" Hail said, summoning his sword and his ice blades to surround him.

Chapter 8:
Water and Ice

The tension around the lake center was as thick as ice. Dew droplets fluttered in the air, adding a chilly, particle breeze when the wind blew. Hail stood there, unmoving in front of Led Zmaja, the infamous monster that slid out of that hole in the ice. Its base was black, with black scales and light blue scales randomly scattered throughout its hardened hide. Extending far out of the hole, the serpent towered over everything. Its abdomen was about 3 -4 feet outwards, with no arms or legs: just a long tail that slithered under the water, keeping it afloat. Shining blue glazed over eyes, a long tapered snout, and jaw armed with razor-sharp teeth sat on top of its thick neck. Small, winglet-type fins sat on its back. Mist seeped out of Led Zmaja's open mouth as it eyeballed its opposition. Void and Sky stayed with Diana.

Blaze grumbled on the sidelines next to Gaia and Volt, watching as Ocean climbed on the platform and stood next to Hail. "I can't let you go at this alone, this is my homeland too." Ocean held up his palm to the sky. A single water droplet fell out of the air and landed on Ocean's hand.

Instantly Ocean's hybrid weapon materialized. His weapon was split into two parts. The base piece had a soft grip and a pointed metal tip on the hilt. On the center portion was a metal holster, either end branched off to a flat blade that was curved on the ends. The piece that fit in the center had its own hilt as well. The blade edge was circular, shaped more like a skinny lance. The end was detachable, made

140

with a shiny blue metal. While gripping it and swinging the blade off to the side Ocean readied himself for the incoming storm. Hail slowed his breathing as much as he could to get his rapidly beating heart under control. He looked over at Ocean, trying not to let the sweat cover his eyes.

Zmaja's eyes flashed for a moment causing the ice in around their footing to spiral unnaturally.

"Watch your feet!" Sky yelled out, alerting them to the spikes of ice that shot out of the lake, directed at Ocean and Hail. They both avoided the array of ice spikes coming from below.

"Thanks, Sky!" Ocean yelled out, regaining his footing from his hard dash. Hail's dodge wasn't as clean. When he regained his footing, it was on a weaker area of ice.

"Shit." Before he could refreeze it, the ice beneath Hail gave way, sending him plummeting into the ice-cold lake.

"Hail! Damn, man." Ocean carefully walked over to the new hole created by Hail's drop. Without hesitation, Zmaja seeped back down into his own hole and confronted Hail.

Under the water, Hail flailed around, looking up for the hole he dropped into. Looking around, he noticed just how deep it was in here, and dark. The bottom could not be seen from this point. Just as he saw a place he could swim out of, Zmaja fired a blast of ice, freezing over the surface before Hail could get there.

From on top of the ice, Ocean banged on the ice, looking for any sign of Hail. From under the ice, the serpent swam straight for Hail.

The master of ice was nailed in his chest at full force, knocking the air out of his lungs and sending him tumbling backwards. Zmaja turned around and continued his stride back towards Hail. In a last-ditch effort to free himself before he lost consciousness, Hail quickly charged his mana, summoning a score of ice swords, and sent them shooting up in a straight line. The blades crashed into the ice, one by one, in quick succession. After a moment of his blades breaking away at the thick icy surface, the last blade in line was able to break through, poking up on the surface and alerting Ocean.

"There you are!" Ocean quickly ran over and pulled the sword through. He used his mana to manipulate the water and pull it through the hole the sword left like a geyser. The breach began to expand from the pressure. Hail came blasting several feet into the air, and tumbled next to Ocean. "I gotcha buddy." Ocean patted Hail as he sat up, coughing water and heaving. Finally, regaining his breath, Hail rolled over and got to his feet. The water reverted back to ice as it dripped off of him and onto the surface below them as a sign his mana had begun flowing normally again.

Hail grumbled and wiped his face off. "Thank you. I might've been a goner there. Watch out!" Hail shoved Ocean away creating immediate separation between the two. They landed on either side of the center of the lake. Just as they were about to get up, a barrage of ice spikes shot out from below the ice, splitting the surface, a streak of calm water separating them.

"You should have the advantage underwater, right?" he yelled across at Ocean, who nodded. "Well, get ready to help me keep him down there. Hail gathered his mana again as Zmaja spun out of the water before letting out a low grumble. Pointing his hand to the area above the serpent's head, he spawned a large circular, mirror-like sheet of ice in that position. "When given the power to lay judgment, attack with the fury of all five kings!" The sheet of ice grew and began to glow while Hail chanted. Zmaja turned its head up slightly, but it had already started. "Scatter and pierce, Ledeni raspršeni napado!" In an instant, slender shards of ice shattered and rained down on Zmaja's head. Its head was forced down with the intense pressure of the blows. The monster retreated, blood now beginning to trickle down the back of its head. The sheet of ice turned and began to shoot ice at the Zmaja's face and chest.

Zmaja's thick hide stopped the shards from getting too deep. The barrage did serve to weaken him, though.

"Do it, Ocean! I'm almost out of mana," Hail called out.

Ocean jumped into action. He siphoned water out and trapped it into the shape of a very long whip. "I got it."

Ocean swung around his water whip and wrapped it around the neck of the weakened serpent as it was still getting pummeled; it couldn't retaliate. "Gotcha, now get over here!" Ocean jumped into the water, tugging the serpent down under, as well.

The ice sheet disappeared, and Hail gathered mana once more. His hands glowing a bright light blue, "go get em Osh. Frozen graveyard!"

With a spinning motion, Hail's mana spiraled around him, reaching out in a circular path, and freezing everything in its path, stopping at the barricades of the lake. The lake was frozen solid with Ocean and Zmaja underneath. On the blockade, a giant wall of ice formed around the entire perimeter and high up into the air, obstructing vision for the rest of the knights. Hail collapsed into a sitting position and looked around observing his work.

"I'm beat," Hail panted, exhausted.

Under the ice, Ocean stared down his foe while sheathing his weapon. Next, with the swipe of each arm, water claws materialized around his wrists. These large claws resembled ice, but were actually made of his own hardened mana. "It's just us now, haha," he said with a large smile.

Ocean's mana surrounded his body, causing him to glow blue. He could also breath freely, and moved much more swiftly while under water.

Zmaja charged at him full force. Ocean swiftly dodged and floated away.

"Yeah, this feels much better," Ocean smirked at the frustrated serpent as it tried continually to bite its way into his chest. "Too slow, ha-ha!" With his mana surrounding the blades on his claws, Ocean slashed away at the sides of Zmaja after each dodge, chipping at its strong hide. Its sides were littered with claw marks before long, adding a hint of red to its otherwise rich black and light blue scale color scheme.

After a loud roar, the serpent abandoned the sensible approach as it couldn't hit Ocean; instead, it began shooting ice spikes at Ocean from its mouth. These spikes scattered about in plentiful amounts like bullets, forcing Ocean to turn up the speed. "Haha, still not enough!" Ocean said as he moved the water with his mana causing the spikes to miss and shoot off to the side. "Think it's about time we close this up, what do you say?" Ocean put away his claws and pulled out his hybrid weapon, pointing it at Zmaja. It noticed and began swimming for Ocean immediately. "From the future to the past, erase our foes with a blast!" The center lance piece on his weapon began to gleam in the lake water, growing brighter by the moment. "Hydro bomber! Wahoo!" The lance went shooting off like a rocket towards Zmaja just as it got close, connecting fully with its nose and causing a massive explosion afterward. Ocean danced around to himself as the smoke and debris filled the area around Zmaja's head. Its body was cocked back slightly as it floated there.

"Well, that's that." Ocean turned around to face the icy surface and swam up. The smoke cleared to reveal an enraged serpent dragon, mist fluttering out its mouth. In an

144

instant Zmaja spun around, smacking Ocean with a vengeful tail strike with incredible force sending him crashing through the ice and high into the air. "Wha- how did this happe-." Ocean was frozen solid from a long-range ice beam coming from the water.

"Oh shit, Ocean!" Hail noticed Ocean's frozen body tipping over the ice barricade he made and over towards the knights.

There was a hassle on the other side before Sky yelled over, "don't worry Hail, we caught him. Just beat that thing, okay!"

Hail got up and summoned his ice blades before yelling back, "Gotcha," and punching his palm. The ice below his feet began to rumble and crack. "Here we go."

In one motion, Zmaja came crashing out of the ice in an angry rage flailing his head about and shooting ice beams in every direction. Hail dodged the aimless ice beams, keeping a close eye on his foe. He studied its body to notice the deep claw marks all along with the scales, traveling as far down as he could see. "Hmm, maybe that's why it's raging; I've never seen it like this." Hail studied himself. "Ocean bought me some time to regain a bit of my stamina, and I've got to use this opportunity. Good thing I already covered the area with my ice; that makes this easier." He focused his energy and held out both of his hands at his ice graveyard; his hands shaking shortly after. "Hmph, let's see how you handle this," an ice beam flies past his face as he speaks. "Infinite. Ice. Works." As Hail raised his hands into the air, ice blades of varying varieties began rising out of Hail's ice all around the lake's surface. The weapons poked out of the ice like old war grounds, disheveled, and uneven. "Not perfect, but eh, it'll do." Hail grabbed two of the ice blades close to him, his mana radiating as a very noticeable sky blue aura surrounding him.

Hail zoomed off towards Zmaja at an enhanced speed. He used and broke multiple ice blades along the way; blocking and parrying sporadic ice blasts and beams. He had to move faster and faster, the closer he got, wearing him down. "C'mon just a little more." Hail's ice glowed brighter as he zoomed; his swordplay even more masterful as he went from dual wielding to using up to seven interchangeably. The spares he had suspended in the air around him for added protection. After a considerable effort, he finally got in range of Zmaja, who started to rapid-fire nonstop. "Hmph, let's finish this." In his rush he began to slash at the injured sides of Zmaja while surreptitiously tossing ice swords into the air above its head in various places all aimed at weak spots. As he threw his twelfth blade, he messed up and got his right foot frozen by an ice beam. Hail was caught with his back to Zmaja, on one knee; his frozen foot holding him down. He put his head down. "Guess no more dodging for me…" The serpent stalked Hail, charging a large amount of ice mana right behind him in its mouth. Hail smirked while crossing his forearms, the ice blades above Zmaja's head hardened and enlarged ten times their normal size. Zmaja chuckled a bit as it unleashed the massive ice blast at Hail. Hail kept that smirk the whole time as he encased himself in a thick block of ice made of pure mana. "Ice. Coffin… Bitch."

Hail's voice faded away as he locked himself in, allowing the ice blast to crash into him. During the attack, the enlarged ice blades jerked, then shot down, finding their mark on Zmaja's neck, head, back, ribs, and other weakened areas around its scaly hide. Mana began to seep and spurt out of its neck and back as it let out a single shriek of terror before collapsing forward; eyes rolled back into its bloody eyelids.

The ice coffin shattered, Hail still on one knee. His aura had calmed itself, as his body was drained, but he was laughing to himself. Hail's ice graveyard that surrounded the perimeter of the lake faded away, revealing him back to the knights. The holes in the lake surface also returned. Hail turned back over his shoulder at the bloody ice monster behind him, grumbling. "Ugh, a little too ugly for my taste, but you deserved it, didn't you." Zmaja's body shattered into an icy mist, revealing a shiny light blue orb that floated in place. "Hmmm...What's that?" Hail asked curiously, forcing himself to his feet using his original sword.

Sky and Volt's eyes lit up when they saw it. "Hail, that's an elemental orb, grab it and put it to your chest. It's what we are searching for in our journey, and you found one here..." Sky yelled up to Hail.

Hail shrugged his shoulders and started towards the orb. "Doesn't that mean he's one of us, Sky?". Volt whispered in Sky's ear. Sky laughed out loud, "yes, I guess it does, ha-ha."

Hail's attention was caught by Ocean and the others as they were still frozen in Zmaja's ice. "Hmm how odd." He got a foot away from the orb, hand-stretched out before it disappeared on him and the ice particles in the air around him began clumping up together and reforming. "What is this...?" Hail yelled out with a hint of frustration, then stopped and saw Diana over next to Void, hope in her eyes. He had done plenty in his show of strength, but now was the time to confirm the kill. He had to finish it. The precious mana had come together in five separate groups, mana spraying light rays all about. In a flash it was over, and out came five smaller ice dragons, mini Zmajas. They each floated in the air, 'swimming' through it like seals. "Oh, come on!" Hail struggled forward, using his sword primarily as a cane. "Shit, man, I'm drained. The mini Zmajas sensed the weakness and surrounded Hail, taking bites from him on all sides. Hail struggled to protect himself, unable to block all of the attacks, and out of mana.

Suddenly a ring of fire surrounded Hail, warding off the attackers and protecting him momentarily. "There, bought you some time, think of something Hail, Diana is here watching," Blaze said, causing Diana to look over at him, smiling.

Hail lowered his head as the fire melted the ice around him and died down. He was on an island of ice now, the water surrounding him about five feet out. A small block of ice was all he had as footing. "Thanks, Blaze…" Hail calmed himself and got down into a low defensive stance, his sword out in front of him. "Guess I can try that move I saw Hepheaus do…it might work if I can do it right."

All five of the serpents flew towards Hail at once, colliding with him at the same time. Only one was actually blocked by Hail's defense, the rest bit his body in his legs, arm, and ribs. "Ack! Damn, this hurts." Hail stood there as their teeth remained there buried into his body, drawing copious amounts of blood. "This better work…Mana drain!" Suddenly as blood came out of his body, mana replaced it as Hail's body linked to all five of the mini's, sucking mana out like a vampire. "Ahhhh much better!" Hail exploded with mana, throwing back all of the mini Zmajas and summoning his array of ice spears to surround himself. "Watch this, Diana, this is for you!" He pointed one of his floating blades at each of the serpents as they charged back at him. The blades, sensing the threat, flew forward and stabbed each of them in the head, stopping them in their tracks. "Ice Pulse." Hail moved his hands melodically, dancing in place as the blades pumped his own ice mana in their heads. Every passing second, more and more of the mini's bodies were engulfed. The pulses eventually covered their targets in ice, turning the mini Zmajas into oversized popsicles; though they still floated in midair. The ice mana pulsed through the ice surrounding them, violently. Hail posed as through the end of this process, his hands up flailed to the sides. The ice

148

explodes, shattering each of the five serpents; it resembled fireworks slightly with the icy mist it created. Diana clapped eagerly, tears in her eyes.

The ice surrounding Ocean and Diana's parents melted away; they were unharmed. Both of the rescued were met with attention and warmth from Diana. Hail collapsed on the ice in the middle of his island. "Guess the adrenaline is gone, haha, I'm still messed up." Hail stared down at the blood, squeezing out of his legs and his torso. Blaze walked up onto the lake, reaching out and grabbing Hail when the ice island floated over in his direction. He tossed Hail over his shoulder and rejoined the rest.

Once there, Blaze focused his flames on his fingers and cauterized Hail's open wounds to stop the bleeding. Hail winced and fidgeted as his new partner ran his hot fingers across his body. After a slew of curse words being rang out from Hail, Blaze finally finished. Blaze was shoved away for his efforts but brushed it off and just nodded. "Hmmm. Good job, that was reckless, though. I can't always be here to patch you up." Blaze said while watching Hail rub away at his new scars..

"Well, hey, it wasn't for me, also I've got this. What the hell is it?" Hail pulled out the light blue orb and held it up in front of his face. "I figured you guys would know something about this right?" Hail asked Blaze as he was being helped to his feet, though limping.

Blaze pounded his chest. "Just become one with it, man, easy as that. It's what we knights are searching for at the moment, actually."

"Those are the elemental orbs we will use to help fulfill our potential. They are relics from the Gods. Go ahead and listen to Blaze, place it into your chest, you'll see," Sky said reassuring him.

"Hmm, Uh, Ok, I guess. Here goes nothing." Hail held the orb with both hands and slammed it into his chest.

As it shattered over him, the sphere melded into his body, which glowed afterward. "Woah, what a rush." Hail said as his hair spiked up further. "I guess…I guess I am one of you guys, huh?" He shouts as his eyes light up.

Ocean, still dazed and freezing, shook his head. "You guys ready to head over the main island? We got Hail with us now."

"Hey! I didn't say I was coming with you guys yet!" Hail retorted.

"Well, are you? Your powers could help us, brother. And they did come to help you." Gaia turned to Hail, staring at him with eyes open wide.

"Eh, fine, fine. I'll join you guys, damn." Hail said breaking eye contact with her.

Sky walked past him, feeling back to normal now. "Good, and if Ocean and Diana's parents are any indication, I think the people here are going to be just fine now." Sky looked over to Diana, who was hugging all over her parents, in a real sight of happiness.

She returned the look and waved at them as they walked away. "Thanks so much, guys, especially you, Hail!"

"You be a good girl now, okay D?" Hail pet her hair with a large, genuine smile on his face.

"Hmph I was there too," Ocean mumbled to himself. The rest of them waved and walked out following Sky, who was helping Blaze hold up Hail. They departed from Bora and headed right across to the main island of Eodon. The docks were deserted when they arrived in western Eodon. Only a snowy path uphill into the forest welcomed them there, and so they went.

-Year 276 Frosty Forest Main Island Eodon, Sylindra-

The knights arrived at Eodon's main island and immediately began the trek through the dense and harsh snowy forests towards Ula, the sacred home for Ocean's family for generations. No signs of life awaited them along their journey through the woods, leaving them with their own thoughts. Hail limped up next to Ocean, who was leading the walk. Almost the entire day had passed as they pushed their way through, trying not to allow fatigue to stop them from the hope of warmth on the other side. The night crept closer and closer.

"Okay guys. I know we want to press on, but let's set up camp for the night!" Sky ordered, creating an immediate response from the knights. They quickly ran around and collected wood for fire and camp. Gaia and Hail worked together to create small shelters for the knights to sleep in, made up of the earth and ice itself. This large encasement helped to protect the fire from the harsh winds outside. Blaze sat right next to the fire, keeping it burning strong all night.

Hail pulled out a few large trout from a bag he kept with him, and plopped them down next to the fire. "Heh, if you're hungry, I've brought fish!" he snickered.

"Trying to buy us off already? Sorry, it won't work!" Void said with a small smile on his face while picking the fish up. He began prepping it to be cooked on a small stump made of ice.

"Won't work, huh?" Ocean jested as he helped Void prepare the food. The two started cooking the fish as Blaze pulled out a jug of whisky.

"Got this from the castle before we left, should help us keep warm for the night as well." Blaze said cheesing.

"Hey, that's very expensive! How did you grab that from the castle?" Sky scolded while reaching for the bottle.

"We are the Royal Knights, are we not? I think we deserve the best, or at least this. Not like all of us can get this whenever they want after all…" Blaze trailed off as he took a long swig of the whiskey.

151

"Give me that real quick." Void grabbed the bottle from Blaze's hands and began splashing bits of it on top of the cooking fish. "Mmmm, a new recipe inbound."

"Volt, do you want any of this?" Ocean said taking a swig himself.

"No thank you." Volt waved him off.

"Thank you." Sky came around and grabbed the bottle himself. Taking a nice, long drink himself before sitting back down.

Void finished the fish and divided it up amongst everyone, skewering the pieces with sticks. Gaia took the first bite, burning her tongue in the process. "Ouch! Mmf. Mmm. Mmm, damn Void, this is delicious!"

"Thank you, Gaia." Void calmly grabbed his piece and took a seat near the fire.

"Shit, it really is. Never had my fish taste this good before, and with barely any materials too, I'm impressed." Hail nodded at Void.

"Well, I've been roaming the world for most of my life, so learning how to cook with whatever I had was a necessity for me. It's simple stuff, really."

"Oh right, so Hail, now that we have you here, tell us about yourself." Volt said, garnering the attention of everyone now.

"Oh good idea Volt!" Sky yelled out.

"Eh, not much to tell really." Hail shrugged. "I grew up with Gaia at that port. Met a lot of really awesome people, but overall it just wasn't for me, too hot, haha. I moved here about five years ago."

"Why here? Was it just the…lovely temperature?" Blaze said, trying to keep nice.

"Ha. That was part of it, also, I wanted to be able to use my powers in my element where it'd truly be useful to someone. That's why I protect this town. Those pirates mostly wanted to use me to chill their beers." Hail's tone lowered a bit here.

"Heh, yeah…I can see them trying that." Gaia laughed.

"Anyway…" Hail changed the subject. "So Osh, when was the last time you came back here? A lot may have changed," Hail questioned.

Ocean put his hand to his chin and looked up into the cloudy sky. "Hmm it has been a while, probably haven't been here since I was training to be a warrior and left for a cure for my sisters. Have you seen them, are they okay?"

Hail nodded. "Yeah, they still hold that same innocent smile, your mom has grown cold though. Over the years since you left, it has been rough for everyone. She still puts all her effort into them and their well-being."

"Do you…know her Hail?" Volt asked.

"No, no, no, not personally. Just everyone knows about his family over here. His mother is the only one that makes public appearances though, so that's who we get to admire.

"Admire? Eh never mind. I'm tired now, heading to bed." Ocean laid himself down in the corner.

"Not a bad idea, that meal has me really tired too." Blaze laid back as well, nearly in the fire. One by one the knights all rested themselves by the warmth.

****
**

The knights awoke early in the morning and immediately set off back on the road towards town. Smoke could be seen over the trees in the distance. Ocean took the lead again. "Think we're getting close finally."

Blaze huffed and puffed as he stomped through the full path. "Fucking snow."

Hail got really close to Ocean, whispering in his ear, "Hey man, I think your mom has been getting weaker too. Using her mana to allow herself to walk and function with that disease has slowed her down over the years. You know how little damage those of your family can take. Though not as bad as her, I'm sure even you have noticed your lack of sustain." Hail nudged.

Ocean sighed, "I guess...doubt any amount of training will surmount that weakness. I just need to be as strong a water magus as my mother, though I've never seen it myself, I've just heard about her conquests. No one has been able to touch her in battle."

Hail pushed some brushes out of the way to go forward, a small path, and a clearing appeared in front of them going further uphill. He turned back at Ocean. "You know why that is right? Because she probably can't afford to."

They finally reached a thinner part of the forest, the end had to be up ahead. Ocean nodded calmly as they all walked up the tall hill, a trio of shadows awaiting them at the top. "Yup."

Light hitting them from the back, it was impossible to identify the figures in their path at the top of the hill. In approaching, however, the glare faded, revealing the three that stood before them, though the one in the middle gained all attention. The knights stopped at once, Ocean out front, his jaw dropped to the ground. Still gazing forward, Ocean turned his eyes to Hail next to him, "Hail...she...she looks like...me," he stammered.

"That's her, man. Hepheaus Farriage. Your mother in all her glory.". The knights were dazed by her beauty.

"My lord, she is beautiful," Sky said, resulting in an elbow by Gaia. Hepheaus had long, flowing, silver hair, positioned all to her right side as the other was shaved. Glowing markers were on this side of her head though, along with black war paint going across her eyes. These made her light green eyes stand out above all. The markings stemmed down her neck and saw traces on her arms and legs, branching out into different symbols for each part. A metallic black choker garnished her neck matching the light metallic purple lipstick and high colored armored crop-top breastplate. Broken up with cloth in the center, silver around her bust, and on her shoulder guards, her breastplate stopped at her stomach, showing the more glowing symbols but this time in a circle around her belly button. Her gloves were a jet black, encased in an engraved silver gauntlet on her right hand. The fingers of the gauntlet only went down to her pointer and middle finger, the rest were left open. Around the waist area, silver side and butt plates connected to black pants. Lightweight silver grieves armed only her left leg and foot, while the right side only had knee guards. Attached to her waist guard on the back sideways were two long weapons, one sheathed, the other tied up. The sheathed was a wrapped up katana weapon with an extended blade, about as long as Void's claymore, except much skinnier. There were sacred engravings with silver writing along the hilt and the sheath. The other weapon was a spear with a short blade and a long bow staff. The same carvings went down this one, as well as it is positioned higher on her belt. Hepheaus side-eyed all of the knights before stopping at Ocean, which caused her to raise an eyebrow and walk closer.

She approached Ocean calmly and ran her hands through his hair before grabbing him by the chin and getting a good look at him. Ocean was dazed, not able to move or say anything. The rest of the knights watched intently. After about a minute of surveying Ocean, she released him, satisfied. "You came back, my son," In a cold, but heartfelt way, Hepheaus grabbed Ocean and pulled him in, hugging him tightly; a tear falling down her face, her war paint staying intact.

155

"Haphe—…mom…" Ocean hugged her back, equally as tight. The two behind Hepheaus stood like rocks. They were fully armored with light mail and silver armor, armed with large lances. Hepheaus finally let go and backed off a bit. "You have a lot of explaining to do Ocean. But I'm glad you're here, follow me guys, and son. We're gonna head into Ula now." She led them up the path and into town.

They soon noticed as they approached the town, how different of a place they were arriving than what they were used to. Extensive irrigation like paths of water traveled throughout the city. Bridged connected different sides of the street, hovering slightly over the water. Special silver encasements on either side guided the water through every street and into every home the lines branched to. The tall, narrow buildings were made with a particular silver metal that allowed the water to circulate and travel throughout, defying all logic and physics in their upward paths. Water could even be seen circulating up some of the roofs. This metal also made the stream immune to freezing as well, allowing the water to move freely even through the harsh weather in Eodon. The irrigation sparkled and shone, adding to the beauty of the town with snow piled on every building, and every structure expertly crafted to withstand anything.

The center streets they walked through had all shops and businesses, with the housing being located on the outer streets that opened up after every few shops or eateries. As they around town, people got up and cheered, giving all their attention to the celebrities walking through their homes. "What's all this?" Ocean said to his mom while he gazed around at people coming out of the shops to ogle them.

"Hey guys! Welcome to Ula!" A shopkeeper shouted at the knights in a friendly tone while waving. A few kids ran across a bridge just to see the knights, excitement in their eyes.

"This is…different…from what even I'm used to actually." Hail said looking around. *Is this what it's like to be a Royal Knight?*

"So many people, and they all look so happy!" Sky said waving back at the people cheering towards them.

Hepheaus turned to Ocean. "Maybe they are proud of what you've become out there. Word does travel fast over here, after all. I, on the other hand, have still not forgiven you for leaving." Her face went from playful for a moment, then back to serious as she stared at Ocean.

He blushed a bit and looked away. "Uhh…Mom, I had to."

"Yeah well, how has your search gone then 'hero', have you found any leads?" Hepheaus paused for a moment as he stood silent. "I thought so."

They continued walking through all the shops on the block along one side of the street before eventually they arrived at a pair of enormous gates. They had walls that were wrapped around the entire area ahead of them. The guards accompanying Hepheaus rushed forward and unlocked the gate, then opened the heavy doors. An extra-large line of water traveled under their feet and into this area via the silver pipeline.

Directly in front of them was an open courtyard. Guards lined up around along both sides, weapons and an extra reinforced square stood center stage of the yard. Behind it were the large doors of a castle that towered and provided shade over the area before them. To the left and right were dining sets with chairs and tables used for entertaining guests for events and parties. The castle was made out of a mixture of the silver, and large dark stone bricks as well. The water lines traveled throughout the surface on every level, adding an appealing aesthetic to the castle, which also was snow-capped.

157

They all walked inside into the courtyard, with the gates closed behind them. Hepheaus stopped short and turned to Ocean. Just then, her aura flared, and the powerful shockwave knocked everyone back, except for Ocean, who blocked but was unaffected. He looked up, confused as hell. "Ocean..." Hepheaus grabbed his arm, and judo tossed him far into the center of the square at the center of the courtyard.

Ocean spun and landed on his feet, looking back at her sideways, "Whaa?" Then she reached back and grabbed her katana grips.

"What was that!" Blaze started forward but was cut off by a trio of the guards, who held out their hands to stop him.

The rest of the knights got the message as most of the other guards looked into their direction. They stayed still and watched. She faded away into a mist and reappeared inches away from Ocean, spinning around with her blade slashing at him. He quickly summoned his hybrid weapon to block but was still pushed back in the clash. She looked into Ocean's eyes, passion, and strength in hers. "Fight me, son, I must see for myself how far you've come in your training." She completed the slash and forced Ocean back. "Show me your worth to be my son, and I might consider forgiving you!"

Ocean sighed and split apart his weapon into both separate parts. Ocean gathered his mana as his aura began to radiate and show.

Hepheaus did the same with hers, though hers was much brighter and expanded more to the areas around her. She sheathed her sword and got down into a low fighting stance, her hand still on the hilt. "Come."

Ocean watched all this and sighed again. "Fine." A crowd of servants, townsfolk, and soldiers began to gather around in the courtyard to watch. The knights get comfortable and ready for what should be an exciting exhibition between mother and son.

Chapter 9:
Mama Ocean

Ocean and Hepheaus stood across from each other, weapons ready. "Let's see what you've got, son," In an instant his mom rushed him with an onslaught of sword strikes.

Ocean blocked some of the quick strikes, narrowly dodging others. "Whoa, you're really serious!" Ocean said, stammering back.

Hepheaus narrowed her eyes at Ocean. "You better start, or I'll put you on your ass." She lowered herself into another low stance, though her mana radiated more. The mana turned into a large puddle of water, sliding down and splashing on the ground next to her. Then, like it had a mind of its own, the pool bubbled, then rose into the air and melded itself into shape. The blob finished changing and hardened, resembling the same form as Hepheaus. This clone made of water moved freely and went down into the same stance as the original. This process repeated itself, with the blob breaking away from Hepheaus and forming a clone, three times.

The four of them all stared down Ocean, who was taken aback from the new targets. "Oh, how is this fair," Ocean grumbled and held his hybrid weapon towards the group of them. He fired the centerpiece at them. All four darted around the explosion it caused like ninjas and darted towards Ocean full force. "Shit!" Ocean jumped up and shot a blast of water the ground for extra propulsion. The clones

160

reached Ocean's location, and then one got down on a knee and gave another a boost into the air. The clone flew at him swinging her sword swiftly. The original Hepheaus stalked the ground for him to land.

"Hmm, water clones, eh, that's smart. It must use a good bit of mana to keep up, though," Hail said to himself watching the bout. The town's people that showed up began cheering for their queen, while the knights rooted for Ocean, trying to out-talk the masses.

Ocean dodged the swing from the clone midair while his mana whip came slithering out of his right hand. He tossed it out, wrapping it around the clone's neck and positioning to toss it into the ground. A small blast of concentrated water mana came shooting at Ocean's chest, knocking the air out of his lungs and causing him to release his whip. He went crashing into the ground while the clone landed safely on its feet. "Uhhh, Gah, sheesh. Ok, ok, we got this," Ocean mumbled to himself while trying to breathe. The clones and Hepheaus surrounded Ocean, one hand out towards him. Mana began to shimmer and glisten on their hands. "Oh, fuck off, mom!" Ocean slammed his fist into the ground, gushing a large amount of his mana into it, liquefying the ground in a puddle directly around them, interrupting their attack. This caused the clones and Hepheaus to sink into the ground to their shins and get trapped.

"What's this?" Hepheaus yells as the ground hardens around their legs.

"Gotcha!" Ocean molds his water mana into dual short swords, both still resembling water but as hard as steel. In a whirlwind spinning motion, Ocean slashed   through two of the clones, turning them into the water as they splash away into a puddle.

Ocean pointed his newly formed aqua blade at his mother, who retaliated by throwing another concentrated ball of mana at Ocean. "Nope!" He deflected it this time, but it exploded in his face, the thick mist blinding him temporarily.

Hepheaus grabbed her spear, twirling it around a bit for momentum, and crashed it into the ground beneath her. This powerful strike shattered the very earth beneath her, and her clone created a small crater just big enough to free them both. They jumped out, flipping back into position across the hole towards Ocean. The crowd went crazy with their cheers of 'Hephy' repeatedly. Ocean shook his head at the group as he walked out of the mist, his blades at the ready.

Hepheaus sheathed her sword and held up her spear. "You know that torpedo move you do, who do you think originated it?" Her spear began to glow brightly.

"Oh, nope nope nope," Ocean charged forward, laying a rain of blows on his mom, who blocked them using the side of the spear. The clone attempted to stop him but was unsuccessful. During the onslaught, Ocean swept one of Hapheus's legs, causing her to fall onto her back, and continue blocking. In a desperation move, the clone ran behind Ocean and grabbed him around his waist, pulling and tossing him back. Ocean flipped around and landed on his feet, but it was too late.

Hepheaus had used this opportunity to knip up, stab her spear into the ground, pull out her katana, and lower herself into a low Finestra guard stance. Mana gathered from all around her body and traveled until it reached her sword. Active water mana, almost resembling translucent blue spirits, began to spiral around the tip of her sword. Ocean noticed and tried to run back in her direction. "Too late!" She yelled as the cute water spirits were released out of the tip of her sword towards Ocean. He attempted to dodge, but it was a faulty effort as the spirits surrounded him and expanded. In moments Ocean was trapped inside of a large water prison and suspended into the air. Ocean struggled, punched and kicked, but was unable to break out. Hepheaus calmly walked back and pulled her spear out of the ground.

She slowly spun around to face Ocean, her spear glowing. "From the future to the past, erase our foes with a blast!" Hepheaus spun her spear in circles before arching back into a better tossing position.

Ocean's eyes widened as he heard those words. "What? No way."

"Hydra bomber!" Hepheaus tossed the spear at Ocean at high speed. Ocean put up his guard, but the spear pierced the bubble and exploded in a burst of super concentrated water. The remaining smoke was very light, resembling a cloud, but it still expanded and impaired everyone's vision. The crowd covered up while the fog and mist blew in all directions. It smelled like fresh rain as the smoke cloud wet people. Everyone was silent from the crowd of civilians to the knights as they waited for the outcome. The dust took an unnaturally long time to clear, Ocean's mom waited with her sword at rest to her side.

Suddenly from the smoke came a sharp point of mana traveling towards Hepheaus' face. This caught her off guard, and before she could react, her water clone stepped in front and took the hit for her, getting speared in the neck and reverting to water. The smoke cleared to see a severely injured Ocean, barely able to stay on his feet. Blood and scorch marks littered his arms and chest. His clothing was tattered, and he stood breathing heavily, his hand still up with his mana whip attached. "Dammit…" Ocean summoned his aqua blades back, charging at Hepheaus afterward. She stood in her stance, untouched. In a single swing at their clash, Ocean's weapons went flying off to the side, his hands a bloody mess from her sword blow. Hepheaus had disarmed him making him drop to his knees afterward from a compilation of damage and exhaustion.

163

Ocean sat on his knees, his arms down, motivation is gone, a small smile was on his face.

Hepheaus swiped her sword over at his neck. "I win."

Ocean lowered his head in defeat, unable to do any more. The crowd went crazy in their cheers for both Ocean and Hepheaus. She sheathed her sword and helped him up, putting his arm over her shoulder, and they began walking back towards the castle. The knights walked over and followed behind them. In the middle of the trip, however, a spark was released on Hepheaus' left knee, causing her to drop entirely on her chest, Ocean following. A slight static began to surround her body, causing her body to jerk and twitch, but unable to move.

"Haphe—, er, mom! You ok?" Ocean rolled on his side and tried to shake her. The knights rushed up and gathered around as the guards filed the crowds out of the courtyard.

"It seems my mana has given out on me; I can't walk at the moment. Here take me inside if you will," Hepheaus said in a low voice to the knights. Void promptly lifted both Ocean and Hepheaus over either shoulder and carried them according to her orders.

-Year 276 Farriage Castle Underground Springs Eodon, Sylindra-

The knights ended up in a large room hidden away underneath the castle. Four large circular pools in this dimly lit room shone and glowed with an otherworldly aura about them. The water bubbled and simmered as one got close to them, steaming up on all sides. Hepheaus led them in and

164

gestured for them to throw her in. The water splashed slightly as Void laid her into the one closest to them. "Ahh, there we go." Hepheaus sighed as the mana radiated around her; her nicks and dirt washed away instantly, she was good as new. Even her armor was polished in this mystical liquid. "These are our sacred mana pools. Just lying in them for a moment restores your mana and heals your injuries. It helps me survive through multiple battles with my weakened body." She gestured for Ocean to come to join her as she stood up freely in the pool, restored.

Ocean slid himself into the pool, barely able to take his top off, and diving himself entirely under the water. When he reemerged, his injuries had magically been erased from his skin. His mana radiated with the same glow as his mother, and he popped up reenergized. "Wow! This is amazing; I don't remember this being here before."

Hepheaus laughed as the knights one by one began stripping and getting into the different pools. "We didn't let you come down here as a child; this is a very special place. Couldn't risk you telling anyone. And I still hope you'll keep this to yourself, all of you." She gazed around as everyone relaxed and looked back, guilty looks on their faces. They nodded in unison, not to tell anyone about it.

Hepheaus took a long breath and put her head down. "Now that we're all relaxed, I have a good idea as to why you came back here. You're here to get your orb, aren't you, son?"

Ocean leaned back and nodded at her. Everyone else looked over, paying attention now. Hepheaus pushed herself up and sat on the edge of her pool. Water dripped down her hair and down her body, making sure not to miss a crevice. Her hair was let free and dipped down over most of her face. "Well…" she said, flicking her hair back behind her head, sending water flying in front of her. "Now that you are nice and refreshed, I wanted to teach my son a couple things before you go away again. Come with me." Surprised, Ocean got up and followed her through a door in the back of the room.

"Uh, so do we wait or?" Hail shifted in the water.

Sky looked over at him. "No idea at all."

"Well, I won't be sitting here bored while we wait, imma go look around." Blaze said getting out of the water and redressing.

"Hmmm, I'll join you. Sitting around like this makes me restless." Volt ran after Blaze.

"Yeah, uh, me too," Gaia said not far behind.

Sky sat back in the water further. "You guys go ahead, I'll just sit here and enjoy this." Void and Hail shared his sentiment and stayed put.

-Year 276   Ula Town Center   Eodon, Sylindra-

Blaze, Volt, and Gaia made their way past the courtyard and across the bridge, back towards the main shopping center. They arrived at a large plaza with an open area in the center, with shops of different types all around them. Weapon shops, clothing dealers, multiple fish stands, they had a lot. The people looked at them with the same reverence and excitement as before.

"Hey! I know you'd like another weapon to go with that, come check out my shop!" An elderly man approached the group, directing his attention at Blaze.

Blaze raised his hands. "Oh no, I'm fine in that regard, thank you."

"Aw, darn. Well that's okay. Head on over if you change your mind!" The old man walked away.

"So…nice…" Blaze said with his eyes widened, shocked.

"Hey, Blaze you hungry? This shop here looks great." Gaia pointed to the eatery right on the end, the man out front was pulling out a pot of some fresh noodles. Next to it was a dark broth, with such a strong aroma.

"Yeah, you know what? I can eat!" Blaze responded now excited. Volt nodded and joined along.

The three grabbed a table outside and were greeted by a middle aged woman wearing an apron and tongs in hand. "Hey guys, welcome to Fisochu, my names Maria. You folk been over here before?" she said in a friendly, but weathered tone.

"Thanks, hey we haven't, but honestly just give us whatever you think is good," Gaia chuckled.

"I'm fine with that too," Volt nodded. Blaze just shrugged his shoulders.

"Well, that's what I like to hear, sweetie, I'll be right back!" The woman headed back inside. She returned quickly with three waters. Behind her, another man came out with three large bowls and placed one in front of each of them.

"Mmm, this smells great, what is it, Maria?" Volt said in a soft tone.

"This is our specialty, Seafood miso ramen! Enjoy." She bowed and walked back.

Chopsticks appeared next to the bowls spontaneously. Inside the bowls, local fish and steamed shrimp sat atop of a fantastic broth, eggs, corn and spinach. The sheer aroma from the meal put a smile on each of the knights faces. They all attempted to eat with couth and dignity, but it didn't take long for the taste of the dish to hit. Starting with Blaze, and moving to each, they began slurping down the ramen without remorse. Within minutes, they were all gone.

Blaze leaned back far in his chair, rubbing his stomach. "Ughhh, wow that was the best meal I've ever eaten."

"Yeah, I don't know what came over me, I've never eaten like that," Volt said checking himself.

"I'm so glad you enjoyed it! Do come back to eat again, knights!" The lady came back out with a smile.

"What do we owe you Maria?" Gaia spoke up.

"Oh no no, we could never take your money. We take pride in our food, and having that reaction from the Royal Knights is all we could hope for!" The owner came from behind inside and offered his thanks waving the knights off.

The three bowed back at the shop owner and made their way across the street. "Hey, Volt, come help me pick out some new clothes!" Gaia drug Volt into a clothing store on that side of the street. Volt groaned the entire way but reluctantly followed.

"Hmm. Guess I'll just check out some armor or something then," Blaze said out loud to himself, mostly. Gaia and Volt spent the rest of their time going around the small shop, and trying on clothes. Volt forced to be her main critic. Blaze spoke to the armor smith, learning more about the form and function of different types of armors, along with the weakness affiliated with them.

-Year 276 Farriage Castle Underground Springs Eodon, Sylindra-

Back in the springs, Void, Hail and Sky redress and wait for everyone to come back. One of the guards from outside came in to check in on them.

"Hey man, what's your name?" Sky said as he stopped the guard.

The guard looked young, having only mildly, heavy armor and a long spear in hand. "Uh, Ryan?" The guard nervously responded.

"Hmm, no need to be so nervous, we don't bite." Sky said with a chuckle. Void shook his head.

"Come sit with us, Ryan." Hail waved him over.

Ryan reluctantly came over and sat a bit away from the three, on the ground. "Y-yes, knights?"

"How are things on this continent?" Void spoke up first. "Everything seems very energetic and happy...too happy really."

"Oh you're worrying over nothing in that regard. We are enjoying life, everyone supports Hepheaus and believes in her with their lives." Ryan's previous nervousness was replaced with conviction.

"What of her health? She has that bone disease after all," Hail added.

"Well of course everyone knows about that, but she defies it with her strength and mana control. Ocean will be lucky if he inherits even half of her strength." Ryan nodded to himself as he continued. "She is already incredibly smart as well, how she's helped set up this town and make it what it is today, this entire continent is grateful to that woman."

"Heard that, sorry for doubting you." Hail satisfied nodded in place.

"Oh no no, I'm sorry for my outburst. It's unlike me," Ryan apologized, regained himself.

"It's okay, Ryan. Think we know what we need to." Sky got up and began his mental communication. Just then, Volt and Gaia came busting back through the doors.

"Volt! Why'd you have to drag me out of there like that?" Gaia shouted, pouting.

"Because...you were embarrassing yourself!" Volt yelled right back.

"Ugh, like a married couple already, get in there." Blaze pushed the two fully inside and walked in behind them. Ryan ran back outside to resume his post.

"Uh, you guys have fun?" Sky threw a loaded question out there.

Volt blushed for some reason, but didn't respond. "Yes, we did, thank you!" Gaia said grabbing his arm.

"Highlight, we had some amazing ramen from a place in the shopping center. The people here are very nice as well, " Blaze responded for them properly.

"Thank you Blaze. We had an interesting conversation ourselves in your absence. I think Hepheaus would make a great ally for us going forward," Sky said, trying to sound as serious as possible. He clearly wasn't used to it.

"I wouldn't mind. They seem very organized here. I'll let Father John know," Volt responded regaining composure.

****
*

After fifteen more minutes had passed, the door in the back had slowly creaked open. Out came a winded Hepheaus and an Ocean with mana surrounding his body the way it does his mom usually. In his arm was a folded up outfit, similar in look to his previous minus the tatters. There were also silver engravings that circulated around the uniform, especially the knees and elbow areas. Mana was visibly seen linking each of his joints, with slight electricity radiating along the streams. Ocean's hair was also spiked up and sweaty or wet, it couldn't precisely be differentiated. He holding his ribs, and noticeably limping as he walked forward as well.

"Whoa, what happened to you, Ocean?" Blaze asked as he watched Ocean slide himself into the water gingerly.

"Go rest yourself in there, then make me proud out there...son." Hepheaus walked up the steps and stopped at the door. "It was nice meeting you Royal Knights, good luck in your journey. Keep Ocean safe." She walked out the door after winking towards them and closing it behind her.

Ocean sat up after taking a nice long dip in the water, "Man, I feel so invigorated!"

Sky walked over and bent over next to him. "So what did she teach you exactly? All that cool stuff she did to you in your fight?"

Ocean laughed softly. "Ha-ha, I guess you will have to find out. Either way, are you guys ready? She told me the way to get to the trail site." They all stood up and rushed over.

"We've been waiting for over an hour; we are beyond ready," Void said in his low, slow tone. Ocean got changed into his new garb and lead them out.

-Year 276 Frosty Forest East Ula Sacred passage Eodon, Sylindra-

The knights traveled out of town, through the southern exit and back into the forest. Their path was marked by the mystic water ingrained into the ground and flowing downwards through the woods. Although the snow was on the grass in some places, the water still did not freeze and remained draining down to…something. Ocean led the pack as they made their way towards the eastern edge of the island.

"Apparently, this path leads through a sacred silvery pond that's said to be a portal to another dimension or something. It's called the reflecting pond." Ocean said as he walked.

"That certainly sounds interesting," Volt said, nodding.

Ocean shook his head. "Nope, we can't go near it. I was warned of its inherent danger."

Blaze chuckled lowly to himself. "By your *mom*? Hopefully, if something does come after us, you can wow us with your new abilities." Blaze said, trying to keep a straight face.

Ocean, turned away, trying to ignore him while still trudging forward.

Another hour passed as they walked. The sun had faded, leaving only the bright moon as the light source for their journey. Thankfully, this part of the forest was a lot less dense than the others. "You thinking about setting up camp for the night? It might be easier to see if we start again in the morning."

Ocean shook his head. "It doesn't seem to be too much longer before we reach an area we can stop at." As they walked, the scenery slightly changed under cover of night. More and more trees and plants were dead and rotting as they progressed. Slight hints of silver were splattered on the ground, on top of the snow. A mild light shined beyond the trees in front of them.

"What's that light?" Sky asked while he slowed down a bit."

"I-I'm not sure, nothing should be out here," Ocean stammered. They all slowly approached the clearing in the trees that was illuminated by a bright light.

"Whoa, this is…" Blaze's eyes gaped open when he saw what awaited them on the other side of the trees. There was a clearing surrounded by dead trees and brushes. Snow-covered the entire area cleanly, except in the center. There lay a lake, made of a mixture of silver and water, but it glowed with a magical shine that made the entire clearing appear to be daytime. Aside from the glow, the pond was entirely calm. On the opposite side was an oddly placed stairwell embedded in the ground. It led downhill from there and out of sight.

The knights stood still as they stared at the pond simultaneously. There was an odd feeling in the air. "Do you guys hear that whispering?" Volt said, taking a step forward.

Void grabbed Volt's arm and stopped him, "I...would not go near that man."

Volt's eyes glazed over clear as his body moved him forcibly forward towards the pond. "You don't hear that guys? I feel like it's calling to m——..." His legs moved on their own now.

"Volt, stop!" Sky yelled. "That's an order!"

Volt kept going, and before anyone could react, the pond rumbled a bit, and parts of the silvery water came shooting out towards him like a liquid hand, grasping Volt's body from all sides. Void lunged forward, grabbing Volt's ankle, holding on tightly to the only part he could reach. In one motion, Volt's body was jerked forward and down into the pond, Void right behind him stopping the movement with a tight grip on Volt's ankle. He was pulled to the edge of the water as he struggled to keep Volt's body from being lost in the pond. Void looked back at Ocean and Sky, who were frozen in shock, along with everyone else. "Ocean!" Void yelled loudly, snapping Ocean out of his trance. "I can't hold this for long ok; I'm going to go in with Volt...keep him safe. You guys stay away and go down those steps. Ocean you have a job to do, don't worry about us...I'll handle this." Void was pulled further forward, his toes sliding into the water.

Ocean sighed and nodded. "You can count on us, I'll believe in you, Void," he said.

Sky put his hand on Ocean's shoulder in agreement. "Void, use our link to tell me what happens. We will move forward. Be safe." Void sighed and grumbled as his strength gave way, and he was pulled into the pond along with Volt. The surface grew calm again moments after they went in.

173

Sky stared at the pond for some moments before motioning for the rest to follow him down the stairs. Sky's head was sagging the entire time they walked down the obnoxiously long stairwell through the trees. The bottom couldn't even be seen from where they were. Everyone looked away, not wanting to acknowledge what they had just seen.

It was Gaia who finally broke the silence. "I, uh, hope they'll be alright," she said, voice trailing off mid-sentence.

Sky looked up into the air. "I'm sure Volt will be alright; he's got Void with him. Very dependable, he is." Sky looked over to Ocean, who was still sulking to himself. "So... tell us what we have awaiting us at the bottom of this stairwell. She should have told you, right?"

Ocean shook himself back into action. "Well, she wasn't able to describe to me what it looked like or anything, but she did say there was a shrine of sorts at the bottom of this stairwell, and the beast resided in an underwater city."

Blaze smirked at Ocean. "That doesn't really sound very safe for the rest of us. I know you can breathe underwater but..."

Ocean chuckled and looked over at the rest of them. "Well, I hope you can hold your breath and swim then." Blaze looked away, embarrassed.

After about an hour and a half of constant movement down the stairs, the bottom was finally visible. A small, outhouse sized building stood there, barely visible with the high tree's coverage blocking out the moon. Gaia stopped short as everyone began picking up the pace down the stairs with their destination finally visible to them. "Maybe we should make camp for the night before going into that cramped looking shrine because I don't know about you, but I don't fancy a battle for our lives underwater... *in the dark*."

174

Ocean trotted forward more, looking back slightly. "Don't worry, we can do that. We'll set up right in front of it and hope nothing comes out and bites us, haha."

Gaia's face changed to frustration, but she soon calmed down and began running down the steps to catch up with the others. By the time she got to the bottom, the rest of the knights were already chopping up wood for a fire and readying themselves to rest. The knights promptly cleared the snow in the area. Gaia rose the earth to create a small fire pit in the center of their newly secured camp area in front of the table. Ocean tossed a large pile of wood inside. Blaze snapped his fingers, lighting a fire in the middle, creating a second light source for them to see what they were doing. One chopped down tree later, and they all had logs to sleep on. Void carved each log into a flat slab for comfort.

It didn't take long for most to drift away under the warmth of the flames before them. Sky sat to watch on top of his log, staring into the fire. The silence was deafening, only being broken by eerie winds that occasionally blew through the barren trees that surrounded them. A small spark broke away from the chirping flames and landed on Gaia's cheek, gently waking her out of her sleep. She raised her head and looked at Sky, his back towards her.

"Too worried to sleep, Sky?" she said.

He didn't move, and it took a few moments for him to finally respond. "That...and I sincerely do not trust that temple. I couldn't sleep either way, haha."

Gaia crawled over and sat up next to Sky, staring into the flames as well. "You've known Volt for a while, right?" Gaia asked.

Sky crossed his right leg over his left and began shaking it. "Yeah, why?"

Gaia sighed. "Well, he seems a bit cold at times, I don't quite know how to explain it, but I feel like if I throw myself at him, I'll end up getting hurt."

Sky chuckled a bit to himself. "You do like him, don't you?" He stopped, shook his head to fix his composure. "That'll be a tough road to go down, he hasn't really felt 'love' per se. Doubt he would understand the feeling even if he did have an interest in you like that."

Gaia blushed and looked away. "It's not like I have the most experience myself, I'm no harlot! I've been trained to fight since I was a little girl. I just know I favor him quite a bit," Gaia sarcastically trailed off.

"That girl couldn't land a man if she was the only woman left on Sylindra, haha." Hail chuckled still half asleep.

"Shut up!" Gaia grabbed a rock and pelted it at Hail. It bounced off of his cheek, waking him up.

"Hey!" Hail said rubbing his cheek. "Just…don't get yourself chasing 'church boy' over there. Just trust your big bro."

"Do you guys all have to be so loud?" Blaze said still groggy, but already annoyed.

"Ah shut up. We all know no one's gonna wanna marry your angry ass either." Sky chuckled.

Blaze opened his eyes fully, his mouth open. He was shocked, if not a little hurt. He brushed it off though, shaking his head. "Never mind, I'm going back to bed," he said laying back down.

"Oh come on, I was kidding bro. You know we love our Blaze. We wouldn't be here without ya, man," Sky said attempting to be genuine.

"You comment on my anger issues, then you say shit like that. Everyone always wonders why I go off so easily." Blaze scoffs before closing his eyes.

Gaia looked at Blaze through the exchange, sensing the hurt he felt, but kept her words to herself. Sky laid back down as well; the awkwardness made any further interaction too much.

176

"Anyway, let's all try to get some rest, a lot of fighting to come tomorrow," Sky added.

"Ok, you're right." Gaia laid her head back down. Hail had already fallen back asleep. Ocean never budged throughout the conversation.

-Year 276 Ula Sacred Passage Under the pond Eodon, Sylindra-

Volt and Void sank into the pond, but they didn't drown, nor did they gasp for air. They drifted to the bottom and landed softly on the dirt. Volt's body sat there as still as a stone, while Void looked around mystified as to why he could breathe right now. A pure white orb appeared from beneath the dirt and hovered in front of Volt for a few seconds. A flash of light exploded from the sphere, eventually materializing into a barrier of sorts surrounding the two knights and a semi-circle seven meters out in all directions. The wall shut out all of the water, and only a translucent shining white circle could be seen around them, but they could breathe normally now with air as the water was sucked out.

After some awkward coughing, Void regained his voice. "What the hell is this?" The white orb pulsated a few times in front of Volt's face, snapping him out of his trance, and then backing up two meters into the center of the barrier.

Volt shook his head, his right hand massaging his temples. "Uh Void, you want to explain what happened?"

Void turned around and looked at Volt sideways. "You really don't remember?"

Volt innocently shook his head.

The orb that stood before them began to shake violently, then as if coming into existence, a beautiful woman appeared in the place where the ball was previously.

She appeared with her hands together and her head drooped. Long silver hair trailed down just past her shoulders, but she didn't look a day over twenty-five. With light, pale skin, an innocent smile, and all-white cloth clothing only covering particular parts of her body. She didn't even wear shoes, but her cloth covered her breasts and her crotch area barely. "Maybe I can help with your confusion a little," the woman spoke with a soft, calming voice. Her lips didn't budge, but her voice echoed inside the minds' of Volt and Void.

They both winced at the violation inside of their minds. "Who are you?" Void looked at the woman as she strolled forward towards them. He stood tall, looking down at her, his senses itching with each step. With a sharp glare from the woman, Void's body was forcibly dragged down to a knee, his body surrounded by red mana.

"Watch your tone." The woman's face went from marvelously murderous intent than back to innocence.

Volt got up himself, looking curiously at the woman. "What is your name, miss?"

The woman smiled. "My name is Luvia." Her head cocked to the side after her response. As she strolled over, Volt's body was forced to his butt simultaneously. When she arrived in front of them, she bent her knees to get lower to their new eye levels. "I want you both to understand something now before we begin this conversation. You have no power here, I am in control." She switched her sights between Volt and Void as she spoke, keeping her tone as calm as possible.

Volt and Void sat as still as possible, the sinister mana surrounding them, causing great pain at even the slightest budge. "I've been waiting for a while for this fated meeting to come to pass, you know. Ah, I got it! How about I tell you a little story since you must be so curious about who I am and why I summoned you here. Well, Volt anyway."

Volt turned and looked at Void, sensing the gravity of the situation they were in now. "Yeah, he's uninvited, but he'll have to sit and watch for now. But either way, is that story ok with you?" she questioned them with a large smile on her face. They both nodded, figuring they had no choice either way.

"Go ahead," Void said shortly.

Luvia clapped "Alright, lovely! Let's get the place set up."

She sat all the way down and crossed her legs. The orb that they currently resided in turned all black, the interior acting as a projector into Luvia's mind it began to aid in her storytelling with a visual recap.

"A long, long while back, closer to the creation of humans, the deities began getting very curious about the day to day life of humans. The way they interacted with each other differed from most other races they had created. Like any other strange being, they made a way to test it out for them. By mimicking the forms of humans, and taking professions that interested them, they were able to blend into different societies around Sylindra. Now during this process, a young, purposeless girl grew more and more curious about this process. This girl was made from the shadows of Lucinthis and molded into being by Nefula's hands. Though made from them, but not one of them, this girl never had any guidance in her life, not from the Gods, no one. Growing equally curious about the humans, this girl began to test out her powers on them. She found she could control the minds of some and even make herself a physical body as well. She had quite a bit of fun messing with the silly humans, though her 'fun' might have been a tad too sinister for some. One drunk man forced on a young queen, and the tempting of war between feuding magi clans was all it took to sway the attention of the Gods. They finally noticed her, but they weren't happy, of course. Quite a bit of anger and fighting

179

later, the girl was stripped of her physical form and trapped in a hell of sorts. The girl was too strong for this to stop her, though. Before she was sent away, she did another experiment. A spawn of hers was formed, a human boy. Of course, she couldn't take care of him being in this hell, so she was forced to give him up to the noblest person she could think of, a man named John, I believe." Luvia took a deep breath and a long pause as she looked up into the air. Her thought projections stopped as she looked at Volt, who was frozen in place, his mouth gaping wide open.

"Wh-who are you?" Volt stuttered with a single tear rolling down his cheek. Void nudged Volt's shoulder and whispered in his ear. Volt broke away from Void, his sanity fading. "All this time I've wondered and…no way." The restraints on Volt faded away. He stammered as he paced back and forth, pulling at his hair. Void tried to calm him down but was unsuccessful.

"Yes, it means what you think it means, Volt, you are technically my spawn." Luvia let out a small smile. Volt immediately dropped to his knees, floods of tears running down his face uncontrollably. Luvia rose up and stepped in front of Volt, placing her hand on the top of his head, ruffling his hair. "Sorry you had to find out in this manner but I did find out something else too." Luvia switched from messing with his hair to grasping the top of his head tightly. "I found that the power struggle between you knights, who hold power gifted from the Gods, and the evil demons who threaten your world, actually make me stronger. With each enemy you defeat, the closer I get to reclaim my physical form, hahaha." She then got really close to his ear and whispered softly, "Then all I need is one of your bodies to become a vessel for me. Will that be you, sweetie?"

At this, Void decided he had had enough, breaking free of his restraints. Void threw a swift strike with his claymore, separating the two. Luvia backed off a bit and

180

began laughing maniacally. She held out her hand towards Void, surrounding him with her devious mana again, constricting his movements and causing him to drop his weapon, and to his knees. "Damnit," Void said.

"I'll make you a deal Volt since you claim to be such a good duelist, as I've seen. If you can land a single strike on me, I'll grant Void the ability to teleport you both to your own sacred areas. A bit of a shortcut for the both of you if you will. If you can't, I'll just use your body as a vessel now and be done with it," Luvia said with outstretched arms a couple feet away from Volt.

Volt looked back at Void, who was trapped still and nodded. He wiped his face off and summoned his spear, stabbing it into the ground and using it to rise back to his feet. "Sounds like a deal to me...Mom." Volt arched over to the side and threw up on the ground. When he popped up, his expression was all the more serious. "It was a shocker, but it could still be a hell of a lot worse. We'll get this done, then go to defeat Scourge!" Volt said, wiping off his mouth, looking back at Void again, who nodded at him.

The smile on Luvia's face grew and grew. "There's that confidence I expected!"
Void gave Volt a side-eye stare, "I know she might be your mom, but for both of us, you better kick her ass!" Volt nodded back as he spun his spear in place.

In a quick motion, Volt tossed his spear at her head, teleporting to it shortly afterward. Luvia slightly moved her head to the left, allowing the spear to pass before grabbing it and quickly tossing it into the ground. A seemingly misplaced kick into the air caught an incoming Volt in the stomach just as he teleports.

After a large gasp for air, Volt collapsed into the ground. "Ack, wow," he said as he cracked a little smile.

Luvia held out her hand and sent him flying back with a shockwave. "Try again, heh." This is when Volt summoned his spear back and rushed at Luvia, throwing a barrage of blows at her. She easily dodged and parries all of them as noticeable green mana appears around her. This mana made her translucent and caused Volt's attacks to go right through.

"Wait…that's Sky's…" Volt stopped and stared at his opposition. His yellow mana began radiating in his hands. The mana drifted down until it engulfed his spear. "I'll get you this time!" Volt spun his spear again and started swinging. Luvia dodged his blows entirely this time instead of letting it phase through her.

"Ha, you think I didn't see your fight against that phoenix on Laix?" she said.

Volt backed up a bit, looking at her sideways. "But how…if you were trapped here all this time," Volt asked. The orb surrounding them turned black again as Luvia closed her eyes.

"This orb we reside in allows me to be all-seeing in the outside world and project my consciousness as well," she said as the visuals changed to an overhead view of the remaining knights approaching the beach with a stairwell awaiting them down into the water. Shortly after the image, it turned back to normal as Volt swung at her again using his fists of lightning mana this time.

"You were watching us the whole time?" Volt yelled. Luvia nodded as she deflected Volt's fists with streams of water mana now. The green mana around her soon changed to a blue one. With each parry, Volt's own electricity began building up and shocking him. "Damnit," Volt said as he stumbled with his movements slowed. He dropped to a knee, "How do you have those abilities?"

Luvia chuckled to herself. "Maybe you'll find out if you can hit me."

Volt stuck his spear into the ground and rested his arms by his sides. Slowly and calmly, he began to breathe. "Ok, let's

182

get serious then." Like mockingbirds, electric mana began to chirp around his hands. Electricity jumped and circulated around his hands before rising up his arms and taking homage there, and orbiting it. His arms even glowed bright yellow as well. Volt's head was down, his voice low, and his tone soft. "Erupt and eradicate, shatter their hopes for they failed to embrace the goddess…and I will punish them...*Inazuma*!" The calm lightning exploded into a rage with large agitated sparks around his hands when he punched his palm. He clapped his hands, causing a massive thunder shock wave that encompassed the orb they were in. Luvia surrounded herself back in her regular mana, "This should be interesting, eh?"

"We'll see how interesting this is for you!" When Volt separated his two hands, a sphere of pure electric mana was revealed. He caressed and held it softly as he looked up at Luvia. "Boom!" As if delivering dueling palm strikes into the air, Volt thrust his hands forward, and an enormous release of electric energy blasted towards Luvia. The blast soared across the room, closing the distance in an instant. Mere inches away from her, though, Luvia hopped over out of the way of the blast. It crashed into the walls and fizzled out, the wall was unfazed.

Luvia looked back at where the blast hit and smirked, "Hmph, figures."

Volt's arms were still surrounded in thick mana. "Hit you? I'll fry you, Luvia!" With another clap, Volt sent forth another blast wave.

Luvia dodged and mocked Volt's hand movements. "Not going to hit me like that hun."

"Agh!" Volt let out a scream of rage and began shooting off blast after blast to no avail.

"My, my, are these getting weaker?" Luvia commented on the smaller waves each time.

Breathing heavily now, Volt stood up straight again and clapped his hands together. "Fine then, dodge this." Volt charges the energy in his hands for a few moments before he separated them this time. The blast he now released was twice the size of the previous ones, leaving little room to dodge.

Luvia held up her hand before it reached her; a large dark portal extended out of her hand, catching the blast wave. A hint of static was heard in Volt's ear as he stopped in shock. A twin portal opened up to the right of Volt and Void with the blast burrowing out towards then. Volt turned over quickly. "Shit! Void!" He rushed over and dived in front of Void, who was still chained down. "Ack!" Volt blocked the brunt of his own attack with his back as he covered for Void. They both were pushed back and slammed into the wall and tumbled to the ground. Volt eased himself up to his feet, holding his right arm, of which was bruised and burnt through his armor. A piece of metal from his boot lay next to his foot. After a struggling couple of moments, he dropped back down to a knee.

"Man, Void, I haven't seen you use your portals like that before, quite a surprise there, Luvia," Volt said with one eye open as he winced with pain.

Luvia pointed at Void. "You'll find that I can use your powers better than even you can. It's why I swell with joy at the thought of using your body to its full potential." She smiled.

"Don't count on it." Volt hoisted himself up and walked back over to his spear, which he grabbed and held up at Luvia.

With an eyebrow raised, she expressed her confusion, "This again? Didn't you already try this and fail?"

Volt spun his spear around in place, "I got you this time!" With a sparked liftoff, Volt underhand tossed the spear at Luvia, disappearing shortly afterward.

With a smug, confident look on her face, she smacked the spear away, punching forward to where his path would lead him. But she caught nothing but open air. Below her, however, came afoot materializing in a streak of lightning. In a thrusting kick from underneath, Volt pushed himself forward with his electricity and connected with an unprepared Luvia, directly under her chin. With enough force to lift her off her feet. Volt finished the kick with a combination of successive kicks. With each kick, they both raised higher into the dome, and higher still. A final mule kick sent Luvia's skull crashing into the ceiling of the dome and propelled Volt back into the ground. Volt knelt in place for a moment, as Luvia unpleasantly splattered behind him. "Told ya," Volt said with a smirk.

Luvia's body instantly popped back up unnaturally. "Good job, Volt," she snapped her neck back into place and patted him on the head to his irritation.

Volt turned around to face her, then over to Void, who was silently celebrating to himself. She looked back and noticed the piece of metal at where her feet were before she got kicked.

"Ahh, I get it now, smart. Your powers may have evolved without my knowing. Fantastic." With a snap of her fingers, she released Void from the chains. A couple of grunts later, and he walked over to join Volt. "Guess I owe you a bit of information, huh?" Luvia chuckled a bit lowly.

"More than that, but that's a good start," Volt said, crossing his arms.

She opened her arms and backed away a few steps. "Ask away, hah." Her entire body seemed to angle over to the right as she spoke, almost ominous was her stance.

185

"Fine, I'll start with a big one then, what events in the lives of the Royal Knights have you had something to do with?"

Luvia laughed hard for a moment before cutting it off quickly. "My my, what a question. Fine. Well, I did quite a bit of meddling over my years of finding myself. One of the first things I tried to do when I studied humans was to see what simple words would do." Volt looked at her cautiously. "A young Sky might not remember as much, but his clan has been at odds with a rivaling magi-clan since before his birth, though they always avoided contact; until me of course. I descended unto your world and paid the rival leader a visit to his chambers, had a small conversation with him. Next thing you know, he's attacking a home village of Sky's, and the rest is history. They've been at war ever since, and now grown Sky is tired of being surrounded by fighting." She stopped to notice Volt's eyes open wide, but his mouth shut tight, Void had the same straight face on though.

"Shall we move on?" she said.

Volt nodded solemnly.

"We move on now to a young queen, husband recently lost, but that didn't stop her from stepping up and being a leader for her people. Strong in will she was, but with my curse flowing deep in her blood, her body was weak. That was an earlier endeavor, the curse. Revenge for that damn family defying me. Cursed all of the females with a bone-eating disease, eventually causing this bloodline to die off. Either way, we were talking about his mother, weren't we? So, she was on a simple stroll down the street with her guards to clear her mind one night, or so she thought. This is where I was testing out my ability to control human actions." Luvia took a breath.

Volt was shaking his head at this point, slowly. "You. You are the reason for all of his family's hardships."

186

"A lowly homeless drunkard going nowhere in life, I took control of his mind and body because it was easy. I wanted to see how strong I could make him with my powers, so I pushed it. Moments later, he came out of an alleyway, killing a guard and forcing his way onto a currently defenseless queen. Defenseless against my might flowing through him. Just under a year later, everyone was introduced to the young bastard Ocean, the first male heir in ages. But of what circumstances? Wonder whatever happened to his father after that. Probably dead, oh well," Luvia snickered.

Again, Volt was shaking in place, unable to really say anything. Only a tear that rolled down his cheek.

Luvia smiled softly. "I remember a young demon mercenary who was so powerful and talented at killing he even caught the attention of Demise himself. I latched onto him with my mana link early, I saw his potential."

Volt stopped her. "Wait, what's this mana link you have?"

The biggest smile yet was on Luvia's face as she put her hand to her heart, "My links transfer power to me constantly from whomever I have linked. More-so the stronger they get, and if they were to perish, all of their residual energy goes right to me. This is how I still grow more powerful even though I am locked away. This is why I am happy when you guys have your little rivalry with Scourge, you build each other up, and me in return."

Volt held his hands up defensively. "Woah Woah Woah, Scourge is not our rival. I don't know why he messes with us, but don't disrespect us like that."

Luvia bursts out laughing. "You are lucky I'm giving you that distinction, Scourge is far more powerful than any of you right now, and he knows it. It's sad really, he is such a specimen, but he wastes time on those weaker than him. Everyone."

187

Volt walked up to Luvia, getting in her face. "We will catch up to him in short order, as soon as we can get our elemental orbs."

She held up her hand in his face, letting out a simple shockwave that sends him skidding back. "Hence rivals. And don't get in my face Volt, I can end you both right now on a whim I don't care if you're my son."

Volt was taken aback but held his ground. "Well, are you gonna help us or what? It does look to benefit you as you have this link on all of us right. The orb makes us more powerful." Volt nudged towards her multiple times in a row before she responds.

Luvia scrunched her face up and grumbles a bit. "I guess," she said with a smile. Luvia held her hand out towards Void. His body began to be forcibly pulled towards her.

"What the hell?" Void yelled, trying to resist unsuccessfully.

"Oh, shut up and take it like a man." When Void's body reached her, she grabbed him by his head and forced him to his knees. After a few moments of mumbling to herself, mana began to leave her hand and enter Void, whose entire body was glowing white at this point.

"What is this…sensation?" he said.

Luvia looked down at him, "This is me using my mana to unlock some of your potentials. Shortly you will able to use your portals to travel very long distances, like right near your orb's sacred sites per se."

Void silenced himself, and Volt nodded curiously at her. "Well, since you are so intelligent, where are our sacred orbs located on our continents?" Volt questioned.

Luvia nodded, the room going dark again as she closed her eyes. She reopened them shortly afterward with a visualization of a map of Sylindra being shown reflected off all sides. Kayard was shown on the wall to Volt's left.

"That's actually quite accurate, Luvia," Volt said, looking

over at Kayard. A bright red marker appeared on the spot around the southeastern part of Kayard, marking an ancient swamp town.

"You'll find what you're looking for there. And Void for you-" Luvia spun the map of the world around to put the focus on Basonali. A marker appeared at the end of the Nasol Ruins on the northern end of the continent. "For you, Void, your challenge is to get to the hidden town of Malervia. There's no set place for it, not even I can sense it. All I know is that it's through the Nasol Ruins, there's a really dangerous cauldron you have to go through to make it to the other side."

Void nodded to himself a few times. "I've heard about that town, there is something they are protecting there. It's why there is a magical force field that masks the mana there so no one could search for it."

Void walked over next to Volt. "Either way, are you ready to go? Make sure you link with Sky to let him know what the plan is. The portal to Armageddon should be on Repshira. So that is a good place to meet for all of us after we finish."

Void closed his eyes for a moment and clapped his hands together. "This better work Luvia."

Luvia stood there, her arms crossed, a small smile on her face, "Just get out there already and give me a good show. I'll be rooting for you guys, for obvious reasons, heh." Void's eyes opened wide suddenly as he raised his right hand into the air before slamming it into the ground. A burst of mana flooded into the field, spiraling around into a much cleaner looking portal on the ground. It expanded and expanded until it had encompassed the area surrounded by both of their feet. "This one's for you, Volt, good luck, brother." Void said, holding up his fist.

Volt pumped his fist as he walked past, spear in hand. "See you on the other side, I'll try not to take too long." Volt hopped into the center of the portal, disappearing. The portal dissipated; Void repeated the process with a new entrance at his feet now. He took a few steps towards the center before stopping short.

"You know. No matter how powerful you get from us, you won't win; we will defeat you, Luvia," Void threatened.

Luvia leaned back onto the wall of the room, crossing her legs now. She looked up and shook her head disappointingly at Void. "You know, I really do not like you Void, maybe the next time we meet, I'll just kill you off sight, just to get rid of you."

Void took another step forward. "You better do it now then because it won't be so easy next time!" Void stared Luvia in the eyes as menacing as possible as he walked forward into the portal. He kept eye contact the entire time. Void disappeared as well, returning Luvia to her solitude

Chapter 10: Water Beast

-Year 276 Unknown area under the Eodic Gulf Eodon, Sylindra-

While Volt and Void were trapped with Luvia, the rest of the knights went down to the shrine and opened it; the shining light that incurred transported them all to a mysterious area underwater. They all appeared at the bottom of the ocean gasping for air, surrounded by rubble. Soon afterwards, a translucent mana force field surrounded the entire area, allowing the knights to breathe underwater. They stopped choking and realized they could actually breathe underwater.

"Gah! What the hell?" Blaze said coughing and cursing loudly.

"Are w-we underwater? Why? How?" Gaia said looking around her. She noticed the dome also helped them to stay easily on the ground with minimum effort.

"Hmm. I guess your orb *would* lead us underwater, wouldn't it? It's kind of hard to move down here though," Sky said waving his hand almost moving in slow motion.

"I'm perfectly fine, its *easy*," Ocean said with a cocky smile, swimming up in place.

"This is terrible," Blaze mumbled under his breath.

"You okay, man?" Ocean motioned over to Blaze, who had yet to make it to his feet.

"Yeah, don't think you can count on me much here." Blaze shrugged.

"I know, don't worry." Ocean chuckled.

"Hey, start searching around guys, so we can get out of here. I don't enjoy underwater much either," Sky said as he moved forward to look around. The knights nodded and followed.

Upon a little exploration, the area appeared like a sunken city sitting on what used to be a fourth island in the Eodon territory. Around the perimeter of the town, the mana from the barrier occasionally flashed, showing the active area they had to work with. The city had been abandoned for decades by the looks of it. Roofs were caved in, the innards of the buildings and homes could be seen of those that still stood. Most left only the foundations, paths between different areas of the small city remained through copious amounts of rubble floating from one part of the city to another. This would make travel more difficult if they weren't underwater. The mana surrounding the city held everything together like gravity, keeping the city from being blown away into the ocean.

"Oh, look at these guys." Sky ran over to the rest holding a dilapidated wooden figurine that resembled a man, but it was too darkened and worn to make out any features.

"I wonder what kind of place this was, and how long ago," Gaia questioned to herself.

The knights walked along the main road of the city, searching around for any clues to the sacred orb's location. "What's that?" Blaze pointed out a large sign broken up and laid against what was left of a wall off to the side. He ran over to it, looking at it sideways for a bit, unable to make it out. "Hey Ocean, uh, you able to make this out?"

Ocean came over, everyone else behind him. He got lower to look closer, trying to piece it together. "I think this says Alantos. Maybe the name of this city? I don't remember any teachings of this place growing up, so I have no idea."

He turned around to Sky's face all scrunched up. "Hey, you ok, Sky?" Ocean said.

Sky put his hand over his ear, which seemed to be bothering him. "Yeah, think it's a mana link from Volt. He's trying to use my connection to him to contact me, hold up." He closed his eyes for a moment; the tension in his face seemed to fade away. "Yeah I can hear you. Ok I'm glad, though we'll have to talk about the how later. Ok we will head there afterward, Good luck, Volt."

The rest of the knights looked at Sky curiously as he appeared to have been talking to himself. "Um, what was that?" Gaia finally spoke up.

Sky chuckled. "The link worked; I got a message from Volt. First of all, he is ok." The knights cheered a bit, fist-bumping and such before turning back to hear the rest. "Also, he met some odd woman, details of which he'll have to fill us in later, but the important part is that she upgraded Void's portal to allow him to transport himself and Volt close to their sacred orbs to avoid the travel from here. He wants us to meet him on Repshera when we finish up; we'll all go to the portal to Armageddon together."

Ocean looked up in anticipation. "Awesome if we could ever fin—"

Screeeeeeeeeeech! A loud, ear-splitting sound echoed throughout the city. The sound stunned the bodies of the knights, paralyzing them temporarily. Gaia was the first mobile again.

She pushed the knights behind cover and kneeled next to them while looking around. "What the hell was that?" She whispered trying not to draw attention. They all peered up beyond the rubble and noticed the glorious beast that made the sound. Long in stature, and with a burly, hairy outer hide. It resembled a grizzly walrus, but ten times the size, and had an angry demeanor. With a permanent snarl and rows upon rows of razor-sharp teeth, this water beast

194

was very unapproachable, to say the least. The creature swam back and forth in a predictable and repetitive pattern above them. "We need a plan for that thing, it looks *huge*," Gaia whispered as the rest of the knights were coming to their senses.

Ocean shook his head and tapped Gaia and Sky for their attention. "If this is the same beast of 'legend,' I think I've heard of him. I heard of a great battle in the past, and I heard of a weakness that I may be able to use against him." Ocean said with his finger up like he got a fresh idea.

Blaze tapped Ocean on the shoulder, "Hey uh…do you see the beast? Think I lost it."

Ocean's eyes widened as he heard a rush of water going in his direction. "Shit, get down!" Ocean yelled as he is pushed back by an invisible assault. The shockwave from the impact sent everyone else to their backs. Ocean got shoved further back into the ocean waters, off the ground. The figure of the beast faded into view with its giant teeth clasped around Ocean, who sprung up his aqua claws and blocked teeth from impaling him, but not the jaws from crushing him with sheer force.

The pressure became overwhelming as his claws started to bend and scrunch, the mana behind them wavering. Sky was the first to notice the predicament Ocean found himself in. In an anxious attempt, Sky tried throwing a streak of air mana at the beast, as sharp as steel it was, but it caused no damage as it brushed off of the monsters back. Ocean screamed in peril as the jaws came closer and closer to crushing him. Sky tried to use his wings, soon realizing they were waterlogged and heavy. He decided to just swim to Ocean's aid. Blaze sat behind cover, frustrated at his lack of water mobility. Gaia and Hail prepared something to help for real as they charged their mana. A few feet before reaching the beast, Sky flinched as huge shards of ice and even bigger giant stalagmites forced their way past the ice spikes like snakes in the water. The rocks hit first, just under the jaw of the beast, forcing it to relinquish its grip on Ocean.

In a small roar of surprise, the ugly monster wobbled in place, giving Sky enough time to pull Ocean away to safety. After they were clear, the Ice spikes slammed into the beast's body, and slid off, surrounding it in a small prison of ice. When finished, the shape the ice formed looked like an ice sculpture with the beast as the ornament. Hail tossed a couple of ice swords at Ocean's feet. Sky and Ocean swam down to the bottom to join the others. "Whew, thanks, thought it was going to crush me like a grape," Ocean said, releasing his aqua claws and grabbing Hail's ice blades.

"Thank the siblings over there." Sky looked back at Gaia and Hail's poses in tandem as they regained their composure.

Ocean walked over next to the two wrappings his arms around them. "You know, we could actually do this, with you two helping to support me. Sky can't fly, and Blaze is pretty much useless under here, so I think it's up to us."

Gaia and Hail nodded. "Yeah, we got your back, Ocean. The sooner we can get out of here, the better." Hail shrugged.

Ocean took point with an ice blade in either hand and his hybrid weapon on his back, a rocket set inside already. Hail and Gaia stood behind him, charging their mana continually. Moments later, the beast began to wiggle and shake violently, breaking away from his ice prison. Another screech echoed throughout the waters, temporarily paralyzing the knights, who all fell to their knees. The beast used this opportunity to strike and rushed at Ocean, mouth open full and watering. "Gahh damn this, I can't move," Ocean grumbled, trying to get to his feet. The beast picked up speed as it got closer to Ocean, Ocean's eyes widened with the teeth mere feet away from tearing him apart.

Flashbacks of his life rolled past his eyes, the good, terribly sad, and even his fun journey with the knights was shown to him.

Before long, Ocean realized his eyes were closed, and a hot burst of breath and exhale smacked him in the face, then trailed off. Ocean opened his eyes to see the beast tumbling in the sand to his right and a stiff, horizontal rock formation to his left. It was Gaia; he had saved him in the last possible moment. Sand and debris that the beast fell into shot up into the water, then floated back down slowly. Ocean, got up to his feet, able to move ordinarily now. "Hail, we've got to knock out its vocal cords to stop that screech, otherwise, it'll keep paralyzing us."

Hail nodded, then began to charge his mana. "I'll keep it still. You've got one shot at this, though, can only use my Icy graveyard once," he said.

Ocean chuckled to himself. "That's alright, my aim is impeccable." Ocean grabbed the weapon from his back and held onto it with both hands.

Sky walked up and put his hand on Gaia's shoulder. "I'm so glad the paralysis doesn't last as long on you, you really saved Ocean's life there."

Gaia smiled. "Yeah, I'm staying back here to watch their backs, and to make sure y'all don't get eaten either."

Blaze sighed to himself and sat in a corner. "Don't think he likes being dependent," Sky chuckled to himself before paying attention to the action again.

Ocean put his hand on his own heart, causing it to pulsate. With each pulsation, the aura around his body changed colors, from blue to orange to red to white. As this process happened, a light in Ocean's hand started forming as well. When it turned to white, Ocean crushed the fire in his hand. In a spontaneous chain reaction, Ocean's likeness was split at that moment into four separate beings. Each of which looked exactly alike. "Wow, mom, that was easy after you

197

explained it," Ocean said to himself. Each of the clones bared a different colored aura, with the blue marking the original Ocean. The knights looked at Ocean in shock.

"What the hell? When did you learn that?" Sky yelled across to them.

All of the Oceans looked back and snickered as they each held up a hybrid weapon with rockets intact.

Hail shook his head. "This is gonna be so weird but whatever." The beast began to stir, and stir it did as helpless building debris was flung around in its rage. Hail took a deep breath, then began. "Gaia! Gimme a barricade!"

"Yep!" Raising her hands into the air, Gaia rose the earth surrounding Ocean, Hail, and the beast in a rough cylinder. They were now barricaded off with a tall layer of soil surrounding them.

A huge smile grew on Hail's face as he spun in place, his mana exploding off in all directions. "Frozen graveyard, bitch!" Just as the beast was preparing himself for another rush, Hail's mana froze everything within the perimeter of the earth walls. His powerful mana turned the area into an enormous block of ice. The beast and even the Oceans' were frozen solid.

Hail had his arms down to his sides, now drained of mana he shook away the ice from himself and walked over and touched each of the Ocean's shoulders. All of which were then defrosted with his touch. With a cave-like path carved out by Hail, Ocean now had a clear way to the beast's throat.

The original ocean shook him off. "Thanks, Hail, now it's my turn." Hail simply nodded eagerly and fell backwards, exhausted. The Oceans now rushed down the hollowed out path towards the beast, eager to get this done quickly while they had time. When they reached the spot, the creature was elevated, making them aim their rockets up to hit it. "Hopefully, this just kills it." A mana charging party began as the line of Oceans began to aggressively gain energy into their weapons. Loose mana began to scatter out and chip away at the ice like sparks from a flame. The clones started to all yell simultaneously, "from the future to the past……..erase our foes….with a blast!" A massive, concentrated blast of power shot out the rocket on each of their weapons, propelling them into the neck of the beast with incredible speed and force. "Hydra Bomber!" In a flash of silence, the rockets all exploded at once. The explosion broke away all the ice and sent shockwaves that flash melted the surrounding areas too.

All that was left after the blast was a cloud of dust and tiny ice shards hovering in the open water. Sky rushed in following the explosion and dragged Hail away from the action to safety next to Blaze. "Good job, man, leave the rest to us now," Sky said to a barely conscious Hail. Over near the beast, the dust was beginning to fade, and the Oceans all stood at the ready. What came from the smoke surprised Ocean. The creature swam in place, but it maintained a position at a bit of a slant. A gaping hole so big a horse could fit inside was gushing blood out of the beast's neck. The blood left and trailed down alongside the body of the creature, who was noticeably having trouble breathing.

"Hch, looks like it worked nicely, great now's a good time then!" Ocean and his clones rushed up towards the beast, hoping to finish it off. The beast tried to scream, but only a small squeak was let out. This caused Sky and Gaia to snicker as they overlooked.

Realizing the peril, the beast opened his mouth wide as the Oceans approached. In a quick burst of energy, the creature gathered mana and expelled it from its mouth in a blue blast wave towards the Oceans. "Shit!" With no room left to dodge, the clones all got engulfed by the blast; Ocean himself barely slipping away. When it opened its mouth, a disgusting release of blood and tissue splattered out of the

199

beast's neck. This caused it to wobble in place and shake, taking evident damage, even in a small victory. Ocean landed back onto the ground, his left leg burned severely from contact with the blast.

"Ugh damn, this is bad." Ocean looked down at the burnt tissue on his leg. "Looks like he's not doing the best either." Ocean and the beast stared each other in the face, wavering in conviction with every passing second. Ocean summoned his aqua claws again, bouncing on his right leg to propel himself forward towards the beast. In another quick motion the beast exploded another blast wave towards Ocean. "Nope!" Ocean swam to the side, dodging the blast, but placed his claws in the ensuing explosion and rode the mana up to the beast's mouth as if grinding on a skateboard. "Take that!" A quick claw strike later, the beast's face was slashed up by a passing Ocean. More blood was flung up into the water with deep claw marks on the beast's nose and cheek. A small wale later and it turned away from Ocean. "Ha, that's what you ge—." A cocky Ocean was smacked back to the ground by a surprise tail shot as the beast spun around. He landed flat on his face; dust tossed into the air when he fell.

Gaia ran to Ocean while he got up. "You ok?" she said, attempting to help him up.

"Yeah just didn't see that coming." A slow trickle of blood began to run down Ocean's forehead.

"Do you need help?" Gaia said, holding him up.

"Nah, I'll be fine; this is my figh—." A beast blast wave came and flew past Ocean, nailing Gaia and pinning her to the ground. She was left in the center of a small crater in the ground. "Gaia!" Ocean yelled as he limped over to her body, then looked up to the beast. "Just you wait! I'll end your ugly ass." Moments passed by as the two stared at each other in place again. A spark of mana flared up behind the beast and began expanding. It began spiraling into a portal

200

eventually. In a faded screen, the portal revealed a dark city on the other side. Ocean stood up and looked back at his comrades. "Where do you think you're going?" Ocean said as he focused his attention back at the beast before swimming at it full speed. The brute backed up into the portal, with an eager grin on its ugly mug.

"Shit! Get back here!" Ocean swam into the portal after the beast, disappearing into the new world.

"Ocean, wait!" Sky grumbled, looking at the portal, then to Hail and Gaia, and back to Blaze.

"Shit, we have to follow him, you know," Sky directed at Blaze. He nodded, then walked over to Hail and then to Gaia, placing one of them over each of his shoulders.

"I got them, just give me a lift to the portal," Blaze said. Sky began thrusting his arms into the water repeatedly until the tide pushed Blaze and his passengers up in the water. He was elevated all the way up into the portal by the current. Sky was all that remained underwater.

"Tsk. It's always something with these damn beasts." Sky swam up to and into the portal, disappearing just as the portal closed behind him. The remains of the underwater city floated about peacefully in the now calm waters.

-Year 276   Farriage Castle Conference Room
Eodon, Sylindra-

Back at the Farriage castle, Hepheaus gets a surprise visit from an old friend in Father John while she is relaxing in her conference room.

"Hello, princess. Oh, sorry it's queen now. How are we feeling?" Father John says bowing as he appeared out of a pure white portal.

"Rise up, you were always like another father to me. Has it really been that long?" Hepheaus smirked while crossing her legs.

"It has, I see you've grown into quite the woman, and leader. I'm proud of you." John smirked back.

"Enough of the flattery, what brings you back here unannounced?" The queen said getting serious.

"Why of course." Grandmaster grabbed a seat near her and focused his attention. "This…journey the knights are on is not the only thing we have to worry about. The dark forces are making moves of their own. I feel as if a great number of wars and battles are upon us," he finished.

"What do you mean? Are you saying the forces are moving *because* of the formation of the knights?"

"Well, that and because they are getting stronger as well. Demise has been gathering strong demons from all across Armageddon in anticipation of them. Scourge is just the beginning unfortunately," He continued, shaking his head.

"I heard about what happened with him at Kegos. You say this is just the start? It'll take a bit of time, but I certainly can mobilize my forces. How big do you expect this to get?"

"Well, I have to gather as many allies as I can. Scourge is the priority now, but we are going to need a lot more if we hope to defeat Demise." John said shaking his head.

Hepheaus shifted in her seat and held up her hand. "Woah, one thing at a time okay. I'll get my people ready to help, especially if the repercussions will come back to hurt my land. What are you going to do?" she asked getting closer.

"First off, if Scourge is able to draw out the power of Wendy for himself, or worse yet, Demise, it'll effect more than just Eodon. All of Sylindra, and even Ardin will be under his rule. Not even I will be able to stand a chance. I don't think the knights realize how important it is to get Wendy back, let alone their orbs right now. As for me, I'll be making rounds to other lands, trying to grow our allied forces. Just be ready when I make the call." Father John bowed again before creating another white portal.

"Hmph. Don't worry about me, old man. Tell that elderly war coot, King Hiyama, I said Hey too. Not that he will show up." Hepheaus chuckled as she waved him off.

John nodded. "I'll be off now, good luck," he said disappearing into his portal."

"Eh. Guess I'll have to train my own body more as well," Hepheaus said while the mana linked around her body begin to glow. She got up and stomped out of the room.

****

While the knights continue their journey, many pieces of their backup begin to come together slowly but surely. Jax got back home to find Kegos in shambles, nearly destroyed, but his people still alive. No sign of Wendy anywhere as they heard of her kidnapping by Scourge. By the time John got there, they were more than happy to accept his offer for revenge and to get their Wendy back. Sky's parents finished their current war just in time to get Father John's message as well. Things were heating up in Sylindra. The last couple days of the year quickly approached as the knights suspected the New Year to be filled with many hardships and triumphs.

Chapter 11: Judgement!

Void arrived in his homeland on the outskirts of Perasma. He could only teleport to places he had been to or could see. Without knowledge of the location of his trial grounds, he went to the familiar place in Basonali to get information. For years since its rebirth, Perasma had been the location for underground dealings and bounty hunters. A lot of people crammed into one place. Basonali, this time of year, was unbearably cold, but too cold and dry for it to snow most of the time. The land was barren, frozen solid without the company of wildlife or green. Only a depressing gray and brown scenery next to the shoddy sign at the entrance of the city.

Void gave a long, relieving sigh as he stood there taking in the land. "Well, I made it in one piece. Good." Void stopped and looked before him as if from the shadows themselves, a figure in a black cloak appeared, leaning on the sign. "Who the hell are—."

"I see you've kept good care of my sword, Void," the man interrupted and pointed to the claymore on his back. Void's eyes opened wide as he froze, having flashbacks of his fight with a great, but evil warrior in his past. He shook himself out of it and held tightly onto his sword's hilt. "Whoa, now, I'm not here for revenge." The man held up his hands, which were covered with black gloves. His head was also hidden by the length of his hood.

"What brings you here conveniently at the same time I arrive then?" Void asked.

The guy shrugged. "I'm here to help, let's say. I have a good feeling I know why you're here."

Void's eyebrow raised. "And what is that?"

"Well there have been dark disturbances to our north in Paradise city, more so than usual. I think this might be part of that wild journey you were referring to the last time we met."

Void shook his head. "And how and why are you helping me right now?"

"I...I don't really know; some force is compelling me to be here right now." He shook his head, vehemently. "Ugh, so let's get this over with then, shall we?"

Void released his grip and calmed his hands at his sides. "Is there any reason why I can't go into town for information?"

The man nodded. "Uh, I wouldn't recommend that. The town has changed since you were here last. I fear the negative influences would not be good for you, especially since your incoming journey will test everything you are."

"What do you mean?" Void asked.

"Just...trust me this one time and head right towards your next destination." The figure pointed off in the distance. "You are looking for the Nasol Ruins; it has the jaws of a giant, dragon skeleton as the entrance."

Void's eyes squinted a bit as he thought back. "Wait. I think I've heard about that as a kid. I have to go through it to reach the city?"

"Yeah, Malveria or Paradise city is hidden away and isn't on any map. The only way to find it from the outside is those ruins, so good luck. Off to the Northwest ya go!" The helpful stranger waved him off.

Void turned around. "Thanks...I guess. This better be the right way, or I'll be back." Void turned back towards the city, then walked away, in the direction of the rising sun, and eventually the Nasol ruins.

****

Void trekked on for hours in what seemed like a straight shot towards the horizon. The sun was in the center of the sky, and with it came the frost fog, a phenomenon where the mist became attracted to any sources of mana, engulfing it and lowering the temperature until they froze. The mist could materialize out of nowhere and ice over entire towns at times, causing rapid flash freezes without warning. As Void walked, the fog tried to impede his progress multiple times, but he held it back from attaching to him. Coming down from an icy hill, Void's path led through a small settlement of locals. Sporting a wagon, four tents, and many other supplies they dragged along with them. In front of the cart, a short man wearing an extra-large jacket jumped up and waved when he noticed Void's tall figure sliding down the hill.

"Hello! Hello, there, sir!" The man did not stop jumped until he saw that Void noticed him. Then he waved him over. "Can you come here for a sec?" His two partners were doing some work in the tent behind him.

Void tried to ignore him and walk past, but the man came running around the stand and went to tug on Void's arm, pulling him towards his position, to a death stare reaction from Void. He was fearless though. Void was taken aback from the look of his dark, almost frostbitten face. The hood on his jacket hid most of it, but a close inspection from Void had him realize the origin. This man had survived an attack from the frost fog; it was all over his face. From the frost hanging on the tip of his nose to the sparks of mana fizzled out all over his body. "Uh, are you okay?"

206

"Maxon. Kye Maxon at your service. And yes, I just...came out on the good side of frost fog. It came and froze over the town I was operating out of." Maxon turned back to his two helpers. "I was lucky to save these two when I did. Their families were all killed in that town as well." Void lowered his head a bit and closed his eyes, as his way of paying his respects.

Maxon raised his finger at Void; his hand so cold the glove had frozen solid onto his skin. He would probably never be able to take it off with his skin intact. "But enough of that talk! We have a business to attend to, my friend."

Void opened his eyes and cocked his head to the side. "How so?"

"Well, I'm glad you asked!" Maxon turned and began to dig in his wagon and pulled out a pair of worn, but expertly crafted battle iron knuckles. He held them up in front of Void, they were clearly used, with dried blood on the tips of each spike.

"Whoa now, I think I'm okay with my current weapon, I'm not really look——." Void started,

"It's okay! All the best warriors use more than one weapon. These can help you when you don't feel like swinging around that large, cumbersome claymore on your back. Just one good punch and *boom* they're gone," Maxon punched his own hand comedically.

Void turned his head away, shaking it.

Maxon held his hands up. "Whoa whoa whoa, I'm not done yet, my friend!" Maxon tossed the knuckles to the side and dug back into his wagon, pulling out a short rapier, with royal embroidery on the hilt. It was in a much better condition than the knuckles. "What about this beauty. Totally not taken off of a dead prince, it was crafted to last, it's beautiful and deadly."

Void actually chuckled, "Man, do I look like I would use a rapier? Although I think something like that might suit

Ocean…and his birthday is coming up, I think. I don't have any gold on me, though."

"Oh, that's totally okay! I was gonna say you could always pay in mana. I'm running a bit low; I don't know how long I can last…fighting off the frost…" A piece of the skin on his face, cracked and broke away shattering when it hit the ground. "I need to protect these two still." He looked back at the two workers.

Void nodded, "I think I should have extra to spare."

Maxon handed Void the rapier. "Thanks. You ready?" Void said, holstering the weapon on his back next to his claymore. He put his hands on either of Maxon's shoulders. Mana began to radiate on his hands, creeping into the short dealer. Void closed his eyes to help his concentration. The last thing his eyes saw was the helpers clapping along as the process continued. (Man I hope this helps him, he is looking horrible. Wonder how much mana I should give him for it to help hi —.) Void's inner thoughts were interrupted by a stinging cold on his hands. He jerked away from Maxon and opened his eyes. "Ahhhhh!" Void screamed as he opened his eyes to the horrific sight of everything frozen solid around him in a smoky haze. Maxon and the helpers were both solid ice, along with the tents and the wagon, everything.

"Hey, Max…c'mon man!" The fog surrounding them he noticed came towards him now. "No!" With a burst of mana around him, he blew the mist away. Void lowered his head as he looked around. "The fog might have been drawn to my mana. Dammit, I should have known…" He put his hand on Max's shoulder softly. "Sorry." Maxon's body shattered and turned to a cloud of frosty dust at this touch, blowing away in the wind afterward. Void's eyes opened wide, then he turned away. "I need to get off of this damn continent."

As Void turned towards the hill in the wagon caught his eye. "Hmmm, what's this feeling?" He quickly went

208

over and peered into the frozen cart to an exciting sight. Two very similar almost possessed looking Dao swords. They both had dark blue blades on the shorter side, which were quite broad in comparison to others of the same type. There was a mysterious aura surrounding them, and hideous growths engulfing most of the swords. Darkened growths expanded down the back of the blade and down near the hilt; each held a pulsating gemstone in the center, one red and one green. The two swords were the only two things in the wagon not frozen.

Void reached out his hand, hesitatingly. "Something tells me... I'm going to regret this...dearly." As Void reached his hand closer towards the swords, loud shrieking screams jolted through his head and body like a bloody warning. He continued however, the screams getting louder, and his focus fading. Finally he grasped the hilt of the first sword softly. The screaming stopped all at once. He then grabbed the second and held them both up next to his face. Void took a deep breath, "Who   " His breathing was broken up by a staggering rush of dark mana from the swords throughout his body. It was shook, and made his body twitch and jerk. Void's eyes turned red, and the ordeal culminated with him coughing out a hefty glob of blood and collapsing to a knee. The new swords held him up. "What was that? Damn." Void barely able to muster out between his heavy breaths. "I think these things just restored all of my mana...the rough ways. These are evil; I would be smart to only use them as a last resort." He got to his feet and settled both swords onto his belt on the left side. He wiped the blood from his mouth and noticed an unknown figure at the top of the hill in front of him.

"Now, what in the hell are you?" Void yelled at the thing. It was short, cloaked in black, with a tall hood on shadowing out its entire face. It had odd mana surrounding it, which made it hard to decipher if it was a ghost or a real

209

entity before him. The figure didn't respond at all, only slowing backing up down the other side of the hill. "Hey! Get back here!" Void ran up the mountain to see the figure waiting on the other side of a small barren valley. "Hmmm. Maybe it's leading me…I still don't like this thing, though."

-Year 276 Te Whatitiri Wapu City Southeast Kayard, Sylindra-

On the other side of Sylindra, Volt arrived in the sacred swamp town of Te Whatitiri Wapu near the coast peninsula on the southeastern part of the continent. Volt landed right in the middle of the city as it was in the thick of destruction. The swamp city, for the most part, was supported by wooden foundations that elevated off of the swampy, green waters underneath. It was a small city, only consisting of a couple dozen homes, with dilapidated shops in the center; overgrowth of vegetation taking over a good majority of the sights. A freshly destroyed temple sat on the edge of town near the oceanside. A chalice with golden embroidery was on the ground beside a dark stand at the back of the temple. The majority of the city was evacuated and destroyed by the time Volt arrived. A single figure remained, hidden in the shadows under a bridge, watching their home burn away because of a roaring beast in the skies.

Volt stood there soaking in the land, the atmosphere for a moment before moving any. He tracked streaks of lightning going across the sky as well the ones striking low to objects in his area. "Well now, I guess it's time to test myself against this great and holy being from my teachings as a child. Father, I hope you're watching," Volt said as he summoned his Sigrun and impaled it into the ground. It started sparking and sputtering shortly after. "Cause this will be the fight of my life!" Lightning began to strike closer and closer, hitting the roof across the marketplace square from him, then a garbage bin in the center, then one last one on his spear. This strike was more significant than the rest and caused a quick flash after it hit, blinding Volt for a second. When he regained his sights, he was met with his opposition. "O-Oh…" Volt's recovering eyes were introduced to the castle-sized lightning dragon that is Tarakona Tapu, or Thadrado in the common tongue. This massive being's body resembled that of the wind phoenix as its structure was made of a darkened skeletal mass engulfed in lightning mana to give it a figure. Massive wings eclipsed the buildings behind it, while a long, snake-like body stretched down the empty alleys. With two arms on either side, but no legs this monster spends all of its time in the air. Massive and large jaws were at Volt's eye level, forcing him to stare into Thadrado's ugly, but ferocious grin. A line of spikes going along the back began to wobble and shake as a clot of lightning mana gathered at the base of Thadrado's opening mug.

"Wait. Is this…" Volt immediately used his spear to teleport himself off to the side corner of the square as a blast wave of mana came exploding out of Thadrado's mouth, annihilating every piece of the city behind Volt in a vast range and width. Making himself small, forced against the wall on the corner of the square, the edges of the blast wave was just ahead of his nose. The blast kept going past the beach and continued into the ocean and on. The docks and any buildings were disintegrated or filled with massive holes through these centers. After it finished, Thadrado shocked away back into the sky, leaving a crater in its wake. Volt let out a heavy sigh of relief. "That's just like my Inazuma blast except, so much more impressive. What kind of monster is this I have to deal with?" Volt looked up into the air trying to track strikes again. "Let's see if I can learn from this thing." With his left hand up, Volt closes his eyes. His spear in his right hand. "C'mon wor—"

Volt's body linked to a lightning bolt and teleported to it. This landed Volt in free-fall high into the air. Surrounded by lightning. "Ha, it worked!" Volt exclaimed as he continually linked himself to lightning bolts to slow his descent while looking around. Volt noticed something and put his spear on his back. "Found you!" Volt got into his stance, and clapped his hands together, mana gathering there now. "Erupt and eradicate, shatter their—." Thadrado appeared out of a thunderbolt interrupting Volt with another blast wave. "Damnit!" Volt dodged into nearby flashes, stopping himself. "You quick bastard, that was close!" With a fancy spin, Volt recovered his spear.

"Lucin, grant me the power to strike down all who oppose you! Ringa Uira *and* Tao Uira!" Both Volt's hand and his spear began to radiate with his lightning mana. His spear tip resembled a large drill and his hand with an overflowing surge of mana. "Let's see how you handle this!" Thadrado charged at Volt, causing him to dodge in mid-air using the accompanying thunderbolts, then he threw his spear at the side of the beast. Thadrado shifted his body off to the side, but not enough, and Volt's drill contacted in the higher end of its tail. The creature staggered in the air, and Volt began to free fall; his spear stuck inside of Thadrado. Lighting and mana began to spill out of its side as the spear stopped drilling and stayed there. "Shit!" Volt yelled as he began to drop out of the air quickly. Volt stopped yelling and closed his eyes, and his mind. After a quarter-mile of concentration, Volt opened his eyes. "C'mon!" With a jolt Volt's body was transferred to his spear, his right hand still brandishing the energy from the Ringa Uira. "Whew!" Volt went for a ride on the side of the electric dragon as it wobbled through the air.

"Let's finish this aye!" Volt said as he held on tight to his spear; his body flopping about in the wind. Volt propelled himself up and used his spear as a foothold to jump up onto the back of Thadrado. *Rawrrr*! As he ran, Thadrado flew crazy paths and jerked around to throw him off. "Not gonna work!" Volt lowered his lightning fist hand over the conducting spine of Thadrado as he ran up it's back. His mana growing in size every second. Eventually, he reached the neck and stopped. "Think that'll do, ah!" Volt charged the mana in his palm and lowered it to strike the back of Thadrado's neck with his hand. Lightning came spewing out of both sides of Thadrados neck as it called out in pain. Its flying grew slower as Volt continued, eventually they both dropped elevation past the clouds, Volt still damaging it the entire way.

After the buildings below were not ants anymore, Thadrado regained its senses and pulled a precarious roll with its entire body. Volt was slung into the air and smacked with the tip of Thadrado's tail. This sent him crashing through the air and into a building with a low ceiling below them. "Ack!" After tumbling through the floors, Volt landed at the bottom, looking up through the holes he went through at an enraged beast. Attempting to move proved futile as Volt tried to wiggle his limbs. "This isn't good." Thadrado was seen half a mile into the air staring down at Volt, lightning still letting loose from its neck. Eyes flustered, Thadrado charged mana in his jaw and directed it towards Volt. *Roar*! With a release, the dragon let out another powerful blastwave towards Volt, so vast it took over the entire building he was in.

"Ahhhh!" Volt was taken over by the blast as the building was incinerated around him. In the aftermath, Volt lay in a pile of rubble, his garments as tattered as the building now was. He was unconscious. Under the bridge, the figure finally began to move as it seemed the battle was over. Cloak over their head, they sprinted out from the bridge as it spontaneously fell apart. They ran and hid behind a building leading into the Marketplace area where Volt crashed. Thadrado, still damaged, lowered himself to just above the ground, snarling at Volt's body, which began to stir. "Ack!" Volt coughed and rolled over to his side. "Damnit, that was rough," he said wobbling and struggling to get to his feet while holding his left arm. Turning to face Thadrado slightly, Volt's already tattered arm started to glow. Afterwards, mana resembling black lightning started to flicker about on his entire arm. He winced in pain when it started. "Eh dammit, I did not want to use this move, but I guess big and flashy won't work on you. I've gotta shut down your mana. Tsk." Volt fought the pain in his arm as the black lightning grew more and more ferocious. After a deep breath, he calmed his breathing. "Pouri Uira." The black lightning on Volt's body grew out of control now, branching out and hitting nearby objects now. *Roarr*! With a stiff, pained roar, Thadrado shot out an array of beams of mana at Volt's chest. Volt powered up and endured the blows to his chest as he gingerly walked towards the dragon. "Stay calm, your end is at hand."

Many failed blast attempts later, and Volt stood directly in front of the Thadrado's jaw. It opened its mouth wide for a point-blank blast. Volt sighed. "Just die already, please." He slowly raised his left hand up and placed it on the tip of Thadrado's jaw. Immediately the lightning on his arm discharged, along with Thadrado and Volt himself. A shockwave was also sent out that cleanly sliced through the buildings that surrounded them. Volt's mana was dissipated, and he dropped to rest on his shin. Thadrado got the worst of it though. Thadrado's mana had stopped, causing it to plop lifelessly down onto the ground in front of Volt. The remains were a darkened skeleton encasing a dark mass in the center. It didn't move for several moments as Volt waited and did his best to get himself together.

Volt finally struggled to his feet and took a step towards the heap. "Hmmm. If you're dead then give me my orb already." Volt summoned his spear and poked the dark mass. "Uhhh…" Around the heart of the weight, it cracked like an egg. This crack spread all the way to the sides and underneath the belly. Volt cautiously took a few steps back as it began to split open, mana exploding out of the opening. This didn't last long. However, the mana stopped as a humanoid figure stepped out of the slimy mass. His body was surrounded by the same dark weight that was on the dragon. Soon after he emerged, his body was too surrounded by lightning mana. He stared at Volt with red devilish eyes, sporting a dark bone inspired sword in each hand. Volt looked down at his burned and useless left arm, then back at the being now opposing him. "Well, I don't think this is going to end well."

The being's eyes flashed as he opened a mouth not defined before on his face. "Thados. My name. You've gotten further than others. Now you die though. Sorry." Volt stumbled backward with Thados approaching. "Heh, this isn't fair, you know." Volt held himself up with his spear, calming himself again shortly after. "Fine." His mana rose again as he powered up. "I guess you'll get everything I have left!"

Suddenly Thados teleported like a flash of lightning right in front of Volt. What came next was a constant struggle as Thados rained down blows from his two swords on Volt, who took every bit of himself to block and deflect the strikes. Volt was pushed back despite his efforts, though only suffering minor slices to his arms and legs. Back against the sidewall of a home, Volt looked back quickly then dived forward, dodging simultaneous swings from Thados. Now with the sides swapped and Thados taking a moment to turn around to face Volt again, he saw the opportunity. "Tsk, take this! Tao Uira!" The tip of Sigrun began to spin like a lightning drill." Thados lunged at his prey but stopped short as Volt sliced a giant crescent-shaped gash out of the ground right underneath Thados. Falling a bit, Thados stopped himself and floated there for a moment, catching himself holding onto the sides of the wood. He came to his senses as he was eye level with Volt's incoming foot. "Take that!" A stiff, lightning charged kick sent Thados sailing into the house behind them. It came tumbling down on top of him afterwards. Volt stood there, his legs wobbling from the seeming small slices, now stinging. "What is this sensation? My arms and legs are getting numb. Are his blades...poison?" Volt almost collapsed but caught himself and stood back up.

By now, Thados was shooting back up from the pile the rubble, dusting himself off; no apparent damage on him. "Oh, come on! Not a scratch?" Volt labored but hopped back as Thados jumped into the air, twirling around and releasing a couple of crescent mana streaks. The two streaks sliced through the foundation, opening another hole into the rushing waters below. Volt smacked his leg, which was becoming unresponsive, along with his spear arm. "Crap," he said as he looked up to see Thados jumping at him with both swords from high in the air. The impact between Thados and Volt defending with his spear with one arm caused a shockwave that echoed underneath them. Volt glanced down as the area under him began to crack with Thados pushing down on him harder and harder. "Oh no!" Volt crashed through and plopped into the water, getting caught in the rough waves carrying out towards the ocean. A fading Volt was carried around the canal past the bridge where the mysterious figure was hiding before. One eye open, Volt looked up near the marketplace as the figure was looking at him. Their eyes met as Volt saw those red, almost

216

reptilian eyes hiding under the hood. Line of sight was broken, though, and he had shoved around in the water near the boardwalk. Volt let out muffled grumbles as he raised his spear out of the water and stabbed it into one of the supports of the dock, holding on tightly. This caused him to fling up into the air and land on the dirt beach, five feet away from the shore.

"Thank goodness." Volt raised himself up to a knee, his body nearly giving out on him. Suddenly everything went white all around him. "What's this?" Volt said looking around, confused. An eerie whisper in his ear caught his attention. "F-father John, is that you?" All of his attention was up in the stars as the words brought back memories.

-Year 270 Lastera Holy Church Far East Kayard, Sylindra-

A younger 18-year-old Volt met with Father John at the entrance to Father's church after Volt's coming of age ceremony. The rain outside was falling nonstop as Volt arrived at the front. The church was empty, only a whistling wing made sound inside of the church. Large windows decorated the top of the church, with a giant statue of Lucinthis at a centerpiece at the back end behind the podium. Volt wiped his feet off and walked inside the front entrance, Father met him there. "Volt! Congratulations, my boy." Father John reached over and pulled him in for a big hug.

"T-thanks," Volt said, getting squished.

John released him and waved him over to follow him as he walked towards the back of the church. "Come come, we must do this now. Time is not on our side!" Volt ran behind him.

"Wait, close the door, son!" Father turned around and waved him off. Volt turned around promptly and shut the door, then met back with Father at the podium. "Now, what you are about to see I've been preparing since the day I received your blessing on my church steps eighteen years ago."

Volt looked at him, curiously. "Is this why you had me rush over here after the ceremony?"

"Yes, watch closely." Father turned around and placed his hands on the statues in a praying position. He remained in this position for a moment until slowly, mana began to drain out of his hands and into the sculpture. Father broke away, his demeanor appearing a bit weaker.

"What was that?" Volt asked.

After catching his breath, he looked at Volt. "That was using some of my life energy to activate this."

The entire church began to shake as the statue slid backward, revealing a hidden stairway leading under the church. The stairs led deep into the basement, the bottom out of sight currently. "Uhh?" Volt looked down the opening.

"Come on." Father walked down the stairwell with Volt close behind. "Hurry, not much time left, son!"

At the bottom of the steps, not much remained except a carved rock with a long, slender box on top. The box was shining brightly on top of the stone. Father walked over and placed his hand on it. It was wooden and cheaply made, light shining through the cracks in it from all sides. "This case, son, this is Sigrun. The ancient spear that the original Volt of legend used while he was alive." Father turned around to check that Volt was paying attention, and he was all too well. Volt was staring at the box like he was calling to him. "It's drawing me in almost. That box…is speaking to my soul," he said Father nodded. "Sigrun links to your mana, allowing it to seamlessly become part of your fighting style. It learns, and teaches you new abilities as well as you go along." Father lifted the top of the wooden box to reveal the

218

spear. The entire thing was shiny and glowing. The tip was two-pronged, with one longer than the other. The majority of the handle was a metallic teal, except for the dark grey handle. The weapon did not match any other in the entire continent, specially crafted to meld to its users' mana. Volt took a couple of steps forward and picked up the spear. A blinding light flashed as mana was absorbed into Volt's hands.

"Whoa. This sensation. This mana, it feels like it's attaching to me," Volt eked out with pain on his face. "Hold that spear close; it is extraordinary. Also, I want you to listen to it. When it feels you are worthy, it will whisper the enchant words for new skills to you. The last skill it teaches you, it will give you the eyes to read it right off of the side of the spear. But that's much later, don't worry about that." Volt was busy staring at the spear in his hands. "Uh, huh," he said absentmindedly.

The church shook violently as a piece of the ceiling caved in and crashed onto the ground. The rain pounded on the exposed floor right above them. "What was that?" Volt said as he looked up at the ceiling. Father looked around, then sighed and peered at Volt. "Oh well, I guess time's up." Father John gathered mana in his hand and opened a portal on the ground behind Volt. The eerie ringing of darkness and footsteps echoed from above them. Volt looked up at Father John cautiously. He averted his eyes. "As my last coming of age gift to you, I leave you my castle. The Royal Castle. It's located in its own dimension, safe from the shadows. That'll be the base for you and the other incoming knights. Decorate it how you will, protect it, and help Sky lead the knights to victory against Chaos." Volt nodded eagerly. "I won't let you down, Father. I'll treat your most prized possession with care." Father John snicked and cracked a smile as he put his hand on Volt's forehead. "Silly Volt, *you* will always be my most prized possession. You'll

know me as Grandmaster going forward though, call it a
promotion if you will, I'll be looking after you knights as
you mature and grow into the world's saviors." A tear began
to roll down Father John's eye. Simultaneously, one ran
down Volt's eye as well as he sniffled. "You'll always be
Father John to me." Father John shoved Volt back and into
the portal head first. He shook his head and ran upstairs.
Volt drifted through the portal hearing bits and pieces from
the other side. "Get out of my damn church demise!" That
was the last he heard of Father John for years.

-Year 270   The Royal Grounds   ??? -

Volt landed on his back, smacking against a wooden
floor, Sigrun in his lap. He opened his eyes. "Whoa! Uh..oh.
Where is this?" Volt looked around the room he was in. It
was the foyer of a very large mansion. A giant dragon statue
sat on a finished rock as a centerpiece. There were doorways
leading to rooms to either side of him. Ahead of him, behind
the figure, was an empty room filled with a dozen boxes.
Two grand staircases led up to the second floor which
housed more rooms, chandelier lighting the way from the
very top. Right above him on the second floor was a massive
painting depicting all of the mana elements meshing
together. Volt got to his feet and turned around to the door
behind him. He took a deep sigh and opened it. "Let's see
what's out here." Outside he saw what would be his home
for the next few years. There was a pathway leading down to
a center platform. That platform branched off in three
directions. One to the housing quarters, one to an enormous
castle with a floating barrier around it, and one to the shore.
Water surrounded the area on the ground under these
platforms like a mini sea. The shoreline included a mountain
with an awkwardly placed door on the side of it. A metal
barrier rose out of the water surrounding the castle.

"Something's off….about that sky." Volt looked up and noticed how it was dimmed out from everything in the horizon and past the mountain. There was a unique aura surrounding the entire area. "Is this what he meant when he said it was set in a different dimension? Is it in Sylindra, just a piece cut out from the rest of the world? Interesting." Volt walked forward and started down the path towards the castle. "Whelp, this will be my home for a while, might as well look around, right?" And off he went as he awaited the arrival of the remaining knights…

-Year 276 Te Whatitiri Wapu coast South Kayard, Sylindra-

Volt looked up into the air calmly, the white mana blinding him from everything except his spear. Thados appeared at the end of the boardwalk, zapping closer with each passing second. "Sigrun!" Volt's spear wobbled and released itself from the post as Volt called to it. His spear landed in the ground directly in front of him. Thados was merely ten meters away now. "I-I can see it," Volt said, looking at sacred writings along the side of the spear. All but hidden before. Thados was right in front of Volt's prone body now, his blade soaring towards Volt's chest. "When we acknowledge…that all of life is sacred…and that each act is an act of cho—" Volt stopped to cough up blood as Thados's first sword pierced Volt's stomach on his life. Volt breathed deeply realizing his peril, but still calmly continued to read. "Choice and therefore sacred, then life is a sacred dance lived each moment consciously. When we live at this level, we participate in the creation of a better world—Ahhh." Thados stabbed Volt again in the right side of his chest. Volt's lung collapsed and made breathing, let alone speaking, difficult. Mana from Sigrun began to radiate and

221

surround both Volt and Thados like a spotlight. Releasing another gasp of blood from his mouth, Volt eeked out the rest. "Rise and cast your ultimate judgment Lucinthis!" Volt and Thados' feet were covered in Volt's blood.

The sky and clouds above them opened like a shining light from the heavens. The thunder and lightning that plagued the air stopped. An abundant light shined from the new hole in the sky. Volt's body flopped over to the side as he looked up at Thados with his one open eye. "Mission accomplished." Volt closed his eyes. A thunderous and gargantuan sized beam of mana fell from the sky. Thados looked up, unable to pull his swords free from Volt in time. The massive beam fell faster and faster with each passing second colliding with the ground right on top of them with the force of the gods. The crash sent shockwaves for miles, blowing everything in the vicinity in all directions. The mysterious figure stood frozen behind the building, staring at the massive beam smashing into the ground without quarter.

After thirty seconds of constant fury, the beam finally stopped and faded away. Volt's body was sitting in a crater two feet under where he was initially lying in a puddle of his own blood. Thados's body and swords had disappeared, and only a glowing yellow orb remained in his stead. Volt lay motionless as residual mana sparked all around and his spear stood in the center of the crater, untouched. Volt's eyes, glazed over, opened meekly to see the cloaked figure sliding down the sides of the cavity towards him. They closed again, and his mind went blank.

Chapter 12:
Paradise

Void came stumbling over a steep, icy hill chasing after the shadow. The other side revealed a large cave opening protruding diagonally out of the ground, nothing but darkness past the entrance. Around it was a plethora of bones resembling different races; demons and humans. On the top of the cave rested the gargantuan skeleton of a Udalton type beast. Though slightly smaller than Udalton, the bones still spanned at least twenty meters down the back of the cave. The perimeter of the cave was surprisingly devoid of ice, though the earth was cracked and decrepit. "Hmm, I guess this is it, huh," Void said as he watched the shadow sprint into the cave and down. He walked forward, into the territory of the cave; he heard a whistling in the air, too clear, and too melodic to be just the wind. "What is that?" Void looked around him and attempts to discover the cause. His searches led him towards the cave. Counting the two blades on his back and the cursed ones on his hip, Void walked into the darkness with a heavy sigh.

Void could not see anything once entering the cave. Trusting his senses, the dark knight blindly walked forward until he rested his foot on a dip. It was old, shotty steps that led down to a room below. "Ha, that coulda been dangerous." Void caught his footing and eased his way down the steps until he reached the floor below, which actually had limited visibility. Reaching that floor, he saw where the light came from. Shiny gems decorated an intricate door at the back of the room. Nothing else was lit except for a bit of the path leading him to the door. "I hope this whole place isn't this dark." Void arrived at the door and got a closer look at it. It was segmented into four sections. The top left and bottom right sections had the gems while the bottom left and top right sported carved animals praying; a horse and a wolf respectfully. "Hmm there isn't a handle on this door, how do I open it?" Void looked deeply at the carvings. "Maybe..." He stepped away from the door, heading towards the darker corners of the room, searching around with just his hands. On the ground in a corner near the steps Void came across a small foot long statue. He picked it up, unable to actually see it and continued looking. The piles of rocks and rubbles that were hidden in the dark made this search more difficult. Surprisingly he found the second by nearly tripping over it. On the right side of the room, he caugh himself and picked up the second statue.

"Hmm, let's see what you are." He walked up and held the statues at the door, waving them even. "Hmm, these look like the same things...but what do I do?" He sat them at the base of the door and placed them into their corresponding animals, but nothing worked. "Ugh, this isn't working, whoops!" *Crack*. Void accidentally dropped the dog statue and shattered it on the ground. The dog carving on the door lit up and a mana line from the two adjacent gems connected to it. "Oh. You destroy them. Of course, right." Void tossed the horse statue down and shattered it. The door lit up again with the horse carving. It shook, and light spread from the center as the creaks opened to reveal a lit room.

"Oh, this is what I'm talking about." Torches along the walls lit up the room, but it was empty. Void walked inside, and the door shut behind him. He noticed an opening on the opposite side of the room. "Not this again!" Void took a couple steps forward and was greeted with shadow beings coming from all of the walls surrounding him. They oozed off of the walls and materialized around Void, twelve in total. They were hunched, wielding short daggers, entirely engulfed in the dark. "Hmm... fine then! Come at me!" Void reached back and pulled out his claymore. The shadows came at him in waves. Three to four at a time, they charged at him. Void, outnumbered, dodged most of their advances and used his wits to find the perfect time to swing. His claymore splashed through the shadows like bubbles. Moments later, the crew of shadow beings were dispatched.

"Well...that was interesting." The door on the opposite side was opening as he spoke. More darkness awaited him on the other side of the door. "This gets so tiring..." Void sighed as he walked through the door. A couple steps outside, his feet were waved over a gap he couldn't see. "Woahhh!" Void pulled his foot back. "That was close. I can't see the ground, so getting to wherever the other side might prove dangerous." Void kicked a rock off the ledge and waited for it to land. Five seconds passed. Another five. Another ten, before finally a crack as it landed with a very faint pop. "Yeah, definitely dangerous." Void inched his feet to his sides to see if the path was walkable.

Finally, he found a way that led forward in this room, but he still walked gingerly. After about six steps ahead, he again couldn't continue. A couple of sword taps later, it was determined that there wasn't a connecting walkway. "What the hell?" Void looked around in frustration before stopping, an idea coming to his head. "Hey, let's see if this works." Void picked up a couple of rocks and started throwing them in different directions. A loud popping sound echoed and finally, he was blessed with a response. The rock hit the side and slid off, down into the deep crevice. "Eh, it seems like two sword lengths. And that's if it isn't elevated higher than I am." Void gathered mana in his hands. "Wish I could see where my portals go." Void opened a portal in proximity to where he threw the rock. He spent a few moments psyching himself up before attempting to go through it.

Void created another portal under himself and jumped in. Moments later, Void found himself in the open air, unknowingly a foot away from the ledge. "Shit!" In what was almost instinct, Void reached for his side and yanked out the top cursed blade. With the sword over his head, he stabbed it forward with all of his might, praying to hit something. Void's strike wasn't for naught as his blade pierced and dug deep into the side of the cliff, easily. This slowed his descent, dragging and flopping his body against the rocks until he stopped. Holding himself up with only one hand on the blade's hilt. Two seconds after he halted, however, something spectacular happened. With a surprising explosion of dark mana, the cursed sword seeped into the earth and crumpled it in a large, ten-meter diamond directly around the blade. The surface disintegrated, leaving an open, cleanly cut indent and dropping Void's body on the edge, his legs still dangling off.

Void pulled himself up and promptly sheathed the sword. "What. The. Hell…is this sword?" He said, looking down at his waist. Void's attention was then drawn to how low on this side of the gap. There was also a line of black flames surrounding the areas the sword cut, emitting powerful dark mana. The path ahead was lit by the mana, but lighting was still deficient, but with the slight light from the flames, he could see how high the giant walls of the earth on either side of him were, too high for him to jump. With nothing but a gap down to nothingness behind him, he looked forward, noticing small glowing spheres in front of him, assuming it was the door out of here. It was like twelve meters above him, though. "Let's hope that's the end of this…" Void started forward, soon realizing the diagonal upwards incline from the back half of the diamond.

Trudging up the steep path, the walls on his sides that eclipsed him before now became a lot less intimidating.

At the top now, Void faced the door stiffly; ignorant of all the hardships he missed in this room. Void shoved in the door to reveal another area. This one was smaller, though, with only one dimly lit candle in the middle of the room, resting inside of a stand. Quickly, he walked over and picked it up, holding it up to brighten different areas of the room. It was empty, but there were two openings on his left and right sides. With the light on the left side, strange feline beasts were primarily drawn with blood on the walls around the door. They were depicted attacking humans and angels. The opening on this side had a rocky pathway leading downwards and spiraling off. Void shook his head and shined the light on the right side. The path was traversing up on this one. Around the door, paintings of water, little squiggles, and people in conquest were drawn in clay this time. "Hmmm, which one, eh?" Void looked back and forth as he thought.

During this process, Void noticed the figure appear behind the door on his right, just waiting there. Void grumbled at the site when he saw it. "Hmph, nice try, not falling for your little trap." Void turned and started down the path to his left. The road curved wide, carved out like a tunnel from a worm. Eventually, he reached the bottom, which culminated in a room that sat below the previous one, much further below. The room was closed off by a thick stone slab, blocking the entrance. As he approached, it slid up, revealing a small opening into the room. The room was completely black. No light left the room, and it was impossible to see how large it was. "Of course it's another dark room. So tired of the dark, ugh." Void ducked and entered the room. The slab came crashing down behind him, closing him inside.

Void reached back and pulled out his claymore, expecting opposition. Red eyes opened and closed in the depth of the blackness. Void gripped his sword tighter. "I feel so much malicious intent. Are these really simple beasts?" He twitched back as something quickly swiped past him. "I can't even tell how large they are…" Claws were heard scraping on the stone floors, coming towards him. The red eyes got closer and closer. Void closed his eyes. "Guess I'll have to try to and feel their mana since I cannot see them." To his right, Void felt a heavy presence coming towards him. Sword up to block, Void gets impacted by one of the large felines. It pounced towards him, heavy claws clashing with his sword. He spent the next few moments holding his sword above his head to stop the paw from crushing him.

Bright red eyes glared open, illuminating the feline for only a moment. It had a dense and long body, resembling a tiger. The head was longer, though, like a dog's snout, long tentacle like whiskers protruded from the sides of their cheeks. The claws were long and curved like assassin daggers. They even secreted a dark substance that dripped off of the tips of the claws. With a burst of strength, Void temporarily pushed off the cat to the side and jumped to the side, breathing hard. "What am I up against here?" He stopped to take a breath and gazed around. "Those claws look dangerous too, I have to be care— Ack!" Void was caught off guard by one of the beasts behind him. It brushed past him, slicing him deeply on his right side, just under his ribs. His blood was thrown forward in the impact, and it even jerked Void forward. He dropped to one knee and held his side. "Tsk. Damnit, Void, look what you did. This actually kinda hurts. Wow." Void struggled back to his feet, a dark aura surrounding his wound. The felines all began to pounce at once. Dodging and blocking most of the advances

229

on him now, Void struggled to avoid contact. He couldn't attack in his current predicament.

"I have to start killing these things!" Void held his claymore horizontally above his head. Out of the darkness, two of the beasts came leaping at his sword. They both clashed him and pressured him, shoving him back and forcing him to use all his strength to hold them up. His side began bleeding more, the more pressure he put on it. "Grrrr!" Void bumped up his sword, causing the felines to get stunned and open themselves up. With a quick spin, he slashed low at their ankles; this toppled them to the ground in front of Void quickly. Something crunched just then. "Ahhh!" Void looked down to find his left leg overwhelmed by the teeth of one of the felines. The entire area above and below his knee was bleeding profusely. With a crack and a messy gash, Void stabbed his claymore into its skull. "Damn cat," he said as he bent down to pry the slain beast's jaw from his leg.

"Ack, what the hell am I doing?" Void looked down at the swords on his hip as dark energy illuminated them in the darkness of the room. The bottom sword on his hilt shined this time. This one was shorter than the one he used previously and was separated in the middle. The two beasts in front of him caught his attention as they began to stir and crawl towards him. Multiple bright red eyes started to pop up in the short distance behind them. Void gingerly sidestepped to the right, unable to put much weight on his left leg at all. Wincing in pain, he removed his ripped up undershirt and wrapped it around his leg, which would not stop the bleeding on his ribs anyway. With his shirt off, the deep gashes in his side were freshly bleeding, trickling down his leg. Scars of varying sizes from multiple types of weapons littered his entire chest like skin-colored tattoos. The more Void winced in pain, the brighter the glow from the cursed weapons.

The felines drew closer now, starting to stalk and surround their prey. Void felt their combined hunger and rage aimed toward him. He shifted his body to the side and grasped the hilt of his sword with one hand, his claymore in the other. "Let's see what you can do then. Shadow slicer!" With a spin, mostly on his one healthy leg, Void swung his swords across ahead of him, sending giant dark mana shockwaves forward. The shockwaves soared through the darkness in front of him. Most red eyes disappeared as only splatters of blood were heard, forcing their way against the wall and floor; small squeals followed. The darkness from the cursed blade began to travel up Void's arm and up to his head. Soon Void's eyes began to glow red as well, his skin growing even paler as he peered around. "Hahahaha! That's what happens when you step to Void. Now come and get skewered like your friends." Void laughed maniacally as he moved around normally and sheathed his claymore on his back, the energy from the sword giving off a burst of adrenaline, which he still held in his right hand. A few of the remaining beasts in the back opened their eyes and charged at Void full force. "Come!" With long strides, they reached Void rather quickly as he stood there with his arms open, in an accepting stance. Void's eyes flashed as a new ancient scripture read itself to him, implanting deep into his mind. Just as the three felines were all within a small radius around Void, he snapped his fingers. Suddenly a dome of darkness surrounded him resembling the mana he used for his portals.

Void's body was even more lost in the dark, but the felines still rushed into the dome. They stopped, however, after getting their heads and a limb or two inside. Void's hand was up, and his eyes were closed. "Boy, oh boy, have I wanted to try this, hahaha!" The felines struggled in place to free themselves before the portal dome disappeared suddenly, cleaving the beasts into pieces. The part that penetrated the dome splattered on the ground, severed from their other halves. "Mercy's shift," he said with a snicker.

The room began to shake violently, and in the next breath, the room was illuminated. Torches that sat all along the walls all had come on at the same time. Void looked around at the hordes of dead beasts and copious amounts of blood all along the walls in this makeshift den of sorts. It was a dead-end without a door to lead forward. The freshly sliced heads and body parts had rolled at his feet now. "Wow, that is gros—." Void cut himself off as in a struggling motion, he grabbed the hilt with both hands. Wobbling the entire way, Void grabbed the cursed blade and sheathed it back on his hip. The dark mana surrounding him faded away, and his wounds began to bleed again. Void lowered himself onto his knee.

"Woah...I have to be careful with those. I can feel the dark influence trying to take over me just by wielding it." Void limped towards the door before stopping and surveying the scene again. "So much destruction. I definitely need to limit my use of these."

Void hobbled his way back of the spiral path and back into the room above to find the figure there still waiting for his return. "Damnit, maybe this was the right way," Void said, looking away, then at his leg that was dripping all over the floor. He walked forward, and the figure disappeared into the shadows. The dark warrior dragged himself up the hill of a path and up to the room ahead. It was open, but of course, there was no light. Just tiled rock floors that he could see from standing at the entrance. He took a deep breath before continuing. "Something tells me I'm going to regret this…"

Traversing towards center of the room, Void cautiously looked around, waiting for something to jump out, but it didn't. Just as he reached the center of the room, a loud cracking rock sound could be heard originating from the corner of the room. Soon the cracking sound followed to his position and past him to the other side. Void stood utterly still and looked around, not seeing anything. "Oh damn!" Suddenly the floor that held him crumbled away all at once and began to drop down a hollow corridor directly under the room. "I knew it!" Void yelled as he fell over twenty feet and splashed into an icy cold pool of water in the room below. After landing, he immediately went under to dodge the impact of the stone from the floor above. Under the pool, Void struggled to swim effectively with the weight of the weapons, and with one ineffective leg. Void looked all around him as he slowly sunk down the pool.

The extreme dark still impaired his vision, the ice-cold water numbed his other senses, and Void was indeed trapped in the situation. Void didn't even shiver, but he knew he was losing it. Losing his mind, consciousness; air. In a frantic rush, Void began to reach out and swim, trying to find something, some kind of opening to release the water. After senselessly swimming back and forth right above the bottom, something inside Void stopped him. Air beginning to escape out of his mouth, but he still managed to calm himself by slapping his face. Void closed his eyes and began to meditate deeply. However, already numb, he closed off the rest of him at that moment. His mind was blank. His focus was on anyway out of this predicament. Any little nook. In his serenity, there it was. A tiny whooshing sound across along the ground he heard. Then he felt the subtle tug of water going in that direction. Void aimed the tip of his cursed sword at a small hole that seeped out water below.

Seconds before he passed out from lack of oxygen, Void stabbed the sword towards the area he felt the opening. Void's body hunched over as his mouth finally opened. He was out. The sword was thrown with such force that not even the water slowed it. The tip of the sword jammed into the hole; this stopped the water for a bit. Moments later, a small square of the floor in front of the sword was lazed out and blown up. Water began rushing out of the hole, down into the room below. The sword rattled but didn't move much as the area was drained through the hole. Void's body splattered on the ground face down, his mana weapons clanking in the process.

After the water all left this level, a door on the wall just ahead of Void, on the ground level, began to shake open. Behind it, finally, light shone into the darkroom, creating a path that illuminated his unconscious body.

Void's body lied motionless for a while before he began coughing. "Gah! Dammit…hmmm, I'm alive." Void heaved as he threw up a good bit of water; his back arched over on all fours. He stood all the way up but was immediately reminded of his useless leg, stumbling and catching his balance. He then started dragging his body towards the door. The cursed sword was grabbed in passing and sheathed back at his side. Void gave a sigh before entering the doorway, "I'm not looking forward to this at all," he grumbled.

-Year 265   Machi Rock, Soros   Central Basonali, Sylindra-

In a shallow valley off of the outskirts of Soros, the capital of Basonali, two men stood face to face with swords out. Skeletons, weapons, and old rusted armor were tossed about in piles around the valley. Slash marks slid up and down the valley floor as the cold, hard stone curved up around them in all directions. This left them an irregularly small battle area. Twenty-one-year old Void stood across from a man in an all-black cloak, a long and skinny bladed sword in his hand. His opposition stood with Void's future Claymore over the back of his neck. The icy cold wind blew

234

past them softly. The sky was as gray as the scenery was. Void was much skinnier, wearing a baggy and cheap-looking brown shirt and soft, cotton pants. Void tapped the sword on the ground repeatedly. "I'm taking my sword back. Neither of us is leaving until I get it," Void snarled as he took a step forward.

"Wrong. The sword is mine, you know the rules. To the winner go the spoils." The man took his hood off and tossed his entire cloak to the side. This revealed his scar ridden body with sword and bite marks going up and down his chest and arms. He was slim, but a bit more muscular than Void. His eerie smile was filled with rotten and golden teeth.

"Orgi…I can't believe you murdered them…just for that sword." Void lowered his head, looking at the ground.

"Void, you may have been in line to inherit it. But I couldn't let someone so weak be granted such a blessed sword." Orgi patted the sword on his back a few times. "Only the strong deserve these blessings! Ignore your aspirations to become a knight, they don't bless those who've done what we have! Embrace the darkness!" he said, lowering the sword to his side and running at Void.

"For my father, and all of your pupils, I will kill you, Orgiii!" Void raised his own sword and charged at him full speed.

Void and Orgi clashed in the middle, crossing blades. Void was immediately pushed back with the massive claymore. He quickly bounced back and swung again, but was met with harsh opposition. With his overhead blow being deflected, Void backed off a few steps.

"Give it up, I left only you alive for a reason. Don't make me overturn that decision," Orgi said, shaking his head.

"And what's that?" Void spun around twice and swung his sword at Orgi's head. Orgi dodged and shoved

235

Void to the ground from behind. Void rolled forward and turned around, regaining his stance.

"You know, I think this sword is alive. It fought back and forced me to hesitate when I tried to kill you. I chalked it up to fate, I guess." Orgi pulled up the sword and held the black in his hand. "This is a very interesting blade. It can feel it needs to feed my bloodlust as I hold it."

Void smirked and looked up at Orgi after this, pulling himself fully up with his sword. "Do you not remember the given name of that blade?" He rushed Orgi with a bunch of rapid swings. Orgi dodged while keeping the claymore lowered for easy maneuverability. With a tight grip, Orgi lifted the blade with his left hand in the middle of Void's combo, catching him clean in his side. He found Void's weaker strike with his right hand. Void cringed, but kept his pain to himself, blood leaving his body and soaking the blade in his side. Orgi's hand bled slightly under the pressure as he held Void's sword in position.

"No, please enlighten me, Void." Orgi pulled the claymore towards him, slicing up at Void's side even further until it is freed of his body. He then lets go of Void's sword, which drops like an anvil into the dirt. Void lowered himself to one knee as he caught his breath. Void is still within range of Orgi, but he rested there.

"That sword was crafted by my grandfather's personal blacksmith. He wasn't a normal blacksmith, though." Void paused for a moment and spit off to the side. "He was an outcast for his habit of messing with dark forces and infusing them into his weapons." Void smirked and stood back to his feet. "The one he made for my ancestor was one of his most significant accomplishments. He trapped a demon inside that black blade, this demon is spiteful, but still lives to fulfill it's wielder's desires."

Orgi's eyes flared as he lifted the claymore above his head, "So if I want to cleave you in half, it'll help me is that right?" He yelled as he lowered the bloody blade towards Void's head. Void simply looked up and stared at the sword, his eyes starting to radiate with a red aura. The weapon abruptly stopped an inch away from Void's forehead.

The force pushed back Void's hair like a sharp breeze. Void smiled and slowly and softly put his hand around the blade. Orgi pushed and pushed, but he could not make the blade budge an inch. "What is this?"

"I feel like I told you, this is *my* sword. His name is Fonos, the blood blade. He likes to kill, but now that he has tasted my blood, he knows who I am. He will not hurt me." Void released his hand on the blade and opened it. Fonos slowly forces its way out of Orgi's hand and floats over into Void's. Orgi was stunned, unable to move because of this shock. Void turned the blade in Orgi's direction and thrusted it towards him, piercing his chest. "Oh, look, no problem with hurting you."

Blood trickled down Orgi's mouth as his arms fell to his sides. "Tsk. Damn. Looks like I underres—."

Void's other blade pierced his chest on the other side. Blood flung behind Orgi by the second stab. "Shut. Up. You. Damn....traitor!" Void placed his foot on Orgi's chest in between the swords. Orgi is already out at this point, his head bobbled behind him. Void held tightly on the hilts of both swords. "I don't care what you think. I will be a knight. I *will* atone for the sins of following your ways all these years. I *will* make something good of my life. And. I will *not* allow the darkness to consume me, as you've shown me the dangers of that... In one last lesson. Thank you." With plenty of force, Void kicked Orgi's body off of his blades and back a few feet before he landed and plopped onto the ground; his eyes rolled back into his head. Void stared down solemnly before turning around and walking away, towards the exit to the battleground, blood still coming down his side. "Ugh, I hate these feelings. I need to find that annoying guy with the wings again, I have a lot of thinking to do."

-Year 277 Te Whatitiri Wapu Southeast Kayard, Sylindra-

The end of the year came by, and the first day of the New Year arrived, but there was still dismay. On the edge of town, just outside the city, a small shack housed the unconscious Volt and the mysterious figure who saved him. This shack was barely two hundred square feet, crafted with cheap materials, old leftover wood, and straw, there wasn't much to it. Inside were a single cot and a large pot for cooking on one side, and in the center was a large wooden table with cursed symbols carved into it. These glowed steadily as they made contact with Volt's body, which was lying on his back in the middle of the table. His Sigrun was lying off to the side, along with the majority of his Royal Knights garb. A long black cloak sat next to his stuff, hastily thrown there. Volt's chest was bare, and two very large, lightly sewn together wounds quivered as mana from the symbol underneath continually healed him, infusing its mana with his own like dark lightning with a mind of its own.

"Come on, stranger, you can do it. Wake up. Please?" A strange woman stood over Volt with her hands clasped together, as if in prayer. She had ashen skin, an off grey even. Her long red hair was in a ponytail, a black choker around her neck. She wore a one-piece top that was cut low, showing a majority of cleavage from her sizeable bust. On the bottom half, jewels decorated the bottom portion, which cut off like a skirt just over her butt. She had long black boots, with razor-sharp edges around the heel and toe. This woman had a beautiful, innocent face, but razor-

238

sharp teeth. It had been days upon days that she had been looking after Volt as he recovered, sitting for hours just staring at his face, wondering what kind of man he was, what the fight she had witnessed was about. Her meddlesomeness was so hard it became a selfish need to know as she waited for Volt to awaken. And then it happened.

Volt's eyes creaked open, but his body remained still. His eyes glanced around, unable to move his head. The woman peeked over and noticed his eyes open. "Ooo, are you awake? " She came across and started to poke him in the cheek. "Hey! I saved your life. Say something."

Volt parted his chapped lips and eked out something indistinguishable, "Ehr egllo." Volt cleared his throat and licked his lips. "Um, hello."

The woman jumped for joy and squeezed Volt's cheeks. "Yay, you're alive!" she screamed.

Volt winced in pain, and the woman was forced to stop. He meagerly opened his mouth again. "So many questions…"

She put her finger up to his lips. "Save your energy, I'll tell you everything," she said as she backed up and pulled a chair over next to Volt. She sat down right in front of him, her bust at his eye level; hands softly placed on her lap. "Dear, my name is Scatha. You are lucky; you are."

Volt bent his neck and peered down at himself, then nodded. He looks over and saw a yellow orb on a desk behind Scatha.

Scatha focused on Volt and nodded as well. "I was in town when everything happened. You fought a dragon, then a warrior. You saved the city. But you were hurt. I was too shy to approach, but you looked so…so…" Scatha blushed and stopped herself.

Volt cocked his head to the side a little "Hmm?"

"C-cute. I haven't seen a human — I mean someone who appeared as you do." Scatha turned away.

Volt's eyes widened. *First Gaia, now her. What's going on with me?* "Um, so, I noticed your skin," Volt said. Scatha shook in her seat and stiffened up. "Are you a demon by any chance?" Volt asked.

"W-why do you say that?" She turned around in her chair, facing away from Volt. "Why…"

Volt shook his head. "No, it's okay if you are. You saved my life; I couldn't fathom looking down on you." He squinted over and saw her still turning away. "If it helps. I think you're cute as well, Scatha." Volt coughed.

Scatha scurried around, her face a mix of red and grey. "Really? R-really?"

Volt nodded at her and tried his best to smile without hurting himself.

She got close and hugged his face, her chest nearly suffocating him. "Thank you, uhhhh…"

"V-Volt!" he managed, trying to catch his breath.

Scatha backed off. "Volt, thank you. No one's ever told me that. Only hated ridiculed. That's me."

Volt turned his head to look at her eyes. "I'm sorry to hear that. Is that because you are a mixed race?"

Her mouth shot open. "How…how did you know that? I don't tell anyone that."

Volt's hand slid off of the table and hung in the open. "I can tell because, me too. I recently found out who my true mother is, and she is an insane bitch. Now I have to live my life knowing that I'll have to watch my back for my own sole family member." A tear rolled down his left eye.

She came over and held his hand with hers. Tears in her eyes. "Worry not. My father is a terrible demon. Please. We should stick together. We are the same."

He shook his head. "No, the path I'm on in a dangerous one. Can't risk anyone else getting hurt. Just look at me."

"I'm a healer, *please* let me help you. I need this…" She smiled while rocking his hand back and forth.

"I can't risk that. Why are you living out here anyway? Seems a bit meager." Volt questioned.

Scatha turned her head towards the door. "Um, actually. I'm here hiding from a group I was with before."

"What do you mean? What happened?" Volt said, trying to sit up, but failing.

She pulled him back down. "I uh… I had to do what I had to. To survive. After my mom died, the only one who would take me in was a small group of demon mercenaries. They are cruel, harsh, and merciless. They constantly terrorized me for who I am. Made me their healer, no love, only hate." Scatha had her head down, moments from breaking away into tears again. "One day, my group was contracted to kill this family, but mostly the parents. They were rebels. There was a small child among them as well. Defenseless. She didn't do anything wrong. She was innocent, hadn't had the chance to form an opinion of her own yet. So I saved her."

Scatha began shaking her head. Volt calmed her by squeezing her hand. "What happened after that?" he said.

"They did not like that very much. Hated it even. They are big about not showing weakness. Very big. The leader said that if I didn't kill the baby myself now, he would kill me. I took her and ran. They have been trying to kill me ever since. So I am here." She turned back towards the door as she heard some noise outside.

"What became of the kid?" Volt questioned.

"Hate in their hearts but still. I was able to find a family that could take care of her." After this, Scatha turned

241

and looked outside the window behind them as she heard noises again.

"That's good. Wait, what's that?" Volt turned to his side.

"Oh no, oh no, oh nooo. They are here!" Scatha screamed as she hi behind the window. Suddenly, something banged on the door.

Volt looked at the window, then over to the orb on the desk. "Hey Scatha, quick, take that orb and smash it on my chest!" he said, nudging at her.

She looked over at the orb and back at Volt. "But why? Wouldn't it hurt you?"

"Just hurry; it'll make sense!" Volt said, straining himself. Something banged on the door again, shadows appeared outside.

In a rush, she grabbed the orb as it burned her hands and sprinted over to Volt. "Ouch!" she shouted.

"Woah, I guess only we can touch those safely," Volt commented. The sphere dropped and landed on his chest, breaking and releasing mana everywhere all over Volt. The mana was so intense it destroyed the magical table he was resting on and radiated around him. Volt landed on his feet, crouched. His eyes are glowing a bright yellow. "Ahhh. That feels great."

"You're okay! My healing worked?" Scatha was shocked and dancing to herself. She stopped when the banging got louder. The door was so punished it began loosening from the hinges.

"Open the door, or I will break it down!" A voice boomed from outside.

Scatha went over to Volt, who was still crouched, trying to assess his body. "One more thing before...stuff starts happening. You were very hurt, so I had to use some very dark arts to heal you. Dark mana, evil mana. I'm so sorry, Volt!" she said, covering her face.

"Why so sorry? What does that mean for me?" Volt said, looking at his body.

Scatha looked around. "Well, I gave you a second chance, and there are consequences. The darkness may threaten to creep up on you eventually. You're strong though, right?" she said with a smile.

Volt finally stood up, holding his chest softly as he winced in pain. "Eh. So I'm not fully healed. At least I can move though." Volt eased over and got dressed.

Boom! Suddenly the door came shooting across the room, slamming into the pot on the opposite side. Approaching them, were three menacing demons armed with light armor and jagged-edged swords. "Open up!" The lead demon with large horns protruding from his head yelled, busting open the door.

"Eeep!" Scatha jumped, and then looked towards him. She nudged at Volt, who wasn't ready and quickly ran over to the entrance. "Er helloooo, guys." she said, putting up a face loosely resembling a smile.

The lead demon immediately grabbed her by the neck and lifted her into the air. "I should crush your neck right now! Mind telling me why I shouldn't, you little wench?" he said, cocking his head to the side.

Scatha kicked her feet in the air and grabbed at the demon's hand. "Haiza, please...I...can't." She was losing consciousness quickly.

A massive blast of lighting mana came soaring across the room and blasted everything behind Haiza's elbow, including him and the two demons behind him. The shack's roof and the other half was also blown away as the attack devastated everything. Scatha dropped to the ground, unharmed, and the demons were all on the ground burnt to a crisp. Scatha's home was in shambles.

"Because I'm here, that's why..." Volt said as he collapsed back to a knee. "Wow that was more powerful than before." Volt looked at his hands. He got dressed and placed his spear on his back. Scatha was on her knees, bawling. Volt approached and gave her a tight hug. "Come on, you can come with me. Grab what you need. Don't say I didn't warn you."

In her tears, Scatha stared at Volt with endearing eyes, nodding. "R-really?" She muttered out between her tears. Volt got up and started for the doorway, or what was previously the doorway. "O-oh, okay!" Scatha grabbed her book of dark arts and a spiked staff from the corner and ran after him, holding his arm tightly as they walked out.

-Year 277 Malveria, The Paradise City Basonali, Sylindra-

Malveria. For decades, the hidden city had been known as 'Paradise City,' serving as a refuge for many types of people. Malveria hosted a very diverse cast of characters from demons to outcast mix breeds to warriors of differing tribes. The ninjas that founded it wanted to make it a place of peace, hidden away from the world. Over the years, Malveria housed outcasts but also became a place for many underground dealings. The most infamous mercenaries, dealers, assassins, and treasure hunters found peace on these grounds.

The founders were monks and ninja warriors that made their way through the Nasol ruins together to discover this holy land. The city was located on the very tip Northeastern part of Basonoli. That edge of the continent is more elevated than the rest. Coming out of the exit of the ruins, an ingenious contraption made by the monks took you straight up to the ground level of the city from underground.

The city itself was separated into four different districts. They were split by wide streets intersecting in the middle. Each region was home to a diverse assortment of people. Benevolent demons, human outcasts and criminals, warriors from every continent, even a few angels had found an area to call their own. The layout of the city allowed for each ground to live without interacting with too many other groups if they chose to. In the back of the city laid a dock. Reasonably unknown, this secret dock served as the second entrance into the city. Also, a plethora of underground dealings go down over there with minimal attention. In the middle was a large square and a sacred temple in the center housing a dark orb of very malicious energy. The first monks found this evil orb sitting in this same spot. They built around it and set up barriers to protect it. They also felt if they surrounded it with the positive energy of people that the orb would remain dormant for long.

For years it worked without issue, but today was different. The orb began to agitate. Black ooze seeped out and began to spread around the temple unbeknownst to the monks guarding it. Before they knew it, the black ooze was everywhere, and outside the surrounding areas as well. The monks finally began to scatter out of the temple and started to spread the word. Before long. The city's populace was gathered at the docks, but those that could fight gathered around the temple.

The ooze had melted the temple's walls away at this point, leaving only the roof. It spiked out and spread further with each passing moment. Bounty hunters and monks stood side by side as they awaited this unknown that threatened all of their homes. Of the usual ragtag group of fighters, a group gaining traction began to inhabit Malveria. Led by Alex, a tall dirty blond-haired warrior, Keith and Kerri blend in the crowd. Keith had long, spiky, all black hair tied back. He had a head wrap that surrounded one of his eyes. The one still visible was bright green. He donned a baggy white and black thin oriental robe, a hidden short sword on his hip.

Two small holes were on the back of his cloak as a single beautiful white angel's wings stuck out on his right side. The left side was wingless.

Next to him, super close in the crowd of people was Kerri. She had dark red hair with a bright yellow streak going right through the middle. She had a tight fit all black assassin grade light armor on. Overtop was a flailing cloak, blocking out the top of her body. Many daggers and short swords were hidden under this and in various pockets on Kerri's pants. Her primary weapons were on her hands, though. Katars, with a large center blade, dressed her hands. The main one lining up with her middle finger. She was about five feet tall, getting shoved back in the crowd.

After expanding past the temple, a few feet, it calmed and jiggled in place. The fighters began separating and readying themselves to pounce. The ooze contracted back around the orb and floated there for a moment, dripping itself on the ground. The sphere's surface kicked and rumbled in place like something was trapped inside. It expanded again, but this time into a figure. An average-sized form with horns and nothing much else of note came about this. Only in shape, though, as the ooze made up its body entirely. The body dripped onto the ground as it stood in place, head down.

"Ha! Look at that little thing, we were worried for nothing." Some cocky bounty hunter out front said with seven different swords sheathed around his body. "I got this, guys." He walked forward while unsheathing two of his swords.

The being made from the ooze stood still as the confident man ran at it full force. He swung at the being with two swords, jamming them in its side. "H-huh? It's stuck; I can't get it out." The man said as he pulled and tugged, attempting to dislodge his swords from the thick, absorbent, and sticky ooze makeup of the being. The center of its head lit up, around where eyes would be, and two sword silhouettes came bursting out of its hands. Grasping the new ooze-made blades, it turned attention at the man attempting to harm it. The man nervously pulled his hands back, letting go of his swords, but the ooze sprung out and attached to his hands, not letting him free. "Ahhh, dammit someone help." *Sloosh*. The odd being had stabbed both of the newly formed swords into the chest of the man. His eyes rolled back behind his hand, and he fell to the side, dead.

The remaining warriors gasped, watching the first victim plop onto the ground. One by one, they rushed at the being and were cut down. From monks to bounty hunters, they all got victimized and sent down into a pile of bodies. Keith and Kerri stood there, as the last two remaining alive. "Man, where is Alex? We seem to have an issue on our hands," Kerri said, looking around.

"Don't worry about it, I will handle this thing myself. Holy light!" Keith shouted as he slid out his sword. It was surrounded by holy mana, making the shape and size of his blade not visible. Only a bright aura was seen in its place. The same effect was on the one wing on his back. "Fragarach, let's do this." Keith dashed forward.

At this point, the being had gained access to plenty of different weapons. It had grown a dark armor, and a face mask. It now held akimbo axes, and it moved with the movements of a martial artist. Keith looked at him for a moment, then gathered a small amount of holy mana in his hand. "Let's make this quick, so I can get out of here." He threw it at the being's feet. When it reached the ground, it created a large flash, blinding everything in a wide range. The creature was stunned and open, clearly suffering from the effects of the mana. Keith slid in, and with a spinning slash, he slashed at the being, slicing its body in half from the hip. The top half crashed into the ground as the bottom half dropped to the ground, knees first.

"Wow, Keith, I didn't even see anything," Kerri said, rubbing her eyes.

"Heh, it was that easy." Keith brushed off his shoulder and sheathed his sword. The ooze that remained attracted and melded together, creating another ball. The ball tumbled around and expanded again, this time creating an actual being more massive than the previous one. It had more defined horns on its head and had large vicious claws instead of weapons. "Why, I thought it was done, ugh." Keith pulled his sword back out as he faced the new foe staring him down, as tall as the buildings around him it was.

-Year 277 Nasol Ruins Northern Basonali, Sylindra-

Hungry, pained, and at the end of his rope, Void made his way through many rooms of monsters and deadly traps. He now sported a bleeding gash on his forehead and bruised hand on top of his injuries on his side and leg that wouldn't stop bleeding, still. Void dragged himself up to the most enormous door yet. It sat on the top of an inclined path leading from the previous room. The trail was actually finely paved, as opposed to the rocky paths before. The door spanned from the bottom to the top of the twelve-foot tunnel. It was made of a dark onyx colored stone with symbols carved around the rim. The symbols were hard to identify in the dimly lit pathway. One part was easily visible, though. On the left side of the door was a Sun; on the right, a large moon indented into the stone.

"Oh dear, is it finally over. Have I reached the end?" Void pleaded in front of the door. Void sighed as he pushed open the door. "As if I'd be that lucky." The heavy door creaked open. Void limped in, a trail of blood following him. He squeezed his leg tightly. The room he found himself in was wide open and square, mana stones on all of the walls to light the room. In the center, the cloaked figure stood there calmly waiting. There was an eerie feeling in the room, but Void didn't notice it initially. "Hmm, I guess it would be you as the final boss here. It's like you lead me here just to end me."

The doors slowly shut behind Void. The two stood utterly still, Void staring, but his opposition focused on the ground. The lights flickered for a moment, and a quick flash of a terrifying grim reaper appeared before Void in the moment of darkness. This shocked Void, causing him to back away. "What the hell was that?" Void yelled.

The lights stabilized, but Void remained skeptical. The figure's body began to stammer and shake in place. The lights started to flash on and off again, in longer intervals now. That image showed itself again and again, while the original figure began to grow in size slowly. Void pulled out both of his cursed blades. Dark mana from the sword flowed through Void and radiated around him. "No time to think, regrets come later." Void said as his eyes glowed red. All of the pain in his body was muted. His thoughts and feelings replaced with an overwhelming rage. "Ahhhhh! Die!" Void screamed as the cloaked being morphed into a towering reaper with a triple-bladed scythe equally as massive. As soon as he was fully formed, the lights shut out entirely.

Void stood there impatiently in the dark. A high pitched and loud scraping sound approached Void. It sounded like a blade scraping against concrete. He was at the ready, swords cocked to the side. "Come on!!" Void couldn't wait any longer and swiped both swords in the dark, letting out a ruthless streak of mana in the dark. For just a moment, the reaper could be seen off to the side of the attack, floating in the air. Void rested his swords, and the lights flashed back on for a moment. The reaper was directly above Void swinging horizontally at him by the time it was lit again.

Void ducked all the way down, dodging the swing. He then leaped into the air and rushed at the reaper. With a single, bony hand up, the reaper stopped Void in place with just his mana, holding him there. Void struggled against it with all his might as the reaper raised his scythe again at him.

"This can't hold me!" Void forced his way out of the hold just in time. He landed on the ground, mana exploding all around him violently. "Grah!" The lights shut off again, and Void went on the attack. What happened next was a flurry of clashes between the giant scythe and Void's cursed blades. Each encounter sent sparks that lit the area for only a moment, and the cursed blades sent shockwaves towards the surrounding walls with each swing. The room shook and began to crumble from the opposing forces.

"Bahahahaha!" With each clash, Void's strikes were faster and grew more oppressive. His body was still bleeding, but it did not slow him. His face was covered in blood at this point; he looked like a true savage. With the impending force, the reaper eventually began to back up. Void used this opportunity to leap himself up into the air, above the reaper, and come down with a heavy strike that landed across the chest. The reaper staggered back, and a dark explosion insured afterward.

Lying on the floor, on its back, was the reaper. The lights turned back on. "Come on, is that all?" Void chuckled as he walked towards his enemy. The darkness in Void's aura had slowly risen throughout the battle. He stood over the fallen reaper with both cursed blades raised, ready to strike. "Die!" Void lowered his swords, but the reaper raised his hand simultaneously. The lights shut off simultaneously, and spears made of dark mana tore out of the shadows and skewered Voids' body in multiple areas. His body was lifted into the air higher with each spear shot. As it was finished, Void had seven separate spikes in him, and he was so high

250

that his back was just under the ceiling. Void coughed up blood and passed out. His blood quickly traveling down the spikes. The mana around him had calmed as well; his body hung limp.

The reaper eased himself up, followed by a sinister, bone-shaking cackle. Void's eyes shot open, his mana restored ten-fold and bursting out more than ever. "I'm not dead, damnit!" With a swipe of his swords, Void broke away from spikes and begun to fall towards the reaper. Void lifted his sword high as he approached and pierced the surprised reaper's chest with both swords. The reaper was forced back onto the ground, mana draining from the reaper and into the swords and Void. As the mana drained, the holes in Voids chest, and even his leg and chest wounds that wouldn't cease to stop bleeding, began to close and heal one by one. "Ahhhhhh, beautiful!" Void's body quivered as it was repaired. The reaper slowly shrunk back to its previous small cloaked body during this process.

Void pulled his swords away, and a massive dark explosion erupted on the chest of the reaper blowing a hole through it and sending shockwaves into and through the floor where it lay. The reaper tumbled through the hole and down beneath the room. Void, now breathing very heavy, struggled to sheath his swords. He pushed with all his might, but his tainted mind fought against it.

He finally succeeded, and the mana surrounding him faded away instantly. Voids eyes returned to normal, and his body slowly was drained of its energy. After struggling with his weakness, Void made it to the door, practically crawling on his knees. "Damn, that was berserk. I couldn't even control myself. And my body… It healed me, but it took every ounce of my strength. I guess this is my punishment for messing with the darkness. At least it is over." The door before Void creaked open, only to reveal another room

251

afterward. It was similar to the previous, and only a single, small enemy awaited him.

"Damn…o close." Void forced himself to his feet and walked into the next room. The door shut behind him. "Least it's small," Void said as he looked at what appeared to be a turtle without the shell, standing upright in the middle of the floor holding a type of machete. It patrolled back and forth, knee-high it was almost cute with its chubby face. This "turtle" wore a bright crimson shaman robe and brown sandals. "Whew. Ok, let's get this over with." Void inched forward with Fonos dragging along next to him.

Scraping on the ground as he dashed forward, Fonos shined the closer it got to the enemy. Void noticed this and stopped short. He skidded to an ugly pause, and caught eyes with the turtle a couple feet away. It had stopped walking and focused on Void, weapon readied. Void cautiously broke eye contact to look at Fonos. "What's going on with you? You haven't done that before. Is this your way of warning me?" Void said, looking at his sword and back in front of him. He patted the side of Fonos, then started forward again. "Don't worry, it'll be oka—."

"Ack!" Void was spontaneously sent flying into the wall behind him. He gasped for air as his body plopped out of the crater in the wall he created and slammed into the ground. Fonos clanked on the ground next to him. Void was face down on the ground. "W-what in the hell happened, I didn't even see anything," Void said, lifting his head, gasping for breath, sweat on his brow. The turtle had only moved a couple steps forward. Void shook his head. He then looked over at Fonos curiously. *Is my body too weak for this fight?* Void lifted himself up to his feet and grabbed his sword.

After twirling his sword around a few times, Void released a horizontal swing that let out a streak of mana at the turtle. The turtle simply nudged his blade forward and a much more impressive vertical streak of mana. It was massive, slicing at the ceiling and floor in its path; Void's attack didn't stand a chance. His was torn apart, and Void dived to the side to avoid the same fate. "This. Is. Unsettling," Void said as he saw the destruction behind him. "My legs won't even let me walk near that thing. I feel as if my death is assured if I do that." Void said, staring into the eyes of a cute demon.

"OK, look, I know you want to be antisocial, but I need you to talk to me. After being with me all this time, you haven't said a word. Well look, your master is about to die. It'll behoove you to help me out. What is wrong with my body right now?" Void held Fonos up to his face for a moment, then gave up and dropped it down to his side with both hands. "Fine. Nothing? Here goes then." Void aggressively took a couple steps forward towards the turtle.

"It's because…" A voice booms from the sword.

Void stopped hard. "Did you just?"

"Just shut up and listen. Your body has absorbed too much darkness, Void. Going berserk took a lot out of you and overloaded you. You will need to release that darkness if you want any semblance of normalcy," Fonos said.

Void looked at his hands. "How would I do that? I doubt just firing it off would do anything to that thing."

"Give me control. I'll use a secret forbidden technique to release it. Should also help you with that…thing you're fighting," Fonos said as it began to surround itself in dark mana.

"How can I trust you with control over my body? This is our first interaction," Void questioned.

"You asked for help, did you not? This is me helping. I'll go through all the motions, just remember the sensation for if you need to use it on your own." The hilt of Fonos began to glow white. "Just grab it, and I'll take over."

Void nodded. "I…I guess you're right," he said as he grabbed the glowing hilt. The sword immediately turned into pure mana and entered Void's body. Afterward, his sight was temporarily taken from him.

Fonos held both of Void's hands out in front of him. Mana began to incrementally release from his body like steam from a kettle. The mana did not leave his radius though, torrential amounts of dark mana started to orbit him swiftly. In increasing speeds, the mana spun around his body on different paths resembling a small spherical atmosphere of darkness a meter off of him. "Hahahaha, there it is; it's been so very long since I've felt this sensation," Fonos said as the mana began to get violently fast. Lashing out off path and scraping away at the ground. "Let's start then," he said, closing his eyes and squatting down; his hands still out in front.

"Ack! Filled with rage and anger, my curse is turned into a blessing from the hands of the Gods that deemed me worthy to wield the ultimate darkness." Suddenly the ball surrounding Void began to expand, the violent mana shaking the room as it tripled in size. Fonos started laughing maniacally as he continued. "Feel my pain, my struggles, and shatter from the weight of my spirit!" After this, the ball instantly shrunk into a super-concentrated ball right in his hands. It jerked left and right as Fonos struggled to control it. After a moment of centering it, he was ready. "Keni Bala!" At match speeds, the ball sped across the room towards the turtle, who dashed to the side instantly, still dodging it. Mana from the ball linked to the turtle's body just in passing and pulled itself to and into it. The turtle was stunned and shocked by the mana flowing through his body now. After six seconds of torture from the Keni Bala, the turtle dropped the weapon and fell to its knees. The energy stopped flowing afterward, there was nothing. "Hmph. I've done my job, your welcome. You owe me one," Fonos said as he left Void's body and reverted back to the claymore on his back.

Void now was able to see again normally. "Woah, what was that? It's still alive though, Fo?".

"Just deliver the final blow, damnit! Do I have to do everything?" Fonos yelled from his back.

Void inched forward towards the turtle, who was on all fours now, in a completely weakened state. "What's wrong with him?"

"The Keni Bala, also known as the dark shock. It is a forbidden move that attaches to and destroys the mana chains throughout the target's body. This means they can no longer use mana at all from that point forward. Those chains really cannot be repaired either. It weakens opponents indefinitely." Fonos said. Void shook his head as he continued forward. "You know you were facing a strong opponent because any weak enemy would be torn apart immediately from their mana chains breaking down alone," Fonos explained as Void reached the turtle's body. It was quivering in place, unable to move.

"Wow, such a depressing ability. I can move well again, though." Void pulled out the rapier he got for Ocean and held it above the head of the turtle. "I didn't want it to end like it did, but I need to get past this. So. Sorry." Void lowered the rapier into the back of its neck, creating a small splatter of blood. The turtle went limp and was still now. He lifted his sword back up and wiped it off on his pants, resheathing it after. Void looked down at his exposed chest, admiring his new scars. "Ugh, that was such a hassle, and it's not even done yet. I've got to kill this fiend."

The room began shaking as a secret exit opened up in the far corner of the room. Light from outside shot inside like a ray from the heavens. Void started towards the door, taking a second to look back at the devastation he left behind before rushing out of there.

Year 277 Malveria, The Paradise City Basonali, Sylindra-

The sky was darkening evermore by the moment. The smaller being had been defeated and evolved. Now, a giant fiend shrouded in darkness took its place and towered over the city of Paradise, threatening its very existence. Dark lightning struck, ever frequently, the closer you got to him. Keith, exhausted from the consecutive fights, lied face down in the center of the street, the fiend mere meters from him rampaging, but paying him no attention. His sword was laying next to him. Keith's body started to twitch slightly as his pitch-black hair started to run white, pearly white streaks rapidly developing.

"Keith!" Kerri comes running down the street, trying to remain hidden from the field while searching for the spot where Keith had fallen at the end of the last fight. She hugged the wall of the building and slid over next to Keith. The fiend stomped around, firing blasts of dark mana at the crumbling remains. Kerri picked up Keith and started shaking him about. "Keith, c'mon, I need you to snap out of it!" Keith's hair stopped its transition.

"Uuuuugh," Keith moaned while clutching his head. He then recalled his situation and slowly got up to his feet. "Thanks, Ker, though I," Keith stumbled a bit, and regained his composure, "I thought I told you to stay put. You knew the danger that this would put us in."

"Come on now, what would you do if I wasn't here?" Kerri retorted while she helped him up against the wall. Keith ran his hand through his hair with his left hand while picking his sword up with his right. "That thing's hide is way too strong for me to penetrate it, I'll have to leave it up to you, but I can contact Alex, see if he's thought up something to help put a stop to this monster," Kerri said, eyes never leaving Keith.

"Sounds good. I can buy us a bit more time then, but tell Alex that if he doesn't hurry up, then his ass is dead." Kerri nodded in approval, and a smile cracked on her face. Keith snapped his fingers, and his wing of energy reappeared. His feet, hands, and wing glowed, as did his blade. In an instant, he took off towards the hulking fiend. By this time, it had sensed the burst of mana and noticed Keith once more. A boisterous, evil laugh echoed through the ruins. The energy surrounding the demon reformed along with his focus; in his palms, a giant fiery whip appeared. He began his assault once more.

The initial swings of the whip failed to make contact, as Keith gracefully dodged, but the fourth caught him, and the fiend sent him flying into a nearby building. He got up and went back on the attack, targeting the monster's head. One good slash to the eye would be enough to cripple the demon, stop his attacks long enough for Alex to come up with the solution as to how to put the monster away. The trick was getting there. Keith poured more mana into his wings, quickening his pace as his mana drained. Who would have thought he'd have a third form. This was definitely unexpected, but the thought of this monster destroying the surrounding innocent areas sickened him.

Keith started pouring energy into his left hand and aimed for the monster's whip hand. "Ileun Flare!" A wave of fire and holy light surrounded the monster's hand and caused him to drop the whip, as it dissolved into the air. When the light subsided, the monster's hand was charred, and the smell of burning flesh and tar filled the air. Keith took this opportunity to charge towards the beast, pouring more mana into the wing for another speed boost. He lunged towards the monster's eye, but flinched, and missed his mark. He slashed the cheek of the beast, which started to ooze black blood.

Unflinching, the fiend grabbed Keith and began to squeeze him without mercy. Harder and harder it clenched, till he felt Keith's body go limp. He laughed and threw him to the ground. His body bounced slightly before resting. Keith barely moved, and his hair was almost white as snow in this onslaught.

The fiend poured a rain of dark mouth blasts into Keith's back. After a few minutes, he disappeared. Keith reappeared behind the demon, blood slowly coming down his head. He unleashed a surprise slash of the divine wind, slicing off the fiend's left hand. He reeled in pain as dark-colored blood shot out like a sprinkler, and Keith used this opportunity to continue the assault. A few flicks of his sword later, and the fiend fell to his knees from the sheer volume of attacks alone. Keith charged towards the creature's eye again but got stopped. The fiend used the stump of his left hand to block the attack, the sword getting lodged into the bone in the process. The fiend summoned his whip with his right hand and wrapped it around Keith. Keith reeled in pain as the whip absorbed his mana. After several moments of draining, a figure flashed upwards, and cut the whip, causing it to vanish again. Keith fell to the ground from the sky.

Kerri smiled in midair with her successful save, but before she could celebrate, the fiend whacked her with his nubbed arm and caused her to crash towards the ground.

Void leaped into the scene, catching Kerri as she was about to connect, before rolling and sliding into a pile of crates. "Whew, barely made that," Void said wiping his brow.

"Uh, thanks? Kerri said as she released herself from Void's grip.

"I'm Void, would you mind explaining the situation to me?" Void got up and brushed himself off and looking at the body behind them, twitching.

Kerri got up herself and looked up at the Fiend as it cracked its whip at the two of them. "That is some monster that came out of the temple in the center of the city. It kept growing and growing every time my partner defeated it. Now it's huge and ugly."

Void put his hand on Kerri's shoulder, "Ok, think I know what this is. The dimensional fiend. It's something I have to defeat...something I've been through a lot to get here to bea—"

Suddenly there was a flash of light, and a dark mist filled the area. "Dammit. Too late, he changed into Adrian already," Kerri commented.

"Huh?" Void said, coughing as the thick mist entered his lounges.

Keith's body arose once more, his hair had grown, and was pure white now. "Ha, I'm back!" Keith said. "Been a while since I could be myself." Adrian laughed and jumped back.

Void looked back at him, confused. "Did he just change personalities?"

Kerri rolled her eyes, "It's a long story, just know. That's Adrian now, with the white hair."

The fiend planted its feet and began to suck up the mist that exploded out of Adrian, pulling up many other things in the process. Boxes, dead bodies, everything felt the suction. Some of the darkness surrounding Adrian quickly got sucked up. As the demon sucked it up, Adrian planted his feet and willed the thick, remaining darkness around him like a cape. He quickly manipulated it and stabbed it into the ground, securing him in place. Adrian saw Kerri getting pulled towards the fiend, despite a lot of resistance. He rolled his eyes and snapped his fingers. Tendrils of dark mana sprung from the ground on his will, wrapped themselves around Kerri, and strapped her to the ground as well. Void watched quietly, shoving Fonos into the ground to keep him still.

Suddenly, darkness sprung from the ground and lifted Adrian into the air. He fired more of the dark mana towards the wicked beast, in the form of dark spears, feeding the large dimension in his chest. Then, with a smile, Adrian snapped his fingers. "Light Extinction." Within seconds, the trail of darkness that was being consumed was replaced with giant explosions of energy.

"Nice!" Void yelled as he could stand normally again. He pulled Fonos out of the ground and swung out one of his cursed blades as well. Using both, he swung and sent a streak of dark mana flying towards the fiend right behind the explosions.

The fiend noticed the trail of destruction coming towards him, forcing him to deactivate his void and jump back. The explosions extinguished in the open air, along with the streaks. The Fiend toppled buildings as his large mass leaped back a city block. "Heh, wow, didn't know his big ass could move like that. I hope people evacuated that area already." Adrian chuckled. He then looked over next to him at Void. "On that note, who are you?"

"The name's Void. Let's save the explanations till after this thing is dead, ok?" Void nodded.

"Fine. Thanks, by the way." Adrian looked away.

"For what?" Void questioned, creating a portal in front of him, and switching his long-range cursed blade for the close one.

"For Rosalie-er Kerri to you. My other self would appreciate it." Afterward, Adrian formed a giant dark wing on the opposite side of his back, completing his set, and flew towards the behemoth, faster than the eye could see. A trail of dark mana flew behind him. All that was left behind were mere shadows of his form. A tendril of darkness grabbed the

Fragarach, his magical sword, from the ground, and it flew to Adrian's hand.

"Uh yeah, sure." Void said as he hopped into the portal.

Adrian charged forward, his body surrounded with a malicious purple hue, and he rapidly swung his sword. The fiend swung at him, unsuccessfully, as he was caught with simultaneous swings from Adrian and Void, who spawned in from his portal and immediately began to slash at the fiend as well.

Each sword swing from Adrian left behind a small detonation. "Infernal Assault!" He yelled as he flew up and down his enemy, leaving a minefield of explosions. Voids slashes were less frequent as he traveled through his portals in midair to keep himself airborne, but his cursed blade still left a more gigantic blast every time it connected.

The demon grabbed Adrian in a rage and threw him, but Void managed to stop his momentum mid-throw with a well-placed portal. Adrian tumbled out a few feet back and nodded at Void. He then slapped his hands together, and a wave of mana expanded in all directions. From the fiend to Void, everything inside was slowed as if time stood still. Adrian's movements improved significantly in this new 'slow zone.' Adrian began chanting with his hands, still clasped together. The flesh on the surface of the fiend was charred and torn from the onslaught of attacks. The fiend slowly attempted to offset the slow effect and began to move slightly towards Void.

"No mercy; innocent or guilty. Bring down their lying sun. Blood a sweet silver black by night. Upon their faces pale white. No longer will the people have to wait for days, my cruel moon will bring the end. The dawn will never rise, and slaves of the light we shall end. Rise, Lunar Princess, bring darkness eternal. Protect us in your everlasting Night. Nocte Aeternus!"

Darkness immediately consumed the area, taking the place of the aura he set initially; the fiend was stuck for even longer in this new environment. Even Void was clouded at this time. Upon Adrian was a shimmery see-through cloak. He donned two daggers of new twilight mana, they glowed a sparkling white and black with shining specs. The dark spellcaster swung his arms several times, and giant red streaks of mana appeared, unmoving. He flew around the behemoth, and continually turned, leaving the red stripes of mana stationary with each swing. The demon was frozen in the mana as all around him, an army of mana was ready to devastate.

Adrian flew back elegantly and snapped his fingers once again. "Lunar Tempest!" All at once, time went back to normal, and the streaks went flying towards the fiend, leaving deep gashes wherever they struck. It was pulled from side to side as, from all directions; minor attempts to block were thwarted. The demonic blood gushed at the ground, leaving a pool of black in its wake. The fiend dropped to a knee as suddenly, the blood came flying towards Adrian, and started to swirl around his arm like a satellite. Void and Adrian looked down curiously and saw Kerri's hand stretched out, giving her last bit of energy to Adrian and collapsing afterward.

"What is going on with you?" Void said as the blood around Adrian's arm pulsed, and he placed his free hand on his arm in question. Darkness imbued within the blood and drew itself to his palm. The cluster of blood and darkness swirled in an orb and got bigger by the moment, soon expanding to the size of Adrian, ever getting bigger and bigger.

"Muahahahaha!" Adrian laughed as soon, the gathered mana was the size of the surrounding buildings. And held steady. The demon, still reeling from his damage, started to make its way towards Adrian. It was too late, however, as Void blocked its path. The energy in Adrian's hand ascended into the heavens, and hovered overhead the demon, growing larger. Adrian gave a smile and started laughing malevolently, rivaling even the demon's laughter. "Kerri, I must say you are a damned good woman. Your mana allowed me to combine the powers of demon blood and darkness for my own personal use. You shouldn't have. Heh." Adrian looked down to see a soft smile on Kerri's face.

Void landed himself on the roof of a nearby building after being pushed back by the fiend. Now he watched, curious about the outcome of the fusion.

Adrian teleported into the sky above his energy ball. With a quick thrust, he jammed his hand into the dense energy, and shouted "Unhallowed genesis: Profane indignation!" There was suddenly a pillar of darkness where the mass once was, aimed towards the fiend. A giant hole through his chest was left as the pillar intercepted it. After the excess hit the ground behind the fiend, cutting through like butter, the energy bounced and rose into the air in a wide area surrounding the entire city block. Mana pulsated and was forcibly driven upwards, violently, shredding apart everything from debris to skin as it travels towards the heavens.

Everyone in play was damaged by this sudden upwards rush of mana, except for Adrian. It felt good to him, like a cold fire. All his wounds were healing, and he felt stronger than ever. The fiend's body was still as mana tore through his hide and sent more of his blood and flesh soaring into the air as well.

"What the hell is this?" Void yelled as his entire body felt like it was being torn apart. Void focused his mana on keeping himself together, creating a barrier around himself like when the frost fog hit. His face winced in pain as his body was shot from all over as bullets of mana came

263

from the ground. After what seemed like an eternity for him, the darkness finally dissipated. The remains of the fiend were an empty shell, stuck in a position in reaction to the pain. In its eyes was nothing; all signs of life were gone. The body stood there, arms at their sides like a glorified statue.

Adrian then chuckled as he walked over to Kerri's body, who was conveniently out of range of his last attack. "Try not to die until I've perfected this, please," he patted her unconscious head then snapped his fingers again. The color came back to Adrian's hair, his eye colored in green, and his body slumped over. He had returned control of the body to Keith, where he slumbered on the ground peacefully. His sword collapsed next to him as the mist that followed him quickly faded away.

Void stumbled on the ground, crawling forward; His body was in agony as he angrily looked at the direction of Adrian, now Keith. "Damn you."

In the wake of the destruction, a giant portal opened up behind the fiend. The fiend's body remained unmoving as the portal's perimeter wobbled and misshapen in the time it stood there. "Shit. It's just me now, what is going on now…" Void pushed himself up to sit on his butt, meditating and regaining his strength while he waited.

Chapter 13:
Return!

-Year 277   Malveria, The Paradise City

Basonali, Sylindra-

The field of battle was silent as Void, the only one still conscious, waited to see what would become of this portal in front of him. The lining of the portal oscillated at quicker paces until something squeezed out, something great. A monstrous beast came swimming out of the gateway at high speeds towards the fiend. "Huh?" Void yelped as the creature was drawn to the fiend's body like a bee to honey. It was oddly graceful.

Inches before the beast hit the fiend, a fascinating phenomenon happened to the two. The fiend's body disassembled and broke apart into small sparkles of mana that still shaped to form the same figure as before. Its body appeared more like a constellation of stars located in the same area. As the beast got closer, its body began to share the same qualities. Instead of colliding, their bodies meshed mana like atoms and rearranged into a new form, a fusion between both beings. The terrifying head of the beast sat in place of the fiend's head. The fiend was recovered and regained his limbs, gaining size even further. As a whole, the new being had grown another story, tall and bellowed so all could bear witness.

Void scooted himself back as quickly as he could. "Whelp, that is unexpected."

As he backed up, the portal continued to push out empty air for moments before finally, a group of figures came shooting out of the entrance, directly towards Void.

266

Void held up his arms just in case, and Gaia comes crashing into him, hard. Void's air was forced out by the impact, but he nodded as she patted his shoulder in thanks. One by one, the remaining knights with her began crashing into the ground all around him, especially Blaze, who fell extra hard. Sky tumbled out of the portal last, using his wings to slightly soften his fall. Void got up to his feet and caught his breath, looking around him in the process. "I see you guys somehow made your way to me."

Sky dusted himself off and walked up next to him, staring at the ugly combination in front of them. "I'm glad you're safe man," he said as he put his hand on Void's shoulder and nodded at him. "It uh looks like the thing we were fighting somehow fused with the thing you were fighting."

Ocean and Blaze got up next and posted up next to them. "What in the hell is that!?" Ocean scratched his head.

"Looks like you in twenty years," Blaze chuckled, getting a smack from Gaia behind him in retort. "Hey, I was talking to Ocean," he said, stretching.

"Doesn't matter, I guess," Hail murmured from next to Blaze as he held Gaia up, barely.

"It was rude." Gaia fell back asleep after this, and Hail struggled to hold her up in his own weakness.

"I feel like something was up with that portal though, it feels like it's been days everywhere else, but time stayed still for us as we traveled. My mana should be restored by now, but it's not. But the time we were stuck was suspect," Ocean whispered in Sky's ear.

"Yeah, I understand it, but we have more important things to deal with right now." Sky shoved Ocean back in position as the ground began to shake in the wake of a massive influx of mana that was gathering in the monster's mouth.

"We might need to move, guys!" Blaze shoved the group down through Sky as a beam of mana soared by them and melts through buildings behind them.

"Thanks, Blaze," Sky snickered as he raised himself back to his feet.

The monster began sprinting at them now, at ridiculous speeds. "Is that thing running!? What!?" Ocean grabbed the other side of Gaia's shoulder and helped Hail hobble her in the opposite direction of the monster.

"Knights, scatter!" Sky bursted out his wings and flew up into the air. The rest began to run out in different directions, Blaze and Void at opposite sides of the approaching enemy. Within seconds the monster had reached their position and stood in the middle, raising its arms high into the air.

"Get ready for it!" Blaze yelped as he put his hands up to guard.

The monster slammed its fists into the ground, creating a harsh shockwave, but mana also began to pour out in a circular motion in all directions around them. It was a portal, but it trapped things in the opening like quicksand. Blaze and Void were the first couples caught, Ocean Hail and Gaia were next, unable to get away in time. They all stood their waist-deep in this black ooze, slowly drifting down.

"Eh!? What is this?" Ocean pounded against the ooze pointlessly.

Sky hovered above the monster, looking down at the peril. "Guys! The long-range now! I'll distract him" In a quick motion, the beast stood up and smacked Sky away; far. Sky soared backward, not hitting anything for miles.

The monster now focused its attention on Ocean, who defended Hail, and Gaia, still weakened. It charged another beam of mana and sent it towards them. Ocean held up his hands to block the incoming attack.

"Badong Pa!" Out of safety and into the ooze, Keith came leaping in front of Ocean. His hidden sword swung at the beam. After a short clash, the laser was reflected back towards the monster five times the size. Keith collapsed into the ooze afterward, looking sideways with one eye open.

"Whew! Thanks, man, whoever you are," Ocean said as he sighed.

With both large hands, the monster caught this beam and held it there. While holding it in place, it charged another beam and blasted the beam with more energy. This created an even more massive and menacing blast combining the two. Keith buried his head into the ooze. "Whelp, that was all I had in me."

Just as the blast was to hit them again, a giant portal was created in front of them; large enough to encompass the beam. "Don't worry, I got you!" Void yelled as he had both hands up keeping the portal stable. The connecting portal appeared behind the monster and aimed off into the distance. When the portal opened up, revealing the head of the beam, the beast instantly leaped high into the air, allowing the laser to fly directly under him and off into the distance. Void's mouth gaped open. "Just how nimble is this thing now?"

While it was still in the air, beginning its descent back towards the ground, a searing sound was heard at his level. Cutting through the air at insane speeds, Sky came flying towards the monster, his God slayer scythe equipped. A foot off of the ground, Sky crashed into the beast with his scythe; this caught it off guard and caused it to dip back neck first into the ooze. "Take that!" Sky yelled, clearly irritated.

"Woah, go, Sky!" Ocean said, fist-bumping the air.

With the flick of his scythe, Sky created a funnel of air mana that surrounded the monster, resembling a tornado, but it spun backward. "Xi Qi!" Mana and oxygen began to suck away out of the twister up into the air. The monster swung and roared in frustration but was unable to shake free of the attack.

"Guess now's a good time, Void." Blaze winked at Void, who proceeded to create a small portal under Blaze, inside of the ooze portal. This compounded the dimensions and created a disturbance. Blaze slowly eased his legs free of the portals, and when he got clear begun to charge his mana, standing purely on Void's portal. "Nova wings!" Blaze grew two flaming wings on his back and charged a small blast below him. This blast destroyed the ooze and Void's portal in his spot. Blaze regained stable footing afterward. He stomped on the ground and used his wings to soar him into the air high above the monster surrounded by the funnel. "I'll free you in a sec Void, okay?" he said as he gathered mana in his hands.

Void brushed it off, "Whatever."

"Oh, great lords grant me the power to create the ultimate destruction, kneel before the power of lord Verafelt. Molten Nova!" Blaze's mana grows above his head as his Nova formed and towered over the monster. "Heh! You should've never left the water!" he said as tossed it down towards the beast. The Nova touched the top of the funnel, and moments later, the entire thing was absorbed and swirled around the monster like a flaming tornado. "Oh, that's new," Blaze huffed, clearly winded now.

The flaming tornado damaged the monster, singing it from all sides and causing massive damage, but this did not last long. Inside the funnel, the beast had crossed its arms and gathered mana this entire time. In one move, it expanded its massive body, and with a shell of water mana, it dissolved both attacks at once. A wave of water and mist flailed out all around him. Even the monster huffed and puffed now though, with burn marks and boiling ooze littering its arms and legs.

"Guess that wasn't enough then. Blaze, free Void, and Ocean, I've got an idea to finish this." Sky nodded at Blaze, who was barely staying afloat with his nova wings wearing out quickly.

"Gotcha," Blaze stammered while he sent blasts at Void and Ocean's positions. Before it goes there, though, the oozing portals dissipated, freeing all of them.

Void looked over at the monster curiously, "hm, it must be running out of mana."

Ocean cracked his knuckles and walked forward. "Think I have an idea of what your idea is. Want me to hold him, Cap?" he said.

Sky nodded and pointed his scythe downwards, charging mana into it. The more that gathered, the brighter the golden shine became, almost blinding levels. "Y-yeah, hold him nice and steady." Sky troubled through while holding his scythe still, it shook like a boiling teapot in his hands. Mana from the air and that was released from the funnel began to draw to Sky's scythe. The entire area became a sort of catalyst for Sky as everything in the area opened itself up to send him mana, everything except for the knights.

"Mana whip!" Ocean created a long whip of mana from both of his hands and poured more mana into them to make them larger. Blaze came over and landed next to Ocean.

"I'll assist with the pulling." Blaze opened his arms.

Ocean nodded and proceeded to swing and wrap the two whips around the monster's chest. "Yeah, appreciated." The lashes spiraled around and tightened in one motion, clenching around its rough carcass trapping its arms as well.

The monster tugged and pulled with his arms trapped. The two were towed and slung around back and forth as it flailed about. It then focused itself and stopped tugging, but instead began charging mana inside its mouth.

He faced and targeted Blaze and Ocean as they both met eyes. "Um. I don't like the look of this. "Ocean said, stuck in place holding the mana whip. The fiend began firing rapid-fire mouth beams of dark mana on a direct collision course with the who arresters.

In a moment of quick thinking, Blaze leaped over in front of Ocean, with his back to the fiend. The beams centralized on him and pelted him continuously, creating a minor smoke cloud around him. Ocean was shaken as he watched Blaze wobble in place but stay relatively upright, barely. "Eh, shit. Can't have you losing consciousness, or these whips go, right?" Blaze said, cracking a smile.

"A little help here, Void!" Ocean yelled over as the fiend began charging up again. With a
simple nod, Void acknowledged. This time, when the array of beams came forth, Void's portals saved them, rerouting the rays off into different directions, away from Blaze and Ocean.

"Okay, about ready now, ready yourselves for the shockwave. If this is anything like the others, the orb should be in its center. When I cut it, Ocean and Void, I need you to hop in and grab your orbs. That should make it so it shouldn't recover," Sky commanded while he raised his scythe to his side. It was now glowing brighter than ever like he was holding a star in his hands. The holy wind mana that radiated from his weapon sliced through the air randomly. "Ahem. Hear my calls as I display my blessings. O' Ardin, grant me the power to slay your demons and your angels. Xi...Neng!" After his chant, Sky's God slayer scythe wobbled and shook in his hands. Sky spun around and darted in the air towards the monster. After getting right in his face, he turned again, this time with his scythe raised. With a deep slash, Sky cleaved through the monster's abdomen with one clean swing. The impact created a massive shockwave of light and a streak of mana that soared

272

into the ground behind the monster, forming a crescent-shaped crater as massive as the monster itself. The shockwave was like a gust of wind, but not strong enough to move them.

The knights stood still as they watched the monster's top half glide into the air away from its bottom half. The life in the beast's eyes faded away as both the orb of darkness and water slipped out of its ooze and fell. Ocean ran forward, tapping Void on his shoulder to jolt him into action as well. They both ran and jumped to catch their respective orbs. The top half of the monster plopped on the ground, ooze leaking out slowly. Void and Ocean stared at each other, orbs in hand. The slime began to move and reattach itself. Void looked down at it and immediately crushed his sphere in his hands, Ocean followed suit. Mana from the orbs seeped into their bodies, causing them to glow for a moment. The remains of the monster fizzled and dissolved away at that moment, prompting the two to high five each other.

"Good job, you two." Sky walked up to Ocean and Void, his scythe back to normal. The rest of the knights gathered around Sky and started making camp. By the time they finished, and had it lit, Gaia was awake and on her feet. "Well then, looks like everyone, but Gaia has their orbs now. Any ideas where yours is?" Sky questioned while sitting down next to the fire.

"No idea." Gaia shrugged her shoulders as she looked around, embarrassed. "Uh, any idea where Volt is?" she said, directed at Void.

"Eh, I'm sure he'll be at the portal in time when we get to Polkera," Void said, looking away.

"You don't know? You should go get him now before we find a boat and sail over to our next destination." Gaia's face was slowly getting redder as she spoke. She sat down next to Sky.

"Who knew you fancied him so much?" Blaze walked over and tapped her shoulder while he snickered.

Gaia turned and punched Blaze full force in his arm. He hopped back and shook out his arm, which was numb. "Don't act like you don't care, damnit!" She yelled.

"He-" Blaze started.

"Of course, we care, we just have to believe in him now. It would not be a good idea to go back and not know where he was. He might already be there waiting for us at this point. As the only continent, we haven't been to, it could also be the place to find Gaia's orb." Sky interrupted. "Right, Gaia?" he nudged.

"Yeah, fine whatever let's go already," Gaia protested while crossing her arms, noticing Keith up again.

"I think we could all use a bit of rest, that battle was…very taxing." Void said resting next to the flames, his war-torn body shown in the light.

Keith was still sitting on the ground, cross-legged, where he had fallen. He had his head down, bobbing it back and forth like he was trying to stay awake. Kerri walked over to him, holding her stomach. She stopped right behind him and wobbled there for a moment, afterward dropping down to hug him from the side. She squeezed tightly, causing him to wince in pain.

"I'm so glad you're okay…and that you're still you," Kerri said, nudging her face against his. Keith just nodded silently, his hair flailing over his face. He rubbed the top of her head softly to convey what words could not.

Kerri helped Keith up to go sit next to the fire, next to Void. Void looked up at the two of them as they get comfortable. "You gonna be an okay man? You did a lot of fighting before I got out of that underground hell," he said, turning his body to face them.

Keith nodded again, but this time pursed his lips. "That thing, it had different forms. The first killed off so

274

many priests and bounty hunters before I took it out. I fear after this fight, it'll take a while for the economy and personal here to recover."

Void got up to sit on his knees. "Keith, how long have you used this city as a refuge? I've lived on Basonali most of my life, and I've never been able to come to this place."

"Our group has been using this as a base for about five years. Alex suggested it when we first got together," Kerri interrupted.

"Alex?" Void asked.

"He's kind of like the face of our group, I guess?" Kerri said, looking at Keith. "Keith doesn't like the spotlight too much. He's more of the heart and our muscle." She chuckled.

Keith shook his head, "Alex is our archer and a fantastic artificer. He crafted this sword I have here, and Kerri's blade as well. I'll be okay though, this is nothing. Alex should be around soon to get us out of here." Keith ran his hand over the side of his blade as he spoke.

"I'll have Father John look into getting this place back in order, but in the meantime, we have someone we need to kill." Void holds out his fist towards Keith. "Oh, and thanks for your help too. You're very strong…uh, both of you in there."

Keith cracked a small smile and fist bumps him back. "It's just— Worry not, knowing fate, we'll meet again."

"I guess you guys have to go soon huh?" Kerri said shaking her head.

"Yeah, after we rest up a bit. I'm kinda tireddddd." Ocean said falling out next to the fire as well.

"Don't dry yourself out too much over there Ocean." Blaze chuckled.

"I'm sure it'll take a lil more than a lil flame to do that, for both of us." Hail said slightly aggressively, towards Blaze

"Heh, is that a challenge?" Blaze raised an eyebrow at Hail.

"I still owe you a beatdown now that ya mention it!" Hail shouted starting to get up.

"Will ya'll chill out!" Gaia yelled while throwing a rock at Hail's forehead, causing him to tumble backwards. This sparked a laughter from everyone in attendance, even Keith snickered a bit.

"I know everyone's tired, but we don't have long to stay here. Take a couple hours to recoup, and we are heading out, got it? Also...good job guys, we are almost done our first mission!" Sky said laying back. The knights all nodded along and collapsed for a much needed nap. Even Keith and Kerri took the time to relax for a couple hours.

****
*

Sky was the first to awaken three hours later, getting himself prepared to head out. "Aright guys, wake up! Let's go," he yelled as the knights all jolt up one by one. The Knights gather in the open behind where the fire was.

"You guys be safe now alright? Thanks again for everything," Void said to a still groggy Kerri and Keith as he headed to rejoin the knights.

Kerri waved bye to Void as he walked away. Sky was the first to come up to him. "You expressed our gratitude, I'm sure?" Sky nodded at Void.

"Yeah, he's solid, and there's a lot to learn about him. He seems like a good guy, too, so we might have made ourselves an ally." Void peered back at Keith. Kerri was rubbing Keith's back. "Oh, that reminds me!" He pulled out the rapier he was holding on his person and tossed it at Ocean. "Here, happy birthday."

Ocean awkwardly caught the rapier and looked it up and down. "Woah, you remembered? And hold up…this sword where did you get this?"

"I, uh, picked it up from some guy on the way here. I thought it'd remind you of home." Void shrugged his shoulders.

Ocean nodded as he continued to stare at the sword, a tear rolling down his eye. "Yeah, I know this sword very well. The royal guard's commanders used these when I was training there, years ago. This is an old model, but still so very beautiful. I wonder how it came into the hands of whoever you got it from."

"No idea, but you better take care of it, let's see if it'll bring back some of that old Ocean," Void winked.

"Thanks, Void, I love it," Ocean said, clipping it onto his belt.

"We ready?" Void looked at the knights.

Sky nodded at Void, who proceeded to create a giant portal underneath the knights, they all began to slowly drift downwards. "Onwards to beat the hell out of Scourge, and get him to cough up Wendy," Gaia said, shaking her fist in the air.

"It's still a long road ahead of us guys, this is just the beginning," Sky said, waist-deep in the portal now.

"I really hope Volt is okay, though…" Gaia sighed as she went under.

"Tsk, he'll be okay. I know Scourge won't be, though, when I get my hands on his ass." Blaze went under as well.

The knights all disappear into the portal, and it closed behind them. Keith and Kerri still sat there waiting for the arrival of Alex, who was very late at this point. Moments of silence passed as the two share a moment.

"Muahahaha!" A heart-crushing laugh echoed through the city ruins. "My my, I thought they would never leave." A muffled voice calls out as a dark portal opens up behind the two. Scourge stepped out, holding his mask and staring directly at Keith.

Kerri immediately noticed the bloodlust and turned around with her weapon poised at Scourge's neck. Keith eases himself up, still drained.

Scourge flicked his finger in Kerri's direction, sending out a powerful shock wave that sent her flying back into and through the side of a store. She was knocked unconscious from the impact. "Get out of here, wench," he snickered. Kcith pulled his sword and swung it at Scourge, who caught his hand. With his other, Scourge grabbed Keith's head and began to squeeze. "I have been watching you for a very long time, Keith." Scourge pulled Keith's head close to his own, as he whispered in his ear. Keith struggled and kicked, but he didn't have the energy to truly fight back.

"L-let go…" Keith let out as he was lifted off his feet.

"I want what is inside you. I want Adrian for myself. So you're coming with me so we can rip him out, muahahaha." Scourge opened up another portal and dragged Keith on the ground behind him to enter it. They disappeared into the darkness.

"N-no…shit," Keith whispered as his voice faded away.

****

"Kerri! Kerri! Wake up!" Alex shakes Kerri and pulls her out of the wreckage in the building. He sat her down softly as she tapped her face to wake her. Alex was skinny, wearing a fancy, royal purple robe, and skin-tight white pants. On his back was a long, handmade bow and arrow. Alex takes off his nice jacket and places it under Kerri's head. This revealed two small daggers on his hip and a pure white t-shirt.

"H-huh, Alex? Alex! Alex!" Kerri waked up, and her emotions went from surprise to sadness as she recalled what happened, and began crying.

"What's wrong? Where is Keith?" Alex questioned, trying to calm her down.

"H-he was taken. He was taken from me...my Keith..." Kerri stopped crying but sighed there, her emotions written all over her face.

Alex looked down at her and hugged her tightly. "I'm sorry, who was it? How could they take Keith? He wouldn't let that happen."

"It was after a huge fight, he didn't have any energy left to fight back. And I couldn't protect him." Kerri started crying again. "It was some really powerful demon with a mask on."

Alex rubbed her forehead, "Okay, well, that's our next move. We are gonna find out who this demon was, and we are going to get Keith back."

Kerri nodded, tears coming down slower now. Alex and Kerri both got up and headed towards the docks together, leaving behind a mass of destruction known as the city of Paradise.

-Year   ??? ???   ???, Sylindra-

The wind rustled harshly, blowing the few trees around till their branches broke. A sizable grassy field, filled with mostly dead grass, was interrupted by the bodies of Volt, Sky, Blaze, Void, and Ocean. Blaze and Volt laid face down sprawled over wide tree stumps. Before them stood

Scourge, in all his rage, laughing maniacally at his feats. Of the knights, however, only Blaze was conscious enough to hear it. He slowly raises his head off the stump, looking directly at Scourge, then to the other knights. They were all beaten up, with Void and Ocean sharing grave injuries. "Eh, wha?" Blaze said as he finished surveying the scene.

Scourge, who was crouching on one of the stumps, stood and noticed Blaze is still awake. Blaze blinked and Scourge was gone. A few more times, he blinked, but no Scourge. He looked around, thinking he's crazy, even lifting himself up a bit to help. The next and last thing he remembered was a dark-colored foot cracking into his face. Everything went black after that.

-Year 273 Ryon town Kegato, Sylindra-

Blaze's eyes shot open. He was asleep against a wall in his home town of Ryon. The air was different, though. The usually happy atmosphere was replaced with a pure, eerie silence. "Damn, why do I keep having that damn dream? And who are those people with me?" he said while scratching his head. Blaze soon noticed the silence and rose to his feet. "Hmm, that's odd. It's quiet. I smell the smoked meat, but something else… Is that blood?"

His demeanor suddenly became a lot more cautious as he walked down the street and turned the corner to the left, where the food vendors are. "W-what is…this?" Blaze's mouth gaped open as he saw the massacred remains of his townsmen and women. Dead bodies and blood littered the street. Many shops were absolutely obliterated, with people inside. Bodies were tossed onto the grills used for cooking meats, creating a disgusting burnt hair and skin smell that reeked over the scent of blood.

Blaze peered around in disgust and depression as he was forced to step over the bodies of acquaintances and

280

friends he saw not even half an hour ago. At the end of that street, he heard a loud slosh coming from the square, around the town bank. Blaze dashes around the corner quickly to find the demon that would come to be known as Scourge with his hand through the mayor's chest. The mayor wore an all-white suit, which was a crimson red now as he was face down, hanging from Scourge's hand penetrating his chest.

"Hmmm, he's from my dream…" Blazes said lowly to himself as he watched Scourge toss the mayor's body to the side into a bloody heap.

"Found ya." An ecstatic but creepy smile could be felt from beyond Scourge's mask; he noticed Blaze standing on his presence. "And how marvelous, you're the last one left too," Scourge said, hailing at his work.

Blaze's face changed from a soft sadness to complete anger. "Who are you? And what the hell have you done here?" he said as his anger was received by his mana, and his entire body was engulfed in flames instantly. With a single step for momentum, he sent himself at Scourge like a giant flaming bullet.

Scourge smiled again and punched Blaze in his ribs and knocked him out of his flames; through the bank. A massive hole was made in his wake. Dust and debris flying out of the bank like a dust cloud. "Uh, what?" Blaze whispered as he crashed into the wall.

"Come on you have to try harder!" Scourge yelled as Blaze sat up, blood coming down the sides of his head. Blaze wobbled in place, being held up by the remains of the wall he went through. "You're quite weak, are you sure you were chosen?"

Blaze huffed and puffed while he picked up his head and looked at Scourge. "What are you talking about?" In between breathes, he managed to get out.

"Huh, has no one explained it to you yet? I guess I got here first, no matter." Scourge gathered mana in his left hand as he shook his head at Blaze. The darkness created a sound resembling a loud wind as it accumulated. Just as he was nearly done gathering mana, an echoing clink sounded as Scourge's hand was pierced by Sigrun's lightning charged stab. Scourge peered back as his hand bled profusely, and saw Volt standing a few meters behind him. "Oh, it's you again, here to save the day, I presume?" Scourge chuckled sarcastically.

Volt stood there unmoving as a devastating bolt of lightning came from the sky and struck Scourge. With purpose, Volt ran over and grabbed Blaze out of the rubble and began helping him out of the area. "Who and what are you doing? I have to kill him!" Blaze said with anger and rage.

Volt pushed Blaze along as he fought back. "Just trust me okay?" Volt yelped. After a few moments, Blaze silently nodded and followed Volt out of the town, loud raging yelps coming from behind them.

-Year 277 Scourge's Castle Basement Shadow Path, Umbra-

A dark, dimly lit room with a single swinging torch in the center housed Keith, strapped down to a medical bed, sat all the way back. The torch swung back and forth directly above him, revealing more pieces of the darkroom with each rotation. Surgery intruments were on a table on one side, enchant books and scrolls were on another table on the opposite side. Jars, cursed weapons, and various tools sat on a third table five feet from Keith's feet. Keith awoke as calmly as possible, using his eyes to look around, realizing that his head was strapped down as well.

"Hmm. What is this?" Keith clenched his fist, feeling a noticeable difference. His power was sapped from his body. "I couldn't move even if I wanted to. I haven't felt this sensation before, it all feels numb."

Just then, the door on the far side of the room busted open. Scourge and another figure came walking cockily into the room, talking to one another. The man with Scourge wore a long black medical coat of sorts, with the sleeves rolled up. There were odd markings and insignias carved up and down his arm. His spiky, gray hair was tipped in black and slicked back on his head. A pair of goggles helped his hair sit upon his head. Scourge and the doctor had finally arrived at the side of Keith's bed, standing over him at his feet. The doctor stood with his legs spread wide and his arms behind his back, a big smile on his face. Scourge approached first.

"My my, sorry for my rudeness before when we picked you up. I never introduced myself," Scourge said as he actually removed his mask and did a short bow with it. Scourge's face under his mask was beaten and burned, most of the top layer of his demonic skin burned away. His smile was big, as were his long sharp teeth. His voice was much less muffled and muttered without his mask. Looking at it was hard, though, the amount of raw tissue present. Even Keith avoided eye contact while his head was still forced in one direction. "My name is Scourge. Demon mercenary, positive role model, and proud father if I do say so myself." Scourge replaced the mask on his face.

"Hmph. Yeah okay. Sure. What am I doing here, Scourge?" Keith said, annoyed already.

Scourge put his arms behind his back, "Oh, why I am so very glad you asked. I have been watching you and the other you for quite a while." Scourge began waving his finger in Keith's face. "I like how you…change. No offense but I don't really need *you*, I need the other one. The evil one, I want him on my side." Scourge rested his hand on his own chest.

283

"I think you're mistaken. There's only me." Keith smirked.

"That's not what I've seen, or what I've been told. A mutual acquaintance of ours actually, Edgar? I believe you know him?"

A sweat droplet formed on Keith's forehead and traveled down the side of his head. "Um. W-what?"

"Heh. There's that fear you've been trying to hide." Scourge rose up and patted the shoulder of the doctor, who hadn't moved the entire time, that same smile on his face. "I enlisted the best for this process, though. This surgeon is a master of the dark arts as well. He also studied with the mana in Polkera as well. All that crazy stuff that goes on there, I'm sure if there is a way, he will find it." Scourge laughed and started towards the door, leaving the doctor and Keith alone. "Can't promise it won't be painless!" Scourge shouted across the room, slamming the door behind him as he left.

"Oh, we're going to have fun! I've learned so much about your seal from Edgar." The doctor slithered out in a creepy and uneasy voice while he twiddled his fingers.

"It won't work." Keith stammered; his eyes open wide at the mention of Edgar again. "Not him, anyone but him…" His face turned white.

"Yep, it will. Edgar Wiley told me so much about your seal. Scourge showed me so much in the way of torture. And I've experienced in everything else. We're gonna have so much fun. Hahahahaha!" The doctor cackled as he began sharpening his tools.

It was a hot summer night, and a frightful storm was headed towards the Kingdom of Albon, a small kingdom in Northern Kayard. The weather forbade the things to come on this night. All was quiet in the kingdom; the food and jewelry merchants had packed up their merchandise, the residents had gone to their homes and locked their windows and doors. The streets made of worn stone were all that were left, barren, and dry. Not a sound could be heard, save for the whistling of the wind passing by through the cracks in the wooden houses, and the rustling of the trees. All the animals, dogs, cats, chickens, and even the rodents had found a place to stay for the night, to protect them from the impending storm.

The magi in-town had called for a severe thunderstorm, with whipping winds and stinging rain. It was the calm before the storm, and the only light in the whole kingdom to be seen was from the castle standing in the middle of the town. A giant beacon stood lit at the top of the castle at night, providing a slow flickering light. Standing six stories tall, and made of the most elegant blue marble, imported directly from the Kamas mountains, the castle's beauty could be seen for miles around.

The rulers of the kingdom, King Basile the Proud and Queen Riona, were well-known, as they were one of the few rulers of Albon who had no known enemies; save for the Hiyama's who feuded with everyone. They were even friends with the Giants, who were driven to live entirely in Armageddon by the humans. The Giants, who inhabited Sylindra long before the humans, hold a grudge that lasts throughout the generations. Small statues of famous giants decorated parts of the castle to honor this.

The silhouette of a man could be seen in the castle, walking up and down the hallways lantern in hand. The butler, Genji, had been in the service of the King and Queen since they first took the throne, having been the personal butler of the previous rulers for nearly thirty years. On a night such as this, Genji made sure that all the windows and doors had been shut and locked. It was nights like this that he had to help the guards keep watch, for it was the kind of night where someone would try to break into a castle and steal precious artifacts, or worse.

He was making his final rounds in the castle before he would head off to bed when the storm began. It came quickly, with nearly no beginning, it had immediately started pouring down rain, with bright flashes of lightning and the cracks of thunder sprinkled into the storm. The rain pounded on the windows, and lightning flashes illuminated the entire hall. In between the claps of thunder, there was a faint noise to be heard, the sound of something breaking, which seemed to come from the floor above Genji. He decided he would go check it out, and walked briskly to the nearest flight of stairs.

The sound was loud enough to wake a little ten-year-old boy who was sleeping soundly in his bed. Keith, abandoned at the castle doorstep as a babe, was adopted as the son of the royal family they were never able to have. His entire life, he was never able to figure out why he was so different or how to control the majority of his mysterious powers. Keith kicked off the embroidered blanket that had been covering him, made from the wool of golden-fleeced lambs, and ran to his closet. The boy grabbed his trusty sword, a little two-foot blade that he had made himself, with a little help from their personal master blacksmith. He also made sure to grab his cloak that he had gotten for his birthday from Queen Riona.

After hiding the sword under his cloak, the little boy rushed downstairs, trying to go as fast as he could, yet trying not to wake his parents up. The kid made it to the fourth floor, and stopped to catch his breath, and heard another smashing sound. Keith tried to locate the origin of the noise, but it could have come from anywhere on the third floor. This was the biggest floor in the castle. He peered out the window on his way down, and shifted his black hair out of his eyes to have a good look. The boy saw nothing but rain and lightning, with the occasional branch or hay fly by.

The storm was so loud that Keith was surprised he could even have heard anything other than the wind, rain, and thunder. He finally continued back down the steps, and he peered down to the end of the corridor and saw the broken object, a bright blue vase with gold trimming that his mom had bought for over 800,000 Gold. The boy went down to the vase and tried to pick up the pieces so that he could later ask the magi to piece the shards together before his mom saw it was broken. He cut his hand on one of the pieces, which caused him to wince. The blood from the cut landed on his light blue pajama bottoms. Not wanting his mother to be angry for the potentially ruined pajamas, he began thinking up excuses for the origin of the blood. Maybe Genji or Maria, the new maid could help cover it up for him. Either way, he finished picking up the pieces and put them in a basket nearby.

Suddenly, another noise could be heard, the sound of someone walking up the steps behind him. This caused the boy's heart to skip a beat, as there shouldn't have been anyone awake at this time. He drew his sword out from under his cloak and walked towards the stairs from whence he heard the noises. They were drawing closer with every step, and the possibilities of what was on the other end of those footsteps raced through the boy's mind. It couldn't have been a monster of any sort, there was a definite magic barrier protecting the kingdom that he lived in, and an even stronger one guarding the castle. No robber would be so bold, not in this community.

Then suddenly, Genji's face poked up from the set of stairs. "Young Master, what are you doing up? You should not be up this late at night. Oh dear, look at your pants, you have blood on them. Shall I clean them for you? It'll just be our little secret, before your mother finds out, eh?" He bombarded with statements ending with a quick deep chuckle.

"Yes! That would be awesome, Genji, you are the greatest." Keith said, putting his sword back in his cloak. "There was something or someone up here. The vase that used to be over by the fourth guest bedroom broke, and there were no windows opened."

"Yes, unfortunately, that is what I was here to check out. This storm is almost deafening, but I am thankful for that wonderful stone that is protecting us from this monstrosity. My bet is it was a neighborhood cat, who somehow could have gotten in before we closed the doors and windows, but it still would be safe to check things out. Shall we discover who the devil is making all this noise together?" Genji asked as he pulled out a vial from his vest. He knelt and poured it on the boy's pants, and in an instant, the stain was gone.

"Yes, I want to know! And then I can tell all my friends down at the sword-arts school," the little boy said.

"Well then, let us go, but don't forget to be quiet, we don't want to alert whoever is making all this noise. Though I doubt they could hear much over the sound of this storm either," Genji said.

So off they went, back up two flights of stairs that Keith had just come from, and up to where the parent's bedroom was. The thunder was getting louder and louder as the storm neared. The rain drowned out the sound of the footsteps of the two, and the wind made a violent hissing noise as it blew through the cracks all throughout the house. Genji chanted something, and his lantern grew brighter as there were hardly any windows on the fifth floor, as per the advisory's direction. Too many windows could mean an easy kill for an archer on the outside. They walked down the hallway, which seemed to take a lifetime. The constant repetition of purple and black, which made up the carpet covering the hall, was slowly lulling the little boy back to sleep, but he knew he couldn't fall asleep. He had to help protect Genji and Maria. They finally made it to the end of the hallway and found the door to the bedroom open, but not a single sliver of light came out of the door.

"Stay here, let us see what is going on, oung master," Genji said to the little boy. He proceeded to the room, and Keith gripped the hilt of his sword. He wasn't sure what was in his parent's room, but his sword-arts teacher always taught him to be ready for anything. Genji peered into the room, and then put two fingers to his ear. "Tch, no response," Genji mumbled under his breath and started to go in.

The little boy tried to follow, but Genji told him to stay there and wait for him to come out. After a few moments, Genji came running out of the room. The little boy could see the look of horror on his face and rushed to see what was wrong. He was too late, though, for, at that moment, a giant shroud of darkness covered Genji and sucked him back into the bedroom, closing the door with a loud slam! There was a lot of screaming, and the sound of things being thrown everywhere. Then, there was silence. Not a peep to be heard.

The little boy's mind raced to try to figure out the situation. His knees grew weak, and he almost wanted to run back to his room, hide under his covers, and wish that this had never happened. But he couldn't do that, he had to remain stable. He put his hand to his chest, which under the pajama top bore the seal that Basile said was a symbol of his strength, and to never fear. "I can do this!" Keith said to himself. Genji would have run in without a second thought and try to rescue me if I was in trouble.

The little boy fought back the tears of fear, and rushed to the door. Keith chanted a small incantation, and his eyes glowed a faint yellow, allowing him to see in darkness, if only for a little. Frantically, he hacked at the door with his sword until it was weak, and knocked the rest down with a hard tackle. The kid knew that his side would hurt in the morning, but didn't care about that at the moment. He got up waving around his sword, and looked around the room, seeing nothing but blackness. No sign of his parents, nor Genji. Where could they have gone? Where were his mom and dad? He had no time to think, as suddenly he heard a noise, looked around, and barely dodged an incoming attack. "Whoa!" he said, cowering to the side.

Two daggers had been thrown at him and landed behind him, in a chair in the corner of the room, creating an unusual thud. He looked up and saw two figures hanging from the ceiling. He couldn't see who they were, because they too had been covered in darkness, but he could vaguely make out their body types. One was a hulking muscular figure, and the other a more slender figure, most likely a guy and a girl. They slowly dropped to land on the ground, rising back up in front of him.

"Ok, ok, this is it!" Keith grabbed his sword and quickly lunged at the two figures, which dodged and slithered behind him. He turned, and lunged again, this time the two didn't dodge; they pulled out swords from seemingly nowhere, and clashed swords with Keith. The boy pulled back and swung again and again, but to no avail.

One of the blades from the shrouded figures connected with the boy, leaving a gash on his arm. "Is this the power of the darkness?" Keith questioned to himself. The feminine figure snapped its fingers, and a few thin blades of ice appeared in her fingers. "An ice user reminds me of mother. But you're nothing compared to her," the little boy mumbled. Thankfully, he knew the counter to ice, which was fire. He muttered under his breath, and a blaze of orange flame encircled his sword. The shadow threw her ice needles at the little boy, but the boy saw it coming. He weaved in and out and used the flame from his sword to ward off any that would hit his body.

He rushed towards the feminine figure and melted any ice that was thrown at him with the flames, but it was then that the other appeared and stabbed Keith's shoulder. It didn't go very far into him, and the character just cocked his head to the side, almost as if he was curious as to why it didn't go through. What he didn't know, was that it had hit a pocket of pure mana, right by the seal placed on Keith's chest. He retracted his sword and jumped back next to the female shadow. They cocked their heads together and then proceeded to charge at Keith.

Keith was seemingly in a trance, staring straight forward at the assailants. What they didn't notice, however, was that the boy's faint yellow eyes had started to glow blue, keeping only a hint of the yellow. The figures swung at Keith, who, still in his intrinsic state, instantly dodged, and tightly gripped his sword. He swung his sword with a ferocity that the figures could do nothing except block against. The fire on the sword burned bright, and pretty soon, it was the only thing you could see of the sword. He swung his sword several times, and the flames fired out of the sword in waves. The figures, on the pure defensive now, only dodged; where there may have been an opening before, it was instantly greeted by a wave of flame. Keith gave a flick of his wrist and created a massive wave and then disappeared into thin air. The figures dodged the waves but were then greeted by surprise with the blade in Keith's hand. In one critical strike, they crumpled to the ground, and didn't get up; they only oozed black darkness that seeped out of their pores and slithered out of the door like a snake.

Keith's eyes reverted from blue back to yellow. He took a few moments, looked around the room, and then felt the two figures at his feet. "They are dead, I killed them. I actually killed something. Woohoo!" The little boy yelled, doing a little victory dance, "I got them! I killed them! But hmm. Where are mom and dad? And Genji?" Then suddenly, there was a burst of light in the center of the room with such force that it knocked the little boy back into the wall, and immediately extinguished the flames. The light died down, and he opened his eyes slowly, but once they were fully open, he couldn't believe what he saw. The black veil was slowly going away from the room. The chairs in the corner were occupied by Genji and the new maid, Maria, each with multiple daggers sticking out of their bodies, crimson blood oozing from their wounds. Their glassy eyes no longer held life in them. The room itself was stained with the same crimson color that covered Genji and Maria on that note.

"Was this the work of that shadow?" It wasn't until that point that the little boy noticed the two figures in the middle of the room. The darkness had gone from them as well, but what the boy saw he couldn't believe; under the remains of the shadows were his parents, lifeless and lying in a pool of red velvet.

"M-m-mom? D-dad? Wake up! The darkness is gone! I saved you! Wake up. Please," the boy cried. His parents wouldn't move, nor would they ever. He ran over to them, knelt down, and hugged them. It wasn't until then that he noticed the big sword mark streaking across their backs, the source of the hue that now stained the marble floors of the castle. It suddenly hit him. He did it. He had killed them.

His face contorted into a grotesque shape. He killed his parents. He lost everything in one night. Furious with anger and rage, Keith knocked over the flower pot that was behind him on a study table his dad used to study botany. He swung his sword at anything that could be cut, and once he ran out of energy, he proceeded to cry. The tears streamed out and didn't stop. He wanted to climb back up in his bed, and go back to sleep, and wake up, and have everything back to normal. It was going to be his birthday that coming morning.

A little while later, the little boy heard a shuffling noise coming from outside of the room, but couldn't pinpoint where it was coming from. He grabbed his sword and slowly got up. As if a puppet, his legs dragged him in the direction of where he believed the noise was coming from. Upon approaching the door out of the room, he heard a voice call out to him from down the hallway.

"What's wrong young one? Hey! You don't look so good." This character was a very unusual looking person, wearing a dark purple coat and green slacks. A light blue dress shirt and a black top-hat decorated his head. The man took off his hat and gave a small bow. Keith saw he had black slicked-back hair. "What's your name, kid?" the man asked.

"I'm Kei…" The boy began but was immediately interrupted.

"Wait wait wait wait wait. Where are my manners?" The man put back on his top-hat and walked towards Keith. He kept walking all the way till he got to the doorway where Keith stood. "I am Edgar Wilcy, but just call me 'Ace.' That's what everyone calls me anyway. Why don't we play a game? That'll cheer you up! Won't it?" Edgar said, holding out his hand for a shake.

"Wait, how did you get here?" Keith shyly asked with his head down.

"Worry not about that. One thing at a time, right?" Edgar said as a smile crept on his face.

"Yes. What game?" Keith asked, but there was no emotion in his voice. It was as if he acted on instinct alone, but wasn't mentally there, still scarred from what had just occurred.

"Let's have a little duel. If you fight me and manage to hit me with your sword, I shall give you powers beyond your wildest dreams. Powers, which might just be able to reverse what happened tonight." Edgar looked in the room, grabbed Keith's chin, and pointed it towards the place that began to stink of iron.

"And if you lose, you will come with me. Nobody is going to believe you when they see your dead parents, dead servants, and you, alive, with their blood on you. I'll teach you things you wouldn't believe were possible and will become so powerful. I know there were always things you wondered about yourself. I can help you with that. Now, that sounds like such an honest game. In fact, you have the advantage, seeing as how skilled you are with a sword, and me being completely defenseless. In fact, I'll let you have the first shot. Easy enough, right? All you need to do is beat a completely defenseless person. Should be easy enough for *you*, at least, right?" Edgar teasingly made an imaginary circle around his stomach, signaling an invisible target on him.

Keith didn't hesitate and immediately started running towards Edgar. He lunged with his sword. He didn't quite make it, as he curiously fell to the ground. It looked like Edgar's shadow had tripped him, but that had to have been his eyes playing tricks on him. Just as he was sitting up, Edgar squatted down and flicked Keith on the forehead with such force it toppled Keith back. "I win! I win!" He started clapping and dancing around.

Keith sat up and held his head with both hands. He started to feel tears well up into his eyes, as the emotions he had been holding back began to flow freely again. "I don't want to be here anymore. What do I do?" he said, lip starting to quiver.

A smile beamed on Edgar's face. "Why you just come with me, that's all there is to it. If you would like, I could let you sleep while we traveled to my home, give you time to forget everything that's happened here," Edgar said, nodding his head.

Keith nodded his head back. "I... I have voices inside my head that say mean things. My powers sometimes change too, but my butler says I'm not myself when it happens. I don't want to hurt you, Edgar, after you're being so nice and helping me," he said, wiping some of the tears out of his eyes.

Edgar shook his head. "Worry not young prince, I am powerful, you cannot hurt me..." He stopped and snapped his fingers like a light bulb just went off in his head. "I've got an idea, Keith! Would you like to hear it?" he asked with a big smile on his face.

"Mhmm." The young boy nodded.

"If you come with me, I will help you to learn to control your powers", Edgar came over and waved his hand across Keith's head. Sparkles flew out, and Keith was out like a light. Edgar picked him up, muttered an incantation, and disappeared into thin air. He and the little eleven-year old boy. Keith left his precious sword and his slain family behind, along with the peaceful path that could have been.

As quickly as the storm came, it went, and there was naught but peace and quiet throughout the kingdom again.

Luvenesyar

Ardín

Armageddon

Kritie Jungle, Sylindra

Kanatas Port, Sylindra

Ula Town Center, Sylindra

Chapter 14:
Chaos Clouds

-Year 277 Polkera open lands Repshera, Sylindra-

The knights arrived in what felt like a land of wonders. The ground was hard and barren, but magic filled. From the clouds to the fog that dropped down at waist level, small electric charges pulsed through them with mana from many different elements. It looked like a light show when the different colors fluttered across the sky, right in front of them like neurons in a brain. Reds, blues, purples, yellows, greens, all flew past and around them. When an element matched one of the knights, it would sting them slightly before moving along.

"Wow. What is this place?" Gaia looked wide-eyed at the wondrous mana cloud they had to walk through.

"Welcome to Polkera, Rapshera," Void said aloud, his arms open wide. "I've only been here once before, as a child. I guess that's why I was able to actually take us here. Don't know much about this place, but I would be careful touching the different manas flowing through these clouds, though." Void's words fell on deaf ears as the knights began waving their hands through the clouds for the sensation, like children. They resorted to playing with it while they continued.

Void led them through the seemingly never-ending path of clouds, visibility very limited. His time in the cave seemed to have improved his senses. Sky had tried flying above the fog, but to no avail. "It just never ends, I guess, even trying to push the wind forward doesn't seem to make a difference, the air is too thick." Sky flew lower, trying not to lose sight of his companions.

302

"There should be a cabin around here somewhere. I remember Grandmaster telling us it was important," Blaze said, looking around aimlessly.

"Hope it's around here soon, this is getting ridiculous." Ocean was dragging a bit behind, his affinity to the mana was more sensitive than the others so it weighed him down.

As they continued, randomly, a dark brown elemental orb in the same style as the others appeared in front of them. They all stopped and stared at it. "Uh, Gaia, there's no way it's gonna be that easy for you is there?" Hail looked back at her while she stepped up towards it.

Gaia stops in front of it and looks the orb over as it floats there. "Should I?" she asked, looking up at Sky, one of her arms already outstretched towards it.

"It's probably a trap." Sky and Void both said simultaneously.

"But, we haven't gotten this far by being scared, go for it. We have your back." Sky nodded at Gaia, who grabbed the top of the orb and pulled it out of the cloud. The ground began shaking violently as soon as she touched it.

"Oh dear," Gaia looked down at the orb, then back up to Sky as the shaking got worse. "Hehe, maybe you were rig-!" Before she could finish talking, what resembled a large snake's tail, made of a mixture of different types of rocks wrapped around her and pulled her down. Gaia was shoveled through an open area underground. It was a sizable capsule-shaped opening with digging holes in multiple places along the walls and the uneven ground. These giant holes signified something huge burrowing down here. Puddles were littered about, signifying an underground spring was located somewhere nearby.

Gaia fell on her face after the tail released her. She took some time to wash her face in a puddle near her, and looked forward to seeing the gargantuan snake made of rocks and mana towering over her. The figure of a snake was smoothly mimicked by different types of stones, even the long fangs were carved out of stones. The being still hissed at Gaia convincingly though, somehow. She could feel the massive cluster of mana holding the rocks together.

"Well, hello to you too!" Gaia punched her hand aggressively at the snake that opposed her.

The snake hissed at her again, causing her to charge at it, mana enhancing her hands; this caused them to glow brown on her skin and yellow in the aura around it. The snake dodges her initial swing gracefully, slithering to the other side of the room. Its tail got hold of Gaia's ankle and swept her off her feet and into the air. After a slam into the ceiling and a nearby wall, Gaia was slammed into the ground. "Ooff." Gaia exhaled as her chest was devoid of oxygen. She punched the ground and pushed herself back up, hyperventilating in the process to get air back. As soon as Gaia lifted her head, a horde of stalagmites rushed towards her, a gift from the earth snake.

"Hmph, no thanks!" Gaia punched the ground again, this time manipulating earth with her mana to shoot up a small wall in front of her. The spikes crashed and broke against the wall. Gaia heard hissing approaching quickly, and before she could react the snake came from around the right side of the wall, jaws wide. In one motion, the snake lunged at Gaia and clenched its jaws around her. Gaia used her mana to gather earth to reinforce her arms to block the jaws from crushing her. "Ahhhhhhh!" Gaia shouted as she struggled to hold the snake's mouth open.

After steadying the jaws, Gaia slid her arms out and let them slam shut. She held the snake's mouth closed afterward as she leaped into the air and let off a stiff, sturdy, kicks that launched the snake's body back, rocks flying in many directions along the way. After she settled herself back on the ground, Gaia took this time to change her stance. Her left fist was out in front of her, her right hand was open above her head, elbow bent. The lower half had her weight focused low on her back leg, as he left was outstretched. Gaia let out a massive sigh as the snake regained composure and began charging at her again. "Hmph, let's break em' Kirici," Gaia smirked as a shiny, brown, and long bo staff was summoned into her hands.

Just in time, Gaia twirled the Kirici, the breaker bo staff, and slammed it into the lower half of the snake. It was then spun into the air and crashed into a corner. Before it could recenter itself, Gaia swung the staff and summoned earth stalagmites of her own that spiked out of the walls and pinned the snake in the pile it's in. Only its head was free out front and upright. The spikes formed a web of sorts, skewering the rocks in the snake's body and kept it in place.

The snake hissed loudly as Gaia approached, twirling Kirici back and forth aggressively. "Kötülük için merhamet yok. Crack ve şut, kırıcı sürücü! No mercy for the evil. Crack and smash, Kirici. Breaker drive!" The tip of Kirici shone brightly as mana spiraled around it, and Gaia rushed at the snake's head, who hissed even louder the closer she got. With a last spinning combination and a spin move for momentum, Gaia swung at the snake with an uppercut motion with her bo staff. She connected just under the snake's chin, severing its head and sending it crashing directly up through the layers of earth and towards the surface. A thick pillar of stone followed, sealing the hole the skull was sent through. Gaia sent Kirici away as the remainder of the snake's body that was trapped, crumbled away into pebbles.

"Ugh, now I gotta go back and find the others," Gaia said, swiping her hair back and punching the ground. Gaia's mana created a small platform that rose with her, through one of the travel holes the snake created, back to the surface.

Gaia ran up and stopped behind the others out front of a mysteriously placed wooden cabin. It was rather sizable, with metal bracing the wood logs that ran along the sides. A long lightning rod stuck out of the top of the cabin. This rod created a force field twenty meters in diameter around the cabin. This barrier blocked out the mana in the chaos clouds, creating an area free of the troublesome fog. The orbs in the knights glowed as they walked past the mana barrier and lined up next to each other out in front.

Gaia eased up in line next to Sky. "Hey sorry I'm late. Least, I finally found my orb," Gaia said as her orb glowed along with the rest of the knights now.

"Good job Gaia," Sky said as he fist-bumped her.

"Oh my, company. Don't get that often around here." A voice was heard as the front door of the cabin swung open and a woman walked out. It wasn't easy to tell as she had a Scourge-type oriental mask on, her blond hair tied back in a ponytail, and wore a long white cloak that was opened in the front. Her skin-tight, black pants folded perfectly around her curvy, but slim legs. Large heavy-duty, dark-colored boots dressed her feet. The woman leaned on the open door with her arms crossed. "You must be the knights ol' John told me about. I can see the shine in those orbs a mile away, even in these chaotic clouds." She smiled at them as she raised her mask over her head, reached back, grabbed a bowl of food, and began munching. She had pale skin and beautiful blue eyes. "You'll have to excuse me; been working all morning. Haven't had time to eat."

"Cute," Ocean mumbled under his breath.

Hail jabbed him in the ribs with his elbow and smirked at Ocean, "what was that, buddy?"

Ocean shook his head and played it off. "Nothing."

Sky shook his head and stepped forward, changing the subject. "So how do you know Father John, and what are you doing out here?" He questioned.

"Also, what's your name?" Void interjected.

The woman smiled and finished her chewing, lowering her bowl. "Come, let's talk inside. It'll be a little less chilly." She waved them over as she turned and walked back inside, leaving the door open behind her.

The knights all looked at each other and shrugged. They followed behind Sky as he led them up to the door. "This better not be another trap," Gaia said, following behind them.

Once inside, the door shut behind them. The entire cabin was assembled in a single room. In the back corner was a cot for sleeping and a small table. The other end had a fire pit and an oversized pot for cooking. In the center of the ceiling, a hole led to the chimney. A thick pole dug into the floor over a magical circle. This gave the barrier outside its power. Closer to the door, however, were all the alchemy testing kits. Vials of different elemental mana in different sized containers were marked in line. Large books of notes, full of scribbles and doodles, were on the table to the left with the vials. Mini pots with accompanying fire pits were on the right side of the room, five of them in total, spaced out well. Suspended above them were cups of mana that boiled violently. The woman turned around to face the knights, her hands clasped together at her chest. "My name is Sierza, welcome to my workshop." She said, letting out a half-smile.

"Wow, this is insane. What goes on in here exactly? Mixing mana?" Hail asked, looking at the pots boiling.

"Close, actually!" Sierza raised a single finger into the air. "Father John and I discovered this place had begun emitting that odd mana about five years ago before you guys got together. He helped me to set up here so I could study and figure possible uses for such an anomaly. And. That. Is. What. I. Did." She was shaking with excitement, obviously enjoying this.

"So. Cute when she's passionate about something," Ocean thought out loud.

"What was that?" Blaze jabbed at Ocean. Ocean shook his head and looked away.

Sierza waved at them to all follow her over to one of the desks; it had dishes with different mana dropped on separate sides of the same square plate.

"This is fire mana, and this is lightning mana," she said pointing to the mana on either end of the plate with a metal mixing tube. The knights all gathered around the table to take a look. "Now, I pre-balanced the amount of energy in each sample of mana for this demonstration, but it is normally tough to level out the mana in different elements to match each other. Also, if I try to mix them when they aren't equal, there are unexpected consequences." She was focused on drifting the two puddles of liquefied mana closer together. It was a soft goo that was mostly a dark gray with hints of other colors, though only slightly. It coagulated like eggs after condensing into a liquid and left a residue as it slid across the plate.

Sky looked concerned as he looked at Sierza. "Uh, what exactly happened when you mixed it incorrectly?" he asked.

Sierza chuckled to herself. "Oh, I just almost blew up the lab a couple times. When that didn't happen, one element held more influence in the final product than the other, anyway! Shall we?" She inched the two even closer to each other until the tips of the mana touched. The contact

308

created a reaction that produced a flash, and the entirety of mana on the table morphed into one, with properties of fire and lightning. The change was almost instantaneous, and it emitted a stronger aura than both previous mana on their own. It also slightly pulled everyone in while it was releasing energy, another side effect of the reaction. The blob that resulted in pulsated and radiated with energy in place.

The knights were frozen in awe and amazement, opening Sierza up to continue. "The same type of mana exists in all of you as well soooo…theoretically…it should work on humans as well. Of course, I have no idea how it'll work or what would happen, heh heh. So, uh, who's ready to try it?" she asked, looking around at the room.

Hail waved his hand at this with rejection. "Wait, wait what? You expect us to do this uh fusion, with our bodies?" When he finished, the blob had powered down and slowly separated into both of the individual mana samples, gaining the attention of Hail for the moment.

Sierza reached over and grabbed a piece of diced meat out of her bowl and put it in her mouth. "Yes, yes, I do. From my tests, it is a temporary merge that gives a large boost in strength while active. Now how long it'll last with you guys is for you guys to determine," she said still chewing. "I call it Contact *Fusion*. When your mana gets in a certain vulnerable, malleable state, it can meld with other elements in that same state. And luckily for you, I know how to do it." Sierza smiled widely, it wasn't as genuine as her others, though, and it was noticeable.

Ocean looked at her sideways. "Is it…safe?"

"Totally." Her smile began to crack at the seams. "I mean, I haven't done it with humans before, of course, but it should be okay. Come on, step outside with me." Sierza said as she grabbed a bucket of vials and walked back into her lawn."

"I am not sure about this at all," Void said under his breath as he followed the knights back outside.

The knight's file in front of Sierza, each taking a vial from her and making space for themselves. They look at and shake the dark liquid that housed itself in the bottles. "What is this, Sierza?" Blaze asked, sniffing it and cowering away.

Sierza pointed to the vial. "That is a substance I created to make the mana in your body unstable."

"What?" Blaze yelled, pulling it back away from his mouth. The rest of the knights followed suit and looked at her, confused.

She chuckled. "Yep, it is the only way for the contact fusion to work. Don't worry, your mana should stabilize after your first fusion. So! Don't act like a wuss and just do it!"

Ocean stepped up a moment, holding his vial. "She's right! Let's just trust her and do it. She did all this work to help us get stronger," he said as he scrunched his face and took back the vial with a single gulp. "Ahhh, see, totally fine." Ocean's face was scrunched in disgust as if he had just sipped medicine. His mana flared for a moment, then settled with a calm aura around him. Sierza smiled at Ocean, causing him to blush a little, even with his current ugly face.

"Ugh, screw it! I can't let ole wet willie over there beat me." Blaze chugged his vial vigorously and tossed it to the ground. His experience was different, though. Blaze immediately hunched over in pain as his mana flared out in random directions around him, singing the earth and the air.

Sierza pulled out a notepad from the bottom of the vial container and began writing. "Hmm, interesting, so Ocean's stronger control of his mana is prevalent here," she mumbled out loud. Blaze grumbled in pain in the background.

One by one, the knights began taking the vials like shots and attempting to get their mana calm again. Only

Void and Gaia had adverse reactions, though not as bad as Blaze. Void, after sipping the vial began having issues controlling the sustainability or size of his portals. They wobbled and failed constantly, making them very hard to control. Gaia simply could not maneuver the earth at all how she did before, causing her great frustration. Blaze, on the other hand, had troubles adjusting the strength of his flames. They would burn bright like volatile explosions, making it dangerous to train directly near the other knights.

"Hmm, that wasn't too bad," Sky chuckled and received a stiff punch to the arm for it from Gaia.

"Ow. Guess you're still working on controlling your new boost in power with your orb. Sorry. I understand Blaze's lack of control, but why you Void?" Sky asked.

Void was hunched over in pain. "Eh, there's a lot of foreign darkness that has been through me lately. I'll be fine, though." The day went on as the knights trained with controlling their mana in this new state. An hour after everyone else had finished, Blaze was finally able to bring down the strength of his flames. He walked confidently up to the group afterwards.

"Ahhhh! Let me fuse already," Blaze called out. Sierza was still taking notes throughout the process for all of them.

"Woah now Blaze, you only just got a handle on things. I'm just glad none of you are dead. John would have killed me ha-" She stopped as a bright holy light shone behind her. The light soon materialized into a portal behind her, blowing her hair and clothing all over. Out came Father John with his glistening armor standing directly behind Sierza. "O-Oh, hello there?"

"I'm glad they aren't dead, too," John said with a smirk.

311

"That's him...it really is... I've heard so much about the famous Grandmaster." Hail said, bowing his head to Father John.

John patted Hail. "Wendy has told me so much about you and Gaia growing up. It's nice to see you all grown and with my team of warriors." He looked around at the knights, noticing the absence of one. John swiftly walked over to Sierza and grabbed two of the vials. He drank one, then held out the other. "It seems we are missing one," Father John said, holding his hand out ahead of him.

Sky sighed. "Yeah, we were forced to come here first and wait for his arrival."

Void shook his head to himself. "Yeah, I kick myself, but I was forced to send him there alone, it's worried me because I couldn't even finish my own sacred beast on my own."

Father John waived his finger at the knights. "Disappointing. But that is why I'm here now. To bring you guys together again before this next chapter in your journey. In the future, be sure not to leave your fellow knights behind. That is not how we do things." He outstretched his fingers as his hand began to glow with his holy aura. White lightning started to scatter and flicker all around his arm and in front of him. "Come to me, my son," John said as a horizontal white portal appeared about six feet off the ground. It pulsed with electric fury, more oppressive with each passing moment.

Gaia held her hands together, happy to see Volt again. Blaze was rising back up to his feet, converting the pain to rage. The rest of the knights wait patiently. Sierza walked over and stood next to Ocean while they waited. Ocean noticed, but purposely avoided looking over at her.

The portal was now in full swing as the center opened up and down-dropped Volt and Scatha, surrounded by a white mist. They plopped down, coughing and looking

312

around, confused. Scatha's demonic aura was summoned as she landed, her pale gray skin glistening with slight sweat droplets. Blaze noticed the demon girl and immediately ran over, summoning his sword and swinging at her face in one motion. Volt, mist still in his eyes sensed this and blocked his strike with his spear. The shockwave from the clash exploded and cleared the fog. They stood still, struggling there for a moment. "Who is this, Volt?" Blaze yelled, his rage reaching critical levels, and his mana expanding in all directions, holding the others back.

"Blaze! What are you doing?" Sky called out to him.

"Who...is this girl?" Gaia quietly said to herself while she tried to look away.

Father John looked at Volt as well, curious. Sierza has walked over and whispered in his ear. "Let this play out, it might help things," she said. John calmly backed away as well.

Volt forced Blaze's sword back and got up, pulling Scatha back with him, and holding her behind him. "Stay back here, okay." He calmly said to her. Scatha cowered back, shyly. "Blaze! Stop this, she is the one who saved my li—" Before he could finish, Blaze dodged past Volt and lunged at Scatha. Volt tripped him and kicked him off to the side. Blaze caught himself and kipped up before approaching again. Volt sped off to the side and stood between Blaze and Scatha. Blaze ran at Volt and kicked forward, connecting with the side of Volt's spear as he blocked. Blaze stepped up on top of the spear and propelled himself into the air towards Scatha. "Shit." Volt tossed his spear back at Scatha's feet and teleported to it just in time to parry Blaze's sword strike. Blaze angrily rose back up and now began swinging at Volt, who dodged and blocked conservatively.

"Why is that demon with you Volt!" Blaze unveiled a flurry of sword strikes and finished it with a blast of fire.

Volt dodged, but the explosion still burrowed towards Scatha.

"Shit!" Volt quickly spun around and stuck his spear into the ground. He clapped his hands together facing the blast. "Erupt and eradicate, shatter their hopes for they failed to embrace the goddess…and I will punish them. Inazuma!" Volt rushed through the line and let out his own mana blastwave that destroyed Blaze's. "Blaze! Stop! Let me explain." Volt got caught by Blaze while his back was turned as Blaze wrapped his arm around Volt's neck and suplexed him.

"You have burned my trust Volt; never thought it'd be you; you know what they did to me!" A tear in his eye, Blaze aimed Volt's head for the ground as he tumbled them back. Before they hit the ground, Volt teleported to his spear to avoid the impact. Blaze plunged back on the ground and rose to a knee.

Volt grabbed his spear out of the ground and spun around vertically, his heel clad with electricity. "Spiral Tap! His heel connected with Blaze's shoulder, stunning his entire body. "Now, give me a moment to talk," Volt said as Blaze struggled and grumbled to get up.

"Stop them, Sky! Or you, Grandmaster!" Gaia yelled as she was held back by Hail.

"Just let them be, it'll settle itself out." Sky said, peering back at Gaia.

"Why is he so angry?" Gaia said, finally calming herself.

Sky sighed. "Well…"

Void put his hand on Sky's shoulder. "Blaze lost everything to demons like Scourge. His entire hometown was wiped out, his parents were ripped apart, just about everything bad that has happened in his life was caused by demons. He felt Volt should understand this more than anything because Volt saw firsthand what Scourge did to his people," Void said, directing attention back to the fight.

John tossed the spare vial at Volt, who caught it with his free hand.

"What's this?" Volt shook it at Father John, who simply motioned to drink it. Blaze's struggles began to work, and he fought his way up through the shocks. Volt took the vial to the head and tossed it down. "Bleh, what is that?"

Blaze turned his attention to Scatha, then his eyes opened wide. "Volt. Her eyes…they look just like his. You can't tell me you didn't notice!" Blaze's rage started to seep out of his body again in the form of a flaming mana storm. All of his mana began to gather in his left hand as it shined bright. "I'm sorry, Volt, I cannot allow her to live." From his forearm to his hand, Blaze's arm began to resemble a torch's flame. "Take this. My rage, my anger, and all of my fury!"

Volt tossed his spear to quickly teleport himself in front of Scatha. As he skidded over, he began gathering energy of his own in his right hand. Lightning chirped and skipped around his arm as mana raised rapidly. "Didn't want it to come to this Blaze, but I absolutely cannot allow you to kill her."

Father John waved over to Volt, "Volt. On the upcoming clash, make sure to say 'contact,' okay?" Volt looked over at him funny, but shrugged his shoulders. "Just trust me," John said.

"Sure." Volt held his arm to control his mana as it began to destabilize.

Out of nowhere, a stream of water came slithering out of the air like a snake and splashed on Blaze, temporarily putting out his flames. "I can't let this go on; Volt stop him!" Ocean yelled.

Blaze looked absolutely furious, and wet. Steam was everywhere around him, heating up constantly.

315

Volt ran at Blaze with his mana fully charged. "Lucin, grant me the power to strike down all who oppose you! Ringa Uira!" His hand exploded with lightning mana, and he aimed it for Blaze's body.

"This is unacceptable, and no one gets it!" Blaze lit up again, flames exploding from him like a bomb. Moments before Volt got to him, Blaze took a step forward, his hand flaring up again. "Searing finger!" Blaze and Volt's hands were on a collision course, each with a considerable stake of mana behind them.

"Graaaaahhh, contact!" Volt screamed just as their hands met.

Their clash sent out a dome-like shockwave that blew everyone back. The giant orb of energy that was created shot out lightning and flared periodically as the energy in it began to expire. The knights dusted themselves off as they watched the orb leave behind a crater in the earth as it shrank. Sierza clapped in place as she got out of Void's lap, who happened to catch her. "Ooo, lovely! It worked!" she said, happy.

"What the hell was that?" Hail said, picking Gaia up off the ground.

"Here he comes," Grandmaster said, dusting himself off. The orb now disappeared and left an utterly foreign figure in the center of the crater.

Neither Blaze nor Volt were present, but the figure that was, stood there staring at his hands; traces of lightning and fiery mana swirled around his body. He had spiky yellow hair, with red accents that were longer in that back and slicked back on the top. The base of his outfit was black with armor that was a meld of yellow and red metal as well. From the shoulder plates to the chest and leg plates, and over to the lighter gauntlets and grieves, the shiny metal glistened with mana constantly pulsing through it. His weapon was a mixture of a spear and a sword. The blade was very long, and curved back like a hook, a red streak lined through the center of the edge. There was even a blade that rose out of the top of each of his boots. He remained there, staring at his hands.

"It...actually worked!" Sierza happily smiled at the man in the middle as she comes a bit closer. "Plasma, I'll call you Plasma. A mixture between Volt and Blaze," she said at the man in the middle, who looked at her, confused.

"V-Volt, where'd you go!?" Scatha crawled towards the man, crying.

"I-I'm right here, I think?" He looked at her, so unsure of himself. "What is this feeling?" The man said, holding his head.

"Why is Volt in my head? Gah." Blaze's voice rained in the background of Volt's head.

"Blaze? Is that you? Why can I feel your mana all around me?" Volt asked.

"I think we just fused, somehow my rage has also been calmed. And somehow, I can see everything," Blaze said.

"And what does that mean? Get out of my head, please." Volt, as the main driving force for their fusion, smacked himself in the head.

"I mean I can see everything! Your past, your hopes, your dreams, It's like reading a bo— Volt...that lightning dragon. So much blood. Wow. That demon...nursed you back to health?" Blaze began looking at the experiences that Volt went through on Kayard while inside his head.

Volt sighed. "Yeah, she's a really sweet girl, and I decided to bring her with us, I think we can really use her healing. She is also shunned away by the demons herself, so I wouldn't be afraid of her turning on us. Please just give her a chance," he pleaded.

"Fine. But that's it. One. Chance. That's what I'll give her to keep the peace and for her saving you. This

317

fusion mess, we'll have to work together to perfect it too. I can feel the power coursing through us, this is amazing. For now, though, you'll be the voice for both of us," Blaze said.

"It seems as if our bodies and manas have merged, but our spirits both float in limbo until one of us takes the reigns and controls them. We both need to work together though," Volt said analyzing the situation.

"Well, you are better at controlling mana so you take this lead with this Volt. I'll manage the rest."

Volt nodded and moved their body to face the knights and John. "Looks like this fusion worked, so I guess the new name is Plasma while we are together. Don't worry, uh...Sierza? We heard you. I just needed to have a conversation with Blaze first."

Sierza unconsciously held Ocean's hand tight in excitement. He happened to be the closest person, and blushed hard at the contact. "So, Blaze. I know you're in there, how do you feel now? Does it still hurt?" she asked Plasma.

"I feel fine now. Mana is all under contr—" In a flash of light, their bodies were unceremoniously separated from one another. They diffused and were thrown down to the ground on their butts. Blaze and Volt stared at each other blankly for a few moments before fist-bumping and laughing hysterically.

Scatha ran over and hugged Volt tightly. "Oh thank goodness, you're okay." She then diverted her eyes to Blazes. "Uh."

"Don't worry, I won't try to kill you anymore. For now." Blaze attempted to reassure her with his hands up.

Gaia meanwhile was clenching her fists tightly at Scatha's embrace on him. Hail was continually holding her back in an attempt to cool her off. Father John shook his head with a smile on his face looking at the middle of the crater. "Just what happened inside of there I wonder," he says clapping while approaching the two. "Good job, you're the first two to have used contact fusion. Be sure to master it to keep yourselves together longer and be able to add more than one knight to the mix."

"Contact fusion?" Volt said, still confused.

Sierza somehow found herself next to Volt without anyone noticing, especially Scatha. "Yes it is a phrase I coined for how you two just melded together. Anything with mana can do it, demon, angel, humans, anything. That drink he gave you helps to open up the links in your mana. You just need a less wild catalyst the next time you fuse." Sierza said with a smile.

Blaze and Volt helped each other to their feet, and they stepped out of the crater to join the others. Scatha calmly walked behind Volt the entire time. "So guys, sorry for the, uh, late introduction, but this is Scatha. The woman who saved my life after my grueling fight with my sacred beast. She is also a great friend of mine now." Volt was staring into Scatha's eyes while he said this part, making Scatha blush, and Gaia fume.

Sky stepped up ahead to greet her. "Now it is odd to have a demon join our ranks, Volt trusts you, so I will as well. Nice to meet you Scatha. My name is Sky, and this is Ocean, Hail, Gaia, and Void. I believe you have already met Blaze, and over there is The Grandmaster." Sky shook her hand with a smile.

Scatha simply nodded and shook Sky's hand back. "You too."

Grandmaster clapped his hands together, then slowly separated them. Mana traveled like lightning between his hands rapidly. "So, time to get some practice in my knights.

"But how would we have time? We have to make it to that portal soon.

"Way ahead of you." Grandmaster spread his hands fully and mana expanded out in all directions, pouring out like a waterfall. Eventually the mana created a dome inside of the one already in place around the lab. Inside of this new space, the environment was entirely white. Nothing outside of the dome could be seen, it resembled Luvia's realm.

"Woah, what is this?" Ocean looked around at the inside of this dimension.

"This is my timeless zone. Like the name suggests, time does not pass normally inside of here. A day in here amounts to maybe an hour outside," Grandmaster said with a smile.

"This is perfect for us. We have the time and room to practice now," Volt said, his eyes lighting up.

For the next two days inside of the timeless zone (or two hours real time), the knights practiced fusions continuously… Scatha used her spells to help them recover after violent failures and to recover mana as well, allowing them to train without rest. "Hey Volt, do you want to practice with me next?" Hail called over.

"Hold it, we aren't done yet." Blaze said stopping him short.

"Just let them go on a little longer, Blaze needs a partner much more versed in mana control to control all that energy he has." Void cut in; he was practicing with Gaia at the time as they both needed to master control as well.

"Hm, that'll probably take a while, looks like he has his hands full over there!" Sky snickered.

Volt sighed out loud. "Is it my turn to talk yet?" he said shaking his head. "Hail, try working with Ocean for a bit. You both heavily excel at mana control too, so you guys will undoubtably be vital in one of our fusions in the future."

"Fine, let's try to match our levels Ocean. I'm sure we can create some pretty powerful attacks together." Hail turned to Ocean and started practicing.

Sky flew up above the ground, and began sensing the mana of all his knights. Sky's mana meshed well and served to enhance the powers of every knight. He simply needed to practice fluctuating his own mana to match any of his teammates he was to partner with, a very tough task indeed.

"Hey Volt," Blaze started while attempting to match Volt's stable mana. "Do you think we'll be able to fuse all of us together at the same time?"

"Hmm. Who knows. We have enough trouble with just two of us. It's going to take a lot of work or a lot of help to make that work. For now, just focus on this. When all else fails, this is our chance to get ahead of Scourge and hopefully get strong enough to defeat him." Volt's mana raised slightly as he finished, throwing Blaze off his concentration.

"Hey, careful! If I'm off sync my mana can explode and damage both of us. I know you have your little girlfriend here now, but I'd rather not use her power if we can help it." Blaze shook his head but was hit with a pebble out of nowhere. He looked around but didn't find the culprit.

The knights used this time to also experiment with the compatibility of each element to one another. After practice, Ocean, Volt, Hail, and Sky were shown to have the best mana control, while Blaze, Void, and Gaia had the largest pool of mana. They weren't able to successfully contact fuse all that often, but when they tried combo attacks using one knight from either side of the list produced the best results.

After the first day, everyone had improved their mana control enough to even fight while in that altered state. They began sparring with each other, testing the limits of how long they could keep their mana concentrated under pressure. Sierza oversaw the process to give tips and also make sure they didn't kill each other with bad fusion attempts. At the end of the second day, Sierza came to them and shared the knowledge she picked up from watching them spar and train. She informed them how when they were injured and stressed and kept control over their mana, it was at its strongest form. This led her to believe if used at the latter end of fights it could create even more powerful fusions with time. The scientist also noticed that if proper teamwork while in the fusion was maintained, it could last longer even when mana was low when initiating. Lastly, she also noticed when the elements were combined the resulting mana was so powerful that it could possibly even heal both users.

After they had finished training, Grandmaster took down the timeless zone and released them. After the dome disappeared, an odd wave of energy passed throughout the knights; almost as if the time was syncing up for both zones.

The knights stood in place stretching after their two full days of hard work. "That was more necessary than I thought it would be," Blaze said, sensing his improvement in his mana control.

"Still needs work, but at least we have the process down. We can probably contact-fuse without killing ourselves." Volt shrugged his shoulders.

Sky peered over to Father John. "So, we can fuse, though a bit iffy, we have our orbs too. What is next for us?"

John let out a big smile. "Hmph. I'm so delighted you asked. Now's time for an all-out assault on Umbra, The Shadow Realm," he said, almost giddy.

"A what?" Volt said from behind Sky.

"You heard me correct. We have an army made up of allies from all around Sylindra. And we are going to siege Scourge's castle and get Wendy back. We need you to get through the portal on this continent and confront Scourge. With him distracted, we'll be able to sneak the army into place. Scourge has an army of shadow soldiers of his own, so it's going to be big." Grandmaster looked into the eyes of the knights as he coached them.

"Woah, we are…ready for this right? I feel like everything just escalated quickly. Very quickly." Ocean said shocked.

Hail and Gaia were especially happy when he said they were going to get Wendy back. "Wait, how do you know where she is?" Gaia pushed her way to the front.

"Because of…who she is, I can sense her mana just as well as I can sense yours. It's how I'm able to materialize wherever you guys are. Once you get there, you'll be able to sense her mana again I'm sure, at that point you'll split up. One team to sneak her out, the other team to go after Scourge. All the while, the armies are battling it out to destroy Umbra and open up a path for you." Grandmaster began gathering his mana as he spoke.

"What exactly is Umbra anyway?" Ocean asked. "I've heard of Sylindra and Armageddon, but not Umbra."

Father John nodded his head. "The Shadow Realm is the midway point between any dimension and Armageddon. You simply must go there first. It is home to a tremendous amount of demons and monsters that are too proud to serve under Deces' and Ruin. A hell of a lot of prisons also find their home there. Demon prisons. Our presence there won't destroy all of it, but we need to make an easy path to Armageddon. Scourge, having won Demise's trust, owns a huge castle there that can be used for that purpose."

"Will you be joining us, father?" Volt asked while looking off in the distance.

"I, unfortunately, cannot enter Umbra. As long as I am a Holy Knight, I can only project myself there to contact you guys. I cannot physically step foot even in that portal." Grandmaster's hand was glowing brightly now. His mana was ready. "Any more questions? It is nearly midnight, the portal will open soon."

"Just one, where exactly are these armies coming from?" Sky said in a doubtful tone.

"Heh. Well one is from your father Sky. Hepheaus and Jax also have brought forces to help you fight as well. Trust me, you will be fine, and they will be waiting for you on the other side." He swung his hand across all of the knights and Scatha. "Be safe. We'll talk after you make it back safe and sound. I'm counting on you guys." With a snap of his fingers, the knights were all sucked into a white portal that opened up above. In moments they were gone.

"Bye, guys! Good luck with your new powers, okay!" Sierza yelled with a large smile as they disappeared before her eyes, leaving Sierza back to her solitude.

Chapter 15:
The Portal

-Year 277 Scourge's Castle Basement   Shadow Path,
Umbra

Scourge walked down a long corridor with jail cells lining the walls. They each had a large door made of mana enhanced black steel. The only way to see in them was by the light of a small barred window in each cell. Scourge casually passed many as he walked all the way to the last cell on the left. He stopped and turned towards the door, peering into the window for a moment. The sound of dripping and creaking could be heard from the walls around him as he stood there.

"Oh Wendy? You're still alive in there?" Scourge said, waving in front of the window.

"Yes sir, I'm not dying in a place like this. You'll die way before me, even though I've been alive for over a century, hehe." Wendy was sitting in a chair with her arms chained behind her back. "Also, can you guys loosen these a little, you really do not know how to treat an elderly lady." she said as she was struggling with her chains.

"Good to see you're still so lively, maybe you just haven't lost hope yet. I'm almost there. I'll be so disappointed if I lead them all the way here, and they just die too easily." Scourge holds his mask and shakes his head. "Everything I've done is to make them stand a chance when they fight. No one in this damn place can take me. It's been so long since I've been forced to go one hundred percen—"

"Hey, no one cares Burnt Face. Here, toss me that ugly ass mask of yours, maybe I can use the horn to pick this

326

lock." Wendy called over to Scourge. "I know you have me trapped here, but that doesn't mean I have to listen to your muffled voice talk to me, do I?"

Scourge's mana began to boil in obvious annoyance. He clenched his fist, and mana surrounded the chains, tightening them around Wendy's chest. "Let's not forget where you are, Wendy." Scourge took off his mask and spoke clearly to her.

"Ouch! I don't know what hurts more, my old bones crunching or your disgusting face!" Wendy smiled through the pain and the darkness. Her breathing began to get troubled as the chains squeezed her even harder after she spoke. Scourge's face was writhed with anger as his eyes beamed almost through Wendy. "Nope nope, definitely the chains now." Wendy eked out.

Scourge turned away and replaced his mask on his face. He relaxed his hand and released his mana from the chains. "And here I just wanted a nice, calm talk with my prisoner. I hope you do realize that the knights are definitely not going to be coming to save you. They'll be dead long before they get here, so I wouldn't hold my breath." Scourge turned and took a step back the way he came.

Wendy sent out a large wad of spit at the bars in the window on her cell door. "Those knights have a damn huge amount of potential. The Gods will not let that be squandered by someone like you," Wendy yelled.

"Hmph, we'll see about that. You don't even know the kind of things I have awaiting the knights here on Umbra. I guess I'll have to come to tell you how it goes." Scourge scoffed and trotted his way down the corridor.

The knights land at the foot of an enormous mausoleum. The chaos clouds didn't stretch this far, but there was still an eerie mist that surrounded the area. The shrine was just as secluded as the research cabin was, one would only find it if they knew where it was. A large, heavy, double-sided door sat at the entrance. Sacred symbols were carved into the door depicting different times of day, and in four separate sections, it showed the different areas that matched with the positions of the sun. The structure of the mausoleum was built in a gothic style, with a long pointy roof. The majority of the building looked old and dilapidated, but the door was still as sturdy as ever.

"Woah, this is. Wow," Volt said to himself as he peered at the structure before them.

"Yep, welcome to the Sylindra World Mausoleum. This is the site where they sealed Chaos's spirit," Void said as if he were a teacher on a field trip.

"Wait, wait, like *the* Chaos? The one who threatened the existence of everything on this and other planets, Chaos?" Blaze exclaimed.

"Yes," Void replied coldly.

"Should we be so close to this thing? And why isn't there a large lock on this door?" Blaze asked frantically.

"Well, Blaze, this acts as more of a gateway than anything else. It allows for travel to Umbra, which leads to Armageddon, Ardin, somewhere I don't know, and to space where Chaos is trapped," Sky responds, while running his hands over the markings on the door. "Also, the entrance to Ardin and Chaos won't even open unless someone with ungodly power stands worthy before it. Not even Demise was able to open it, so I think we will be okay." Sky

328

chuckled and went up to the door along with Void to shove the door open.

"All of these gravestones on the ground around this mausoleum...they belong to the old heroes, here to help protect this place, even in death," Volt said, looking around at the seven gravestones that surrounded them.

"Come on, time is wasting, midnight has to be here by now," Void said as the door began to budge from his and Sky's efforts.

Gaia tried to smack confidence in herself in the back of the group. "Whew this is it, I can do it. A long journey led us here today, Can't turn back."

"We also gotta get back Wendy." Hail patted her on the back, and she nodded at him.

"Look! It's activating!" Ocean yelled as the portal began to form in the open doorway. The stairwell down to the tomb could only be seen for a few seconds before the portal blocked their vision. It reeked of darkness, sucking and clawing away at the air as it spun around in place.

Sky walked back and stared at the portal. "Think it's probably good to say that there is no going back after we walk through this doorway." He turned around to see the range of faces from determined to worried. The knights gathered around him.

"There is no turning back, regardless of how we feel. This is our duty. We have to get rid of Scourge, and we have to get sweet old Wendy back too." Blaze put his hand on Sky's shoulder.

"We will know nothing if it isn't a victory. We must continue on our path." Volt stepped up with Scatha holding his arm tightly. Gaia, watching, cringed.

"We still have so much more to learn and many ways to grow." Gaia punched Volt in the shoulder blade as she said this. He winced and cracked a small smile at her.

"I must. I must atone for my sins. I will use everything that I am to protect you guys." Void coldly spoke into the portal.

"Don't forget, guys, we have people back at home who are we must protect. We all have our own goals, but they lead us on the same path." Ocean punched his hand confidently.

"I thank you guys for allowing me to join you on this journey. It has opened my eyes to so much, and I will lay my life on the life to protect the world behind us, and to protect the future before us." Hail raised his fist into the air.

Sky held his scythe up into the air above his head. "Royal Knights! All our lives, we have been nurtured, taught, pushed, or had been fated into becoming what we are today. We might not have been doing this too long together, but we are full-fledged knights. We are a team. We have the blessings from the Gods that got us here, but our determination and teamwork have kept us here, alive, together. The trials that await us on the other side of that gateway will be none like any of us have ever faced. But! We. Will. Be. Okay. We have our power, we have each other, we have our grit and experience. Notice a pattern here?" Sky paused to wait for a response.

"WE!" The knights all responded in unison.

"Exactly. We. Now let's go in there and kick Scourge's ass! Knights onward!" Sky led the knights into the portal, cheering and determined.

Scatha stopped short of the portal and tugged on Volt's shirt to stop him. They were the only two remaining at this point. "Volt," she said very softly.

"Yeah, Scatha? What's wrong?" Volt turned around and put his hand on her shoulder.

"I'm scared, but...I can't tell you why," she said, putting her head down. "It's just a feeling I have."

Volt pulled her in close and gave her a warm hug, squeezing tightly. "Well, whatever it may be, you can count on me to protect you from it. I promise," he whispered into her ear.

Scatha began to cry softly. "I don't think there's anything you can do..." She mumbled to herself as she wiped her face.

Volt ceased his embrace and grabbed her hand. "Come on now, we have to get in there before we get left behind again." He pulled her into the portal after him; her eyes fixated on his warm smile as they disappear after the others. The massive doors shut behind them; the portal faded away as well. The knights embarked on the next part of their journey towards Umbra, the Shadow Realm. On the other side, friends and foes awaited the arrival of the Royal Knights as an all-out, full-scale battle was about to begin.

-Year 277 The Portal

The knights found themselves in a vast, nearly empty space that connects Sylindra with Umbra. The only noticeable details they could make out in this dark expanse were the subtle trails of mana flickering throughout the void, and the two doorways of light, which illuminated the space. The first portal—the one they had just came through—stood directly behind them, while the other was situated about a quarter mile ahead of them.

As soon as they landed on what appeared to be a ground of some sort, though it was just part of this space, they all collapsed to their knees instantly. "Woah...this sensation, I've felt it before when Scourge kidnapped us." Sky said as he struggled to get up unsuccessfully.

"I think I know why..." Void said, getting sucked to the ground himself.

331

"Shit, I feel so drained right now. What's going on?" Ocean said as he was face down on the ground.

"This area must be under the light of the Chaos moon as well. The Chaos moon orbits around Armageddon, draining mana from all forces under the blessings of the deities while strengthening the darkness. It's one of the reasons why Grandmaster cannot travel here," Void said as he pushed against the gravity that was to hold him down to criss-cross his legs.

Blaze peered back at Scatha. "I guess that means she's free from this hell, oh joy," he sarcastically mentioned.

Scatha, who was indeed unaffected, was forced to stand around awkwardly while the knights were in peril.

"Either way, these orbs should kic—" As Sky spoke, his orb's light from within him began to shine. The silhouette of a green sphere was seen on him. Soon the weight was lifted, and he was able to stand normally again. "Ahh, there we go." He let out a long breath and watched as one by one, the knights were able to stand via their own orbs.

"Oh, so much better!" Hail gets up and stretches, his light blue orb the last to activate.

Volt brushed his hand through his hair, "Father John told me the reason getting these orbs are always the first mission for every iteration of knights is because of their ability to help counteract the effects of the Chaos Moon," he said, gauging his mana.

"Yeah, it's not perfect, I'm still only at about half strength," Void said, looking at Volt gauge himself.

As if like vultures, hundreds of mini portals began opening out of the space surrounding them. Shadow soldiers of many shapes and sizes began popping out like ninjas, laughing to each other like hyenas. Average soldiers, shamans, archers, even new, more gigantic beast-like shadows joined the fray. They got into formation and readied themselves to attack.

"Like moths to the flame. Don't let them catch us off guard guys!" Blaze shouted while summoning his sword.

One by one, the knights summoned their weapons, Sky's scythe, Ocean's new rapier, Void's claymore, Gaia's bo staff, Volt's spear, and Hail summoned a mini-army of floating ice blades. Even Scatha brought forth a small staff.

"What? I didn't know you could fight?" Volt asked, confused.

"Hehe, it's not much, but I'll do my best," Scatha said shyly.

Suddenly, from behind the army of shadow soldiers, a monster of a demon ported in. The field was over seven feet tall with large, bulging muscles in place of armor. His muscles were so thick and massive, it was debatable if he could move his arms normally. His neck was at least a foot across, a bit smaller than. He had a dark grey skin with red markings down his arms. Black spiked brass knuckles stuck on his fists along with spiked cleat-like boots seemed like his primary weapons. "Hah. Hah. Hah. Name Braugg, y'all ready die," he said in a deep voice and muscling a few shadows out of his way.

"Uhh, who's the big guy?" Ocean said, backing away slightly.

"I'm surprised he can speak our language," Gaia said, his speech being the most surprising part to her.

"We all learn since young your puny language. Our king uses us demons to intimidate, conquer. We need to communicate with you people for that." Braugg tapped the side of his head as if to make a point.

"Is it just me, or does he still sound dumb?" Gaia retorted in jest.

"Yeah…not it!" Sky said as he spread his wings and flew into the middle of the pile and begun the fight against the shadows. He flew past shadows with his scythe low, reaping their heads off. The archers began to aim at Sky as their new moving target.

"Oh no, you don't!" Hail said as he shot ice spikes at the arrows to deflect them. Shadow soldiers surrounded and started to lunge at Hail as he was distracted. Volt, on the other side, tossed his spear through a shadow and into the ground. This created a shockwave that took out a few more shadows as well.

"I gotcha back, H, just focus on covering Sky," Volt said as he grabbed his spear and started battling them back.

Blaze began going wild on the shadow beasts and Summoners, taking on large amounts at a time and bursting them down with explosive blasts from his sword. All the while, Braugg was still pushing the soldiers to the side as he burrowed towards the knights. As the knights battled and destroyed the soldiers, more and more, we're continually spawning in from portals in the air.

"Guess the big guy's for us, then, huh?" Gaia said, patting Void on the chest.

Void rested his claymore on his shoulder with his right hand and pulled out his explosive dark blade with his left. "Yeah, guess so," Void said as Braugg had made their way to them, tossing an archer practically into their laps.

"Heh. New victims." Braugg dashed at Gaia and swung at her face. She caught his punch and guided it up, proceeding to deliver one of her own. She punched his crotch, which was hung halfway down his leg. Her blow was full strength but sounded like she hit steel when it landed.

"What the hell!" Gaia exclaimed, looking up at Braugg's face. She was met with a broad, creepy smile.

"You're gonna die, bitch!" Braugg reached down and grabbed her by the head.

Void dashed in and slammed the butt of his cursed sword onto the wrist of Braugg, forcing him to let go of her head. Gaia flipped back and spun out kirici. "Thanks, he is as hard as a rock." She said.

Void went in with both blades, aiming to stab him in the chest. The tips of the swords clanked and bounced off Braugg's eight pack. "Holy sh——." Void is cut off by a stiff punch to his chest that knocked him back and on top of shadows. They all fall out.

"Void!" Gaia yelled as she dodges the advances of Braugg who threw punches at her violently. She avoided and swung kirici at Braugg's chest more, amounting to no damage at all. "Ugh, I need more power." Gaia blocked a punch and skid back next to Void, who was still down.

Void touched his chest and noticed the blood come off on his hand. "Eh." He grunted as he forced himself up using his swords.

"That doesn't look good at all." Gaia peered back and looked at him.

Out of nowhere, Scatha ran over from helping Volt and over to Void. She held her staff up in front of him, and it glowed green. Void would close up quickly after this, and Kirici stopped burning. "Thanks for that. Your healing is very helpful," Void said with a slight bow.

"Um, yeah. I can't do much, but I can heal, I guess." Scatha ran back over to Volt's side.

"Yeah Scatha is awesome!" Volt yelled from across the battlefield.

Gaia clenched her fist. "I do not think I like her."

Void brushed off his chest. "Why, she seems nice enough."

"But m-my Volt..." Gaia trailed off.

Braugg slowly stomped over towards the two, laughing calmly.

"Eh, no time for that. Do you want to try that fusing thing? We need a burst of power, and if it's anything like what happened with those two, it might help us actually do some damage to this guy," Gaia pleaded.

Void sheathed his cursed sword. "Sure, sounds like a better idea than I had."

"Uhhh, how does it work again?" Gaia said, gathering mana into her hands.

"I believe we have to slam our mana together and yell contact," Void said, mana already gathered.

Braugg senses the mana and switches from a trot to a sprint right for them.

"Contact!" Void and Gaia yelled as they crashed their hands into each other. An explosion of energy was released and blew Braugg and half a dozen shadows back in its wake.

The result was slightly shorter than Void, with tan skin and dark, almost painted on rings around his eyes like a mask. The lining of their armor was all black, missing the purple or brown shades. Long silver hair went down his neck but was accented with brown highlights. The weapon that materialized in his hand resembled a nagita with both a long blade and a smooth blade handle that extended twice the distance of the blade.

"My my, a much-needed surge of power," Void said as the lead of the fusion. His mana flared out holding the shadows back from charging in. "Hmm, I think Dark Gaia works as a name for us, hehe," he smiled as he stroked the end of his new weapon.

"Woah, nice guys!" Blaze said, holding off multiple shadows but all his attention on the newly formed fusion.

Braugg fought past the waves of mana still coming from Dark Gaia and swung at him, knuckles glistening in the wind. With a swift parry, Dark Gaia spun their blade around and slices off Braugg's right hand. It went flying into the air separating from the knuckles in midair. "Aghhhh!" Braugg shouted as his hand plopped on the ground behind him.

Dark Gaia smirked as dark mana began to engulf him. "Hmmm, let's go with...Dark Rush!" With weapon tightly in hand, he dashed at the stumbling Braugg, grasping at the nub on his wrist, and let out a flurry of blows with a style similar to Gaia's bo staff attacks. Each strike let off a mini dark burst on Braugg's body. After a couple moments of clean shots, Braugg covers up to block. "Hmph. See how long that lasts," Dark Gaia said while increasing the frequency and power of his attacks.

Braugg got pushed back while he defended, unable to block everything. At the end of the combo, Dark Gaia spun low and swept Braugg off his feet with the hilt of his weapon. He slammed onto his back, hands up over his face; a blade rose right above it, ready to drop down and have his brains diced. "Ahhh!" Braugg yelled while Dark Gaia begins dropping the blade.

Halfway down and a tremendous explosion of mana was let out above Braugg. Smoke spread all around him, blinding him. When it cleared, Void was collapsing to the side, and Gaia was shaken, standing over Braugg alone.

"Damnit, out of mana so soon..." Void groaned as he crashed into the ground, unconscious. A horde of shadow soldiers immediately ran over and jumped on top of him, restraining him.

Sky noticed the smoke and flew over in that direction. "Dammit! It ran out already!"

Braugg smiled maliciously from under Gaia, "Luck's out, bitch!" he said as he blasted her with a pulse of mana. She flew upwards, right past Sky. She dropped down and caught a robust and stiff left-handed punch from Braugg's knuckles, straight to her face. Blood sliced from her face in four places as she slammed head first into the ground. Shadows ran over and leaped on her as well.

Sky nose-dived towards Gaia. "Volt! Help, Gaia is —." Sky got caught by a blast from Braugg and hits the ground, face first. He slid over his face and saw Hail getting overwhelmed and jumped from across the battlefield. Sky's eyes slammed shut as Braug's fist collided with the side of his head, causing a twitching shiver through his body before it sat still. Scatha scurried and hid behind a pile of bodies, hoping no shadows see her.

Braugg triumphantly sat on Sky's back as he watched Ocean, and Volt got surrounded and beaten down as they run out of mana. Blaze desperately tried to hold back the waves on his end and on Volt and Ocean's. "Volt, I can't… I'm out, my mana is all drained." Ocean said in a defeatist attitude as his mana whip disappeared, and more shadows surrounded him and started to attack.

Volt looked over at his own spear as lightning mana stops radiating around it. "I don't know, I'm about done myself…" Volt said lowly to himself.

"No!" Blaze yelled as he burrowed past the shadows gathering around Volt roughly. "It's not done yet. Give me the rest of your mana, and we can contact. Use that explosion of mana to power up our attack. Think I've got enough for one Nova," Blaze said, nodding at Volt.

Volt sighed then nodded. "Yeah, let's try it, there's only us now."

"That's the spirit!" Blaze smiled as he released the last of his mana. "Oh, great lords grant me the power to create the ultimate destruction, kneel before the power of lord Verafelt." Mana began pouring into a giant molten ball above Blaze, whose hands were up to control it. It gained size but was still smaller than usual.

"Contact!" Volt screamed as he slapped his hand on Blaze, and in another release of mana, the two were one.

The fusion between Volt and Blaze, known now as Plasma, was formed again. He began blowing the hair out of his face, still holding the ball of mana. After the transformation, the mana had tripled in size, also sporting a

338

layer of lightning around the outside. "Okay! Get erased you damn shadows!" He threw the ball high into the void, and it lands in the center of the battlefield, creating a big bang like effect and sending powerful waves of mana everywhere. These waves destroyed many shadows upon contact. Moments later, the field was very different. Only select shadows survived, but they were still knocked out. The knights were still unconscious, but no shadows were on top of them.

Braugg still sat unscathed on top of Sky, laughing hysterically. He didn't say anything, though. Plasma instantly reverted to normal, Volt out cold right away hitting the ground hard. Blaze fell to his hands and knees. "See, look at that; we did it…" Blaze said, breathing heavily in between words. His sight was leaving him as he tried to stay conscious. He stared directly at Braugg.

Approximately fifteen seconds afterward, seven large portals opened up on the side of the Void, and shadow soldiers poured in, filling up the battlefield once more. "…Damn…" Blaze said as he collapsed to the ground. His last earshot was of Braugg's laughing, and shadows trotting up around him and the rest of the knights.

Chapter 16:
Escape!

Nearly half a decade before the new knights were bestowed with power from the Gods, Scourge was making a name for himself in the underground ranks of Umbra. Whether as a mercenary or an assassin, Scourge was well known for his efficiency, tenacity, strength, and potential. After slaying the Emperor of Umbra in a vicious duel, Demise demanded that Scourge came to see him. Afraid of retaliation, Scourge agreed to meet with the master of Armageddon, in his castle.

So here they were, in this massive throne room, Scourge at the feet of the three enormous seats housing Demise, in the center, and Scarlet and Ruin to each of his sides. Their thrones were carved entirely out of onyx, with sacred carvings running across and down the sides. Skulls and swords were carved and welded to the back of Demise's chair. Demise sat there with one leg casually crossed over the other, both arms firmly placed on the armrests. Scarlet and Ruin's seats were perched upon a pedestal higher than his. The room they were in was huge, A small path led from a circular platform that held the thrones, and it extended towards the entrance. To either side of this pathway were mini paths that led to the sides of the room. Stairs led up to a second floor that had more rows of seats overlooking the thrones. A semi-circle of chairs sat on this floor directly over the entrance and through half of the room. Ambiguous shaped shadowy figures filled these seats, all eyes on

340

Scourge in the center. Underneath the main floor of the throne room, a hot pool of lava almost six feet down; this heated the room immensely as the areas not covered by the pathways were completely open. No barriers, of course, so one wrong step, and you'd be tumbling to your death. Along with this threat was a constant veil of darkness that expanded like fog around the ground, and the lava underneath as well.

Demise beamed down at Scourge with evil intent, the pressure of his mana nearly suffocated Scourge and held him in place. Scourge had his head down while he knelt there, taking this visual abuse. Scarlet and Ruin remained quiet at this moment. "So." Demise's voice boomed and echoed throughout the room. It demanded the attention of everyone in earshot. His deep voice rattled through Scourge's body. "I've heard of what you've done over these past few years, Scourge. From assassinating four heads of my armies on assignment to your performance against the angels in the great war. Then most recently, you murdered my dear friend and emperor of Umbra." Demise took a moment to allow the echo to stop ringing through the room.

Scourge nodded his head, calmly, "Yeah, that was me. All of it. Sorry, your friends were unlucky enough to cross my pa—" He was cut off by Demise's ax as it flew across the room and slashed into the ground to the right of Scourge. The floor there split and left a crater about six feet wide in its wake. Demise summoned his ax back and cleared his throat; Scourge lifted his head up and stared at the hole wide-eyed. Scourge's face was gnarled, raw, and fresh with burns and exposed flesh. His smile was just as big, but the wounds were more recent.

"Respect Scourge, It just might save your life." Demise said, cracking his fingers at Scourge.

Scourge cracked a half-ass smile, "I came here expecting you to just kill me anyway. Dark Overlords don't

341

usually take it lightly when you kill their people." Scourge's smile was bright as ever as he began to sweat a bit.

This caused Demise to start smiling. "Well, I did not call you here to kill you, Scourge. I could have killed you at any time I wanted. I'm actually quite impressed by your skills. I called you here so you could work for me."

Scourge's eyes lit up for a moment as he looked at Demise sideways, then over to Ruin and Scarlet, who kept their blank stares. "What do you mean?" he asked, curiously.

Demise chuckled with a deep, hearty pace, "Yes. I want you to be my personal mercenary. My personal assassin. I want you to fight for me, Scourge! Help me crush my enemies!" Demise clenched his fist up into the air.

Scourge thought to himself for a moment then lowered his head again after giving a sigh. "Fine. I guess no isn't an option anyway, huh?"

Demise's face got serious for a moment. "No, no, it is not." His smile returned. "So, I'm glad you see it my way."

"Mhm." Scourge simply nodded, knowing his life would change now. Freedom quickly became thoughts of the past for him. He understood that he couldn't dream of facing Demise, not yet anyway."

"Deces', tell him." Ruin spoke up for the first time in a cold, lifeless tone.

"Ah, right. One of the main things I need you for is the Royal Knights." He said with his hand on his chin.

"The who?" Scourge looked up, confused.

"The Royal Knights, a generation of warriors who got hand fed powers by those damn deities. They should be forming up in the coming years, and I want you to throw a bit of a wrench in the plan. Maybe get there early and knock them off before they can become one?" Demise said, tapping his chin. Scourge got off of his knee and stood all the way up, dusting himself off.

"Do you think these novices will be able to give me any sort of entertainment?" Scourge laughed out loud for a moment before catching himself.

"At the moment, no. Just don't underestimate em' and end up dead. Also, your face is disgusting, let's cover that up." Demise snapped his fingers, and immediately the large doors at the entrance to the throne room creaked open. The screeching sound of stone on stone was rough, but it finally opened fully. A triplet of servants came in holding a large square wooden casing with a fancy velvet pillow on top. Sitting on the cushion was something hidden with a cloth on top.

"Tsk." Scourge looked over to the side, slightly annoyed. He tried not to show it, though.

The servants walked over past the narrow, dangerous pathway and stopped directly to the right of Scourge. Demise gave them a nod, and they gingerly placed the set down and made their way back out the way they came. Scourge reached over and removed the cloth, tossing it off into the lava. Underneath was a white mask with red and black markings painted down from the eye holes and swirled down at the bottom. Large curved white horns erected from the jaw as well. It was Scourge's iconic mask, the cleanest it's ever been. Mouth wide open, Scourge calmly picked it up and looked deep into the mesmerizing eyes of the mask. For more than a few moments, he is almost stuck there, staring in silence.

"Well?" Demise asked to break the silence, his booming voice shaking Scourge out of his trance.

"It's…beautiful," Scourge said, getting himself together. "Thank you, Deces'. I'll wear it always in your honor as your personal mercenary and assassin," he said, rising to his feet and bowing, the mask firmly in his hand. Scourge raised it up again and softly placed it on his face. A line of mana traveled around the rim of the mask, adhering it

343

to his face. Scourge breathed in deeply and exhaled with passion as if he was reborn anew. A loud, muffled laugh rang out afterward.

Demise joined Scourge in his laugh, causing them both to just stand there awkwardly smiling afterward. Ruin peered over at Demise angrily, causing him to stop and clear his throat. "Glad you like it, Scourge."

"Ahhh, yes, it feels great. Who shall be my first target, though?" Scourge responds.
Demise nodded up to Ruin and got a nod back. "Well, the Royal Knight, who was passed down the moniker of "Blaze," has yet to fully realize his powers. He is also alone at the moment, so the perfect time already has arisen to take out one of the knights early."

"And where shall I find the poor bastard?" Scourge chuckled.

"Kayard. In a small town called Ryon. Go show them what your arrival means to that world." Demise stopped, then a second later held his hand up. "One more thing. When you get back to Umbra, I'll have a castle for you to live in. Don't. Don't let me down, or it'll be your head and that fancy little mask on the ground, detached from your body. Got it?" Demise started caressing his ax as he spoke.

Scourge nodded a few times after this while he opened a portal behind him. "Off I go to ruin some lives." He backed up into the portal and disappears.

Scarlet scoffed. "You know he liked to play around with his prey. Why would you send that guy to fight the knights?" She stopped to push her bright red hair out of her face. "You have to know he likes fighting worthy opponents, and that the knights at the moment are not even close." Her last word was cut off by strands of hair getting into her mouth.

"Oh, I know what he is like, it should be all the more fun to watch from up here as the knights struggle against Scourge's might." Demise ended it with a loud and hearty laugh that the entire castle was probably able to hear.

-Year 277   ???   Umbra

The knights woke up surrounded by dark walls on all sides except one. Some hard, cold stone walls with minor cracks suffocated them. Slightly glowing circular insignias were carved into the walls. Light and mana were steadily sucked into these carvings like mosquitoes. This made visibility low, even though the dark metal bars in front of them. There was nothing inside of the cell, only a hard cement floor, so they just sat there cross-legged in a group. On the same row as them were eighteen other cells, and across from them, they could see cells with varying monsters and demons sleeping or just grumbling there. One wondered how they all ended up there, and how they ended up in prison for demons.

The cell the knights resided in was across from a long stairwell off to the right. Beyond the stairs was a large gap leading to the level below. The stairs were very worn down with warped and bent metal rungs to walk on. Cleary very heavy beings have walked on them. The walls echoed a sorrowful song, singing of all the demons that have found themselves in here over the years. Off in the distance, beyond the lower level, was a massive thick door chained and sealed tight. Before the door, multiple translucent man-made walls were lined up on the pathway approximately five feet apart each. Seven walls were set up all together; each could only be destroyed by a powerful burst of mana. This is the last resort set up to prevent escapes.

Right in front of the first barrier, a large open area was partitioned off as a community area. If featured a cold floor as hard as concrete and a single table in the center, nothing else. The different types of demons and humans gathered in groups to entertain themselves. Probably plotting various escapes, but nothing usually pans out. Sometimes fights broke out, but the guards typically let it happen gladly. Deaths occured all the time, evident by the stained blood on the cold ground, and the walls. Guards lined up constantly surrounding the open area as well as patrols up and down all the rows of cells. Their movements were very meticulous and serious. Each guard was a shadow soldier, but they were more humanoid than usual, resembling a muscular human with no other real features, only shadows. They were equipped with long swords, extra-large shields resembling riot shields, and dark mana whips housed on their hips. On the ceiling of each level of cells was a small lantern to provide the lowest possible amount of light. It even flickered as it swung on the short rope it was tied to. There was no breeze, but the movement of mana could sometimes cause the lanterns to sway back and forth, becoming the difference between light and darkness.

The knights gathered around Blaze, who was the only one still out cold on the cold ground. Their usual garbs were replaced with all-white one-piece uniforms. Mana was drained continuously from within this building so they couldn't muster up much of anything, no matter how much they tried. Weapons won't spawn, auras won't appear, everyone, for the most part, was virtually powerless here. The only beings retaining their power were those of higher class demon bloodline and the shadow soldiers, of course. As they waited there, the awkward silence started to get to them. Gaia, who was kneeling next to Volt. punched him in the shoulder. "So," Gaia said, trying to hold back her emotions as much as possible.

Volt rubbed his shoulder and looked Gaia in the eyes. "Yes, Gaia?"

Gaia cleared her throat about three times but still couldn't find the words. It's like he doesn't care that I'm upset. I hate him so much! "So. Tell me about this demon woman. What is she to you?" She finally let out.

"Oh, Scatha? She's really nice and sweet. She helped me when I really needed it. Glad to have met her when I did honestly," Volt said with a big smile on his face.

Gaia grumbled and mocked Volt's words off to the side. Oh, so you aren't happy you met me? Did I not help you guys at all!? Look at that smug look on his beautiful, beautiful face... "And me?" Gaia questioned while nudging him slightly, a forced smile on her face.

"You've become a pretty good friend, Gaia, though a little aggressive at times." Volt put his hand on Gaia's shoulder.

Ocean, who was looking over at the entire exchange, just shook his head in disappointment. "Is now really the time for these guys?" he questioned.

"He's right; you guys need to focus on our current predicament," Sky said, raising his voice over the two of them.

Gaia's mouth gaped open with shock and annoyance; she remained this way for an awkwardly long pause. "W-what?" She sighed. "You know what, never mind, forget I asked." Assholes. She got up and walked to the other corner of the cell, face to the wall.

Volt, noticeably confused, looked around for assistance from everyone else. It did not come. "Gaia, wait! What'd I say?" he said, reaching out. It was too late though, the damage had been done.

"Terrible," Hail said, running his hands through his hair.

Volt attempted to get up after Gaia, but he was stopped by Void, who pulled him back down. "Come on,

Volt, don't you think we have other worries at the moment?" He motioned over to the ugly demons chuckling at him from across the hall. He then pointed down to Sky, who is looking around outside the cage, attempting to come up with a plan.

"Yeah, I guess you're right. We should probably wake up Blaze so he can listen in." Volt leaned over and shook Blaze a bit; he doesn't budge, though. The knights gathered back around Blaze and stared at him.

After another couple seconds, he started to stir finally, but Ocean impatiently got down and shook him until he opened his eyes forcibly. "Huh, Woah, what!?" Blaze yelled, sitting up fully. "Where the hell are we?" he said, looking around frantically.

"Oh, joy, you're awake!" A dark portal opened up from the ground about six feet tall and giving a face to the voice, Scourge came stomping out right in front of them. Scourge's dark armor was different than usual, though; it was quite thick and plated all around. In the cracks of each piece, it glowed bright red, and he wore a full head mask now as well. A pitch-black cape fluttered on his shoulders as well. His cursed blade was the same, sheathed horizontally on his back, near his waist.

"Shit." Blaze scooted back while he continued to shake out the cobwebs. Immediately afterward, the knights popped up to their feet, and regular fighting stances replaced the summoning of their weapons. Gaia stayed in the corner, though, not having any of it.

"Ha. Ha. Do you fools really think you pose any sort of threat in your current state? You can't even get out of that cell." Scourge chuckled to himself.

Sky smirked at Scourge, a droplet of sweat falling down his head. "What's got you all dolled up, Scourge?" He spit at Scourge's feet.

Scourge laughed again. "Disrespect, huh. Ok. Well, if you must know, some of your friends decided to bring their armies to my front door." He stopped to clench his fist. "So, I donned my armor to go crush their pathetic existence with ease." Scourge caught his breath and sighed angrily. "Then I'll plan your public execution for all to witness. And! After that, I am going to waltz up to your little castle and burn it to the ground. Lord Deces' will reward me with great power; power that I can even destroy him with!" Scourge's tone calmed again as mana began to radiate around him.

"Well, it seems like you got big plans." Hail said.

"Too bad, you'll be dead before any of those dreams get realized." Void stepped up to the cage to threaten. He put his hands on two of the bars and shook them slightly.

"You will not touch him, or your execution will come early." A young, evil voice rang out. Another portal opened up next to Scourge and out walked a demon warrior armed up and down with blades. He had two long and thick swords sheathed across his back in an 'X' shape and a couple of battle axes on his waist. His armor was a mixture of white and black plates with blades on the back of his gauntlets and under his grieves. A black 'X' was carved into the white chest plate.

"Who the hell are you?" Blaze yelled.

Scourge put his arm around the demon and pulled him close. "This is Strike. One of my new apprentices! He'll be assisting me in the disposal of your allies," Scourge bragged. Strike reached up and began twirling a strand of his spiky black hair. The calm, straight face of his didn't budge while he did this. His skin was a cool grey, similar to Scourge's, but he had fewer blemishes and scars. "I'll let him finish intimidating ya, I'll see ya on the big day!" Scourge disappeared into a portal laughing maniacally.

When Scourge disappeared, Strike stopped twirling his hair and grabbed one of his blades out. After obnoxiously holding the long katana type sword in Sky's face, he whistled at Gaia in the corner. "Aye! You gonna join the conversation, girl?" Gaia doesn't budge.

"Don't worry about her, you're talking with me now! Let me out this cage, and I'll show you how to talk to someone with respect." Sky stepped up to Strike's face, only the bar between them. The air was still for a moment as they had an old fashioned stare off. Strike eventually looked away first, replacing his sword in its sheath.

"Whatever, I want *you* to try and escape. If I see you out of that cage, you'll be the first one I cut down. Someone needs to do something about that mouth of yours." Strike scoffed before taking a survey of the knights in the cell.

"That's what I thought." Sky crossed his arms and plopped back down, satisfied. Blaze patted him on the shoulder, chuckling a bit off to the side.

"Hmm. Where's that other one you were with?" Strike pondered, stopping his gaze directly on Volt. "Hmm?" He cleared his throat.

"I have no idea what you're talking about," Volt said firmly, staring directly at Strike.
Strike grasped his chin. "Really? You don't know where Scourge's little cursed spawn went?" Strike cockily put his hand on the bar and looked at him sideways.

Volt's eyes shot open, his head cocked to the side slightly and turned toward Strike. "W-what did you say?" he stammered. Blaze and everyone else in an earshot looked over as well. A bang was heard from the back of the cell. Gaia had punched a hole into the cell floor with her bare hands with enough impact to shake the cell. As a whole, the knights tried their best not to notice, sweat dripping down their brows.

Strike noticed the crowd of onlooking eyes and starting bursting out laughing, still holding himself up with the bar. "Yeah, that girl is Scourge's biological daughter. Scourge dropped her off in Sylindra and kept an eye on her from afar. We lost her on Kayard, and recently we saw her with you on our portal. So, where did she go?" He struck his hand against the cage.

"There's no way...the conscience of that..." Volt shook his head. "It doesn't matter where she came from, we'll still accept her. We have no idea where she is, and even if we did, we wouldn't tell you!"

Blaze looks at Volt then over to Gaia, who is slowly grinding her fist further into the ground in the other corner. I KNEW it. There was no way she just happened to have the same eyes as him. She even has that incredible potential, shit. I think I was thrown off by her ignorance. I don't think even she knew who her father was, let alone how powerful he is. That's right, there's no way she knew.

"No matter, when we get our hands on her, we will take her back to our side. We're gonna twist her and warp her until she is just as evil as the rest of us. No one can resist Scourge's influence, especially not his own child!" Strike said with a large smile.

"You will *not* touch her!" Volt said face to the bars now, fist clenched. If he had mana, it would be flaring all around him now.

"Volt. Volt!" Blaze punched Volt's shoulder. "Get yourself together, Volt. You have much more couth than this. Leave the angry stuff to me."

Strike shook his head at Volt. "So sad. After such a small threat, you lose your head. Gee, that must mean you must have had quite the relationship with that demon. I wonder...have you guys had se-." Strike was cut off by a mass exodus of the air in his lungs. A fist had appeared buried into his chest and causing him to skid back a couple feet, gasping for breath. Strike held his chest plate in place. "W...what the hell...what that?" he said, taking pauses to breathe in between words. He looked up to see Gaia's fist sticking through the opening between the bars, clenched

351

tightly. A cold seriousness was on her face. The knights around her noticeably took a step to the side. Volt stopped as well to pay attention to Gaia. "How!? You have no mana!" Strike yelled.

"Or leave it to her." Blaze backed away, pulling Volt back with him.

"The base strength I have is enough. You just needed to stop talking. I couldn't take hearing your voice anymore." Gaia said in her same cold tone. She looked over to Volt now. "That was for you too. I'm allowed to be mad at you. But no one else is to mess with you. Got it?" Gaia went back behind Hail and sat down. Volt nodded and regained his composure again, as simple as that.

Strike turned and trotted off down the stairwell, "You'll pay for that one. Don't worry," he grumbled angrily. His footsteps grew softer and softer, and he got further away.
"Ha ha ha badass brown-haired beauty." A fat demon laughed from the cell across the hall from the knights. A wide black cloak was covering his skin and face over the top of his prison clothes. He clapped as well, rocking back and forth while he sat there in his dark cell.

Gaia wrinkled her face up in disgust at him, "What?"

The brute removed the cloak from his head and opened it up around his chest. His skin was darker than usual for a demon, it was almost black. Upon closer examination, his skin was actually burned and scabbed viciously. Even his face was mortifying. You could practically smell the burning flesh from looking at his face. It was gross. A vile mist of hot air left his mouth as he took heavy breaths. "Woah, woah, watch it now, I may be able to help you escape. For a price," he said, letting out a stomach curdling smile.

Volt looked at him closely from across the cells. "Hey, wait. Haiza, I think it was. What's your crispy self-doing here?" He smirked.

Sky stood next to Volt, looking at the demon as well. "And how do you think you can help us get out?" Sky pointed at him.

The demon chuckled, letting more hot air out. "Well, I've been in this stupid prison ever since you took Scatha away from us. Scourge felt the need to torture me here instead of just outright killing me. So it's your fault, Volt!" Haiza yelled, then immediately coughed up afterward. "So you owe me!"

Volt rolled his eyes. "Fine, whatever we'll let you out too. Just help us out of here, we have to go kill Scourge." Volt punches the cell bars to try and intimidate Haiza.

Haiza coughed and chuckled at the same time. "I refuse to let myself die in here. I don't have forever to live, these injuries and the internal ones from Scourge will have me dead in no time. I don't want to die like an animal in a cage." Haiza picked up the cloak and sniffs it. "This cloak. I'm sure you noticed the tacky prison uniforms we are forced to wear in here, and how it should be odd that I have this thing with me," he said, twirling it in his hand. "In reality, Scourge gave this to me as it has mana stored in it, a constant stream of healing mana. He wants me to stay alive as long as possible so he can use me for his experiments. In a place where mana is scarce, this right here is a goldmine. You want it?" Haiza held it out in front of him.

Volt waved him over. "Yeah, find a way to throw it to us, we'll find a way to absorb the mana and bust out."

Haiza held his hand out. "Wait, I'm not finished," he said, adjusting his butt in place. "There isn't enough mana in that to do anything offensively. But maybe enough to call for help!" He now held the cloak in one hand over his head. The parts of the sleeve covered bits and pieces of his face.

"What do you mean?" Sky said.

"Mmmmm, that Scatha is here, you know. I was with her for so long, I can recognize her mana anywhere. She

should be able to bust her out even with her feeble mana."
Haiza breathed in deeply.

"That could actually work. Better yet, she can revitalize our mana long enough for us to get out before it gets sucked out again." Ocean chimed in.

Haiza shook his head as he just realized something. "Actually. The way out of here is behind several mana barriers. They each need a large explosion of mana to break them. There is no way we'll have that much mana. Not enough to get through all of them anyway."
Hail got up from next to Gaia. "We won't know till we try, right? Hand it over, we'll handle it."
Haiza snatched it back to himself, smiling again. "Well, if this does work, I want one more thing," He said, holding up a single finger.

Sky sighed. "We are gonna let you out of your cell, what else could you want?"

The demon's laugh bubbles up again uncontrollably. "Hahaha! I want a nice tender kiss from that beauty right there!" Haiza pointe at Gaia.

Volt punched the cell bar again, "What?"

Gaia's face scrunched up again as she gets up and walked towards the bars. "Oh, I'll give you a nice tender kiss, alright." She said, talking through her teeth and punching her palm threateningly.

Haiza scooted back in his seat, sweating. "Heh. Heh. Fine! Forget about that. Here, it's yours. Just make sure to make it work." He manipulated the mana in the cloak with his hands, stretching and rolling it, forming it into the shape of a homemade arrow, as tough as steel. He arched the black arrow back and launched it through the bars and across to the other side. In the knight's' cell, it crashed into the wall, remaining stuck there for a moment, then reverting back to cloth and falling to the ground.

Sky looked at the cloak curiously and picked it up. "What the hell?"

Haiza smiled, proud of their shock and awe. "Yeah, that's my ability. Manipulating the mana of things is something that was passed down into my group," he said, but everyone was already preoccupied with the cloak.

Void placed his hand on the cloak as Sky was holding it. "Let us absorb it together. We can combine your mana link with my portals to just bring her straight here. We want her to be able to help us before the guards find ou—" Void stopped and tucked the cloak behind Sky's back as he heard footsteps coming from the left of the cage. His instincts were served well as a few seconds later, one of the guards came stomping by their cage and off to the right. "Ahem, like I was saying, let's do that."

Sky nodded at Void. "Yeah, sounds good. The boost should help me locate her better as well." Minutes passed as Void and Sky seemingly meditated over a black cloak with the remaining knights overlooking with anticipation.

Suddenly, a dark aura surrounded Volt. His eyes rolled back behind his eyes, and he collapsed to the ground, a seizure followed. Volt's body began shaking and convulsing as he laid on his back. "Volt! Volt!" Gaia noticed first and immediately goes over to check on him, turning him on his side and rubbing his back. "Come on, Volt, what's going on with you?" Gaia said, almost crying in fear.

Void and Sky remained focused, but everyone else gathered around Volt now in concern. "What is this aura around him, it couldn't be mana, could it?" Blaze said, trying to feel the energy coming off of the mana.

Haiza peered over from across the cells at Volt. "That one. Yeah, he's cursed. That damned Scatha used something forbidden," he said, shaking his head in dismay.

Gaia looked up at Haiza as she began to squeeze Volt's arm. "W-what?"

There was a fierce rain on the dark fields of Umbra. From the aura to the depressing appearance, everything seemed to dull senses and suck the energy out of anything, not a demon. The grass even slowly absorbed mana in the air like nutrients. A soft fog of dark mana hovered over the top of the green. A weird and unique ecosystem the Shadow Realm was, but it all served to strengthen the darkness. The current field was called Shadow Path, the centerpiece of Scourges territory as a strip of monuments to his success and pull in the Shadow Realm. With vast battlefields, a personal prison on one side, and his castle and armory and training grounds on the other, his area screamed 'I love fighting.' The outskirts of his territory transitioned into bone dry lands and deserts with small demon settlements in place at the border.

A young warrior rushed away from an explosion that echoed in the background, towards the prison. He ran and ran, pushing himself beyond his limits to escape recapture. Short silver wings hung low on his back, his right a bit lower than the left with a large gash on the muscle connecting the wing to his back. The open wound flapped back and forth in the rain as he ran. The blood and footprints in the grass left a perfect trail leading to his position.

Young Silverwing was a hybrid, half-demon half-human. Scourge and his forces chased him to experiment and eventually use his body as a mule for a cloned army with his likeness. His blood was unique and served to be an excellent fit for a warrior. The human side gave them the passion and drive they needed, as humans have always had a natural way of overcoming their weaknesses. The demon side gave them the longevity, longer lifespan, and an exceptional recovery from enemies.

Only fifteen years young, Silverwing began to feel the darkness closing in on him, and his life. Suddenly in the middle of his stride, upon reaching the front of Scourge's castle, Silverwing stops. His feet slid on the wet grass, causing him to finally stop a few feet past where he intended. He looked around frantically, sensing but not seeing the threat.

Sheeeeewww! A cursed blade came flying through the air and sliced into the ground in front of Silverwing. "I told you there was no way you could escape from me, young Silva'." A familiar, muffled voice echoed.

Silverwing lowered his head and sighed. "My life hasn't been long, but I realize now that the end has come. For me," he said softly, grabbing the top end of his wing on each side.

Scourge walks forward out of the darkness, a large group of shadow soldiers followed close behind, weapons and chains at the ready. They strafed sideways and surrounded Silverwing as he stood there. "I'm glad you now realize your fate. Give me five years, and I will make your likeness into the greatest army in all of Umbra, or Sylindra even! Just you wait! My discoveries will lead me to prominence. Haaaa, I simply cannot wait!" Scourge said, almost giddy with excitement.

Silverwing shook his head solemnly. "I may not be able to escape, but I'll do my best to make that dream a lot harder for you!" He took a firm grip on his wings now. SPLAT! "Aahhh!" With one sharp tug, Silverwing ripped his wings from his back. Blood splattered everywhere from the action and from the nub that remained. His arms flail off to the side as life fades from his eyes. Silverwing let out a confident smile at Scourge as his last conscious action. Scourge's face dropped as he watched blood leak viciously out of his back. "Noooo! What have you done!! Get him! Stop the bleeding now. We need him," Scourge ordered

357

while Silverwing drops to his knees, now unconscious from blood loss. The shadow soldiers grabbed Silverwing's body as a group and teleport him elsewhere.

Scourge looked straight up, the rain runs down into the cracks of his mask and onto his skin underneath. "I will not allow this to phase me. My destiny has me as the king of all of these worlds. Valiant effort Silverwing, but we will still use your body to clone the greatest army. I will crush everyone...especially him…" Scourge finished by harshly grasping the mask on his face and squeezing it. "No one disrespects me. Especially him," he said in rising anger. Scourge opened a portal and teleported away, his head still in the cloudy skies.

-Year 277   Scourge's Prison   Shadow Path, Umbra-

"Volt! Volt!" Gaia screamed as she squeezed both of Volt's arms and shook him slightly. Slowly the seizure stopped, and his eyes drug open a moment later.

"Eh…ow. My arms are numb," Volt said, groggy with his eyelids still low.

Gaia noticed how hard she was holding him, letting go of both his arms and sending him plopping onto the floor. "S-sorry!"

Volt rubbed the back of his head and sat up on his own. Blaze and Ocean let out a sigh and rubbed either shoulder. "You had us worried there," Blaze said, shaking his head.

Ocean lowered himself to a knee and got near Volt's ear. "What was that, man? Did you have any thoughts while you were out?"

"Hmm. Actually, I don't remember what led to me being out, but I did have sort of a flashback in there." Volt put a couple of his fingers on his temple as he thought.

"Hm, what happened?" Ocean questioned.

"I think it was an insight of Scourge's army. Something about Silver-something and how Scourge experimented with cloning in the past. Don't know how it works, but it might have been a sort of call for help." Volt shrugged his shoulders.

A dark portal opens up behind them, followed by a dim light as Scatha drops down out of the portal clumsily on the ground. Sky and Void's endeavor was successful. "Whew! It worked. All of that gifted mana is gone now, though." Sky said, releasing a loud sigh.

Scatha popped back up to her feet, staff in hand, looking quite distressed. She looked around the cell as the knights all turn around to discover the cause of the noise. "Oh, it's you guys, wait, how did I get here. One second I'm sneaking around, the next, a portal catches me, and I'm teleported here." She looked back at Void and nodded her head with an ahh.

Volt looked at Scatha silently, letting out an awkward smile. "Welcome back." Gaia stared at Volt from behind solemnly.

"Ugh, we don't have time for this." Blaze picked Volt up to his feet and pushed him forward. "Come on, Volt, talk to her lover boy. We have to go."

Volt stopped himself just short of running into Scatha and cleared his throat. She looked back at him startled but innocent as she waitsed for Volt to speak. "U-um. So Scatha, we need to escape this prison to go battle Scourge. Problem is, this cell and this entire place constantly drain our mana so we can't do anything. Do you have any spells that can revitalize our mana and keep us going while we fight our way out of here?" Volt quickly averted his eyes away from looking directly at her after he spoke.

Scatha's eyes light up. "Ah, yes! I think I do actually." She dug in a small bag she had around her waist when she got here and pulled out a little book. She flipped through the pages and stopped around the middle. "Anything for you, Volt. I hope you're okay though, you're acting a little weird." She waved everyone to gathered around her. "Come on guys, get close, I want to get everyone with this." They listened and surrounded Scatha. Gaia made sure she was as far back as possible, though, not wanting to touch Scatha.

"Now is not the time," Hail said, pulling his sister in closer to the pack.

Scatha watched this silently, then refocused herself. "Ok, then!" She finished the reading and put the book back into its pouch. Both hands grasped around her short staff, she held it out ahead of her vertically. After a few embers of mana, it began to flow out freely. Mana seeped from the staff and plopped on the stone floor in the middle of everyone. "Rise from the depths of obscurity, rise from weakness. Cheat your death with mana from the dark lord!" A pulse of yellow energy radiated from this mana, and it instantly expanded and stabilized into a mana circle on the ground just big enough to encompass everyone. Mana resembling thin lightning flashed up and attached to each of the knights all over their bodies like spider webs on prey.

"Ahhh!" The spell attached to their mana sensors, causing them great pain. Nearby guards start noticing what appeared to be a fancy light show happening inside of their cell and began to head towards the bars to see what's going on. The spell stopped, and the mana tethering prevented cold. The knights collapsed to their knees to catch their breath. Residual yellow static from the mana in the spell circled the bodies of the knights slightly.

"Hey! What's going on here!" Four guards had gathered around the cell bars, weapons ready when they saw it was mana causing the light show.

360

Blaze smirked and let his mana run free around him, flames surrounded his body and a small area around him as well. This caused the rest of the knights to back up to avoid getting burned. "Let's test this, then shall we?" Blaze yelled. A small flame slowly floated up to his hand, changing into his blade with a brilliant flash. He then spins around towards the cell bars and keeping the momentum, Blaze swings his mana infused sword swiftly. An 'X' shaped streak of flaming mana soared towards the doors twirling wildly through the air like a drunk bird. The streak crashes into the bars and immediately explodes violently. The bars are singed to a crisp, and the guards went flying in different directions. One hit Haiza's cage across the hall and bent the bars, two went flying to the left, and the last was sent down the stairs into the main area. A large cloud of black smoke loitered around in front of their cells in the aftermath.

"What happened to stealth!" Gaia called as she smacked Blaze in the back of the head.

"Ow! No one said anything about sneaking out of here. No way!" Blaze retaliated.

Sky jogged up to the area that was previously locked off with bars, exiting the cage. "We gotta go, guys! Come on," he said as he looked, either way, to see the guards mobilizing towards them.

The knights nod and joined Sky out into the smoke, trying to decide which direction to go first. Haiza calmly sat in his cage, knocking onto the bars to get their attention. "Ahem. Are we forgetting something, guys?" Haiza said with a half-smile on his face.
Scatha put her head in her hands with a gasp. "What is he doing here?" She backed away behind Volt.

Volt looked at Haiza, then back to Scatha. "We owe him for helping us get to you. Unfortunately." Volt sighed as he summoned Sigrun and sliced the bars on his cage in half with a single strike.

Haiza dodged the bars that fell towards him. He rolled over and finally pushed himself up to his feet. "Heh. Thanks," he said, brushing his legs off and stepping out of his cell. "Now, it's time for my true reward!" Haiza said with his tongue hanging lowly out of his mouth and looking directly at Gaia.

Without words, Gaia turned in his direction and shut him up with a stiff punch to his oversized gut. He crumpled over himself, out of air. Hail shook his head at him. "Shoulda saw that coming," he said.

"I-in all seriousness. You should…go, get your proper armor back," Haiza said, coughing afterward. He pointed off far past the stairwells that went down to the main level, and at the very end of the current hallway. A big stiff door sat there all alone. "We just need to get there. They keep our clothing and weapons there, for us who don't have our weapons connected through mana links." Haiza was back to his feet now, just as they had gotten surrounded by shadow guards coming from all sides.

Sky looked at the far off door then summoned his scythe. "Easy enough, let's tear through them, knights!" He said, spinning around and catching a guard in his shoulder with the sharp point of his scythe and dragging him to the ground. "These guys are a bit tougher than your average shadows. Hmmm," he said as the shadow guard forced his way back up to his feet with the scythe still inside his shoulder. After a shock of mana that Sky shot through his scythe, the guard dissipated, the blade slicing him in two. "Of course, it takes extra mana to take them out."

The knights began battling the shadow guards in this area right near the stairs. One by one, the shadows got sent packing after bursts of mana. Haiza used the fighting to steal a guard's key and snuck past and made a beeline for the door, unlocking random cells along the way. "I'll meet you guys there, okay? Just uh, take care of those guys!" he said,

362

slowing down after the short sprint. Demons began leaving their cells and attacking the shadow guards around, some even jumped to the main floor and started dropping the guards there with their bare hands. It was chaos everywhere as the prison was in an uproar. Demons and prisoners on other levels began hollering and banging on the bars to get released as well. Promises of obedience and debts were screamed at the top of their lungs.

The pandemonium allowed Haiza to get to the door quite quickly, unlocking it and rushing inside the maze of demon personal effects. The knights finish with the wave of guards and rush towards the door as well. "Um. Be careful guys, the mana I gave you will still drain in this place. Don't go overboard." Scatha said, running slightly behind the rest.

"Yeah, I can already feel the mana getting sucked out of me, we have to hurry." Blaze said while stretching his fingers, testing his strength. When knights got to the door, Haiza was tossing weapons over the railing to the released demons below. The knights stopped and looked at him for a moment, but decided not to pursue the elephant.

"Did you find them?" Sky asked, getting Haiza's attention.

Haiza nodded and dragged out the box with the knights' clothing and armor in it. "Yup, get dressed so we can break out of this bitch!" He kicked the box towards them. The knights took turns changing in front of the room and keeping watch for more guards to come towards them. When they finished, they all looked over the railing with Haiza.

"Go ahead and hop in there, the demons should help keep the majority of the guards distracted, use that time to destroy those mana gates blocking the exit. Don't worry about me, I'll find my way out when it's clear heh heh." Haiza coughed a gross phlegmy cough and held a thumb up.

"We won't. Don't worry. But thanks." Gaia side-
eyed Haiza and jumped over the railing landing on the back
of a guard and joining in the fight on the main floor. The
other knights followed suit and began taking out guards one
by one. More kept joining, though, but they were met with
more demons getting released by Haiza above.

"I see the mana gate, barely, but it's there," Volt
said, looking down the long hallway on the main floor. A
row of clear, thick plates blocked the path to the giant door
at the very end. Volt claps his hands together. "One hundred
percent of this first gate belongs to me." He gathered mana
in his hands as they're firmly placed together.

"Go for it!" Blaze encouraged as he fought off a
couple of shadows. "Just know you'll probably be useless
afterward." He nodded at Volt

Volt shrugged his shoulders. "Erupt and eradicate,
shatter their hopes for they failed to embrace the goddess
...and I will punish them...Inazuma!" He thrusted forward his
electrically charged blast aimed at the first gate. Crash! The
Inazuma wave, after a couple of moments of struggle,
shattered the first gate. Volt nearly collapsed afterward, out
of mana. "Whew, I'm so glad that worked because I am
beat." The next gate flashed almost as a dare to attack it.

Sky sliced down a couple of shadows at once and
stepped up next to Volt. "Guess I'll go next then." He tapped
his scythe softly. "Okay!" Sky swung his scythe off his side
and gathered his mana. "Cut down the holy to protect the
precious, cleave and devastate! God Slayer!" Sky's scythe
grew and glowed that crisp golden sheen. His new enlarged
scythe gets raised into the air. Slowly, the mana in the air
began to gather into his weapon instead of the prison's
absorbers. The longer he held it, the more it shined. The
other knights guard Volt and Sky while he gets prepared to
attack. "Ahhhh this place is a goldmine for absorbing mana.
Hear my calls as I display my blessings. O' Ardin, grant me

the power to slay your demons and your angels. Xi...Neng!"
Spinning around, Sky swung his God slayer scythe at the
gate, releasing a wide streak of destructive mana that sliced
through even parts of the wall holding the gates up and
eventually right through the second gate with ease. It
shattered, and the streak also damaged the third gate as well
before it stopped.

"Nice! Sky. "Volt said watching.

"Ha ha. Yep, all I can do." Sky collapsed back to his
butt. "Man, that mana really does drain quickly.

"Mind if I clean up?" Gaia hopped over with kirici
already in her hands. She eases down into her low stance and
calms her breathing. "Crack ve şut, kırıcı sürücü! No mercy
for the evil. Crack and smash, Kirici. Breaker drive!" Gaia's
bow shined and crackled with destructive energy as she
eased back up to standing straight. "Okay!" she said as she
took one last breath and rushed toward the gate with kirici.

"Watch out!" A voice boomed from behind Gaia. As
she focused on the gate, a giant menacing figure stepped out
of a portal focused on her. This shadow was at least fourteen
feet tall, with six arms equipped with a blade in each. The
top of the shadow soldier guard's head were three horns
resembling a dark crown. This monster was clad entirely in
darkness and oozed a pungent aura as it moved. Its arms
crossed back and forth as it sliced at the air approaching
Gaia. A foot away from Gaia, she finally felt something
behind her; she slowed her stride and began to turn her head
behind her. She heard the scraping of the blades against each
other, inches from her body. It was too late. She was caught,
and the remaining knights didn't notice in time to act. That
shadow had gained on her that quickly.

"Oh, no." Right as she was to get cut by the blades,
she was shoved, landing on her butt.

"Move beautiful!" It was Haiza! He had somehow
come to the rescue, saving Gaia's life. After shoving her, he

simply lowered his head, realizing what befell him next. A mere moment later, Haiza was instantly sliced into eighteen different pieces, blood spraying in all directions, even on Gaia, who was closest. Haiza's sizeable slabs of meat made a splat as they slapped onto the cement-like ground.

Gaia sat there, stunned as the monstrosity refocused its attention on her. "Dammit Haiza, why'd your sleazy ass have to go and save me. How am I supposed to hate you now…" Gaia got up, wiped the blood from her face, and grasped her bo-staff. It was still powered up and hungry for prey. "Time to pay for that you ugly…thing!" Gaia rushed at the shadow, unleashing a flurry of powerful blows. The shadow soldier parried and blocked the blows with sword strikes of its own. A power struggle soon started as the two gained and gave up an advantage when one's attacks were harder or faster than their opponents. Back and forth they went, Gaia, pushing herself to keep up with all six arms at the same time while trying to create an opening for herself. "Tsk damnit, someone help!" Gaia pleaded.

"What is that the damn warden or something?" Blaze said, finally finding an opening in the fight with the lesser shadow guards. The demon prisoners had finally had enough to overwhelm the guards and keep them busy enough for the knights to focus. Ocean and Hail looked at each other at this moment.

"You want to try what we practiced in the timeless zone?" Hail said, nodding at Ocean.

"Yeah, sounds good." Ocean held his hand out, mana softly radiating around it.

"Heh. Nice. Contact!" Hail slammed his hand into Ocean's starting the process and causing a small flash of mana right around them. Mana and a watery mist peppered onto everything around them as they emerged from the fusion as Mist. He had long spiky frozen hair down to his shoulders. He retained Hail's fur jacket and had Ocean's

366

water claws attached to either forearm. A soft icy mist floated around his body at all times. He even breathed ice-cold breathes as if he was outside in the snow. "Ahhh, this is nice." Mist, with Hail as the lead, ran his hands through his frozen hair. It melted to the touch but refroze as soon as he let go.

"Any day now, bro!" Gaia yelped on the full defensive from the shadow's nonstop flurry.

"Right right. Well, let's do something about his movement first." Mist stomped his foot onto the ground in the direction of the two battling it out in front of him. A small puddle of water rose up just around his foot. The water was gifted life and began slithering on the ground towards the shadow, creating a trail of water from Mist's foot, and its target. Soon the liquid arrived and circled around the shadow's feet. Gaia was pushed back by a forceful strike skidding back almost into the wall. The water at the shadow's feet began to rise and expand as Mist controlled it through his mana with his hand as the guide. "Ice coffin!!" Mist closes his hand, and the water instantly is pulled up into the air and freezes solid, leaving a gigantic ice block that encased the shadow.

As soon as it was frozen, Gaia leaped up and swung at the two middle arms that were outstretched forward, shattering them into many small pieces of ice on the ground. "Whew, thank goodness." Gaia backs off and catches her breath, mana running low for her.

Mist opened his arms wide and spun around, releasing his water mana along the ground like a growing lake. Soon a shallow puddle of water filled the entire main floor of the prison. "Icy graveyard!" The pool again flash froze to create a new winter-themed zone for Mist to use. He watched the ice block with the shadow soldier guard shake in place and rumble. "Not much time now." Mist raised his hands into the air. "Infinite. Ice. Works." Various ice blades began shooting out of the ice all over the main floor and the walls, wherever his ice graveyard had touched. Mist's sky blue mana flared as his domain was set. "Now, I'm ready." Almost like clockwork as soon as he finished the monster before him had broken out of his ice coffin.

Immediately, the shadow charged at him with his four remaining arms. The top two arms lowered blades aimed directly for his face, but Mist didn't move. The edges connected, but not with Mist himself. A thin sheet of ice appeared in front of him. It shined when the blades traveled through them, stopping the momentum. Mist placed a single finger on the tip of one of the blades. "Thanks for the mana." He calmly said as his mana left his finger and clenched onto the sword, draining mana from the shadow and into Mist. "Mmmm, I needed that, now back off!" Mist grabbed an ice blade in either hand and slices at the shadow's leg. Black ooze flew into the air as the shadow limped backward, leaking from behind his right knee. Blaze settled himself off to the side and began to gather his flaming mana into his right arm.

Mist drug two swords on the ground on his way to attack the shadow. "See if you can handle this!" he said as he began a flurry of his own using the two ice blades in his hands, swapping out with the many all around them as well. The shadow was on the full defensive blocking the attacks with his now four arms. "Faster, faster, faster!" Mist sped up his movements, and his attacks as more and more blades were sacrificed to outdo the shadow. The speed slowly began to be too much for his opponent as Mist's blades began to nick and slice away at the sides of the shadow creature. In a moment of desperation, the shadow swung all four swords at once, forcing Mist to block and be blown back a few feet. The shadow's back was now facing the mana gates with Mist and the knights in front of him. "I guess you're done with me playing around with you then."

Mist raised his right hand into the air. "Fine then." Mana began to spiral around his arm. The icy graveyard began to shake and rattle as the collection of swords rosed out of the ice and into the air. They all balanced themselves and point directly at the shadow. An army of ice blades now stared the shadow and the gates down. A large smirk was on Mist's face now. "You should have never shown up today."

"When given the power to lay judgment, attack with the fury of all five kings! Scatter and pierce, Ledeni raspršeni napado! Ice glass barrage!" Mist sent the blades soaring at the shadow at incredible speeds. One by one, they slammed into the shadow's guard, shattering and pulsing on its arms afterward. Eventually, the pulses and the continual swords began freezing the arms of the shadows. "Ha, doesn't look like you'll last much longer!" As soon as mist spoke, the shadow's arms all shattered at once from the ice. The blades now hit his chest directly, slowly digging into him, one by one. Grumbles and roars could be heard from the shadow in pain, but Mist continued laying the nearly endless amount of blades into him. The black ooze soon began to splash out of the shadow's chest, and soon enough, the blades pierced his chest and all followed through him and towards the mana gate. The hole in its chest widened before the ice started to crash into the mana gate mercilessly. The rest of that damaged gate shattered now too. The blades stopped flowing now, falling back to the ice around the shadow, who stood there lifeless. After a few moments of watching this, Mist stepped up again. "Heh, now that is how you do it. I guess it's about time I finish you of-." Mist gets cut off by Blaze rushing past him and getting face to face with the shadow.

"Why do you get all of the fun, it's my turn!" Blaze's arm was shining brilliantly from the gathered mana. He jumped up into the air, right in front of the shadow's body. "Take this! My rage, my anger, and all of my fury! Searing finger blast!" Blaze held his fist out, and instead of touching the shadow with it, the mana in Blaze's arm gathered in a small orb directly in front of him. He then readied his fist and punched the sphere, causing a concentrated blast of mana to fire out directly through the hole in the shadow's chest. It blazed through and destroyed another mana gate. Right after it was destroyed, Blaze reared back with both arms as he gathered what mana he had left into another orb over his head. "Agh! I'm not done!" The globe of mana proliferated above his head. "Oh, great lords grant me the power to create the ultimate destruction, kneel before the power of lord Verafelt." He reached back and tossed the destructive ball of molten mana ahead of him. "Molten Nova!" Blaze's mana annihilated what was left of the shadow's body on its path down the corridor and into another gate. Four down. Blaze collapsed backward onto the ice. "Whew, I did too much. I'm dizzy," he said, closing his eyes.

Mist rushed up slightly past Blaze, staring down the next gate. "You're not showing me up today! I've still got some more in me," he said, gathering more mana in his hands. Gaia drug Blaze over to where Volt and Sky were resting. The demon prisoners had finished cleaning up the remaining shadow guards as well, so they waited in anticipation as well. They now owed the knights their lives and would follow them to their deaths. "Ahhhh! I'll put everything into this next one." Mist summoned nine of the mana rockets that Ocean usually has on his hybrid weapon and hovered them in mid-air around him, facing the gates. "From the future to the past, erase our foes with a blast! Hydro bomber barrage!" All at once, the array of rockets soared down the corridor and burette the gates with explosion after explosion. The entire prison shook from the impact. A cloud of smoke and mist came seeping out to reveal not only was one of the gates destroyed, but the other

370

was severely damaged as well. Mist gave one last smirk, "Beat that." Mist collapsed and reverted back into Hail and Ocean, each with a smile cracked on their unconscious faces. The damaged gate crumbled on its own, falling apart onto the ground soon afterward. One more barrier to go.

Void finally got up and readied himself. "I guess it's just me now, huh," he said, releasing his claymore, Fonos. As he prepared himself, dark mana from the remains of every defeated shadow in the entire prison began to gather in a single sinister sphere in the center of the main level.

"What's that?" Gaia pointed to the sphere as it grew and grew in size. Soon it began sucking dark mana from Void himself when it ran out of shadows.

"What the hell is that? Hmph. No matter if it seems dangerous." Void raised Fonos into the air and charged at the now person-sized sphere floating there. CLANK! "What?"

A large black spiky and bony demon hand appeared from the darkness of the sphere and caught his blade. The area cracked, and the inner mana expanded and formed into the rest of the demon. His head cleared at least the first floor and a half judging his height. Its body was long and lanky, dark spikes decorated its entire body. Its hands and feet had long, sharp claw-like fingers and toes. His eyes were slanted and glowed a bright red, a menacing jaw full of razor shape teeth awaited as well. Last to spawn in was a twelve-foot tail that slammed into the ground and the steps behind him. The demon growled at him after completing his summoning, "I am the warden, Raizen, not that damn weak shadow before. I just absorbed all of the shadows here to make my arrival. Now feel my power!" The demon boomed from a mouth three stories up. His mana was enraged and shook the prison only by flaring it up.

"Uh…you can do it!?" Gaia said reluctantly.

371

"Goodluck, Void. It's just you with mana now, remember." Blaze said, looking away.

Void put away Fonos. "I guess I'll have to go all out immediately if I don't want a quick death." Void pulls out both cursed blades simultaneously, instantly the dark mana began circling around him, overcharging his body and warping his mind. "Time to go...berserk...ahhhh!" Void's mana reached a fever pitch and began to rattle the prison in a way similar to Raizen's. The two stared each other down with white-hot intensity.

"Be careful, Void." Sky said seriously.

"Shut up, Sky!" Void barked back.

"What is this mana coming from Void, it's so sinister," Gaia said, covering up from the dark winds threatening to push her back. The knights watched intently, waiting for the first move.

It was Void, he dashed in zipping around in a complicated path on the way to the demon's legs. Both swords in hand, he slashed at the ankles and calves first. The swords clanked against Raizen's hide but did not break his skin. Void in frustration continued the onslaught traveling up to the first floor with single mana powered leap and slashing away at the impossibly tough chest and arms. Nothing was working. "Grahhh!" Void bellowed in frustration. He crossed both swords and swung them, creating an 'X' shape streak of mana headed for Raizen.

"Ha. Ha," Raizen chuckled as he blocks the attack by merely holding his hand up. The streak exploded on his palm, creating a smoke cloud, blinding Raizen.

Void opens up his hands and creates a portal around the wrist of Raizen. "Mercy's shift." Void closed the portal, severing Raizen's hand from his wrist. The limb crashed onto the ground, nearly smashing onto Blaze's head.

"Gaaah, damn you!" Raizen grumbled as he waved his nub around in pain.

372

"Hmph." Void smirked as he disappeared into a portal. He reappeared in midair right in front of the handless arm, stabbing into it with both cursed blades.

"What are you—" Raizen starts.

"Let's see how much pain you can take!" Void feeds off of the dark mana in the swords and swung one blade up and the other down, splitting Raizen's lower arm like a piece of celery. The streaks from his blades had traveled up the sleeve, giving it extra range. Both slabs of the demon's arms flailed in different directions, and Void stood suspended in the air before he fell.

Before he had the chance to fall, Raizen swatted Void into the ground with his other arm. Void created a crater on the bottom floor upon impact. "Damn you, human! Hope you've got tricks cause that won't work a second time!" Raizen roared.

"Void! You okay?" Gaia came over to the crater made from Void's body in the cement. He was already getting up; blood was trickling from his head and body. The enraged energy kept him up on his feet, even though his entire body was damaged.

"Graaaahhh!" Void called out, spitting out blood afterward.

"Void..." Gaia said, her voice getting lower as she realized he couldn't hear her. Talking to him now was pointless.

"Die!!" Raizen rose his foot and lowered it right towards Void and Gaia. The demons foot rumbled towards the ground like an asteroid. Suddenly a giant portal opened up in the path of the foot blocking Void. Raizen halted his foot just short of the entrance, leg suspended in mid-air. "Told you that wouldn't work anymo- ahhh!!" He yelped as everything below his knee ungraciously fell to the ground, black ooze splattered out like a water hose.

Void was then spotted on the first floor back to Raizen, both blades bloody as hell and glowing with evil dark mana. The big portal near the crater and another near Raizen's other leg both closed then. Void's wounds began healing then, his body revitalized from absorbing mana with his last strike. Void turned around slightly, staring directly into Raizen's eyes. "Hah Hah Hah!" He chuckled with a sinister, pure evil smile.

Raizen was forced onto his arms and knees as he was off balance with one leg. He looked up in anger at Void. "Ugh, get over here!!" The demon plants his hand and his nub onto the ground. Dark mana begins to bubble and come to life on his back. "With the mark of the dark lord, escape is futile. Grab him and never let go, Death's grip!" Suddenly, the mana on Raizen's back materializes and comes to life as dark tentacles spread out from his back and traveled towards Void in a frenzied group of twelve.

"Is this desperation?" Void said, jumping back and slashing at the two dark tentacles that got there first. The first two were sliced up and off Void went, running down the path on the first floor back towards the cells. Right before he got there, Void skidded to a stop and back flipped onto the stairwell going up. Two tentacles speared into the ground, aiming for him. "Do these things not have a range limit? Maybe I will try it myself." Void continued up the stairs and onto the next floor as the pursuit continued.

"There is no escape!" Raizen yelled.

About halfway through the second floor, Void spun around, sending multiple streaks of mana towards the tentacles. The first two were able to dodge, but the next two that were just making it to the second floor were sliced in two. Void smiled at the mild success, but four other tentacles had snuck around the railing behind him; all six now dived for him at once. Using his enhanced instincts, Void leaped into the air, upside down, using his long-ranged blade to

374

balance himself. All six pursuers collided in the middle, only managing to knick Voids' lower arm.

With his other hand, Void came down with his other blade slashing one of the tentacles and releasing a brilliant explosion at the same time. All six were caught in the crossfire as Void skidded back on his feet from the impact. Both of Void's swords fly out of his hands as well, landing on the floor in different spots. Out of the dust, the final four tentacles speared into Void, shoving him back into the wall at the end of this floor. One pierced either shoulder and both thighs. "Ha! I told you there was no escape!" Raizen yelled from the first floor as the tentacles began to drain the life force from Void.

Void simply smirked quietly. The dense dark mana surrounding him diminished and disappeared. Void lowered his head and closed his eyes. Let's see if this works.

"Shit Void, are you okay!" Blaze called upstairs, not able to see Void.

"I'm starting to feel his presence less and less." Sky said, trying to sense him, his eyes closed.

The flow of mana and life force stopped cold. There was a chilling gasp as the knights all stood there in silence, trying to sense Void now. Raizen's face transitioned from determined to a gaping smile as he sucked the last of Void's mana dry. Hot air seeped out of his mouth as he gleanced confidence. "Bahaha, now it's time to skewer the rest of yo-."

"YOU THINK I HAVEN'T BEEN THROUGH WORSE THAN THIS!" Void's eyes shot open as the flow of mana reversed, filling Void's body with hordes of dark mana. His body quivered with power, almost like a few hundred shots of caffeine. Void jerked in place, and the tentacles all removed themselves from him at the simultaneously.

"Tsk. How is this possible! No matter, I'll get my mana back through them!" Raizen looked over to the remaining knights, pulling his tentacles back to him as quickly as possible.

Void's feet finally touched the ground again. He walked forward, allowing the new mana to heal his injuries. Both cursed blades get picked up and sheathed again. A cloud over his head seemed to have calmed as he took a moment to calm his mind, his eyes closed. "Let's do this, Fonos, gotta hurry." His eyes open again, but glowing a bright white. A thin layer of dark mana began exhausting out of his body and hovering around him like a cloud. Void grabbed Fonos off his back and leaped over the railing, traveling down to the first floor the fast way. He twirled and spun in midair to change his trajectory and soar closer to the tentacles. The knights stood there still, full faith in Void. About a foot before the pointy tips of the tentacles reached them, Void's cold hard claymore sliced the first three like cucumber, and Fonos sent a streak of mana towards the last. It traveled along the ground curving and exploding on the tentacle right in front of Gaia. She rose up and summoned Kirici back as soon as she saw Raizen shift. Void's claymore was stuck in the ground from the impact.

"Gah! Dammit, you! Raizen positioned his hand like a spear and directed it at Void. Gaia lept over and blocked the attack with her bo staff, pushing against the force that Raizen still put into his hand, trying to skewer Void. "What? How are you so strong as to oppose my might!" Raizen yelled, confused.

"Pfft. Get over yourself, dammit!" Gaia said, talking through her teeth as she skid back slightly, trying to hold back Raizen's arm. She now held Kirici with both hands, horizontally, holding him back with all her might. "Ok Void, hurry up! If you've got a plan, do it now!" she pleaded.

"I won't let you!" Raizen said, pushing against Gaia.

All this time, Void has been standing there, back to the action, in silence. He's been concentrating his mana; the white aura had grown along with the dark fog of mana around him. It expanded several feet in all directions and began to spark like a nucleus and agitate with a life of its own. Void turned around slowly while the mana surrounding him started to orb around him very quickly. He squatted, both hands in front of him, this seemed to make the mana travel even faster. The knights watched in silence at the spectacle happening before their eyes.

"Whew, I can do this. Filled with rage and anger...my curse is turned into a blessing from the hands of the Gods that deemed me worthy to wield the ultimate darkness." The mana began expanding even further now, spinning at mach speeds around Void. The mana started to shock and hit at the knights as they were inside the range. In its rotation, the mana began to resemble a giant dark sphere around Void, more massive than the biggest molten nova from Blaze. "Feel my pain, my struggles, and shatter from the weight of my spirit!" The mana instantly condensed into a head-sized orb of mana in front of his hands.

Raizen looked nervously at the concentrated mana before him. He pulled his hand back. "Hey! Let's rethink thi—"

"Keni balaaaaa!" Void sent the orb forth, only moving slowly at first, but as soon as it sensed Raizen's mana, it exploded forward, cutting through his chest like a bullet. It zoomed past the hole in Raizen's chest and blew towards the last mana gate. The gate was destroyed with so much supplemental force that it blew open the gigantic locked door that lay behind it. The doors swung open, allowing the chilly fresh air from the outside to breeze in. The demons that were previously imprisoned began to jump and celebrate. The knights get up and run over to Void and Gaia excitedly

"Look at him," Gaia said, looking at Raizen's body. He was unmoving. The hole from Void's attack had begun to petrify Raizen's body from the inside out, traveling throughout quickly.

Void nodded, the white glow and dark mana both missing from him now. "I guess it affects all beings differently," he said.

Sky put his arms around both of their shoulders. "Good job, you two. We now have the climax of our journey waiting outside of those doors. We better be ready for anything." Suddenly as he spoke, the demons all came over and bowed at Sky's feet. "Um, what? So, unlike you demons," Sky said in reaction.

One of the demons stepped forward. He was quite chubby with skin resembling cooled molten lava all over his body. "For us demons, loyalty is life and death. You have saved us from the torturing exploits of Scourge. Our lives are now yours. Whatever lies ahead, you can rely on us to back you up as well," he said, bowing again.

Hail's eyes opened wide. "Wow, that's surprising."

Sky looked at the faces of the knights for confirmation. Void and Blaze just shrugged. Volt mouthed 'Why not?' and Gaia plainly shewed him over. "Fine. I supposed we wouldn't mind some extra help. You guys made good work of those shadows in there, you may be useful." Sky smirked.

The same demon nodded to his other demons, and they all picked up their weapons. "Thank you." He says, raising a club into the air.

Sky, the knights, and the demon prisoners all walk out together, and into the brisk winds of Scourge's battlefield. The second they exited the prison doors, their mana began to restore on its own. This next walk was a short trek as they worked their way up to the front of Scourge's castle, where their allies are undoubtedly preparing to launch an attack.

Chapter 17: Climax

The scene in front of Scourge's castle was a tense one. Scourge's sizeable castle loomed in the background, the top reaching into the clouds. Many levels were lit through the windows, together with the chaos moon, giving the battleground some illumination. The castle was in a high gothic style, spiked tips for all ceilings with an eerie aura surrounding it, of course. The front gate for the castle was wide open, showing Scourge's confidence in his defense today. On his side, directly out ahead of the fence was his over two thousand strong armies. Grey skinned demons clad in full armor, and a spear and shield combination for weapons all looked ahead of them with red eyes filled with vicious intent. Each was a clone of Silverwing, except pumped full of dark mana to push the potential to the fullest. Shadow soldiers surrounded and backed them up, filling out other classical roles. A line of archers and large shield shadows were out front, setting up the Silverwing clones as the main fighting force. This evil army waited in anticipation for their leaders to arrive.

Opposing them was a medley of different warriors with different backgrounds and origins but one single goal. Take down Scourge. Pirates, Aqua Knights, and the Hiyama army were all standing side by side with Hepheaus, William, and Jax out front to lead them. Together they had nearly one thousand five hundred warriors put together, mostly made up of the Hiyama army. Hepheaus, Jax, and William crouched in the front strategizing while the rest of the army waited in anticipation for orders.

Jax stood tall with his captain's jacket sitting on his shoulders, the sleeves flailing in the wind. A slightly tattered tank top was all he had on his chest. He also wore sleek black pants and tall brown boots as his attire, making him probably the only one without armor on. Jax donned two unique black machetes, though. The blades were longer than usual, as well as having a serrated edge along the backside. He excitedly tapped the back end of one against his shoulder as it rested there. He was ready to get to work.

William himself had the flashiest armor of the group, of course. It was themed after an eagle, but it was so thick and bulky it made Will's usual small stature appear huge. The helm resembled an eagle's head, with mostly white and green plates around the neck. The helm was connected directly to the shoulder plates in one piece. The heavy feather-shaped plates sat over the shoulders, and almost down to the elbows, loosely. It could be lifted as the arms moved around. This piece wrapped around even to the back and had a lining of real feathers underneath the metal ones. The silver chest plate had golden lines down the side, and a green pinwheel with a blade behind it symbolized as the mark of his regime. The bottom of the chest plate extended into the side and butt plate as well. The Gauntlets were asymmetrical, though. His right hand had a thick, clawed gauntlet, the talons on each finger were as sharp as an eagle's talon, shaped the same as well. The left was much smaller, using an expensive glove instead, much better suited for holding his weapon. A gigantic golden lance, modified with a blade's edge running along the bottom, cone-shaped elsewhere. The edge extended from the tip to the guard in front of the grip. His shiny lance was dug headfirst into the dirt in front of him, his arms crossed as he talked to the other two captains.

Hepheaus wore armor similar to when she first met with the knights. She held two long, curved katanas sheathed on her back this time, though. Mystical symbols ran down the center of the blade, their families crest was laid on the handguard. The mana channeled throughout the symbols lined up and down her body, freely. She wore a silver helm resembling a water dragon's head. Glaring red eyes sat in the center of the helm, bone-white horns curved around both sides of the jaw. This marked the bottom of the helm as it left her mouth open, scale plates running down the sides of her jaw and her neck. The top of the helm had five white spikes shooting back on the head, sitting on dark blue scales. When it connected to the sides, it turned back into silver. Her soft, long hair flowed down under the sides of her neck and down her back. Her armor was slightly heavier this time as well, where the armor actually covered her body. Thick silver and blue scale plates wrapped her arms, razor-sharp blades ran parallel to her forearms on these gauntlets. Her breastplate stopped just below her solar plexus, allowing for plenty of movement. Her tall, lightly plated grieves and skimpy bottom armor remained, extra sheaths wrapped around her waist for the new blades she dawned. Hepheaus stood with her hand on the butt of her sword, tapping it softly, ready to draw it at a moment's notice.

Just then, the massive doors of Scourge's castle creaked open as Braugg, Strike, Scourge, and Adrian came stomping out next to each other. The doors shut behind them on their own. They crossed the bone graveyard that served as the courtyard and made their way through a dirt path and the front gate. Black tombstones and bones scattered randomly over uneven mounds surrounding the castle. Surrounding the creepy courtyard was a tall, thick, and solid onyx colored gate, tall spikes protruded out of the top. It looked almost like a cement wall around the castle.

The four generals of this dark army walked forward without pause as the demons split like the red sea to let them pass. Walking in a straight line with Scourge leading now, the four arrived at the front of the formation and huddled up in the center. Braugg had a fresh arm and armor from the damage taken in the last battle. Strike had a nasty smirk on his face always, he showed a lot of movement as he huddled in place. He fidgeted back and forth, very eager for some reason. Scourge flexed through his new armor as he directed his attention towards the other three, explaining plans and such very quietly.

Adrian was his own form now. He had successfully been separated from Keith through Scourge's experiments and swore his loyalty to the dark mercenary for releasing him. Scourge's influence and teachings helped Adrian to better control the mana channels in his new body. His massive amount of mana was brimming at the seams waiting to be released. He also donned a new set of armor gifted from Scourge and based on Demise's old armor set from before he was seen as a God. This set was a dark grey and black with red accents under the plates on the joints. It was quite simple overall. Large oval shoulder plates with a single curved spike coming outmatched the slim gray greaves, which also had a spike on the top of the foot. The armor around the chest had tightly wound plates crisscrossed to look like medical bandages. This configuration made for a light armor with some movement but a lot of protection. Adrian's style isn't one of a lot of movement or physical, but by letting his mana do the attacking for him so Scourge figured the armor set would protect him in a vast battlefield type environment. The sword Adrian wielded wasn't the same as Keith. This one was more like a broadsword with an extra-long blade edge and a hollow inside to help conduct mana. The blade guard near the handle was large and curved downwards, black but still slightly shimmered under the chaos moon.

Calm, eerie winds blew as dark clouds began to form above the battlefield. The Captains of the Knights army finished their meeting just as Sky came over the hill to their right, a determined coalition of fighters behind him. Hepheaus jubilantly jumped into the air in excitement from laying eyes on the knights again. She jogged over and met the knights, while Jax and William waited in front of the army. "Ah, darlings, I feared you wouldn't make it!" Hapheaus opened her arms wide and hugged as many knights as possible. Hail and Gaia ended up getting left out.

"Hey, mom, we made it," Ocean said, smiling in the center of the embrace.

"What happened since we last saw each other knights?" Hepheaus backed off and peered at the dark forces, just to check that they hadn't moved yet.

Sky scratched his head. "Eh, a hell of a lot of things happened Heph."

Hepheaus looked at Sky sideways, waiting for him to continue. Sky just stood there awkwardly, not wanting to get into it. A single sweat droplet came sliding down his forehead. Void finally saved him, moving Sky to the side and positioning himself in front of Hepheaus. "Long story short, we were all separated after we left Eodon. Volt and I went to Kayard and Basonali, respectfully, to get our orbs. We ended up meeting back up in Paradise and traveling to Repshera and here together. We lost our powers and got captured in the portal on the way to Umbra, and we actually just broke out of Scourge's prison. Now we are here ready to kick Scourge's ass, with your help, of course. Will that suffice?" Void said, brushing his hair back with his hand.

As he was talking, Hepheaus had slowly started to trail off her attention, but when Void said 'Paradise,' she immediately perked back up. She held her left hand up, waving it in place while she was trying to find the words. "Did you just say Paradise?" She finally got out.

"Yeah? What of it?" Void responded.

384

"It actually didn't look too bad a place before a fiend laid waste to much of it," Blaze said, shaking his head in shame from Void's right side.

"Paradise? Paradise? In what universe is that a good place to visit? Way too early for you to go there!" Hepheaus said, raising her voice.

"Woah, what do you know about Paradise that we don't? You aren't making sense!" Ocean said, trying to calm her down.

"Paradise?" Hepheaus scoffed. She gave the Royal Knights and the different demons who stood before her a dead look. The demons silently got very interested in what she had to say. "That area is cursed. Has been since the times when Lucinthes's spawn threatened Sylindra's very existence. It is believed that Chaos is, in fact, sealed there somewhere as a cause for all the anomalies. Time does not flow there, snowfalls endlessly; chilling winds freeze you to the core." Her face began to get very serious as her audience's faces got more and more confused. "That place is a graveyard. Many generations of knights, those who came before you are buried there." She said, lowering her head, sighing softly.

Volt raised a brow. "You mean…" Before Volt could finish, Hepheaus cut him off.

"Yes…The true heroes of the Gods. Their bodies even in death do not feel the effects of time." She trailed off for a moment.

"That's horrible…" Gaia gasped covering her mouth.

"A cruel gesture from Nefula…they are stored there so that their dead bodies will be undisturbed, forever locked in time. Dead, but also still forced to suffer, alive at the same time. Such a depressing place. How they treat our chosen warriors. I pray that peace finds your bodies when your time comes." Visible shock, disgust, and disbelief awere written all over the Royal Knight's faces. They'd never heard such a story about their gods and previous Royal Knights before. "You see now why I find it odd that you speak of it with such grandeur?" She questioned.

"Hmm. I feel like that kind of story we would have heard about. But no one spoke of that on Basonali while I was there." Void pondered with his fist placed directly over his lips.

"Wait...Basonali? The place I'm referring to is southern Eodon." Hepheaus squinted her eyes at Void.

Ocean placed his hand on his mother's arm. "We went to a hidden city up north; I think there is confusion here."

Hepheaus nodded her head. "Yeah, maybe you're right. Sorry for losing my cool. Either way, I want you guys to visit that grave and pay respects when you can." She started walking back towards their army and waved the knights and company to follow. "Anyway, come on, guys, we just finished strategizing. This battle for Scourge's castle will begin soon. We need to be prepared."

Hepheaus and the knight's party finally joined William and Jax, who had waited there so patiently. The two groups made their reunion, catching up and greeting each other after their long break apart. Jax, William, and Hepheaus took turns describing each of their separate armies' strengths and abilities, and the current strategies for the clash preparing to occur. They first looked at the pirates.

Wendy's pirates wore light cloth armor, so they could move around effectively. Simple extra padding was added to each piece. Most chose to wear cloth vests and jackets for their chest, each dawning Wendy's Jolly Roger. Their arms and legs are where most of the padding was. Blade resistant shin and arm guards. Each was equipped with a machete and mana crossbows used to fire small amounts of mana over distance. Circular cases carried the arrow-shaped hardened mana used as ammo. Next, they checked out the new garb for the Aqua warriors.

The Aqua warriors were heavily armored with shiny silver armor, powered further with lines of water mana that ran along mercury encased throughout. It resembled Ula's water irrigation. This water mana helped them to transfer mana around their bodies efficiently, and even transfer mana to their weapons easier as well. On top of their massive mana powered armor, they were equipped with oversized mana shields and lances as well. The guards could surround the user with a dome of mana to protect them from damage when activated. Making up for the majority of the army, the Hiyama warriors were next. They exhibited the most poise of the group, showing their experience in many high stakes battles before.

The Hiyama warriors were by far the most balanced. Their armor was mostly silver and green, with golden insignias marked down the sides. The metal plates were thick enough to protect but had enough room in between the pieces to allow for proper movement. Half of the warriors had the traditional sword and shield combination, and the other half was sword and spear.

Sky and Volt took care to commit this information relayed. They were the captain and commander of the Royal Knights, after all. The knights chose the groups they were going to battle in, attempting to cover all bases. Sky and Volt would stay back initially to direct the forces and go in to help out when someone needed it. Hail and Jax would lead one group of mostly pirates and Hiyama forces as well-aimed for the left area, hoping to use their speed to find an opening to flank. Blaze and Gaia took the released demons and the rest of the pirates off to the right side. Ocean Hepheaus and Void would charge ahead directly for the gates with the vast majority of the Aqua warriors. Scatha was to start a medic tent of sorts on the hill to treat the injured along with the few nurses they actually had. Some forces would stay back to help protect her and the path to getting the wounded to her. William stayed back with Volt and Sky to protect the rear with the rest of the massive Hiyama army. This was the plan anyway. The discussion went on until Hepheaus looked over at the opposition and saw Scourge and his generals lined up in front of his army, appearing ready to initiate the conflict.

"Looks like time is nearly up," Hepheaus said, positioning her weapon for the charge and adjusting her helm. Scourge's clone army got into low stances ready to charge at full speed.

Sky slid over next to William as the armies entered formations in front and around them. "So." Sky said, summoning his scythe. "Why don't I see my father here to support his son in his time of need. Why must I have you instead?"

William was taken aback by the sudden statement from Sky. "Woah, Woah Sky. Try not to hurt my feelings, okay? It's been a while since I've needed to dawn this ol' armor, but I've still got plenty of fight in me," he said with both hands raised into the air and a huge smile, you could just 'feel' beaming through his massive helm that covered his head.

Sky must have felt it too as his annoyance showed on his face again while looking at Will. "Hmm," he grumbled.

"As for your father…" William trailed off. "He is taking care of other matters. They ended up losing that battle they were in before you left. They were on the verge of taking over our own land. He still sent me with a portion of our forces to help you out regardless. I think that is still quite generous, right?" Will shrugged his shoulders as he lost Sky's attention. "Hey, I'm just the messenger. Don't be mad at me, Sky." He reached for Sky's shoulder but missed as Sky moved out of the way.

"It's still disappointing. So tired of the war. Let this be it for this family," Sky said, looking ahead of him towards the sea of enemies laid out before him, waiting for the go-ahead to charge. Sky sighed and flapped his wings, hovering a few feet into the air, turning around to face his army now.

"But Sky, that's impossible for our family…" William sighed.

Sky ignored William and held his scythe high up into the air above his head. "Knights!" he yelled. Every pair of eyes ahead of him was glued to Sky. The knights, Wendy's pirates, the Hiyama army, the aqua warriors, Hepheaus, William, Jax, Scatha, everyone. They looked up to him as the Captain, friend, leader to charge forward in this perilous life to come. He wasn't perfect by any sense, but he had the passion and care for his underlings . His quick wit was all he needed right now. Volt stood next to Scatha, staring up at Sky, silently holding hands. As the second in command, Volt was brought up to be a natural leader by Father John. His technical sense for battle makes him not only a great one on one fighter but also essential for changing the flow of large campaigns as well. The perfect commander for the Royal Knights.

"That's our captain, heh." Void smirked while running his hands along the side of Fonos calmly.

"Knights…" Sky said a lot softer this time. "What lies before us is a force unknown to us all, and that makes it unsettling, understandably. What we DO know is Scourge…He is devious and spiteful and dangerous, but that does not matter! We are going to take everything that makes him a threat, and we are gonna shove it, up. His. Ass!" His voice gains volume as he continues and balls up his fist as cheers rang in front of him. "For all the people's lives, he has terrorized, for every death by his hands, for Wendy… He deserves the payback that's coming to him!" A ring of

389

'for wendy' chants went throughout the army, originating from Jax and the pirates. "This is Scourge's final stand, and no way some little army of clones can stop his punishment. We are going to kick his door in, take Wendy back, and kill his ass!" Sky yells. "Now, let's go! Allow us to march towards our destin-." Clank! Sky got cut off by a dark arrow gushing through the top tip of his wing and bouncing off of one of the Aqua warrior's large shields. Sky immediately landed as he heard a roar and the sound of boots tearing through the damp grass and dirt behind him. Anger and disgust in his face, Sky turned around, pointing his spear at the incoming charge. "Knights! Charge!" He screamed at the top of his lungs.

With that, the battle had begun. Scourge and generals stood still as his army of shadows and cloned Silverwings charged forward around them, leaving them behind in front of the castle. The hoard of evil split off into different directions aimed at different parts of hero's formations. Their run was so erratic and wild; it was hard to determine their path. Three rows of the shadow archers stayed behind, raining down dark arrows on the other side of the battlefield. The knight's forces slid behind the massive shields of the Aqua warriors as they took the brunt of the bolts while also preparing for the incoming contact. Those out front immediately activated their domes for protection. All at once, the Aqua warriors out front were impacted by the wild charge of demons. They held ground, stopping them from losing footing with a cramped army of warriors behind them. The demons had covered so much ground; the knight's troops didn't have the chance to advance as much.

"Push back!" Sky yelled from above while simultaneously deflecting the incoming arrows.

"Gotcha!" Blaze and Void let out a blast of mana together, blowing away the Silverwings clumped up against the Aqua warriors' shields. The arrows stopped for a moment. Void, Hepheaus, and Ocean used the opportunity to force their way through the middle of the Silverwings, making a beeline to the castle.

"Watch your flanks!" Volt said as a hundred and fifty shadows of different varieties stealthily teleported to either side of the knight's army and started by murdering warriors on either side caught off guard. Volt on the left and William on the right immediately jumped into action to hold back the shadows. Volt slashed and stabbed through the shadows with the help of the pirates around him. "Tsk. This is ridiculous, hurry up Void we have no room to go!" Volt said, back to back with Jax, while they fought for their lives against a stream of shadows.

Scourge and his generals stood still watching this first turn in the tide of battle. The shadow archers let out another row of dark arrows, forcing everyone to look up to block. Even the front line had to divert their attention upwards as bolts struck their armor, breaking through unprotected areas. Using the opportunity, the Silverwings began stabbing away in the soft areas of the Aqua warrior's armor. Necks, under the armpits, waists, wherever they could find, they stuck away. The knight's army quickly lost a large portion of their front line from this rush. The frenzied frontal assault from the Silverwing clones and attacks from the side from the shadows kept the knights busy.

Just as things seemed bleak, Void and company broke through the Silverwings and made it to the open field, nothing but the archers and generals in their immediate path. As soon as Void was clear, he snapped his fingers. "Demon's Shift!" Just then, Voids mana opened many small portals directly under every remaining Aqua warrior sucking them in, and opening room for the pirates and Hiyama warriors to battle. With space, mana pistols in hand, the pirates started to shoot away at the archers on the opposing side.

The Aqua warriors appeared up from the ground in a single, large portal, directly behind Void, who had skidded to a stop in front of Scourge. This tactic made the slow-moving Aqua warriors get into position faster. Scourge simply smirked and snapped his fingers, summoning a horde of thick, heavy shadow soldiers to match the aqua warriors. The Aqua warriors cautiously held up their shields in preparation. Scourge waved his generals off. "Go. I can handle this myself," he said as Void, Ocean, and Hepheaus all got into battle positions. The aqua warriors and the heavies that Scourge spawned began to battle in a wide around the four, giving them a bit of space in front of the gates to face off.

"Very confident, I see," Ocean said with his rapier pointed in Scourges direction. Void and Hepheaus both got to either side of Scourge.

"As you wish," Adrian said as he lowered his head and teleported away with the rest of the generals. The battlefield, through all the chaos, had evened out a little more at this point. The knights had backed up the Silverwing line and fought off the flanking shadows, giving them actual footing to battle back from behind. As they pressed forward, a familiar mug greeted them.

"Oy! You ready to get beat again, girl." Braugg stood before them, aiming his massive, spiked fist at Gaia.

"What was that?" Gaia halted her advance on the right side of the battlefield with Blaze and peered over at Braugg. "You want to get your ass beat?" she yelled convincingly while she punched down a Silverwing with her bare hands.

William and Jax both held their weapons ahead of them, at Braugg and spoke simultaneously. "Worry not Gaia! We've got this one!" They shouted while battling the line of shadows set in front of Braugg. Braugg casually clapped in place while he waited for his victims to approach.

On the other side, Gaia was pulled along by Blaze while they made their way around the right side of the fighting with the prison demons as cover.

"Where do you think you're going?" A voice echoed from inside of a portal that appeared in front of the two. The demons that accompanied Blaze and Gaia were busy dealing with shadows and couldn't help. Out of the portal stepped Adrian, calmly, with his hands clasped together around his belt buckle. His sword wasn't even drawn.

"Damnit!" Blaze said, skidding to a stop from the wet grass, stopping right in front of him. "Adrian, what is this?" he let out angrily.

"Yeah, I thought you were on our side!" Gaia pulled out Kirici and spun it to her side, at the ready. "What's the meaning of this!"

Adrian peered up with a smirk. "Keith was. But his and my ideas aren't the same."

"But...you're the same person!" Blaze yelled, irritated and confused. Flames surrounded his body incrementally as his mana begun to overflow. Gaia struggled to avoid the random flares flying off in her direction.

Adrian snickered again, then let out a short evil laugh to himself. "Ah, that's right, you wouldn't know." He gestured back towards Scourge. "Due to Scourge's experiments, I was able to be freed from that Vessel. Now I control my own fate, and I owe a great debt to Scourge for that." Adrian nodded to himself.

Gaia held up her hand to interrupt. "Wait...wait...what became of Keith after those experiments?" she asked.

Adrian smiled and shook his head at Gaia. "Who knows." At this moment, Adrian spread his hands apart to either side of him, and mana at the boiling point inside of him immediately released itself, spreading a veil of dark mana across a large chunk of the area on the east side of the battlefield. Only the smallest amount of light was allowed to shine through the mist. The mist was an extraordinary spell that immediately clouded the minds of all those caught inside as well. The actual effects per person remained unknown, but Blaze and Gaia, along with all of the pirates that followed them into battle, all collapsed, holding their heads like they were trying to squash a watermelon.

"Ahhhh damnit, what is this...Why do I feel like chopping my own head off!!" Blaze yelled, kicking his feet in place while he rolled around on the ground. "G-Gaia! Are you okay? How are the pirates-" As soon as he finished, the screams of the pirates and demons collectively overshadowed his voice while they screamed in agony. Outside of the strange mist, no one could hear or see what happened inside. The shadows slowly began gathering around the pirates in their vulnerability.

"This...hurts," Gaia said to herself as she tried to calm herself and concentrate on her head, not exploding. She sat up, then immediately collapsed forward onto her hands and knees.

"Shit. This is bad. "Blaze was wincing so hard he couldn't even open his eyes.

"Hahaha. This is just my initial spell, Mávro péplo. Upon unleashing my powers, this black mist travels in all directions to make any area into my 'zone.' How do you like it?" Adrian snickered out loud while he watched everyone in pain in front of him. "This mist is a part of me. My own fears, anger, hate, anxiety. All of my negative emotion is channeled through my mana and forced onto you. Now you can feel what I feel every waking moment. It's too much for your puny minds. Pretty soon, your heads will explode!" He laughed.

"Fuck. Off." Blaze in defiance pushed himself up to his feet, using his own blade to hold himself up. His legs wobbled in place, trying not to fall again. His own flaming mana flickered slightly around his body like embers on a flame.

"Hmph. Well then. This is my second spell! Darkness incarnate." Adrian shouted as suddenly the darkness behind him twisted and warped, concentrating until it was solid. The darkness tucked itself in around Adrian's back like a cape with a frayed bottom. It even materialized a high popped collar around his neck, the mana constantly flowing with a heartbeat of its own. Adrian calmly walked up towards Blaze and stopped a foot away.

Blaze just stared into Adrian's eyes with a furious passion; as if at any moment he could swing at Adrian. "Do it."

Adrian smiled his dark cape rumbling behind him. The bottom left edge twirled up into the air and formed a sharp drill shape, pointed directly at Blaze. "See. My darkness incarnate reads my emotions automatically. I don't even need to tell it to skewer you." The edge reared back and shot forward towards Blaze's face. Blaze didn't or rather couldn't move an inch.

Out of the corner of Adrian's eye, he noticed a bo-staff swinging towards him, but it was too late. Gaia's Kirici came crashing into his chest with impressive force, sending him sliding back three meters but keeping his composure. The cape's sharp edge, a bug's length away from Blaze's nose, was pulled back as well. Adrian stood back up straight, pounding his chest. "Didn't feel a thing, my what fantastic armor Scourge," he said to himself.

"Back off!" Gaia screamed with a mix of frustration and overcoming her own pain. She breathed heavily for a moment before the pain stopped miraculously. With this hit, though, the pirates had also stopped screaming but were unconscious instead. Blaze, able to move freely now, went to check to make sure they weren't dead.

"Damn Gaia, you freed us from the spell. Nice. Also, they are just unconscious." Blaze got up and readied himself towards Adrian, the mist still messing with vision.

Gaia breathed a sigh of relief. "Good. Now I can focus on this traitor." She spun Kirici around and pointed it at Adrian.

Adrian ran his hands through his hair, attempting to calm himself. "How many times must I tell you, I was never your ally!" His darkness expanded more now as his rage grew. He also pulled out his special blade as well, confidently. Blaze and Gaia braced themselves against the shockwave of darkness that approached.

On the other side of the battlefield, near the castle, Scourge stood firm facing Void Ocean and Hepheaus. Other than the Aqua warriors that came with them, no other Royal Knight forces had made it that far, getting intercepted by hordes of shadows, creating the perfect opportunity for an uninterrupted fight.

"Double, triple-team me, I don't care. You'll all fall by my hands all the same." Scourge chuckled as he revealed his own cursed blade. A grotesque demon eye sat inside the side of the black blade, right above the hilt. The sword was a longer than both of Void's cursed blades, but shorter than his claymore. The evil mana that radiated off of Scourge's sword cursed and rotted the grass and plant life in the vicinity. He swung it around liberally, killing off all in its wake. "Void. Would you like to know about those two swords you hold?" Scourge said.

Void had his arms crossed, a hand on each of his cursed blades now. "Hmm. If you must, I guess I can hear you out," he said with a small, forced smile, sweat dripping down his brow as his fingers fluttered back and forth against the hilts of the two blades. The rain stopped at this point, leaving a wet, muddy mess in its wake.

Ocean and his mom both looked at Void confusingly. "Really?" Ocean finally said out loud.

"Yeah. Curious about the power that comes with this blade." Void said while shrugging his shoulders.

Scourge stopped twirling his sword to shove it into the dirt. As soon as it pierced the wet earth, the ground dried up and was sucked of all life in a thirty-meter radius around him. Eerie cracks began to form where there was once a muddy mess, grass replaced by a thin dark aura directly over the ground. "First off, these three blades we own...they are part of a set, all crafted for the dark lord, Deces," Scourge said while staring tenderly at his sword.

Void's eyebrows raised at this, but he didn't say anything out loud, opting to listen instead. Hepheaus looked at Voids swords as if trying to decipher what made them tick. Scourge pointed at Void with his right hand, his left still on the hilt of the sword. "These swords. They were crafted to enhance the strength of a young Demisc. Well, his dark mana anyway." Scourge started. "It all started on Luvenesyar, a few centuries before the collapse." Scourge began painting the picture of another world much different from Sylindra.

-335 Years Before Expansion   ???   Osândă Sierra, Luvensyar-

Osândă Sierra. Home to a majority of the great battles and wars between the Guardian Deities armies and Chaos. Close to the mana core at the equator of Luvensyar, Osândă is an area of excellent mana concentration. Warriors on both sides were able to use this concentration to become more and more powerful over the centuries. This escalated the scale of the wars, taking a toll on what was formerly a beautiful, serene sierra. Now, the very earth is scared and sickly from the abuse. Mana doesn't even flow as easily as it once did. Before these wars, Osândă, meaning doom, was formerly Natură, for life in nature. Large, expansive fields of many different kinds of grass and small brushes of trees lined out the area in between low mountains for miles. Patches of Fierra grass mixed its bright orange and red hue with the singed and burnt green grass to create what appeared to be a sea of flames. The wild spotted deer and Fierra mountain lions once made this beautiful place home now had been forcibly relocated to further away lands along with the rest of the animals. The only way to preserve them, as though by the Gods.

Chaos, through the countless mana intensive fights against his makers, incurred grave injuries. Weakened and without his physical form, Chaos still pursued nothing but infamy and destruction. He now floated there unable to access all of his power as a lively shining orb next to his new lead general, Demise. Demise, before he was known as Deces' before he was feared as having the power to rival a God before he ruled over all of Armageddon, he was an only child of demon royalty.

When Lucinthis cast the first shadow on this world, along with Chaos, Rygen, the light Snuffer, and Scarlet, the Soulless also emerged from this influx of demons and dark beings. As the name suggests, Rygen could suck mana and life out of anything he touches on an enormous scale. A single touch to the ground, for example, could kill off an entire continent if he wished. Scarlet could control the minds and hearts of people by stealing away their very soul and free will. They soon came together and joined their interests to rule over a vast majority of the demons who arose with them.

Before long, they had a child in Demise to entrust the future centuries. With an enormous empire under them, Rygen and Scarlet grew very cocky and arrogant. Realizing

398

they would never indeed be the leader of all demons as long as Chaos was still alive, they challenged Chaos with all of their combined might and forces. It did not end well for them. After a decisive, world-shattering battle, Rygen and Scarlet were both Slain by Chaos. Their powers were absorbed into Chaos's, and their young son, Demise, was also taken as the apprentice to Chaos. He would still be groomed to lead, but as Chaos's second.

Now that Chaos was the sole leader of the demons on Luvenesyar, with his combined power, not even Verafelt, the "Evil God" could keep him in check on his own. Chaos was never satisfied with any mild form of destruction; he regularly pondered paths that would lead to the destruction of Luvenesyar. Chaos dreamed of creating his own world in his evil image. He wanted the Gods to create his own world for him.

During the fierce battles with Chaos, the Deities, on multiple occasions, have enlisted humans and angels to halt the advances of the demons. It was ineffective, with Chaos only taking over more and more of Luvenesyar for himself. The final straw came when Verafelt came down to confront Chaos on his own. Taking the form of a giant warrior wielding two menacing axes with Viking-type light armor. Leather straps being the only protection on his chest. Tattoos ran throughout Verafelt's body as insignias of his name in the ancient text.

One night, after another rough skirmish on the Sierra, Verafelt snuck onto Chaos's camp in his human form unbeknownst to the other Deities. Chaos noticed who it was immediately, and teleported both of them to a remote location so they could speak. Apparently, Verafelt called Chaos to take things into his own hands. A one on one battle to settle things, Verafelt thought. The battle lasted throughout the night without interruption. After a night of explosions and massive displays of mana visible for miles, the struggle finally ended just as the sun was beginning to rise in the new day. Verafelt had lost. A bloody mess and vulnerable in his human form, all that was left was for Chaos to deliver the final blow. Verafelt lowered his head, accepting his defeat and his mistakes.

As a gift for ascending to the top, Chaos has crafted a unique and powerful spear known as Twilight. It was said to be a perfect accent for Chaos.

Chaos raised his long Twilight Spear high into the air, aimed for Verafelts heart. The light from the sun reflected off of the spear-like mirror. Just as he began to lower the spear, a clank rang out loud; a sword was thrown at his spear, causing Chaos to miss. Upon looking up, he notices a young warrior with wavy hair shaken, but angry still, staring at a hole into Chaos.

Verafelt looked back now at this young, brave warrior. Knowing what could have been his last action while a part of this world, Verafelt instantly gained great respect for him, seeking to further his life past this moment. Before Chaos could direct his rage towards the warrior, Verafelt put the rest of his strength into teleporting to his position and then teleporting both of them far far away. That young man would one day be promoted to the first Royal Knight Blaze from Verafelt.

After making it back to the other Gods, they finally understood the real strength of Chaos and decided more had to be done to protect this world. They had underestimated him and would grow to regret it. Shortly after, they formed the first class of Royal Knights, together with defeating and sealing away Chaos. As the second at the time, Demise was quickly promoted to the Commander of Chaos's army. Still lacking in his potential power, Chaos, reduced to a floating orb, directed his Demon blacksmiths to craft three cursed weapons using the raw mana and rare metals used in Chaos's spear.

A full year they spent crafting in the dark depths of Umbra in its infancy before Armageddon was created. Deep underground, an outcast group of three worked around the clock, using twelve innocent sacrifices to activate each weapons' unique ability. Devora the Soul Eater, Tăia the Cleaver, and Izbucni the Rage, the three weapons birthed from Twilight. Devora, as the name suggests, absorbs the mana and the soul of its victims. The stronger the enemy, the more it consumes, giving the access mana to its owner. After a while, this cursed mana warps the mind of the wielder into craving stronger prey. Tăia excels at cutting through targets at any distance. Based off of the old demon lord, who was overly obsessed with not letting destinations escape him. Whether it's a real hit or the mana streak that's released when you swing it, Tăia is very hard to stop once it's active. Izbucni is a more close-ranged sword but is very dangerous when the hits land. Once engaged, Izbucni let out a terrifying hard to avoid explosion on the target.

Each weapon individually is dangerous, but together their potential is limitless. They cover up each other's weaknesses' make each other more powerful as if a supportive family. While the strength increases, so does the effect on the user's mind. Demise quickly became a powerful tyrant leading his army to many victories over the Deities, only getting more powerful after each battle. Eventually, his thinking and focus lined up with that of Chaos as his care for the current world fell. Again, the world began to fall apart, leading to an early end to the war as the planet was nearing its last days.

If things stayed as they were, all of the demons would die on the planet as it exploded, but the council of Gods knew the balance of the world would be thrown off, so they made a deal with Demise. They would give them their own planet in exchange for capturing and sealing away Chaos. Without much choice, Demise agreed, vowing to free his master one day. With that, Luvensyar was destroyed, prompting the creation of separate worlds for each race to preserve peace. Sylindra for humans, Armageddon for demons and Ardin for the Angel's. Specific areas in each of the planets were created that mimicked the concentration of mana on Luvenesyar. Demise ruled over all of Armageddon while continuously planning ways to free Chaos from his prison and absorbing the souls of humans to make him and his army more powerful.

-Year 277   Faith Hill   Shadow Path, Umbra-

"And in walks Scourge who now holds Devora. Bestowed to me by the Demise himself because of my will to take down strong enemies. Though he isn't too happy about how long I've kept you alive.," Scourge said as he chuckled, still stroking the side of Devora after he finished his long-winded story.

"Hmm. So that certainly explains a lot about my two blades and why they affect my mind the way they do." Void shook his head while looking at his own two cursed blades. "Uh, thanks, I guess, Scourge, it's a shame we're gonna have to cut you down now!" Void pointed his claymore at Scourge.

"Not really! Been waiting for his annoying ass to finish talking." Hepheaus rushed in with her blade ready.

Ocean summoned two mana whips and rushed in after her. "Finally!"

Scourge simply laughed as the three rushed at him aggressively. "Hahaha. I hope you paid attention! Because I'll soon cut you all down and absorb your powerful souls!"

"Hope you're prepared to work for it!" Hepheaus said, disappearing from sight.

Powerful shock waves spread as Scourge and Hepheaus clashed for the first time. She appeared before

Scourge forcing him to immediately go on the defensive. The shockwave was so strong it stopped Ocean and Void mid-stride, skidding them back slightly. "I'll take the brunt of this. Just back me up, okay!" Hepheaus yelled back at the other two.

In the center of the battle, another battle was unfolding. With the veil of darkness from Adrian as the stimulus, William and Jax both charge at Braugg simultaneously. The shiny, sharp point of a lance and the curved edge of a black machete both clanked against the palms of Braugg as he defended both attacks with ease. Jax and Will were both shoved back, promptly. "Humph." Jax scoffed, trying to shrug it off.

"Do better!" Braugg stood up straight and pounded his chest.

Jax unsheathed his second black machete and scraped them against each other threateningly. "I heard what happened; don't make me cut that arm off again!" Jax let out in a cocky fashion. It clearly worked cause Braugg immediately charged him, leaving two small craters at the feet of the dodging Jax. Jax leaped back to Will, nervously, then they both swung back. Braugg blocked the strikes this time, stopping his backward momentum by swatting his arms out, breaking the guard of Jax and Will. Before they could react, two large, burly hands had their heads crashing into the ground. Showing off his strength, Braugg started jogging forward with both faces squished into the dirt, Will's heavy armor forced his side to move a little more labored than Jax's. Taking it for a ride with him, Will spun his lance around and stabbed the point into Braugg's ankle. They stopped suddenly, and Jax was tossed into a crowd of knights fighting off shadows.

"Aghh. Ow!" In an instant rage, Braugg ripped William off of the ground from his collar and held him there. After another grunt of anger, he relayed a powerful short jab

403

to Will's heavily armored stomach. The blow shredded through the armor as his spiked knuckles smashed into bare flesh with so much momentum it knocked Will out of Braugg's grasp. A small shockwave echoed as Jax landed on his feet before nearly collapsing, his lance holding him up.

"Gah!" William gasped for breath as his spit and choked in place; his legs resembling spaghetti noodles more by the moment.

Braugg's outstretched arm was pulled back quickly as two black machetes narrowly missed him. Jax followed through and stumbled forward before spinning around to defend Will. "Geez, I felt that man, how are you feeling?" Jax threw back at Will.
Will coughed a couple more times, his lance glowing slightly. "Gah."

"Huh?" Jax tried to focus on Braugg and Will at the same time.

"Jiaqiang." From the point of his lance to around his entire body, Will was surrounded in a dark green aura. The aura moved on its own and clumped up on certain parts of his body, like his exposed stomach, for example. "Ahhh, much better. I excel at reinforcement spells. So I'm fine now." Will says as he stands up straight, seemingly unhurt.

"Hm. Nice." Jax shrugged. Will joined him at his side as they faced down Braugg again.

"Heh. So tough now? Let's see if that'll do." Braugg's fists both now surrounded themselves in dense dark mana.

Will shoved Jax behind him and summoned his oversized shield. "Oh boy, just stand back and prepare for a counter-attack," he said, holding it ahead of the two.

Braugg walked up cockily while shadow boxing in the air. The swings started getting quicker and quicker, and before long, his fists were lost in the vast array of blows. "Gatling Darkness!" he said as his swings became wild and unkempt but generally in front of him. William held his shield steady as the pounding began. Staring at ten punches every couple seconds and increasing incrementally, soon, Will started to have trouble maintaining his guard up.

"Damn, this is…actually a lot." Will mustered out as he slowly got pushed back with the punches raining down on the shield-like hail. The sounds of fists pounding into the shield could be heard from across the battlefield, catching the attention of Sky and Hail, who kept close attention to both sides as they dealt with shadows and clones in the Knight's territory. An evil figure traveled in the shadows assassinating warriors undetected.

"I got this, don't worry." Jax, serious now, tossed his captain's jacket off of his shoulders. And gathered mana into his two blades. He then ran and used Will's back as a stepstool, lifting himself up into the air.

"Hey!" Will yelled.

"Take this!" Jax swung both blades and released a thick steak of mana at an angle down at Braugg's head.

In an effort not to get beheaded, Braugg stopped his onslaught from catching the streak of mana and breaking it in his hands. "Not ba-." Clank! Before he could finish, Jax had landed with both blades clashing against either of Braugg's sides. "Grrrr," he grumbled.

Using the opportunity to rest his shield, Will lowered his guard to regain his energy. Jax and Braugg began clashing now, fists and blades flying into the air as they each attempted to get the upper hand. Each heavy fist that Jax blocked slowed him down little by little. "Be careful, your body can't take many hits from that monster!" Will yelled, getting back to his feet.

"I know! O—" Distracted, Jax stops as a fist soars towards his side. With minimum time, he is only able to hold up his knee and his blade to defend himself.

"Grahhh!" Braugg's fist breaks through the shoddy defense, punching a hole in his blade, and nearly one in Jax's ribs. Jax tumbles to the ground holding his side; both blades fly out to the side. Braugg walks up to Jax's body menacingly. "Night night, pirate." He says, cracking his knuckles.

"Jax!" Will yells as he taps his lance back into the ground, surrounded by that same green aura as it travels towards Jax on the ground like a rushing river. Jax noticed the massive standing over him and points his damaged machete at Braugg's face. Braugg reared his right fist back, aimed to shatter the rest of that sword before shoving his fist through Jax's chest. Inches before the spikes on his knuckles reached the tip of the blade, the green aura had reached Jax and surrounded his entire body, including the tattered sword.

"AGH!" The reinforced edge of the blade had gone through Braugg's hand between his ring and middle finger. Braugg stopped as the blade reached the middle of his palm and retrieved it quickly. Blood splattered wildly as he held his hurt hand. "Damn you!" Braugg screamed, waving his hand back and forth.

Jax looked over and winked at Will, looking more like a wince than anything. Will rose his shield up and charged at Braugg, his mana trailing off the massive shoulders of his armor as his speed increases. "Let's see how you handle this shield charge!" Will's momentum increased to its max just before reaching Braugg, who instinctively held up his right hand to defend, a dangerous mistake.

Upon contact, Braugg's hand began shaking and quivering in place as the strength in his arm was enough to hold off and stop Will completely. "Urghhh!" He grumbled, skidding back a bit in the dirt. After a short lift into the air before settling back on the ground, the shield charge was stopped. Braugg's hand bled profusely now with the added pressure.

"W-what?" Will exclaimed as his energy left his body.

"Hmph." Suddenly blood began spraying violently in all directions. The origin, the fresh nub on the right arm of Braugg. Jax stood over this nub with victory in his eyes, and demon blood soaking his black blade. He lowered his sword near the limb, flopping around on the ground and stared into the eyes of Braugg. The blood loss was clearly starting to show its effects as his eyes were glossed over. The rage didn't leave them for a second, though; as Braugg met Jax's stare.

"You...think...win...I'll crush you!" Braugg, barely thinking now, brought up his left arm and palmed the top of Jax's head firmly. "I'll squish...melon." Braugg managed to get out.

Jax rolled his eyes as he got slowly lifted into the air from his head. The blood coming out of Braugg's arm increased in frequency, the more he squeezed. "You just refuse to learn, huh?" he said, swinging some of the blood off of his blade.

From the corner of his eye, Jax sees Will's massive shield being tossed to the side and Will lunging forward with his lance. He dug his golden weapon directly into the center of Braugg's bicep. Jax was dropped immediately as the hole in his bicep grew the more Will thrusted. After about two seconds of thrusting, Will ripped his lance to the side and took the lower half of Braugg's arm with him. He then retreated back, out of Jax's way. "Finish this," he said. Suddenly a shadow along the ground came rushing in from across the battlefield towards them.

Upon hitting the ground again, Jax spun his sword, holding it like a dagger, then he turned in place clockwise and with the added momentum stabbed Braugg deep with his machete; blade up. Now stuck, Braugg coughed up blood all on Jax's face, who looked quite upset afterward. He now had blood coming from both arms and his mouth.

"S-shit," Braugg breathed out as he lost consciousness.

"That's it then." Jax's machete began glowing white. He then raised his blade up through the rest of his body, exiting right in between his eyes and slicing everything in the middle in half. Blood sprinkled into the air like rain with this quick motion, but in another second, Jax turned his blade to the side and decapitated Braugg's already separated head. Jax caught one half of Braugg's head in his hand and left the rest to collapse and separate onto the floor. "Whelp. That's one down, aye Wi—"

"My thoughts exactly. A mysterious voice echoed. Meanwhile, Jax suddenly couldn't speak. His throat was clogged, he felt as if he was choking. So spontaneous, it actually scared him. Jax looked around, left and right in a panic. He examined his hands after dropping the head and his sword, they were shaking as Jax's oxygen levels were lowering.

"Uh, you okay, man?" Will said, looking at him curiously while picking up his shield and lance.

Jax cautiously shook his head no before coughing. An eruption of blood came exploding out of his mouth, but he could only cough once. Jax still could not move. As Jax shook his head at the cup of blood he just coughed out, two blades materialized already penetrating his torso. They each came from underneath, hitting him from below the ribs, up into Jax's lungs, crossing each other for an 'X' shape. The blades slowly began sliding themselves out of his back as a figure shrouded in darkness begins stepping out of the shadow behind Jax ominously. He wipes both blades of Jax's blood and beams at Will. Jax crumples to the ground bleeding profusely.

"J-Jax…what the hell…just…happened." Will stammered, raising his shield in front of him.

Chapter 18:
Fire vs. Darkness

The dark shroud surrounding the figure faded away like a fog. It cleared to reveal Strike standing there stoically with a sword lowered to each of his sides, black mana densely covering both blades tightly. He stared at Will silently for an awkward five seconds before smiling and laughing slightly. "You're next." Strike uttered before reverting back to a shadow and disappearing. He was gone.

Will peered over his shield nervously looking for Strike but to no avail. He checked the ground for ominous shadows, but everything appeared normal. He took a couple steps back and started looking again. A nearby shadow hanging under a rock to the left shot out towards William with incredible speed coming from the side. Sensing the murderous intent, Will was able to shift his body to his left; the shield followed suit. Strike came gliding out of the shadow as he dashed towards his target with blades at the ready. A meter away now, Will's legs shook slightly, his mind still trying to wrap his head around the shock that he just experienced. Strike's entire body was now out of the shadow as he swung his swords at Will's shield with no hesitation.

"Ice coffin!" Strike's body was instantly frozen in a solid block of ice with his blades inches away from Will's shield. Hail then comes blasting in the area through clones to Will's side, sliding on a stream of ice like a surfer. "Sigh. You cannot defend against attacks from this guy. His swords will go right through and tear you apart. Luckily I showed up when I did." Hail motioned him over at Jax.

410

"Well, thanks. Guess I missed that bit of information at the meeting." Will said, putting away his shield and lance. They both rushed over towards Jax's body. "Do you think that ice will last?" he said, looking back for a moment at Strike.

"Not even a little bit, he's way too strong. That's why you're gonna take Jax over to Scatha and have her try to heal him." Hail said, noticing Jax still breathing, barely.

"What about yo-" Will started.

"I will take care of him. Now go, and be careful." Hail picked up Jax's body and laid it on Will's shoulder. "Follow the ice." A trail of Hail's mana ice led back into the battlefield and off to the left. Will didn't try to speak anymore, just nodded, patted Hail on the shoulder, and dashed out of the area of open space they had been fighting in. Hail summoned his array of ice blades in the air around him, with two in hand. He faced the ice block at the ready, his conserved mana waiting at the brim to spill over. "Alright now, Strike, shall we do this? I saved up some mana just to kick your ass. I owe you one for my sister." Hail smirked.

The ice block, with barely any rumbles, just shatters, and Strikes walks up casually up to Hail while licking his blade. "Hehe, yeah, shall we?" Strike said, cracking his neck in both directions. He scrapes his swords against one another and gets in a low stance to face Hail. A short stare down later, and it was on! Strike rushed at Hail with incredible speed, dodging and parrying the ice blades sent after him on the way to their clash. Two on two, a sword in each hand for each of them. They began swinging faster and faster as they tried to one-up the other in swordplay. Hail used his ice to slide in and out of the way, Strike just grew more and more nimble as they crossed swords. "You cannot keep up with my speed Hail, why try?" Strike chuckled.

411

"Shut up!" Hail slammed the hilts of his ice blades into those of Strike, causing a shockwave that separated them. He begins gathering mana in his left hand while summoning five small ice daggers in his right. "See if you can handle this!"

"Bring it." Strike feigned left and right before he started to rush again.

"Ugh! When given the power to lay judgment, attack with the fury of all five kings! Scatter and pierce, ledeni raspršeni napado!" Hail let out his ice glass barrage towards Strike. His razor-sharp ice crystals shot out like a gatling gun and homed when they got close, but still, Strike dodged and slashed away at the mana that came towards him. When Hail missed his shots trailed off and hit shadow soldiers in the background, tearing through them instantly. Strike slowly made his way closer and closer to Hail. Two meters out and Hail finally tossed those ice daggers aimed directly at Strikes ankle. Still trying to dodge the barrage, he was only able to avoid two. The other three knives jammed into the side of his thigh, calf, and ankle like darts. He jerked slightly when they penetrated his skin, but right after ice began pulsating from the daggers, slowly freezing his entire leg over ten rough seconds because Hail was still firing off the whole time. "Ice pulse. Heh." Hail smirked as he began to really lay the barrage into Strike, whose leg was frozen solid and could no longer dodge.

"Tsk. You think you're so tough." Strike scoffed as he could no longer parry but could only block with the sides of the blades protecting his vitals. He was pelted by thousands of tiny shards of ice so hard it lifted and pushed him back and down into the ground. The stream was constant and nonstop for a minute as it unloaded into Strike's body on the ground. This created a dust cloud eventually. By the time Hail finally stopped, a dust cloud resembling an explosion had gathered in the area around Strike's body.

"Heh. How do you like that!" Hail said, breathing heavily, trying to keep himself together. "Damn, that was a lot of mana...hope it worked." He mumbled to himself.

"Too bad it didn't, huh." Before the dust cleared, a wild explosion of dark mana exploded from within. It flared out and raged like the flames of a forest fire before calming down and surrounding the body of the risen Strike. Through the darkness, the damage could be seen. His swords were shredded, small holes had been forced throughout, making them now useless, so they lay on the floor for either side of him. The earth surrounding Strike was littered in small holes as well, like hundreds of little meteors had landed there. He was no better either. Blood was trickling down his arms and legs and forehead. The armor that Scourge had passed down to him appeared to have been granted with cheese. Dinks and small holes tore into every part not covered by his swords. He was alive though, the armor had done the job, and he was ready for revenge. "Now then. You'll pay for what you did to this precious armor." The mana that covered his body now transitioned to his left hand as he reached to his back and summoned his favorite weapon, Oktar. An extended bladed katana with a beautifully crafted handle. Four black swans ran up the side of the grip, and the beaks formed the handguard.

Strike was stagnant for a moment. His leg still damaged from being frozen earlier. Moments later, he disappeared into a shadow. Hail, having the moment to get himself standing normally, looked around cautiously. "Dammit. Not this shit." Hail gathered mana while he looked all around him, knowing one good blow could decide this battle. He then widened his stance. "Ha. I know a way to find you!" Hail spins around with his hands out, releasing his mana in all directions. A lining of ice mana layered around the perimeter of their battle area. Shortly after, everything within began to freeze solid from the outside in.

413

Hail also dropped to a knee and encased himself in an icy shell in the center. "Icey Graveyard! Ice Coffin!" he said as he protected himself inside the ticking bomb that was the battle area.

Rocks, the ground, shadows, and Silverwings that found themselves inside the circle all fell victim to the icy graveyard. The circle of ice grew smaller and smaller by the second, but the shadows remained still around Hail. Soon the ring was three meters out. However, no movement. It was quiet surrounding him, except for the crackling as the ground and grass froze. Slight drizzles remained of the storming earlier. The droplets that entered the zone also froze instantly before plopping on the ground softly. Hail nervously waited there for everything to freeze, knowing as soon as it did, he had the advantage. Not long now, one and a half meters before the circle reaches the center. Crack. Hail's eyes shifted quickly to the left, where a large break formed in the ice on the ground. He stared and stared, and nothing had happened. He calmed himself for a moment. One meter left. He had done it! Hail thought to himself. He had taken out one of Scourge's disciples on his own, he would get so much respect and praise for his efforts. There's no way he could lose now; it's over! As the last meter closed, he let out a sigh of relief. One. Second. Too. Early.

Hail's eyes suddenly widened. He held his breath and froze. The shadow cast by Hail's block of ice slowly lifted into the air, peeling itself off the ground and rising into the air above Hail. Moments later, with added volume, it materialized into a shrouded Strike, long blade aimed down at the block of ice, behind it, Hail.

"Good effort. But sorry to say that." Strike then thrust his katana into the ice. The dark mana around his blade cut through the ice like butter and led the blade through Hail's back and into the icy ground on the other side. "But that won't work." Strike smirked as he peered back at the ice incoming that stopped short of his face.

Even quicker than it appeared, the ice that surrounded them all shattered at once into a sparkling mist of mana. Hail's ice coffin was next to go, breaking in the same fashion and leaving Hail there still on one knee. Hail coughed up blood, and his entire body was shaken, but he generally kept his composure, even managing to bring a smirk to his face. Strikes blade still radiated that dangerous dark mana while piercing through the center of Hail's back and into the ground at a downward angle. Strike stood quietly while Hail looked up into the air, getting his thoughts together. An eerie smile found its way on Hail's face when he closed his eyes. "Damn. What a dumb mistake. This is on me." He lost consciousness after this. Strike makes quick work of pulling his blade out and ridding it of Hail's blood. Hail's body laid face down on the hard earth. A puddle of blood growing more and more by the second lay under him now.

"Hail!" Out of the corner of his eye high in the air, Sky saw Hail drop to the ground and immediately began his rapid descent towards Strike from behind.

"Oh, no!" Will fought his way back and arrived at that same moment to find Hail fell at his feet. He got down to check his pulse and put pressure on the wound in his back. "Shit, he's barely alive."

Cutting out of the air Sky arrived with his scythe low aimed to decapitate Strike, who was staring at Will. Will looked up directly at Strike then Sky, who caught his eye over his shoulder. Strike, without looking, pointed his sword into the air behind him and grabs Sky's scythe in the center of the arc as it's nearly surrounded his head. He then ducked and tugged Sky and his scythe down to the ground forcibly in front of him. Sky tumbled into the ground Before getting caught by Will's shield. Sky got up and readied his scythe

while he stared a hole into Strike, who was exceptionally calm and lax. His sword was on the ground, and Strike danced slightly side to side for a moment before lifting his blade directly in front of him. "Are you sure you want to step into this fight, Sky? I'm a master assassin, already taking out two of your own." Strike chuckled.
Sky looked back at Will, then back to Strike. "That's precisely why I must be here! No one messes with my knights, you'll pay for that." Sky beamed at Strike with intensity.

"Oh?" Strike waved his sword back and forth slightly.

"Sky! Don't. That's how Hail got this way. I don't want to lose my cousin because he didn't think and evaluate at the moment. Let us retrea—" Will tried to get out.

"No! I will not retreat or falter. I will win. Take Hail over to Scatha, you should know the way by now." Sky broke off his stare with Strike to side-eye Will.

"Sky…" Will was speechless, but he picked up Hail, holding him upright under his arms. "You can count on me, don't die."

Sky sighed and calmed his tone a bit. "Look, during my scope, I saw Ocean, his mom, and Void taking on Scourge directly. Gaia and Blaze are battling with Adrian secluded from the rest of the field, and Volt is fighting off shadows around Scatha. Speaking of whom, she has a bit of a healing circle started with injured warriors. She's using all of the mana she can get to keep the healing going between all of them. I'm sure you already know that part, though. Also, overall, our forces are doing quite well against the Silverwing army, but I need you to take the reins and command our forces. Hephaestus and I are both about to be in tough fights, so we won't be able to manage as well. That's the status of the fight as I see it, now go…please. I must focus." Sky turned his attention back to Strike, who waited patiently.

"Fine, Sky. I'll lead the army, you handle business here. Don't be too reckless." With that, Will dragged Hail out of the circle, using his reinforcement to protect them on the way back to Scatha.

"One more thing." Sky directed at Will without moving his head. "Keep Scatha safe. Something tells me we're gonna need her later."Sky said. Will stopped to nod, then continued on his way.

"So you're done, I presume?" Strike said, getting antsy now.

"Yeah, sorry about that, have to lead everyone as the captain, right? Don't worry, it only delayed your death." Sky said, smiling now.

"Hahaha! Shall we then!" Strike said, disappearing into a shadow as his first move.

As soon as he disappeared, Sky stomped onto the ground, creating a gust of wind that first soared up then horizontally all around himself. Seconds later, with his scythe cocked, Sky lunged at a random shadow and dug in. In one motion, he scooped and pulled Strike up from the shadow by his right shoulder and tossed him back. "You will fight me straight up! No tricks." Sky yelled, flapping his wings in the wind.

Strike flipped and landed on his feet, clutching his bloody shoulder. "Ah. Guess mine was the only nonmoving shadow in all this grass and rocks. Oh well, straight up, it is." Sky and Strike both stared each other down again in silence. The wind blew softly now, blowing some of the still frozen crystals around the outer edges of their fighting grounds.

Back off to the right of the battlefield trapped inside of a giant dome of darkness, Blaze and Gaia still found themselves defending themselves from waves and waves of deadly attacks from Adrian. A game of attrition it had turned into while the knights, through the pain and persistence, still manage to continue against Adrian, who flexes his immense mana pool. They both now stand facing him, attempting to catch their breath long enough to mount a comeback.

"Just let me know when you've had enough. I won't stop! Hahaha!" Adrian laughed as he charged his dark mana in both hands again, another wave of evil blasts incoming.

"As if I'd let you!" Clapping both hands together, Blaze shoots out a blast of flames soaring towards Adrian. The fire lit up the darkness like the light on an angler fish. At the same time, Gaia dashed at Adrian with Kirici in hand, trying to close the distance quickly.

With his mana still charged in his hand, Adrian spun his sword around, holding it like a dagger and twisting his body until his blade was behind him. His knees were bent in his low stance; eyes focused on the stream of fire mana before him. In a single motion, he twisted his torso and led with his shoulder like he was throwing a ball, his blade directly in the path of Blaze's attack. "Skoúro kýma," Adrian said with a big smile. Blaze's mana was engulfed in darkness upon touching Adrian's blade. Little by little, the flames began turning and morphing into coal-colored embers, suspended individually around him, moving to his will. "Hahaha. If you've ever seen Keith's Badong Pa, you'll get the general idea of this move. But mine. MINE is much more powerful, and I have complete control over my opponent's mana. See!" Adrian gloats as he starts shooting the mana back at Blaze in multiple streams of dark flames, each the same size as Blaze's initial attack. With each flash, Gaia gets closer to Adrian.

"Shit!" Blaze yelped as he dove out of the way as the flames crash into the ground behind him. They didn't extinguish, though; instead, they were pulled back like a whip and fired back at Blaze. "What the hell is this guy?"

Blaze canceled out one of the blasts with one of his own and pulled out his blade to defend against the others.

Suddenly Adrian shot his head to the left. "And don't I've forgotten about you, missy!" The dark mana on his 'cape' extrudes out like an army of tentacles and begins to assault Gaia.

"Damn, both of us at the same time." Gaia stopped her dash short to fight off the mana and avoid getting skewered by the sharp points flying at her in the dark. It took until they got very close for Gaia to see them, visibility is still low. With his hands, he fought off Blaze, and his mana fought Gaia off to the side. The confidence in his eyes grew as the fight dragged on.

"Dammit. This is frustrating, I'm tired of this." Blaze leaped back, slightly out of range, and waved his sword down towards the ground, blade in his right hand. "I know I haven't used you much on this journey. I wanted to do everything with my own strength. But now." Blaze's sword began lighting up. The large red plates on either side of his blade suddenly separated, leaving an open partition on either side of the blade and hot, black smoke began flowing out of these openings. The temperature of the sword started rising rapidly as well. "Now, I realize we are in this together. That we both can show off together. Alright, Red Chariot. Let's win this!" An explosion of flames crashed out of the open areas on the blade-like an exhaust and continued to stream out like jet boosters. Blaze calmly grabbed the hilt with both hands, raising the blade and tilting it to the right slightly. His left foot led the stance, pointing directly at Adrian. "This'll be both of us, together." Blaze stopped for a moment to take a deep breath. Then he smiled slightly. "Nova divide!" The Red Chariot was swung to the ground heavily like it was being weighed down by boulders. Connecting the burning tip of the blade with the ground caused the exhaust on both sides of the Red Chariot to shoot out a thick straight line of concentrated flames on each side. These walls of fire shot out diagonally from the point of the blade. One aimed behind Adrian, and the other shot in front of him, in between himself and Gaia.

"Hmmm. What's this?" Adrian said as his dark mana attacking Gaia was severed by the flames, causing his full attention to shift to this attack surrounding him. "Oh…" Adrian said as he witnessed the earth directly in front of the tip of the Chariot getting absolutely obliterated by a fiery explosion. Adrian shifted back a bit as the explosion chained into another, and another all within the confines of the two concentrated flame walls and rushing towards him swiftly. "Shit!" With the time remaining to him, Adrian gathered the dark mana from his back and clumped it in front of him, trying to brace himself for impact.

The next sequence saw the explosion catching up to him and shredding through layers upon layers of Adrian's defense. The remaining energy hit him directly, and with the angle coming from below, it lifted him a few meters into the air. He crossed his arms out in front to protect his face, but the rest of him was smoking and warping with apparent signs of damage. While still in the air, Adrian let out a loud gasp followed by a grunt as sturdy wooden staff cracked into the back of Adrian's neck in the darkness. A few moments later, his head was crashing into the dirt inches away from the crater created by the nova divide. Gaia lands on her feet behind Adrian.

"Hmph. How's that!" Gaia said, boasting and tapping Kirici against her shoulder.

"Go get em, Gaia!" Blaze rose his smoking blade out of the dirt before spinning it around and shoving it point first back into the ground. He began to gather mana now, channeling it between his body and Red Chariot.

Gaia stands before Adrian's body cracking her knuckles. A single flare from Blaze flickered in the darkness in between them, offering a bit of light. "It's my turn now," Gaia said as she quickly dropped to a knee and passed her mana into the ground slightly aggressively. "Listen to my calls like you did in the past, help me defeat this foe to make this world last," she called, causing a seven-meter diameter circle of mana along the ground to surround the two of them. The area of soil destroyed by Blaze's attack was recovered inside of this circle, making the ground even again. "Dünya baştan!" Gaia shouted. From this lining of mana, the earth shot up high into the air enclosing them in the center of a thick, rock-solid perimeter of mana and the surface itself. It was like a small coliseum for the two of them.

Adrian began stirring and finally grumbled his way back up to his feet. "What is this?" he asked, looking around at the encasement around him.

"Your defeat." Gaia spun Kirici around and pointed it back at Adrian.

"We'll see about that." Adrian surrounded his body in his own shadow mana as armor and held his blade at Gaia in turn.

Gaia's entire body slowed slightly just then, pulsating every few seconds. Rocks and earth began to rise out of the ground and form into plates of armor to cover her body, solidifying on contact. "Kaya Zırhı." Gaia slapped her new plates, testing its strength. "See I can do that too. Prepare yourself," she said rushing at Adrian with a fury of staff blows. Adrian was successful in countering and parrying the majority of the swings initially, losing only a small amount of ground.

"Heh!" Adrian snickered.

Gaia remained to her convictions and swung without mercy at Adrian's head. He ducked, bending both of his knees, causing Gaia to overshoot and miss. Strike veered back his blade before shoving it through the air towards Gaia's midsection. Before he could fully start the action, a stalagmite of the earth came spiking out of the ground catching him in the side, spearing through his guard and piercing into him slightly. The body of the earth spike quickly proved itself very flexible as it slithered around like a snake lifting him into the air and crashing into the ground, still trying to dig deeper into him. "Gah!" In frustration, he cut off the tip of the spike, causing it to 'die' where it stood. Adrian then leaped back a few meters to get a bit of distance from Gaia, his side now bleeding a bit from the stab. Before he could even land, there was a rumble in the wall a meter away behind him. A gang of spikes then shot out of the wall with particular vigor and rage as if they were alive.

With half a second to spare, Adrian landed and immediately spun his shadow cape in front of him like a matador, wrapping his entire body in a dark sheet of armor in a cone shape. At the end of that half, a second, the two dozen snake-like spikes of earth mercilessly pelted into his dark cape-like oversized hail. For at least a minute, this continued, finally ceasing as Gaia approached Adrian. "Had enough yet? I made this little enclosure so you couldn't get the space you desperately want," Gaia said, tapping Kirici on her hand.

As soon as the spikes stopped, Adrian collapsed out of his cape, breathing heavily on his hands and knees; his dark mana his used as armor in tattered holes. He now bled through many small holes around his body. "Tsk. You think this is it?" he asked, spitting off to the side, blood in the loogie.

Kirici began glowing in Gaia's hand now. "Finish time! No mercy for the evil. Crack and sm—"

"No!" Adrian's cape of mana regained its composure and punched into the ground propelling him up and to the left. At the same time, in his hands was an armful of hand-sized black balls of mana. He held on tight as he traveled through the air, guided by his cape, still dug into the ground.

"A gift for you, Gaia!" he said, releasing his arms and tossing the flurry of black balls in all directions towards Gaia. Some stuck and snuck their way into the ground upon contact, but the rest exploded when they hit. There was a medley of dark explosions on the ground like fireworks, whereas Gaia gets was caught off guard by the sudden actions. The entire area within the cylinder of earth was rocked and shook from the force of the explosions.

"Damn…I hope she's okay in there…" Blaze calmly said to himself as he charged his mana. His blade was now rumbling with power, shaking in place, making it hard to grasp. The fiery mana surrounding Blaze soon became furious with rage as it flared out nondiscriminatory around him. His eyes glowed bright red as well, hints of fire in the corners of his eyes.

Back inside the walls of stone Gaia stands wobbly in the center of an army of hidden dark mines as the smoke clears on the explosions. The stone armor she sported now crumbled nearly all away, burns underneath on her arms and legs. She gingerly breathed in and out, trying to contain the urge to scream outright as the pain riddled her body. Her arms both rested at her sides, Kirici nearly dragging onto the ground as she struggled to hold it up. "Gee. Didn't…" She took a second to catch her breath as another pulse of pain waved past her. "Whew. Didn't know you'd still have so much mana left." Gaia winced.

Adrian finally landed himself back onto the ground, a couple meters in front of the wall on the eastern side, staring down Gaia. "If nothing else. I'll never run out of mana, you can count on that." Adrian smirked as he showed off his cape flailing with mana.

Gaia stood up straight and breathed through all the pain with one forced scream. She then looked up at Adrian and stomped her foot on the ground. "Toprak Hapis." Earth spikes came shooting out again, but this time from the field and the walls swiftly ensnaring Adrian's body in a web of stalagmites from all around him.

He wasn't even allotted time to move his blade up, so his hand was stuck lowered to the ground, his sword still tightly in hand. The rest of him was so trapped that he couldn't even move his head in any direction, forcing him to stand there staring at Gaia. "Urgh. What is this!?" Adrian shouted nervously, trying to break away at the stone shafts crossing between his limbs with his shadow cape, to no avail.

Gaia stared down Adrian with silent rage. "Now then! Where were we!?" She said emotionally as her bow began to glow again. Adrian returned her glare with shaky confidence. "Crack ve şut, kırıcı sürücü! No—" boom! Gaia takes a single step forward, her food landing directly on a dark mine, causing it to explode. The direct hit left a massive smoke cloud around Gaia.

"Ha!" Adrian let out while still trying to wiggle free. His smile quickly faded as he saw Gaia's face leaving the smoke. It still holds all of the intensity with even more rage. Her right leg was poorly burned, but she again trotted forward.

"Ahhhhh!" Gaia let out before regaining her composure again. "No mercy for the evil. Crack and—" Boom! Boom! Boom! Getting closer to Adrian, she stepped on another mine with her left leg this time. This caused a chain reaction causing three explosions to release on Gaia. Her staff's bright glow the only thing seen through the smoke. Adrian gulped as he saw the glow still getting closer, her voice echoing through the smoke. "Crack and smash, Kirici!" Boom boom! Two more explosions set off directly in front of Gaia, but she still crept closer, under a meter away from Adrain now, the mana around Kirici growing violent and untamed. "Kötülük için merhamet yok!"

"Dammit, you!" Boom boom! The smoke cloud was immense now as Adrian set off two more mines himself directly in between both of them, using his cape.

"Breaker drive!" Gaia shouted, Kirici now inches away from Adrian, both of them invisible to each other through the smoke.

"Die, Gaia!! Skoúro kýma!" Adrian retorted. The next thing anyone heard was a loud clunk and then nothing. The sound simple echoed, and reverberated. On the other side of the wall, facing Blaze, Gaia came crashing through the thick walls she created, head first and tumbling into the ground her and Kirici flopping on the ground until she finally slid onto the ground face down at Blaze's feet. Kirici disappeared along with the wall of stone she created as well. Bruises and blood splattered through the shredded skin and armor all along her arms, legs, and back. Her head was concussed, and she was bleeding from the top of her head. Blaze looked down at Gaia then up at the towering cloud of smoke, finally clearing out in front of him, then back to Gaia, confused.

Gaia lifted her head, her hair covering much of the blood on her head. "I-I'm sorry, Blaze, he's got a major set on him, I couldn't get it done. Who knew that reflect could work on...physical attacks." She faded away into unconsciousness as her head dropped back down into the dirt.

"Gaia ...damnit..." Blaze said, welling up with rage again, his mana almost charged. He looked back ahead of him as Adrian stood there in the middle of scorched earth, smoke whisked away now.

Adrian's legs were shaking in place, barely holding him up. Two significant burns were on either side of his chest, tearing away at his armor entirely, showing his bare chest underneath. His whole body was in shock, it was taking everything in his being not to pass out from the pain

425

himself. "Goddamn, that bitch was scary…" Adrian said to himself, breathing heavily. "Wait, what is that mana I sense." He looked up ahead of himself to see the monstrous mana Blaze had gathered around him. "Oh…"

"Out of the raging bitch and into the fire, Adrian. Get ready!" Blaze grasped the hilt of his blade with both hands, lifting it the ground and high into the air. The mana that he had gathered around his body began flowing into the tip of Red Chariot. A ball of fiery mana began to gather and grow at this tip, doubling in size every second. "Let's see you reflect this!"

"No rest for me, I guess. Shit." Adrian used the cape's mana to wrap around his limbs and give himself a helping hand in moving around. He waved his blade around before lowering it to his right and getting back into his stance. Pain in his body with each assisted movement. "Give me your worst peasant!" Adrian gathered mana of his own in his blade.

The mana above Blaze was now the size of a house still growing. "You'll regret trying me," he said, balancing the mana. The surge began to crack the ground he stood on, loosening his footing. The ball of mana lit up the field of the black mist like a rising sun. "Oh, great lords grant me the power to create the ultimate destruction, kneel before the power of lord Verafelt!" A quick sheen wiped through the ball of mana over his head as it reached max size. As large as to eclipse them from the chaos moon in the sky, the Molten Nova had reached a size larger than any other attempt; this caused difficulty for Blaze as he tried desperately to control it. "Ahhhhhhh!" He let out, holding the Molten Nova above his head steady. The mana surrounding it swirled and cut through the air aggressively as if trying to propel itself into the air. "Whew. Full power now. Here goes everything." Blaze looked at Adrian, then up at the bottom of the Molten Nova above him before smirking.

"What's this? Done already? C'mon, throw it over here, see what happens!" Adrian laughed.

Blaze closed his eyes, still with a smirk on his face. "Verafelt. Quell my rage to rid me of my demons. Calm my soul so I may live on without hatred and regret. Suck away my fears, my anger, and my sorrows lest they prevent me from absorbing your love. Let your overwhelming feelings and power rain. Down. On. Me." Blaze finishes the enchantment with his eyes still closed, his voice calming to a whisper. Mana began to leave his body like evaporating water. Larger chunks faded away from his resembling red lightning bugs, flying sporadically and up into the air. After the mana vacated his body, his arms both dropped to his sides, his head lowered as well. His Red Chariot's blade slung into the ground with his lifeless hand somehow still gripped the hilt, barely.

"Huh?" Adrian said, confused. He still charged his mana, but cautiously started inching forward.

After the last mana ties were severed, the Molten Nova began to descend slowly. Blaze stood motionless as in one motion, the mana all dropped onto him at once with devastating weight. The Nova sank into the ground and twirled in place, Blaze's body all but disappeared from sight in the vicious mana storm he was in the center of. Sporadically lashing out with fiery mana in all directions, the ball sat there for at least a minute, gently spinning.

"Oh...uhh, okay then." Adrian leaped back to avoid the flares and still stood in wait, not understanding what was happening before him. He only saw an impressive power and knew he had to be wary.

"Phoenix mode." A voice echoed from the center of the storm of mana. The twirling Molten Nova soon began to reduce in size faster than it gained mass. The outer surface wobbled and pulled in like it was being sucked on from the inside. Eventually, after just a few seconds, the form of Blaze's body revealed itself behind a layer of flaming mass. From this mass came two flaming wings sprouting out of Blaze's back. The flames formed into feathers and structured like a phoenix's wing, flapping and letting loose phoenix feathers left and right. The mana also hardened into bright red and orange armor over his body. Each piece had an aura of fiery mana to itself that made it shine in the darkness.

The Red Chariot received the most significant upgrade, though. The blade had doubled in length and changed form to become claymore like. The hand guard and hilt reformed to resemble feathers, shining in a golden finish and wrapping down the side of Blaze's hand. The aura surrounding the Red Chariot extended twice the length of the blade, resulting in a three-meter long-range from swinging the sword. As the mana finished forming into a golden phoenix helm, the last piece of armor, Blaze's form was finally visible again. The aura surrounding his body was just as furious as when the Molten Nova was above him. The ground itself trembled in fear as he stood there, the sheer amount of mana was felt to even soldiers who were just outside of the dark mist.

"W-what is this?" Adrian shouted as he forced his weary legs to trample forward towards Blaze. "No matter! You'll still fall to my blade!" Adrian's blade shook as the mana orbited it quickly. "Ahhhh, Skoúro kýma!" he yelled, now running towards Blaze.

Blaze smirked and simply raised his blade into the air towards Adrian before quickly swiping it down vertically, harshly connecting with the dirt. "Phoenix Divide." A wave of light was sent forth in the blade of the blade, getting longer with each passing second. It moved faster than Adrian could react, phasing through him on his right side from his shoulder to his leg and into the mist wall behind him.

Adrian stopped short as the wave finally took effect. The wave of light had sliced across the mist wall above and through to the other side cleanly. Light shone into the dome again, though not much, through these new openings. A look of confusion was stuck on Adrian's face as he peered down and watched the right half of his body cleanly separate from the left.

"H-Huh..." Adrian's body collapsed back to the ground in two parts now. There was barely any blood either. The light had categorized the wound instantly in its intense heat. "I'm...not...ready...Please don't take me...over." Adrian stared up into the crack in his mana mist as he lost consciousness, eyes rolling back into his head. The fog suddenly faded away, releasing everyone from its capture.

Blaze stood silent in the center of the tortured earth around him, his mana still exploding off in all directions. "I guess that's it then," he said calmly.

Around the battlefield, with the mist cleared, the other knights felt Blaze's energy and mana, slightly interrupting their own battles. Almost as quickly as the sinister mana disappeared, an eerie feeling was restored in the area surrounding Blaze. Blaze noticed this and looked around for the cause, finally ending his search onto the body of Adrian. Dark embers began to bubble and fester on his chest like the last spark of a campfire. The mana felt different from Adrian's though, it was darker, purer evil, and even less rational. Before he knew it, a puddle of evil mana had begun to expand underneath of Adrian's body, growing more by the second.

"What is this energy?" Blaze said, walking a bit closer to Adrian's body.

As he stared at Adrian's lifeless body, he overheard a ghostly voice echoing around it. The voice sounded drained and labored. It kind of resembled Adrian's voice, but it was a bit different; muffled like Adrian had a mask over his face. At times, it even sounded feminine. "No mercy, innocent or guilty. Bring down their lying sun. Blood a sweet silver black by night. Upon their faces pale white." After the enchantment, Adrian's body was drug down into the puddle of darkness that spread underneath him. His body disappeared with the pool returning to its original position. Soon after, the dark puddle absorbed into the dirt, destination unknown.

"What is going on...I have a bad feeling about this." Blaze in a rush enlisted other warriors to grab the injured that got caught in the mist and take them to Scatha. A few simple sword swings would be sufficient in covering them as each swing annihilated dozens of shadows. He began to sense the hint of dark mana surrounding the area. "Everyone move back no—" Blaze stopped himself at the realization that he didn't make it in time.

Out of the ground, at points around a fifteen-meter circle with Adrian's previous resting place at the center, came darkness shooting out of the ground like a geyser. Eighteen pillars in total, anything that was under them, was destroyed along with those who were sprinkled by the acidic dark mana. Blaze was only able to get a barrier around Gaia's body before it occurred. Even Silverwings near would get damaged by this. In the air, at the top of the geysers, the splashes began to connect in the center. The sides started stretching to merge with one another with lives of their own. The vision from the sky and any light ceased to exist for those caught under this new dome forming.

"All will know the wonder of my eternal lullaby. Say goodnight at this, the final setting of the sun, tomorrow dawns in darkness, the eternal night has begun! Nocte Aeternus!" The almost angelic voice echoes once more before the gigantic dome of darkness is completed once more, shutting out all light. Not even the light from the flames emanating from Blaze were allowed to shine inside of here.

"Whoa. It's very…dark in here. This is unnaturally dark. Even that mist, we could light up a bit, but there is no visibility here at all!" Blaze grumbled, looking around. Shortly after, a scream reamed out from the darkness somewhere off to his left before a quick silence. What sounded like a gooey explosion going off multiple times is what incited this silence. "What was…" Blaze started. He immediately realized what it was. Not all of the warriors were able to get out of range in time and lost their lives.

"Guess they were too weak to be invited to my special place." It was Adrian's voice, except it wasn't echoed, and it sounded normal. Somewhere in the darkness, Adrian floated around.

"Adrian!? How are you alive. And what is this?" Blaze yelled into the dark.

"Hmm. That damn minor deity tried to take advantage of my weakness to take over my body again. That bitch repaired my body by using her own mana but underestimated me. My mind isn't as weak as Keith's, Ha. She also activated a forbidden spell. If my mist is me giving you a taste of my emotions by forcing them onto you, then my Nocte Aeternus is like stuffing you inside my black heart. It rejects those who are weak, it absorbs all but the brightest of lights. My heart also heals my body, granting me invincibility. You can't win Blaze." Adrian shouted before laughing maniacally somewhere in the darkness.

"Phoenix divide!" Blaze swung his sword in the darkness, releasing another powerful wave of light. The light was still invisible in this overwhelming darkness. A splatter creaks out in the distance followed by a shockwave, seemingly when the wave crashed into the dome.

431

"Ha Nice. You actually got me. Too bad, though."
Adrian's voice is drowned out by the sound of wet sacks
slapping together. "If you weren't in your little special
mode, I'm certain my darkness would eat you alive." Adrian
went silent again as he roamed in the darkness.
Clank! Blaze raised his blade and spun around to block an
incoming sword strike from Adrian. They both stood there,
clashing blades for a moment. "Ooooo." Adrian whistled.

"Good thing, I can still smell you, Adrian," Blaze
smirked. "Ack. What?" Blaze winced as something had
pierced his stomach on the right side and spun in place like a
drill. He couldn't even see what it was.

"Hmph. Bitch. Could you smell that?" Adrian
gloated as he drilled the mana from his cloak of darkness
through Blaze's midsection.

Blaze flapped his flaming wings forward and pushed
himself back, out of Adrian's range. The wound on his
stomach was instantly engulfed in flames and healed. "Heh,
see, I can do that too," he said as he skidded back onto the
ground.

"Heal from this then. Unstoppable darkness!" Adrian
shouted.

Unable to see, Blaze held up his guard with his Blade
and hoped for the best. The barrage finally started. Drill
tipped arrows of darkness rained down on him from the air.
Blaze shifted his wings to the front to try to block more of
the attacks, but each one broke more and more away from
his defenses. Soon the arrows broke through and started
piercing through Blaze, who would heal after each blow.
This barrage lasted for several moments and became even
worse when arrows that hit the ground would move again
and fly back into Blaze from behind, causing even more
damage for him to heal.

"Muahahaha, how long do you think you can last? I
have unlimited mana, can your mana hold up healing all

those injuries? One way to see!" Adrian laughed as he increased the rate of the arrows.

Blaze growled and looked up at where the voice was coming from. "Yeah, you're right." In one motion, Blaze turned into flames and phased to the left out of the way of the arrows. He then spun and threw the Red Chariot at Adrian's voice, cutting off the flow of arrows.

"What the—" Adrian got hit right in hand and got weighed down into the ground with the blade skewering his right hand into the ground. Ten meters off of Blaze, Adrian stood on his knees trying to free himself from the Chariot's dominant force.

"Good. I got you!" Blaze said, lowering his left hand, and bending his knees into a low stance. Mana begins to charge in this hand.

"Uh, heh. Let's talk about this, shall we?" Adrian nervously said while trapped.

The mana in Blaze's hand began to flare out like lightning as his hand glowed, though it wasn't visible. The flames that surrounded his body before all radiated around his left arm and phoenix wings. This left the rest of his body without any aura. "Deities of the elements hear my call. Verafelt replenish my rage so that I may not fall. This fist of mine will hold my soul and my passion. Let it burn bright in the night to incinerate everything in sight!" The mana surrounding his arm shone in the darkness for just a moment before going out. Then Blaze disappeared altogether.

Adrian lost him. He couldn't find Blaze in his sights. Then a flash again off to the side before disappearing again. "Ugh. I didn't want to have to use this level. But good job, you've left me no choice!" Calm white mana began to surround Adrian, replacing his dark mana. It pulsated and began to even light up the darkness as the whitest white possible. It was blinding also. "No longer will the people have to wait for day, my cruel moon will bring the end. The dawn will never rise, slaves of the light we shall end. Rise, Lunar Princess, bring eternal darkness and protect us in your everlasting night." A great flash of light was shone surrounding Adrian at this moment, halting all movement in the dome. When it finished, Adrian's entire body was glowing white, and his hand was free as he stood straight, admiring his newfound strength. White mana trailed down his body like veins, even encasing around his existing armor to make the pieces all bright white.

Blaze flashed back into sight again directly in front of Adrian, his glowing arm reared back, ready to fly towards him. "Phoenix fist!" Blaze's left hand led his body as he lunged towards Adrian full force, his mana cutting through the air.

Adrian starred as his hand until mana of his own was gathered there. He turned quickly towards Blaze and reared his own left hand back. "Shining Fist!" He lunged as well and connected with Blaze in the center. The clash between the two erupted a shockwave that lit up the dome. Like the light of a lighthouse, the dome was illuminated for only a moment before descending back into darkness. Blaze and Adrian stood there still, clashing their attacks. Periodically the lights from the clash would release from their hands, lighting up the area temporarily.

"This is the end!" Blaze said, pushing harder, flaming mana shooting out behind his hand as he pushes Adrian backed a step.

"Ha. Your mana will never hold up! You're already fading," Adrian said as he powered up his shining fist as well. He got closer, bending his elbow, trying to force Blaze back.

Blaze bent his elbow in turn and pushed back against Adrian with all his strength. With his right hand, he reached it under his left arm, palm up. A small flame appeared in the air about a foot above his hand. It slowly drifted back and forth down towards his palm. Adrian locked his eyes on this flame, not understanding what it meant. "This is my win." The spark softly landed on his hand, and the Red Chariot spawned into the grasp of Blaze reared back, the blade on the path of Adrian's side.

"What?" Adrian shouted as he watched the blade break his skin on his right side and tear through his stomach, exiting on the left. At this moment, Adrian's body went into shock, his powered arm still connected with Blaze's. Time seemed to move very slowly. Adrian's lower half began to slightly drop out of the sky, and his top half arched over to the side

Blaze released the hilt of his blaze and retracted his hand to his side swiftly. Mana radiating around it right away. "Take this! My rage, my anger, and all of my fury!" He quickly chanted as his powered up right-hand charged forward and connected with Adrian's chest. "Phoenix finger!" A gust of flaming mana funneled out of Adrian's back, destroying most of his body with one quick, concentrated attack that continued past Adrian and into the wall of the dome behind them. It actually broke through, creating a circular hole in the wall behind Adrian. Adrian's eyes went blank as his head floated into the incoming light shining in from outside. The mana coming from his hand flickered away, and Blaze took over. The mana from his left-hand carried all of his phoenix mana through Adrian. Everything except for his head and shoulders disintegrated from the immense power. This stream of mana left a large hole in the dome as well.

Blaze's arms were crossed over each other, both smoking and empty of mana. Blaze's body was also drained of mana and returned to normal as a layer of ash falls to the floor around him. Adrian's head slowly fell downwards, visible as it passed by both holes in the dome, the light from outside showing his dead face for just a moment.

"Hmph. Should've aimed for my head, so unfortunate." Muffled voice echos. Dark mana from the floor rises up like drips upside down and engulfs Adrian's head, dragging it back into the ground afterward. Dark mana smoothly dripped over the holes on the dome as well, returning Blaze to the complete darkness again.

"What the…shit, I'm out of mana too." Blaze leaped back, scrambling to grab his blade and ready himself to defend.

Suddenly directly in front of him, after a flash of blinding white light, Adrian reappeared as good as new, looking even stronger than before. His bright armor forced Blaze to wince and look up. "That's why I say it's unfortunate. I was just beginning to enjoy someone with your strength. But of course, your mana could not hold up. I told you this much." Both of Adrian's hands were now up, glowing as his mana gathered into little spheres in his hands. He looks over to Blaze, struggling to hold up his sword in defense. "Oh aww, and your sword went back to normal too. You won't survive that way. Shining slicer!" he said as he pointed both hands at Blaze. Out of the balls came large streaks of mana that rushed forward and sliced away at their target, not being easy to halt. The first one crashed into Blaze's blade and broke his guard. The bottom tip nicked his forehead as he propelled it up and away from him. The victory was small, however, because the streaks began to shoot out like bullets, growing to the size of a sword flying towards Blaze.

After a few more streaks, Blaze's hand was hit, and he lost the Red Chariot, effectively disarming him. "Damnit…" Blaze sulked as he watchede more of the streaks soar towards him, each one super bright white. They all attacked at once, causing a small dust cloud when they hit the ground. Blaze dove out of the way at the last minute. Splatters of blood rose up into the air, where a couple of the streaks connected with Blaze. Blaze skidded on the ground on his knee and examined the damage. "Tsk, damn," he said.

A bright flash of light appeared next to Blaze again as Adrian teleported directly next to him. His fist was into Blaze's cheek before he could even react to the bright light. Blaze's face crashes into the dirt. He put both hands under himself to slowly start picking himself up. "This is a pathetic Blaze. This makes me so angry!" He started to pummel Blaze with his fists over and over now, not letting up after many cracks and crunches are heard in the process. After a moment of lying motionless on the ground after getting massacred with fists, Blaze starts to stir again. Blood trickled down his head and cheek, and his breathing was very labored, ribs had to have been broken on that left side.

"What's pathetic is how light your punches are. Yep pretty sure Gaia hits harder than you." Blaze said with a face full of fake confidence and spitting up a bloody loogie to the side.

"Agh!" In a fit of rage, Adrian begins rapidly punching Blaze in the face back and forth. More and more blood is released with each punch.

"D-damn, think I'm losing consciousness. Not good." Blaze mouthed to himself while his face was getting pelted on. Soon after, Adrian changed targets from just his face to his entire upper body. Blaze was on both knees, everything else on him was vulnerable to get punched.

"Ahhhh, you're losing it. Only a little bit further, and I'll have you. Then I'm going to go finish off Gaia and the rest of those pesky knights. Haha." Adrian laughed as his fists glow brighter the longer he keeps up the barrage.

Blaze's torso wobbled back and forth as a mixture of getting hit and passing out. *Dammit. I can't even speak anymore. Is this it for me...I can't. No. I have to protect Gaia and others...I must.* Adrian doesn't care, though. He is determined to get his revenge for the comments earlier. The unconscious Blaze's body was punching bagged for several minutes, at least.

"Ha. Are you dead yet? It doesn't matter. I won't stop, either way, muahaha!" Adrian said, upping the rate of his punches. Blood and pieces of armor flew freely as Blaze's body was pummeled. Face, chest, arms, nothing was exempt from getting hit. Large welts began to expose themselves on his face and chest. The force of the punches was all that kept his body upright, his legs grew limp and wobbled as his body bobbled up and down, every new punch jolting him up again. This continued for a bit longer until Adrian got tired of punching and finally stopped.

Blaze's body slowly drifted off to the side, drifting towards the ground. Adrian reached out his hand and snatched Blaze up from his head, holding him from falling. Blaze's knees drug against the field as Adrian maneuvered him and sat him down on his knees. Blaze's head arched down, his arms dangled in the air, his back hunched over as well. He was still out cold. Blood began to pool under the surface of his skin, where the welts formed. His internal organs had clearly taken a beating. Blood also began trickling out of his mouth, which opened slightly under the weight of the puddle forming in his mouth.

Adrian bent down to look at Blaze's lifeless body. "Pathetic. I'll finish you off now, I guess," he said, taking a few steps back and opening his hands. The mana surrounding them seemed to shift and vibrate. In the deep darkness, a slight twinkle could be seen in various places on the walls. The shining mana around him illuminating Blaze's face even a few feet away. "Under the will of darkness. My light snuffs out the twinkle in your spirit. Come, show me your soul as I rip it out for the Goddess to witness!" The lights that twinkled now shone in full force like headlights, but from all directions surrounding Blaze. "Shining Lance!" The lights all flashed once.

"Come." A small voice whispered in the darkness. A small platform of the earth underneath Blaze suddenly lifting him into the air before jolting him off to the side. In the second afterward, in another flash, The entire area around where Blaze was infested with a lattice network of shining white lances coming from the wall and spearing to the other sides of the dome. Were Blaze still there, he would have at least thirty holes through him now. In another flash, the lance disappeared again. Removing the illumination in that area, except for Adrian himself, of course. After a second, it stopped, sending Blaze tumbling to the ground. The hit to his head actually waking him up for a moment. He landed on his chest and looked over to this left, noticing it was Gaia there next to him, struggling to rise up to all fours. She eventually gave up and just landed closer to Blaze, reaching around until she found him and wrapping her arm around the back of his head. "I got you." She said, resting her face into his shoulder.

"T-thanks, Gaia," Blaze said, only able to see from his left eye. His right was completely swollen shut.

"Aww, and here that would have been such a fitting end for him. Gee, thanks, Gaia?" Adrian said, walking closer to the two, visually annoyed. They both lay there, unable to move, the reality settling in for what was now before them. Dread.

Crash! A hole opened up in the top of the dome, and a body came smashing into the ground. The light from outside was seen but did not travel into the dome. "Ouch. Why's it so dark in here...The hell is going on?" A familiar voice echoed in the dark.

"Is that Void?" Gaia shouted.

"Gaia? What's going on? And uh...who's this shining guy in here?" Void said, finally noticing Adrian walking towards Blaze and Gaia, who were in between the two. At this point.

439

"Void. What are you doing her—" Adrian was cut off by the giant slice and rip in the side of his dome, coming from behind him. Volt came stepping over the opening he made with his spear. He was surrounded by a storm of his lightning mana, though he wore many injuries, he stood inside with poise and stature.

"Hmph. Knew, I felt a ridiculous amount of mana in here." Volt said, staring down Adrian, who now had Void in front of him, Blaze and Gaia to his right and Volt behind him.

Adrian stopped and looked around him. He smirked, but blood vessels on his head still bubbled and popped. "Ugh. I will not be disrespected!" He said as his shining mana began spreading and doubling in intensity. "You think a few more knights will change anything?" He shouted.

"Damn. He's gone mad. Such power." Void said, pulling out Fonos.

On the other side, Volt held up Sigrun. "Let's crunch em Void! Can't see much else but just meet at the shining beacon over there." Volt ran his mana charged hand along the back of Sigrun, transferring mana. "Lucin, grant me the power to strike down all who oppose you! Ringa Uira!" The mana from his lightning fist now resided in his spear. He rushed forward at this point, towards Adrian and his surge of mana.

"Gotcha!" Void said, gathering mana of his own. With even more darkness surrounding Fonos, he rushed forward as well.

Adrian spawned an orb of shining mana to surround him like a bubble. It spun and lifted him slightly off the ground while Adrian gained mana. "Try as you may, but you won't stop me! I'll eradicate all of you at once with my coup de grâce. My ultimate technique!" he said, laughing away.

Void and Volt both slam into Adrian's bubble simultaneously with their powered-up weapons. Both Volt's

440

Ringa Uira and Void's Fonos dispelled and returned to normal upon contact, stunning and shocking them both. "Ow. What was that!?" Volt said, taking a few steps back.

"Don't think this is gonna work." Void said, unsuccessfully pelting his sword into Adrian's mana. The bubble had grown larger, and the mana stronger by the moment. The raging storm of shining mana shaking the entire dome.

"Hahahaha. Your struggle won't amount to much. Your end is still guaranteed!" Adrian gloated as intense flares of mana were released, attacking his enemies.

Volt dove in front of Blaze, diverting a flare inches away from landing with Sigrun's long-range. He then skidded to Gaia's side. "Damn. His capacity for mana is insane. If this happens, I don't know if we can survive." Volt said, troubled.

"There is one thing we could try," Blaze mumbled, picking up his head. "We need to absorb it somehow. We need a LARGE boost in mana." He nodded while turning to his side.

Gaia struggled and finally flipped over to her back. "Think I get what he's saying," she said, getting her breathing back in order.

"Do you mean to try contact fusion Blaze?" Void's voice is heard as he leaps out of a portal behind the others. "The four of us?" he asked.

"Yes, it's the only way!" Blaze said, raising his voice.

"Sounds dangerous for us to try that with so many people. We barely completed it with two as it is." Volt said, dodging stray flares that headed for his head.

"Volt, between the four of us, we all have fused at least once. We may need this, or we'll die." Void said, peering back up at Adrian, the shining mana nearly illuminating his entire face in the darkness.

441

Adrian spun his floating bubble to face the knights. His twisted mug smiling at the crew with ultimate confidence. "I hope you're discussing your last words because the end has begun," he said. The dome began to rumble fiercely like they had danced on a tectonic plate. They all knew why, though. Adrian's mana was so powerful that it shook the very ground they stood on. The reality of this realization dawned on all of them at the same time. "I call upon thee, demon lords of the plane." Adrian began his enchant.

Void and Volt scurried over to get behind Gaia and Blaze respectfully, joining hands and crouching down behind the two. Blaze turned to be fully on his back and stared at Volt's outstretched hand. "Oh, now you're all for it?" Blaze smirked, attempting to muster up some mana in his beaten and worn body.

Volt nodded. "Yeah, we have to try it, I guess. You and Gaia try to gather all the mana you can in your bodies. Void and I will match you and pray this works," he said, priming his mana to transfer to his right hand.

"Embrace me in your arms and lend me your powers once again." Adrian continued his chant. The shaking became more violent, and even broke split the ground into a few areas under the dome.

"Ok ok ok, sounds good, hun, ooo." Gaia squealed a bit as she tensed her body to gather what little mana she had left. Her body shone dimly, then a small amount more as time progressed. Blaze's body also had the same progression as he realized just how drained he really was. Void and Volt varied the mana they released to their hands as their partner's mana fluctuated. After a few moments, they were finally all in sync.

Adrian's voice seemed to get louder as he went. "I offer you blood, pain, and torment in exchange."

"Ok, now's the time we ready?" Void said hurriedly. He looked around and got all silent nods; the knights were clearly nervous, sweating even. They knew this wasn't the time for hesitation, the time was now. Volt and Void held hands, then they each reach down and touch the outstretched hands of Blaze and Gaia softly. "Contact!" They all yelled in unison.

"Pour your wrath upon my sword, and now prepare yourself for my bane. Profane Indignation!" Adrian finished his chant just as the knights began their fusion, causing a hell of a light show. A giant flash temporarily extinguished the darkness while it engulfs the area that the knights stood under its holy grasp. The dome of night opened up from the sky to reveal a gargantuan beam of shining mana lowering from the sky. It covered the entire span of the dome, slowly crashing through the air like an asteroid, straight down onto them. At the same time, shining mana also started to bubble from underneath the earth as well, soon shooting up out from below in the form of towering pillars of light. From below and above, light massacred the area inside as the two collided. More and more pillars from below slammed into the one from above and joined as one. "Now be crushed by my ultimate light!" Adrian said as he and the knights all disappear into the light. Only sight visible was a cylinder of light emanating from the dome and going off into the heavens. Shadows and warriors alike fighting just outside of the dome were both forced back by merely being near this massive amount of mana.

All eyes left on the battlefield were on this light. For a moment, the fighting had paused. It was simply too much power to ignore. This mana remained there for several moments before suddenly, a soft suction sound was heard. The sound grew louder and louder as the moments passed. The perfectly straight beam of light began to wobble and waver. "God's shift." Instantly the pillar of mana was

443

sucked away from both sides into a gigantic portal in the middle. The portal pulled in the light like a black hole. With the light gone, Adrian was revealed again, along with a single figure who stood where the four knights resided.

"What…no way…that was my…" Adrian, now out of his orb of mana and freshly on the ground, backs away a few steps. A mix of confusion and rage was worn on his face, trying to grasp what had just transpired.

Across from him stood the figure controlling the portal. With both hands, he grasped the portal and began to absorb the mana inside of himself. A mix of light and dark mana began to awaken and flow around him. His aura raged on as well as the mana absorbed into his skin like lotion. The man stood about six feet with red-tipped long spiky black hair flying down the back of his neck. His skin was tanned, and he wore armor resembling molten rock. Each piece had a subtle flame surrounding the black stones. His blade was a massive claymore, appearing to be a mix of Fonos and Red Chariot, a giant black sword with red plates on the side. "Hmmm. I think Molten Voltage works as a name, eh?" he said to himself.

"Yeah, that works, Woah, this is weird. Don't think I'll get used to having my consciousness inside of another," Gaia said in the form of counsel with Volt and Blaze as Void taking the reins for control of the fusion.

"I can feel a large amount of mana flowing through us right now. It worked, guys," Volt responded.

"Yes, I can feel it, too. This is amazing." Molten Voltage said, taking a deep breath, finally finished absorbing the mana from the portal. His mana stormed off around him before stopping and all rushing outwards. His feet slowly rise into the air as he begins to hover in place. Back arched and his hands at his side, Molten Voltage started to expel the massive amounts of mana from his body as he screamed.

The mana exited his body and hovered around him like a mist.

Adrian flailed his arms in full on frustration now. "No! Who are you, and where are those damn knights? Did you save them?" He yelled.

"They are me, I am them. We are one now." Molten Voltage said, smirking as he squeezed the mana out. The mana soon gravitated into a growing ball above him. "And now, with all this power, it's time for checkmate," he said. The extra dark mana from the dome was even absorbed into the ball.

"Come then! I have infinite mana, I cannot lose, never!" Adrian grasped his blade, now shining with mana as well, and held it to his side before getting into his low stance.

"Yeah, keep that same energy after this." The ball above Molten Voltage finally fully sharpened and started to spin as it grew. "Filled with rage and anger...my curse is turned into a blessing from the hands of the Gods that deemed me worthy to wield the ultimate darkness. Feel my pain, my struggles, and shatter from the weight of my spirit!" In three pulses, the orb is condensed into a small ball of mana in his hands, pointed at Adrian. The lightning flares off of the ball as it sits there in his hands for a moment. The mana wiggles left and right as if demons were trying to break free from prison. "Kení bála," he said as the mana warps across the field in a blink of an eye, appearing in front of Adrian before he can react.

"Skoúro kýma!" Adrian yelled in a rush as he stared down the orb. He swung his powered-up sword into the sphere as it approached, but to his chagrin, it went right through. The dark orb phased through Adrian's blade and his chest and attached deep into his soul. He paused and looked around. The fear set in as soon as his eyes didn't land onto the orb. A second later, the shocking pain surrounded Adrian

445

as his body was filled with dark lightning and tore through the mana chains inside of him. First, his shining armor disappeared, then it was his cloak of darkness. Mana began evaporating off of Adrian, and it drove him to all fours. His arms and legs quivered in a mix of pain and exhaustion. His eyes nearly popped out of his skull his they were open so wide. The mana next completely dispelled, leaving Adrian's body dry and devoid of mana. In a cough that turned into a bloody cough, he nearly toppled over. "Bleh. What is this...where...the hell...is my mana…" Adrian said, slamming his hand into the ground.

"I took it. I took it all away from you. You're done now." Molten Voltage said, spreading his arms and opening both of his hands on either side.

Adrian struggled to his feet using his sword, barely able to stand now. "I'm so weak! Damnit. Scourge help!" He looked over to Scourge, still in a fight of his own.

"This isn't time for help from your daddy." Molten Voltage, who scraped his feet into the dirt and spread his stance out as he gathered mana in both of his hands. His right carried fiery mana, in his left lightning mana. Aura from all four of his elements spiraled around him as he gathered mana and transferred it to his two hands.

Adrian lowered his head. "Guess this is truly it for my freedom, then, huh?" He got up and sat up with his legs crossed. "Least it was fun to let loose a bit here. The most fun I've had since Edgar accidentally let me out in that internal battle with that damn angel. So glad we were able to use her mana, though. Oh well. Scourge granted me my freedom, the least I can do is to see this out until the end," Adrian said, closing his eyes and placing his sword at his side.

"Alright, Keith, now just stand right there," Edgar yelled from across the brightly-lit room. The room was fifty meters below the ground, down a very dark and long shaft. This shaft was connected by a ladder on either side all up way up to the surface.

A plethora of books lined the walls on tall bookshelves. Every niche in the lab held a diamond gem, the power source for Edgar's experiment. Twenty three long years, he waited for this, and his ambitions were finally coming to fruition. Even among his strict face, Keith detected what could be called a smirk every now and again. Edgar furiously darted about making sure everything was perfect for the experiment, all of the incantations were prepared, with their corresponding diamonds aligned. Keith sat slumped in the chair. Watching his masterwork at this was boring, as he had been at it for nigh eight hours now.

I suppose it's not every day you get to summon a living, breathing deity, lesser or not. Keith surmised to himself. He couldn't help but feel pangs of anxiety in his core, not knowing what to expect. If it wasn't for the coup at the capital to the north some years ago, they would never have found the goddess artifact from an ancient time when the angels lived with the demons. With these times being dead for an eon, the lesser deities would be near powerless if they did still live. But an impotent lesser god is stronger than the strongest living mortal. The fact that they battled within the back of their minds throughout the process.

"Keith! It's ready," Edgar bellowed out, as he came down the brief stairs next to Keith. "Now, I'd like to apologize ahead of time. What's about to happen was never my intention. This method is best to protect us both. As I mentioned before, I will tell you once more. I will have you die briefly, while the power I generate through the gems pours into the artifact and you simultaneously." Edgar stopped for a moment to look into Keith's eyes to see if there was any last-minute regret there. "It will revive you at the same time the summon to go through. With the artifact being directly connected to you, it should cause the summon to go through you like a conduit. Should all go well, the summon will go directly through you before the physical manifestation, and the essence should cling to you as a physical host. You will likely have to battle wills, but the deity should be surprised enough to have a weak will initially. Do NOT lose to her. I will not hesitate to kill you at that moment. Are you ready to proceed, my dearest protégé?" he asked, bowing in front of him.

"Yes, I am quite ready. Just make sure to kill me before I kill you." Keith sat up straight and emptied his mind and channeled his mana out slowly. Edgar closed his eyes, and discreetly mumbled multiple incantations at once. The room lit up in bright flashes, as one by one, the diamonds started to light up. The energy that was gathering sounded like cracks of lightning and birds chipping through the air. The sound lowered to hum, as all diamonds were lit bright, glowing in radiance. Keith picked up the ring and put it on his annularly. No sooner had he done that, *zing* went a small dagger straight towards Keith. He did not budge, as the knife pierced straight through his heart. It was all darkness for Keith therein. Before his limp body fell to the floor, the diamonds' energy shot out and pierced Keith. One by one, they entered his body, with no exit in sight. His body glowed with a massive brightness as if seconds before exploding.

Sometime after, the room dimmed to its normal light. As Edgar opened his eyes, all he saw was Keith's lifeless body on the ground, in a pool of his own making. He stared long at Keith, and as time passed, the more worried he got worried that the experiment went wrong. Then, moving on his body, was a long string of blue-tinged white energy, weaving back and forth all along with his remains. It was then that Keith stood straight up, eyes still unopened; the mana started to mold together. Keith's dark-brown hair rapidly turned white, and the mana began to take form. The more the energy enveloped Keith, the more violent it became. Out of his back sprouted giant aethereal wings, knocking equipment around as they spread wide. Once the aggressive mana had fully enveloped him, he remained motionless, and the berserk energy subsided. And it stayed that way for a few minutes, which turned to hours until finally, Keith's eyes shot open. Edgar had been patiently waiting and watching his disciple's stiff body stand there motionless. It was at that point, Edgar knew something was wrong. Keith's usual green eyes started being enveloped in blue. Keith levitated slightly into the air, and speechlessly looked around the room. He swatted his arm to his side and thrust up. Within moments, there was a large breach in the ceiling leading forty meters up, reaching outside. At that same moment, he was gone.

Edgar swore under his breath, pulling out a roll of parchment paper from one of his pockets. The article had dark writing that could be seen faintly glowing even while closed. He ripped the paper in half, causing the mana within to release, suddenly enveloping his body and pulling him up through the hole as well. After they reached the surface, Keith continued to fly upwards, his mentor not far behind. Edgar snapped his fingers, and a scythe magically appeared in his hands. Edgar increased his speed to catch up to his target, swinging his scythe rapidly when he got there. Without even looking down, Keith disappeared and reappeared 1 meter away. He bobbled a bit in the air, likely rusty after having just awoken. Edgar used this opportunity to swing his scythe as a long streak of dark energy came flying towards Keith. "Gotcha!" Edgar shouted with a smirk on his face.

It hit Keith square on, which sent him plummeting towards the ground. Edgar dared not let up his onslaught and continued swinging his scythe around gracefully as energy flew down and hit the field below. Dust flew upwards as the mana collided with the dirt. On and on, he continued before stopping to let the smoke settle. He landed on the ground and looked around. After a few seconds, a silhouette appeared behind the smoke. Edgar looked up just in time to see Keith leaping into the air and laughing with a female voice overlapping on his own.

Keith's arm was stretched out, and a ball of bright white energy came flying down towards Edgar. He jumped out of the way, but a small piece grazed his leg and left an abrasion in his suit. Edgar fell to one knee and clasped his hand on his wound. Residual mana rose from his hand, and when he removed it, his leg was healed. When he looked up, his impending doom awaited him. "Shit," Edgar said with a deep sigh. A giant black orb was high in the sky, drawing energy from Keith. Edgar threw his scythe at Keith, which he deflected effortlessly. Upon deflection, the cutter spun back around and came flying towards Keith. It made a direct hit to Keith's arm, leaving itself embedded in his flesh. He flinched, and it was at that moment, Keith's eyes started to revert from blue to green. Edgar paused when he noticed and jumped back, attempting to keep his distance. After a point, the black mist started to flow out of Keith. The mana that he was gathering above him quickly dissipated as well at this moment.

Edgar was horrified at sight, as he knew exactly what that meant. Adrian had awoken from his decade-long slumber. But how? The seal was supposed to hold him at bay. It was at that moment he realized that the power from the lesser deity's energy would have erased entirely any charms or seals, meaning Keith and the deity had been fighting Adrian as well inside. Adrian had to of defeated

Keith, leaving the goddess to take control. He had to of just took over with that moment of weakness. "This has to end now!" Edgar shouted. He didn't want to use it, but he was going to have to. He reached in his bag and pulled out a small charm. He chanted in the magical -tongue, causing the one charm to multiply into ten. He threw the charms at Adrian, who swiped his arm, ripping the papers in half with ease. The ripped pieces of the charm all flew towards Adrian and stuck to various parts of his body, exploding one after another.

As soon as the charms were destroyed, Adrian's body contorted. He collapsed down to ground level. The blue celestial mana that outlined his body started to crack, and the aetherial wing on his left side fell off, softly crashing into the ground. Adrian yelled out in pain, overlapped yet again by a female voice. It was then that Adrian sensed Edgar dash towards him, but it was too late. Edgar's index and pointer fingertips were glowing purple, and within moments slightly breached the skin on Adrian's chest. Edgar twisted his hand as if his fingers were a key, erasing all mana and clothing in a small area around his fingertips. Adrian was undamaged, but a small sigil could be seen now on his chest. Edgar continued this process on his head and stomach. Three masses of gray mana blew out of Adrian's body and erupted into the night sky. The mana that surrounded Keith had disappeared entirely at that moment. The mana then took the form of three pointed stakes. They flew down and pierced Adrian, where the sigils had formed. Mana had begun raging again on Keith's body, but only in those specific points. The sigils glowed, the mana arranging to form a seal. The deity mana instantly dissipated again, along with Adrian's. Only his left eye returned green. Edgar noticed that the remaining aethereal wing had also taken physical form. "Thank goodness. You're still with me." Edgar sighed again as Keith collapsed forward into his arms.

A week later, Keith awoke with a jump and noticed he was in his bed. Next to him sat Edgar, who was sipping on some tea, and reading a book. "D-did we do it?" Keith gasped out, looking back at his new wing, a new permanent addition to his back.

"No. We didn't. But do not worry." Edgar put his book down, set down his teacup, and stood up. He bowed a deep bow, and stood right up, boasting a huge smile. "We completely lost our objective, but the objective has changed!" He shouted with glee, "I believe we have ended up in a position that's even further than I would have thought possible." He grinned, and Keith smiled slightly, as he laid his head back down. He was still exhausted, and so he closed his eyes and drifted off to sleep.

-Year 277 Faith Hill Shadow Path, Umbra-

Back on the battlefield, Molten Voltage had gathered the massive amount of mana needed for his final attack. Third time's a charm, I guess. We could NOT kill this guy with all that mana. Blaze sighed within the fusion.

"Oh, great lords grant me the power to create the ultimate destruction, kneel before the power of lord Verafelt," Molten Voltage said, looking at his right hand. The ball of mana seemed to grow but is instead kept condensed in a small fiery orb, only a few times larger than his hand. He now looked towards his left hand. "Erupt and eradicate, shatter their hopes for they failed to embrace the goddess…and I will punish them!" The lightning mana in his left hand did the same as the right and now stood as a condensed ball of lightning mana. "And now, both together! Plasma cannon!" he said, slamming his hands together, colliding the two differing mana and causing a massive and large blast wave of mana to fire out towards Adrian. The beam was fiery mana continually being orbited by a stream of lighting mana. It got bigger as it traveled, scraping against the ground while it closed in.

Not stopping for anything, the blast wave swallowed up Adrian and continued on, eradicating shadows and Silverwings in its path. Adrian's body was torn apart and destroyed by the waves, leaving only his blade behind. The air was still after the wave concluded. This earth they fought on had received a lot of punishment, the wind has been shaken up as well. Moments after the end of the attack, Molten Voltage had separated in another bright flash. Their bodies were sprawled out as they caught their breath. The terrible injuries to Blaze and Gaia were healed for the most part, but everyone's mana was very low. They sat around there, regaining themselves for a moment while fighting still continued all around them.

Considerable casualties on both sides could be seen from the bodies littered around them. "Man, that's finally over." Blaze said, letting out a massive sigh. The wind and clanks in the distance filling in the background sounds.

"It's not over, yet unfortunately, we still need to destroy Scourge and find Wendy to make all of this worth it," Volt said, standing up fully.

"Shall we go beat his face in as well then?" Gaia said, getting up to her feet for the first time in a while.

"Let's go check in with Scatha and the injured first before we confront him," Volt said, looking off into the battlefield.

"Fine. Let's do that." Gaia looked away from Volt, almost pouting. She stuck behind Volt as he made his way through the fighting off towards Scatha and the medical area. Blaze and Void simply nodded and followed, trying to conserve their energy for the real fights to come.

Chapter 19:
The Queen's Power

Before Volt and Void were able to join Blaze and Gaia in their triumphant effort against Adrian, the two had their own battles they had to overcome first. While Blaze and Gaia were still in the dome alone, and the generals of each side fought, the momentum on the battlefield had significantly shifted. Shadows had begun to fall more quickly without as much direct leadership. The Silverwings still fought, cornering groups of pirates and prison demons to their death. There still stood a circle of fighting enclosing Sky and Strike as they battled to the end. After losing Braugg, Scourge's forces in the middle of the battlefield began to lose ground, giving Sky and Strike a more open area to fight in without interruption. The Hiyama warriors stood guard around the region to make sure shadows didn't approach.

Over to the other side, Scatha was busy with healing up those brought to her injured. Hail and Jax were on the top priority, but so many warriors were injured. It became a draining task. After a while, she brought out her forbidden mana to gather the mana needed. Aqua knights stood guard along with Will to protect the medical area. Will brought in nurses to help care for the injured upon seeing how the bodies piled up. Some of the wounded elected to transfer their mana to Jax or Hail to help them stay alive, selflessly. This process would continue through the fighting, without a shortage of injured. Will, while stuck here, took up the role to lead the army. The medic bay for the knights sat on top of

454

a small hill. From this position, he could see a lot of the movements of both sides and led them to better outsmart the Shadows and Silverwings.

"Doesn't look like you're doing too hot over there, Strike." Sky said, skidding back after the two of them clashed their weapons. Strike had pulled out the third set of blades he had on his body, along with fighting with his injured leg from his battle with Hail. These blades were shorter and quicker than his previous sets. As time went on without him taking damage, Strike slowly began to heal all over his body.

"Oh no, I'm fine, just being patient," Strike said with a small smile on his face. As he said this, a cut on his forehead mended back together in eyeshot of Sky.

"Hm. That's interesting, you sneaky shit." Sky frowned and flapped his wings, soaring towards Strike now. He caught Strike's guard with his scythe just under the hilt of the blade and lifted him up high into the air.

"Damnit," Strike, in free fall now, tried to use his mana to disappear into a shadow.

"Xi Qi!" Sky created a wind tunnel around Strike, canceling out his mana and trapping him in there, oxygen slowly leaving but not returning inside of his personal prison. Sky quickly closed in at high speeds up into the air, and shoulder thrusted Strike higher and higher into the air every time he catches up. After reaching a sufficient height, Sky wrapped his arms around Strike's hips, closed his wings, and arched them both back down towards the ground. They then began the dangerous descent, Strike still unable to breathe in the tunnel. As they dropped backward, Sky started to spin their bodies soon resembling the bottom of a tornado touching down to land. "Fēng Fěnsuì!" The ground approached faster and faster as they twirled through the air at high speeds.

"Tsk. Yeah, right." Strike partially broke Sky's grip and stabbed forward with his short blade, cutting through the tunnel and dispelling it. He then jabbed the hilt of his sword into Sky's right side repeatedly, who was having trouble holding on as they tumbled down. With one final labored jab, Strike created separation from Sky, causing them to drift apart and wobble in place. Before they got too far apart, Strike swung and slashed away at Sky's right side, drawing blood and pushing him higher into the air behind Sky.

"Gahhh, shit." Fifteen meters from the ground now, Sky faces the ground holding his bloody ribs with his left hand. Wind mana quickly radiates around his entire body before lifting off and spiraling around him. His body becomes translucent and fluttered in and out of view in the wind. "Windbreaker mode," he says while rearing his right fist back. Seven meters from the ground now, unbeknownst to Sky, Strike is stalking him in the air above him as they fall. All of Sky's attention was on the ground. At this speed and position, opening his wings would have only caused them to get lifted up, nearly tearing them off. His fist now held the focus of his mana, slowly glowing more brightly green as the seconds passed. Three meters now. "Windbreaker fist!" Under a meter off the ground, Sky punched his mana straight down with so much force that it stopped his momenta instantly. This punch suspended Sky in the air for a moment. After a second long pause, a sizable crater was formed in the ground beneath him around his fist's position on the ground. Sky let out a sigh as he avoided crashing into the ground.

"Gotcha," Strike said as he landed on Sky's back, his blade leading the way targeting that same spot-on Sky's side. His short blade pierced Sky's back, nearly missing his kidney, but the impact smashed his body onto the small patch level ground in the center of the crater. Both of them went sliding down into the hole. Sky's blood painting the walls of the cavity along the way. Once at the bottom, Strike created a bit of distance and waved the blood off of his blade. "You underestimate me, Sky," he said, smirking.

Sky, being temporarily knocked out of windbreaker mode, regained composure and surrounded himself in the wind mana again. He still held his side, though, as the bleeding was much worse now. With his left hand, he swung down and summoned his scythe. "How did you go through both of my wind skills?" Sky said, spitting off to the side.

"My blades and my mana don't only go through physical defenses. It goes through any type of mana one uses to defend themselves. That means your wind, Hail's ice, Void's portals, Gaia's earth, everything. All of you are on my list, and I will take you out one by one until none remain in Scourge's way." Strike snickered while licking the backside of his blade.

Sky's scythe began to glow now. "Oh, you know what, that reminds me." The mana around his scythe raged in a small storm now. "I need to pay you back for your little display against Gaia while we were in prison, don't I?" Sky said.

Strike danced back and forth in place. "If you think you can, come on then! I'd like to see your faulty attempt at redemption. Someone else will be looking for revenge against your dead ass when I finish with you!" Strike charged cockily at Sky with both blades in hand.

"Cut down the holy to protect the precious, cleave and devastate! God slayer mode!" Sky's scythe grew in size and glowed bright gold, emanating unique spirit mana. He swiped the ground before him with his scythe causing an explosion of mana that sent the approaching Strike up into the air and back onto the ground level above the crater. He flapped his wings once and lept out himself as he watched Strike tumble back onto his feet. "Oh, I'll get revenge, worry not." Sky flew at Strike, scythe ready to decapitate.

Strike regained his footing and clanked his two blades together. Afterward, thick dark mana coats them and extended the length of the swords three times over. The mana ran across the edge of the blade like a saw's teeth. "Umbra tăiată." He chanted, holding the blades directly in front of his face, staring deep into Sky's eyes.

Sky stares back, still flying full force, but as he reared back, his scythe for the clash, something deep within him stopped him from swinging. He didn't know why, but his body wouldn't let him turn. A deep fear within him had held him back. Close to Strike now, Sky only managed to rear up the hilts slightly as he tried to curve out of the path of Strike. It was too late, though. Strike lowered his blades, phasing through Sky's scythe without touching it and going right for his head. Sky had shifted enough that the edges missed his head, but sliced away at his right-wing badly, causing him to tumble away and crash into the ground. Sky pops up, confused, holding his bloody wing now. He was tried but was unable to raise it up from its fragile state. The cut on his wing left residual dark mana, cursing and damaging it further. "What the hell was that?" he said to himself, realizing if he had gone full force to swing at Strike that he would have a blade in between his forehead now.

"Hehe. It looks like something stopped you from making the last mistake of your life. Lucky," Strike said, shaking his head.

Sky attempted to fly with one wing, but after a few failed attempts, he gave up and committed to his being a ground battle now. "It's not over yet, Strike!" He dashed at Strike using his one wing to increase his speed at least. His scythe was raised fully now as he charged.

Strike stood still as Sky approached, his blades at the ready. Sky swung his scythe as Strike swung one of his swords. There was no clash; however, Strikes blade phased through the cutter as he dodges the swing at his head and retaliates with his second blade aimed at Sky's leg. Sky stayed true and came back to jab Strike in the chest with the back end of his scythe. Strike's blade gashed into the side of Sky's left calf. The curse slowly flowed into his leg from the injury. Strike ate the blow without a flinch. "Is that all Sky? Ha," Strike said with a big smile on his face.

"Shit." Sky noticed the curse while flinching slightly. He then pulled his left leg away and lept up with his right leg-spinning his body in place and swinging his scythe at Strike. The massive blade on his God slayer scythe catches Strike's right arm and back, propelling him forward.

Strike caught himself with his left hand and rested himself as he soaked in pain. "Ahhh, not bad," He said as he felt mana seeping out of his open wound into the air. He sheathed one of his blades and held just the one in his left hand. His right was left swinging lifelessly.

Sky breathed heavily as the curse on his leg, and his wing slowly spreads. His left leg became more and stiffer as the seconds passed, and he could barely stand or put any weight on it. "I have to end this quickly, or this will get bad quickly." He scoffed.

"My thoughts exactly!" Strike said as they both went at each other again. Sky leaped forward with his right leg swiping his scythe twice. He actually clashed with Strikes blades both times, causing him to think, but then Strike went in for a third swing of his own. Sky lifted the side of his scythe to defend out of habit.

"Woah!" Sky remembered at the last second, ducking his head back as Strikes blade phased through his scythe and released a small dark streak of mana as he nearly missed Sky's head. Sky jumped up and using his right leg pushed off of Strike, sending him back and causing separation. Sky lands on his back and immediately kipped up to his feet, landing on his right leg. The impact caused him to wince a bit from the damage to his side, but he persevered and swung at Strike, who was still caught off guard. Strike was able to get his sword up just in time to stop the scythe from piercing into his neck.

"Heh. Sheesh, that was close, huh?" Strike said, still smiling, but struggling to hold back the scythe with just arm. His arm wobbled in place from the force.

Sky gritted his teeth through the pain in his body and continued to force his scythe down. "Agh! Now you'll feel MY rage, my scythe won't be denied by that pathetic…shit!" Sky yelled as he broke through Strike's guard and the top of his scythe sliced diagonally across Strike's chest. Strike pushing the weapon up at the last moment to prevent himself from getting gashed deeper. Sky's massive Godslayer scythe rammed into the ground from all the excess force Sky put into it, pulling his body in closer. Strike, whose blade was pushed down in the struggle, flipped his blade around, holding it backward now. He reduced the extra length granted by his mana and stabbed his sword into Sky's right shoulder, hitting his wing on the other side as his blade went through and through.

"Ugh. Get out of my face!" Strike said, pulling his blade out and smashing the hilt against Sky's face. Sky was jolted back and to the ground, his scythe falling to the ground. His windbreaker mode entirely dissipated, revealing the bloody hole in his shoulder. As he sat upon his knees, just breathing. Through the blood, the curse started to spread and stiffen through his right arm, chest, and his wing now. The gash on Strike's chest began to leak mana as well, the pain making movement very difficult for him at this time. His frustration and rage made it possible for him to keep going.

Sky sat there for a moment trying to will his way to his feet again. The curse was raging through his leg and his chest, and blood was still trickling down his side as well, his body was in a bad way. Sky summoned his scythe to his left hand and used its long handle to force his way up to his right leg. "Gaaaaaaahh!" Sky screamed to himself. "I'll end this now!" Sky said, holding his Godslayer scythe above his head. The shine glowing brighter than ever before as mana slowly began to drift towards the scythe from everywhere around Sky. The air, the ground, fallen warriors, and even from Strike's open wounds were unsafe from getting mana absorbed.

"What is this!?" Strike said as he peered down at the mana, leaving his body forcibly. "This can't go on," he grumbled to himself. He hasn't been able to heal from any of the attacks from Sky's scythe yet. Probably because of the mana not being able to get there and leaving his body instead. He didn't know what this scythe was, but it was proving to be very dangerous for him. Mana that had gathered around Sky's cutter now spiraled around Sky's body as well, creating a barrier of mana storming around him while he balanced himself with all his weight on his one leg.

"Hear my calls as I display my blessings. O' Ardin, grant me the power to slay your demons and your angels. Xi...Nen-" Sky is cut off by a streak of blood slicing diagonally across his back. The blood sprayed out violently as the curse began spreading immediately. Sky looked around in front of him but had lost sight of Strike while he was chanting. "No way. So...close." Sky got out as his consciousness began to fade.

A mysterious shadow bobbled around behind Sky, and up came Strike fully revealing himself after the shadows faded. He twirled his blade around in his hand and slashed Sky again in the opposing direction on his back, creating an 'X' shaped cut. It also caused even more blood to spray out. Sky collapsed to his knees and lowered his head as he passed out. His scythe reverted to normal, releasing all the gathered mana softly into the air like dandelions. Strike

461

stood behind Sky with his blade rose high above the back of Sky's head. He was breathing heavily, even sweating while he stood there. Using his shadow ability had clearly taken a lot out of his body with his injuries. "Almost ...but not close enough, clearly. I…win." He struggled to get out as he lowered his blade towards the back of Sky's neck.

"Sky!" A voice echoed as Sigrun soared in out of nowhere and landed at Strike's feet. Rushing in like a ball of lightning, Volt teleported to Sigrun catching Strike's wrist as his blade was inches away from Sky. The two struggled there for a moment; Strike not willing to give up his kill. Volt's other hand was on the back of his spear. He stared into Strikes, frustrated eyes. "Sorry to disappoint, but not gonna happen," Volt said with rage in his own eyes. He conducted lightning through his spear and shocked Strike through his wrist. Strike was forced to drop his blade and leap back. "I'll be your opponent now. Got it?" Volt said, lifting Sigrun out of the dirt and twirling it into his battle stance.

"Goddammit. You people keep coming out of nowhere. Fine. I'll kill you both then." Strike pulled his other short blade back from the sheath and gave it his aura boost just like the other one. As soon as this happens, though, one of the Hiyama warriors slid into the battlefield and picked up Sky's body, dragging him away out of the fight. Strike's mouth was stuck wide open as he watched his prey getaway. "You're gonna pay for that, you know that?" Strike said, twisting his face with anger. The wounds on his body now finally began to heal, starting with his arm and then his chest, slowly.

"You will not be defeating me, sorry to disappoint," Volt smirked cockily. He then lifted his spear up above his head and chucked it at Strike's head.

"Nope!" Strike swiped the spear down with his sword in his left hand.

Sigrun rammed into the dirt at his feet. Volt teleported to Sigrun, appearing up in the air with a kick aimed at Strike's head. Strike raised his blade to block the kick, stopping Volt's momentum as he was suspended in midair, his hands on his spear to hold him up. Volt then let out a few extra kicks that also get blocked before pushing off of Strike's sword with his foot. Volt pushed himself back, straightening out the spear in the ground and suspending Volt's body straight up as well. Mana gathered around Volt's right heel as he held himself up. "Spiral tap!" Volt lowers his electric heel with a stiff ax kick towards Strike.

"Aghhh!" Strike yelpped as he blocked the kick, but electricity flowed throughout his body directly to his spine, stunning him and forcing him to drop his sword. Strike's arms tensed up and retracted near his chest. His legs wobbled in place as he was stuck getting electrocuted.

"Too easy." Volt leaped down to the ground, grabbing Sigrun in the same motion. He's back now to Strike, Volt spun the point of his spear to the right towards his opposition. "Tao uira huaki!" he yelled as lightning spun around the tip of Sigrun like a drill, and he let out a barrage of thrusts towards Strike. The first three land on his shoulder, his chest, and his stomach before he was drug down into his shadow and pulled away out of Volt's range. The rest of Volt's thrusts miss, and he waved Sigrun off to the side, returning it to normal.

Strike popped out of the shadow off to the side, laying his back on a facedown, dead Silverwing. He put his head back and groaned; blood started seeping down his torso and right arm. Diamond-shaped stab wounds were revealed. "Aghhh. Just as I was starting to heal," he said, putting pressure on his chest with his left arm. "Think my bodies at its limit after all these fights. I don't have the stamina to draw this out." The shadows on the ground around Strike began to bubble and gather around him. Even shadows of other fighters in the area started to break from their shackles and gather around him.

"You aren't done yet are ya? Volt said gathering mana. Lightning sparked and sputtered around him as it began striking outwards randomly. He then clapped his hands together and bent his knees, getting into a low side stance. "Erupt and eradicate, shatter their hopes for they failed to embrace the goddess…and I will punish them!" Volt aimed his body at Strike as he lied there, his left foot lined up perfectly with Strike's body. "Inazuma!" he said as he thrusted his two hands forward, releasing a gigantic wave of electric mana towards Strike.

"Mmm already? Okay," Strike said to himself. The puddle of shadows under him now activates on its own, and parts of the blob rose out of the ground, attaching itself to different parts of his body and slowly dragging him into the field. His entire body was then drug into the ground right after the lightning wave passes over his position. The puddle of shadows then soaked into the ground and disappeared, zooming off somewhere.

Volt's hands still glowed with mana as he surveyed the area looking for Strike. "Hmm. Come on out now." He whispered while he looked around. Just then, a shadow rose out of the ground like an empty black cloak. "*Boom!*" Volt released another wave of mana from his hands towards the shadow, but it merely phased through it, soaring past their battle area and taking out Silverwings. "Damnit," he said as the shadow went back down into the ground. It swirled around and came out at another area to Volt's left. "Boom!" Volt sent out another towards this new shadow, but this one got filled out with the shape of Strike. Strike raised up his darkness covered hands as the blast approached. Suddenly a large release of shadow mana directly at the lightning mana. Upon contact, the shadows began to swallow and engulf the

464

explosion as the shadows moved down the wave on the way back to Volt.

"What the hell?" Volt stopped firing and leapt back just as the shadows reached his side of the blast. The shadows all retracted after it shrunk, effectively swallowing Volt's mana then rejoining Strike's body. The mass of shadows surrounding Strike nearly doubled in size after it got back to him. His actual shadow on the ground grew to twice its size. Strike's face was the only part of him revealed as the rest of him was engulfed in these very lively shadows. His face was blank as if he was possessed, and he didn't utter a single word the entire time.

"No words, huh?" Volt said, looking at Strike curiously and breathing a bit heavy from the adrenaline of almost getting swallowed up. "Something tells me I shouldn't let that touch me." He thought out loud.

Strike raised his right hand, releasing a mob of shadows that rush after Volt like they're hungry. "Oh, no." Volt dashed and flipped back as shadows fly after him in the air and the ground. Strike's darkness on the earth crept out, attempting to contact his legs, reaching out and grabbing at him multiple times. Volt, nearly getting caught, leaps into the air to avoid, but the mass of shadows coming from Strike's hand was still there to feast. Volt lifts his spear in front of him and twirls it in place to create a makeshift shield, lightning spiraling around his spear as it spun. The shadows simply pushed into his spear's defense, pushing him towards the ground where a puddle of shadows was waiting for him to land. "Humph, think again." As he fell towards the ground, he flicked his spear downwards first. Sigrun landed straight up, and Volt grabbed ahold and stood on top of the spear, crouched low like a monkey. "Whew, now what are you gonna do?" Volt stared down the blob of shadows in front of him, stalking him and swaying back and forth to match his movements.

Volt lowered his right hand as he crouched there. "Pouri Uira," he said as black lightning started to spark and sputter around his hand as mana gathered there. "Let's see how you like a little dischar— huh?" Volt was cut off as a shadow on the ground lifted out of the land and opened up like a mouth, closing around his hand. The mana in his hand is immediately eaten away and he struggled to stay upright as the shadows tried to pull him towards the ground and certain doom. "Ugh. What. Is this?" Volt said attempting to pull his hand up as the shadows crept up his arm. With his left hand in the air, he charged more lightning mana aimed down at his other side, but suddenly this too was dispelled. The shadows that were stalking him had made its move and ate away at the mana in his left hand raised up. He now had shadows eating away at both sides, still trying to balance himself on Sigrun.

"Goodness, so hungry ugh. I can feel the mana draining from my body," Volt said as he pulled the shadows closer by crossing his arms. Volt's eyes lit up as his ancestors' words speak to his soul. "Eat this!" Volt gathered mana all over his body at the same time and kept it just under the surface of his skin. "Porohita, marama!" Suddenly Volt released a wave of electricity around him in all directions, creating an electric bubble that surrounded him and killed off all the shadows in the vicinity. "Hmmm, nice that one's new." The balloon doesn't last long, but Volt used the opportunity to throw Sigrun directly at Strike. As the shadows crept back in, Volt transitions into electricity and follow after his spear.

Strike simply stared at the spear as it approached, raising his left hand up and releasing shadows formed in a donut shape along the path of Sigrun. As soon as Sigrun entered that path, Strike closed the donut, effectively stopping the spear short. Volt teleported to that spot, with his hand along with the handle of Sigrun, but his body met with eight blobs of shadows coming out of the side of Strike's body. While he was stuck le in midair, these blobs began pummeling away at Volt's body like a punching bag. Volt put up his arm there to defend, but he was beaten up viciously for a while there, like a predator wearing out its prey. "Porohita, marama!" Volt said, regained composure enough to release another wave around him, thus freeing his spear and halting the onslaught on his body. Volt lands on the ground, ignoring the pain in his swollen body and rushes forward with Sigrun in hand.

"Agghhh!" Volt started stabbing at Strike's body rapidly with his spear, but Strike's body opened up upon contact, creating holes to make the spear miss. The shadows clearly had taken over his entire body, temporarily stripping him of his human form. None of Volt's attacks were connecting, and it slowly frustrated him. "Hmph. Try this then!" Volt said, pulling his spear back and enhancing it with his lightning mana. The new tip resembling lightning drills. "Tao uira hunki!" Volt started his new enhanced barrage this time, going quicker than before. Still, however, Strike's shadows were able to avoid all of the damage, no matter where he aimed. Strike opened his chest extra-wide after one of Volt's thrusts, baiting him to stab there next. In his rush, Volt took the bait and aimed for the open area, but Strike's body closed around Sigrun, trapping it inside of him.

Shadows twirled up the spear next, quickly grabbing at Volt's hand and arm. "Wait, wait, wait. No." Volt pleaded as he got sucked into the vortex of shadows before him. Sigrun is dropped off behind Strike, but Volt was being sucked inside. The shadows even reached out and grasp at Volt's legs as well, pulling him from both sides. "Nooooooo!" Volt struggled as his mana is drained harsher and harder with each passing moment. He couldn't even use his electric wave anymore, so he only pulled away feebly, trying to avoid the inevitable. "Not…like this," Volt let out as the rest of his body is swallowed by Strike and his shadows. His eyes began to glow with a dark purple hue just before he disappeared. After Volt was fully inside, the shadows grew in size considerably, seeming supercharged with mana and even dancing around in place. Strike's cold face even let out a small hint of a smile after his victory. His shadows all returned to him, creating a large mass of darkness underneath of him.

Suddenly though, Strike's stomach of shadows began to rumble and boil like the surface of molten lava. Long and meticulous bubbled popped in the momentary pause of action. Strike, still not speaking a word, patted his stomach in a silent but nervous laughter. Seconds later, a point spiked out of his stomach, flickering with electricity. It then reverted back to normal, visibly freaking out Strike, who held the spot that spiked out with both hands. Strike then began convulsing in a place like he was trying to resist the urge to hurl. A few moments later and a flurry of points began spiking out of him from points on his body not covered by his hands. Strike tried to adjust his hands to the incoming positions but wasn't nearly fast enough.

The surface of his body had calmed again soon after, granting him a reprieve from the added stress. Strike still held his stomach, rubbing and patting it like a pet. He couldn't hold back the surge of mana that was sent out in a shockwave originating from his center, however. This mana shook his core and attached it to his mana in the form of black lightning. Afterward, another explosion of mana opened up the side of Strike's stomach from the inside like a grenade. A giant ball of dark lightning then floated out of Strike's center and hovered over a meter or so away from him. Strike's upper half flung up into the air, being supported just by a sliver of shadows that held his torso together, his arms flailing wildly in the air.

It didn't take Strike's plastic body long to sling down and reattach entirely though, the shadows making up for most of his mass at the moment. He reassembled and stared at the ball of mana, disgruntled. A handful of spiraling shadow mana in each hand, waiting for the conclusion of what awaited him.

The body-sized orb of dark lightning mana spun in place for an extra few moments without pause. "Uira Te Rewera." A mysterious voice called out from inside. After a fight seemingly broke out inside the orb, a figure finally emerged and landed on the ground before Strike. It wasn't Volt, though. At least it didn't look like him. The character that came out was tall and slender and was entirely covered in that black lightning. As spikes formed on its back and head, it hunched over with large claws made of mana, and a spiked tail trailing along behind it, he slowly began to resemble a demon. The transformation was complete, and the ferocious creature stood there. In front of Strike, parts of the coarse and cold demon skin breaking away from the black lightning coat he wore. The demons bright red eyes beamed out at Strike, who met eyes instantly. Spikey wings then burst out of the demon's back, black veins pulsed along the inside of the wings as the lightning caught up and cloaked them as well.

Strike looked at the demon with disdain, the shadow mana in his hand grew as did his anger. He stared at the beast very intently, not taking a moment to even blink. Just then, the demon disappeared, no trace left behind. Strike looked around frantically before he began shooting out flurries of dark orbs in all directions from his hands. The spheres swallowed the earth where they landed, creating head-sized craters in the ground and any unsuspecting warriors or Silverwings who happened to be around. The fights around them were interrupted as both sides fled the area for fear they were next. None landed on their intended

469

target, however, as the demon was nowhere to be found through this barrage of attacks. Strike continued firing indiscriminately though in a fit of frustration and determination. Stopping him in his tracks was a single, large bolt of black lightning striking from above and simultaneously discharging Strike's mana. The orbs he controlled were all instantly destroyed as he was hit with the incredible jolt of mana.

His body was jolted and tensed up immediately after getting struck as the black lightning coursed through Strike's body, canceling out any mana he even attempted to produce. The black lightning even affected Strike's shadows, which melted away into the ground as he lost control. The shadows also released themselves away from Strike's head and mind, returning him to normal again. "What…the…hell?" he said, regaining consciousness under the bolt of lightning still. Now feeling all of the pain in his body all at once, Strike noticed he was again speechless. Upon trying to scream, nothing was heard. Before he could try and utter another word, the demon appeared before him in an instant flash of lightning. Its hand reared back with black lightning racing back and forth across his palm.

"Pouri zumaaaa!" Hand pressed forward, the demon sends forth a thick, concentrated beam of dark lightning mana towards Strike with incredible speed.

"Fuc—" Strike was struck through his core with a beam that blasted through the majority of his chest and stomach. The attack even managed to lift him into the air with the sheer amount of force is produced. As the beam continued it shoved strike into the air, sending him flying across the battlefield with a hole in his torso. Moments later, a small pool of shadows followed Strike's path in the air like a lost child racing after him. A massive crash was heard in the distance, around the graveyard.

By this time, the demon's enhanced form had faded away into the air, revealing Volt on his butt looking straight up and gasped. His garb was torn and tattered, but otherwise, his body had been restored to perfect condition. Sigrun spawned next to him just as soon as his mind returned to him. "Woah. What that I wonder. Feels like I was in a dream." Volt said as he grabbed his spear and rose to his feet, looking around. Just then, a large crack opened up in the large dome off to his right, and he watched as thick darkness seeped out of the opening. "Hmm. I think Volt and Gaia went over in that direction. Probably a good idea to give them a hand, that looks dangerous…" he said, rushing over towards the dome of darkness, cutting his way through shadows along the way.

****

Over in front of the castle, a wild battle was being raged. Hepheaus and Scourge had been clashing back and forth, coming to constant stalemates. Ocean and Void had been incapacitated off to the side by Scourge's dark aura to prevent them from interfering. His dense, gravity-like aura forced them chest down into the ground. They continually struggled against this force so that they could help. They knew of Hepheaus' weaknesses, but it seemed as if Scourge was still in the dark. No significant blows had been landed on either side, yet as the defensive abilities of both were on full display. After another clash that sent Scourge and Hepheaus both skidding back to their sides, Hepheaus looks down at her son, cracking a smile.

"Don't worry, Osh, I'll show you the potential you hold in that blood running through your veins. I won't let this ugly mercenary's plans come to fruition. Just sit there and watch. I won't let you down," Hepheaus said as she stabs her katanas both into the ground. A puddle of mana slowly grew on the ground around her feet. It began to

471

sparkle and glow under her. This made Hepheaus look magical as the wind blew up through her hair, the mana below her created a glitter of water droplets in the air around her.

Scourge scoffed as he pointed Devora at Hepheaus, dark mana was coating the blade, nipping at the bits for a victim. "Ocean, I hope you are prepared to be disappointed and horrified because I am going to kill your mother in front of you, and you'll have to watch as my blade here eats her remains and absorbs all of that glorious mana she holds," Scourge says laughing a little as he finishes. The mana had now taken over his body as well, as this sinister aura escaped into the air. The earth and dying grass were finished off by the presence of his mana.

"Yeah, right! I'll get out of this and come beat you down myself!" Ocean said, struggling to get up, fruitlessly.

"You must keep your emotions in check Ocean, especially if you want to control your mana to its ultimate potential," Hepheaus said calmly, lowering her head to the ground and closing her eyes. The mana in the water attached to the special lining in her armor, lighting up as it travels throughout her body. Every symbol and every coating of silver and mercury was lit. This mana seeped into the linings on her katana's, traveling up along the blade and wrapping around the hilt. Finally, the mana reached the coatings on her helm, completing the cycle, and it flowed throughout her armor steadily like a river. The mana in the air and aura around her sparkled gently as if hesitant to stray away from its new master.

"Hmm. What is this form?" Scourge looks curiously as he watches the mana orbit around Hepheaus softly. "The mana is following her...on its own, without her having to force it at all," he said.

"Lucinthis. Verafelt. Nefula. Sylindra. Ardin. You, the five deities that govern our existence, I pray to thee now

472

for your blessings. Grant me the aptitude to transcend all and call upon your mana at my will. I offer thine body and my soul in penance for my sins of this life so we can rendezvous in the next." Hepheaus opened her arms wide as the mana glowed brighter and brighter with each passing moment. "Let us merge, our wills converge, unto darkness, we will purge. Zivotno Majstorstvo!" She finished as the mana surrounding her spread like wildfire in the air in all directions creating a sweep of blinding light that absorbed mana of all types from everything it touched before pulling back in around Hepheaus. Her entire body was glowing, mana radiating in and all around her. He lifted up her two blades from the ground, and they too began to glow. "Ah, it's been a while since I've felt this power. Scourge, I hope you've prepared yourself!" she said, looking in his direction. Just from this, it felt like a hundred thousand eyes were all staring in Scourge's direction at once. An absolute pressure was forced in his direction.

"Such power," Scourge said, covering his face from the bright lights with his hand.

"Ocean. This is mana mastery mode, an ability passed down throughout our family as we were blessed to be more favored by mana than others. Watch closely," Hepheaus said, disappearing into the air leaving glitters of mana in the air in her wake. Ocean simply nodded and watched. Moments later, a puddle of water spawned underneath of Scourge, just large enough for a person to lay horizontally across. Scourge lifted his foot slightly to adjust with the new lubrication underneath of him.

"What is this?" Scourge said as four Hepheaus's rise out of the ground, surrounding him. In one swift strike, he swung Devora around, slashing all of them in half. After the slash, all four of the Hepheaus's reverted to water and splashed onto the ground, creating a larger puddle around Scourge. The water rumbled a bit in this moment of pause.

"Hmmm." Scourge thought curiously as nine Hepheaus's now surrounded him. They all rose out of the water and held up a single katana in the air with both hands, aimed at Scourge. "Just in case." Scourge raises his blade above his head and lowers his stance to block incoming attacks. Clank. All nine blades collide with him simultaneously, creating a loud noise and forcing Scourge lower and lower under pressure. "Tsk. What marvelous clones. Substance and strength…but…" Scourge quickly gathered his dark mana along the outer edges of his body like a shell. He then released all of mana at the same time, shooting out in the form of a dark force field that exploded all of the water clones as it expanded. The puddle nearly doubled in size now, even reaching Void and Ocean. Scourge looks down now to see the area of the pool directly under him glowing for a bit before returning to normal.

"Wait. Is this mana drain as well?" Scourge lept into the air slightly to get out of the water, but as soon as he cleared it, twenty-two Hepheaus clones shot out of the water after him. The first three leaps up and slammed Scourge back first into the water with vertical strikes in tandem. Scourge's back bounced off of the puddle as he looked up to a horde of Hepheaus clones diving towards him. He raised his blade to block the initial strikes to get upright again. Scourge then battled to fight off the clones twenty-two to one. His fight spanned the entire circle of water as he used his dark mana and his sword to slash away at his attackers. Every time he took one out, another was ready to take its place and attack.

"Wow, she actually has him on the defensive," Ocean said to himself, slowly feeling the pressure of Scourge's mana lifting, ever so slightly.

"Very impressive, indeed." Void nods, able to lift one arm up in front of him.

Scourge stood in the center of the puddle after finally destroying all of the clones, sucking wind a bit as he breathed heavily. He had a few knicks, and a small crack appeared on the top right of his mask, but otherwise, he was untouched. "Sheesh. Where did you get all this mana? Summoning all of these clones to have to be rather draining." Scourge said, swiping his sword to the side; the puddle shined again and grew. Ocean and Void were now thoroughly wet. The small waves on the top of the pool drifted them back further, out of the way of the fight. With Scourge somehow ending up in the center of the puddle, he is suddenly surrounded by forty-seven Hepheaus clones. Scourge let out a massive sigh. "We are not. Absolutely *not* doing this again." Scourge said sheathing Devora and holding his left hand down. Dark mana began to spiral and gathered around his arm.

Before the clones could react, Scourge slammed his foot onto the ground and lept up high into the air, splashing water everywhere in his wake. The mana in his arm gathered into a large ball offset slightly from his palm. The clones didn't chase after him, but instead, all rose their blades into the air, aimed directly at Scourge. Water mana oozed out of the tips as they glowed bright blue and white.

"Dark impact!" Scourge said as he sent his mana crashing towards the surface. Out of the swords of all forty-seven clones came an aqua spirit in the form of a water dragon, all determined to charge directly at Scourge. Like a ray of light, the water dragons all dodged around the darkness of Scourge's attack and somehow found their target all at the same time. Having just released his attack, Scourge was unable to properly defend himself as the barrage of spirits all exploded on impact, creating a massive mana explosion in the air above the puddle. Scourge's attack also collided with the ground, creating a powerful shockwave that separated the pool and destroyed all of the clones all at the same time. The impact created a giant cloud of smoke and mist that blinded all in the area for a moment. Water that was thrown into the air rained down on top of the fog.

When the smoke finally cleared, the puddle was gone, Scourge was on his back, and the real Hepheaus was in front of Ocean and Void's bodies, protecting them from the impact. "Hmph. How was that, Scourge!?" Hepheaus said, holding her blades tight, scars in the ground off to either side of her. She had sliced the wave of mana in half to protect the two of them.

Scourge rolled back and got onto his knee. He had burn marks all over his chest and arms. On his armor anyway. He was still breathing heavily as he rested on his knee. "Ah. I see now that little transformation allows you to use less mana with your attacks, doesn't it?" Scourge questioned.

"Mhmm. Hope you're ready for even more ass-kickings to come." Hepheaus said, inching forward now.

Scourge chuckled at this and got back onto his feet. "Think I've already figured how to beat you, actually." He smiled, looking at Hepheaus, then to Ocean, then back again. Ocean and Void rise up to their feet, the dark aura losing its strength over them.

"Ahh, finally," Ocean said, pulling out his rapier and pointing it at Scourge. Void also summoned his claymore to his hand and held it out before him.

Scourge chuckled there as he got back up to a vertical base and held his hand out, mana gathering in his palm. "I'll sit you two back down now," he said as he let out a small orb of mana that shot forward towards Ocean. A portal appeared in front of the mana, though, sucking it away into its space. Soon after, another portal opened behind him and out came his ball of mana. Scourge, with his expert instincts, dodged it, allowing it to shoot down towards the ground. Another portal opened, however, and the ball disappeared again. Suddenly an array of small portals opened all around Scourge, orbiting him. The ball left one of them but is dodged again and returned to another gateway. This continued repeatedly, faster and faster as Scourge dodged his own attack rapidly. Soon the orb sped to such levels that only a black streak could be seen zigzagging inside the confines of the portal. "Done with your games?" Scourge yelled as he finally caught the orb with his left hand high up behind him. The sphere was sparking and jittering in place, trying to escape from his grasp.

Void had dug Fonos into the ground and had his hands taken up with the portals around Scourge. Ocean watched as Scourge had gathered the mana for another orb in his other hand and collided with the two. He sent this new orb forward, crashing through the portals and burrowing towards Void. Ocean quickly summoned his hybrid weapon and dashed over. "From the future to the past, erase our foes with a blast!" he chanted while running and pointing the edge of his weapon towards the orb approaching. The mana rocket tip shot out and exploded on contact with the orb, which was rather close to them at this point, so the shockwave knocked both of them back.

Hephaestus dashed off to the side and up towards Scourge, using the explosion as cover. Her mana from mana mastery mode was still shining bright, even in the smoke. Clash. Hepheaus is met with Devora on the other side as she tries to go for Scourge's head. Scourge overpowered her in this instance and swung his sword fully, pushing her back. "Tsk." She scoffed at how close she was.

"Always gonna have my eye on you, Hephy." Scourge chuckled heartily as mana spiraled around his blade again. "Die!" He swiped his sword, and a quick and deadly streak of dark mana zoomed out towards Hepheaus. This wave sliced through the body, which turned to water and splashed into a puddle below. "Huh? Another one?" Scourge questioned.

The water shined for a moment then separated into two streams that quickly ran along the grooves of the tile below and got around behind Scourge. This happened suddenly, only taking about a second and a half before the puddle lifted out of the ground, two blades popping out first, the rest of Hepheaus following shortly behind. Scourge quickly spun around to block the attack. Hepheaus, wet, fully appeared to Scourge's rear, clashing against Scourge's blade. As they fight for an extended time now, each trying to get the upper hand, Devora's mana seeped out and infected the edge of Hepheaus's swords. The very tip of the blades were slightly rotted before Hepheaus backed off and created an inch of separation to save her blades. "Got you!" Scourge used his opportunity to lower his sword horizontally under her hands and popped them up. With her hands now at his eye level, he knocked her swords away with one swipe of his blade. He then raised his sword high above him, lined up ideally in between her eyes. "Swallow her, Devora!" Scourge yelled as the mana returned to spiral around his blade, but this time it formed a large extension, making a dark blade that extruded several stories up into the air. Scourge held this massive dark blade there for a moment before he began lowering it her direction. Hepheaus looked up with wide eyes, almost in shock as she stared at the edge of the blade aimed her for her face.

Hepheaus took a slight step back, almost tripping backward. A portal opens up behind her as she slips, catching her and closing up. She pops back up next to Ocean on the other side. Scourge lowers his blade, creating a large 'V' shaped crater in the ground that extended out of the castle grounds and onto the battleground, dividing much of the fighting area in half with the extra mana that streaked out further than the blade actually landed. The earth and grass that touched the mana dried up and died on contact. Any soldiers or Silverwings that happened to fall in or move into the area as well. Their manas were all sucked dry.

"Whew." Hepheaus looked up into the air and sighs. She looks over to her right to thank Void, but somehow, Scourge had already appeared before him, who was still on his knees getting up from the blast before. "Void!" She yelled.

Void looked up to Scourge's blade dragging along the ground towards him. "I. Am. SO." Scourge said, scraping his sword up towards Void. Void could only raise his hands to protect himself. "Tired of youuuuu!" Scourge swung his blade up into the air, taking Void with it and sending him high off into the air, across the battlefield. His trajectory measured up correctly with the giant black dome that was out there. "Ahhh, that feels much better." He sighed.

"Void…" Ocean said, looking back at him flying. Suddenly Ocean's head jerked forward like a gust of wind had brushed past him. Water and blood also splattered onto the back of his head with just as much force. Ocean, hesitantly turned his head around to find Hepheaus standing over him with her arms spread out, her mana fading in and out. Her head was shaking, and her back was struggling against the might of Scourge's blade.

"P-pay attention damnit, Ocean." She stammered out.

"M-Mom?" Ocean turned fully around both hands out in front of him. Two mana whips came shooting out of his hands and pelted against Scourge's chest from around Hepheaus's body, sending him skidding back slightly. Scourge brushed himself off and looked at the edge on Devora. Hepheaus's blood gets absorbed, almost as if it had been drunk up. "Hehehehe." He smirked at the two behind the cover of his mask.

Hepheaus lowered herself to a knee, trying to resist the pain in her back, as the deep gash started bleeding badly. Her mana wavered more and more with each passing moment. "Damn this cursed body of mine." She shook her head at her own predicament.

"I'm so sorr——." Ocean began.

"No time for that. We have to finish…this." Hepheaus said, struggling up to her feet. She put her focus into revitalizing her mana throughout her body and into her two blades, which now shone pure white. The aura surrounding her was brought back to life as well as it raged and flared out around her. "Back me up," ahe said, looking over her shoulder at Scourge. Ocean got up himself and nodded.

Crash! Just as they were to start up again, a body went crashing into the ground at the doorstep of the castle. Scourge, annoyed, looked back to see who it was. "Strike? What are you doing here?" he shouted.

Strike rose out of the imprint he made on the ground holding a gaping wound in his chest, among other injuries all over his body. "I...Gah…" He stopped to cough out blood then catch his breath again. "My mana has been sealed...I need to ...heal...or I'll ...Grrr screw him, he got lucky." Strike spit out again, then got up and used the handle of the front door to pull himself inside. Leaving his blood on the ground and the grip along the way.

"Ughhh," Scourge grumbled while shaking his head, all his focus on his disappointment in Strike.

"Now!" Hepheaus said as Ocean tossed a dozen mist bombs at Scourge. They all disappeared into a giant cloud of heavy mist that blinded Scourge.

"What?" Scourge said, holding up his hand to cover his face.

Hepheaus started spinning in place counter-clockwise with her blades out to her sides. Faster and faster

480

before soon, she looked like a spinning top with white edges. She twisted herself towards Scourge in the mist. Scourge only saw something white approaching him, so he held out his blade in defense, Devora's mana front and center on edge. It didn't take long for Hepheaus to reach Scourge as she came at him full force. Her spinning attack clashed and knocked away Devora off to the side at the same time as the blade that connected shattered. Scourge's body was now wide open with his sword knocked down to his side and his arms open. Hepheaus grabbed her other sword with both hands at the end of her spin and begun a single, vertical turn before coming down with the blade aiming at his chest. "Checkmate!" she yelled as she landed a full-powered slash on Scourge, slicing him from his shoulder to his waist on the opposite side. She landed on the ground, low, as a crescent moon shaped streak of blood exploded out of his chest, and he arched back.

"Gaaaaaahh," Scourge yelped as he dropped Devora and leaped back, right near the impact Strike made on his landing. Scourge stands there, holding his wound, desperately trying to catch his breath.

"How's that?" Hepheaus said, standing in the center of the mist as it cleared up, with Ocean next to her. Her legs began twitching slightly as she was trying to keep herself upright. Her and Scourge stared each other in the eyes relentlessly for a minute, at least. No one moved a muscle, but blood was still coming out of Scourge's chest, and Hepheaus's back.

"Hmph." Scourge lowered his head for a moment. "Not bad, Queen Hepheaus. Not bad at all, hehe," he said, summoning Devora to him.

"Tsk." Hepheaus held back the sweat that was near falling down her head, she gripped her single blade with all her might.

"If your precious knights would like to finish this fight properly, they'll find me in my throne room at the top of my castle. If you can make it there, that is…" Scourge disappeared into one of his dark portals. The front door to his castle slammed shut on its own shortly afterward.

"Whew." Hepheaus sighed as her mana dissipates.

"Wait!" Ocean lunged forward but is stopped by Hepheaus to grab ahold of his arm to hold her up as she nearly collapsed onto the ground.

"No, don't." she said, holding with both hands now. Ocean stopped to help her ease to the ground. "Wait here on the others, you guys need to go finish this together…" she says, breathing through her words.

"I guess you're right…" Ocean said, calming himself.

"We are...lucky...he didn't call my bluff. Hehe, I'm drained just keeping my body moving at this point." Hepheaus chuckled.

Ocean nodded before putting his arm around his mother's shoulders. "Thank you, I learned so much from watching you. We're going to go kill that demon now." He whispered in her ear before getting back up and looking out towards the battlefield, trying to send a signal for others to meet up there.

Chapter 20:
Syuri the Element
Dragon

-Year 277 Faith Hill, Scourge's castle gate

Shadow Path, Umbra-

Ocean, Blaze, Volt, Void, and Gaia all stood in a group at the front gates of Scourge's castle. The battle still raged on behind them, but without leadership, the shadow forces were struggling to keep up. Will stood as the sole commander of the army as he fought alongside them. An extra thick wall of soldiers surrounded Scatha and the other medics to protect their growing number of injured from the waves of Silverwings who approached. She now watched over Sky, Jax, Hail, Hepheaus, and at least two dozen warriors from the various armies and demons. The prison demons all held guard around the medical area as well, making sure their fallen friend was safe. The Knights readied themselves for the next stage of their battle, while the old would have to find it's a conclusion without them. Ocean related to the other knights what happened, and what their next move would be.

"Hm, your mom going to be okay?" Void asked, looking at the medical bay.

"Yeah, it just really drains her a lot to fight. I'm more worried cause you said Sky and Hail were over there too?" Ocean responded, shaking his head solemnly.

"Scatha is very exceptional with her healing, especially with terrible wounds, I think they'll be okay," Volt said, holding his chest. Gaia, from behind Void, just

484

shook her head at Volt, mumbling under her breath. "Actually, she said that Sky would be able to join us soon, his injuries weren't as bad as she thought. Hail will be a while, though, along with Jax. Both of them received terrible, life-threatening injuries." Volt continued.

"We'll get our revenge for that, don't worry." Blaze punched his fist, flaring his mana for a moment. "Scourge needs to get his too." He looked up to the top of the castle.

Void was staring at the closed door before them the entire time they talked. "You sure you don't wanna wait on Sky to get better before going forward?" he said.

"I think we need to go now." Volt summoned Sigrun. "According to Ocean, both Scourge and Strike are in there healing up as we speak! We need to make sure they have as little time as possible to recoup." Volt said, slightly raising his voice.

"I agree! Let's rush in there." Blaze said eagerly while he dashed left and right.

"Well, we have to make a decision now. We still have Wendy to save as well guys, and Keith too if they have him locked up here somewhere." Gaia got louder than Volt to gain the attention of the group.

"Wait, Keith? Why would he be here? Didn't we leave him back on Basonali?" Ocean replied curiously, thinking to himself for a moment.

"Well..." Blaze stopped pacing to look over at Ocean.

"Apparently something happened to him after we left. Scourge got his hands on him and, through his experiments, was able to split Adrian away from Keith. Adrian fought on Scourge's side and-" Gaia starts.

"And he got his body destroyed by us in the process!" Blaze interjected.

485

"Yes, and I think they have Keith, the original host body, locked up here somewhere for insurance." Gaia finally finished.

"We'll look for him while we're in there as well, but for now. Open up!" Volt held his right hand out towards the door letting out a massive blast of electricity that busts the doors wide open. The two tall doors nearly fell off of their hinges from the force. "Shall we?" he said, walking forward.

"Anyone else notices the edge on Volt there? Where'd that come from?" Ocean said, peering his eyes at the other Knights.

"Don't know, but I like it!" Gaia walked forward after Volt.

"Well, come on, Void. We've got work to do." Blaze walked behind Ocean into the castle.

"This better not be a mistake." Void sighed before finally following after the rest.

-Year 277 Scourge's castle, Foyer Shadow Path, Umbra-

Beyond those doors was the massive Foyer of Scourge's castle. To their left was a long curling stairwell that led up to the next level. In front of them was a shining white orb in the center of the room, floating there in place. In the back of the room were a pair of spacious mysterious elevator shafts. The one on the left had an up arrow posted beside it, a down placed on the right one. The area in front of the elevators was also vast and open; decorating on the floor was dreary at best. The lighting was low, with the torches that lined the walls, the primary source of light. Black flames fluttered off of the torches, continually threatening to blow out at any moment. Ripped, black drapes covered the tall windows along the wall behind them. Slight cracks in this wall were illuminated occasionally when the light decided to reach that far. An ominous aura wreaked along this floor, almost as if a pool of darkness was at their feet. This aura moves throughout the castle like a fog, sapping mana where ever it can find it, including the knights. On top of everything else, a loud creak echoed through the foyer every few moments just to add to the creepiness.

"So, this is nice," Gaia said as sarcastically as possible, looking around at the ominous decor.

"Yeah, how are we going to do this? Half of us take the up elevator half of us to take down?" Blaze said, pointing at the pair of elevators on the other side of the room.

"First off, what are thos—" Suddenly, everything had stopped. Volt had taken a step towards the glowing white orbs in the center of the room; time within the castle then stopped. The knights had stopped moving, the fog had stopped flowing, even the flames on the torches had paused.

As they stood there, frozen, the elemental orbs came softly floating out of each knight's chest. They each eased out like they were rising out of water. After every sphere had left its host, they all floated merged with a corresponding shining orb in the center of the room. Out of the open door behind them came a light blue and bright green ball floating to the middle as well. After all of them had gathered in the center, a bright, blinding light was released. When the flash was finished, the knights were seemingly moved into another area. There was nothing but a whiteness all around them in all directions. No sky, no ground, everything was one. The seven orbs were now a single mesh, with a medley of colors running throughout.

"Those? Huh?" Time had resumed, and Volt continued.

"What is this? Weren't we just in the castle? When did we get pulled into this dimension? Think I would remember that." Void questioned.

"Yeah, wait are those our— ouch." Ocean stopped and grabbed his chest as pain ran through everyone.

"Tsk. Yeah, why are our orbs over there? We worked damn hard to get those!" Blaze shouted, holding back his own pain.

The collection of orbs in the center slowly began pulsating now. The mana within them pushed and pulled its own aura like waves of the ocean. The intertwining mana ran across the surface of the orbs faster, and faster with such force, they all began to shake.

"Get us out of here, Void!" Volt yelped.

Void held his hands up to make a portal, but he rested them back at his sides shortly afterward, in disappointment. "I can't. I don't know if it's anything to do with my orb absent from my body or not, but I can't use my Demon's shift." Void said, staring at his hands.

"Hmm. You're right, my energy field won't come out either. Looks like we're stuck here to deal with this, whatever it is." Volt said, summoning Sigrun to his hands.

"Right, we got this, though. I have full faith." Blaze released his chariot, unlocking it's powered and creating a small cloud of smoke.

The orbs in the center of the area created another blinding flash of white light, causing all of the knights to look away. What awaited the knights as they regained their senses, seemingly immediately lowered spirits. At their eye level, all they saw were the massive, thick, tree trunk-like legs with scales but made out of lightning mana, with the rest of the dark mass beneath it. "Roaaarrr!" The beast let out a booming roar of hot air that shook the very souls of the knights before it.

Blaze and the rest of the knights stood there, avoiding visual contact with the towering beast in front of them. "Whew. So. Guys?" Blaze said, his eyes glued to the ground.

"Uh, yeah?" Ocean responded.

"So if I raise my head right now, we definitely won't have what I think is in front of me. Right? Right?" Blaze uncharacteristically stammered.

"Even if that were the case. You took out something similar to get your orb, right?" Ocean said, staring at his boots.

"I'll tell you right now, this thing in front of us is at least twice the size of that Deogrith that I defeated." Blaze retorted careful not to look ahead of him.

"Yeah. Well, you've got to be at least twice as powerful now, right? Heads up now knights, we can't afford to fall here. We're fighting our fate right now!" Volt said, raising his own head to get a glance at his fate. One by one, the knights all looked ahead of them to shiver at the monstrous being before them.

What stood there, truthfully twice as tall as the Deogrith, was a gigantic dragon, sporting the combined elements of all of the knights. It's thick, electric clad legs resembled those of the Thadrado. The torso was a mix of hardened ice in the front, and rock armor on its back. Aqua claws made up for the arms he sported, thick but also very maneuverable as they flowed like water. His menacing head was made of molten rock, and continuously on fire. Even his simple breathing released spurts of flames. The being's wings were nearly invisible, only being seen because of the white background behind him. They were made with the power of the Wind Phoenix. It flapped its wings a few times in place. Each flap threatened to topple over the knights with the surge of force. Finally, the aura this massive dragon surrounded itself with was made of pure darkness. The mana

489

from this aura was so powerful, it could be felt from across the room clearly. The dragon winced its eyes over at the knights, and immediately his dense mana's influence fell upon them, weighing on them like gravity and forcing them to strain just to stay upright. The dragon then made a mental link with all of the knights, causing a little pain in their heads, but allowing him to speak to the knights through their minds. "Good morning Royal Knights; my name is Syuri, the Element Dragon." He spoke directly into their heads.

"Woah, did he just...speak?" Blaze looked around in astonishment at the other knights.

"So proper for such a beast." Void said lowly to himself.

"Boys, focus!" Gaia yelled as Syuri flapped his wings and slowly rose into the air. With the white in all directions, no one knew exactly how high or far this dimension went. Volt simply looked at her and nodded.

"Thank you for visiting me in this dimension. And thank you for this beautiful power. Unfortunately, I must use it to destroy you." Syuri spoke again as he increased the pressure of his dark aura. The knights were all forced to their knees or on all fours.

"His mana is so...strong...shit." Volt struggled against the aura as best he could to look up. Syuri had somehow flown up high into the air at that time. His mouth was open wide and pointed upwards. Mana quickly gathered into a giant molten ball at the base of this opening in his mouth.

"That's..." Blaze stammered, forcing his head up to look at the familiar move. Blaze quickly shook his head to focus himself again. "Red Chariot!!!" He yelled with his blade dug into the ground to hold him upright on his right knee. His Red Chariot began shaking in place, waiting impatiently to unleash it's pent-up mana. "Release!" On cue, Blaze's sword released an explosion of mana propelling him

490

roughly into the air, breaking past the dark aura's field of effect and soaring directly towards Syuri with his sword held back ready to strike. He attempted multiple times to gather his own mana on the tip of his blade, but nothing came. Shit. I can't use my molten nova. I guess moves we learned from our beasts can't be used either. Oh well, change of plans. "Guys help!" Blaze said as the heat coming from Red Chariot rose again, causing its entire blade to catch fire. "I need your power again, Nova Divide!!" The edge extended with the help of the flaming mana and glowed like hot coals in a blacksmith's forge.

While Blaze soared up at Syuri, the dragon had finished charging his ferocious ball of mana and readied it directly at the knights. "You're too late! Molten Nova!" Syuri spoke again as he fired the shot directly in Blaze's path.

"Tsk. Don't. Threaten me with flames!" Blaze suddenly got very angry as he grumbled off almost at the outer edge of the gigantic ball in front of him.

"Toprak başak!" Gaia yelled as she created spiraling spears of the earth that twisted up towards the dragon. They seemed to spawn out of nowhere, using only her mana instead of the environment to summon them.

"Hmm. This is one I learned from a past foe. With the mark of the dark lord, escape is futile. Grab him and never let go, death's grip!" With both hands into the ground, Void gathered his own mana and spawned a small armada of dark tentacles out of his back that zoomed up, matching Gaia's speed. The tips of each limb flashed and contracted as it tried sucking mana out of even the air.

"Don't leave me behind now, mana whip!" Out of Ocean's hands came eight mana whips from around the sides, headed towards Syuri as well.

Blaze peered through the molten nova right in from of him now, and into the fiery eyes of Syuri. "See, my knights always have my back! Who's got yours?" Blaze said in a rage as his nova divide sliced the molten nova entirely in half, causing both halves to drift off into the ground to either side of the knights on the ground. Blaze, now suspended in midair for a moment, staring directly at Syuri with ultimate confidence.

One by one, the attacks racing towards Syuri connected all over his body, except for his torso. None of the tentacles or spikes could attach to his chest, but the rest was fair game. Syuri winced as the spikes penetrated his lightning coated legs, and the dark tentacles attached to his aqua arms. The dark tentacles that attached slowly started absorbing mana for Void. When the mana whips got there, they immediately wrapped around his wrists and ankles, two each, and tugged him down a bit lower to the ground. "Blah. Your confidence sickens me, you kno—" With Syuri's momentary loss of concentration from the damage, Volt had made it to Syuri's head and stabbed his Sigrun directly into the back of his neck. The dark aura had faded from the knights and a portal from the ground, and one above Syuri's head both closed simultaneously.

"Spiral tap!" A tremendous shock of lightning traveled through Sigrun and through Syuri's back. Volt grimaced as he dug his spear deeper and deeper into the dragon's spine. An eerie crackling sound echoed across the dimension as Sigrun stopped. The lightning kept going for a few moments before stopping. Volt stayed suspended there as the lightning dissipated, without so much as a flinch coming from his target.

Syuri's face hadn't changed the entire time he stood there and withstood Volt's attack. "I don't need friends or help. I'll show you." Syuri actually smirked and pulled his limbs altogether, curling himself into a ball. The mana whips and tentacles get stretched and drawn closer as well to match. Mana quickly gathered to the edges of his coarse skin. Syuri then spreads his arms and legs aggressively, causing a release of dark electric mana to expand in a sphere around him. Blaze, Volt, and all of the attacks connected to him all were immediately discharged of mana. Volt was knocked temporarily unconscious and fell off of the top of Syuri, pummelling towards the ground.

"I'll show you the difference in our strengths!" Syuri reached out with his water claw, his limbs now free to move about, and wrapped it entirely around Blaze's head, aiming it towards the ground.

"Aghh, let. Go!" Blaze said, squirming under the pressure of the hand wrapped around his head. Giant clouds of steam began to form as Blaze's body heated up against the water-based arm of the dragon.

"Blaze!" Gaia yelled as she caught Volt's body but still looked up to see Blaze's head getting grasped.

Syuri then started to drop, straight down, towards the ground and the rest of the knights using Blaze's head like a meteor. They all scattered in different directions to avoid the impact. Gaia runs still holding Volt's body. Void, after getting out of range, turns around and creates a giant portal in the path of Syuri to divert him. "You underestimate me!" Syuri's booming voice jolted the head and ears of Void, throwing off his concentration. With his free hand, Syuri slammed his palm into the center of the portal, causing it to immediately dissipate. He then shifted his weight again to force the side holding Blaze ahead of him just as he approached the ground. In the same motion, he slammed Blaze's head and body into the ground with impressive force. A cloud of steam and smoke erupted from the ground where they landed. The white barriers of the dimension were unaffected, but Blaze's body immediately showed the damage. Blood ran down the sides of his forehead and neck and onto the ground. He lay there motionless as Syuri stood back up straight. Smoke drifted out of his heat, emitting mouth as he turned towards the rest of the knights who now surrounded him from their separation earlier. "Ahhhh, who's next?" Syuri asked seriously while looking around him.

"Shit," Ocean said wide-eyed, looking at the conditions of Blaze and Volt.

"Blaze…" Gaia trailed off, still holding Volt. She let his feet ease onto the ground now, bending her knees to make it easier. His body flopped over the side of her arms like a wooden doll.

"No one? Okay, I'll choose then." Syuri said, looking in Gaia's direction, his gigantic wing's flapping behind him.

"Oh, no!" Ocean called from behind the dragon. He had noticed Syuri's intentions and gathered mana back into his hands.

Gaia looked up to see the monstrous beast dashing towards her at incredible speed. "Uh, w-wait a minute!" Gaia stammered.

"Here, I come!" Syuri dashed towards Gaia, covering half the distance in only a second. Before he could get closer, however, four mana whips wrapped around his arms, his stomach and his neck, slowing down his pace but not stopping him. Syuri pushed forward, taking long, heavy strides towards Gaia and Volt.

"D-damnit, s-so strong," Ocean said, getting pulled forward behind Syuri.

"You think this will stop me? Ha." Syuri gloated as he trudged forward.

Ocean's heels drug along the ground while he pulled back with all his might. He did activate the mana draining properties of his whip though, changing the flow of mana towards Ocean. The mana went from a solid teal blue water to white particles traveling through it like a stream. The mana of Syuri. This worked very quickly with the large mana pool of Syuri, thus giving Ocean a quick boost in mana.

Suddenly, Syuri stopped and stood straight up. "You really think you're slick, don't you?" he said, obviously angry. The now furious dragon turned around to face Ocean, grabbing all of the whips with his right claw. He then snapped all of the lashes with one grip of his hand, severing the connection. "I guess you've volunteered." Syuri's tone had changed again, much calmer now.

In this distraction, Gaia had crept away further and placed Volt down softly. She then summoned Kirici and held it out before her. "Welp now's the time, I guess," Ocean said, lowering himself to one knee and placing both of his hands on the ground. A circle of mana soon appeared on the ground around him, flashing every few seconds.

Syuri charged at Ocean now full speed. Within seconds, he had swiped his massive claw at Ocean's body, but to his chagrin, his target turned into a puddle of water. "What!?" He grumbled angrily. The circle on the ground grew in size, covering a bigger radius now. The pool also increased in size. Seconds later, out came two dozen Ocean water clones slowly easing their way out of the puddle. They each had their hybrid weapon out and pointed at Syuri. "Hmph. I'll just squish each one of you individually then." he said, holding his right claw into the air.

"From the future to the past, erase our foes with a blast." All of the Ocean clones said in tandem as they fired their mana missiles directly at Syuri.

"Oh." Syuri instead pulled his arms back to cover up himself as the point-blank missiles explode on contact, creating a heavy mist and smoke cloud around him. Visibility was next to none during this time.

"Take that!" The Oceans yelled and jumped for joy.

"It's not enough, Ocean!" Gaia called towards Ocean.

"Ahhhh! I'll crush you!" In an instant, with the swipe of Syuri's hand, all of the mist was blown away. He raised his claw into the air then dug it into the puddle of water where the clones resided. One crackle after another ice began forming and overtaking the pool, freezing clones stable as soon as the ice reached them. Off to the side, the real Ocean leaped out of the puddle just as the clones were all frozen. With his other hand, Syuri reached over and snatched Ocean right out of the air.

"Shit!" Ocean said as he was swung around like an action figure.

"Toprak hapis!" Gaia yelled, summoning an array of skinny earth spikes that ensnared Syuri's left claw that held Ocean, trapping it in place.

"Mercy's shift!" Void came out of nowhere with a finely placed portal that opened on top of Syuri's wrist, effectively cutting it off from the rest of his arm. The claw reverted to water and released Ocean, who landed safely on the side of one of the earth spikes.

"Thanks," Ocean said with a sigh.

"You'll pay for that!" Syuri said, pulling his handless arm back towards himself. He grumbled as his nub banged against spikes on the way back.

"You won't get the chance!" Gaia smacked the end of Kirici into the ground, and she immediately shot up in the air on a platform of earth. Bending into the sky, the platform lets her off above Syuri's head. In midair, she put Kirici on her back, and gathered mana into her right hand, quickly sucking mana from even her own earth structures she's formed. "Dünya pençesi!" Gaia reached down with her powered upright hand in a palm strike aimed at Syrui's face. He lifted his other arm to block, though. Gaia's palm connected with Syuri's forearm sending devastating shockwaves throughout the dragon's body. When they finally reached the ground, massive earthquake level

496

shockwaves were radiated outwards aggressively, knocking Void and Ocean down.

Syuri smiled in Gaia's face for a moment, thinking he had successfully blocked the attack. That smile was wiped away quickly, though, as his water arm exploded into water droplets. Cracks were even sent through both the ice and earth parts of his torso. "Ouch, that was some atta—" Crack! He was cut off by Gaia's bo-staff cracking into his forehead`, Syuri having no limbs to protect himself.

"Crack ve şut, kırıcı sürücü!" Gaia's bow shined with might in the breaker drive mode as another shockwave was sent through Syuri's body, releasing onto the ground. It was Syuri's forehead that cracked his time though, the hard molten shell was damaged. "How's that?" Gaia yelled, putting her all into that swing.

"Hmm." Lava trickled along the side of Syuri's mouth like blood. His eyes peered up at Gaia with anger as he struggled against the force of her bo-staff on his forehead. He pushed and pushed until finally Kirici was flung high up into the air, leaving Gaia wide open.

"Uh oh," Gaia said, putting up her arms to cover up as Syuri sends out a blast of fire mana blowing Gaia towards the ground. She tumbled to the ground, next to Volt and Void, her body smoking. Void gets down and begins gathering mana in his hands as he peers up at the enraged dragon.

Syuri put his head back and rereleased his massive aura, charging up his mana and reforming both of his water claws. The dark aura was also unleashed again, snapping Void's momentum and forcing him to the ground once again. "Do I have your attention yet?" Syuri, his head still cocked back, starts gathering mana in front of his open mouth. He flaps his wings and floats, hovering in the air in front of the Knights.

"Oh, great lords grant me the power to create the ultimate destruction, kneel before the power of lord Verafelt," Syuri said while he kept his mouth open. The mana grew and grew until finally, the molten nova sat there in the air, ready to annihilate. "Dieee!" He yelled, firing the massive ball of fiery mana directly at the knights with convictions. As the ball gets closer, Void stared deeply into it, still struggling to move his body. Gaia had regained herself long enough to lay her body over top of Volt's before the aura affected them. A tear left her eye while she held his unconscious body close. A few meters out it was now, the end seemed all too near. There was no wind or outside sound in this dimension, it was only them. No one would see or hear the end from the other side. There's no way this could be the end, could it?

"Xi Neng!" Suddenly a massive wave of light soared from behind the knights and easily sliced through the molten nova, destroying it and rushing towards Syuri. The hesitant dragon immediately rose high into the air to dodge the mana wave, which continued on past him forever. In this distraction, the dark aura was again lifted, allowing the knights to move.

Gaia got up gingerly, her body still in pain, and turned around to see a familiar face. "Sky!" She limped over and embraced Sky with a big hug.

Sky hugged her back, "About the time I save ya'll, my precious knights, for once," he said with a smile looking up at the dragon, slowly lowering himself to the ground. "Think it's about time we turn this around, Void, bring Blaze over here." He nodded.

"Are you okay now, Sky?" Volt said, finally waking up, holding his head.

"I'll be fine, Scatha really did wonders on my body. Hail's wounds were worse, so he'll still take some time to heal, but I'm here to help now." Sky looked down to see

Blaze's body coming up beside him. "Thanks, Void," he said.

"Glad to have you back, Captain." Void nodded.

Smack. All the knights looked over to see Sky smacking the back of Blaze's head. "Time to wake up, Blaze, nap time's over." Sky chuckled.

Blaze's eyes open, rage in his eyes, but his body wouldn't move. "Sky! You asshole. Tsk, I'd slap ya back, but I can't really move in my current state," he said, shaking his head.

"That's fine, I've been watching the whole time while I was healing. I think I have an idea on how to beat him." Sky said looking around to his other knights.

"Wait, how could you see the fight? We're in another dimension." Gaia said, looking around.

"Via my mana linkability. Not only can I contact you guys, but I can also look through your eyes to see what you see. I just discovered this part of the ability admittedly while I was unconscious myself. There were a lot of struggles going on within my dreams, and on the other end, I saw it. Your fantastic struggle with this thing," Sky explained, finishing by pointing at the dragon as his feet finally clasped back onto the ground.

"Looks like we have a new person joining for the slaughter," Syuri chuckled while clapping his hands together. Each clap sounded like someone splattering face-first into the water.

Sky looked up at Syuri for a moment, then diverted his attention back towards the knights. "I think we need to try an ambitious four-person fusion to overcome his ability to counter us at every turn. I noticed he could outdo any one of us separately, but together, we just need to have more power than him in this one moment. That's all we need." He stopped to look at the knights, all giving him their full attention. Nods were shared all around. Even Blaze and Volt looked up to listen. Volt's head somehow ended up getting hoisted upon Gaia's lap.

Volt sighed. "Thanks, by the way, Gaia, I felt your body protecting me back there, I really appreciate it," he whispered to her. She simply smiled and stroked the hair on his head.

"Volt, Void, I want you two to try your own fusion because I don't know how fusing all six of us would turn out on the first try," Sky continued. "Blaze, can you muster up even half of your strength?" he said.

"Yeah, I've got plenty of mana left, I just can't move my body." He smirked to himself.

"Awesome, we'll go on your lead then, raise your mana as high as you can, and we'll follow suit," Sky ordered. Void was already picking up Volt's body so Gaia could get up to her feet. Volt and Blaze both started gathering mana simultaneously while the others waited to gauge and monitor their own levels. They still kept an eye on Syuri as well, who seemed almost too intrigued to intervene.

"I don't know what you're planning over there, but it's not going to work! Go ahead! I'll let you finish your last struggle before I wipe you all from existence." Syuri crossed his arms and waited patiently for the knights to finish.

Sky looked up at Syuri. "Thanks! That's very kind of you," he replied sarcastically.

"What won't be kind is the way I rip you apart," Syuri grumbled.

"About ready, Sky," Blaze said, his mana radiating around his prone body.

"Same, Void." Volt's mana was shocking Void as he held his body.

"Good, my turn." Void replied with a dangerous mana of his own.

"Aaaaaahhhhhh!" The remaining knights all charged their mana as well, trying to match each other as much as possible. One after another, flairs of different elements sputtered into the air as they stopped charging. It almost looked like a rainbow, the number of different colors flying around in one area.

"Ready!?" Sky said, struggling to keep his mana calmed.

"Contact!" All six knights said in tandem, sending out a bright flash and a shockwave of mana so massive and powerful that it even pushed back Syuri several hundred feet. The mana in the air seemed afraid of what was inside of that mass of shining light. The mana pulsated in the air as it exploded out but was then pulled back in. After a moment of total blindness, there were two figures in the center, being orbited by mana like a planet.

"What. The. Hell?" Syuri said, covering his face from the flash of light.

One of the figures had red, blue, green, and brown mana swirling around them before it finally calmed down and just radiates like a typical aura. It was a mixture of all four elements being pushed up towards the sky. He stood there, looking at his hands. His black hair was long, spiking up wildly into the air, never having the chance to settle. Bright flaming wings flapped behind, while a single, long engraved zweihander was holstered at his side. Water claws were attached over his hands, and spiked armor fitted his body. "Hmmm. This feels awesome. I think I'll steal a bit from you and call myself Syaris," he said, looking intently at his body before looking up to Syuri. He then looked over at his partner, who was also checking himself out.

This one was calmly playing with an overlaying part of his long white hair. His hair didn't spike up but instead was straight and sat down to his shoulders, bangs coming down over his face. His armor was entirely black, and slender, contrasting this white dimension very well. In the ground next to him dug a giant ax bladed halberd that radiated with its own dark lightning mana. Altogether the halberd was at least twice his height, the blade taking up a third of this space. A pointed edge on the top stuck into the ground as it waited to be wielded. "Hmm. Dark lightning, I think Impulse works as a name, what do you think?" he said, talking to himself. I like that a lot actually, haha. Volt told from within, taking a backseat in this fusion.

"Don't know if you were talking to me, but I like that too," Syaris said, Sky as the head of the fusion.

"Ahem! What the hell did you just do? Why is your mana so much higher in that weird form of yours?" Syuri grumbled to break up the conversation.

Syaris looked directly at Syuri, "All I'm saying is, you should not have allowed us to do this. It'll prove to be your end."

"Yeah, okay!" Syuri said while letting his massive amount of mana run wild, his aura not contained within his body.

Suddenly without warning, Syuri was kicked on his head, causing him to slide back a few feet. Only a second later did Syaris's body appear in the air where he was kicked, and his after image disappear from its original spot next to Impulse. "Guess I might as well start as well, huh." Impulse reached over and lifted his halberd out of the ground. He spun his heavy weapon above his head with just his right hand. Moments later, he disappeared into a single bolt of black lightning that traveled horizontally towards Syuri.

"Gahhh, so fast!" Syuri said, holding his hands up before him letting out artillery of mana whips from his water claws. They dashed off towards Syaris, wobbling around to coincide with his movements in the sky. This would prove futile, though, as Syaris easily dodged every single whip as he soared towards Syuri at massive speeds and delivered a stiff kick upon his jaw, sending his head flying up. The lashes all disappear on contact.

Just then, the black lightning representing Impulse had reached Syuri's torso summoning back his body, his halberd at the ready. The tip of the blade swelled with darkness, while the rest of it radiated lightning mana. He reared it back and took aim. "Shadow Boxing." As soon as he finished, the darkness reached out, engulfing all of the lightning on the halberd to create a perfect fusion. The aura surrounding Impulse himself was the same way, flaring out with lightning and darkness in all directions. "Tao uira huaki!" Impulse said calmly as the darkness on the tip of the halberd spiraled into the shape of a drill. He then rapidly thrust this point into Syuri's chest countless times faster than the speed of light, hitting him over a hundred times a second. The sharp streaks from the attacks shot through Syuri's chest, coming out far on the other side. Holes now pierced through his body all over. He looked like a beehive.

"Gaaah! What? H-heww, blahg?" Syuri shouted, spurting out more lava blood, unable to process the amount of pain he just endured in a second. He couldn't even hold his arms up any longer. "My....armor....shit..." He gasped, trying to catch his breath.

Impulse then took a step back then fully leaped backward, passing by Syaris in the process. "Your turn," he whispered mockingly as he landed behind them.

Syaris smirked at Impulse as they crossed paths. He then held up his single right hand, gathering a vast amount of aqua, fire, air, and earth mana at the same time. They all swirled around each other and gained size and momentum. After a moment, a giant orb of elemental mana sat in his hand as he floated there in the air. "Always wanted to try this since we first learned contact fusion." Syaris chuckled, then his face got serious. "Luven Vorldo." The ball of mana suddenly shrunk to the size of a fist in his palm. "Feel a little taste of the origin world's power. Try not to die too soon, alright?" Syaris said as he drifted the mana towards Syuri, who, in his damaged state, was still trying to catch a breath from the last attack.

The orb slowly drifted over towards Syuri at its own pace as if it had a mind of its own. The mana eventually entered the dragon's right chest area and immediately had an adverse reaction with his mana, exploding and taking a large chunk of his chest with it. His arm down to just above his stomach was lost. Syuri's eyes were wide open as his body slowly drifted off to the left side. He let out a single breath as he fell. Right as he was to completely crumple onto the ground, he caught himself with his left knee. "Graaahhhh no!" He roared, shaking his head, breathing heavily. "No! I refuse to lose to you humans. I'll destroy you all, I'll take you with me! You'll get blown away! Just. Just. Die!" Syuri flapped his left-wing and what was left of his right-wing and lifts himself back into the air.

"Heh, look, he's rambling now. I think we've got him. Looks like something big is coming, charge up your attack now I'd suggest. "Syaris said while looking at the weary dragon. Impulse nodded back at him.

Syuri had summoned an orb of mana representing all of the spheres he had inside of his body using his left hand. These orbs spun in place in front of him, the circle aimed at the knights. His hand then began glowing as he slowly brought it closer and closer and eventually placed his hand into the ring made by the orbs, which surrounded his massive wrist like a bracelet. "Haha. Ha, haha. Hahahahahahaha. This is it, guys! I'll rid Scourge of you before you even have a chance to get to him. One by one, the orbs lit up around his wrist to match.

Meanwhile, both Syaris and Impulse were gathering vast amounts of mana themselves. Syaris was collecting it in

his ancient zweihander; he gripped with both hands. From
the tip of the blade to the hilt, the entire thing shined with
the lights of all four elements. Impulse gathered his mana all
over his body. He released a single line of electric mana
straight up into the air and then started to gather a ball of
dark mana directly in front of him. He hovered above the
ground as he primed this mana, almost as if the gravity
around the orb was defied. Syaris's blade was on his side
drug along the ground with the weight of the concentrated
mana it held. "With the mana control of Ocean and Gaia to
make this possible, with my precision and Blaze's incredible
destructive power, whatever he does, I'll be ready to counter
it in the most dramatic way possible ha. Just be ready to
finish him off." Syaris turned to Impulse again. The mana
was soon unable to be contained just in the blade and started
to rage around it as well.

"Don't worry. I just thought up a combination that's
sure to destroy him entirely." Impulse smirked back at his
fellow knights. The mana in front of him was primed and
ready. It sat like a mini black hole, waiting to suck.

"Don't worry, I'll spread the word of the famed
'Royal Knights' that fell into my hands. Gigantesco
Vigore!" The mana Syuri had all flashed at the same time as
he thrust his one hand forward. From this circle came an
overpowering humongous blast of elemental mana at least
twice the size of Syuri himself aimed directly for Syaris, and
closing the distance fast.

Syaris stared down the frightening display of power
with ultimate confidence. He even cracked a smile while he
gripped the hilt of his blade tighter. "Xi...Neng...Divide!"
He said as he swiped his sword up into the air in the
direction of the blast, and only one swing was all it took.
The massively concentrated mana sent out a vertical
crescent-shaped streak of mana that began slicing through
the explosion cleanly. Seconds later, all of the mana was cut

in two and destroyed, the wave slicing through even Syuri as well. At this point, the dragon spoke no more words into their heads. His eyes were simply wide, his expression blank, and cracks and lava blood began to explode out from different parts along the center of his body. His head, chest, even down to his crotch, began to slowly separate as his body lowered towards the ground. "Hmph. Your turn." Syaris said, lowering his blade back to his side.

"K" Impulse looked up to the sky, where he released the light. "When we acknowledge that all of life is sacred and that each act is an act of choice and therefore sacred, then life is a sacred dance lived each moment consciously. When we live at this level, we participate in the creation of a better world," Impulse chanted to himself as the sky of the dimension breaks apart directly above him. Out of this opening comes a rumbling sound as the castle shaking can be seen through this hole. A massive exhaust of lightning mana came crashing down through the ceiling and into the dimension through the hole. Syaris lept back far, and the lighting dropped down directly on top of Impulse but just stopped there.

Syuri's mouth gushed lava blood, but his mind allowed him to speak one last time. "This...isn't the end. I will be back for my revenge, I'll be...back…" And that was it, his eyes rolled back into his head.

The orb of dark mana he has before him catches it in its own gravity and forces the powerful mana to circulate around it, and Impulse. "Heh looks like it worked. Filled with rage and anger...my curse is turned into a blessing from the hands of the Gods that deemed me worthy to wield the ultimate darkness. Feel my pain, my struggles, and shatter from the weight of my spirit! Keni Ékrixi!" He chanted, causing the concentrated ball of mana to expand slightly almost as if being activated. It circulated with dark and lightning mana, and Impulse grabbed it with both hands.

"This is the end. Thank you for helping us to improve further before our final fight with your boss. Farewell Syuri, the element dragon." He sent forth a blast of dark lightning mana only slightly being rivaled in size by Syuri's own. It shot out with so much force that it actually pushed Impulse back while he fired it. The blast was so devastating that it immediately overtook and desecrated Syuri's body, even traveling off for miles inside of the dimension. Impulse landed back onto the ground after the blast had run its course and rested his arms back at his sides. All that remained of where Syuri stood was the collection of orbs that had been stolen from the knights.

Syaris walked back up next to Impulse and held his fist out. "We did it, guys," he said with a smile.

"Yeah...let's hope this power is enough to defeat Scourge." Impulse said, looking off to the side.

A concerned look made its way onto Syaris's face before being quickly wiped away. "It will have to be, ya know?" He nodded.

"Guess you're right, as usual." Impulse said as a flash of light from each of their bodies ended the contact fusion.

The knights all fell out on top of each other but soon got up, generally healed from their wounds before. Even Blaze and Volt could get up on their own now. The orbs all immediately shot towards their corresponding knights and rebound to them. They jammed into their chests, and after a quick glow, the knights were once again one with their orbs. Even Hail's orb jolted off through the opening and off towards his body.

"Aww, did you miss me? Haha." Ocean said, rubbing his chest where the orb returned. "Well, me too."

"Man, it's amazing what that contact fusion can do. I can actually move again from all those injuries." Blaze said, clenching his fists.

"We still have much to learn about them, but we are getting better at combining our mana and abilities. Frankly, this is awesome." Volt smiled.

"Well, are we ready to storm the rest of this castle, guys? We aren't done yet, guys!" Sky said, scratching the back of his head, scythe in hand.

"Yeah!" The knights all cheered in unison as the dimension that surrounded them began to crumble away around them.

"I...hope, Hail is okay," Gaia said, thinking about her brother again.

"I'm sure he'll be fine. He should be here to join us soon. You've got to believe," Volt said, messing with Gaia's head.

Gaia let out a small smile, trying to hold back her emotions. "I hate you, Volt," she said while throwing a light jab at his side and looking away. Not wanting him to see the look on her face.

****

Chapter 21: Scourge's Castle

After the grueling battle inside of Syuri's dimension, the knights land back inside of the Foyer of Scourge's castle directly in front of the two large mana powered elevators. The left one is going up, the right going down. The eerie aura was still there waiting for them, the dark mist making visibility harder than it should have been.

"Yep, this place is still creepy," Blaze said, shaking his head.

"Even I second that," Void said, standing to his left, also looking around the foyer.

Sky walked ahead of the group and stared at the two elevators up and down. "You know…we're probably going to have to split upright?" Sky's voice whistled as a window in the background blasted open from the action outside.

Gaia crossed her arms and stood behind Sky. "You're right." She sighed. "We need to find Wendy and Scourge. Chances are they will be in different directions, and we've got to get to both quickly. Who knows what kind of conditions they have her in," Gaia said, trying to hold back her emotions as much as possible.

Sky looked down at Gaia's face. "Which is why you'll be going down there to find her," he said, looking at her then over to the other knights. "Take Void and Ocean with you too. If there's a dungeon or a deep basement down there, Void should be good in the dark. And you three work together well from what I've seen with Syuri."

510

Void nodded at Sky. "That's fine with me."

"Yeah, count on us to protect her," Ocean said, walking over to the side with Void and Gaia.

"As for the rest of us, we have a date with Scourge, and we can't be late," Volt said as he looked up at the left elevator.

Blaze's hands set on fire, and he punched his own fist in a display to sike himself up. "Yeah, I can't wait to pay him back tenfold for what he's done to my people!" he said, very eager.

Volt walked over and banged on the doors of the left elevator before tapping on the button and waiting. "Let's get this over with then, shall we?" he said as the mana run elevator shaft shook until the doors finally opened abruptly. It was so dark inside the elevator; the only thing visible was the spider webs along the bottom edges of the walls. Inside it was actually pretty wide, about two meters long. Volt stood guard at the side of the elevator, waiting for someone to enter first. The Sky and Blaze both looked at each other wide-eyed then looked around, waiting on the other to volunteer first. An awkward silence later neither had taken a step forward. Volt gestured towards the door again. "...well?" he said, waiting still.

"Fine. I'll go first then, goddamn," Blaze said confidently strutting forward towards the open doors. He took two light steps onto the steel floor of the elevator before putting all of his weight down. "Whoa!" Blaze shouted as the elevator shook violently for a moment before settling down. His face had almost lost color that quickly. Volt and Sky both had their hands out just in case but rested themselves after they realized all was well. "Whew. All good guys come on," Blaze said reassuringly.

Sky nodded and joined him inside, followed by Volt, who turned around to face the other knights as soon as entering. "Ocean, Void, Gaia, you guys be safe down there. We'll see you on the other side," Volt said, shaking his head.

"Good luck, alright. Get Wendy back to her extended family, then join us up top to help us kick Scourge's ass," Sky said, holding up a thumbs us.

"Don't worry. We got this down!" Ocean said, retorting with a thumbs up himself.

"Sky, whatever you do, keep that mana link open, so I can sense your position," Void said seriously.

"Course," Sky responded.

"Volt— er…you guys. Don't die. Save some for us, okay?" Gaia said with a slight hesitation in her voice. Volt looked into her eyes and nodded at her. The doors then shut them off and up they went, towards the top of Scourge's castle.

"Whelp, our turn." Ocean hit the button for the right elevator. The doors opened immediately, revealing another web infested room before them. Ocean got on first then waited on the other two to join him.

Void and Gaia both looked at each other before Void held out his hand towards the shaft. "Ladies first." He said with a small smile cracked on his face.

"Mhmm," Gaia smirked back before joining Ocean on the elevator. Void followed shortly after, and the doors shut behind him. The sounds of screeching all that was heard afterward as the elevator raced downwards towards the basement.

-Year 277   Scourge's castle, basement   Shadow Path, Umbra-

Slam! The right elevator aggressively and loudly slams to a stop at the bottom. The knights are jumbled on the ground after the sudden drop from the base floor. The door slowly creaked open to reveal a corridor full of doors, but still just as dark as the floor above it, so it was impossible to tell how large this area indeed was. One light was on around the corner on the right side, though, where footprints could be heard going up and down cement could be heard. Talking could be heard in one of the rooms closest to the elevator, but suddenly it stopped.

"Shit, why's it always so damn dark in these places?" Gaia whispered, getting off of Ocean's chest with her butt.

"Shhh. I think someone just heard the elevator." Void put his hand over Gaia's mouth to stop her.

"Hey! Did you hear that?" A deeper voice echoed from inside of the room on the left.

"Huh, what are you talking about?" Another smaller voice said.

"Sounded like it came from the elevator. No one should be coming down here right now." The original sounded again.

"Well? Go check it out then!" A third voice boomed at the other two. The door soon busted open and out walked two demons armed with serrated blades and basic plated armor looking directly at the open elevator shaft.

"Hey, I don't see anything?" The deeper voiced demon said, looking into the darkness. The three had backed up to the furthest corners of the elevator to be hidden in the dark. The shorter one moved up to the front of the shaft to take a look as well. He then jerked up and started pointing.

"Hmmm. Wait, what's tha—" He was cut off by a spike of earth skewering his neck and his body. In an instant, both demons were full of holes from a web of spikes from all of the walls. Their dark green blood sparkled against the slight amount of light coming from the open door behind them.

"Toprak hapis," Gaia said, putting Kirici away and walking towards the spikes in front of them. She softly rested her hand on one of the spikes, and then all faded away back into pure mana. The two demon's bodies both collapsed onto the ground like wet sacs. She walked up now towards the open door.

"Damn..." Void whispered from behind Gaia, following closely.

"Hey! What's all that noise out there, Sarin?!" The commanding voice yelled from inside the room.

"Sorry, I don't think they'll be responding anytime soon," Gaia said as she kicked the open door off its hinges and halfway down the hallway. She walked into the small room to confront a surprised Strike in a chair with four healers surrounding him with their mystic mana steadily. His wounds from Volt were closed now, but he was still significantly weakened. "Hmph. I knew that voice sounded familiar." Gaia cracked her knuckles by merely flexing her fingers, all without losing eye contact with Strike.

Strike's healers continued healing him the entire time, not batting an eye at the threatening aura that Gaia currently displayed. "Bitch...it's you..." Strike retorted, holding eye contact.

"Oh shit, it's Strike," Ocean said, tumbling in on the severe moment inside the room behind Void. He shut himself up when he noticed the tension, though.

Void put his hand on Gaia's shoulder to try and calm her a bit. "Remember, we want to conserve mana for the final fight to come to Gaia," he whispered in her ear.

She shrugged his hand off of her shoulder and refocused her attention at Strike. "I'm only going to ask you this once, and you better answer me." She said, cracking her fingers still. "I have to kill you for what you did to my brother, but I'll make it very quickly if you answer me." Gaia's mana unconsciously began to rise around her pushing

514

up her hair as it gusted upwards. Her mana soon spread to the floor and the walls around them.

"Heh, oh, that fool was your brother? He caught me off guard and did a good amount of damage. Too bad, he was an idiot." Strike said, smiling, even chuckling a little bit.

Gaia clenched her fists so tightly she made her own palms start to bleed. "Where. Is. Wendy?" she stated firmly. Ocean and Void both decided to take a step back towards the doorway.

Strike's face got serious for a moment. He stared into Gaia's eyes for a moment, as if he were looking deep into her soul. After the moment was up, his smile returned to his face. "Fuck. Off. That old woman will die down here," he said as he summoned a portal made from shadows that reached up and grabbed him and his healers inside before pulling them back down, out of sight.

Gaia immediately looked down at the ground, an ugly expression creeping up on her face. Pure rage.

"No, no, no, Gaia wait!" Ocean said, but it was too late. Her mind had been made up, and the chase was on.

"You will not get away! Dünya pençesi!" Gaia's right hand raged with mana quickly as she leaped into the air and slammed her hand into the ground in the center of the room. A large chunk of the floor was obliterated, but the shockwave of her attack was so powerful it continued to demolish floor after floor downwards until it hit the dirt on the final floor five stories down. Debris from the holes all tumbles down at the bottom into a large pile. Gaia jumped down the hole afterward without an inch of hesitation.

"Damn. This basement goes down deep. This is ridiculous. "Void said leaping down after Gaia.

"Don't worry, Wendy, we're coming," Ocean said, looking down the hole through multiple rooms. Commotion and confusion were heard from below by the demons that resided here. Crumbs from the debris still drop along the edges of the hole regularly. The room they were in was a makeshift medical bay, Strike had gathered a large number of supplies to treat wounds and gemstones to aid with mana healing inside of this room for his own treatment.

At the bottom floor, Gaia landed on the pile of rubble before sliding her way to the ground. Limbs of Strike's healers were seen buried underneath the piles. They wouldn't be healing anytime soon. Soon after, Strike bursted out of a collection of rubble in a rage of his own. "Grah! Damn, bitch!" he said with rocks and debris flying all around him. "I hope you're ready to die!" Strike said as his dark mana slowly creeping around him. He looked down at his body now, seemingly trying to gauge where his injuries were. A crumbling sound emits as Void and Ocean then slid down the pile next to Gaia.

"Don't forget about us," Ocean said, pulling out his hybrid weapon.

"Doesn't matter. He's mine." Gaia summoned Kirici into her open palm and pointed it at Strike. "I'll break all his bones and make him beg for forgiveness. I'll find Wendy myself; he no longer has an opportunity for mercy. Just death," Gaia said as her mana begins to run wild.

"Gaia…" Void said, noticing her anger running ramped.

"What do you want from me, Void? He nearly killed my brother, and Jax, AND Sky, he's got Wendy locked up here somewhere, probably suffering. They tortured Keith and did inhumane experiments on him. This type of evil, we cannot afford to let live. He needs to die." Gaia turned to face Void.. "And if you won't give me your support, both of you, then stay out of my way."

"Damnit. My mana hasn't fully recovered yet, and my body is barely healed yet. What a lovely bunch to bump into right now." Strike says lowly to himself. His shadow mana still slowly crawls onto his body, covering him like armor.

"Fine then." Gaia scoffed then looked away from Void, back to Strike. Gaia's rock armor had formed around her body as her mana rose.

Ocean stared at Gaia for a moment as she readied herself to go and had a change of heart. He traded his hybrid weapon for his royal rapier and dug the blade into the ground. "I'll support you then," he said as his aqua mana seeped into the ground here, creating a layer of water along the entirety of the floor they stood on.

"What is this?" Strike said curiously as he lifted his feet out of the water. His shadow mana had encompassed his body entirely at this point. "No matter. Your mana can no longer reach me in this stat—Huh!?" Strike peeked down to see water mana rise out of the puddle and wrapped itself around his feet and legs. He tried to rise up out of the water, but the grip of the mana grew tighter the more he pulled. "What is this?" He cut at the mana, gripping him only to create more links with everyone his cut down.

"Go get em, girl!" Ocean said, leaving his rapier in the ground and pulling his hybrid weapon back out. He crouched down into stance with the tip facing the struggling Strike.

"Gotcha." Gaia nodded as she dashed off to the side but in the direction of Strike.

"Get off!" Strike said, still slashing away at his binds.

"From the future to the past, erase our foes with a blast!" Ocean chants as his mana rocket fires off towards Strike.

As Gaia ran forward, a portal opened in front of her, causing her to disappear. "Guess I might as well help," Void said while pulling out both Izbynci and Taia, his cursed blades. He immediately felt the dark sensation as extra dark mana filled his body from his two swords, creating a thin film of darkness on even his head.

Just as the mana rocket was to hit, Strike manipulated his shadow engulfed body, opening up his torso and leaving a hole for the blast to simply glide right through, exploding against the wall behind him. This shook all of the walls, causing rubble to come tumbling down that massive hole in the ceiling. "Ha, you missed!" Strike chuckled as he slowly reformed his body. A portal opened up behind him though, the long end of a bo-staff jabbed out and placed itself right where Shadow's body was before. His body floated around Kirici, causing his top half to wave around in the air like a ghost, unable to return to form. "Uh… Shit." Strike said looking at his chest then finally to his legs still trapped by Ocean's puddle.

"Got you." Gaia smirked as she walked fully out of the portal, Kirici fully blocking Strike's ability to reform.

Out of a portal for himself, Void appears above Strike's mass of shadows with Izbynci the rage aimed down at him. With one direct slash through the shadow mana that was Strike's body, Void landed on the ground, his back to Strike. A moment later, a giant dark explosion erupted on Strike's body, blowing him back into the wall and collecting into a pile of shadows. These shadows reformed to make Strike whole again. He still sat in Ocean's puddle though, the mana reaching up back to grab him. "Ouch…" Strike said frustratingly as he pounded his fist on the ground. After doing so, a pillar of darkness pops up out of the puddle across the room. "How dare you think you can turn this into your domain. This is MY area!" Strike yelled as more and more pillars shot up out of the ground. It took only moments for the aqua mana to be swallowed by these pillars and replaced with the cloud of darkness. It sprayed up into the air like a mist, and before long, the light was shut out from the lanterns. They all sat there in the darkness. The only semblance of light came from what shone through the hole in the ceiling. Strike's body disappeared into the night of the room, leaving only eerie laughs behind.

"Hmph. What is with you guys and the excessive darkness." Void said, shaking his head, his two cursed blades wobbling in his hands in anticipation.

"Void, you should know more than anyone." Strike's voice echoed in the darkness. "What makes shadows even more powerful? Simply removing all the light that constricts it!" Strike chuckled.

"Ocean," Void said seriously.

"Yeah?" Ocean's voice called from his right.

"Fuse with me real quick, I'm going to need a boost in mana to absorb all of this darkness." Void said, jumping a little when Ocean's hand quickly finds its way on his shoulder.

"I'm ready when you are okay," Ocean said, already allowing his mana to radiate.

"Like I'll let you!" Strike yelled as the sheen of a blade was heard in the darkness, rushing towards them quickly.

"Please make it in time," Gaia said, troubled and gathering mana in her hands. "Listen to my calls like you did in the past, help me defeat this foe to make this world last." In an instant, Gaia creates a dome of rock around where she heard the voices of Void and Ocean. "Hurry up!" Gaia called.

"This dome cannot stop my shadow, mana!" Strike yelled, very close to the two now. A sharp gust of wind blows by, followed by crumbling and the wheezing of mana, all in the same spot. "H-huh?" Strike could be heard clearly now.

"Hmm. I guess Abyss works for me." A new voice said from the center of the action. "Focus your mana drain on draining this darkness mana surrounding us." Void as the lead in this new fusion, says to Ocean, who resided in his head.

"Whew, they made it." Gaia breathed a sigh of relief.

"Hmph. You think combining your body is going to make a difference? Couldn't defeat me apart, can't defeat me together. It's truly that simple." Strike taunted in the darkness.

"You keep dancing in the darkness. I'll bring all your sins to the light." Abyss gathers a head-sized ball of aqua mana in his hands and holds it above his head. "Mist bomb!" He says as the bomb explodes, sending his mana in all directions. The walls, rubble, Gaia, Strike's shadow self, everything was splashed.

"Hey!" Gaia yelped waving her arms to dry them off.

"Hmph, what's your plan to get me wet?" Strike stared at Abyss curiously.

Abyss simply smirked and arched his back, his mouth open, and his arms on either side, hands clenched. He started to inhale mana aggressively now, from everything that was in the air, and from those his mana touched. The room lightened up as the darkness gets sucked up into the mouth of Abyss.

"H-hey, what are you doing!?" Strike murmured while death gripping the shadows that surround him. His body partially reverted to normal as he was pulled forward too.

"Damn. Me too," Gaia said, lowering to a knee as her mana was sucked out as well.

Moments later, it was done. All of the mana in the room belonged to Abyss. Strike's shadows had left him, and the light in the room had returned. Abyss stood still for a moment, his body quivering like he was on a caffeine rush. He gave out a loud sigh. Every muscle on his body contracted at the same time, and dark mana erupted from him like an explosion. It took all of Abyss's might to contain the mana and keep it contained in the aura around him. Strike took a couple steps back, holding his chest like he was naked. Gaia sat in the same spot, she slowly tried to regain her mana from the earth.

"M-my shadows! Give them back, you curr!" Strike yelled with great fury and rage.

Abyss, while containing the massive amount of mana he currently possessed, looked over to focus his attention on Strike. "Don't worry, I'll give you that and more! Be careful what you ask for!" He threw out with a smirk. With both hands out, he began to channel the mana that he possessed and the mana that he acquired all out in front of him. A seeping ball of darkness began forming, shadows lashing out, trying to escape continuously. This ball of mana was alive and growing more and more by the second.

"I'll regain my mana just in case," Gaia said as her hand was still in the ground absorbing mana from the earth around and under them. "Don't know how this will work out," she said, looking at the eerie ball of mana.

"Woah Woah Woah, let's just talk about this, huh?" Strike said with his hands up in front of him. Strike's back was to the giant vault doors in the back of the room, he took a slow step after step towards Abyss.

"Too late!" Abyss yelled, the ball of darkness as powerful and refined as it would get. "Filled with rage and anger. My curse is turned into a blessing from the hands of the Gods that deemed me worthy to wield the ultimate darkness. Feel my pain, my struggles, and shatter from the weight of my spirit and your own darkness! Keni...bala!" The mana immediately compressed and condensed into a smooth small sphere of sinister spirits. His hands still held out before him, the ball slowly drifts from his hands, towards Strike.

Suddenly the fear in Strike's eyes disappeared as a large smirk appeared on his face. "Hehehe," he chucked in an ugly fashion.

The Keni Bala then stopped in its path about halfway between the two and started to reverse back towards Abyss. "What?" He said, struggling to push it forward, to no avail.

"Ha. You forget that this is *my* mana you mess with. My shadow mana has a mind of its own. It fights for me and only me. Now prepare to get crushed by your own audaciousness!" Strike held his hand out to control the mana and help force it towards Abyss.

"Shit, curse my intuition," Gaia said, dashing at Abyss full speed.

"Welp, there goes all my mana, I can't even fight it anymore." Abyss defused and returned Void and Ocean back in the same spot. Ocean fell out, not used to the conditions of his mana in a fusion yet. Void sat there staring deep into the Keni Bala, unable to move. "I guess this is my fate for using such a forbidden move as liberally as I have." Void said, lowering his head.

"Void, quick, how do I activate its full power!?" Gaia shouted off to his side.

"Simply chant Ékrixi, it'll turn it into a blast, but wh—" Void got cut off by Gaia's hand, coated in layers of her mana so she wouldn't touch the darkness directly. Her hand appeared in front of his face to catch the mana just in time.

"Thanks, I got the rest, Void," Gaia said as her shoulder jammed into Void's chin, knocking him back and allowing her to catch her balance on the ground. She stood there with the Keni Bali in one hand and Kirici in the other.

Strike saw this display and summoned two of his jagged edge weapons to his hands. "Oh, you again? Guess I can punish you a little more, girl." Strike coating his blades in his shadows as some of his mana returned to him.

"Kirici, this is it, let's finish this." Gaia charged at Strike with the ball of darkness focused on him.

Strike rose both blades to defend, his mana firmly coating both. "Heh, I'll cut you in half before you have a chance!" he yelled.

A meter before they collided, Gaia leaped into the air, causing Strike to raise his guard to defend. She came down with Kirici, however, aiming for Strike's hands. She stuck her bo-staff above his hands and slammed them down with one stiff motion. Strike's blades were dropped into the ground as he looked up to her, wide open and surprised. "Wow. This bitch is smart," Strike said almost in a defeatist tone as his hands flopped to his sides.

"You sicken me. I hope this hurts!" Gaia said as she drove the Keni Bala into Strike's chest with her other hand, pushing him back as she fully extended her arm. A pulse of mana emanated throughout Strike's body as his body went instantly cold and began cracking. "Ékrixi." Gaia pushed palm even further, and dark mana exhausted from the orb rushing through Strike's chest and even blowing a large hole in the left side of the vault door behind them. For a brief second, as the mana traveled, the light was extinguished. Gaia pulled her hand back, the black mana gone at this point.

Strike's body collapsed lifelessly on its knees, a giant hole in the center of his chest. The gap grew larger as the seconds passed, his body seemingly getting eaten away from the inside out. The disintegrated parts of his corpse turn to dust as he slowly was killed away. "Tsk." He scoffed one last time before his body entirely faded away in the breeze. There was a long silence after Strike disappeared. A clump of shadow mana suddenly drifted up and flew through the massive hole in the ceiling. Gaia put Kirici away as she waited for Void and Ocean to get back on their feet.

"Do you feel better now, Gaia?" Void said as he walked up to Gaia, who hadn't moved from that spot yet. "You did well with my move, too, actually," he said reluctantly.

"It'll only be worth it if we find Wendy and the others," Gaia said in a monotone voice, staring straight ahead of her.

"Hmm. You're right. But hey, what's behind that door in front of us? I feel it's gotta be important to be down here locked up like this." Ocean said optimistically.

Void suddenly turned around as he sensed an onlooker from the stairwell behind them leading up. A demon had peeked around the corner, saw his gave, and quickly ran back up the stairs. He shook his head afterward and continued his gaze forward.

"Yeah, let's check it out, I guess." Gaia finally responded as they walked forward towards the Vault, which took only a small shove to topple at this point.

"Woah...what the hell." Ocean's mouth dropped as he saw what was beyond that door. A long dark hallway lay before them, with jail cells on either side all the way down. At the very end was a single cell on its own. A small figure was chained up inside, their hands forced above their head, connecting to the ceiling.

Gaia stopped and stared as well as her eyes open wide. Tears slowly began to trickle down her cheek as she looked before her. "Wendy!" Gaia dashed forward suddenly, headed towards the back of the hallway.

"Wait, Gaia!" Void and Ocean yelled as they chase after her.

Gaia dashes past the cages with tunnel vision headed right for the one that held Wendy, the boys a few meters behind her. She skids to a stop right in front of the gate and breaks the bars down with Kirici. "Don't worry Wendy, I'm here, I'm here," she said talking to a barely conscious

524

Wendy, her eyes closed. Gaia crushed the chained that bound the old lady and caught her in her arms. She looked down at her with an endearing smile on her face, tears still in her eyes. Wendy shook her head back and forth a few times before easing her eyes open. They were all white and lifeless. Ocean and Void had silently stopped behind Gaia and just watched.

"I-I'm sorry darling, I'm afraid I can't see you anymore. But I know... I know that's my Gaia, I can always sense you." Wendy let out with a sweet, innocent smile. She rubbed her wrinkled finger up against the back of Gaia's hand before letting herself down into a cross-legged stance. Gaia kneeled at her level and looked into her eyes.

"W-Wendy...Your eyes. Did they do this to you?" Gaia's voice got sadder the longer she spoke. Upon further inspection, Wendy actually had a lot of new scars and injuries all around her body. Her tattered clothing revealing old gashes and wounds along her ribs and legs as well as the pricks running down her arms.

Wendy simply smiled at her question and looked down and to the right, her arms rested on her lap. There was an awkward pause now, leading Ocean and Void to shift back and forth while they waited there, just outside of the cell. "These..." she started.

"Tell me, Wendy, please," Gaia said, cutting her off.

"So..." Wendy paused again, looking for the words. "Have you ever wondered why you and Hail, my children, were able to receive the blessings from the Guardian deities even though you don't coincide with the original five heroes?" Wendy said in a calm, low tone. A tear casually slid down her cheek, but she still held a smile on her face.

"Wait, I thought you were over a hundred years old," Ocean interjected impulsively. "How could you be the mother?" he continued.

"Well, Gaia and Hail are indeed my great-grandkids, but because of who I am, it takes a few generations for my genes to be successfully passed down. Technically, they are my children, all of you are." Wendy says, leading to another silence in which everyone looks at each other for a moment.

"Because of who you are…." Void mumbles to himself. "Wendy…who…are you?" he said. Gaia also looked up at Wendy earnestly.

"I am…Sylindra…" Wendy said, the smile off her face now as she got serious for a moment.

Gaia's eyes got very wide as she was speechless at the moment. Ocean's eyes got wide as well as he chuckled a little bit out loud. "I'm sorry, what?" He was raising his voice.

"As in, God? The Goddess of everything from the earth to the sea? The namesake of our homeworld? That Sylindra?" Void said, trying to confirm things for himself.

Wendy reached out and rested her hand on the top of Gaia's head, rubbing it a little. "Yes, that one." Her smile returned afterward.

"But how? I didn't know that deities could visit our world," Ocean said.

"Is that why Scourge wanted you so badly, Wendy?" Gaia said, holding both of her arms and staring at her.

Wendy nodded. "Yeah… He was trying different experiments on me to draw out my Godly power. Of course, they didn't work because there are rules for when us deities travel down to your world," she responded.

"Wait, all of you guys come down to Sylindra?" Void said, astonished.

"We do, but have to live within the confines of that world. We have to set ourselves as regular humans and restrict our powers accordingly. It's actually very vulnerable for us to be here, so please don't tell anyone about me," Wendy said, smiling again.

"Of course not!" Gaia said, giving Wendy a huge, tight hug.

"It can be really rewarding to haha," Wendy said, hugging Gaia back. "Oh yeah, uh, which knights am I talking to?" she said, pointing her head in the direction of Ocean and Void.

Gaia put her hand on Wendy's cheek. "Ma, you didn't recognize the voices?" she asked, sincerely.

"Sorry, hun, it has been a long time since that time. It was closer to the beginning of your journey away from me. I'm glad I could see feel you again before I reincarnated," she said as she tenderly stroked Gaia's face with her old fingers.

"I'm uh, Ocean," Ocean said, slightly offended.

"Void here. And what did you mean by reincarnation? Are you going to restart this life with a new body?" Void asked.

Wendy nodded slowly. "In a sense, yes. I have to go back to my closed world within the infinite canvas. When I return, I have to don a new body as well. I guess this all happened at a good time, after all. Jax can take over for the pirates, and Gaia here won't be lonely anymore. She has found her place. Her stubborn older brother has some growing to do." She ended by shaking her head.

"That's really sad, I don't want to lose you. Especially after all of these hardships to find you." Gaia started crying again.

"It's gonna be okay, darling. Here, help me up. You guys have somewhere to be, don't you?" Wendy questioned as Gaia helps her to her feet. She then started walking towards the exit of the cell. Gaia, Void, and Ocean all follow her out, taking care not to walk over her and her languid pace.

"My my wasn't that cute." A voice echoed from a cell off to their right.

527

Void's head spun around so fast his neck popped. "Keith?" He yelled before slashing down the cell door immediately. "Have you been here the whole time?" He asked, walking inside.

Keith simply nodded, not moving his body an inch as Void approached. The decrepit man's arms were chained off to both sides, simple work for Void's claymore, but the injuries on his body were the real issues. The left side of his face had been burned, presumably by chemicals as his skin was near bubbling. It was so scarred. Skin in this area was black and led down even to his neck. His hair was more gray than white, and it was stained with dried blood, especially on the tips of his hair that overlayed over his face. The muscle tone in his body had mostly faded away, leaving him looking sickly and weak. Both of Keith's legs were injured as well. The left simply had a gash along his thigh, slowly getting infected. The right dealt with its kneecap busted, not like either leg was rushing with strength anyway. The cell was just as dingy and gloomy as Wendy's, dark spots were splashed under and around him on the wall. It looked and smelled like dried blood.

"Keith…" Gaia said softly while looking at the rough state he was in.

"Yeah…a…a lot has happened since we saw each other last…" Keith said, holding back tears by silently laughing to himself.

Void walked up a few steps and knelt in front of Keith. He then broke away the chains that bound his arms and legs. Keith's arms lifelessly flopped to his sides. "I know. We defeated Adrian, your other half. Destroyed his body and everything," Void said calmly.
Keith's eyes lit up for a moment, then they returned to their sad state. "That would mean that his spirit would return to me….but it hasn't. Meaning tha—"

"Meaning that Scourge has it. His and Strike's now too." Void interjected.

"Fuck, Strike…" Keith grumbled.

"Well, good thing we're on our way to go kill Scourge next!" Gaia said optimistically.

"They did…so many experiments on my body to separate Adrian from me forcibly. Being with him for the majority of my life means that without him, my body is so weak and feeble. They only kept me alive to research the seal placed on my body. Chances are, Edgar, helped them to break it," Keith said, shaking his head. "Hey…can I ask you something?" He looked up to Void.

"Yeah, go ahead." Void nodded.

"Can you take me with you? I want to see Scourge's face when you defeat him. I'd like to help any way I can." Keith raised his hand to Void.

"Of course you can." Void reached over and lifted Keith up with both hands. He put Keith's arm over his neck and acted as his crutch. "I got ya, man, let's go." He cracked a small smile at Keith.

"Any word from Sky yet Void?" Gaia questioned as she made her way out of the cell. Wendy was waiting outside of the cell with Ocean already.

"Not yet, it only slightly worries me, though. Maybe it was a long road to get up there. Who knows?" Void shrugged.

"I hope that's all. I guess we'll have to walk the long way," Gaia said, walking back towards the doorway that led them there.

"Hey, wait! Do you want to end this war raging outside now?" A voice yelled from deep inside the cell next to Keith's.

"Who the hell are you?" Ocean said, looking over at the demon yelling at him from deep within the cell. He was grey and smaller, but his wings were torn off. Cauterized

529

nubs were left on the muscles connecting the spine and where a wing would be. He had looked crazed as he shifted around in place, trying to free himself from the chains.

"Kill me! Kill me now!" he screamed while flailing his arms as much as he could while still chained down.

Gaia tapped Kirici against the cell doors. "Hey! Calm the hell down and talk normally. You can manage that, can't you? Or are you too savage a demon?" she barked.

The demon stopped shaking and took a deep breath. "Ok, ok, I'm sorry. It's just been a very long time since I have seen anyone new come down here," he finally let out.

"Good, now explain yourself," Gaia said, calming down herself.

"My name is Silverwing," The demon started. The knight's eyes grew wide upon hearing this name. "Those little demons you've probably fought already were clones made from my body, with some added darkness," he said as calmly as possible.

"Wait, did you just say clones? I think Volt had a dream about you?" Void responded, trying to think.

"If that's the one with the spear, then yes. I entered that into his memories for the hope that it would help in some way. But for now, I need one of you to end my worthless life. If I die, all of the clones made of me will disappear. That should be the victory outside inevitable for you guys, so it's a win-win!" Silverwing said with a smile.

"I... I don't know about that..." Void looked away for a second and set Keith down for a moment to give himself a break.

"Yeah, we can find another way I thin—" Ocean stopped as a sharp spear-like rock flies past him, through the cage and directly into Silverwing's neck. Ocean, Void, and Gaia were all stuck in shock as blood starts squirting out of Silverwing's wound, with his hands chained he couldn't even put pressure on it.

"Thank…you…" Silverwing was able to eke out looking up past Ocean. His head then flopped down, lifelessly, blood flowing freely out of his neck. His body laid cold, dead. A shaking ensued afterward, originating from outside but shaking the entire castle. Moments later, the cheers from humans out could be heard even from the basement.

Gaia looked over at Wendy, whose hand was still up, rock fragments on her fingertips. "Wendy, yo—"

"No one else was going to do it. You all hesitated at the opportunity to end this war right now. Save more of our people's lives or the life of that demon, asking to get relieved from his suffering. I guess I still have to stick around for a little to make the tough decisions." Wendy vented, before starting her slow stroll back towards the doorway at the end of the shaft.

The knights were still silent but just followed behind with their heads down for the moment, leaving Silverwing's dead body where it lay. "You're right, I guess…" Void mumbled to break the silence.

"I know," Wendy responded, finally reaching the broken doors that led them here. "Now that it seems the battle is over outside let's finish things upstairs," she said. Wendy started the slow climb up the stairs off to the side of the lowest floor. The group gingerly made their way up to the next level, which looked like it was the research floor. There were labs and testing rooms on either side, with a couple of sealed-off places in the back corner. From the rooms they could see into, all of the workers were missing at the moment, leading to a completely empty floor, free from demons. In the center was a room surrounded by glass on all sides, with a reclining chair in the center. A giant mana cannon of some sort was elevated over top of the chair, aimed directly at the top. Around it was many smaller tools on tables, from knives to injectors. The floors inside were

531

shiny and white, making it the cleanest looking area in the castle so far.

"He really puts passion into his experiments, goodness," Gaia said, looking at the large room. Keith immediately looked away when he saw it, tears involuntarily trickling down his face.

Ocean patted him on the shoulder. "It'll be alright, man, don't worry," he said, trying to console.

"I know. This is just where…it happened. My body clearly doesn't like it." Keith said, wiping his face off. "Let's just…get out of here," he said, pointing to the next stairwell.

Upon reaching the next level, they noticed that there were still enemies on this floor. Hearing grunts and moans coming from the rooms around. This floor looked like it was used for specialty training for demon warriors. The second they all stepped foot up there, the grunting stopped. A cage of sorts for battle was center stage on this floor, with the adjacent rooms holding equipment and such. Suddenly though, demons came rushing out of every room around them, surrounding them very quickly. These demons were all huge and muscular, at least seven feet tall, equipped with simple armor and swords, and growled with intensity as they prepared to strike.

"Oh boy, that happened very quickly," Gaia said, summoning Kirici and looking around her.

"Yeah…Ocean, protect these two, we got this," Void said while lowering Keith to the ground next to Wendy. He then summoned Fonos and pointed it to the biggest demon he could find.

"Got it!" Ocean said, summoning a giant water barrier to surround them three.

"I can protect myself!" Wendy opposed it while putting up her fists.

"Let us do this, we have got you," Ocean said while swiping his mana whip at approaching demons.

Void began gathering his mana as the demons inched closer, but then he noticed something within himself. "Wait, hold on Gaia, let me try something," he said as he let his aura flow freely. "Sit down!" Void expanded his mana rapidly around him, enveloping all of the demons. Suddenly his mana began weighing down on the demons like a massive gravity, causing them all to get pushed down to the point of even kneeling under pressure. They grunted and fought against this mana with all their might, but were unable to break free.

"Nice, Void! Guess you picked that up from the higher-level demons like Scourge," Ocean said, excited for him.

"Yeah, I guess so..." Void said, keeping the pressure on.

"Hehe...this is perfect..." Gaia smiled devilishly. After gathering up enough, mana herself, she rises up and snaps her fingers. "Toprak başak!" Earth stalagmites pierce through the ceiling and the ground beneath them, skewering all of the demons at once. The remains of the demons looked like hedges around the knights in a semicircle. Gaia's mana then faded away, leaving bloody corpse at their feet afterward. Void later released his aura from the area and picked Keith back up.

"Hmph," Wendy said, relaxing again.

"See, I told ya. Leave it to us." Ocean smirked while getting rid of the barrier. Wendy rushed ahead to lead them forward again.

"Wait." Void stopped and put his hand on his temple. "Sky's finally giving me his location, get closer to me, we're shifting." Void said, placing a large portal underneath of them.

"Finally..." Gaia said.

"Let's go see an old friend," Wendy said, looking at Keith while cracking her knuckles.

The group all disappeared into the portal, which closed up behind them. The basement of Scourge's castle has left a wasteland, dead demons scattered about on top of the already eerie feel. A lot of horrifying memories were left down here for Keith and Wendy that they never want to revisit again.

-Year 277 Scourge's castle, Upper level Shadow Path, Umbra-

Upon the top floor, Blaze, Volt, and Sky walk down a long hallway leading to a giant engraved and jeweled golden doorway. The door extended from the ceiling to the floor with a curved golden handle on each side. The engravings depicted darkness and murder in the form of primitive-looking drawings. The path from the elevator doors to the door in the back was taken up by different memorabilia, and trophies assumed to belong to Scourge. Each item was carefully cased in its own glass dome, on top of onyx colored stones at least two meters tall each. The items were positioned on either side of the walkway in groups as if they were museum exhibits. Around the center of the room, the path breaks off in two directions. Very vain paintings of Scourge occupied the walls overlooking the items in the glass cases. Many different objects were in these cases. One group immediately off to the left of the knights had a collection of three swords, three different types of katana, with dried blood still on the blade. Off to the other side are groups of helms from different warriors he defeated. Any cracks, dirt, or damage was preserved there as well.

The knights walked through this very odd and egotistical display on the way towards the doors in the back.

Sky led in the middle, with Blaze on the left and Volt on the right. They all walked with their weapons out, prepared for whatever happens. "Shit, this guy really loves himself, huh?" Sky said, looking at the pictures of Scourge on the walls.

"I think he's even more proud of himself. It's like he's his own proud father or something," Volt said, chuckling a bit, Sigrun waving back and forth in his right hand.

"Hmm, wouldn't know what that's like," Blaze said mostly to himself. He stopped for a second to peer at a display that held a still-beating heart, black as night, and encased in two separate containers. The first was made of ice mana, the second, in a glass. Blaze then jogs up to catch up to the others.

"Wait a minute. Isn't that?" Volt stopped the group to draw their attention to a long wooden walking stick engraved with ancient writing running down the sides. They all stared off to the left at the staff become more and more familiar. "That looks like Wendy's old walking stick, right?" Volt questioned.

"I think so, but why is that here?" Sky asked.

"Maybe he holds it as a badge of honor. I say we relieve Scourge of that staff. Save it for when we get Wendy back," Volt responded while walking up toward the case that held it.

"Sounds good to me," Blaze said while melting a large hole in the glass case and simply pulled the staff out. A bunch of footsteps then echoed from both corners as they neared the center of the room. A screeching sound followed, sounding like stones rubbing against each other viciously. A stampede of feet trampled onto the cement from around the corner, causing the knights to immediately get into fighting stances and wait for the enemy's arrival.

"If you'd like to keep your lives, I'd suggest you turn back now." The stomping grew calmer as a demon led a pack around the corner to the left. He held a long double-sided spear and wore light armor as black as a knight that covered nearly his entire body. The demon soldiers behind him all had heavier black armor to conform to their burlier bodies. The lead demon was more slender and had blades mounted to the outer sides of his forearms. As soon as his group of demons reached got closer, a separate group of demons came from around the corner as well.

The knights looked around as they were slowly surrounded by the demons, while the demons slowly crept behind them on both sides and began flanking them as well. "Tsk, I guess it wasn't going to be that easy to just waltz in here," Blaze said, gathering his fiery mana around him.

"I'm ready when you are, guys," Volt responded by spinning Sigrun in his hand like a baton. Lighting mana trailed it, soon giving it the appearance of a lightning wheel.

"Yep," Sky said, holding his scythe before him, directly at the leader who also met gazes with him.

"I'll snuff out your light before you can even reach the master," The lead demon said, tapping the blade of his spear on the ground. "Oh, before I forget, my name is—"

"It doesn't matter what your name is," Blaze said, cutting him off, gathering mana in his right hand.

Volt then dug his spear into the ground and began cracking his knuckles, a thin layer of lighting mana surrounded his body like a film. Sky simply snarled at all of the demons that surrounded them. The wind started to push and pull around him, creating a soft vortex that sucked air towards him as he gathered his own mana. The captain then looked ahead at the doorway to Scourge's throne room. Blaze had finished gathering mana in his hand, which had glowed bright orange by the time it had finished, radiating heat. He then nodded at Volt, who nodded back.

"Your next move will undoubtedly be your last, as fair warning," Volt said seriously while staring at the demon intently.

"Hmph. Don't mock me!" The demon growled, raising his weapon into the air. He then took a step forward. "I'll k—." Slam! Before he could say anything else, his head was slammed back into the ground, creating a small crater when it hit. His body was flipped again, legs up into the air, his weapon flipped up into the air. Volt's body appeared a second later as everyone's eyes adjusted, with his arm swung over. He had punched the demon before anyone could even react, let alone see him coming. He then moved to the right a bit and looked over to Blaze, who was in his stance already.

"Uh oh, oh no, you don't," Sky said as the other demons all took a step forward after they realized what had just occurred. All of the demons were immediately swept up into the air by Sky's wind mana and then brought together trapped in a giant ball of wind mana resembling a translucent bubble. The clump of demons growled and grumbled as they struggled to get free right above the knights.

"Take this...my rage, my anger, and all of my fury!" Blaze chanted low to himself as he charged forward. The demon's body had flipped back, and he landed on his knees, upright. He was unconscious already too. Blaze palm connected with the demon's chest releasing his mana in a beam-like form through its body and off behind them. A massive hole was opened in the demon's chest, and he fell off to the side, dead.

Sky flew up to meet the giant ball of demons, his mana spinning around them faster and faster now. "This is a new one for me, so bear with me." He grunted then aim the ball at the doors of Scourge's throne room. "Dàqì!" The entire sphere began to rotate in his hand rapidly. Sky then soared forward swiftly.

"Damn, go, Sky…ha," Blaze said while standing back up, pulling his hand from the demon, Volt to his right.

"Knock knock!" Sky's ball of mana went forward and obliterated the doors, sending debris of metal wood and demons tumbling in the doorway. Sky landed and stood there strong directly inside of the room. Volt and Blaze walked up and rose to either side of him. Volt on his left, Blaze on his right. They looked ahead of them to see Scourge standing there, in the center of the room, waiting for them; his ominous demonic aura making the throne room reek with evil.

Chapter 22: The Dark Mercenary

-Year 277   Scourge's castle, Throne Room

Shadow Path, Umbra-

Blaze Sky and Volt stood at the doorway of the throne room, just staring. A dark figure shrouded in shadows was across from them in the center of the room, around him was dark, but also very well made throne room. This space was huge, absolutely had to be the biggest room in the entire castle, and it was on the top floor. This was only of the only areas in the castle with natural light, as the Chaos moon's line shone through the large, circular openings on the ceiling. They rose above to create latticed domes on the roof. The walls were all a dark brown to the grayish toned stone that was engraved with gold depicting the ancient language. These domes were all along a straight line leading from the doorway to the throne on the ceiling, counting five total. After an indentation on the high up the roof, crown molding and olden styled artwork was painted. This artwork depicted the stories of Chaos of old. The ceiling rose thirty feet into the air, though, making the bottom half of the room quite drafty. Eight girthy pillars sat parallel to the domes on either side, albeit spread a bit wider apart for proper support of the room. Each post had a different battle scene carved onto it in gold that wrapped around and extended top to bottom; until it met with the golden moldings on either end. At the base of each pillar, a small gate surrounded it where flames burned bright and consistently adding a bit more of light to the room. A couple of extra doors were located to either side of the door they came in, where they went, who knows.

The walls were essentially just larger canvases for the demonic artists to work on. Their paintings were shown on a massive display along the entirety of the walls. Their pallets were slim, though, ranging from gold, red and blacks as their primary colors. On the wall described the parting of the infinite canvas, to the rise and fall of Luvenesyar, to the inhabitants of the different worlds in one long, connected piece. Three huge circles with golden engraved Mozaic type designs indented within the lines were positioned at various points in the throne room. Two were on either side of the doorway, and the last was placed right at the bottom of the throne to create a perfect triangle. On the ground mirroring the indentation lines of the dome on the ceiling were carpet like linings that traveling back towards the throne, stopping just before the circle there. On the other side of the ring, were steps that lead up to Scourge's throne. Scourge's actual chair was the creepiest part of this otherwise quite lovely and beautiful throne room. His chair was onyx colored appearing to have been made out of the shadows themselves, then hardened like ice. Jagged spikes and growths extruded out of the sides and back of the chair, almost like they had been alive. A dark aura flared on its own around it. A few secondary chairs were off to the sides. However, they were less fancy and more as regular throne chairs.

The figure that stood in the center of the room had a very dark and profound aura surrounding it as it stood there waiting and staring at the knights. As soon as the two met eyes, the aura faded away to reveal Scourge rising before them, battle-ready. Scourge began to chuckle from behind his mask, quickly revealing his murderous intent. The knights also stood facing their adversary with their weapons on the ready, no one wanting to make a move before the other.

"Alright, guys, this is it." Sky started as he watched Scourge pace back and forth, silently. "I already sent the link to Void to join us, but with the way this castle is, it might take a while for him to receive it, let alone get here," he said in a low voice over to the other two.

"So you're saying we've got to hold him off for a bit?" Volt questioned while looking over at him.

"Eh. Unfortunately, we have to be careful," Sky said hesitantly.

"Hmph. I say we go all out, overpower him before he can make himself stronger," Blaze chimed in flaring his mana up around him for a second. Suddenly Scourge disappeared into a mist of darkness as they are talking.

Volt is the first to notice as he took his attention off of Blaze and glanced to where Scourge's body previously was. "Hey guys, what was tha—" He was cut off as his head jerked back from the reappearing Scourge ramming his fist into the chin of Volt as the dark mist faded away around him. It almost felt as if the punch was done in slow motion, Blaze and Sky's faces of surprise put another smile on Scourge's masked face as Volt flew back behind him and all the way into the wall at the back of Scourge's museum in the previous room. The entire floor shook violently from the impact. Scourge's body disappeared just as quickly as it appeared.

"Guess that settles it, we've gotta go all out," Blaze said, gathering his mana. Sky did the same after a quick nod agreeing. Scourge reappeared in his original spot, chuckling to himself and pacing again back and forth.

Suddenly Sigrun came crashing forward, clad in lightning, digging into the ground angled backward before the handle tilted forward in the field like a switch. In a flash, Volt zoomed to his spear, using it to hold himself up for a moment. His body arched over the handle before popping back up. When he sat up, the damage to his face was shown. His chin was bruised, and the top of his head on the left side was cut open slightly. "I hope that's not the best you've

542

got!" Volt yelled as his own mana levels began to rise to match Blaze and Sky. The three of them stood side by side, gathering mana while Scourge simply looked at them, unflinching. "Because I didn't feel shit!" Volt continued.

"You ready, guys?" Sky said, holding out his hand to Volt.

"Mmm." Blaze nodded and held his hand out to the other side to Volt.

"Let's kill this demon!" Volt held his hands out to connect with both Sky and Blaze on either side of him. "Contact!" They all said simultaneously, resulting in a bright, blinding light that engulfed everyone in the room.

"Ahhhhh, this feels amazing." Blaze's influence came through as the head of this new fusion. The light eventually faded to reveal a tall, slender individual with black wings and a very volatile aura of lighting and fire and spun around him quickly and viciously like the winds of a tornado. "Hmmm Scorch works for this, I guess," he said to himself, looking at his body. His armor wasn't even visible with the flames and lightning, creating its own set of armor over top of his body, purely mana armor. He wielded two spears that he held behind his waist horizontally. One slightly resembled Sigrun, the other looked as if the Godslayer scythe was converted into a spear. His hair was long and white like Sky's with red tips; his hands radiated a strong heat aura around them, almost as if wearing mana boxing gloves. He looked forward towards Scourge with rage. "Get ready!" he yelled.

Scourge only chuckled again and summoned a scythe of his own. Gathering his dark mana around him in anticipation. "Hmm. Odd, he hasn't said anything yet." Scorch said while he watched Scourge gather up mana. Yeah, he usually has a big mouth. Volt said from within Scorch. "Either way, let's go wild!" In a burst of mana, Scorch rushed towards Scourge, landing a powerful fist that pushed Scourge back a few feet. Scourge looked up at Scorch, lowering his guard a bit just to see him before chuckling a bit. This clearly ticked Scorch a bit because the fake smile he put on was accompanied by an aggressive surge in his mana. He collected his mana jointly around his arms and legs, nearly doubling the size of his mana armor in these areas. His limbs almost appeared to be on fire. As he stood there staring at Scourge, a large gust of wind began blowing from behind his enemy, slowly pulling him towards Scorch. "So not enough for ya yet, eh? We'll see." He said as the wind picked up strength. Scorch got down in a fighting stance as his mana finished gathering. Scourge still had his guard up as the strong wind finally lifted him far enough to pull him forward.

At the same time as Scourge's drift forward, Scorch lunged forward with another stiff right hand. "Take this!" Scorch's charged up punch busts through Scourge's guard and lands directly on his face, cracking his mask and jolting his head and body backward. With his left foot, he catches Scourge's head on the way to crashing to the ground. He then kicks Scourge's body up into the air with the help of his wind mana, sending him ten meters up easily. "I'm not done!" Scorch surges up after Scourge with a rush of lightning, punching him in the kidneys this time. Next came a flurry of quick, powerful blows to Scourge's body that he was unable to block effectively. Eventually, Scourge was relegated to just eating punches to the midsection as Scorch used him as a midair punching back, leading him higher and higher up, the opening and dome right above them. The light shining down on their faces as they approached.

When the two had nearly reached the ceiling of the throne room, Scorch flew over to the side and caught Scourge's back with his foot again this time, jolting him up directly towards the dome. Pang! A loud sound rang through the room after Scourge's face, and the body bounced off the metal bars, bending them slightly before free-falling back down. Scourge fell along the path of Scorch who had both hands rose above his head, his fists were combined with a hefty amount of lightning mana, which kept growing as he gathered mana from the air around him. "Lucin's wrath!" With the massive swing of Scorch's hammer fists, he smashed Scourge's back with a large flash. In an instant, Scourge's body crashed into the ground with a tremendous burst and a trail of lightning leading back up. Dust from the rubble flew up into the air, creating a small cloud of smoke and debris.

Scorch flapped his wings, hovering there as he peered down at his damage. As the smoke cleared to reveal Scourge's body twitching in the center of a small crater in the floor, Scorch raised his hand and pointed it at the hole. "Xi qi..." he said as a short twister of wind began spinning from underneath of Scourge, lifting his lifeless body off of the ground and back into the air towards Scorch. In the meantime, he gathered mana into a ball off to his side with both hands. Fire, lightning, and wind mana all combined within this ball, creating a volatile combination. The ball grew larger and larger as the seconds passed. Scourge's body got closer as well, about half the way now. "Haha. Hahahahaha. Haha, I've done it, it's finally over!!" Scorch began to ramble frantically as the mana grew larger than him. The majority of the flame and lightning mana now gathered in the center as the wind surrounded it like a translucent barrier.

Scourge now found himself a few feet under Scorch, the mana facing him would be at least times as tall as he is, but he didn't move an inch. "Mega...ton...surge!" he said as he twisted his hips and pressed his palms down towards Scourge. The mana that exhausted from the ball exploded forward, growing in size as it traveled. It caught Scourge and overwhelmed him, blasting through the floor beneath him as well. The room shook and boomed like a thunderstorm had been born within. After a few moments, the shaking had finally stopped, the mana whisked away as quickly as it began. Nothing was left of Scourge's body; it had been completely obliterated in the blast. The smoke and extra mana in the air took another moment to dissipate.

Meanwhile, Scorch flapped his wings and lowered himself towards the ground, landing softly next to the hold in the field. It had entirely found itself under the dome above. The light from above shone through the hole.

"Hmm. That was…too easy. What was that?" he said, looking at his hands in confusion.

"You're right. I couldn't resist." A presence revealed from behind Scorch, causing him to immediately turn and leap away to the other side of the throne room with haste.

"What?" Scorch said, looking around but not seeing the origin of the voice. He eventually went to land his feet on the ground again. As soon as his right foot hits the ground, his back gushed blood from a deep slash from behind. He went from one foot to immediately on his knees. "How…" Scorch said, tumbling forward and defusing at the same time. Blaze and Sky were able to leap out of the way, but Volt wasn't so lucky. Out of the shadows, Scourge's body appeared stomping hard on Volt's back on his first step. Volt wailed in pain before collapsing back to the ground and remaining still.

"Hahahahaha." Scourge's muffled voice echoed throughout the room. "Sorry for the disappointment, but here I am, at full health." He chuckled.

Blaze and Sky both look up at Scourge, Volt's body still under his foot. "How did you survive that blast?" Sky questioned.

"Easy. I wasn't in it!" Scourge said, opening his arms to either side cockily. "What you destroyed was a clone I was experimenting with, you guys seemed to like the

546

perfect guinea pigs for it, so. Thank you." Scourge licked the edge of his cursed that slashed Scorch when it was formed. "I'll be sure to leave a nice display for your friends when they finally decide to join us," he said, waving the blade off to the side.

"Damn, we used a lot of mana already, that'll be rough, but we've got to last Sky," Blaze said, looking over at his captain.

"Yeah, I know. We need a plan." Sky started. Scourge had disappeared from sight again.

"You think you'll have time for that?" Scourge whispered in Sky's ear, appearing behind him moments later. Sky immediately soared in the air away from him.

"Shit." Sky sighed, holding his chest. His heart was pounding viciously.

"Sky!" Blaze yelled, sending a blast of flames at Scourge, who waved it away quickly.

"I'll have you know, I'm a lot more powerful than that silly clone. Don't mock me —" Scourge raised his hand to send an attack at Blaze but is stopped by Sigrun tucking up under his right arm, from behind him. Scourge peered back at Volt, who had made it to his feet and was staring intensely at Scourge. "Oh, so you *do* want to die first!" Scourge shoved Sigrun out of the way and turned to face Volt.

Volt steadied his spear at Scourge's face. "Do what you have to do guys, I'll hold him off!" Volt stated as his vision blurred, and lightning slowly creeps around his entire body like a jacket.

"Humph. Not for long," Scourge responded, chuckling.

"Hmm. Let's see how this goes," Volt said as the lightning coats his body, and he charged forward towards Scourge darting around at light speeds. "Uira Tikanga." Volt's first attack in this mode had him bouncing from the

547

walls and pillars and colliding with Scourge at insane speeds, attacking from all directions. Scourge shifted his body slightly to block each attack with only his right hand, but unable to counterattack as Volt zoomed back off afterward.

"Flash mode, huh. Too bad, I can still see you." Scourge said as the area around his eyes on the mask began glowing a dark red. Aura began calmly flowing around this area afterward. He backed up slightly as he defended against the constant attacks, not giving him a chance to do much else.

"How do you like that, eh?" Volt said, increasing his speed even more.

While those two had their tussle, Sky, and Blaze and gathered enough mana between them for another combination attack. The two had their mana charging right next to each other off to the side of Scourge. "Ready Sky?" Blaze yelled to his right, trying to hold onto his concentration while pushing his left hand forward.

"Yeah, let's do this?" Sky responded with his right hand, pressed forward.

With a single stiff strike, Scourge shoved his fist into Volt's chest as he passed by and forced him hard into the ground. "What was that?" Scourge let out with one of his trademark chuckles. It created a heavy impact on the ground, but Volt's lightning engulfed body bounced right up and back in an instant afterward. He flipped back and gathered mana from his body into both of his hands while he was still in the air. "Wait, what?" Scourge snapped.

"Kotahi Inazuma!" A loud boom sound as a Giga electric blast released from each of his two hands, combining in the middle and becoming even more abundant. Scourge put his right hand up to defend while he looked over at Sky and Blaze, who also seem to have something coming.

"Flaming tornado burst!" Sky and Blaze chanted simultaneously. A twister spun at Scourge before soon bursting into violent flames and rushing wildly towards its target.

Scourge rose up his left hand and caught both attacks with just his hands. He stood there, his feet planted, holding back powerful attacks from both fronts. "Heh. You'll have to do better than this if you want to defeat me!" Scourge confidently boasted. He then noticed something concerning the electric wave grows in strength.

"As you wish!" Volt said, putting even more of his mana into his attack. The blast fattened to twice as thick after his burst of mana. Scourge's right hand began to wobble a bit under pressure.

Blaze looked over to Sky and nods. "Yeah, let's show em," Sky responded with a nod. They both increased their mana levels as well. The twister began to spin faster and more violent, the flames growing in size. Both of Scourge's hands started to move and lose control.

"Hahahahahahahaha." Scourge laughed maniacally as his dark mana began spiraling around his arms and legs and the rest of his body until a dense aura coated his entire body. The gravity from it started to shake the room. "Dark impact," he said calmly, releasing a quick blast of dark mana from both hands that tore through both attacks with ease striking the knights with a stiff fury. Volt got knocked out of flash mode from the impact and thrown back and slammed into one of the pillars, toppling down on the ground. Sky and Blaze somehow got twirled together and blown into a wall off to the side. They climbed over each other out of the pile and ease their way back to their feet.

"...Ow...," Blaze said while breathing through the pain all over his body, pulling out his Red Chariot to hold him up.

"Yeah, he's tough." Sky shook his head.

Volt got up as well, holding his head where it slammed against and chipped a piece of the pillar off. "Hmph. Thought that was a pretty good shot." Scourge stood in the center of the knights who were sprawled out to different sides of the throne room. He raised his right hand at his eye level. "You know, it's funny you guys think I was done. Ha," he said as a ball of his dark mana spiraled around in his hand. He bent down and placed the orb into the ground. Immediately it began to attract and pull like a strong gravity. "Dark embrace." Soon, the gravity reached the knights and started to pull them across the room towards it.

"What…is this?" Sky said, trying to fight against gravity by sticking the sharp point on the bottom of his scythe into the ground. He was still drug forward mercilessly. Not even his wings would help him repel this force. Neither Volt nor Blaze had any better luck fighting against it, both also getting pulled against their will towards Scourge.

Scourge slowly slides Devora out of its sheath. It immediately covered itself in a dark aura, its own cursed aura that reeked in darkness. "Shadow wave!" Scourge charged his mana in this stance a bit, before swinging the blade around and raising it up into the air just at the three had finally made it to him. The three knights all tried to put up mana barriers, but their mana was immediately sucked away by the dark orb. He lowered his blade cutting through all three of them with the massive amount of mana flowing through the edge. The residual wave of cursed mana flew through and cut into the wall and ceiling behind them. The knights all collapsed before Scourge in different positions. Slash marks on their forearms and bodies. The attack had gone through all of their attempts to defend themselves and landed directly. They all sat there, breathing heavily, blood flowing down their chests, their armor stood no chance.

"Ack...damn, this is bad," Volt said, spitting blood off to the side, his body still in too much shock to move. Neither of the knights could move for the moment.

Blaze's fingers finally let go of Red Chariot as it clunks onto the ground next to him, his arms both at his side. "Tsk. Fine," he said defeatist.

Sky still tried to raise his arm up, struggling, but he couldn't muster the strength. "What is this sensation in my arms?" he questioned.

Scourge raised Devora above his head once more. "That sensation? Ha! That's Devora's cursed mana. It eats away at your mana and your strength, kills away any living thing from the inside out. But worry not! I'll put you out of your misery now, you should thank me," he said as the dark mana is summoned around Devora again. "It was nice knowing you, better luck in the afterlife!" Scourge said, lowering the blade. He stopped suddenly, though, as a portal opened up from behind Scourge.

"Hydro bomber!" Ocean's voice echoed from inside of the portal as his mana rocket fly past Scourge as he jumped up and out of the way. The rocket soared over and exploded on his throne.

"Finally...goddamn!" Sky yelled, collapsing backward. Ocean, Gaia, Void, Wendy, and Keith all come dashing out of the portal like heroes.

"Ahhh, I was wondering when you guys would show up," Scourge said, stroking the back edge of Devora with his fingers. "Oh look, more food for you to enjoy," he whispered to his blade as Devora's mana began to flare up even more seemingly from his words alone. Wendy immediately went over to Sky, Volt and Blaze to start treating their injuries from Devora's poison. Keith stood guard next to her, holding nothing but a dilapidated short sword he found on the way from the bottom floor.

Void, Gaia, and Ocean all stood ahead of Scourge, deterring him from any sudden moves. "Don't even think about it!" Void let out after watching Scourge flinch forward an inch.

Scourge stopped just to look up to Void sideways. "You have some nerve!" he growled before disappearing again. He reappeared again, in midair this time directly in front of Void, with his hand raised above his face. "Întuneric sferă," he whispered as an orb of darkness emitted from his hand and surrounded Void like a bubble, lifting him into the air to match Scourge.

"What's this?" Void said, trying to break free, but with the lack of space to move, this proved very difficult. A pulse of mana flared out from the orb knocking Ocean and Gaia back a few feet. The live darkness inside of the sphere awoke as it noticed Void's presence.

"Feast on his darkness!" Scourge chuckled as small pellets of darkness start to attack Void all over, beating on his body in surprising force. Void could only hold up his arms and crunch his body to protect himself as much as possible. The darkness was relentless, feeding on his dark mana as it attacked.

"Tsk. Damn." Void did his best to defend from the attacks, but he still grew weaker and weaker the longer it went.

Suddenly Scourge turned his body back a bit and held out his hand, catching Sigrun inches from the blade piercing his face. "Good try, Volt," Scourge said, looking over at Volt, who had just recovered from the poison, still recovering his energy. He tossed Sigrun over to the side and spun Void and the orb around, aimed directly at Wendy and company. "Hm. You want him back? You can have him!" Scourge yelled, gathering mana in his hand holding Void, placing his other hand on his own wrist. "Release!" Scourge released the orb, shooting it at Wendy.

552

"Damn, hey you, buy me a second, I'm not done with Blaze yet!" Wendy yelled in desperation at Keith, who nodded and got out in front, his shoddy blade in hand. Gaia and Ocean rush over to try and help as well, but they hadn't made it there yet.

"I got this," Keith said as his mana began gathering around the sword, making it tremble under pressure. The orb holding Void grew closer and closer, limiting the time he had to prepare. Keith lowered the blade to his lower right side once the necessary mana was gathered. His body was arched forward with about two meters separating him and Void. "Badong...Pa!" He chanted, sliding his sword forward and then vertically up into the air parallel to Void's face. At the last moment, he moved the blade to the left slightly and pushed it forward, connecting and piercing the orb-like he was slicing a melon.

A flash of light mana ensued as Void tumbled out of this opening into Volt's waiting arms. The rest of the mana surrounded the orb, causing it to expand five times over and shoot back at Scourge twice the speed it came at him. As Keith finished the swing of the sword, the massive amount of mana shattered the blade into pieces, but it did its job. Keith lowered his hands and dropped the broken blade as he watched the mana shoot forward, the rest of the knights also watched in anticipation. "Whew. That took a lot out of this body. I wish I was at a hundred percent for this fight," Keith said to himself as he looked down at his handshaking.

On the other side, Scourge looked at his mana racing towards him with another laugh. "HA. So silly. You'll be the first to die then, Keith. You should have run when you were freed." He says, raising a single finger and pointing it towards the mana orb. His fingers began to suck dark mana to it as if the tip of his finger was a black hole. A loud, eerie whistling sound echoed as the mana spiraled towards the center of his finger, growing faster and faster as the seconds passed. A devastating beam of dark mana shot out of his finger like a bullet, creating another high pitched sound that pierced eardrums a second passed by shooting faster than the speed of sound.

This concentrated beam of mana blasted forward through the orb, shattering it instantly, and kept going. Before he noticed the mana, Keith had a hole in his chest, right below his left shoulder. Blood spurted out as he made his way to the ground, surprise and pain illuminated his face as he held his wound tightly. "What the hell was that!? Keith said as the dispersed mana disappeared and revealed Scourge with his finger still pointed at him.

"Done!" Wendy yelled, finally finishing with Blaze. Blazes mana immediately raged with intensity as soon as he sat up. The whistling sound started up again, clear that Keith was the target.

"Move!" Blaze tossed an exploding ball of mana at Keit, blowing him off to the side, out of the way of the beam that tore through the floor a second later where he sat.

"Ha, smart!" Scourge said, watching Keith tumble unconsciously up against the wall. "But can you defend yourself?" He said, pointing his finger at Blaze now.

"Knights Scatter! "Sky yelled from the other side. Blaze, Void, and Volt all jumped off in different directions. Ocean stayed and created an aqua barrier around himself and Wendy. "That move mostly likely can't be blocked, do your best not to get hit!" he shouted, lifting himself into the air.

Scourge lowered his fingers a bit and looked up at Sky, who is to his right now. "Smart Sky. No wonder you're the captain. It won't help you, though. I'll still be laying you all out shortly," Scourge finished with another annoying laugh.

"I'll shut you and that annoying ass laugh up, just you wait!" Blaze said in anger.

The loud whistling sound started up again as even more mana was sucked towards him. "Just try!" With his first shots, he laid out a barrage of dark beams towards Sky, who attempted to dodge but was struck on his left-wing and went crashing to the ground right next to Blaze. Blaze immediately rushed over to check on Sky but was caught with the incoming barrage as well, using parts of his body to cover Sky. Scourge, without missing a beat, raised his finger again, but this time towards the knights on the other side of the room who were caught off guard by the quick onslaught of deadly beams. Scourge continued this attack, waving his hand back and forth across the group for a good twenty seconds. A cloud of dust and smoke filled the air after Scourge finally stopped firing. "You had enough yet?" Scourge yelled out into the room.

Suddenly Scourge felt a presence approaching in front of him in the smoke. He instinctively held out his right hand before him. Only a moment later, the smoke directly around him cleared away, and Fonos comes directly towards his face from the air. Scourge's hand entirely caught and grasped the blade as Void's body jerked forward with the sudden stop. His eyes opened wide at his lack of strength to force through Scourge's grip. "Tsk. Damn," Void muttered as his feet land to the ground, Scourge's hand still around Fonos.

"That all, Void?" Scourge said, looking slightly down to him, up close he was only a couple inches taller than Void.

"Yep, definitely!" Void scoffed then looked back up to his blade, which had been gathering mana in the time Scourge held it. "Fonos!" Void said, letting go of his claymore's grips just as the blade released a small shock wave of mana. This shocked Scourge, causing him to let go of the edge as his hand began smoking. Void spun in place to gather momentum as he simultaneously grabbed the two of his cursed blades from their hilts on his way from being face to face with his enemy again. This is my chance! The darkness leaked out as they left their sheaths aimed from a diagonal slash at Scourge's chest. Scourge lowered his left hand to Devora's side and flicked the wrist guard with his thumb, pushing the sword up out of the sheath along the path of Void's swords.

Clank! A loud, dark shockwave issue as they clashed their blades, clearing out all of the dust and smoke in the room at once. Scourge replaced his hand on Devora's hilt so he wouldn't be forced back from the extreme pressure of the two dark blades pushing against his. Scourge took this moment to look at his destruction on the knights, with the room visible again. Blaze was the closest, with his body flopped over Sky, a bloody mark along his right shoulder and through the bicep on his right arm as well. His body was laid over on his left side, face down, with a bloody circle through his stomach and into Sky's stomach as well who was under him. A fiery aura was disappearing around the area where the two were. Blaze had used this to protect from most of the attacks.

Wendy stood on the other side, unscathed, while injured Knights surrounded her on the ground. Ocean's aqua barrier had been torn apart, he was on the ground holding his left leg, which was riddled with laser holes and unusable now. Volt was pelted behind them without any direct hit damage, but a good amount of area damage done to his armor. Gaia was unconscious for the moment, a beam had bounced off of her head as she used her earth armor, knocking her out. Keith had a couple extra holes in his chest as his body was still on his back, where he fell.

"Hmmm, so I should improve my aim it seems, no one is dead from that barrage. I'll have to fix that shortly." Scourge said to himself, slightly ignoring Void's struggle against him.

"You've gotta get through me first, remember!" Void said, pushing forward with his blades, the dark mana slowly absorbing into his body.

"Simple. DEVORA!" Scourge shouted as his blade phased through both of Void's swords and slashed away at his chest. A sputter of blood flew up into the air as Scourge appeared behind Void, who collapsed afterward.

"W-what?" Void pushed himself slightly off the ground to look back at Scourge as blood trickled out of his chest. He was forced to collapse back down.

Scourge shook his head and walked forward, towards the center of the room, passing by Blaze and Sky along the way. "My my, I expected so much from you guys at this point when I let you live many moons ago." Scourge stuck Devora into the ground where he stood as he looked at the laid out Knights surrounding him. "You know. This really does make me angry." Scourge looked over at Sky, who was sliding Blaze off of him but met eyes. "My entire life, I've been fighting. As a young demon fighting to secure food for myself, as I got older, I fought to increase my standing in our world, and now I fight for the whims of Deces'. After a while I started to enjoy the fighting, it invigorated me, gave me life, purpose. It was the only thing I was exceptional at." Scourge broke eye contact with Sky to look down at his clenched fist. He looked dimly downwards like his mind was full of images of another time. At this moment, he was barely paying attention to the current environment.

"When you live a life with as many battles as I, the thrill of a normal fight or a one-sided skirmish becomes very boring. The challenge makes it fun and enjoyable. I could have stomped down you knights the moment I was ordered to, easily." Scourge continued, shaking his hand in the air in front of him now. The knights all began stirring now, trying to deal with the pain from their various injuries while Scourge spoke. "For some reason, I sensed potential in your knights, so I let you live. I allowed you to grow. I gave you a chance to mature!" Scourge raised his voice for a moment but calmed himself soon after. "I-into beautifully powerful young flowers. Is what I thought. I haven't even had to use more than twenty percent of my power so far to crush you knights...pathetic." He started shaking his head now, regret was written all over his body language. "Why did I even decide to keep you alive? Such a mistake...You know what, I should just stop playing with my prey and just finish you off already. Then I'll go outside and finish off that woman and the rest of those fools who opposed me." Scourge began nodding his head and grabbed the handle of Devora, his conversation with himself nearing its end. "Yep. Yeah, that's what I'll do!" Scourge began pulling the sword slightly out of the ground. "Sorry knights, but it's all over-"

"Wait!" Sky cut him off, upon his knee now, using his scythe to help himself up. "We can...get more powerful than this." Sky managed to get out before Scourge pulled his sword out of the floor.

"Oh?" Scourge stopped, curious. "And how is that going to happen? Hopefully, not that shotty fusion that defeated my clone. Because that won't cut it, I assure you." Scourge chuckled a bit, but still gave Sky his attention.

"A fusion, yes, but stronger. We just...need time. Time to prepare. Give us that, and you'll have that challenge you crave," Sky said, nodding meagerly.

"Hmmm." Scourge peered at the pathetic sight of the knights easing their way up, all of which are in pain. "Fine. But no more holding back for me." Scourge said, raising his mana levels just to display how much strength he still had to demonstrate. "If it doesn't match up will cut you down instantly, just know that." He rested his blade back into the ground thoroughly and crossed his arms. "Have your time. My patience is thin already, so don't take too long," he finished.

558

Sky nodded. "Void! If you still can, summon us all near each other! Knights start gathering your mana, as much as possible, we won't have this opportunity again," Sky yelled, stabilizing himself on his knee. This caused to Scourge to nod as well.

Void, still huddled over, holding his chest, nodded and slammed his hand onto the ground. "As you wish." Void opened a portal under himself, Sky, Blaze, and Volt sucking them all in. They appeared shortly out of one large portal right next to Gaia and Ocean. After landing, they all began charging their mana, yelling both in concentration but pain as well.

"You three start, we'll join when we have the mana!" Sky said, gathering his own mana. Scourge watched with anticipation as the knights all stood side by side, ready to provide him with his entertainment.

"Come, knights! Bring me your all!" Scourge yelled with his arms spread wide apart as if gesturing for someone to hit him.

"Contact!" Came three voices as a bright light that surrounded the knights. After the light faded, Void, Volt, and Ocean were replaced by a single ominous figure resembling a grim reaper from the depths of the oceans. He wore a long black cloak that almost seemed to melt off his body. It was wet and constantly dripping down his chest. The face wasn't visible as the hood sat over his forehead, with only darkness poking out from underneath. The cloak melded onto the ground under him, creating an illusion that he genuinely was fusing with the field. Especially as his dark mana dripped down and splashed onto the ground like water. His hands were mostly covered as well by the loose ends of the cloak, but his black gloves were still revealed just enough to see him grabbing the devilish scythe that he held off to his side. The cutter was all black, huge, but only about half the full size of Sky's Godslayer scythe. It was

559

equipped with three blades on end, the top longer than the other two. His entire look resembled that of the water spirits that stalked the seas back in the times of Luvenesyar's youth. But the knights would not recognize this, or why this fusion would afford this form. "Eternal Abyss…yes… that sounds good." An ominous ghostly voice comes out of the figure.

"Woah?" Sky looked up, confused at the odd voice that came from the new fusion. The other knights were still gathering mana as Eternal Abyss walked forward a few steps. How the cloak was positioned, it appeared that he was sliding across the floor.

"Hmm, this looks promisi—." A loud crashing sound echoed as Abyss disappeared, leaving only a single bubble of water where he stood. It popped just as he appeared before Scourge with a mighty swing of his scythe. Scourge caught the blade with his hand but was immediately pushed back. His feet, firmly planted into the ground, dug through as his enemy pushed with immense pressure.

"Heh." Eternal Abyss smirked within his hood as he completed his swing, breaking Scourge's guard. A massive streak of lighting mana slashed diagonally through the wall and down to the floor behind Scourge. Large chunks were indented where the wall was super thick. Before he slid back, however, Scourge snuck and grabbed Devora from the ground, now holding it in his right hand, the opposite side that he had just defended with.

Scourge swung his sword at his enemy with the intent to kill, but to his dismay, the blade phased through a shadowy mist as Abyss had changed positions already, shifting himself over to the right a bit, his scythe already ready to swing again. "Damn, he's fast, haha. Guess I'll use forty percent of my power." Scourge charged back in with a new burst of energy and the two clashed blades this time. Again, and again. Neither was able to land any significant blows as they rushed back and forth, swinging their weapons and phasing to dodge. Eternal Abyss teleported using Void's mana with Ocean's as cover, most of his attacks used Volt's lightning mana for added range and damage. Scourge was unable to curse his enemy with Devora, so he focused on getting used to his movements to catch him off guard. Scourge did look like he was enjoying himself more, though.

"There ya go, guys, wear him down a bit for us." Blaze nodded to himself while he charged up.

"Hmph. Try this!" Abyss stomped on the ground with both feet, propelling himself into the air backward while simultaneously releasing a splash of dark mana onto the ground. The mana came in the form of a mysterious orb but exploded into an ocean of dark mana that waved and flowed like water as it filled up the area quickly like a pool.

"What?" Scourge immediately leaped into the air as soon as the mana was released but was still too late as the mana 'reached' into the air like it had a mind of its own and grabbed Scourge's ankles. It pulled him down under the water like mana. A dome surrounded the knights and Wendy, protecting them from this mana with unknown origin. As soon as Scourge was submerged, Eternal Abyss shot out a blast of electric mana at the pool, shocking everything underneath constantly. Soon, the mana began draining out of the room through the large hole in the center of the floor. When it all cleared out, Scourge was on all fours with electricity surrounding his body. He looked stunned, and his body was shaking slightly. "Tsk...ouch..." Scourge shook his head while he looked at the floor, mana still slowly draining away past him.

Eternal Abyss looked down at Scourge in his prone position with his Scythe reared back behind him. Devora had been washed away to the other side of the room. A second later, he zoomed off like a true grim reaper aimed for Scourge's head. It took only about three seconds for Abyss to close the distance between the two. At the last second shadowy mana emanated near Scourge's hands. Next was a very quick clash that ended with a flash of darkness. Scourge was on his feet with his arms spread, a long thin blade shrouded in darkness in each of his hands. Eternal Abyss was on the other side with his scythe to his lower left, scraped against the ground.

"Gotcha." Scourge chuckled as he peered back at his enemy. The slash marks on Abyss's body had finally shown, one across his right shoulder to his chest area, and the other across his left side of his stomach. He then lowered his head and dropped the scythe.

"How…" Abyss said, looking down at his body.

Scourge turned around fully and started to walk towards Abyss, his two shadow blades along his sides. "Never assume that Devora is my only weapon. I have Strike's soul with me now, so I can use his abilities and his weapons as well. Nothing can escape his shadow slashes. Not even a spirit," Scourge said, within a few steps of Abyss's back now.

"Ah. So that's why." Abyss nodded before a bright flash was released where he stood. Scourge flinched a bit, not expecting the light. In his blindness, he felt pressure on his left and right arms along with his legs. When the light faded, he looked down to see Void and Volt holding his arms, and Ocean grabbing both of his legs still.

"What's the point of this?" Scourge looked down angrily as he pushed to try and move his arms.

"There's more than one way to win!" Ocean said, struggling to keep Scourge's legs still.

"Gaia now!" Sky yelled from the other side of the room before Gaia disappeared into one of Void's portals from her position in the line.

"Without having to worry about wasting mana to keep you still. With the time to charge enough mana to fully

562

release my power. *With* the rage and the help of my fellow knights. I will punch a hole through you!" Gaia's voice echoed loudly throughout the throne room, causing even Scourge to flinch a bit.

"Heh, heh. Now let's just calm down, Gaia!" Scourge yelled.

Just as he finished talking, Gaia popped up in front of Scourge out of a portal. Mana was raging around her right arm. Her hand was glowing bright yellow, as well as her eyes. She didn't wear her usual earth armor; all of her mana was focused on that single arm. She then planted her feet and reared back her arm. The mana had the last chance to expand and flow roughly like the boosters of a rocket. "HOLD HIM, STILL GUYS!" She said, clenching her fist. Her left hand was holding her right steady. Void, Volt, and Ocean all held Scourge as tightly as they could. "Dünya...pençesi!" With that, Gaia let loose the most forceful punch she had ever given in her life, aimed directly for the center of Scourge's chest. Her fist landed on his body with such impressive force that the shockwave it caused blew the other three knights off of Scourge. Her fist shattered his armor in the area where she punched instantly, traveling through his body and releasing on the other side, blasting away the armor along most of his back without ever breaking the skin. Scourge's head reared back slightly before literally throwing up blood in his mask. Blood began pouring out of the bottom of his mask and down his chest, trickling past Gaia's fist in the process.

Scourge's head bobbled back and forth for a moment before he regained consciousness. Both of his blades were dropped and disappeared. The intensity on Gaia's face did not leave for a second as she stood there stoically. "Such...power. I did not expect that at all. I underestimated your hate for me, I guess. Never again," he said, lowering his head to look at Gaia in her face. He gathered mana in his right hand and waved it around him, creating a dark wave that blew back the knights from around him. Gaia landed on her own, but the other three landed near the rest of the knights. When he was bright, Scourge lifted his mask up a bit to get a couple of deep labored breaths. He held his chest tightly, with the other hand, clearly dealing with a lot of pain and internal injuries. "Ouch…" Scourge said with a deep sigh and lowering his mask back over his face, facing the other knights still charging mana.

"Damn…I put my all into that punch too…" Gaia said, defeated against the wall she landed against.

"What a monster, he's still on his feet after that punch." Void said, getting back up and charging his mana next to the others.

"Gaia! You did a good chunk of damage; it'll help us to defeat him in the end. So don't feel discouraged and get over here and get ready for the next fight!" Volt yelled at Gaia as he started up himself.

Gaia jerked herself up upon hearing his voice, nodding. "Y-yes, you're right, hun!" She got off the ground and joined the other knights, gathering her mana as well.

Scourge placed his hand on his mask and began laughing again, even though it caused him pain. "Haha, they're still getting better. This is getting scary hahahahaha! I'll push even harder then! Congratulations knights, I'll be using seventy-five percent of my power now!" Scourge claimed as his mana flared up again, his aura nearly doubling in size as his mana began surrounding his body as extra armor, especially around his chest. His muscles also visibly grew larger as he powered up, causing him to look even more like a monster. His mana began to take a form of its own, resembling a giant demon that shadowed him like a ghost. "Let's shred em up Devo." Scourge said as he opened the palm of his hand and summoned Devora to his hands. Upon arriving, Devora began feeding off of Scourge's dark

mana and went through a transformation of its own. The hilt
and blade both grew twice their original size, with the latter
also employing a razor-sharp serrated edge as well. Each
'tooth' resembled that of a shark's, but infinitely more
devastating. That nasty evil aura returned to the blade as
well, showing at the curse was reactivated. Scourge stood
there now, waiting for the Knights to finish as well.

"Contact!" The knights all yelled as soon as Scourge
looked back up, causing another blinding flash to occur.
Scourge instinctually rose up Devora in front of him while
he was blinded, causing a loud clunk as a blade bounced off.
Scourge leaped back as he regained his vision. It was
Impulse before him who had tried to sneak and spear him
with his halbert. His white hair flowing freely as he floated
in the air for a moment.

"Heh. Not bad!" Impulse smirked as he began to
land.

Scourge's instincts told him motioned behind him
now, so he spun Devora around full force with a low swing.
He caught Syaris's zweihander just as he was to rise it up to
strike, pushing him back. Scourge now stood in the middle
between Impulse and Syaris. He flared his mana again to
deter them from approaching for a few seconds. Hehe, that's
right! My instincts are incredible when I use this much of
my power. It has been a while since I've had to get serious
like this. "ha. Come at me knights!" Scourge proclaimed
while looking back and forth between the two, holding
Devora up in front of him.

"K," Impulse obliged, walking forward with mana
spiraling around his hands. He spins his halbert around in his
hand. "Shadow boxing." He says as he tosses the halbert at
Scourge, slowly. "Lucin, grant me the power to strike down
all who oppose you!" Impulses hands both radiate
concentrated lightning mana before being surrounded by
darkness. Scourge swings his blade up, knocking the halbert

slighting in the air, but out of the way. Impulse immediately phased to his spear as it reached Scourge, sitting him low right in front of his target as both of his hands are in the air holding his sword. "Ringa Uira!" He shoved his hands forward, aiming for Scourge's chest with his dark lightning fist.

Scourge instinctually raised his left knee and moved his body off to the side a bit. His knee caught Impulse's right arm as the mana shoots forward past his normal range, past Scourge. He used his knee to separate the clenched hand with his left a bit and began lowering his elbow rapidly, aiming to break the arm. Inches away from making contact, his arm jolted to a stop as Syaris's sword caught inside one of the teeth of Devora, halting him entirely. Syaris shook his head at Scourge when he peered back at him. Scourge pushed his blade up a bit to throw Syaris off balance before releasing the hilt entirely and reaching up with his left hand. His hand connected with the center of Impulses halbert as he began turning his body to drive the blade towards Syaris, who noticed and immediately dashed back out of range just as he completes the full extension. Free now, Impulse also dashed back before summoning his halbert back to him, out of Scourge's hands. Scourge caught his own blade back and stared the two down all over again. The fight had pretty much reset.

"My my, you have good instincts and speed as well. That'll be difficult still. Perfect," Scourge said to himself out loud. He looked over at Syaris's flaming wings, which helped him to pull himself out quickly, then over to Impulse, who was also very quick with his combination of lightning and dark mana. The knights both readied their blades at Scourge.

"My, my this is intense," Wendy said as she stroked Keith's hair while he lied there, unconscious.

"Hmph." Scourge smirked as he flipped Devora over and digs it into the ground below him. "Curse zone," he said as mana suddenly pumped into the ground, pulsating out a wave of Devora's mana in a circular motion along the ground. It quickly passed under the knights just as they tried to jump back out of its range. "Too late!" Scourge yelled as the mana rose out of the ground and connected into a dome surrounding the three of them. The evil mana pulsated like a heartbeat along the translucent sides of the dome. Dark lightning traveled up and down the dome-like raindrops on a window.

"Argh," Impulse yelped as he bounced off of the lining of the dome, his back singed and smoking. The curse of Devora slowly creeping into the wound.

"What is this encasement? Guys, are you okay?" Syaris said, looking around himself, then over to his fellow knights.

Impulse looked over to Syaris, wincing. "Yeah, for now..." he responded as convincingly as he could.

Suddenly the whistling sound from before began to start up again. Scourge stood there with his head down, and two fingers pointed to the ground. The mana around his sat uneasily in his presence. "There, now there's nowhere to run and hide." He said as he raised his head to look at the two of him. The whistling sound grew faster as the mana gathering at the tip of his fingers became visible. "Now, die!" He pointed at Impulse and Syaris with both of his fingers, releasing the whistling barrage of mana at the two of them.

They immediately began dodging and jerking out of the way of the beams as Scourge kept them both on the run. Syaris burst out his wings and flew up in the air to avoid the attack watching as the beams crashed against the barrier behind him. Even flying around at full speed, he still got hit by the occasional stray ray. On the other side, Impulse used his quickness and lightning ability to dodge back and forth, but Scourge's mental prowess and foresight saw him gain the upper hand. He led Impulse and got used to his patterns, soon landing more and more blows. In both of their upgraded forms, the damage they took was reduced, but the beams of concentrated mana still were deadly if they took too many shots. With his left side, he eventually caught up with Syaris, blowing many holes in his flaming wings, thus causing him to crash back into the ground. On his right side, Impulse speed had slowed enough from the blows to his legs, that he could no longer dodge as effectively. Scourge stopped firing for the moment after he was immobilized, the two of them.

"And for the finish!" Scourge readjusted his posture before clapping his hands together and slamming them to the ground. "Devil Maiden." As he spoke, mana from the ground slowly took over the sides of the dome, before soon, the three of them were encased in total darkness.

"Impulse, we have to do something...now!" Syaris yelled across the room.

"Y-yeah." Impulse stuttered in response. But what damnit!? This is bad.

"Too late for that, unfortunately." Scourge offered his two cents. Small holes opened up in the inner side of the dome, shooting out red beams from all directions. These beams bounced off of the walls and came back to attack the knights.

"Ahhh, Damnittt!" Syaris yelled, trying to protect his body from getting destroyed from the dangerous beams of mana. He and Impulse both but up a protective aura around their bodies to absorb some of the damage, but they were still at their wits end, just trying to survive. Scourge's own body took a bit of damage from the beams, but not as much as the other two. Suddenly the size of the dome shrunk by about a foot, bringing that dangerous barrier a little closer and the beams as well. The pelting grew harder during this time. The inside of the dome sounded like the beating of a punching bag.

"Is that screaming? Damn, I hope those kids are alright in there," Wendy said, looking at the blackness before her.

The only light source inside was the flashing of red from the beams bouncing off of the walls, not enough to discern where anything was, however. "Tsk, if only I could find him, I could send an attack at him in this chaos, but...damn." Impulse trailed off while he refocused on protecting himself. The dome got smaller again by another foot, causing Impulse to take a few steps forward to avoid any further damage from the curse.

"Impulse! Throw a lightning attack down where you think the middle is. I'll light it up for us just a bit." Syaris yelled towards his partner.

Scourge stayed silent, controlling the flow of mana, on one knee in the center of the room. "Fine!" Impulse scattered lightning down through the center of the room, causing his right arm to get damaged badly from the beams as he switched his aura from defending to attacking.

Syaris peered ahead of him, with his own hands at the ready. "There! Take this!" He sent out a small but fast flame ahead of him towards Scourge, who he only caught a glimpse of from Impulses attack. "Flaming vortex!" Syaris said as the fire zoomed forward, connecting with Scourge, who was still kneeling in the center of the dome, and immediately exploded into a flaming tornado that spun at an angle directly on top of him. Even so, the beams seemed to continue firing, maybe even faster now. Syaris's body was damaged more than before as his defensive aura had faded. He stood there for a moment, taking the hits before he flared his spirit up, readying himself for an attack. Blood soon began to break all over his back and arms.

The flames had successfully brightened up the room for the two of them, but they were still in a predicament. Impulse looked over at Syaris getting beat on, as he kept his defensive aura on, holding his right hand, which was unusable at the time. "Hey! You okay!?" He yelled.

"Ahhhhhhh! Let's kill him, nowwww!" Syaris yelled with uncontrollable rage as he channeled Blaze's power to absorb the temper for an adrenaline rush and gather an enormous amount of mana quickly. He punched his own hand and tilted his body to the side. Blood had started coming down his head, blinding him in his right eye.

"Tsk. Fine, I guess now's the time." Impulse lowered his own defensive aura for a more aggressive one as he gathered his mana into his left hand. Darkness began spiraling down his arm, followed by lightning. His body also started to get punished by the beams, but his defensive abilities weren't nearly as high as his partners, so he pushed all of his mana into that hand as quickly as possible and dashed forward.

Scourge still remained in that same position, even with the flames spinning around him. "Heh. Let's see if you survive knights."

Syaris looked down at his right arm as the bright phoenix mana spiraled down it in surprise. This mana was much lighter and more intense than Blaze's normal flaming mana. "Hm, nice, I can access this mana even in this form." With the phoenix mana caressing his arm now numbing some of his pain, he looked straight up, his hands at his sides. "Okay. Here we go!" he said after a deep sigh. "Deities of the elements hear my call. Verafelt replenish my rage so that I may not fall. This fist of mine will hold my soul and my passion. Let it burn bright in the night to incinerate everything in sight!" After the chant, Syari's right arm glowed as bright as the sun, the mana nearly all absorbed into him.

"Hmmm, this might be kind of dangerous." Scourge said, eyes wide, in reaction to the spike in mana coming from Syaris.

Syaris now looked to his left arm, gathering even more mana there, but this time it was Gaia's. "I feel as if all of my mana is heightened now. A new chant just revealed itself to me." Syaris says, his eyes glowing for a moment. "Oh dear goddess Sylindra, mother, allow me to make my body a mere vessel to your infinite powers. Bless me with the powers of nature and the world around us. Bestow this fist with the power to send your enemies back to the dirt that they came from! This divine claw will annihilate all in our path as we are one! Tanrısal pençesi!" Resembling Gaia's earth claw, but a shining white instead, Syaris's left arm now glowed as well. Mana rushed off of his body as he soon rushed forward, both arms positioned behind him as he ran.

On the other side, Impulse was nearly done combining mana in his arm. "Hmm, Syaris is right, I can use heightened versions of my skills in this form much easier." Impulse smirked. "Shadow boxing." He said as his arm flashed and gained an extra layer of darkness. "Erupt and eradicate, shatter their hopes for they failed to embrace the goddess...and I will punish them. Kotahi Inazuma!" he said, holding his hand up towards Scourge as a huge exhaust of lighting mana came burrowing out of his hand surrounded and accompanied by oppressive darkness that slowed it a bit. What it gave up in speed, it gained in a considerable size boost, getting larger the further it traveled.

"Hmph. Okay, let's see if you'll succeed this time in killing me." Scourge said, pouring even more mana into his beams. Impulse's body really took a beating in this barrage, one of them also hit him in his eye, and another went through his stomach, burning a hole through him.

Just then, Syaris came out from beside him and rushed forward with his charged up fists. Scourge peered to

571

his side as soon as he saw him in his peripherals, but it was too late to react. "Take this!" He yelled as he shoved his phoenix fist into Scourge's chest. His fist connected just below his pectoral muscle on his left side. Releasing that built up mana in a rage that tore through Scourge's armor and body from that chunk over to the bottom, leaving a semi-circle opening in his body. Scourge's slight movement at the last second, allowed him to avoid instant death.

The wound began to burn away his flesh that came in contact with the mana still around his arm. "Tsk. Not done yet!" Syaris said as he pulled his right arm over to the side and came around with his left. This time, his punch landed directly in Scourge's solar plex. A devastating shockwave then ensued inside of Scourge's body as soon as that shining fist touched him. It was like an earthquake had just rocked him. All of his armor on his torso cracked and shattered away. Even Scourge's body began to crack and break apart, coming from the small crater left in the center of his chest.

Blood soon began trickling down from behind his mask as well before suddenly even his mask grew a giant crack right through the middle. The beams had stopped as Scourge's body stood straight up, his hands no longer touching the ground. Syaris pulled his hands back and jumped out of the way now. "Blerg. Damn…that was worse than the first one Gaia gave me...by so much." Scourge said, coughing up blood. As soon as he looked back up, he was met with the enormous blast of mana being released by Impulse. The mana immediately overtook him and blasted him back towards the walls of his dome.

"My my, that is a large amount of mana being released in there. It should be over soon," Wendy said, feeling the raging going on inside of that dome.

Just then, Keith eased his eyes open, looking up to Wendy. "Huh? What's going on?" He said, sitting up.

"Oh, so you're finally up! Did that mana wake you up?" Wendy questioned.

"Maybe. I don't really know," he responded, questioning it himself. "I'm guessing they are all in there?" he said.

"Yep, it should be over soon, though, I think," she said as a large crack echoed from the far side of the dome.

"Mmm. I see," Keith said.

A moment later, the entire dome cracked and shattered as Scourge's body was thrown through it from the remainder of Impulses attack. Scourge toppled back and landed on his stomach. His mask clanked onto the ground and spins a bit before eventually resting still and entirely breaking in half, right in front of Scourge, who reached out to it. Scourge's burn and battle ridden face were now exposed. What looked like ground meat and bone made up for his unappealing face in his instance. "My…mask…" He said as his entire body was cracking more and more slowly, light seeping out from below these cracks.

Back in the center, Impulse and Syaris both watched Scourge intently as they try to deal with the pain from their injuries. Both of their armors were beaten up. Impulse was holding his right arm again, his left eye still would not open, and the multiple injuries to his leg and back forced him to take this moment on one of his knees. Syaris stood a little better than Impulse with his added defense, but he too was still drained and hurt from the injuries along his back and head from the beams.

Scourge slowly crawled forward towards his mask. He wasn't without injury as well, with blood trailing the ground, his body missing a chunk of himself, and glowing so bright beneath the cracks of his skin so bright it was as if his soul about to explode out of his shell. "Such a shame, really." Scourge said as he grabbed his mask pieces and sat up a bit.

"Wow, that son of a bitch is still alive?" Wendy exclaimed as soon as she saw him lit up.

"And here I put so much mana into that..." Syaris said defeatist.

"Same." Impulse responsed with a loud sigh.

"It is such a shame you guys did not defeat me there, when you had the opportunity, Because now, now it's my turn." Scourge chuckles while looking into the eyes of his mask. "I know how to unleash my full power, and it's all thanks...to you," he said with a smile. His smile was actually visible now, and it was hard to look directly at his deformed face.

"How?" Syaris said.

"Welllll, hehehehe." Scourge could'nt help himself but laugh at this to Syaris, who looked at him seriously. "I still hold the souls of Strike and Adrian within me. Now, if I use your technique to fuse with them, I will become even stronger!" Scourge finished.

"What!?" Keith blurted out loud.

"Oh no, this is bad!" Wendy shouted upon hearing this. "Knights! You can't let that happen!" Wendy screamed as she gets up to run over there, but Keith stopped her and gets up himself instead. Keith wobbles to his feet and dashed forward a few steps.

"Light Grenade!" Keith threw three orbs of light that exploded on contact directly at Scourge as he ran closer, but it was too late. Two small spheres of darkness, resembling the elemental orbs that the knights all acquired, came out of each of his hands and forced their way into his chest. A gigantic tornado of darkness immediately surrounded Scourge after this catalyst had activated. The orbs hit the twister and exploded, but nothing changed. The mana, along with the evil aura within grew every second. Scourge's hideous laughter could also be heard from inside as the knights could do nothing but just wait. Dark lighting and soon flames began to spiral around the tornado as the moments passed.

Syaris went to stand next to the Impulse as they faced their imminent threat together. "Whatever comes out of there, we got this...right?" Impulse asked. He looked down to take a deep breath afterward, wincing in pain as he tried to get back to his feet, not letting go of his right arm for a second.

"Yeah...I hope so, if not us, then who else?" Syaris said as confidently as possible, trying to hide his own lack of breath.

Suddenly the tornado before them disbursed all at once, sending a giant cloud of dark mana in all directions, filling up the room. The blackness resembled Adrian's mávro péplo, but the mist was even thicker, making breathing harder as well. The knights could see nothing. In this complete darkness, the knights could only hear Scourge's laugh, which seemed even more terrifying now as his new massive aura accompanied it. An eerie screeching sound echoed through the throne room, growing closer by the moment. It sounded like someone was scraping a knife against the floor.

"We need some light here." Impulse said, sparking up his mana in his hand to reveal just enough to see his body. He was still on his one knee.

"Good idea." Syaris unleashed a flare as well. After three seconds, the light was snuffed out by the mana around them. Impulse's mana was also sucked away. "What the hell?" He said in confusion. I guess it is Adrian's mana, as I figured. Blaze added, finally understanding the situation.

"I'll do it once more so we can determine his location before the light gets eaten away." Impulse said, sparking up again. The screeching still getting closer in front of them. He then quickly shoots it off in the air forward, slowly illuminating the room in this path. About six meters out, the knights were introduced to a fearsome sight for just a moment. Underneath the massive shadow aura, Scourge had grown twice his size. He was now over ten feet tall, hunched over dragging a long Scythe along the ground with one hand, an enlarged Devora over his other shoulder, resting evenly over his extra broad shoulders.

After this quick sight, there was a long pause between the knights in the darkness. The screeching was close now, and they still hadn't responded yet. "Ha. Ha. Ha. Ha." A deep, voiced Scourged started chuckling. His voice was extra close now, causing Impulse to jolt back a step and ready his Halbert to toss. With his one good hand, he reared again and leaped into the air.

"Back off!" he yelled, twisting his hips to start throwing his weapon. The next sound heard from that side was a loud bang as Impulse slammed into the ceiling and back down to the ground with a solid thud.

"Impulse! You okay? What was that?" Syaris yelled, firing blasts of fire before him randomly. The small semblance of light showed Scourge's hand up into the air, dark mana smoking off of his hand, and Impulse face down on the ground.

"Ack…my ribs, I-I can't move," Impulse said, talking into the ground, breathing heavily. "It was a silent, dark blast. It was so quick, I couldn't even defend," he continued coughing a bit afterward.

"Remember, try your best not to revert forms now. It is highly unlikely we'll have the power to contact fuse again if we get knocked out of it!" Syaris yelled.

"Easier said than done." Impulse responded while struggling against his pain to get up, unsuccessfully.

Suddenly. Syaris's body tensed up all of a sudden. He grabbed his long blade and held it to his side, his hands slightly trembling. Shit, all he did was focus his bloodlust in my direction, and my body won't listen to me already?

Damnit. "Let's finish this!" he said, feigning confidence. His blade starts glowing bright white as a rock hard earth armor shell began collecting around his body. The size of his blade's white aura nearly doubled in size as mana began collecting around it. As the blade cooled, it slowly started to glow a bright golden color. He rose the sword high above his head. The light that is released from the blade illuminated the area around them. Scourge immediately rushed at Syaris, his scythe drawn to his side; Devora stabbed into the ground. His scythe wore a shadowy and seemed to move way too freely in Scourge's hands. "Divine Divide!" Syaris said as he lowered his blade towards Scourge, slicing at the ceiling along the way.

"Heh, my shadows are too strong for your light!" Scourge smiled as the shadowy mana groped his body as well, allowing him to phase through Syaris's mana with his body and his Scythe as well as if he wasn't there. Syaris's eyes widened more and more, and the blade on Scourge's scythe grew closer and closer to his body. "Die!" Scourge went in for the kill with the edge of the cutter up towards his enemy's chest. Syaris let go of the hilt of his blade and shifted his body to the right slightly at this time.

"Urghhh…mmff…shit.," Syaris grunted as the tip of the scythe's blade easily slipped past his armor and landed itself into his chest, right above his last rib. A loud sloshing sound aired as blood began falling down his side. The noise was so loud, it caused even Impulse to raise his head.

"S-syaris!" Impulse eked out.

"Hmph! You act as if you've never seen this shadow blade technique before. Way too easy!" Scourge chuckled as he watched Syaris's body quiver, his head aimed down at the blade inserting his body.

Syaris slowly raised his head to face Scourge, blood trickling out of the side of his mouth. "Don't worry, I have seen it, which is why I know a way to defeat it," Syaris said with a smile as he wrapped his left arm around Scourge's right, which held the scythe in him. He reached his other hand up directly in Scourge's face. "Now, you can't phase away from this attack while we're connected like this!" he said, gathering mana in his hand.

Scourge raised his free hand up and aimed it at the other side of Syaris, his sharp claws ready to rip him apart. "I hope this was worth it for you because I'm about to tear your body in half!" Scourge yelled, his hand flexing like it couldn't wait.

"Not if I can help it! Mercy's shift!" Impulse managed to raise his hand and create a portal along the path of Scourge's hand before closing it around his elbow, effectively severing his forearm.

"Ahhhh hahaha not ba—" Scourge started.

"Oh, great lords grant me the power to create the ultimate destruction, kneel before the power of lord Verafelt, Molten Nova Blast!" Syaris cut Scourge off with a massive burst of dense fiery mana exhausting in his face at point-blank.

"Hahahahaha." Scourge chuckled as the smoke cleared from the blast. Even more, burns were over his face, but he was still intact.

Syaris was breathing heavily with his hand still up towards Scourge's face. He looked up, noticeably annoyed, grumbling. He then fired another molten nova blast from his hands, then another, and another. After each burst, Scourge emerged laughing at Syaris's face. "Tsk. Damnit!" Syaris yelled, shooting off six more blasts in a row. The ceiling above them had a large hole in it now, rubble tumbling out of the opened after each explosion. Syaris was huffing and puffing at this point, the blood loss making these attacks difficult.

"Are we done yet?" Scourge held up the arm with the cut off forearm as the links of dark mana in his one arm start to rise up and reattach before eventually his hand was recreated. He flexed his hand, cracking his knuckles before rearing his hand back and stabbing his razor-sharp claws into his shoulder. A small splatter of blood came backward, all over Scourge's forearm.

Syaris flinched but kept his hand up nonetheless. "Ek, I still have... one more idea," he said, pausing in the middle to catch his breath. The water mana around his hand, creating the water claw dissipated as he turned his hand palm up, revealing his bare hand. His hand remained in this position for a moment before suddenly, four small sparkles of mana came from his body and floated around his open palm. One for each of the elements that resided in his body. The red, green, blue, and brown sparkles collided together in the middle to reveal a head-sized transparent elemental orb with different manas swimming throughout. "Hope you're ready for this!" Syaris yelled as he crushed the sphere in his hands. The shell of the orb broke, but the mana remained localized around the same area, half of which absorbing into his hand. The rest floated around his hand, moving when his hand did.

"Hmmm? What is this? Some new trick?" Scourge mocked while twisting his fingers in his foe's wound.

Syaris took a moment to hide the pain from his face to look at Scourge seriously. "Luven Vorldo!" The cloud of mana instead of slowly drifting like before locked onto Scourge's mana and zoomed towards him, absorbing into his body instantly.

Scourge chuckled after a moment of no effect on his body. "Haha, what was that? Worthles- Hmm, that's odd." He stopped himself as blood randomly started trickling down the side of his mouth. "What is this reaction? I don't even feel anything, this is odd…" He said as blood came down the other corner of his mouth now. Suddenly small mana explosions started occurring from within his body and appeared on the surface. The finely laid plated scales along his legs began bursting out with blood one after another, all under his armor. This chain reaction brought its way up through his torso, arms, and finally exploding at the top of his neck. When it hit his arms, Syaris released his grip on Scourge's arm, and Scourge's other hand slipped out of the flesh as the small explosions pushed him back a step. "Agghhhh Nooooo!" Scourge yelled as cracks formed on his face and starting bursting forward with blood. Scourge's head reared again in pain, his arms flopping back at his side.

Syaris stared down Scourge as his own arms both dropped to his sides, without the strength to put pressure on his wounds. Blood flowed freely down his torso. Breathing heavily, Syaris raised up his right fist fire mana surrounding it. After an extra deep breath, he punched his own wound in his side with the concentrated flames. He winced, nearly passing out from the pain, but stood his ground. When he pulled back his fist, his wound was burned shut, stopping the bleeding, effectively cauterizing it. He then did the same with the wound in his shoulder, burning that one shut as well. "At least, that's over now," Syaris said to himself, looking up to Scourge's body, which was teetering back about to fall over. The dome of dark mana started to come apart, starting from the top, letting the light sneak back into the area.

Wendy and Keith's eyes both opened wide as they can view the battle again. "Did you get em?" Impulse asked, looking up while still on his chest.

"Knights!" Wendy yelled as the dark mana was nearly gone.

"I… I think so," Syaris said, his arms back to flopping freely at his sides and looking at the still Scourge, unmoving.

"Heh. Sike!" Came from Scourge's body as dark mana started rushing quickly away from him, causing a gust of wind and blowing open the door in the back. "I won't be dying so easily, unfortunately!" Scourge swung his head back to normal and reared back his right arm, pushing it forward with the intent to crush his head. Syaris hadn't the time to even move at this moment as he could only watch as the claws rushed towards his face.

Suddenly, a blade made of pure ice stabbed into Scourge's right hand, coming in from seemingly nowhere at all. Scourge stopped to examine the blade curiously. "Where the hell did this come from?" he said, looking at everyone within the room, noticing no one had made any movements.

Syaris looked up at the blade as well and immediately understood when it started pulsating with mana, absorbing it from Scourge's arm. "That blade…Oh shit," he said as he dashed back a reasonable distance, grabbing Impulse along the way and rejoining Wendy and Keith.

"Mana pulse." A voice said from outside of the room. Scourge looked around to try and find the origin. He also tried to swing the sword out of his hand by waving it around before giving up. "O' great deity of the earth, allow me the use of your mana to surround thy enemies with your cold embrace. Arrest and freeze under the weight of the Goddess's mercy, Krajnji zatvor!" The blade, which was glowing previously suddenly, nearly instantly expanded into a giant block of ice, Scourge's body was trapped inside the block, his mana suppressed and a slight mist of ice hovered about.

Syaris looked towards the door now as he felt a presence approaching. "Hail…" He said, trailing off as the two doors swung open dramatically. A fully healed Hail came bursting through the doors with Scatha on his flank.

"Hey, what'd I miss?" Hail said, surprisingly serious as he reached the rest of the knights. He walked with a different level of confidence as before, whether it was real or fake had still yet to be determined.

Chapter 23: The Ultimate Light

-Year 277   Scourge's castle, Throne Room

Shadow Path, Umbra-

Scatha immediately ran over to Impulse and started healing his wounds first. "Oh, noo hun, you're hurt in there, don't worry, I still have a little mana left to heal you," she said as she released her mana around the two of them without waiting for a response.

Syaris's face scrunched up for a moment at the sight of this, but returned to normal shortly after, almost as if an internal battle had happened quickly. "A lot Hail how is your body?" he said.

Hail felt himself up and down. "Pretty good, actually. Scatha did a good job. She saved me and a lot of other lives out there too," he said, looking over at her with a genuine smile on his face, rare for Hail.

"Speaking of, Sky speaking, what's the situation like on the outside?" Syaris asked in response.

"Well, we don't have much time to talk because that ice will not hold him for long, but I'll try to make it short." Hail said, rubbing his hands together. "And after that, I think I have a way to defeat this thing!" he said eagerly.

"Well, get talking, son!" Wendy stepped in to say as she heard the first cracks of the ice in Scourge's direction.

"Okay, okay, so with the absence of the dark generals, the battle is pretty much over outside. Between Hepheaus and Will's leadership, our forces were able to clean up the shadows fairly easily after a lot of Silverwing

582

soldiers suddenly whittled away," Hail said, looking up to think quickly.

"What abou—" Impulse started.

"OH! And your girl Scatha is amazing! Not only did she save my life by healing my wounds. She also healed Jax, who was also in critical condition at the time as well. Plenty of other soldiers owe their lives to her as well. So, all is well there. We owe Will too 'cause I heard he did help guard our bodies…" Hail started to trail off, but Scatha had already begun to blush.

Impulse gave her a quick one-armed hug after she finished healing him, pulling her closer. "Good job Scatha," he said, making her smile. She could sense Volt in there. The ice cracked again, louder this time, even starting to rumble afterward.

"Anything else? Times short, it seems." Syaris said, looking at the ice.

"Oh, right!" Scatha went over to Syaris to heal some of his wounds as well.

"Heh. Not you, but it's okay," he said, shaking his head a bit.

"Yeah, right." Hail started up again. "While I was in my small coma, Grandmaster came to me in my dreams to relay a message," he said, thinking.

"Uh, huh?" Syaris said with a huge crack splitting down the center of the ice, causing everyone to shake a bit.

"And he said that we all can contact into one ultimate being," Hail said as his right hand started glowing with mana.

"How would we manage that? We are barely able to gather enough mana to fuse four of us together, let alone seven…" Syaris said with Impulse nodding right after.

Hail held up his pointer finger from his right hand, glowing with mana. "Not without a little help! He instilled a symbol to use as a catalyst for the fusion. Apparently, it was

583

used in the past to create the being known as the Knight of Destiny. Each iteration is different, of course, but this one may be the most powerful if we can hone our skills. We need to do it from our base forms, though, so you've got to defuse first," Hail said as another large crack burst through the ice. There wasn't much time left now.

"Why didn't you say that before? It was taking everything in us to keep these up," Syaris said as a bright flash of light ensued, out came Blaze, Sky, Gaia, and Ocean, all drained. Impulse also followed suit, Volt, and Void almost collapsing from the lack of mana. Scatha caught Volt before he toppled over.

"Oh shit I'm beat, how are we gonna find the mana to do this fusion, we can barely even stand at this point," Blaze said, huffing and puffing.

Hail pulled out a light blue gem from his pocket and placed it in the ground off to the side. "One more thing. This is from Hepheaus. She says she uses it to replenish her mana as she uses so much to keep up her movements," he said as the gem glows in place.

"Damn, so she did bring those with her. I think we'll be okay guys; those gems are made by my people. They allow you to gather massive amounts of mana from the world around you in one place. I just can't believe she brought an extra one with her," Ocean said with newfound confidence.

"Oh, it wasn't extra. She gave it to me and then immediately collapsed. She's entrusting us more with it now, so let's not let her down ey?" Hail started drawing the symbols in the ground with his hand of mana. Ocean's eyes went low for a second, but he looked back up and nodded at Hail.

Just then, the ice shattered and exploded as a gigantic roar filled the ears and souls of the knights in the room. Scourge was free and not happy. "Gaaaaahhh! I'm done playing around with you ants!" Scourge screamed; his demonic mana radiated uncontrollably around him as he stomped forward.

"Shit!" Sky said, looking over at Scourge, staring at all of them.

"S-scatha? Is that you!? What are you doing with them?" Scourge's voice boomed like a disappointed and angry father.

"Um." Scatha immediately hid behind Volt, unable to find the words.

"What did you do to my baby?" Scourge was really angry now as he dashed at Volt with incredible speed.

"Damnit!" Hail stopped drawing as he heard Scourge and put six ice barriers up between Scourge and Volt, even dashing in front of Volt himself. Scourge's rush didn't slow a second as he immediately smashed through the obstacles and rammed his fist into the last barrier Hail put on himself. He broke that too, sending Hail flying into Volt and the both of them flying into the wall.

"Are you okay, Scatha? What did they do to you?" Scourge said, standing in front of Scatha. The rest of the knights couldn't even rise to step to Scourge at this point. Scatha silently shook her head in the presence of Scourge.

"Ack. Damn, does no one else have mana left at all? I need to finish this symbol," Hail said, getting up from the pile of rubble holding his side. He had cracked ribs already.

"Guess it's my turn again?" Keith said, willing himself up, with Wendy trying to keep him down.

"Don't push yourself too much, I'll hold him off," Wendy said, hobbling up a few steps. This caused Keith to pop right up and walk towards her. Blaze held up his Red Chariot for Keith to take before getting there. Keith grabbed it and nodded a thank you as he stood at her side. Scourge looked over at the two of them curiously, not taking his attention off of his daughter for a second.

Hail nods to himself as he hobbles himself and Volt over towards the circle. "We don't need that much time, just keep him off of us for a second," Hail said, waving the knights to make their way in his direction off to the side.

"Don't worry, I'll kill every single one of these germs who infected my daughter, and I'll take you back with me." Scourge said, flaring up his mana.

"But, they didn't…" Scatha got out with her small voice.

"Shhh, don't worry. You don't have to say anything!" Scourge said, staring Keith down. "You think you're a match for me now, boy? When you couldn't do anything, those many moons ago could you?" Scourge laughed.

Keith peered back at Wendy, who was behind him slightly now. "Keep her enhancement mana on me, I need to be able to survive his blows for a minute," he said seriously. Keith then lined his own mana onto the Red Chariot before it disappeared in his hand. He spun his now invisible blade in his hand a bit to get a feel for the weight of it.

"You ready, hun?" Wendy said with mana engulfing both of her hands now.

Keith took a big sigh. "Yeah." The knights had now gathered around as Hail drew the symbols on the ground with his glowing hand. The symbol turned into what looked like two seven-pointed stars melded together with a circle around it. As he drew, the gem in the center of it began to glow more and more.

"Kind of rusty at enhancements, so don't blame me if you die!" Wendy said as she shoved her hands ahead of her towards Keith. The mana on her hands transformed from blue to green to brown to white before finally leaving her and surrounding Keith all at once, infusing him with her own aura.

"Woah! This power is insane!" Keith shouted as he summoned his light mana to test his ability. He then created ice armor out of mana along his body. His armor was as heavy as Will's warriors, restricting movement a bit, but protecting his body. His armor glowed an off white-yellow, wholly made of mana. Keith stepped forward with an invisible Red Chariot before him, aimed at Scourge.

"I hope that armor will allow you to last past at least one attack, or this will be a very quick intermission. I don't plan to let the knights do what they want any longer. So stay down, will ya?" Scourge snickered as he charged forward at Keith. Wendy moved over to the side when Scourge made his move.

Scourge reached forward with his massive claw, swiping towards Keith's head, but was blocked by Keith's invisible blade. The impact still pushed Keith back several meters from what was a light attack from Scourge. The sword rattled along with his armor and, in turn, his body afterward. This stunned Keith for a moment eventually, making it so he couldn't move until the shaking stopped. "Oh, boy. He's pretty strong right now. I've gotta be careful not to take any more major damage," Keith said, almost sweating again.

Suddenly Scourge charged again with both hands full of dark mana. "Dark mines!" He shouted as he tossed the mana he held towards the ground below Keith, creating massive dark explosions in its wake.

"That attack…" Keith said, leaping up and out of the way at the last moment to avoid the explosions. The darkness from the explosion like a vengeful ghost even reached up further like it was trying to reach him.

"Heh. Recognize that? It's from the other you!" Scourge said, chasing Keith in the air while he pulled out his scythe in a wave of darkness. The wave flew past Keith as he contorted his body to dodge it midair and held his invisible blade back, aimed at Scourge.

"Tsk. Of course, I do, I'd never be hit by my own move!" Keith shouted as a flash of mana radiated over the invisible Red Chariot, giving it a halo. "Saseon Flash!" Keith swung his blade in a flurry directly down at Scourge, sending out shockwaves of light and wind mana. Scourge lifted his Scythe above his face to block the barrage as it pushed him back to the ground and kept going even after he landed. A small cloud of dust formed around him as the shockwaves that missed crashed into the field around him. On his way towards the ground, Keith tossed the sword towards Scourge's hand and knocked the scythe from his grasp.

"What?" Scourge said, looking up towards Keith with no weapon in his hand. The barrage had stopped, though, so he shrugged off the minimal amount of damage and swiped his claws towards his enemy. He then rested the blade on his back and opened his arms wide. Keith drops towards Scourge with a giant ball of mana gathering in his right hand. The mana was at least twice the size of his head and spiraled more violently the more it spun. The mana also radiated a bright, blinding white light as it turned, temporarily blinding all onlookers, including Scourge. He swiped up at Keith blindly as Keith fell towards him. In the middle of this sequence, Keith teleported at light speed to the ground behind Scourge. The mana in Keith's hand had condensed into the size of a pebble in his palm as he stood back to back with Scourge. It took Scourge a second before he noticed and started to spin his body around.

"Too late!" Keith said, spinning around faster than Scourge, with both hands cradling the mana he held as he pushes it towards Scourge's back. "Ileun Flash!" Keith said as he shoots a beam of energy at Scourge's back. The beam of light burns Scourge's back, but only pushed him forward a few feet. Even so, Keith flips back to make the distance between the two. A few seconds later, a light-based explosion echoes through the throne room, originating from where the beam of light hit him. Scourge flinched forward slightly from the impact, although it was a pretty massive explosion on his back.

"Haaahh. Is that all!" Scourge yelled, quickly recovering from the explosion.

Keith flinched as he felt Scourge's murderous intent being released. He immediately leaped into the air, Wendy's mana still increasing his mana charge time, and defense, facing Scourge with both hands shining white. The mana in his hands quickly radiated with heal like a microwave as he raised his hands up near his face, palms facing down towards Scourge. "Tsk, try this! Solar Flar—" he started with confidence.

Scourge had appeared before Keith in the air, with his hand tightly gripping both of Keith's wrists just as his attack was ready to release. He forcibly lowered both of Keith's hands to the sides as Keith looked at him, nervous. Before he knew it, sweat began dripping down Keith's forehead as the two of them made eye contact. Scourge's ugly mug smiled, and head-butted Keith with incredible force, immediately breaking through the armor around his head and knocking him out before he could react. Blood also sprayed out of his head like a slash wound after the impact. Keith's body went limp as Scourge lowered them to the ground holding Keith up only by his wrists. Scourge then let's go of Keith's limp left wrist and raises his hand to spear Keith in the chest. He pulls his sharp claws back, ready to strike before Keith pops into consciousness, randomly shaking his head.

This sudden action slowed Scourge's reaction time. Keith took advantage and grabbed Scourge's wrist that still held him down with his free hand. He then leaped up with a foot on either side of Scourge's chest and used his mana to blast away from Scourge's grips. "Whew, that was close. Think my head would have been caved in if not for this armor." Keith said, propelling himself higher into the air away from Scourge. He pulled the Chariot from behind him as he saw Scourge gathering mana in the space between his two hands in a dark ball. Keith reared the blade back at his waist while he was still in the air, he was ready. Come on, you ugly fucker, about to send whatever you throw at me right back at you.

"Dark snare!" Scourge released his mana forward, but instead of a blast, his mana sprouted out like a flurry of dark chains aimed towards Keith. Keith, his mana encased around the blade, swung it forward toward the dark chains ahead of him. The chains suspiciously dodged Keith's swing and turned around to his backside.

"No way!?" Keith said, shocked and caught off guard as he missed entirely with his swing.

"Did you think i wouldn't learn from the past!" Scourge yelled. The chains of mana all pelted into Keith's back and arms, drawing blood and propelling Keith forward toward Scourge.

"S-shit...Ouch." Keith released the blade in his pain, not able to move his body at all as he was pulled towards Scourge, who had his massive fist reared back and ready to attack.

A wave of mana pulsed underneath Scourge as he prepared his fist for its target. "Midnight, Fist!" Scourge's fist suddenly spiraled with dark mana as soon as it went on the move towards Keith. In one motion, he stuffed his fist into Keith's stomach, shattering the armor and connected with his body as he focused his body towards the ground.

"Ughhh, ughhh." Keith made noises as his body failed him. The chains disappeared upon contact, and a small flash was released when Keith's armor was broken, but

Scourge fought through the weak light and pummeled Keith's body into the ground. The ground at Scourge's feet crashed, nearly exploding with the impact alone. The effect on his stomach caused Keith to spit up blood as all the air in his chest was forced out in an instant, leaving him breathless and unconscious again.

Keith's body flopped to the ground unceremoniously as Scourge stood over his body, laughing. Wendy's mana disappeared from around him entirely, leaving him unprotected. Scourge shook his head while he looked down at his fallen enemy. "Your effort was nice, but a waste. You can die now…" Scourge raised his hand into the air and summoned Devora, aiming the cursed blade directly down at Keith's chest. "Goodbye, Keith." Scourge lowered Devora towards Keith.

A bright, aggressive light exploded from off to the side of Scourge, effortlessly jerking his body off to the side, throwing him off his balance. The force of the light shot back past him shaking the rest of the room as well. "What the hell is that!?" Scourge looked over to where the knights were previously as a huge, bright orb of mana now resided there. The light was more brilliant and lasted longer than any contact fusion light in the past, causing a sustained amount of damage to his eyes as the moments passed.

"Oh, thank goodness." Keith and Wendy said simultaneously as they breathed a sigh of relief.

"They're still in there? Exactly what did they just do? This looks bad," Scourge said to himself, looking at the light. As the star shone, Scourge noticed everything seemed to move in slow motion. His movements were delayed, the wind even seemed to lag as it blew through the openings in the ceiling.

Even his breathing felt slower, also though he was sure he was breathing normally. Then all at once, everything had stopped. Scourge couldn't move his body, he couldn't breathe, it took everything in him to rotate his eyes to look around. The life in the rest of the room had also paused. Wendy and Keith were also immobile. The debris that had been blowing around from the wind had stopped tumbling in midair. What is this sensation I feel? I need to get out of here. Scourge immediately puts pressure on himself to break away from this trance. He tensed all of the muscles in his body using his massive amount of mana to push forward before sensing something coming from his left, towards the light. The brightness had begun to fade a small amount, but this isn't what concerned Scourge, however. A slight sparkle flashed for a second from the center of the shining light causing Scourge to pour his mana in and around his body rapidly until- Clinkkkk! As if breaking through a single sheet of glass, the effects of the time-slowing were broken for Scourge as he jolted his entire body backward.

A single vertical wave of mana suddenly sliced through where Scourge's body just resided, half a second after he moved. It sliced cleanly through the ceiling and the floor and through the wall and beyond. The powerful mana left an afterimage afterward as if trying to catch up to the quickness of the light. Scourge looked at the destruction the mana caused and then back to the light as it finally receded to reveal Scourge's next fight. What was shown from this light is what could only be described as a majestic being. This new fusion wore all golden armor seemingly made from the mana of the Gods. It glistened so hard it created its own light. From the spiked helm to his two smooth finished gauntlets, which led up to heavy shoulder guards and down to his pristine heavily plated grieves, his armor was engraved in the ancient text. This text ran up and down the sides of the armor, describing different Royal Knights of the past. The knight had grandiose golden wings on his back, rising high into the sky behind him. Their golden feathers occasionally fell off and hovered towards the ground, blessing it with magnificent mana. The top and front of his wings were plated with golden armor as well. The heavy shoulder guards were sat lightly on a lighter chest piece with a single gem in the center, glowing brightly.

"So beautifully done. I almost want to tear up," Wendy said, wiping off her eyes. Her and Scatha helped move Keith over to the side out of the way. Scatha used her mana to create a demonic barrier around them.

Symbols representing each of the knights were also curved into his armor in different places: Sky's pinwheel was on his wing plates, Blaze's flame on the gauntlets, Void's spiral on the chest, and Ocean's water droplet sat on the shoulder pads alongside Gaia's rock. Hail's icicle rested at the sides of the grieves, and Volt's thunderbolt was on the center of the forehead of his helm. The knight was positioned with a massive golden sword dug into the ground ahead of him, mana freshly smoking off of the backside of the blade. His sword had a short hilt with a star-shaped piece on end. Both wrist guards pointed downwards and were very narrow with sacred cloth wraps sashed around the center portion. The guards seamlessly transitioned into the bottom of the blade, which extended out six or seven feet while staying relatively narrow. A silver lining found itself along the edge all the way around. Inside of this, towards the center of the blade, was a small indent that made a rectangle sunken in. On this indent was a dragon carved out of gold flowing down the length of the blade. The entire sword radiated with its own light mana, almost like a pulse. "Ahhhh, I'm surprised you were able to dodge that attack. Good job, but you won't be able to defeat us any longer, I can feel it," the knight said, looking at both of his hands.

Scourge, slightly jumbled, got to his feet quickly, staring the knight down intently. "What...are you?" Scourge asked lowly.

The knight noticed Scourge's question but then focuses his attention back on himself. "I believe I am called the Knight of Destiny, Fatum. For the time I'm able to borrow this body, I'll destroy you and end all of your ambitions, Scourge!" he said, focusing his attention on Scourge now with his fist clenched. I've got to make this quick. I don't think our mana will hold in this ridiculous body.

Scourge readied himself and rushed at Fatum with his sword and scythe in either hand, grumbling in anger. "No matter the new transformation! You're still no match for me knights!" he yelled.

"We'll see…heh." Fatum chuckled while gesturing for the dark mercenary to attack him. And attack Scourge did. A few seconds was all it took for the flurry of attacks to reign down in the Destiny Knight's direction. Clad ultra-powerful darkness, Devora and a dark scythe sliced at the open air as the knight effortlessly dodged out of the way of each strike. Fatum's movements were graceful and light, waving through the darkness like aurora lights. Each feint was at the last possible second, causing his foe to use the most energy.

Scourge, frustrated, slams both of his weapons into the ground, digging the blades through the stone. "Don't mock me!" he yelled, leaping up, dark mana gathering in the area around him. The mana became especially thick and hovered in a cloud around his head. "Unstoppable darkness!" He chanted as pointed arrow tips made from his mana protrude from the sides of the cloud.

"That move…Adrian, huh," Fatum said to himself, mostly. He then pulled his elegant blade before him and stabbed it into the ground. A pulse of light mana radiated outwards, encompassing the entirety of the throne room. This brightened up the area significantly, trumping the darkness Scourge emitted from himself as he was

594

suspended, surrounded. "Infinite light works." He points a single finger into the air. Blades made of his intense mana all rise from the ground within this throne room simultaneously. The swords all glowed like fireflies, and each one was different.

Not wanting to get caught off guard, Scourge sent forth the infinite stream of dark arrows, which rushed forward like little heat-seeking missiles. The knight of Destiny did not flinch at all, however. Instead, the blades that now surrounded both of them wiggled their way free, their target set on Scourge. The two-stream of blades clashed in the middle, but before long, the dark arrows started losing ground. "Tsk. His mana is ridiculous. Can't win this way," he said, converting himself into a shadow and retreating into the ground to avoid the overpowering swords of light. He made sure to suck away his weapons with him as well. The extra blades flew past him and found their way through the ceiling.

"Since when did you turn into a coward, Scourge?" The Destiny Knight shouts as he looked around for his shadow, blades of light at the ready.

"Coward? No." Scourge's voice echoed throughout the room as he traveled through his shadow on the ground behind Fatum. "Smart? Yes!" Scourge confidently rose out the shadow behind the knight, scythe aimed for his neck.

"You so sure?" Fatum said, clenching his hand around Scourge's wrist, stopping the scythe's blade inches from his face.

Scourge was frozen with fear as Fatum grabbed the hilt of his blade and pulled it upwards, severing Scourge's left arm that held the scythe. Scourge's blood sprayed out wildly as he dashed backward out of range. "Aggghhh." He yelped, holding the nub tightly with his other hand. "You'll pay for tha-." Scourge stopped himself in his fit of rage. His enemy had risen the blade directly into the air, straight upwards. He watched the light mana fill in around the sword and phase backward like an echo while it lowered back down towards him. A burst of mana exploded towards the demon so fast that Scourge's last-second dodge still burned the side of his only remaining arm. He skidded to the side and kneeled there a moment, getting himself together. "Shit...what do I have to do? Think, think..." Scourge thought out loud to himself.

"Had enough yet?" The knight of Destiny squatted low with his legs spread, and shifted his arms to the side, his hands slightly parted. In the next few moments, mana began gathering in this area, similar to Volt's Inazuma. The mana here was different, though. Not only was it light mana, but it also spiraled into place with a sort of anger and rush to it. "That'll probably be the end, goodbye, Scourge," he said, almost done gathering the massive amount of mana already.

"Come at me, knights! Give me your worst!" Scourge said confidently, leaving himself completely open.

"As you wish! Eternal light!" Fatum pressed his hands forward, shooting the massive collection of light mana towards his enemy. The strength of the blast pushed him back a few feet. It closed the distance exceptionally quickly.

The dark demon let out one of his signature, evil smiles as he summoned Devora into his hand. "You fool! This is my win!" He reared back his body, almost in a batter's stance, except using only one arm to hold the sword. His dark mana immediately filled Devora, extending up past the tip of the blade two times over. The hilt quivered in his hand from the sheer volume of mana being transferred. The blast of white mana was directly in front of him now, moving was no longer an option. "Skoúro..." he started with the hilt still shaking.

The Knight of Destiny's eyes opened wide when he recognizes the stance that Scourge was performing. "Oh, no!" He lets out, his voice low.

"Kýma!! Scourge yelled as the mana on his blade reached its peak. He twisted his body and swung Devora at the blast of mana. Remnants of mana scraped off as the side of his blade collided with the light before him. For a moment, the two were at a standstill. Neither Scourge nor the blast would give any ground. "Grrr, I will not lose this!" The dark mercenary shouted. The mana from his blade began expanding and shrouding the light mana like the jaws of a snake on prey. This created a dark cocoon around the light that slowly crept down the blast towards Fatum. "T-there we go!" he said, finally gaining ground as he forced the blast backward. The darkness had taken over half of the light in only a few seconds. With a final push, Scourge fully swung his blade to the other side, reversing the flow of mana in the process, sending the light and dark blast towards the knights quickly.

"Tsk. Damn." Fatum put his arms up in front of him to protect himself, having to abandon his own attack. The mana slammed into the knight's arms, forcing him back quickly. His back crashed through one of the pillars and a foot into a wall behind him before he finally stopped. A cloud of debris and smoke fills the area around his impact.

"How do ya like that?" Scourge taunted while walking towards the center of the room.

"Knights…" Wendy said, worried. A couple moments passed as everyone in the room all stared at the smoke.

"Well…" Fatum's voice could be heard from amidst all the smoke.

Scourge raised his sword, making sure he was ready for anything. "Tsk. I knew it wouldn't be enough.

"Can't say I'd like to take another one of those." The knight walked out of the smoke with both of his arms raised up at eye level. The armor around both forearms had been destroyed, even his skin underneath was burned and heavily damaged.

Scourge looked intently at his enemies' injuries before drawing his blade again. The mana crept right back up the sides of the blade as it did before. "Time to finish the job. Shadow Slicer." The mana began flowing down the edge of Devora like black flames.

"My thoughts exactly." Fatum winced as he summoned his blade back into his hands. The pain in his palms was evident, but he pushed past it to grip the hilt of his sword properly. He pushed his own light mana through the blade, creating a streak that followed the blade when it moved. He bent his knees and positioned the edge to the side, in a slashing stance. "Deflect this!" he said, disappearing in a flash of light.

"What? Oh!" Scourge's instincts applied again, seemingly pulling his head and body downwards in an ugly duck attempt. It worked though as a flash of light appeared behind Scourge, with it a giant wave of sharp light mana flew above him and through the ceiling. The Knight of Destiny's body appeared a second later, arched sideways in full swing.

"Damn, thought I had you that time! Fatum landed behind Scourge and starts swinging his blade again, going for kill shots each time. I almost forgot; my mana is practically out for this form. I've got to hurry!

"That all you got?" Scourge said, using his instincts and shadows to effortlessly dodge each swipe of his blade.

"Not yet!" Fatum takes a handoff his blade to shoot out a blast at mana at Scourge's feet, causing him to stumble backward. He then leaps into the air, gripping his sword tightly with both hands. "Divine divide!" He shouted as his blade's mana shot up into the sky, blasting through the ceiling, tearing holes through it further as he soared forward.

Scourge tumbled on his butt and held his sword up hesitantly. He looked around, knowing there isn't time to dodge, or anywhere to go. The realization grew on his face quickly as he realized he would have to take this attack from his enemy. The nervousness turned to determination, then pure resolve. He gritted his teeth and looked up at the knights as they tore through the castle's ceiling on the way to him. "I...will...not...die!" Scourge screamed from the bottom of his tongues as the shining blade of mana lowered towards his level, cutting through the walls like butter. Devora, thank you for the power you've given me over these years. Please, just protect me this one last time. Devora exploded with cursed mana, creating a small cloud around it. The eye on the hilt opened up wide as well, causing the mana to spiral above Scourge in a form resembling a dark shield.

Fatum's blade finally came down and reached Scourge, causing a massive shockwave of light and darkness to echo out in all directions. "What is this power?" he questioned, wondering how the demon was able to stop his blade. Scourge looked up into the darkness, struggling to hold back the light with his one hand. The dark shield above Devora cackled and creaked under the massive pressure. His mana slowly began fading in and out as he pushed his blade forward. "Shit, I've got to do this nowwwwww!" The knights pushed and pushed, and eventually, the dark shield cracked and exploded. The eye of Devora shattered, leaving it's fading pieces of mana on the ground. This happened just as the knight's blade rushed forward, breaking through the sword itself, headed towards Scourge himself. Slush.

Fatum's mana ran out as soon as he broke through, his blade returning to normal. Scourge looked up, unable to see on his left side. Blood trickled down his cheek and neck. He reached up, still in shock, to feel hot steel had run through part of his head, stopping halfway past his eye.

"Oh…" Scourge said solemnly. The two stood there silently for a moment. The knight of Destiny doing everything he can just to keep his form together. Scourge struggled to formulate thoughts with half his head severed.

"Is it over?" Wendy gasped, watching the two clash. Keith did all he could to keep his head upright. "Wait...his mana...is it out?" She continued looking at Fatum with concern. Scatha eased took down the barrier.

Suddenly a dark blast reigns out in between the two fighters. Scourge and Fatum both skid away, separating. The knight holds his bloodied blade down at his side, looking ahead of him. All of his focus was on conserving just enough mana to stay in this form. Scourge held his wounded face with his hand, a crazed look in his remaining eye. "I didn't want to have to do this...it went against everything I stood for." Scourge's mana began going wild. Releasing off of his body with a mind of his own. A dark pulse echoed on the ground below him. After every pulse, the aura around him grew stronger. It wasn't many pulses before this mana's influence reached Fatum.

"This mana… It has life energy in it. Scourge, don't tell me you!" Fatum yelled when he realized the purpose of this mana.

"I drove you guys to the strongest form you could muster up! I've gotten to watch you mature to this point, and it's been so lovely." Scourge looked up, rolling his eyes behind its socket, in a display of his ultimate pleasure. His hand shifted to the top of his head. He let out a sad, but emotional 'mmm' sound afterward. After reaching out as far as possible, Scourge's mana began to reign itself in, slowly. "It's a shame I have to actually do my job before I can die. I was contracted to kill you, after all." Scourge beamed his eye forward at Fatum with bloody murderous intent. His mana also reflected his intentions as it turned a bright red moments before condensing around him.

"How do you still have so much mana?" Fatum shouted, tossing his blade backward, readying himself for what comes next with his bare hands.

The blade lands on the ground, right in front of Wendy. "Keith hun, we're gonna need you to get up, you're gonna be needed again," Wendy said, shaking Keith.

"I can't move my body at the moment, sorry," Keith said, lowering his head again.

"Don't worry about that." Wendy clapped her hands together and then placed her palms on Keith's back. His back lit up a bit as Wendy's mana soared throughout his body. Afterward, Keith's body abruptly stood up with his hands out in front of him.

"Huh, what is this? I don't have control of my body." Keith looked around curiously.

"What is this, mana, Wendy?" Scatha asked.

"Heh. Through expert level mana mastery, one can even control the mana links of others. Like so." The old woman raised her hands up one after another, then kicked her foot forward. Keith's body relayed the exact same movements with his body.

"Oh, that's quite useful indeed." Scatha nodded.

Keith walked over and grabbed the Knight's sword. "Hey, I'm going to need to borrow some mana to pull this off, okay?" he said, looking back at the woman.

"Just trust me, I wouldn't send you out there just for you to die."

Scourge's body had begun to fade slightly, all of himself slowly being converted into mana. "No matter how much light shines down! The darkness will never die!" Scourge yells, removing his hand from his face. The concentrated dome of red mana around him pulsed at every word. Sinister spirits swam along the surface of his mana, trying to be free. "Goodbye! Royal Knights!" Scourge's body disappeared from view as the condensed mana was unleashed, causing a slow explosion, incinerating everything in its circular path. As it tore through the ground on the way to Fatum, dark spirits eked their ideas out of the blast and flew away.

The knight of Destiny stood there, staring at the approaching darkness, breathing heavily and deep. "Just a little more. Let's go," He said to himself as he held out his hands in front of him. His hands clashed with the blast, pausing the path of destruction. The mana pushed him back several feet upon contact. "Shit…it's too powerful, I can't keep this up," he said, struggling. His mana drew lower and lower quickly. "Think I've reached my limit, but...I've got to protect them!" The Knight looked back at Wendy and Scatha before refocusing. His form teased a split multiple times in this exchange, but he somehow takes a step forward; this pushes the blast backward. Suddenly a swift wind pushes past him, right into the attack.

"Bandong Paaaaaaaa!" With a rush of mana, Keith thrusts Fatum's blade against the blast to reflect the mana. The blade wobbled and shook in his hands, as the overwhelming force pushes both of them back.

"What are you doing here? It won't work!" Fatum yelled towards his new help.

"Wendyyyyy! Mana!" Keith screamed before his body glowed with even more mana.

Fatum looked over and grabbed Keith's chest with one hand. "Use that power to protect them! Please…" A tear in his eye, he shoved Keith backward, forcing in to tumble in front of Wendy. The knights put all of their mana before them, pushing back with everything they had left.

"Knights!" Wendy screamed out as they get overtaken by the blast, and it rushed towards her now. Keith got up, the sword slowly disappearing in his hand.

"Damnit! Ugh. One more time." Keith rushed forward with the boost from Wendy and Scatha behind him.

"Bandong Paaaa!" he yelled with powerful mana led swung towards the blast.

The blade cracked the explosion, sending some of the mana bouncing back through a wall off to the side. The sword disappeared after this, though, leaving Keith's body to take the attack head-on. The explosion of mana continued on and overtook the remainder of the throne room, overtaking Wendy and Scatha as well. From outside noticed the giant explosion that leveled the entire top floor of the dark castle. An enormous cloud of smoke erupted in the area as the shock waves shook even the spaces on the ground past the front gates. Everyone on the battlefield was shaken off-balance as their collective attentions all focused on the castle. Tiny remnants of dark mana float above the smoke like a swarm of bees. A wave of silence swayed through Faith Hill as everyone awaited the results of this troublous battle.

Hepheaus sat crisscrossed on the ground next to Jax and William, both were beaten up to hell. The aqua queen sat there to conserve her mana need while idle. The three of them didn't take their eyes off the battle for a second, each wishing and praying in their own ways for victory. The soldiers and pirates all took a knee in unison, beaming up top. Their hope for freedom heavily in the balance.

"You kids better not die up there...or else!" Hepheaus yells up to the top.

"Oh, boy. What would the king think? No, what am I saying, Sky would never fall at a place like this. I've got to believe in his partners as well," Will said, looking up to the sky. He sighed several times in a minute, the smoke had still not cleared at this point. Jax put his hand on Will's shoulder.

"Don't worry, they'll be okay. Aye'?" Jax reassured him. Will simply nodded at him.

"What do you have planned after this fight's over Heph?" William asked curiously, looking down at her for a moment.

"Well… I don't know." Hepheaus responded, looking at the mana in the sky now. "After everyone's healed up, I have to take them to see Paradise. The real one. They need to see where their ancestors rest…at least once," she said, nodding to herself.

"Yeah, that's tru-." Will started.

"That's, of course, if we actually win here first. We need to win here. We HAVE to win here," Hepheaus said, cutting him off. William just nodded silently. The smoke finally began to thin out a bit on top of the castle.

Back in the throne room, the remnants of dark mana spread out throughout the floor, floating in the air. Rubble from the ceiling landed around the outsides of the room, The dark sky looked down on them down. As the smoke cleared, more and more were revealed. Wendy, Keith, and Scatha were all unconscious over to the side of the room. They all had terrible injuries, but for the ladies, it wasn't as bad as it could have been. Between Keith deferring some of the blasts, and Scatha's barrier, the damage was reduced drastically. Keith, on the other hand, was on his back, fighting for his life. Taking the blast head-on with his body already damaged had nearly killed him. He lies there coughing up blood, trying desperately to catch his breath, unable to move his body. In the center of the room, Sky, Hail, Ocean, and Gaia were all sprawled out with horrible burns and damage to every part of their bodies. The initial point of the explosion where Scourge had once stood had a ring around it, ash spread out haphazardly on the other edges. Void, Blaze, and Volt were the only three in the entire room still standing. Their wounds were severe as well, with no shortage of burns and scrapes. They wobbled in place, barely standing, barely conscious even, looking forward like it was the only thing they were able to do.

Void was the first one was to speak up after getting his mind together. He wavered back and forth, focusing on his breathing. The pain was all over his body, along with blood from the burns. "Oh… thank goodness…" he said before collapsing on his back, passing out instantly.

Volt and Blaze look over towards him, chuckling to each other. Something then captures their attention at the same time, the burning ring in the center. The pieces of mana that littered the air slowly began gathering back at that point, creating an ever-growing orb of darkness. The two Knights stared ahead of them in despair. Shaking their heads frantically. "No, no, no, no. This can't be happening…" Volt said, almost angry.

Blaze held up his fist next to Volt. The mana had almost completed reforming into a giant blob on that spot; It then started to radiate with shadows. Blaze took a deep breath and let out a deep sigh, fighting through the pain in his body as well. He couldn't even walk at this point, let alone stand. "One more Volt. One last time so we can finish this. For all those who have fallen and struggled to get us here." Blaze said, shaking his outstretched fist in Volt's direction. Ahead of them, a familiar eerie laugh rang out originating from the darkness, and it formulated into a humanoid figure.

Volt took a large sigh of his own before holding out his fist as well. "Yeah, we'll use what mana we have left to end this!" he said as they knocked their fists together.

"Contact!" They said in unison as a massive flash insured. The darkness and shadow mana had finished reforming as Scourge emerged from the darkness in his original form, very much alive. He arose, still laughing to himself.

"Haaaaa. I did i——. What? How are you still alive!?" Scourge shouted to Plasma, who now stood before him; mana was charging in his right hand. Scourge surveyed his own body for a moment, making sure everything was intact. "Damn. I really reformed myself. I haven't any mana left though, this may be an issue. My body is still so tender, it feels like every cell in my body is screaming right now," he said to himself.

"Scourge." Plasma said coldly. A mixture of lightning and flame mana spiraling around his arm.

The sudden surge of mana somehow wakes Scatha, who lay under a light pile of rubble. She brushes sediment out of her face and looks forward to seeing her Volt still alive before her. "Volt!" she said. A smile etches itself onto her face as she looks back and forth between Scourge and Plasma.

Scourge noticed the deadly intent from Plasma and held his hands up. "Hey now guys, no need to finish me off now. Wasn't the fighting fun for you too? Can't do that again if you kill me, right?" he pleaded, his trademark smile growing larger by the second as his nervousness increased. *I just need to hold out a little until their mana runs out again, then I've won!*

Plasma stared him down, not changing his expression. "Lucin, grant me the power to strike down all who oppose you! Ringa Uira!" The lightning mana around his arm started to glow and gather around his hand. The lightning concentrated there, sounding like a flock of birds chirping in unison. The flaming mana coated around the lightning mana like a mana jacket. ""Take this…my rage, my anger, and all of my fury!!" Plasma finally raises his voice as the red mana enrages around his hand. He then disappeared in a rush of lightning.

Scourge's eyes widened. "Good thing I still have these souls, ehhhh STRIKE protect me!" Scourge dug deep within himself and pulled out an orb surrounded by shadows. Inside was the very soul of Strike, Scourge had somehow kept with him all this time. He helds it out in front just as Plasma appears in a bolt of lightning directly in front of Scourge, his arm reared back. Plasma's mana collided with Strike's soul, destroying it but also dispelling itself. Scourge was blown back after a small explosion occurred. He crawled backward before getting back up to his feet and backing away more.

"Terrible. Your own subordinates. Don't worry, I've got another for you," Plasma said with a smirk on his face. The lightning and flame manas began gathering around his other hand his time.

"Hey, if you think about it, when I die, they die, right? So why not!" Scourge said, still retreating.

"Just die!" Plasma disappeared again before reappearing a few meters forward to attack Scourge again.

"Adrian!" Scourge quickly pulled out Adrian's soul orb and held it out to save himself again. Plasma reached out and grabbed the sphere with his mana charged hand this time, crushing the orb and letting the spirit free. Scourge stared in shock, backing away again. Adrian's soul, free, flying around searching and searching. Eventually, it finds itself entering Keith's dying body. Within seconds, Keith's breathing had returned to normal, his wounds on their way to healing.

"Knew you were going to try and pull that again. Now there's nothing to stop me anymore!" Plasma said, attempting to charge another attack, but nothing comes out. "Huh?" He looked down at his hands in confusion.

This is it! "Or is there?" Scourge chuckled as he rose up and summoned a dark sword in his hand-reared back, ready to stab his opposition. "Checkmate!" he yelled as he thrusted his sword forward.

"Father, no!" Scatha yelled, diving in the way of Scourge's blade. She held her hands out to either side as she stares into her father's eyes.

"Scathy, what are you doing?" Scourge yelled. Scatha lowered her head. A mana circle then appeared underneath of Plasma, slowly feeding him mana quickly.

"Sorry, father, but y—" Scatha got cut off by two raging blasts of fire and lightning mana blowing past her and into Scourge's chest. The blasts collided with each other right before hitting, leaving a large hole in the center of Scourge's torso. Scourge stumbled back a few steps; his arms plopped to his sides, and his mana blade disappears. "You need to die." Scatha finished, frowning.

After the attack, Volt and Blaze immediately defused and nearly collapsed themselves. Blaze caught himself on one knee, while Volt fell on his chest, looking up towards Scourge. Scatha dropped down and consoled Volt while he lied there. All these focus on Scourge to make sure they got him this time.

"Tsk...Damn..." Scourge coughed up blood as he looked down at the fatal wound going through his chest. Blood trickles down his legs onto the ground below. He continually stumbled backward until, finally, he tripped back onto his throne, which somehow still stood in place. He leaned his back on the foot of the seat, tilting his head back onto the chair. He took a few moments here to catch his breath. "Wow," he continued, still catching his breath. "And I'm the evil one...using my own daughter against me? Come on, knights." Scourge stopped for a second to put his hand over the hole in his chest. "Oh well, you got me. Finally. It pains me to say this, but this changes nothing. You're all still going to die. What do you think Demise, the one who hired me, will do when he finds out that I've been defeated? He'll probably go after you himself." He took another break before continuing. "If you can barely. Barely. Defeat me.

You won't stand a chance." Scourge finished spitting then chuckling a couple times.

Volt and Blaze looked at each other for a moment before refocusing on Scourge. "I highly suggest you all go and get stronger. *Much* stronger. Then you should probably launch an attack on him before he goes after you. Word of this battle will echo throughout the shadow realm and Armaggeddon quickly. Let's just hope this test was enough." Scourge slowly lowered his head, his arm also dropped back to his side. "Well...that's all for me. Goodnight Royal Knights, it's been fun...so fun." Scourge's voice faded out as his body withered away into dark ash and flies away with the wind.

Blaze silently nodded and looked down at the ground, tears flowing down his cheeks. "I did it, guys. I got your revenge. You can rest easy now." Blaze struggled and raised himself to his feet, limping towards the ledge on the edge of the throne room.

"Blaze..." Volt said as he watched him collapse and struggle to crawl to the opening and hang over it towards his allies, waiting on the ground level. He threw up a single labored thumbs-up, and immediately a roar of cheers and excitement begins. Warriors and pirates hugged and celebrated together.

Blaze reset himself, resting on his back now; his arm waving back and forth in the wind carefree. He passed out in this position to the sweet sound of celebration from all of the allies they had met to get them to this point.

****

Epilogue

A week after the events in Umbra, the knights find themselves in the tundra at the bottom of Sylindra. Snow fell perpetually here, profoundly affecting the visibility on the bottom side of this mountain range. This area was cut off entirely in the north by dangerous, snowy mountains, helping to block off this area to civilians who would happen upon it. After leaving the base of the hill, a small frozen forest awaited the knights, led by Hepheaus, who trek through quickly. Theey eagerly couldn't wait for what's on the other side, along with warmth. They can't wait for warmth more than most things right now. The knight's and Scatha flanked Hepheaus as they approach the end of the forest. They all sported heavy, thick winter jackets in lieu of their usual armor. Scatha stayed almost attached to Volt's hip, attempting not to get lost in the veil of white they walked through.

"Hey! Make sure you stay on my ass, we're almost there. If you get lost, I will not be coming back for you." Hepheaus boomed, not bothering to look backward to see who was still behind her.

"F-f-f-f-f-fuck. It's s-s-soo cold!" Gaia screamed, sticking close to Void's tall, dark figure. Looking up was painful for her, so she kept her eyes pointed at the ground in front of her.

"Geez, I'm glad I'm used to the cold. Because otherwise, I'd be having a rough time. Right, Blaze?" Hail snickered, looking back at the knight of fire, melting the ice icicles forming on his face again and again.

"Shut up!" Blaze said, trying to keep his focus on warming his body.

Volt and Void were both silent the entire time, focusing mostly on what was on the other side of this forest. Also, concentrating on keeping mana running throughout their bodies, the movement helped a bit with the warmth. Ocean stuck right behind his mother in the walk, attempting to hold back his nervousness.

"Finally," Hepheaus said, spreading the trees before here and walking forward. On the other side of those trees, the forest had stopped abruptly. The storm had halted as well, just in his area. The knights now stood in a broad valley, set in the center of the storm, but still frozen over. The mood became somber when the rest of the knights approached. This 'Royal Graveyard' was just as depressing as they had feared. Two large snowy hills sat on either side of where they now stood. Up and down the mountains, a plethora of stone gravestones were displayed neatly. Each was holding the body of a different hero who risked their lives to keep Chaos sealed away. Before each stone, the heroes' weapon was dug deep into the earth, preserved by the mystical aura that surrounded this area. One of the slabs near the top left side was missing one though, the grave of the original hero Volt, who now shares his weapon with the present-day Volt.

In the center of both sides of the valley sat the most troubling thing about this area. A path led forward up to a stone podium in the middle. On top sat a massive black metallic sphere with black chains wrapped tightly all around and bolted into the podium to keep it steady. The area created a dense demonic aura around it, so black that the chains that encased it was barely visible. Seven translucent mana barriers resembling the ones that kept them in Scourge's prison sat around the ball here as well. These were much more durable than those, however, needing a nearly Godly amount of mana to break just one of the barriers.

Hepheaus led them towards the demon sphere in the middle. "Now guys, this is Chaos," she said in a calm voice.

"Wait, like THE Chaos? The one in all the stories?" Blaze said, clearly shocked.

"The very same. The graves you see on your left and your right are the bodies of your predecessors," Hepheaus responded while waving her hand back and forth.

"I thought I felt odd mana coming from them, why are they here?" Void asked.

"Their bodies are kept here in stasis to help keep Chaos sleeping, well-sealed away. Am I right?" Volt said in a cold stare. His eyes fixated on the grave, missing a weapon on the left. Sigrun wiggled back and forth the closer he got there. "I think that's my..." He stopped.

"Actually, Volt, your guess is pretty close. The previous knights all lost their lives in battle, but they are kept here because they hold our God's mana within their bodies. It's the only thing that can hold back the powers of Chaos." The queen said, moving herself a little closer to the sphere.

"I guess that means we're gonna be here too, eventually." Ocean nervously chuckled to himself.

"Hopefully, by that time, it won't be necessary, but. Most likely, yes, your bodies will find their resting place here when you die." She said, reaching her hand out. Mana began draining out of her fingertips the closer she got to Chaos.

"I see...I guess this is our fate now as well, bro; we better prepare ourselves," Gaia whispered to Hail.

"Yeah, I'll be ready. One thing, though, we have to get stronger," Hail said, looking up into the white sky.

"We all do. We defeated Scourge, but that was such a narrow victory. I don't even feel good about how we defeated him. Now that Hepheaus was nice enough to show us this, we have extra motivation. Because of Scourge, we now have a new focus. We Royal Knights have to march into Armageddon and topple Deces' and his terrifying regime," Sky started.

"And we have to make sure we are strong enough to do that!" Volt said, holding his elemental orb up into the air. Hepheaus turned to face the knights and simply smiled. She had done what she needed to. Scatha held close to Volt's arm, holding him tightly as he spoke. "Let's show them that we were chosen for a reason!" Volt finished, his orb shining brightly now.

Sky also raised his orb into the air. "Well, said, Volt! Knights, are you with me?" Sky shouted.

"Hmph, I'm always ready to kick some demon ass! Let's do this." Blaze said, rising his brilliant flame orb into the air.

"You can count on me to watch your back always; this I'm here for." Void says in a low tone while casually raising his black orb.

"I can't give up on you just yet, can I, Volty?" Gaia winks at Volt and Scatha. Hail snickered next to her as they both lifted their orbs into the group.

"Haha, I'm glad I left and found you guys. I finally found the destiny I had been searching for all this time. Let's go save the world!" Ocean says with a huge smile on his face, but tears in his eyes. Ocean held his orb up, and the knights all clank their elemental orbs together, creating a large flash and a loud echo, heard for miles.

-Year 277   Hiyama Castle   Laix, Sylindra-

After the events in Paradise, Sky finds himself back at home around the same time his parents finally return from their battles. Their armies surround the castle in celebration from the victories on both sides. The Hiyama's throw a massive party, lighting up the skies with mana. Sky's mother gave him a tight hug upon seeing him again, proud of her young warrior son. His father, as stern as usual, simply gives him a nod well done. After the party, King Hiyama takes Sky and Will into the center of the Kritie jungle and trains them to be better warriors. He had heard of the many close calls Sky had been through on his journey, and he was determined to make sure he was better equipped to protect himself. The King had to protect his heir, his son. Sky trained to utilize better his mana link, the skill that was passed down to him and work on defensive abilities. Will improved on his speed and offensive capabilities, groomed to lead an army of his own one day indeed. Sky and his father spent more time together than they ever had at this time. It proved to strengthen their relationship considerably.

-Year 277 Farriage Castle Town Eodon, Sylindra-

Ocean and Hepheaus arrive back home to a marvelous ovation from the entire town. A yearly festival started its precedent this year, honoring all the Farriage family has done for the continent. The mana that traveled through the channels running through town lit up the streets as the townsfolk all left their homes and gathered around the markets. All who could control their mana gathered small, blue, concentrated balls of mana and sent them into the sky. This display represented their thanks to the family by giving back to the Gods, who gave them their powers. The sky lit up with small blue orbs as if it were raining in reverse. Ocean and his mother watched with smiles etched on their faces as they watched the beautiful sight.

Afterward, the town partied throughout the night. The next morning, the two promptly woke up and set off for the training grounds. They would spend their time away improving their fighting ability. Hepheaus guided Ocean towards fully mastering the Mana mastery skill, while simultaneously developing her stamina. She loathed not being able to fight for very long with her weakened body. Ocean longed not to be a burden on the battlefield; he would show them the fruits of his training the next time they would meet. He swore he would be better.

Years later, after Ocean had finally finished his training, he paid a visit to a certain scientist. He traveled to Polkera to finally talk to the woman he couldn't simply get off of his mind. Sierza was dumbfounded when Ocean randomly knocked on her door. The two spoke for hours, days even. He ended up spending the next three days there, garnering a long embrace when he eventually left her place. The two kept in contact afterward. Sicrra eventually visited the castle to 'evaluate ' the effects of the contact fusion on the knights' bodies and provide research to better the process.

-Year 277 Ula Sacred Passage Luvia's entrapment Eodon, Sylindra-

Under the pond in her eternal prison, Luvia sits in the center, legs crossed. Her projected screen turns off as an eerie smile. Then, suddenly, as if unable to control herself, she just burst out laughing hysterically. "HA! Idiots, all idiots! You guys have forgotten about me for the very last time!" She screams. As she finishes, an enormous mass of dark mana begins seeping through the walls of her prison and draws towards her. She absorbs it promptly, her eyes glowing an evil dark red. "I'd like to thank you dark mercenary...Void...and especially you Volt darling. Now I have the power to break these feeble chains that cut me off from the world," Luvia said, standing up, holding her hand up into the air. "Now, I'll be free, just how you feared. And it's all your fault. It's time. Time to get my revenge, prepare yourselves," Luvia said disappearing; The barrier she held herself in shattered behind her, fading away into nothing.

-Year 277   Ula Sacred Passage East Frosty Forest Eodon, Sylindra-

Luvia drug herself out of the silver water in the pond slowly and stepped out into the forest. The rain quickly eased itself down her body as if her body surrounded itself in plastic. She looked around; taking deep breaths of fresh air she hasn't felt in ages. "Now then, where to first!?" she said, concealing her mana so she could walk the grounds of Sylindra in peace.

-Year 278 Sunchaser, Tower of the Heavens Basonali, Sylindra-

Volt, Void, and Scatha arrived at the base of Sunchaser a full year after the knights separated. The three had been spending their time away traveling Sylindra, training around the world in different environments to improve their versatility and teamwork. Void's portals made travel between continents a breeze. Volt also used this time to research the demon that now shared his body. He searched far and wide for the evil scientist, Edgar. If anyone, he would know about this, especially since Scourge was now dead. After months and months of searching and training, the three approached the tower to test their abilities. The tower stood behind a massive mountain range, reaching up towards the heavens, getting lost in the clouds. Warriors trek here to fare against increasingly more powerful floors of enemies. After defeating the final boss at the top level, a gift from the Gods bestowed to the champion. The guardian deities created the tower, and a demi-god awaits at the top. Who knows if the knights will even make it there.

-Year 277 Kamas Desert Kegato, Sylindra-

After the separation, Blaze found himself alone to his thoughts as he walked through the lonely and desolate Kamas Desert on the way to the royal family that reside near the Kamas Volcano, one of the sacred zones in Sylindra. The ebony castle, set on the outskirts of the volcano, was made primarily using the coals broken away from the sides of the mystical mountain. Lava consistently melted and reformed over and over, creating the most potent known building block in Sylindra. Broad, black stairways led around the side of the volcano and up towards a massive opening at the top. The rail less stairwell was made extra perilous with lava and a long fall awaiting any who happened to slip off. Two heavily armed guards stood on either side at the top, a massive gateway behind them. There was only one way in and out of the castle, and Blaze had made his way there, no guarantee they'd let him through. Living in Kegato his entire life, it was his first time visiting the castle, even though he used to be best friends with the prince as a child. After the defeat of Scourge, Blaze received notice that his old friend died in battle and, in his will, requested that he make his way to the castle. The royal family never liked Blaze, treating him like trash as a child when the two would have fun together in his poor town. It's not believed that these feelings changed even after he was chosen by the guardian deities, and certainly not after the death of their son.

So Blaze stood in front of the two guards at the gate, debating on even going inside. What would they say or think? Would they somehow blame their son's death on

617

Blaze? Is he even welcome here even though the son requested it? He decided he should move forward, especially trying to honor his friend. Blaze walks up to the guard on the left while staring at the doorway behind him. "Let me in." He says with a straight face.

"Excuse me, sir?" one of the guards responded while raising his weapon.

"I have business with the queen. Let me pass, please," Blaze grumbled, visibly annoyed already. He was angry and didn't have the patience to deal with anything at the moment.

"Sorry, sir, I can't let you do th——" The guard stopped himself as Blaze's Red Chariot found it's way at his throat. The knight of fire had closed the distance very quickly.

"Wait! Let him in, we called for him, unfortunately. I'd rather get this out of the way. A voice echoed from beyond the doors. The guard simply nodded and backed away. The doors creaked open, slowly revealing the throne room. This area was very spacious, flame torches sat on the walls to light it up. Ornaments and statues made from the onyx colored material decorated this first floor here. Near the back of the wall, a stern woman sat atop a tall throne, beaming at Blaze with her eyes. Doors leading to the rest of the castle were on either side of the wall, behind her chair.

"Blaze." The woman said coldly.

"Saskia, Saskia Forsage`. It's been a while," Blaze said.

"Wish it was forever," she snapped.

"Same, but I hear your son…" Blaze trailed off a bit before continuing. "Well, either way, what happened to Ty?

The queen took a long sigh. "It was a battle. He died, leading our army into victory. His injuries appeared to have been poisoned, and he did not make it past that. Anyway, let's get this over with, bring it in!" Saskia waved over to one of her servants, who walked into one of the rooms on the side and returned with a long rectangular black box. The servant hands the box to Blaze with a bow, then walks away.

"What is this?" Blaze said, tumbling the box back and forth in his hand.

"That belonged to my son. His uncle had crafted that for him as soon as he came of age. Though we should keep it for the next generation, my son was adamant about passing this onto you. With the powers of that along with your own, it should prove to make you even more powerful," Saskia said, pointing at the box in Blaze's hand.

"I see, well thank you for going through with it, I guess I should have had faith in you a bit more," Blaze said, looking deeply at the box.

"Now, out of my sight, if you will. I've fulfilled my son's last wish." The queen shewed at Blaze. The large doors opened up behind him, and he turned and left without a word.

Outside of the castle, Blaze walked up to the base of the steps before his curiosity took over. He sat the box down and opened it. On the inside sat a long, two-handed sword with a beautiful, lava-stoned sheath. It was a shiny black and grey with coals of lava flashing periodically. The blade itself was pristine, almost glowing in the sunlight. Underneath the sword was a shotty hand-written note. Blaze sat the box to the side and took a seat on the first step as he started reading the letter to himself:

Dear Blaze,

If you're reading this, it means I'm already gone. Damn, I miss you, brother. At the moment, I'm on the battleground; we just won the biggest and most important war ever for us. But. You know me, I'm dumb. So dumb. The enemy's leader was strong, but I defeated him on my own. What I didn't count on was his poisoned blade. Fuck me, right? So yeah, I'm dying. But I did want to make sure I got to get you one more message beforehand. Also, I know my family, and I think that this beautiful blade here will do much better in your hands than it ever did for me. Her name is Blare, the sun eater blade. She can absorb all manner of light mana, among other abilities; I was never able to bring out properly. Ha-ha, you were always the stronger fighter of us two anyway. You remember that time I came to town to visit, and we got into a fight with the merchants' twin sons? We kicked their ASSES. But then, my mom came and came down on both of us, ha-ha. Eh, I'm rambling. Sorry. I just. I wish we could've had one last run before...this. Anyway, I'll be heading up to meet our Gods first. Take your time joining me; I'll be here enjoying the show. Anyway, I love ya brother, please live out your potential and be that hero we can always be proud of. Don't forget about me, ha-ha.

Cheers,

Ty.

Blaze looked up into the air after he put down the letter. "Goddamnit Ty, who could forget about you…" he said sorrowfully. A couple of tears came down his cheek. After he left the volcano, Blaze spent his time traveling and honing his skills with Red Chariot and now Blare. He enjoyed the time alone, allowing him to be one with his thoughts.

-Year 277   Kegos Port   Kegato, Sylindra-

Wendy led Gaia, Jax, and Hail back to Kegato to her home at the port. That port had never lit up as bright or roared as loud as they did upon their captain's return. Word of their victory spread quickly as they approached, and one by one, the citizens left their houses, flooding out onto the streets. Applause and cheers were loudest near the docks, where the pirates had started celebrating prematurely with loads of booze. After the parties, Jax attempted to return the captain hat to Wendy, the true leader of the Pirates. She stopped him, announcing to him and the rest of the pirates there that he would be the captain now. Wendy would retire and live out the rest of her days in that body in peace. Before this, however, she took the three of them and put them through a strict training regime to increase both their offensive and defensive capabilities. This intense training took about two years before Wendy was happy enough to leave her home. She would end up passing three years later, looking down at them from above after that point. Jax became a much stronger fighter in this time, leading his pirates through many impressive victories. Gaia's emotions had calmed a bit over the years away from Volt, though she never could entirely forget about him. Hail went from woman to woman while he stayed in Kegos, never quite finding love himself. He ended up returning to Codon after training, meeting back up with Ocean and his mother.

-Year 277   Edgar's lab   ???, Sylindra-

As the knights stormed Scourge's castle, Edgar snuck away; feeling his experiment was done. His faith in Scourge had faded as he watched Adrian's defeat occur from the window. Edgar returned to his lab briefly to collect his research before whisking himself away to the next area for his research. He searched for more examples of angel and demon possessions in the world already so he could use it to perfect his experiments. One day his evil deeds will reach the knights again.

-Year 277   Malveria, The Paradise City   Basonali, Sylindra-

Keith found himself appearing back on the outskirts of Paradise, still injured but walking on his own. Awaiting him were his two best friends Kerri and Alex. After getting nursed back to full health by his crew, Keith decided that he would spend his time training as hard as he possibly could. He told himself that he would never be weak enough to get used by anyone else again. Keith resorted to sneaking away and challenging himself in the gauntlet that is the Nasol Ruins. He used this and Adrian's weak state to take over full control of his own body. He used this power and his newfound control to conquer the darkness.

-Year 277 Exodus Castle Throne Room Armageddon-

In the weeks and months following Scourge's death, word spread quickly around the dark underground. Every demon and shadow stirred with the new opportunity and position freshly open. The many territories under his domain ran amok, clamoring to take his spot. The uproar in Umbra was so great; Deces' was forced to step in himself. The evil emperor descended onto Umbra with the semblance of a God himself. Warring demons and fiends of all types alike bowed instantly upon his arrival. His word was law as far as their chain of command went. Demise appointed Scourge's replacement himself and returned to Armageddon to keep the peace.

Back in Exodus castle, Demise returned to his throne, flanked by Ruin and Scarlet. "Tsk, that fool allowed himself to be defeated by those Knights." He scoffed angrily.

"He probably went easy on them. He was always the type to love a good fight," Ruin said, talking very close to his ear.

"I am so disappointed. I had high hopes for him too. He grew to be so strong. Does it worry you at all that the Knights defeated him, father?" Scarlet approached from his other side, looking at his face.

"Not at all. We are on a different level, all of us. We are Gods, and they are peasants!" Demise shouted, slamming his fist into his armrest. He promptly began laughing maniacally afterward. His deep voice echoed throughout the castle, startling all who resided there.

The Royal Knight's Skill List:

Blaze-(English Based)

Weapon: Red Chariot Blade

Searing Finger: "Take this! My rage, my anger, and all of my fury!" Concentrated mana that pierces a single spot, critical damage, and explosion damage to the target. It can be charged for improved damage or fired as a blast for range.

Molten Nova: "Oh great lords grant me the power to create the ultimate destruction, kneel before the power of lord Verafelt" Giant fiery mana ball that annihilates anything in a wide range. Exhausts a lot of mana to use. It can instead be absorbed for a massive power boost.

Nova Divide: After activating the Red Chariot's pure form, this sword skill is available. After confining the enemy within the confines of two walls of fire, a dangerous and quick explosion travels from the blade to the target to cause substantial damage.

Phoenix Divide: Used while the Red Chariot is upgraded in Phoenix mode. The power to damage even Gods is granted to the blade at a hefty mana cost. The streaks of flaming light cast from the edge either cuts through cleanly or nukes an enemy on contact. If the enemy is more powerful, this is when the cut explodes instead of merely cutting through an enemy.

Nova Wings: Temporarily absorbs the energy from the Molten Nova to gain flaming wings. Useful for hovering or floating more than flying.

Phoenix Mode: "Verafelt. Quell my rage to rid me of my demons. Calm my soul so I may live on without hatred and regret. Suck away my fears, my anger, and my sorrows lest they prevent me from absorbing your love. Let your overwhelming feelings and power rain. Down. On. Me." Blaze Absorbs all of the energy from a fully powered Molten Nova to enter an enhanced state. His strength and stopping power increase 10X, his normal abilities get a boost, and he is in a state of constant physical recovery. His mana usage is increased, however, making his form hard to maintain.

Phoenix fist: "Deities of the elements hear my call. Verafelt replenishes my rage so that I may not fall. This fist of mine will hold my soul and my passion. Let it burn bright in the night to incinerate everything in sight!" Phoenix Mode finishes with a punch that extinguishes all of the flames and mana stored up through an enemy. Very powerful even against strong defenses, but easier to miss than the Molten Nova. One of if not Blaze's most powerful skill.

Mana Healing: Unlock from the orb that activates in times of great peril. A release of mana that reverses even near-death injuries becomes available to Blaze. Long recovery and large mana drain.

Second Sense: A skill gained from the orb's blessing. It allows Blaze to sense an enemy's intentions and evade or counter very effectively. It is something that must be turned on and off as it uses a considerable amount of mana but improves his combat effectiveness.

Phoenix's Touch/ Second Chance: A skill awarded from the orb. It grants the ability to revive Blaze once from death. Blaze is given a jolt of mana and is restored in Phoenix mode.

Volt-(Maori Based)

Weapon: Sigrun Legendary Spear

Ringa Uira (Lightning fist): "Lucin, grant me the power to strike down all who oppose you!" The majority of Volt's active mana is transferred to his hand, which he thrusts into a specific spot, causing piercing and critical damage to his enemy. It goes through guards smoothly.

Tao Uira/ Huaki (Lighting drill/ Lightning drill barrage): His spear becomes a piercing drill of mana that shreds defenses. Its mana does piercing damage unto foes. It can be continually thrust forward for the Tao Uira Huaki, a barrage of powered up spear thrusts from Sigrun.

Pouri Uira (Dark Lightning fist): A semi-last resort move used to sever mana connections in the target. Uses dark mana that pains Volt to use and creates a shockwave knocking out all mana in a wide radius; Even Volts. Leaves Volt at a massive disadvantage if the ability misses.

Porohita Marama (Electric field): Orb unlocks that get more powerful with time. Volt layers mana around the surface of his skin and releases a wave of electricity around him in all directions, creating an electric bubble that blocks attacks and damages those who touch it.

Tao Wa (Spear shift): Volt's body reverts into mana and is drawn to the position of his spear. Grants Volt increased movement possibilities as he can toss Sigrun and teleport to its location. It only works within a specific range, and he cannot be attacked while traveling in lightning mode.

Te Atua Whakatau (Satellite Judgement): "When we acknowledge that all of life is sacred and that each act is an act of choice and therefore sacred, then life is a sacred dance lived each moment consciously. When we live at this level, we participate in the creation of a better world." ~ Scout Cloud Lee, A large and sharp exhaust of mana slams down from the heavens like judgment, causes critical damage for friend and foe in a large radius.

Uira Te Rewera (Lightning Demon Mode): When Volt finds himself in peril deep within him, the newly unlocked demon side of him takes over. Dark lightning mana surrounds his body as his form grows into that of a demon fiend. The lightning demon is dangerous and destructive, destroying everything until his mana runs out entirely, leaving Volt with no recollection of the takeover.

Uira Tikanga (Flash mode): A later orb unlock for Volt. He engulfs his body in his lightning mana enough to change its state. His movements become exceptionally more quick, as he moves at the speed of light. Charge times for his attacks are also instantly allowing him to fire off full-powered attacks with incredible speed. He uses a massive amount of mana to maintain, so he is rarely in this state for very long.

Pouri Zuma (Dark lightning burst): An enhanced, dark lightning version of Inazuma only available while Volt is in his Lightning Demon Mode. Volt teleports in front of his enemy and blows them away with a mostly concentrated beam of dark lightning mana that cancels out any mana it encounters. It's used also cancels out any dark mana consuming Volt as well.

Lucin's Wrath: With the help of Sky's mana, Volt lowers his fists with the power of the Goddess of light. Mana explodes off of the impact with an exhaust of lightning and thunder. Powerful but hard to connect.

Inazuma/ Kotahi Inazuma: "Erupt and eradicate, shatter their hopes for they failed to embrace the goddess...and I will punish them...INAZUMA!" Volt discharges a massive wave of electric mana in a single direction but with great size and range. Takes up more and more mana the longer it is held. It can be fired quickly in succession, but it's weaker each time. Kotahi can only be used in Flash mode. An Inazuma is released from each hand separately using the mana already surrounding him to make the charge time quicker. No chants are needed for this version — results in an overall more powerful attack.

Tuaiwi Oho (Spiral Tap): Volt's foot is charged with his lightning mana for a devastating ax kick that jolts an opponent's spine and entire body; stunning and paralyzing an enemy for a short bit of time

Nihil: Classified

Void- (Greek Based)

Weapons: Fonos Spirit Claymore, Tăia the Cleaver, and Izbucni the Rage:

Skiá Kínisi (Shadow Shift): Void's short-range portals. It can be used in multiples simultaneously, but only in areas he can see or has been before. Works on himself or others. When used on allies, it won't close unless they are clear of the portal's opening.

Daímonas Kínisi (Demon Shift): A future unlocks from the orb's blessing. Void's long-range, continent connecting portals. He can travel much further than his simple Shadow shift, but still, only to areas, he has gone to before. It allows him to transport more people with his portals at the same time as well.

Eleos Kínisi (Mercy's Shift): Void uses his portal as a weapon to trap an enemy or enemy's body parts inside. It can be used to slice off limbs or disrupt attacks. It doesn't hold the same restrictions as the shadow shift.

Orgí Katástasi (Berserker mode): Activated by absorbing his demon swords' mana, or when Void consumes too much dark, evil mana at a time. Prevents stagger while his terrifying mana engulfs and enhances his body. Speed and power are increased 10x, but it alters his mind, causing him to lose control and fall closer to the darkness. Mana and life drain also applies to enemies in which he inflicts damage.

Theós Kínisi (God's Shift): Only used when in a fusion with three of more knights. Sucks mana from an enemy's attack into a portal before absorbing it. It can be used on even the most potent abilities as long as he has the power to control it. It also allows the use of Keni Bala without the need for Dark mana being absorbed.

Shadow Boxing: An enhanced mode activated by absorbing the mana of one of the knights. Their element is used to extend the range of his melee and sword attacks with a corresponding aura to match that element. Gains a strength boost as well if used while in contact fusion

Shadow Slicer: A deadly attack using the long-range cursed blade, Taia. Streaks of dark mana cut through anything in its path mercilessly.

Demon's Wrath: Activated by the close-ranged cursed blade, Izbynci. A short stab or slash releases an overwhelming amount of dark mana in a massive uncontrollable explosion.

Dark aura: An orb unlocks he learns through observation. It allows Void to concentrate his dark aura to impose a heavy sort of gravity on an area caused by the pressure of his mana. Immobilizes or can even crush enemies. Its power grows the stronger Void gets.

Kení bála/Ékrixi(Void ball/Dark Shock/Blast): "Filled with rage and anger...my curse is turned into a blessing from the hands of the Gods that deemed me worthy to wield the ultimate darkness. Feel my pain, my struggles, and shatter from the weight of my spirit! KENI...BALA!!" Void expels all of the extra dark and evil mana from his body and gathers it in a giant ball. He condenses it into a small, mighty ball of mana. When it hits an enemy, it links to the mana channels throughout their body and expands, destroying the links from the inside out. Best used after berserker mode to get rid of the evil mana he has gathered. It can be converted into a blast upon absorbing a certain amount of mana.

Death's Grip: "With the mark of the dark lord, escape is futile. Grab him and never let go." Another orb unlocks learned through observation — tentacles made of dark mana release from his back to spear and drain mana from the opposition. The more mana you use, the more are summoned, and the more relentless they are, not stopping until they reach their target.

Ocean-(Bosnian Based)

Weapons: Hybrid blade, Royal Rapier

Voda Eksplozija (Hydro Bomber): "From the future to the past, erase our foes with a blast!" The mana driven spear of his hybrid weapon propels and explodes, amplifying if it happens underwater. It takes some time to recharge after use.

Mana drain: A Hail and Ocean exclusive ability. Prolonged contact with an enemy with their mana allows them to control the flow of it, draining it from the enemy.

Water clones: Ocean copies himself multiple times with stable clones made of water he can attack and defend. Takes up enormous mana, the more you summon and the more actions they take. The mana usage is more efficient while in Mana Mastery Mode, though, as you gain mana while you use it.

Mana whip: Showing Ocean's mastery of controlling mana, he summons an energy whip he can use to attack or control enemies' movements. Very versatile, and with more practice, he can bring forth more than one at a time, and increase their size and holding ability.

Water claws: Ocean's second weapon set, it's much quicker than his sword and allows him to deliver relentless blows. It can be used to attack or defend. It can be destroyed and resummoned and truly shine when underwater, where their streamlined design moves very quickly.

Water Spirits: Unlocked through his orb, and learned to master from his mother. Works as a last resort move for Ocean where mana spirits from his soul release and immobilize an enemy. It can be detonated at an enormous cost of mana. It can be evolved depending on orb progression and whether he is in Mana Mastery mode or not.

Liquify: Ocean's mana seeps into the ground to turn the earth into a liquid, useful for traps and escape. With increasing orb levels, he can turn himself into liquid and further control the mana within.

Mist bomb: A concentrated ball of mana is thrown then turns to mist to blind an enemy. The stronger the mana he puts into it, the more massive the mist explosion. On higher levels with his orb's blessing, he can create acid bombs.

životno majstorstvo: (Mana Mastery Mode) "Lucinthis. Verafelt. Nefula. Sylindra. Ardin. You, the five deities that govern our existence, I pray to thee now for your blessings. Grant me the aptitude to transcend all and call upon your mana at my will. I offer thine body and my soul in penance for my sins of this life so we can rendezvous in the next." "Let us merge, we will converge, unto darkness; we will purge. Zivotno Majstorstvo!" A late orb skill unlocks for Ocean, learned from his teachings with his mother. An ancient ability passed down through generations; only those in his family may learn it. It allows Ocean to efficiently channel his mana throughout his body's mana link points. This gives him an immense physical, speed, and defensive boost. His mana is constantly regained from nature around him. It also allows him to use any of his abilities without expending much mana. Ocean isn't able to withstand the mode for very long. The amount of time he can use it increases with training.

Hail- (Croatian Based)

Weapons: Mana Ice blades

Ledeni raspršeni napado (Ice glass barrage): "When given the power to lay judgment, attack with the fury of all five kings! Scatter and pierce, Ledeni raspršeni napado!" Hail showers his opponents with a rain of frozen spikes that fly towards the enemy piercing and shredding everything in its path. The barrage lasts as long as his mana does, creating suppression fire when needed.

Bezmjeran Zalediti Mačevi (Infinite Ice Works): Hail can use this ability only while Icey Graveyard is activated. He summons an army of ice blades that rise out of the terrain. The blades are scattered around as if it was a sword graveyard. While within this domain, Hail's speed and physical abilities are boosted, along with his mana regenerative abilities.

Zaleđen Groblje (Icey Graveyard): After a moment gathering energy, Hail uses a massive amount of mana to flash freeze a wide area entirely, either creating a barrier around him or solidifying friend and foe within the range of the attack. Allows for comfortable use of his abilities, and pulls an advantage for Hail. Activates faster and uses less mana, the more his orb's blessing increases in level.

Zaleđen Kutija (Ice Coffin): Hail encases himself or another in a compacted ice block made from his mana. This very sturdy ice protects Hail and allows him to use his abilities while within the ice even though his movements are constricted. They are used to block attacks or immobilize enemies. It can be broken out of depending on the strength of the enemy trapped. Mana drain automatically activates if an enemy is trapped.

Krajnji Zatvor(Ultimate Ice Prison): "O' great deity of the earth, allow me the use of your mana to surround thy enemies with your cold embrace. Arrest and freeze under the weight of the Goddess's mercy, Krajnji zatvor!" An ultimate version of Ice coffin that Hail learns through his orb after a near-death experience. Activates through the use of ice pulse as it takes time to prepare. It flashes freezes the enemy connected with the ice pulse and suppresses their mana as well. It is used for much stronger enemies than the simple Ice coffin. The mana drain is so reliable it recovers most of the mana spent to activate the skill if the enemy is strong enough to handle it.

Pakao! (Spike hell): Used in conjunction with ice coffin, whereas Giant ice spikes are gathered around the enemy and skewer them. Takes time to pick the size

Mana drain: A Hail and Ocean exclusive ability. Prolonged contact with an enemy with their mana allows them to control the flow of it, draining it from the enemy.

Ice Pulse: Activates by contacting an enemy with one of Hail's mana swords. His mana pulsates into the enemy, causing damage and slowly freezing it over time. Multiplies the effect the more swords in an enemy.

Gaia-(Turkish Based)

Weapons: Kirici Bo Staff

Dünya Baştan (Earth/World Seduction): "Listen to my calls like you did in the past, help me defeat this foe to make this world last." Gaia resonates with the environment to change and move large sections of the earth at will. Rearranging the battlefield in many ways from blocking off areas to locking others in are just a few of the uses of this ability. Although it uses a good amount of mana to activate, having her element near increases her mana recovery time and allows her to insert her advantages.

Kaya zırhı(Rock Armor): Gaia uses the earth as armor around her body. It can be recovered after the destruction and dramatically reduces the damage she takes, especially from mana attacks. Her earth mana absorbs damage. She also summons Kirici, her devastating breaker bo staff. Having Kirici allows Gaia to focus her destructive power and manipulation of earth mana better.

Toprak başak (Earth stalagmites): Earth spikes up ground to skewer enemies. They are very agile in travel, resembling snakes as they slitter towards their target. It becomes even more deadly when used in an enclosed area.

Toprak hapis (Earth prison): Gaia swings Kirici and summons many skinny earth stalagmites that come from the walls and ground skewering and pinning the enemy down. The earth is very sturdy and takes a mighty foe to force its way out physically.

Kötülük için merhamet yok (Breaker drive): "Crack ve şut, kırıcı sürücü! No mercy for the evil. Crack and smash, Kirici. Breaker drive!" Kirici shines with might as it enhances itself with the power to shatter crush or sever anything it hits. Best when used in combination attacks for as long as Kirici remains active. After every attack, Gaia's attack power increases. The final hit accumulates the gathered mana of the nature around Gaia and delivers a final devastating blow.

Dünya pençesi (Earth Claw): Gaia gathers a large amount of mana into her right hand, and thrusts the mana through her opponent with the force of an earthquake. This punch sends shockwaves through them, damaging the enemy inside and out and tearing through even the most sturdy defenses.

Tanrısal pençesi (Divine Claw): "Oh dear goddess Sylindra, mother, allow me to make my body a mere vessel to your infinite powers. Bless me with the powers of nature and the world around us. Bestow this fist with the power to send your enemies back to the dirt that they rose from! This divine claw will annihilate all in our path as we are one!" Gaia's ultimate attack using the combined mana of her teammates mixed with her tenacity. This punch hits the opponent with devastating stopping power, shattering defenses, and halting the life force of the target.

Platforms: Gaia can use the earth under her feet to propel herself forward or into the air as her platform.

Sky-(Chinese Based)

Weapons: Scythe of life

Shén Shāshǒu Lián (Godslayer Scythe): "Cut down the holy to protect the precious, cleave and devastate!" His spear grows in size and power, buffing Sky's abilities as well. Getting struck by the Godslayer scythe makes you weaker and frees mana through any open wounds into the air.

Xi Neng(God Cutter): "Hear my calls as I display my blessings. O' Ardin, grant me the power to slay your demons and your angels. Xi...Neng!" Used during Godslayer mode to absorb extra mana from the air and any open wounds on the enemy. This power is gathered in the scythe and released in the form of an enormous streak strong enough to slice Gods in two. It is unstoppable and unblockable and even cuts through the earth itself.

Xi Qi(Wind Tunnel): Created a small wind tunnel over an opponent, depriving them of oxygen. Denys the use of mana while inside of the attack.

Fēng Bāi Zhuàng (Windbreaker mode): Initially activated in times of great peril as an unlock from the orb. Sky coats himself in wind mana that grants his body the same properties as the wind. Physical attacks become near useless as they go right through him. This also increases his speed and allows him to conduct mana quicker as well. Certain mana attacks can break through this form, allowing him to be damaged.

Mana Link: Links his soul with those of his choosing, even across great distances they remain connected. A skill passed down throughout his family. It allows for long-range communication among other perks as he hones the ability.

Fēng Bāi Quántóu (Windbreaker fist): While in windbreaker mode, Sky dashes through the air at incredible speeds and delivers a devastating punch. Hard to avoid because of the pace and increases in damage, the more momentum he gathers.

Fēng Zhuǎnyí (Aero shift): A later orb unlock for Sky. It allows him to teleport short distances in the air very quickly. Enhanced viability while in Windbreaker mode. Fēng Fěnsuì (Aero slam): Mostly a physical move, He grabs an enemy high into the air and spirals them both down, crashing into the ground with heavy force. It Does damage to both Sky and the enemy captured. Extra damage and speed if done in Windbreaker mode, as well as damage reduction for Sky.

Dàqì (Aero Sphere): Sky captures his foe inside of a sphere of wind mana that constantly spins in place. This can be used to hold someone for a while or fired away at impressive speeds like a bullet. Not effective on stronger enemies.

Keith-(Korean Based)

Weapon: Fragarach Wind Blade

Ileun Flash: Energy spins together in Keith's hand, and grows larger, then shrinks to fist size. Keith teleports behind the enemy and shoots out a beam of energy. After a short delay, a massive explosion ensues from the area the beam connected. It can be fired rapidly for more mana usage.

Saseon Flash: Barrage of light mana infused sword attacks and slashes showing off Keith's impressive swordplay. Streaks of mana are sent off after each swipe, increasing the range of his attacks.

Ileun Flare: A culmination of light and fire mana that releases a bright wave of energy that leaves burns and blinds the enemy at the same time. Blinds enemies even if they aren't looking directly at the attack.

Ileun Boon: Keith gathers light mana into concentrated balls he can toss to explode or burn enemies. A bright flash ensues after each explosion.

Absorbed Ability: Keith can use the power of the wind from Fragarach to hide himself or the blade from sight. Using the Fragarach, he can cast a wind spell that grants a speed boost on his sword and casting time.

Bandong Pa(Backlash wave): Using his sword, or any sword-like weapon, Keith absorbs and reflects the mana of an incoming attack, sending it back 5X. The blowback strength can be increased the more mana he puts into it. More mana is needed to send back more powerful attacks.

Adrian- (Sacred Language)

Weapon: Fragarach Wind Blade/Chaos Blade

Mávro péplo (Black Mist): An automatic spell that triggers upon Adrian's awakening. A culmination of the pent-up energy from Adrian being sealed. The mist itself is physical emotion, fear, hate, anger, anxiety, all kinds of bad feelings, taken physical form. It penetrates the mind of those affected by it and stirs up the emotions in the person. If they are mentally stable, then they resist. If not, then they succumb to the feelings and go crazy, usually ending in an instant kill from Adrian.

Darkness Incarnate: Another automatic spell that triggers upon Adrian's awakening. The Black Mist that extrudes from him hardens and can be used to fight or defend. It floats around Adrian like a cape with a soul of its own.

Skoúro kýma(Dark Wave): A dark version of Keith's backlash wave, whereas this one absorbs and reflects an attack at 10X along with giving Adrian complete control over the mana in the attack and shrouding the attack in darkness.

Dark mines: Adrian condenses his dark mana to create hard to see discs that leave deadly explosions on contact.

Unstoppable Darkness: Adrian fires drill tipped arrows of darkness at the opponent rapidly. The arrows tear away at defenses and can be fired indefinitely with Adrian's unlimited amount of mana, enhanced even further when under cover of Nocte Aeternus.

Lunar Princess/ Shining Mode: "No longer will the people have to wait for day; my Cruel moon will bring the end. The dawn will never rise, and slaves of the light we shall end. Rise, Lunar Princess, bring darkness eternal. Protect us in your everlasting Night." Upon this cast, Adrian's darkness is encased in everlasting shining mana as he dons the power of the Lunar Princess. His mana replenishes even faster, along with constant healing and regeneration. All of his natural abilities are boosted with this extra mana along with access to new, shining mana attacks as well. Each of these abilities is supported with limitless mana, making this mode nearly unstoppable.

Shining Slicers: Adrian gathers a ball of mana in his hand and shoots out a relentless barrage of mana with bladed edges. Some are small; some grow as long as a sword's blade, depending on the range of the target. Very sturdy and hard to defend.

Shining Fist: Adrian instantly gathers mana to match his opponents' in his hand and releases his shining mana through a concentrated point to cancel out and repel the enemies' attack, mostly overpowering them even.

Shining Lance: After spreading out small ores of mana, in an instant, Adrian orchestrates a web of shining spikes of mana to skewer the enemy from all directions with no time to evade or defend. The mana is stored in the ores surrounding the area so that the spikes can spawn in quickly.

Nocte Aeternus: "No mercy, innocent or guilty. Bring down their lying sun. Blood a sweet silver, black by night. Upon their faces pale white." The Black Mist expands and covers a designated area. The area is pitch black, not a shred of light can penetrate it, except for high-level light spells. "All will know the wonder of my eternal lullaby. Say goodnight at this the final setting of the sun; tomorrow dawns in darkness, the endless night has begun! Nocte Aeternus!" This chant makes the area expand even further, able to cover miles with total darkness.

Profane Indignation: "I call upon thee, demon lords of the plane. Embrace me in your arms, and lend me your powers once again. I offer you blood, pain, and torment in exchange. Pour your wrath upon my sword, and now prepare yourself for my bane. Profane Indignation!" A beam of darkness descends from the heavens and crashes into the earth, followed by accompanying rays that come from the planet itself; there is no escape. It causes massive magical damage. His ultimate spell is even more effective when sight is erased by Nocte Aeternus, as this spell will then spread over that large area as well.

Made in the USA
Middletown, DE
02 April 2023

28068051R00390